STAR TREK®
PHASE II
THE LOST SERIES

STAR TREK PHASE II

THE LOST SERIES

**Judith and Garfield
Reeves-Stevens**

With a special Introduction by

Jon Povill
Story Editor, *Star Trek Phase II*

POCKET BOOKS

New York   London   Toronto   Sydney   Tokyo   Singapore

Cover illustration

The *Starship Enterprise* depicted on the cover is from a
1977 painting by Mike Minor. It shows the ship as it
would have appeared in *Star Trek Phase II*, updated by its
original designer, Matt Jefferies. A final model was built
according to Jefferies's design, but was abandoned when
the decision to make *Star Trek: The Motion Picture* meant a
more detailed *Enterprise* would be needed for the big
screen. Though the famous starship was updated yet
again, many of Jefferies's design details remained,
including the tapered struts, flattened nacelles, and twin
photon-torpedo tubes on the saucer support pylon. The
other images that appear on the cover are taken from
concept paintings prepared for both *Phase II* and
The Motion Picture, which appear in the color pages of this
book. Digital montage by Mark Gerber, Gerber Studio.

An *Original* Publication of
POCKET BOOKS

POCKET BOOKS, a division of Simon & Schuster Inc.
1230 Avenue of the Americas, New York, NY 10020

Copyright © 1997 by Paramount Pictures. All Rights Reserved.

STAR TREK is a Registered Trademark of Paramount Pictures.

This book is published by Pocket Books, a division of Simon &
Schuster Inc., under exclusive license from Paramount Pictures.

All rights reserved, including the right to reproduce this book or
portions thereof in any form whatsoever. For information address
Pocket Books, 1230 Avenue of the Americas, New York, NY 10020

ISBN: 0-671-56839-6

First Pocket Books trade paperback printing March 1997

10   9   8   7   6   5   4   3   2   1

Book design by Richard Oriolo

POCKET and colophon are registered trademarks of
Simon & Schuster Inc.

Printed in the U.S.A.

C o n t e n t s

A glimpse at *Star Trek: Planet of Titans*—one of the many lost *Star Trek*s developed by Paramount prior to *Star Trek Phase II*. Shuttlebay sketch by Ken Adam. Sketches courtesy of Paramount Pictures.

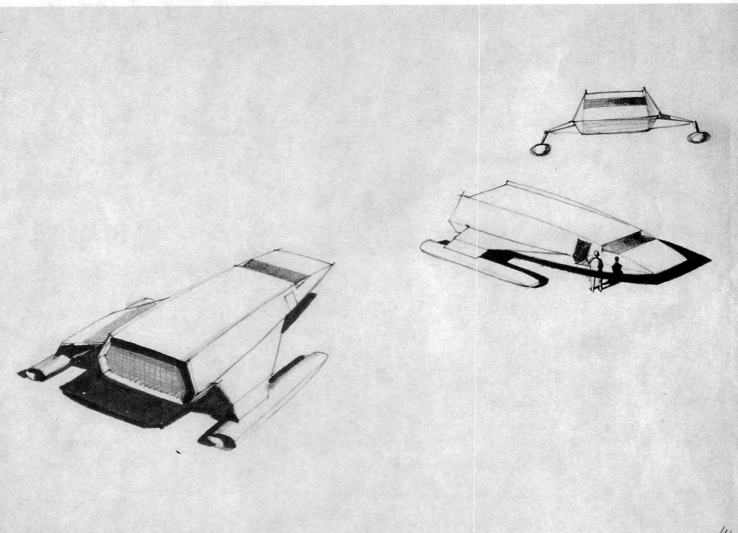

Introduction

by Jon Povill

From January 1976 through early March 1979 *Star Trek* permeated virtually every aspect of my being. In a very real way, even though it is long behind me, it still defines who I am. Those three years felt like an entire career. Hell, they felt like a lifetime. If they *had* been a lifetime, *Star Trek Phase II* would have been the high point.

For me, *Star Trek Phase II* began in the spring of 1975. My first official function on what was (briefly) to become *Star Trek Phase II* was to transport boxes of awards and memorabilia from Gene Roddenberry's garage to his office at Paramount—the very office he had occupied on the original *Star Trek*. He was returning to write and produce a *Star Trek* movie. Though he had told me many times in earlier conversations that he'd had his fill of *Star Trek* and longed to move on to new territory, it was clear to me that this was a moment of triumph in Gene's life. It was a vindi-

cation of sorts, this return to the site of his old battles. I don't remember if he compared it to MacArthur's returning to the Philippines, but he might just as well have done so. Certainly, for the moment at least, his return seemed to be on his own terms.

My situation was, of course, somewhat different. I was still in school while Gene was fighting his wars. I'd been a fan of the show and was filled with excitement at the possibility that I might be involved in some capacity in the next incarnation of *Star Trek*—though carrying boxes was certainly not what I had in mind. I was still fresh out of film school, but felt ready for something big to happen. I'd recently been paid about $1,250 to write a screenplay called "Total Recall" for Ron Shusett, a producer no one had heard of in 1975. But that was small potatoes. This was *Star Trek*.

It wasn't that I didn't believe in "Total Recall," but in 1975, how could it compare to the stature of *Star Trek*? Even now, my reasoning makes sense. If "Total Recall" and Ron Shusett had had the cachet of *Star Trek* and Gene Roddenberry, I seriously doubt it would have taken 14 years and 64 more drafts before it went into production. *Star Trek* was already a legendary series with a huge following. The thought of working on the movie was a definite "Wow!" Reality. Big Time. Trouble was, there was no job for me *except* to carry boxes. All I could do was write, and obviously Gene would be doing that.

But something extremely strange happened that first day as I wandered through the two adjoining reception offices that separated Gene's office from another large office down the hall. Susan Sackett (Gene's secretary) was with me as I entered what I later learned had been Gene Coon's old office. I can still vividly remember the prescient feeling that came over me when I walked in that room. I stood there for a moment feeling the vibe, then turned to Susan and said, "This is going to be my office."

It was no proclamation of a great and glorious goal or plan. I had not the slightest justification whatever to *think* that room would ever be my office. But I *felt* it profoundly. There was mostly amazement in my voice, because I absolutely knew it would happen. It took less than a year.

Paramount turned down Gene's script sometime during the summer, and he invited me to come up with a concept of my own, which he would turn in to the studio if he felt it was good enough. I wrote a spec treatment. He said it would make a great episode if the series were still on, but that it wasn't a feature. In December I got a call from him. He said he had another idea for the *Star Trek* feature and asked if I wanted to cowrite it with him. I said that would be great, then hung up the phone and whooped so loud my neighbors came running over to see what the hell had happened. No doubt in my mind. This was my big break.

I moved into the office I'd envisioned as mine in January 1976, and for the next three years I occupied, lost, and reoccupied that office roughly half a dozen times through the shifting fortunes of the early attempts to make a movie, the breakthrough that was *Star Trek Phase II*, and the series of triumphs and follies that ultimately emerged as *Star Trek: The Motion Picture*.

During those three years I held a great multitude of positions. When the story I'd worked on with Gene failed to generate enthusiasm at Paramount, I continued to hang out in my office until having to vacate it for Chris Bryant and Allan Scott, who came in to write *Star Trek*—the next attempt, which was the version of the feature that Phil Kaufman was to direct. When Paramount passed on their version and on Phil Kaufman's subsequent revisions, I got my office back, though it was unofficial and I was there as much to be an errand boy as a writer. (Though I did get to rewrite a screenplay of Gene's called "The Nine" during this period, and the book is far from closed on this very strange and unique project.)

By now Paramount was pretty frustrated with trying to make a feature version of *Star Trek*. They'd pretty much come to the conclusion that it wasn't possible to write *Star Trek* suitably for the big screen. From this frustration, *Star Trek Phase II* was born.

Harold Livingston arrived, and I was pushed from my office again. But this time the studio seemed fully behind us. The place was buzzing with the activity of preproduction and I was given a new title—assistant to the Producer—and a new official office, a tiny one in the back of the building.

From my little cubbyhole I began insinuating myself into story meetings whenever I could, and I got lucky because Harold Livingston (who was the producer in charge of overseeing the scripts) liked my take on things. In one of the meetings a writer named Jaron Summers pitched a story about space eggs that we were going to reject, but I suggested it could be reworked. Jaron agreed to have me work on it with him, and from that came our draft of "The Child." On the strength of my work on that script, Harold insisted that I be made story editor. It was that promotion that truly turned me from a wannabe into a professional.

Soon I had another, much bigger, office down the hall and my very first secretary, Rosanna—who later married one of my best friends. Now, here I was, giving notes and suggestions to the likes of Richard Bach and Ted Sturgeon—men whose work I respected beyond measure. I was in the thick of it. Some old friends of Harold's who came to pitch stories started to call me the "hatchet man" because I would apply "Star Trek logic" so relentlessly that they couldn't make their stories work for our universe. (I'm still at this. Last year on "Sliders" I was known as "the logic Nazi" for kicking up a fuss every time a story violated the logic of its own setup.) These were very heady times for me and they disappeared all too soon.

The decision to turn our two-hour pilot into Star Trek: The Motion Picture was a disappointment to me, but not a major one. Gene assured me there'd be a job for me on the feature, and I hung around as an unofficial "production coordinator" while the studio sorted out what size feature we'd be making and who would be directing it. Not long after he arrived, Robert Wise grew to appreciate my work and I wound up as Associate Producer on the feature (and got to move back into "my" office for the duration). I was fully caught up in the excitement of making a really big movie and didn't look back all that much at the work we'd done on *Phase II*.

In retrospect, I wish we'd had a chance to make at least some of the episodes we were working on. I believe several of them would have ranked with the best of other renditions of *Star Trek*. Richard Bach's "Practice in Waking" surely would have been a classic. John Meredyth Lucas's "The Kitumba" was a wonderful adventure inside the heart of the Klingon Empire. And perhaps this is just writer's ego, but I believe the version of "The Child" that Jaron and I wrote is far superior to the one that ultimately emerged on *Star Trek: The Next Generation*. You will have the opportunity to judge for yourself, as our script is reprinted in this book.

Star Trek Phase II endures in my life today in the most meaningful and personal of ways. The first woman to speak English in *Star Trek: The Motion Picture* is Michele Billy. We met during *Star Trek Phase II,* and she is now my wife. We have two boys, Andrew and Sean. Until Andrew was about four, he believed that when I left for work in the morning I was going on board the *Starship Enterprise.* His mother's character was killed off after about ten minutes of the film. He's now almost eight, but he still won't watch her die.

It's said that the fans would not let *Star Trek* die. Gar and Judy (the authors of this book) theorize that, had the show not learned to reinvent itself, *Star Trek* might very well have died as its original fans aged and moved on to other interests. They believe that *Star Trek Phase II* was the beginning of the reinvention process, and as such was as vital to all the *Star Trek* incarnations that followed as the original series.

I cannot help being flattered by their premise. As all *Star Trek* fans know, history cannot be changed, so we will never know whether *Star Trek* could have gone forward and prospered in the absence of *Star Trek Phase II.* I can only know that for me, it truly was the beginning of all that is meaningful in my life today, and I will eternally be grateful to it for that.

Star Trek's Missing Chapter

We are confident in stating that more has been written about *Star Trek* than any other television series.

Which raises the inevitable question: Why write *another* book?

For us, there are three good answers.

The first is to further our understanding of the process and medium of television. Our behind-the-scenes association with *Star Trek* has afforded us a tremendous learning opportunity, exposing us to production details rarely glimpsed by those not directly involved in the ongoing life of a series. For all that the *content* of *Star Trek* is unique to television, the framework in which it is made is basically the same for all series. All students of television can find in this book truisms that broadly apply to the industry itself.

The second reason for writing this book is to give credit to those artists, craftspeople, and technicians who have been too long overlooked.

Though it is said so often that we hesitate to say it again, television is a collaborative process. Yet too many times the pivotal contributions of the many are subsumed into the overwhelming onscreen credit of the few. *Star Trek* has had many parents. Given the franchise's unprecedented success and cultural importance, we strongly feel that all of those who contributed to its ongoing creation should receive the credit that is due them.

And third, especially in the case of this book, there is even now still more of the story to be told.

Star Trek Phase II has long been a missing chapter in the history of the *Star Trek* phenomenon. It has been the subject of at least one earlier book, been touched upon in several others, and been discussed in articles in both fan and professional publications. But all of these earlier efforts have been little more than reports by those who have glimpsed the records of the past. Never before have we had the opportunity to actually see these

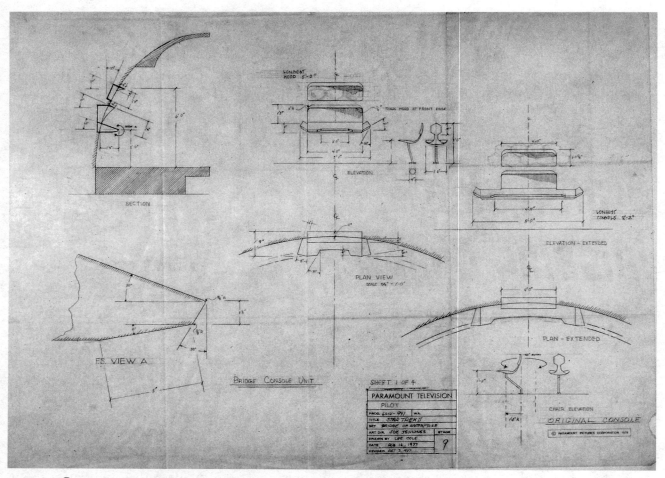

Ⓐ glimpse of the new bridge that would take shape on Stage 9. Courtesy of Paramount Pictures.

treasures for ourselves—from the actual early production scripts included in these pages, to the concept art, blueprints, and even images from never-before-seen test footage shot on the *Phase II* sets while they were still under construction. Only the unprecedented access to the Paramount lot graciously extended to us by Rick Berman and the selfless efforts of Paramount employees and others off the lot who support our work have made these new discoveries and their publication possible.

This book also benefits from the passage of time. Some of the participants in the *Phase II* story have reached stages in their careers where the traditional gloss and logrolling of Hollywood is no longer a guiding, and self-censoring, concern. Where interviews given in the past may have skipped over key events to focus on pleasantries, today the entire story can be told. That is not to say there are scandals and terrible secrets waiting in these pages, but there is a level of candor that has been missing in the past, which helps fill in the curious blanks left by other works, especially in the matter of exactly when the decision was made to change the proposed television series, *Star Trek Phase II,* into *Star Trek: The Motion Picture.*

With much that is new to be told about *Phase II,* we have tried wherever possible not to dwell upon what has been said before.

For the origins of *Star Trek: The Original Series,* we direct you to Stephen Whitfield's *The Making of Star Trek,* first published when the series was in production, and the recent *Inside Star Trek: The Real*

Story, by Herbert F. Solow and Robert H. Justman. As companion pieces, there is little that they do not reveal about television production in general, and the birth of *Star Trek* in particular.

For details on the careers of *Star Trek's* key figures, including Gene Roddenberry and the original cast, during the eight-year interregnum between the original series' cancellation, through the several false-start movies, until the announcement of *Phase II* in June of 1977, we recommend the numerous published biographies available for all. If they are read together, blending the various slants of their viewpoints, a balanced picture can be obtained of the personalities involved in the stop-and-go early stages of *Star Trek's* rebirth.

The long-held inaccuracies in accounts of Harlan Ellison's involvement with a possible story for an early *Star Trek* feature are dealt with in the writer's own book, *The City on the Edge of Forever,* in which he details the writing of one of *Star Trek's* most popular episodes.

As to the events that followed the cancellation of *Phase II,* when the initially troubled and confused production of *Star Trek: The Motion Picture* began, and subsequently succeeded beyond all reason in triggering the resurgence of what would become the most successful science-fiction franchise of all time, they are beyond the scope of this book, and must be saved for another day, and another volume.

There is one additional reason for writing this book, something that occurred to us only after we had digested the sum total of the interviews we had conducted and the memos and scripts we had read. It has to do with the precariousness of ideas in Hollywood.

Star Trek is, without question, a staggering success.

Yet in the course of researching this book, it became clear to us that despite the dedication and talent of the team assembled to produce *Phase II,* had the series actually aired in the spring of 1978, *Star Trek,* as a franchise and a phenomenon, might have died.

There would have been no movies, no *Star Trek: The Next Generation,* no *Star Trek: Deep Space Nine, Star Trek: Voyager,* or whatever other *Star Trek* incarnations are in our future.

We have a simple reason for this conclusion, one that emerges from the complexity of the story that's about to unfold. Study the blueprints, read the scripts and the stories, and then see whether you agree with us.

Like Dr. McCoy traveling back in time to the 1930s, or the Borg to the time of Zefram Cochrane, it's a glimpse of what might have been, one that helps tell us how *Star Trek* survived against the odds to celebrate its thirtieth anniversary, with bright prospects for many more celebrations to come.

Part one

The Road Not Taken

After the Party's Over

Just in case anyone doesn't know this part of the story, *Star Trek* was a failure before it was ever a success, and in the network's eyes, not a particularly noble one.

The series had debuted on NBC in September of 1966 to mediocre reviews and ratings. It had been renewed for a second season only with the help of an unprecedented write-in campaign that confused the network's understanding of the show's audience. In its third season, *Star Trek* had its budget slashed and was relegated to the deepest circle of prime-time Hell—Fridays at 10:00. For the young audience *Star Trek* had been suspected of reaching, that scheduling decision by NBC was the equivalent of putting the series on an ice floe and waiting for it to be devoured by polar bears.

In that last season, *Star Trek*'s fate was so obvious that even the show's creator distanced himself from the production. To no one's surprise, ratings continued to drop. The cancellation decision, when it came, was almost anticlimactic. With the end of *Star Trek*—and the renewal of *Land of the Giants* on ABC—the great experiment of trying to bring thoughtful science fiction to the television audience was over. *Star Trek* was consigned to the same electronic netherworld that had claimed most of the other series cancelled that same year, among them Darrin McGavin's *The Outsider*, Robert Morse's *That's Life,* Don Murray's and Otis Young's *The Outcasts,* and Peter Kastner's *The Ugliest Girl in Town*—all shows of which we have never heard again. *Star Trek* was dead, Jim.

As dead as Scotty in "The Changeling."

As dead as Dr. McCoy in "Shore Leave."

As dead as Captain Kirk in "Amok Time."

Which is to say, in the world of science fiction, the word "dead" doesn't necessarily mean what it does in real life.

What happened next has been elevated to television folklore.

The year after NBC cancelled *Star Trek,* the A. C. Nielsen company began providing ratings not just in terms of how *many* people were watching a given show, but in terms of *who* was watching— *demographics.* This was important information for advertisers because it enabled them to target their advertising to their most likely customers. Why advertise station wagons on shows watched mainly by teenage boys?

As NBC executives told Gene Roddenberry at the time, if *Star Trek* had been rated by demographics and not numbers, it would not have been cancelled. True, the series didn't have the biggest audience, but to advertisers its young-adult viewers were the cream of an eagerly sought market.

The importance of *Star Trek*'s demographic appeal was demonstrated when the series went into syndication on the small, independent Kaiser Broadcasting stations. The schedulers at Kaiser guessed that young males were not interested in watching network newscasts, and so scheduled *Star Trek* episodes to run at six o'clock every weekday.

The ratings success of these repeat showings attracted the attention of programmers at other independent stations. Just as the NBC executives had learned too late, there *was* a strong *Star Trek* audience, and it was growing.

The folklore of *Star Trek*'s resurgence holds that a critical stage was reached at the first *Star Trek* convention in January, 1972, at the New York Statler-Hilton Hotel. At the time, *Star Trek* was being broadcast in more than a hundred local markets in the United States, and in seventy overseas. The convention organizers expected about six hundred people to spend a weekend watching episode films and listening to presentations by Gene Roddenberry and others connected with the show.

Of the six hundred expected, almost *three thousand* arrived.

According to Joan Winston, one of the convention's organizers, among the attendees were representatives from NBC who declined to identify themselves and quickly left so as not to incur the wrath of the fans.

But what they saw during their brief visit obviously had an effect. By March, 1972, Gene Roddenberry was mentioning in his correspondence possible deals for a *Star Trek* feature film, and for reviving the series on NBC.

The first in a long line of dominoes had been tipped.

A market for *Star Trek* existed. Where there was a market, money could be made. The only question was, how could the studios and the networks reach that market?

To borrow a phrase from another high point of television history, *Star Trek* wasn't dead.

It was only resting.

This bold new look for the *U.S.S. Enterprise* of the 1970s was developed by illustrator Ralph McQuarrie for art director Ken Adam during the preproduction phase of *Star Trek: Planet of Titans*. The concept model shown in the photograph became part of *Star Trek* canon when it made a brief appearance as one of the destroyed Starfleet vessels at Wolf 359 in the *Star Trek: The Next Generation* episode, "The Best of Both Worlds, Part I." Sketches by Ken Adam. Photograph by Robbie Robinson. All illustrations courtesy of Paramount Pictures.

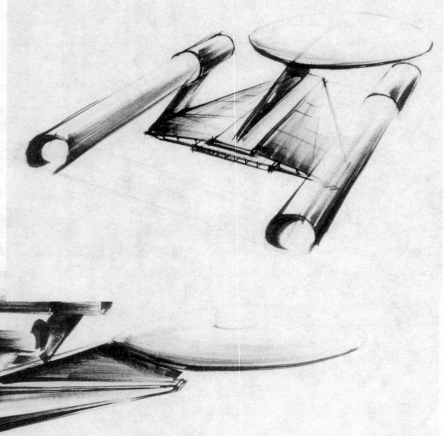

False Starts

In the world of television, producers are lightning rods, channeling the flashes of brilliance from the storm of creativity that roils around them.

In the beginning, Gene Roddenberry had written a 24-page document, called a "bible," in which he had created the spine of what *Star Trek* would become. When NBC ordered a pilot episode of the proposed new series, Roddenberry became its first producer. In time, the creative storm that gathered around him included Co-Producer Robert H. Justman, Art Director Matt Jefferies, Costume Designer William Ware Theiss, and a stable of some of the best television and science-fiction writers of the day, including Jerome Bixby, John D. F. Black, Robert Bloch, Gene L. Coon, Harlan Ellison, Dorothy Fontana, Richard Matheson, Sam Peeples, Paul Schneider, Norman Spinrad, and Theodore Sturgeon.

From the look of the *Star Trek* universe and the words and stories of the scripts, the actors then brought their characters to life, adding depth and nuance that fed back into the writing process. Directors such as Marc Daniels and Joseph Pevney helped focus this broad spectrum of creative effort in some of the series' most memorable episodes.

Flush with the talents of so many creative contributors, *Star Trek* became the series that attracted its important, dedicated, and youthful audience. And with its cancellation, those talents dispersed like windswept clouds, drifting away to other projects and pursuits.

Yet Paramount, the studio that had purchased *Star Trek*'s originating studio, Desilu, and with it the rights to the series, wished to recapture that creative storm in order to recapture the audience it had attracted.

So the first person they went to was the lightning rod, Gene Roddenberry, and they asked him to recreate the magic of what dozens of people had originally brought to life.

During three years of on-and-off-again negotiations and discussions, a third party became involved in the efforts to revive *Star Trek*—Filmation Associates, an animation company. With no sets to rebuild, no costumes to make, no stage rentals or special effects to pay for, *Star Trek: The Animated Series* proved much easier to get into production. The Saturday-morning series debuted on NBC in September 1973, exactly seven years after the *Original Series* had first appeared. Twenty-two episodes were made, it won an Emmy for children's programming, and it ended its run in October of 1974.

In the mid-seventies, children's television animation was an impoverished medium in which cost cutting was sought above all else. Unfortunately, the animated *Star Trek* did not escape the stultifying conditions under which it was made, and unlike the originals, the animated episodes do not stand out as television at its finest. Even Roddenberry discounted them in later years, never accepting them as "real" *Star Trek,* and he claimed he would never have allowed their production if he had known *Star Trek* would return.

In May of 1975, seven months after the cancellation of the animated series, Roddenberry at last moved back into his old office on the Paramount lot to begin writing a *Star Trek* movie script, tentatively titled *The God Thing.* The start date for principal photography was reported as July 15, 1976 (later moved to January, 1977). The budget was estimated at $5 million. Paramount was gearing up for *Star Trek's* return. All the studio needed was a script.

And therein lay the problem. In *The God Thing*, the crew of the *Enterprise* have returned from their original five-year mission, been promoted, and taken on other assignments in Starfleet. When Earth is threatened by an unknown force, Admiral Kirk reassembles his crew, which includes retrieving Spock from Vulcan, and goes into space to confront the force.

The force, by the way, is—or might be—God. Though all of these story elements eventually appeared in future iterations of *Star Trek,* at the time, and in the way Roddenberry had presented them, the story was not what Paramount was looking for. Science-fiction films in which the nature and existence of God was questioned was not perceived to translate into substantial box office earnings.

By August 1975, Paramount's President, Barry Diller, had rejected Roddenberry's treatment. Roddenberry was invited to keep his office, but his development deal had ended. *Star Trek* was once again in limbo.

But even as Roddenberry continued on with developing other projects, he invited his young assistant, Jon Povill, to write a treatment. Roddenberry rejected Povill's story at first, then six months later began collaborating with him on a revised version. This story was a time-travel tale, involving an alternate timeline created when Scotty introduces advanced technology and computers to the Earth in 1937. This results in a future in which humans are enslaved by a central computer, and in which the Federation and Starfleet never existed. The *Enterprise* must travel back in time to find Scotty, and then try to undo what he has done. In the end, Kirk and the others are aided by a "plasma entity" that is really an advanced stage of humanity from the alternate timeline.

At the same time, Roddenberry also invited others to try their hands at developing an appropriate *Star Trek* feature story. Two writers were even paid to write stories—John D. F. Black and Robert Silverberg.

Black had been a story consultant and associate producer of the original series, and had written the first-season episode, "The Naked Time." His new story of the *Enterprise* trying to save the universe from being destroyed by a black hole was not, according to Paramount executives, "big enough." Robert Silverberg's story had the *Enterprise* battling aliens over possession of the ruins of an ancient, advanced civilization. It, too, was declined, though each writer was paid $10,000 for his work. Eventually, these fees were charged against the cost of *Star Trek: The Motion Picture*.

Noted science-fiction writer Harlan Ellison pitched a story to Roddenberry and Paramount that pitted the crew of the *Enterprise* against reptilian aliens who traveled back in time on Earth to change history so that humans did not become the planet's dominant lifeform. Paramount declined the pitch, but in later years approached Ellison about writing *Star Trek II: The Wrath of Khan*, *Star Trek IV: The Voyage Home*, and *Star Trek V: The Final Frontier*.

Other science-fiction writers who, in the words of Roddenberry's longtime assistant, Susan Sackett, had "their brains picked" by Paramount included Ray Bradbury and Theodore Sturgeon.

While Paramount and Roddenberry continued the search for the perfect vehicle for *Star Trek*'s return, a vehicle of a different sort made the news.

The space shuttle.

The first shuttle built was destined never to fly in space—it was an atmospheric flight-test model, originally to be christened the *Constitution*. But that didn't stop thousands of *Star Trek* fans from launching another write-in campaign, this time directing their letters to the White House.

When this first shuttle was rolled out on September 17, 1976, it carried a new name: *Enterprise*.

And at the same time, riding the groundswell of renewed public attention, the first *Star Trek* motion picture was officially in development at Paramount—*Star Trek: Planet of Titans*.

Since few people have ever heard of *Star Trek: Planet of Titans*, the end result of the movie's development should be no surprise. But for nine months in 1976 and 1977, it was a near certainty that *Star Trek* would soon appear in movie theaters around the world.

The key to this particular attempt at bringing *Star Trek* to the big screen was the same as that for *Star Trek II: The Wrath of Khan*: producing the movie as inexpensively as was practical.

In the case of *Planet of Titans*, these cost savings were to be realized by making the film in England. To that end, in July 1976, Jerry Isenberg was assigned as Executive Producer of the film, and the British writing team of Chris Bryant and Allan Scott were hired to write the script.

Bryant and Scott had written two earlier films, *Joseph Andrews*, a *Tom Jones*-type comedy made in 1977, and Nicolas Roeg's classic 1973 horror thriller, *Don't Look Now*, based on a story by Daphne du Maurier.

In September of 1976, the writers began work on the treatment—a fifteen- to twenty-page prose description of the movie's story, broken into key scenes. On October 6, Paramount executives accepted the treatment and gave the team the go-ahead to begin writing the script.

About this time, *Planet of the Titans* was initially budgeted at $7.5 million. Philip Kaufman, at the time director of *The Great Northfield Minnesota Raid* and *The White Dawn*, was hired to direct. Ken Adam, who had won an Academy Award in 1975 for the art direction of *Barry Lyndon*, was hired as the production designer. Adam, who had also been responsible for the sweeping technological sets of the James Bond films, including *Dr. No*, *Goldfinger*, and *Thunderball*, hired noted illustrator Ralph McQuarrie to help redesign the *Enterprise*. McQuarrie, who had just wrapped his work on the still-to-be-released *Star Wars*, brought to the new *Enterprise* a look similar to Darth Vader's star destroyers.

As the movie began acquiring a life of its own, Bryant's and Scott's scriptwriting task was made more difficult by the fact that Paramount no longer had a deal with William Shatner to star in the project. Thus, the first versions of the Bryant and Scott story were written without the character of Captain Kirk. Then, while the writing process was still underway, Shatner and Paramount did come to terms and Kirk had to be added to the mix.

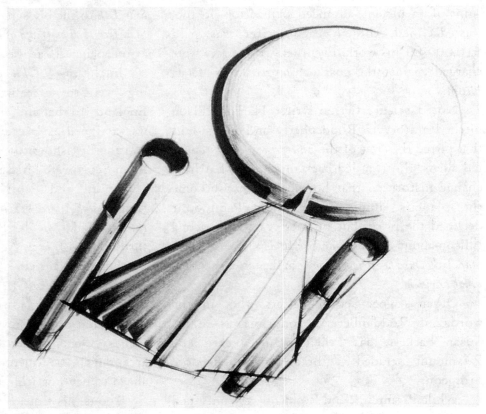

Other possibilities for a 1970s *U.S.S. Enterprise,* based on Ralph McQuarrie designs. Sketches by Ken Adam. Courtesy of Paramount Pictures.

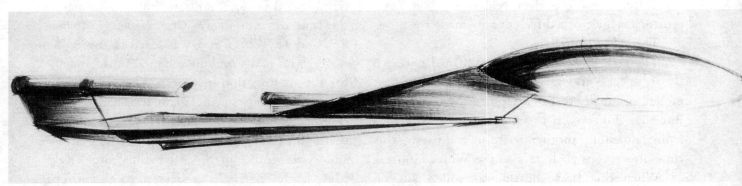

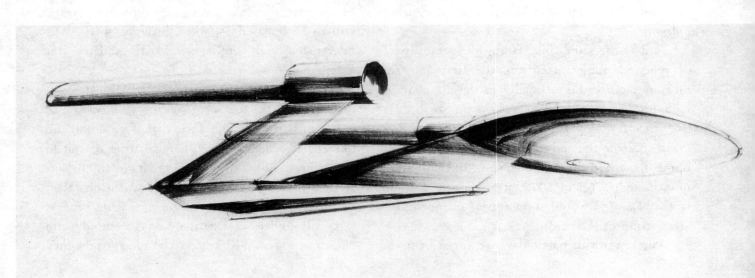

In its broad outlines, the Bryant and Scott script touched on many familiar story elements from *Star Trek.* Starfleet and the Klingons are in competition for a mysterious planet that might be the home of the Titans. As in Robert Silverberg's story, the Titans are legendary—an ancient, though technologically advanced, race that is thought to be extinct.

At the height of the conflict, during which the planet is being pulled into a black hole, further conflict arises with the planet's true inhabitants, the Cygnans, who had destroyed the Titans. To defeat the Cygnans, Kirk orders the *Enterprise* into the black hole. When the ship emerges into normal space again, it is in Earth orbit, thousands of years in the past.

In a nod to *2001: A Space Odyssey,* it is the crew of the *Enterprise* who introduce fire to the primitive humans living at the time, thus giving birth to the technological chain of events that will lead to the Federation in the future. With the abandonment of traditional cause and effect common to time-travel stories, Kirk and his crew are revealed to be the Titans of legend.

Bryant and Scott turned in their script, now including Captain Kirk, on March 1, 1977. In April, 1977, the script was rejected. Though no clear consensus exists concerning the script's potential as a film, an underlying concern for all the people involved, including the writers and director, was what, exactly, is *Star Trek?*

Phil Kaufman immediately undertook a rewrite of the Bryant and Scott script, but by May 8, 1977, his version was rejected as well, permanently. Much to Kaufman's surprise, the *Star Trek* movie, which was now budgeted at $10 million dollars, was canceled before preproduction had even begun. Fortunately for science-fiction fans,

Kaufman's next movie, the 1978 remake of *Invasion of the Body Snatchers,* fared much better.

But why was *Planet of the Titans* canceled? Here, even the folklore of *Star Trek* begins to get murky, though most people agree that the inciting incident was *Star Wars.*

Where *Star Trek* had had a slow build to success, *Star Wars* hit like a colliding asteroid. According to some, when Paramount President and Chief Operating Officer Michael Eisner saw the box-office response to the May opening of *Star Wars,* a film that had come out of nowhere, he smacked his head and said, "That could have been us!"

But with a logic no Vulcan would ever be guilty of following, Paramount executives decided that the success of *Star Wars* was a fluke. True, a large science-fiction film audience *had* existed. But now, each of them had spent their money and seen a science-fiction film, and their appetite had been sated. After *Star Wars,* the argument went, who'd want to see a *Star Trek* film?

Then came inciting incident number two.

Close Encounters of the Third Kind.

That movie's equally phenomenal acceptance by moviegoers finally confirmed for Paramount that the current market for quality science-fiction films was not a one-time affair—it was a legitimate, ongoing market. And Paramount had been poised for years with one of the most popular science-fiction vehicles around, even though they had had no idea what to do with it.

Until now.

Thus it came to pass that *Star Trek* was finally coming back for real, and in a way that no one had ever imagined.

Or, at least, that was the plan.

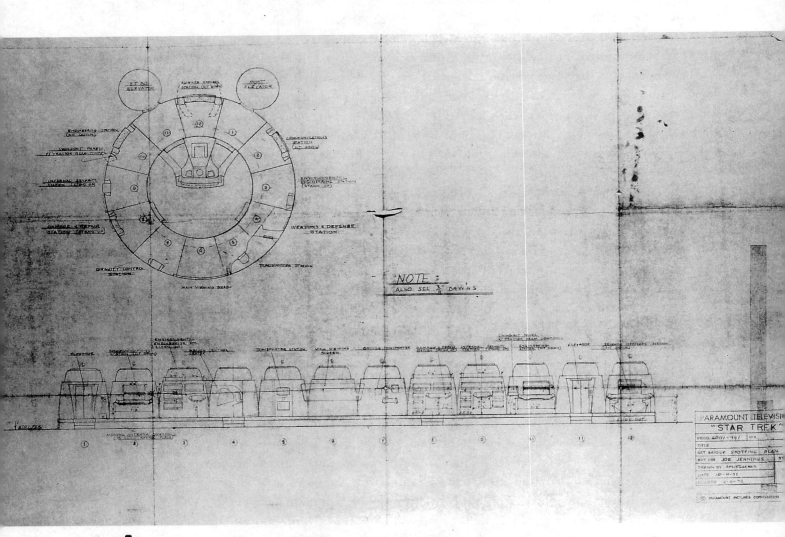

One highlight of the bridge redesign for *Phase II* was the inclusion of *two* turbolifts. However, Gene Roddenberry earlier had made the twin turbolifts part of the bridge in *Star Trek: The Animated Series* in response to viewers' questions about what would happen if one of the lifts stopped working. Courtesy of Paramount Pictures.

We're Back

The official announcement was made on June 10, 1977, six months before *Close Encounters of the Third Kind* was even released.

Paramount's Chairman and CEO, Barry Diller; its President and Chief Operating Officer, Michael Eisner; and Diller's assistant, Jeffrey Katzenberg, called a press conference at which the plans for Paramount's fourth television network were revealed.

Truth be told, it wasn't going to be a *real* network. Not at first. But in its initial year, a collection of independent stations across the country, made stronger by Paramount's recent purchase of the stations forming the Hughes Network, would band together and broadcast the same programming at the same time on the same night. Years later, the fledgling Fox, UPN, and WBN networks would adopt the same strategy, starting out with only a few nights a week, gradually adding to their schedules until all seven nights were filled.

To a studio like Paramount (and 20th Century–Fox, and Warner Bros.), the advantage was clear: They were eliminating the middleman.

As a content provider to the other networks, Paramount would produce a series; license it to NBC, say, typically at a loss; and then watch as NBC in turn sold the series to advertisers at a higher price. Only when, and *if,* the series went to syndication would the studio have a chance to earn extra money from its product.

But, in the case of licensing a Paramount-produced series to a Paramount-owned network, one division of the company would be selling to another, so all the added value and increased income would stay in the family. That offered the heady possibility that a series could at least break even, without the long wait until syndication.

And syndication could be a never-ending stream of income, as Paramount's "seventy-nine jewels" proved year after year. The seventy-nine jewels were, of course, the seventy-nine original episodes of *Star Trek*. Which brings us to the second part of that June press conference.

In 1977, unlike the mid-sixties, demographics ruled the quest for ratings and advertiser support. If a network could guarantee a young male audience, ages eighteen to thirty-four, advertisers would line up to pay a premium for the chance to show commercials to them.

The demographics of the syndicated *Star Trek* episodes proved that *Star Trek* could deliver that all important slice of the television audience.

Therefore, an all-new series of *Star Trek* episodes would anchor the new Paramount network.

Star Trek Phase II was officially a go.

A two-hour *Star Trek* television movie would lead the way in February, 1978, to be followed each week by a brand-new one-hour episode, airing between 8 and 9. The 9-to-11 time slot would then be filled by an original, made-for-television Paramount movie—*thirty* of them in the first year—augmented as necessary by classic films from the Paramount library of hits.

Hollywood's reaction to all this was mostly one of curiosity. The *idea* of a studio owning its own network made sense, but in 1977 it was hard to imagine how *anyone* could stand up to the Big Three networks.

The advertisers, ever eager for a new way to reach their market, reacted favorably, and asked to be convinced that the scheme would work.

And Gene Roddenberry was ecstatic.

After five years of go-nowhere talks and false-start movies, all the pieces were at last in place. Now it was time for Roddenberry to be *Star Trek*'s lightning rod again, and gather his team around him.

Some of the team was already in place. At the very top of the organizational ladder was the executive in charge of day-to-day development of projects for the new Paramount network—Gary Nardino. As the then President of Television Production, Nardino has often been mentioned as the person behind the formation of the network. But Nardino himself confirms it was Michael Eisner and Barry Diller who had made the decision to form a Paramount network prior to his arrival at the studio. "Those two gentlemen had begun planning the Paramount network before I even arrived."

The new *Star Trek* was only one of Nardino's responsibilities. Diller and Eisner had recently purchased the dramatic rights to Herman Wouk's *The Winds of War*, as well as to James Clavell's *Shogun*. In addition to overseeing *Phase II*, Nardino had to ensure that both those miniseries began the long process of development. At the same time, Nardino also oversaw the continuing production of Paramount's existing television product, including the hit series *Happy Days* and *Laverne and Shirley*.

But despite his workload, *Star Trek* had special meaning for Nardino. More than ten years earlier, he had been an agent with the Ashley-Famous agency. Until 1964, agencies had represented only "talent"—writers, actors, directors, and other individuals who worked in the entertainment industry. But just about the time Gene Roddenberry was getting a development deal to write a pilot script for his "*Wagon Train* to the stars" idea, Ashley-Famous took on the task of representing the Desilu studio for its sales of series to the networks. A year later, one of those series turned out to be *Star Trek,* and Gary Nardino remembers "cold afternoons of walking up and down Madison Avenue with Gene Roddenberry and a *Star Trek* presentation, showing it to advertisers to get their support to persuade NBC to put the show on the air."

Nardino and Roddenberry had kept up their friendship, "and over the years we both enjoyed many afternoons of bad golf together at the Bel-Air country club."

So when Nardino showed up as the studio executive in charge of the new *Star Trek* series, he didn't see his assignment as work. "It was fun. Gene and I had a lot of old times to relive, and we spent quite a lot of time together through the process."

As Nardino describes Roddenberry's reaction to *Star Trek*'s rebirth, "Gene was thrilled with the progression of everything because *Star Trek* was his vision of what the world *should* be like, and that's what he always tried to maintain." Nardino, like Roddenberry, had great hopes for the new series, especially because of the improvements in filmmaking technology since the days of the *Original Series*. "People can criticize the rather primitive production values—in the sense of today's productions—for the first series, but what the shows projected was a way of life, and the philosophy that it *can* be a better world if people will only allow it to be." Nardino looked forward to seeing the latest television technology being used to present Roddenberry's vision of the future to a growing market. "Because the hardcore millions of people who are *Star Trek* fans—that's what they look for—that philosophy. And," Nardino adds, "that's what Rick Berman does an incredible job of producing today."

Speaking of today, *Star Trek* has gone far beyond being just the tentpole of the United Paramount Network (in the form of *Star Trek: Voyager*). The entire *Star Trek* franchise, which includes the licensed publication of this book, is a well-respected and intently cared-for tentpole of the entire Paramount operation. But in 1977, that level of appreciation still hadn't been achieved by the studio.

As Nardino says, "I don't think *Star Trek* had the respect that it eventually earned, though at the time it was recognized as an asset they felt they had probably neglected.

"It was worked on. It wasn't ignored. There was suspicion that there was something of great value there. And that suspicion came awake because the figures would come out about syndicated properties, and even in those days *Star Trek* was an enormous leader in attracting male viewers in the syndication drama marketplace. That's what keyed the studio's decision to make a new series, and later a movie. They saw the power of the *Star Trek* pull out there, in the syndication of the old episodes."

Whatever else is said about it, Hollywood is a place of business, and that pull was the bottom line. Roddenberry's philosophy about the future was all well and good. Paramount was—and is—proud to present entertainment with such a positive outlook. But the most important part of the equation was that *Star Trek* made money. That is why, in Nardino's words, "*Star Trek* was absolutely the lead horse of the new network. Because the advertisers recognized the strength of *Star Trek* in the syndicated market."

So what about the other horses in the Paramount network stable—specifically, those thirty television movies that the studio was preparing to make?

In June, 1977, those movies fell under the responsibility of Robert H. Goodwin, at the time assistant to Paramount's head of television production, Arthur Fellows. Goodwin had a development deal at Paramount, meaning he was being paid to find worthwhile properties and prepare them for consideration as projects the studio should produce. When the announcement for the fourth network was made, Goodwin met with Gary Nardino and was given the job of supervising the development of all thirty slots. Going from being a producer's assistant to being a producer in charge of supervising thirty television movies was an exciting career move. (Of course, today, Goodwin is in an even more exciting position as Executive Producer of the stunningly successful *The X-Files*, a series with a core of fans as involved and dedicated as *Star Trek*'s.)

In June of 1977, Goodwin's enthusiasm for the prospect of supervising thirty television movies helped explain why he wasn't disappointed when his first planned meeting with Gene Roddenberry didn't get off to a good start. Goodwin simply didn't want to work on a series.

But Roddenberry was assembling his team, and he knew he needed a strong producer, well

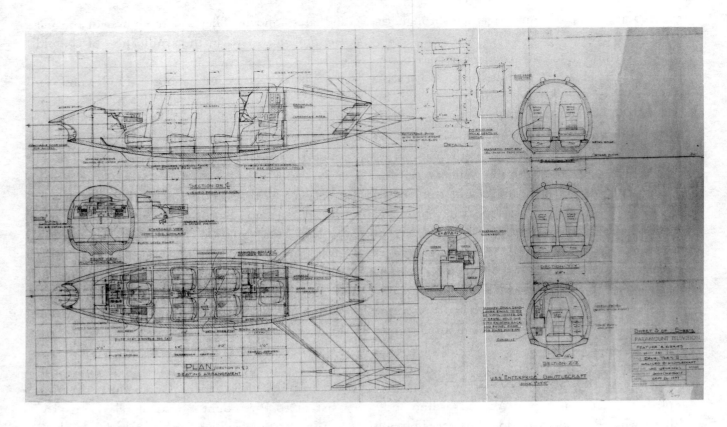

PLAN (SECTION ON Q)
SEATING ARRANGEMENT

U.S.S. 'ENTERPRISE' SHUTTLECRAFT

SHEET 3 OF SHEETS
PARAMOUNT TELEVISION
FEATURE & SERIES
TITLE STAR TREK II
SET SHUTTLECRAFT
DRAWN BY JOE JENNINGS
DATE SEPT. 27 1977

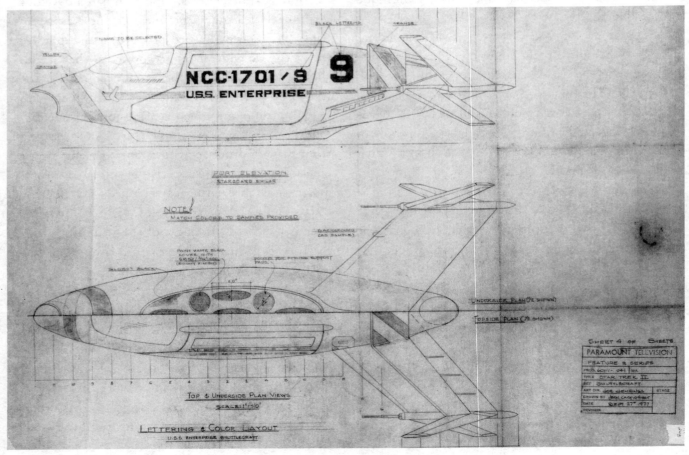

NCC-1701 / 9   9
U.S.S. ENTERPRISE

PORT ELEVATION
STARBOARD SIMILAR

NOTE!
MATCH COLORS TO SAMPLES PROVIDED

TOP & UNDERSIDE PLAN VIEWS
SCALE 1" = 1'-0"

LETTERING & COLOR LAYOUT
U.S.S. ENTERPRISE SHUTTLECRAFT

SHEET 4 OF SHEETS
PARAMOUNT TELEVISION
FEATURE & SERIES
PROD. 6041-041 WA
TITLE STAR TREK II
SET SHUTTLECRAFT
ART DIR. JOE JENNINGS
DRAWN BY DON CARRASQUILLO   STAGE
DATE SEPT 27 1977
REVISED

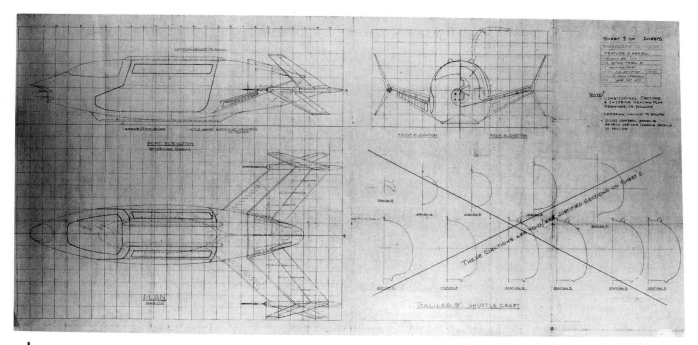

In addition to allowing him to update the *U.S.S. Enterprise,* Matt Jefferies's return to *Star Trek* gave him the opportunity to redesign the shuttlecraft. The original shuttlecraft had been provided by the AMT model company and its flat-walled design reflected the need to keep construction expenses low. Jefferies, a pilot and aviation artist, had never liked the original's nonaerodynamic appearance, and so brought a completely new look to the shuttlecraft of *Phase II.* Though this shuttlecraft was never constructed, see the color insert for an artist's concept drawing of the final vehicle. All blueprints courtesy of Lydia C. Marano, Arthur Cover, and Paramount Pictures.

versed in the technical requirements of keeping a series on track. When he heard of Goodwin's new responsibilities—which was a sign of the enormous regard Paramount held him in—Roddenberry made his decision. Goodwin would be the producer of *Phase II.*

When Goodwin heard that Roddenberry wanted to meet him, his first reaction was, "Why do *I* want to meet *him*? I'm busy." But Paramount executives insisted, and Goodwin dutifully made an appointment.

However, as Goodwin recalls, "It was such a kick because I guess Gene had forgotten to tell his assistant, Susan [Sackett], that he had this appointment. Then I show up, thirty years old, dressed in Levis, very casual, and I guess she thought I was an agent or whatever and she wouldn't let me see him.

"So I said, fine, because I really wasn't interested in working on the series, and I left.

"I remember I was all the way down this long street at Paramount, over on the west side of the lot, and I was just about to turn the corner, and there was Gene, stepping out the back door, way down at the end, yelling at me—'You! You! C'mere!' "

Goodwin laughs as he recalls Roddenberry's reaction to his nearly missing their meeting. "It was so funny. He was such a great guy about it. And in any case, he *insisted* that I produce the series. So I had to give up the movies. I had no choice."

Part of Goodwin's reluctance to work on *Phase II* stemmed from the fact that he wasn't familiar with *Star Trek*. But over the next few months, as he watched the episodes that were screened daily for the production team, he developed a keen appreciation for the series, which led to important contributions to the bible and the development of the scripts.

But Goodwin's main role was as the "producer producer." He would be responsible for all the technical aspects of the series' production. For the writing side, Roddenberry sought out a second producer—noted novelist and screenwriter Harold Livingston.

As Livingston recalls, the idea of having two producers responsible for the two halves of a television production "was, at the time, kind of an innovation, really." Usually, the executive producer would be a writer, and a production manager would handle the "nuts and bolts" of the operation.

Livingston had been an old hand at the Desilu studios. At the time the first *Star Trek* series had been in production, Livingston had written many memorable episodes of its sister show, *Mission: Impossible*. But until he came to work on the *Phase II* production, he had never seen a *Star Trek* episode, or met Gene Roddenberry.

Livingston was brought onto the project by Arthur Fellows, the same executive who had brought Robert Goodwin to the studio. On the surface, Livingston and Roddenberry seemed a good match. Both men had been pilots in the Air Force. Both men had begun writing for television in the early fifties. And both men were experienced professionals.

So much for good intentions.

Over the course of the next year and a half, the relationship between Roddenberry and Livingston would deteriorate dramatically, to the point where Livingston would quit his position on *The Motion Picture* multiple times.

Today, from the more comfortable distance of maturity reflecting upon earlier times, Livingston remembers his run-ins with Roddenberry with wry humor. Pointing out that Roddenberry was 6´4″ to his own 5´4″, Livingston recalls, "It was always masochistic on my part because I felt there was this smoldering anger building up in Gene, and I was always afraid he was going to get wild and whack me one day." But this unsettled relationship with Livingston was still in the future as the team first came together.

Another team member whom Roddenberry enlisted at this time was an old friend already working on the Paramount lot, in the office just above his own—Matt Jefferies, the Art Director of the *Original Series*, who, with input from Roddenberry and Pato Guzman, had designed the original *Starship Enterprise*.

At the time, Jefferies was Art Director for Michael Landon's hit series, *Little House on the Prairie*, and didn't want to give up that position to take a chance on a series with a mere thirteen-episode order.

However, Roddenberry was adamant that only Jefferies could update the *Enterprise*, and with Michael Landon's blessing, Jefferies became attached to *Phase II* as a "technical advisor." Landon, for his part, made it clear that the moment Jefferies's work on *Phase II* got in the way of his work on *Little House*, Jefferies would have to make a decision as to which series he was going to stay with, because he wasn't going to be able to handle two.

"Consequently," Jefferies recalls, "in updating the ship, I did the drawings at night in the Hilton at Tucson, because *Little House* was shooting on location there. But it got to the point where the phone would ring and Gene would say we're having a meeting and we need you back at Paramount. And it just got to be too much." Subsequently, as production geared up for *Phase II*, Jefferies recommended his good friend, Joe Jennings, as the new *Star Trek* art director. Jennings had been Jefferies's assistant in the second season of the *Original Series*, and later went on to distinguish himself as the art director for the miniseries *Roots* and *Shogun*.

Though no scripts had been written at that time, Roddenberry knew that whatever pilot episode was made would include the story element he had already developed for *The God Thing*—that the *Enterprise* had returned home from her first five-year mission, and in the time between the first series and *Phase II* had been refitted.

In discussing the refit, Jefferies recalls that Roddenberry simply wanted the starship "updated," and not redesigned. Indeed, Jefferies's classic design of saucer, lower hull, and twin nacelles remains fresh after more than three decades, still serving as the basis for the designs of the *Star Trek: The Next Generation* starships D and E, as well as for the *Starship Voyager.*

"Basically," Jefferies says, "what I did to it was change the power units, and make a slight change in the struts that supported them. I gave the main hull a taper, then I went flat-sided and thin with the power units, rather than keeping the cylindrical shape.

"Trying to work out the logic of the refit, I knew a lot of the equipment inside would change, but I didn't see that there would be any need to change the exterior of the saucer. Certainly, though, the engines would be a primary thing to change. Part of the theory of the ship's design in the first place was that we didn't know what these powerful things were or how devastating it would be if anything went awry, so that's why we kept them away from the crew. And that meant they could be easily changed if you had to replace one."

Though Jefferies's involvement with *Phase II* had to be curtailed so he could continue his full-time work on *Little House,* he followed through on his assignment to update the *Enterprise.* And here, another unsung hero of *Star Trek* became part of the team—modelmaker Brick Price.

Today, Price is co-owner of WonderWorks Inc., a prominent Hollywood model shop specializing in full-size mock-ups of NASA spacecraft, and renowned for its work in such features as *The Abyss* and *Apollo 13.* In 1977, Price had already established a strong reputation in the industry for building miniature cars with such detail and high-quality paint finishes that, when photographed against real settings, they were indistinguishable from full-size models.

The contract to build the new *Enterprise* was originally awarded to Don Loos, a noted model-maker who was associated with Magicam. Loos later worked for Brick Price, and Price joined him as one of the *Enterprise*'s key builders.

This was also one of the first instances of improved technology being introduced into the production of the new *Star Trek.* Where the original fourteen-foot-long model of the *Enterprise* had been built by modelmaker Richard Datin with a variety of materials—wood for the saucer, rolled aluminum sheets for the nacelles—the new *Enterprise* was made entirely from fiberglass, cast in sections from molds. The new, six-foot-long model would be lighter, stronger, and thus easier to work with. Matt Jefferies, recalling the opportunities he had to see his updated *Enterprise* under construction, recalls that Loos and Price "did a beautiful job." (A second, eighteen-inch model of the starship was also built at the time.)

At the same time Roddenberry was assembling his behind-the-scenes production team, the original actors were also being courted to appear in the new series. Most were favorably disposed to *Phase II.* Most had received "pay or play" money for the last, unmade *Star Trek* film—payments that had been guaranteed them whether the movie was made or not. And now they were being offered a pilot-plus-thirteen-episode minimum to make themselves available for the next planned production, also on a pay-or-play basis. What actor would say no?

Well, Leonard Nimoy, whose disagreements with Roddenberry are well documented, for one.

Roddenberry's first attempt to lure Nimoy to *Phase II* had Spock appearing in the pilot episode, and then in only two out of every eleven episodes to follow.

As Nimoy says, "I couldn't believe it."

Whether Roddenberry made the initial offer knowing that the actor would never accept such an insubstantial role in a series he had help bring to life, or whether Roddenberry felt Nimoy would appreciate the chance of not being tied down by a

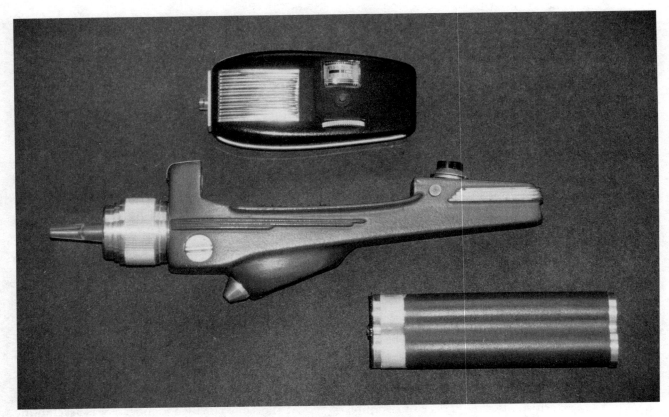

One of the meticulously constructed aluminum phasers built for the new series, based on the original design. This model features real batteries in its detachable powerpack handle that power the working strobe light on the main emitter. Photograph courtesy of Jon Povill.

full-time series commitment, is something even Nimoy doesn't know. But the actor flatly refused the offer. *Star Trek* was returning, but Spock would not.

Thus the stage was set for the creation of a new member of the *Enterprise* crew: a full-blooded Vulcan science officer named Xon, who, we shall see, was the forerunner of *The Next Generation*'s Data.

William Shatner, though he was returning as the redoubtable Captain Kirk, was the impetus for the creation of another new crew member.

Shatner's salary for the pilot and first thirteen episodes was high enough that the studio had doubts about whether the new series could continue to afford him. Shatner reports that contingency plans had been made to either have Kirk's role relegated to a series of cameos in subsequent episodes, for which he would receive smaller pay-

ments, or to have Kirk killed, in which case he would receive nothing.

To pave the way for a second starship captain to take Kirk's place, the role of Commander Will Decker was created. And just as Xon was an early version of Data, Decker was the forerunner of *The Next Generation*'s Commander Will Riker.

Within a month of the press conference announcing *Star Trek*'s return, the preproduction phase of the series had begun in earnest.

A new *Enterprise* had been designed and was being built. Art Director Joe Jennings was overseeing an Art Department that included Set Designer Lew Splittsberger, graphic artist Lee Cole, and Assistant Art Director John Cartwright. (Returning *Star Trek* artist Mike Minor would join the Art Department in August.)

Original *Star Trek* Costume Designer William

Ware Theiss had pulled out his old patterns and was digging through on- and off-lot storage areas, reclaiming costumes from ten years earlier.

Sophisticated new aluminum phasers, following the same design as the original wood and plastic ones, were being built, some with working strobe lights and detachable battery packs.

And as the story meetings with hopeful writers began, producer Harold Livingston, a newcomer to *Star Trek,* was beginning to realize how strong an asset he had in Gene Roddenberry's assistant, Jon Povill. More on this later.

By mid-July, enough preparatory work had been done that it became time to define the new series. In a memo to Robert Goodwin, dated July 15, 1977, Gene Roddenberry wrote:

Would appreciate your preparing a rough draft of new format information on STAR TREK, which we can give to writers during these early stages. This will save us having to say the same thing over and over again to every writer candidate who enters the office. This information will later be included in a new edition of the Writer's Guide.

Please send a copy of your rough draft to Livingston because I want the final information to be jointly his also. Also copies to the others listed below [*H. Livingston, M. Jefferies, J. Jennings, J. Povill, and a position that had yet to be filled—Story Editor*], so that we'll have the advantage of their input, too. I am hopeful that Matt Jefferies will be able to supply us with a fairly comprehensive list of tips to STAR TREK directors, so that the final Guide will be of value to anyone who works on the show.

Your rough draft should include some information on the new characters and also some on how we expect the original STAR TREK characters to be used this time around. Obviously, this will have to be handled generally and diplomatically.

Beyond usage of old and new characters,

here are some of the things which should be included:

We'll use the more naturalistic dialogue patterns of the 70s with sentence fragments, overlaps, etc.

The above should not be construed to mean we will use the slang expressions of the 70s. As in past episodes, STAR TREK should continue to stay away from language which will date the show. No one should ever say "right on, man," "let it all hang out," or "twenty-three skiddoo." If a writer wants colloquialisms, let him invent new ones. But otherwise, dialogue should be pretty much down the middle, semi-formal English.

Describe this being a new five-year mission.

Give as much information as we can about the new look of the ship.

Confirm which old props we'll still use, which have been changed, which have been eliminated.

Same as above on opticals and process, old and new. For example, we should specify that the old-style transporter system will still be used (although we ourselves may improve the optical a little).

Since we will be handing out copies of the original Guide for awhile, your draft should probably include any items in that original Guide which no longer apply.

This will probably be a new and interesting experience for you too, Bob. You will discover whether or not your ego is healthy enough to withstand being rewritten by everyone on the staff.

But Goodwin was obviously no newcomer to the penchant for rewriting in television. On July 19, he replied to Roddenberry's request with the following memo.

Enclosed is a copy of my rough draft for a supplement which will be given to writers along with the original STAR TREK Guide to give them some ideas of the changes in the new series.

Please confine your suggestions for changes to no more than four 3-ring binders.

Among the rough-draft suggestions made by Goodwin were the following:

The Vessel

With its modifications, the *U.S.S. Enterprise* is still the largest and most modern type vessel in the Starfleet Service. The crew is the same size—430 persons, but one third of them is not female (as before) ... now women make up half the crew.

Ship's Weaponry

The weaponry is still the banks of "ship's phasers," although refinements have increased their power. The phaser power is now emitted through the main strut of the *Enterprise,* and not from the saucer section of the vessel.

Equipment

The hand communicator has been updated to serve more functions than just communication. For one thing, it can now be attached to the tricorder to transmit information directly from a planet to the computer banks of the *Enterprise.* So now landing parties can take advantage of the vast array of analytical equipment aboard the ship.

The Viewer (no longer referred to as a Viewing Screen) is no longer a television-like screen, but is actually a holographic image formed within an oval framework in the forward section of the bridge.

Other Changes

In general, the atmosphere aboard the *Enterprise* will be much warmer and more comfortable than before—as befitting a place which will serve as home to over four hundred people. This will mean more greenery—including many exotic plants from other galaxies as well as some from earth. Also, the wardrobe of the crew will offer more variety, ranging from dress uniforms to casual, informal clothes for leisure periods.

The Crew

With the familiar faces, there will be some new, younger ones:

Ship's Commander: Intelligent, appealing, in his late twenties or early thirties. He has had thorough training and some experience in space exploration, but many situations he encounters aboard the *Enterprise* will be first-time experiences for him.

Young Vulcan: A second cousin of Mr. Spock, also half-human and half-Vulcan. In appearance he has the same yellowish complexion and Satanic pointed ears, and the same Vulcanic insistence upon hiding his emotions. He is very young, however (early twenties), and sometimes finds it hard to control his own youthful exuberance.

Yeoman: A young woman in her mid-twenties, extremely bright and well-educated, if somewhat inexperienced. She will be an attractive and charming addition to the crew on the bridge.

A week later, Roddenberry began to have second thoughts about the new female character, for now known only as "Yeoman." In a memo to Harold Livingston, he said:

The three of us should discuss whether our new female character should be YEOMAN or some other higher-ranking female officer with other duties. Simply adding a "flunky" female to the bridge may not satisfy our needs for more sexual equality.

In that comment, we see the beginning of what would become the third new character to be added to *Phase II*: the Deltan navigator, Ilia. However, unlike Xon and Decker, she was not intended to be a replacement for one of the original crew. She was to be all new. But, just like the other two, she was also destined to be the forerunner of a *The Next Generation* character—Counselor Deanna Troi.

It was also in the last week of July that the first writing deals were set for the new series. Arthur Heinemann had a pitch accepted by Harold Livingston for a story that eventually would not be developed. And on July 25, Alan Dean Foster, a young science-fiction writer who was known to Roddenberry for having adapted the animated episodes into a series of successful *Star Trek Log* books, was given a deal to write a story, with an option to write the teleplay as well. The premise he would develop was inspired, in part, by an early Roddenberry story for Roddenberry's unproduced science-fiction series, *Genesis II*.

The *Genesis II* version of the story had been called "Robot's Return."

Alan Dean Foster's version was called "In Thy Image."

And three years later, the world would recognize the story by a still different name.

Star Trek: The Motion Picture.

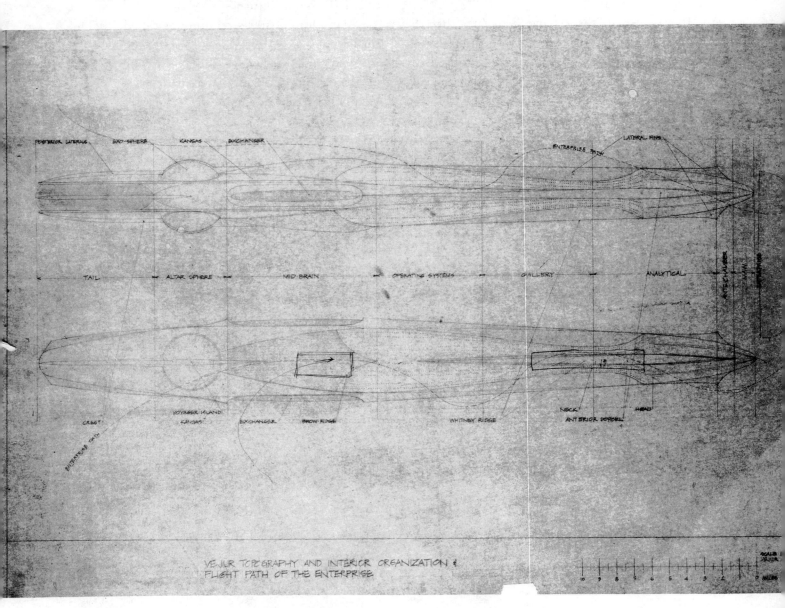

POSTERIOR LATERALS   EXO-SPHERE   KANSAS   EXCHANGER   ENTERPRISE PATH   LATERAL FINS

TAIL   ALTAR SPHERE   MID-BRAIN   OPERATING SYSTEMS   GALLERY   ANALYTICAL   ANTE-CHAMBER MAW

CREST   VOYAGER ISLAND/KANSAS   EXCHANGER   BROW RIDGE   WHITNEY RIDGE   NECK ANTERIOR DORSEL HEAD

ENTERPRISE PATH

VEJUR TOPOGRAPHY AND INTERIOR ORGANIZATION &
FLIGHT PATH OF THE ENTERPRISE

SCALE 1
VEJUR

10 9 8 7 6 5 4 3 2 1 MILES

Star Trek: The Motion Picture's central idea of a staggeringly huge alien vessel returning to Earth was part of Alan Dean Foster's "In Thy Image" story from the first-draft treatment of what was originally planned to be a regular, one-hour episode of the new series. This blueprint of an early version of V'Ger shows the planning that went into choreographing the *Enterprise*'s flight path around it. Courtesy of Paramount Pictures.

4

August

Alan Dean Foster's experiences with "In Thy Image," *Phase II,* and *Star Trek: The Motion Picture* eventually culminated in his decision to leave Los Angeles to concentrate on writing novels, not screenplays. But in 1977, he was a young and bright teacher of screenwriting at USC, eager to expand his *Star Trek* writing credits from books to scripts. Thus, less than a week after getting his story assignment directly from Roddenberry, Foster returned with his story for "In Thy Image," reprinted in Part Three of this book.

In addition to elements of "Robot's Return"—which some say has strong similarities to John Meredyth Lucas's *Original Series* episode, "The Changeling"—Foster had also incorporated Robert Goodwin's suggestion of doing something that had never been done before—threaten Earth. Except for Captain Christopher Pike's illusory visit to Mojave in "The Cage" (which was also included in the two-part episode, "The Menagerie"), twenty-third century Earth had never appeared in a *Star Trek* episode. As Foster's story made the rounds of the production team, it also became obvious that if Earth were being threatened, then it made perfect sense that the *Enterprise* was close to Earth—make that, still in Earth orbit—because . . . it was just finishing its refit!

Though several other stories were in active development by now, consensus quickly favored Foster's story as *Phase II*'s pilot episode. With revisions, of course.

A meeting was called for August 3, to be attended by Goodwin, Livingston, and Roddenberry, as well as Michael Eisner, Jeffrey Katzenberg, and Arthur Fellows.

At that meeting, Robert Goodwin pitched the "In Thy Image" story in great detail, hoping it would receive Eisner's blessing as the *Phase II* pilot.

But the meeting didn't go the way anyone connected with *Phase II* had expected.

Which brings us to the most crucial juncture of the *Phase II* story.

For five years Paramount had tried to put a *Star Trek* project into production. In 1977, they stopped production on *Planet of Titans* before it began, then announced *Phase II*. Then, as far as anyone had known up to now, in March, 1978, another press conference was held to announce that the production of *Phase II* was changing over to the production of *The Motion Picture*.

Part of the reason for writing this book was to track down exactly *when* that momentous decision had been made, and *who* had made it. After all, the whole future success of the *Star Trek* franchise grew out of that change in direction.

As it turned out, Robert Goodwin recalls, *Star Trek's* fate "shifted right at one particular instant." At the risk of being anticlimactic so early in this story, the decision was made by Michael Eisner, and he made it in that August 3 meeting.

It has been well documented that Eisner was excited by the prospects of the "In Thy Image" story. At the end of Goodwin's pitch, Goodwin recalls that Eisner said, "We've been looking for the feature for five years and this is it." Then, Goodwin continues, "Eisner slammed his hand on the table, and that was when it happened."

As it turns out, Eisner wasn't speaking figuratively.

When he said "feature," he meant *feature*.

Because in Paramount's determination, less than a month after it had been announced, *Star Trek Phase II* was already canceled. Before a single set had been built, a single script written, a single frame of film exposed.

The series' fate was not the fault of anyone involved with *Star Trek*. It came about because for more than a month Paramount had been courting advertisers for its fourth network, and no matter how they ran the numbers, the studio had determined it could not generate enough income to keep the network in operation.

By the end of July, 1977, Paramount's network had died, quietly and offstage, and it had taken *Phase II* with it.

But *Star Trek* had left behind $500,000 in expenses related to all the efforts to produce a movie, and hundreds of thousands more dollars in new pay-or-play commitments to the cast, as well as money currently being paid to the production team for their work to date. If there is anything a studio hates to do, it's to write off money already spent.

At the highest levels of Paramount, the decision had been made to salvage whatever it could from the current state of *Star Trek*. Goodwin relates that, though the series was effectively canceled as a Paramount-network show before the August 3 meeting, the executives had "decided to do the two-hour movie with the original cast and use it as a pilot, which they would auction to the three networks, trying to sell it as a series to either NBC, CBS, or ABC."

Paramount already faced the inevitable minor corporate embarrassment that would arise when it eventually would have to publicly announce that its network had collapsed. Added to that, going to the networks to sell what had been planned to be the Paramount series that would have broken the Big Three networks' dominance of American broadcasting would be a daunting prospect. It was more than possible that all three networks might decide to pass on buying the new *Star Trek* series, if only to remind Paramount who was in control. Thus, when Goodwin pitched "In Thy Image," he gave Eisner and the Paramount executives a new way out—one that would fall under Paramount's control, and bypass the networks completely.

Star Trek was going to be a feature.

The only catch was, no one in the meeting could talk about it.

As complex as a movie is, the paperwork that fuels it is more complicated still. New deals would have to be negotiated with the cast, with producers, with Gene Roddenberry himself. New budgets would have to be calculated. Paramount's sales and distribution people would have to estimate how much it would cost to advertise and market the film, and how much the studio could hope to earn.

If one piece of the puzzle didn't fit, the project might not come together. Thus, if anyone announced a new *Star Trek* feature now, and two months later the deals could not be made, Paramount would face another potentially embarrassing moment, and *Star Trek* would be perceived as a three-time loser.

So, even as Arthur Fellows cringed at the money that would continue to be spent, at that August 3 meeting the decision was made to continue the preproduction and development of *Star Trek Phase II* as a series. Business as usual would continue until all the necessary dealmaking for the feature could be completed behind the scenes to make Eisner's decision a reality.

If and when that dealmaking was concluded, then, and only then, would the public—and *Phase II*'s own production team!—be told that *Star Trek* was once again going to go where it had never gone before.

Until then, a group of dedicated, talented women and men toiled on to create a series they and millions of fans could be proud of, never knowing that the studio had little intention of making it. From the studio's point of view, the scripts might eventually prove useful if, after the movie's release, Paramount wished to return *Star Trek* to its television roots. The sets, props, and miniatures might be used in the movie itself. And certainly the "In Thy Image" pilot story would need further refinement to turn it into a feature script. But all the other work that would be done on *Phase II* was already beginning its inexorable spiral into a black hole as voracious as the one postulated by John D. F. Black.

Phase II was dead. But it would be five more months before the body stopped twitching.

One of the people not privy to the results of that August 3 meeting was Jon Povill, still officially Gene Roddenberry's assistant, though taking on more and more of the responsibilities of Story Editor.

On August 2, Povill circulated the following memo, which defined the ramifications of Roddenberry's future. Followers of *The Next Generation* will recognize that, though Povill intended these insights for *Phase II*, they also set the stage for the second *Star Trek* series, as well. Here are some excerpts.

SUBJECT: 23rd century Earth context for *Enterprise* crew members

If the optimistic vision of the future that STAR TREK traditionally depicts is to have a feeling of genuine reality, it is necessary that our characters reflect attitudes that are more highly evolved than those of normal, contemporary dramas.

… Seeing as how STAR TREK presumes that man did not destroy himself, we can expect to see some ways in which human nature no longer is quite as plagued by these negative aspects. After all, we really won't make it to the STAR TREK century if these changes don't occur.

For example:

These men and women have little interest in possession, be they things or lovers. If they do possess something it is likely to be with the attitude of an appreciative collector—ready to share with those of similar proclivities—rather than a jealously guarded hoarder.

…These people are turned on and curious about the unknown, rather than fearful of it. They expect danger. They joined Starfleet at least in part because of the challenge that uncharted space provides. They will generally hit peak operating efficiency in a crisis, rather than fold under the pressure of it.

…Normally, there would be no evidence of ego problems in our characters. They presumably were reared with more love and greater skill than most of us, and so have grown up without most of the difficulties and defensiveness that we are heir to.

Earth itself:

The lifestyles and activities of 23rd century Earth provide the social context out of which our characters are supposed to have grown. But what are they? How do people occupy their time in a world that has solved the problems of hunger, disease, war, and fear?

In our own time, we see that once people have attained a satisfactory level of material security, they begin to turn their attention to the question of personal fulfillment. Thus, we may suspect that the primary pursuits of the 23rd century are of personal growth, learning, and awareness.

... Diversity is a key. To 23rd-century humanity, diversity is welcomed as the provider of fresh stimuli from which one can learn and grow. The differences between people are sources of delight rather than threat.

... In short, Earth has become a world that is at once a playground and a living library. A place where people can feel free to experience whatever activities they want for the sake of their own chosen development as individuals. And if one's personality demands even greater stimulation than all this provides, there is always "Space, the final frontier ... " which tells us a lot about the people who crew the *Starship Enterprise*.

Gene Roddenberry always strove to base many of the technical extrapolations of *Star Trek* on the latest scientific knowledge. *Star Trek*'s appeal among the scientific community gave Roddenberry and his production team access to some of the top people in many different fields, as this memo shows. Courtesy of Jon Povill.

INTER-COMMUNICATION

TO: MARK TANZ

FROM: GENE RODDENBERRY

DATE: AUGUST 8, 1977

SUBJECT: VIEWING SCREEN EXPERTS

Dr. Marvin Minsky of M.I.T. Artificial Intelligence Laboratory has been a principal contact of ours in areas of computer read-out systems. He was enthusiastic about our series and our return to television and can be counted on to be helpful. His wife Gloria is a medical expert and is already doing some thinking for us on what types of equipment we might see in our futuristic sickbay.

Dr. Minsky suggests we might want to talk to Nicholas Negroponte, also at M.I.T., about 1000 line monitors which he uses in color graphics there and which is commercially available.

Minsky also recommends we get in touch with Alan Kay of PARC (Palo Alto Research Center) in Palo Alto, Calif. Kay is an expert on computer graphics, read-out systems and many other exciting uses of computers. If he is friendly and interested in our problems, you should probably consider a trip up there when you've acquired enough information here to be able to ask him the right questions.

In both cases above, Dr. Marvin Minsky allows us to use his name as a reference.

Gene Roddenberry

GR:ss

cc: Harold Livingston
    Bob Goodwin
    Matt Jefferies
    Joe Jennings
    Jim Rugg
    Jon Povill

INTER-COMMUNICATION

TO: GENE RODDENBERRY

FROM: BOB GOODWIN

DATE: 9th August 1977

SUBJECT: Production Status Report

SET CONSTRUCTION

Work is continuing on stage 9 with construction of the Enterprise set. All frames and platforms have been built for the bridge. The plaster mold is almost complete and on Monday we will start casting the plastic skins. There are 12 sections. We will cast 12 skins plus 6 extras. By tomorrow we will have a lay-out on the stage floor for the corridor and by the beginning of next week we will start framing and constructing the corridor walls. Joe Jennings has worked out most of the design problems of the engineering room and has started working on drawings which will be ready for you to see by the end of the week. Having turned over the engineering room to John Cartwright, Joe is now beginning design work on other rooms, the transporter room, recreation room, medical complex etc.

The plan now for stage 8, which will be used as the planet set is to put in the ground row and the backing, but to leave the dirt out until we see if we need that stage space for any extra sets that might be needed for our first show.

CONSOLES & INSTRUMENTATION

Joe now has drawings of the weapons defense station, which are ready for you to see. Once he gets your approval, he will put working drawings out and we can start construction on that particular station. By Thursday he will have several sketches of proposals for the consoles on the other stations.

Mark Tanz, along with Jim Rugg is doing research into various computers and instrument panels etc., which can be used in conjunction with these consoles.

SKETCH ARTIST

We have interviewed Bob McCall, a well-known artist who's worked extensively for NASA. This afternoon we'll be interviewing Mike Minor as two possible candidates for sketch artists to be brought in to work on concepts for the orbital space dock and the 70 km space ship, which will be used in our first two hour show. Whomever we hire will work

One of the first production status reports from producer Robert Goodwin, who is now Executive Producer of the hit science-fiction series, *The X-Files.* Courtesy of Jon Povill.

under the auspices of Joe Jennings, but specifically on those elements that would be going into the two-hour, in order to free Joe to concentrate the work for our on-going sets.

OPTICALS

We have been in discussion with Richard Roberts, who is an expert in the use of an analog computer. Possibly, we can use his services to create computer-type readouts for graphic displays for our bridge and other parts of the Enterprise. At the moment we have to look into the economic feasibility of the use of such a computer, and the advantages and disadvantages in terms of weekly on-going production.

Although our production department is making every effort to secure qualified help, the man-power situation is still extremely difficult. We are still trying to find another set designer. Hopefully, we will be able to secure one in the next day or two.

RWG/hb
cc: Michael Eisner
    Arthur Fellows
    Terry Keegan
    Harold Livingston
    Gary Nardino
    Jon Povill ✓
    Bob Rosenbaum
    Susan Sackett

As work proceeded on the already unofficially canceled series, Gene Roddenberry focused his attention on the "In Thy Image" story. His first notes to Alan Dean Foster were written on August 9. Among them were these comments, which show Roddenberry's concern for remaining true to *Star Trek*'s characters and setting.

...near the beginning of your outline, we reach a point where they have determined that the thing rushing toward Earth is <u>not</u> the nickel-iron of most meteors, but rather is a complex of different chemical combinations hinting at refining techniques. Nevertheless, you have Kirk ordering the photon torpedoes readied for a massive barrage. True, you never use that massive barrage, but even having Kirk ready is really out of character for our captain and ship. Our captain is simply not going to blast an unknown object containing complex chemical combinations hinting at refining techniques. He wouldn't blast it even if it looked like a meteor. At the first hint that it contains refined chemical combinations, Kirk would order the *Enterprise* to parallel its course while the ship's sensors thoroughly investigated the mysterious stranger.

Or, if the mysterious object was so near to Earth that a photon barrage was absolutely necessary, Kirk would be going through enormous personal torment at having to blast it before investigating it thoroughly. If that were our direction, the personal torment would be our principal story excitement at the time.

Any approved STAR TREK story would also require that some attention be given to whether or not the ship's <u>tractor beams</u> could pull something of that size out of its Earth trajectory. About the last thing our people would do is blast <u>anything</u> out of existence. Our optimistic view of the future presupposes that our heroes of the future believe that there is a certain ecological sanctity in all things, even big dumb old meteoroids.

...Somewhere in our story, it seems Kirk will have to learn something about the machine lifeform. Is it possible that Kirk and others could beam themselves into the alien ship lifeform without that alien being aware of it? Being unacquainted with organic lifeforms, it may never have found it necessary to build up a protection from being "invaded" in this way.

...It would be highly exciting if part of our contest could be the typical top-quality human (Kirk) versus a typical top-quality lifeform machine. Kirk is the product of the history of humanity; the alien ship is the product of the history of its machine race. A fascinating contest.

Roddenberry's notes also pick up on one story problem that would continue to plague the script's many contributing writers for months— *why* is the alien lifeform/ship doing what it's doing?

It is hard to buy the great vessel returning the body of its "god" to its home. Why is it doing this? It seems to me much easier to buy the machine seeking out the legendary home of its "god." A burial party isn't a very exciting thing, whereas a quest into the home secrets of a god is exciting.

What happens on Earth when the great machine gets there? I think we need to build in some kind of big danger to our planet.

We have discussed Pioneer 10 and the advantages of using a later NASA probe.

We have discussed also the problem of needing a "black hole" or something to get the NASA probe thousands of light-years away from Earth in a very short time.

We have also discussed the fact that we cannot have the *Enterprise* creating an android Vulcan. If we had that capacity to create efficient androids of this sort, it would affect too many things in our entire series.

...SUMMARIZING, most of our story problems seem to boil down simply to getting to know our alien machine character better. Its abilities, limitations, motivations, needs, and so on. With all that established, it should then be much easier to build a tale which rises steadily in excitement and jeopardies (to the starship _and_ to Earth) to a very exciting and satisfying climax.

By August 16, Harold Livingston had held pitch meetings with almost thirty writers and assigned stories to seven of them in addition to Alan Dean Foster. Among them was science-fiction great Theodore Sturgeon, who had written "Shore Leave" and "Amok Time" for the _Original Series._ Other writers with a _Star Trek_ connection who had requested story meetings at this time included Walter Koenig and David Gerrold.

Within this burst of creative activity in the writing side of the production, the first signs of conflict were arising. Though Alan Dean Foster had turned in a story that everyone liked, he had been given his assignment directly by Roddenberry, without consulting Harold Livingston, who was nominally in charge of all writing assignments. And though Livingston thought Foster showed promise, he wasn't convinced that the young writer had sufficient experience to be given the assignment to write the all-important two-hour pilot.

Also, since Livingston was still becoming familiar with _Star Trek,_ he was depending on Jon Povill's knowledge of the series to guide his decisions as to what was a good _Star Trek_ story. Livingston wanted Povill to be made _Phase II_'s Story Editor, but Roddenberry was dead set against the promotion. He had come to depend on Povill as his assistant, and he didn't want to lose his services to the time-consuming responsibilities of story editing.

On the production side of the series, work continued in those areas that might have a bearing on the still-unannounced feature. As the prelimi-nary artwork reproduced in this book shows, not until Robert Wise was hired as the feature's director was the expensive idea of redesigning the crew's uniforms approved. For that moment, as a cost-saving measure, the original costumes would be reused.

To that end, Costume Designer William Ware Theiss wrote the following report on August 23.

Not wishing to squelch creativity, it should be kept in mind that there are certain budgetary problems involving wardrobe and background extras [_nonfeatured actors in the background of certain scenes_]. Extras are an obvious expense, but keep in mind that aside from the extra's salary, alien and planet civilian extras tend to be more expensive in that they frequently involve pre-shooting interviews to pick particular size and/or facial types. They also generally involve extra pay on the set each morning for wardrobe, makeup, and hair, also involving additional salaries in these departments.

Again, the foregoing caution was not meant to inhibit the writer or director's creativity. Many of our most successful shows have been those that have the visual excitement of unusual aliens and/or planet civilians. Just keep in mind that they come at some cost and it ultimately needs to be balanced out somewhere else.

Costumes in general can be discussed as follows:

We have a stock of:

1. The standard uniform which comprises the majority of our shipboard wear for crew (actors and extras). These uniforms may be redressed (ornamented) for use on crews of other starships and starbases.

2. A substantially smaller stock of dress uniforms used for formal military and sometimes social occasions e.g. court martials, commissionings, changes of command, funerals, weddings, bar mitzvahs, ambassadorial occasions.

3. A very small stock of technical gear and off-duty garb for use on extras or actors involved in unusual work or play on board the ship or elsewhere.

4. There is almost no stock of civilian clothes. All civilians (male or female) in your stories, whether they are on shipboard or on a planet surface, have to be costumed from scratch. Civilian costumes on Star Trek tend to be visually exciting and memorable. If they are not, the audience tends to feel cheated and disappointed. For this reason, it is virtually impossible to use old costumes from an actor in one episode on even an extra in another. These costumes take time to build and last-minute casting will cause production delay. These costumes do not come off a rack. Even the futuristic version of blue jeans must not look exactly like a 20th-century version. If you describe a costume in your script, keep in mind that too specific visual descriptions will be ignored due to the exigencies of:

1. critical limitations of the actor ultimately cast

2. materials available on the market

3. color and other visual characteristics imposed by the set.

However, any generalized descriptions that you can include which will help delineate the intrinsic qualities of a particular civilization or the emotional or characterization qualities of a particular character will be most welcome.

By the end of August, full-scale preproduction efforts were underway. The all-new bridge set had been framed, and the first of the fiberglass "skins" had been molded for its circular wall. Walls were also up in the captain's quarters and the corridors, and walls had been built for the two-story engine-room set. Once the transparent second-story walkways were installed, those walls could be put in position as well.

The details of the instrument consoles were being worked out in considerable detail by Lee Cole, Joe Jennings's briefing room designs were under way, and Mike Minor was hard at work on concept art for the "space office complex" and the seventy-kilometer-long alien vessel that would eventually be called V'Ger.

The *Enterprise* itself was under construction at Magicam.

Director Robert Collins had been signed to direct "In Thy Image," and to begin the screen-test process to choose the actors to portray Xon, Decker, and Ilia.

And, as in the past, the aerospace industry was eager to help *Star Trek* in any way possible.

As Robert Goodwin wrote in his production status report of August 31:

Monday, Mark Tanz took Joe Jennings, Lee Cole, and myself to a lunch and brainstorming session at McDonnel/Douglas. We met with several of their scientists and engineers who are their top people in advanced technology. We came up with several interesting new concepts and ideas, which Joe and Lee are utilizing in their design work. We were given an open door at McDonnel/Douglas. Any further questions we may have, they will happily answer. They're really going all out to put their people at our disposal.

Though August had brought the end of *Phase II,* work on *The Motion Picture* was proceeding apace, a fact still unknown to all but a few.

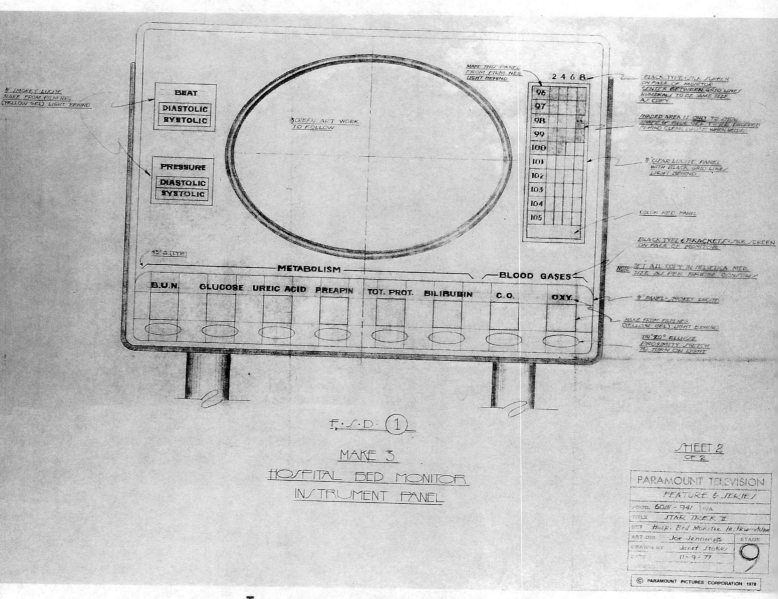

The *Phase II* update of *Star Trek*'s famous medical monitor.
Courtesy of Paramount Pictures.

September

One of the highlights of September was the announcement on September 12 that William Shatner had been signed to return as Captain Kirk. Though the main points of his deal had been agreed to in principle as far back as the June 10 press conference, it had taken that long to finalize the actual contract. Given the complexities of other agreements still to be negotiated for the feature, it was little wonder the studio continued to insist on keeping news of the movie restricted to only the top level of executives.

On the production side of *Phase II,* work continued on the sets, which would be as necessary for the movie as for the series. In his September 8 status report to Gene Roddenberry, Robert Goodwin wrote:

Set Construction

So far we have pulled five skins for the segments of the bridge and by next week we will be finished with all twelve skins. The skins are coming off better than we'd hoped for. The only possible problem involved is an echo effect in certain portions of the set, but Joe Jennings has already arranged with Glen Glenn Sound to go over the set and eliminate any of those problems before we start production.

In the engine room, the steel work has been completed. The ceilings and floors are almost in and the walls are going in today.

Drawings on the briefing room have been completed and work is being started on the construction of the shell. Work is also going forward on drawings for the medical complex, which Joe should have soon for your approval. In connection with the medical complex, Joe will coordinate with Mark Tanz research into the medical equipment and facilities.

The shell for the transporter room is

being built. Soon Mike Minor will have sketches ready for you to approve on the look of the new transporter room.

Models

Mike Minor has completed the various elevations on the orbital dry dock and has turned them over to Magicam. ... Mike Minor and Joe Jennings are now working on the concepts of the drawings for the floating office at the orbital dry dock. [*This would later evolve into the travel pod.*] At the moment, they are working on a concept that involves pentahedrons, that are formed together in a modular shape, and can separate and be used as small working shuttles. After completing his work on that, Mike will go forward with the refinement and additional concepts on the alien space ship.

But though the money and effort being expended on the sets and models would eventually contribute to the feature—or so it was planned—to maintain the impression that a series was in preproduction, work also continued on having thirteen scripts written for episodes that would never be made.

Here was one of the drawbacks of Roddenberry's approach to planning the return of *Star Trek* as a series: the idea that *all* the episodes could be written before a single one had been filmed.

When Roddenberry had decided upon this approach, back when *Phase II* was still to go into production, he could rationalize that the new series would be similar enough to the original that script writers would have no trouble capturing the flavor of the show.

However, as its development process demonstrates, *Phase II* was not shaping up to be the old series. Ten years had passed and the television audience had matured. Censors were a bit more lenient in terms of the story situations they would accept, opening the door for new subjects and approaches for the *Enterprise*'s explorations.

And to the familiar mix of original characters, three new ones had been added, and one had been removed, radically changing the dynamics of the crew's interaction.

In the typical production cycle of a television series, especially in the seventies, a pilot episode was made long before series production began. Therefore, writers who were to be given the first episode assignments had the opportunity to hear how the characters spoke, to experience the pacing of the show, and to see the sets firsthand.

Without a produced pilot, *Phase II* writers still could easily recreate the distinctive personalities and speaking styles of Kirk and McCoy, but how could they know what Xon would sound like? How could they understand how Ilia would really relate to Sulu? And how could they be sure how the supposed father–son relationship between Kirk and Decker would be realized by the actors involved?

Because of the—you guessed it—collaborative nature of television, none of those character dynamics could come only from the pages of the script. In an ongoing series, actors have an important creative role to play in how their characters will be defined and later evolve. The writers and producers, watching this refinement, then feed back into new scripts what they see the actors do.

The core triumvirate of the *Original Series*—Kirk, Spock, and McCoy—did not come about because of a description in the Writer's Guide for that show. Instead, the chemistry of the actors Shatner, Nimoy, and Kelly sparked into life in some early episodes and was noticed by the writing staff, who then wrote to that great strength.

For another example of ongoing character evolution, recall Spock as he appeared in "The Cage," smiling with delight as he encountered a musical plant. Then recall the way he raised his voice in "The Corbomite Maneuver." However, it was also in that same episode that director Joseph Sargent helped refine the Spock character by suggesting to Nimoy that when faced with the terrifying viewscreen image of the alien, Balok, he should ignore what the script called for—a reaction of fear—and simply respond with a single word—"Fascinating."

Not until the middle of the first season of the *Original Series* had Nimoy arrived at the fundamental portrayal of his character—a process that required months of his careful consideration and experimentation, and the input of many writers and directors.

Though efficient, by trying to assign all the *Phase II* scripts at once, Roddenberry was creating barriers for all the other creative contributors the show would enlist, by effectively cutting them out of this ongoing development. As a result, almost all the final scripts for *Phase II*, though they would assuredly have gone through further production "polishes" had the series been produced, feature unfocused characterization. The writers were working in the dark.

So was Harold Livingston.

"I had a different idea for *Star Trek*," Livingston says. "I wanted to make it more universal to appeal to more people. And I just didn't believe in 'the cult.' " "The cult" is how both Michael Eisner and Harold Livingston referred to *Star Trek*'s most loyal and hardcore fans. In the seventies, few shows had such devoted followings, and production people were sometimes uneasy with how seriously those viewers took their work.

Livingston didn't intend to disparage *Star Trek* fans; he simply felt that by developing episodes just for them, the series was limiting its appeal. "I thought this could have a vast audience," Livingston says. And in September of 1977, he felt more strongly than ever that the key to reaching that audience was Jon Povill, who knew not only *Star Trek*, but good storytelling as well.

Here the simmering conflict between Roddenberry and Livingston ratcheted up another notch.

First, of course, there was their ongoing disagreement over Alan Dean Foster and "In Thy Image." Over Roddenberry's objections, Livingston flat-out refused to give Foster the

script assignment. But with a November 1 start date penciled in as the first day of principal photography for the pilot, a script was becoming an urgent necessity.

The pressure on Livingston wasn't made easier when his first choice for scriptwriter, Steven Bochco, wasn't available, and second-choice Michael Cimino wasn't interested.

But the defining moment in what would become a bitter feud between the men came about because of Jon Povill.

Povill, though still Roddenberry's "assistant," sat in on many of the pitch meetings Livingston had with hopeful writers. One writer, Jaron Summers, had pitched a story that Livingston had decided to decline, until Povill suggested a new approach. When Summers turned in a rough first-draft script based on this new approach, titled "The Child," Livingston gave Povill the task of rewriting it to make it match the needs of the production.

Povill's work on the script was the deciding factor for Livingston (and the final script is reprinted in full at the end of Part Four of this book). The young writer deserved to be Story Editor. But, Livingston recalls, "Gene said no, he's not ready. So, I just told Gene that unless Jon was made Story Editor, he could find someone else to produce the show—I was going to walk.

"For whatever reason, Gene felt intimidated and caved in." Livingston adds with a dry chuckle, "And he never forgave me."

The further escalation of the "In Thy Image" schedule crisis became apparent in Livingston's September 8 script-status report.

William Norton was engaged to write the opening two-hour episode. Tuesday the 5th, Norton contacted me to say after considerable agonizing, he had reached a conclusion that he could not write a proper Star Trek script. Although this set us back considerably in time, I think that in the end his honesty and candor and professionalism will prove beneficial. I personally feel this supports my theory that most writers find it extremely difficult writing a Star Trek script unless they have been completely immersed in it for some time. Star Trek stories require special treatment, special handling; the writers really should be well acquainted with the nuance, characterizations, various other colorations that make Star Trek the unique stories they are.

This situation, needless to say, leaves us in a serious state, bordering now on crisis. If we are to meet the November 1st production date, it is essential we receive a script no later than October 1st. We have examined and re-examined and re-examined again the names of writers qualified to write this initial episode. We finally proposed that the following emer-

gency steps be taken: I would embark upon a "crash" program to write a first-draft screenplay in two to three weeks. This first-draft screenplay would then be re-written by Gene Roddenberry. We feel that in the end we would be required to take these steps anyway and at this time assigning to another writer would lose us much valuable time. Time we simply cannot afford if we intend to meet the November 1st deadline. We have presented this idea to the front office and we are awaiting an answer momentarily. We feel this is the only realistic solution and we feel confident that it will be completely satisfactory. It is a step not taken lightly, but as something we feel we cannot avoid and leaves us no choice other than to proceed in this manner.

Star Trek: The Original Series established a reputation for featuring some of the best science-fiction writers of the day, and *Phase II* was to continue that tradition. This memo shows Gene Roddenberry's enthusiastic comments regarding a story and script to be written by Norman Spinrad, an acclaimed science fiction author who had written "The Doomsday Machine" for *The Original Series*. Spinrad's story, "To Attain the All," is synopsized in Part Four. Courtesy of Jon Povill.

cc: B. Goodwin
     J. Povill
     N. Spinrad

INTER-COMMUNICATION

TO: HAROLD LIVINGSTON

DATE: SEPT. 13, 1977

FROM: GENE RODDENBERRY

SUBJECT: NORMAN SPINRAD STORY

This story has exciting possibilities. As Spinrad probably realized when he said he needed "a little input", the tale needs a little straight lining on who wants what and why. Once this is solved or at least made clearer, then a script should give us some great insights into our main characters, i.e. dealing with what tempts each of them the most. What is Kirk's secret desire? Same for all the others. Although not similar, we went this direction in the first season script "The Naked Time" in which all crew members caught a mysterious virus which reduced them to doing what they most wanted to do. (This was where Sulu first became a swordsman).

Suggest that what they have run into is a kind of mental "spider web" left by a race that knew it was dying. They knew that one day, even if it was millions of years away, some starship would have to wander through this part of the galaxy and could be tempted into the trap. Point of the trap is, of course, to provide living bodies in which the consciousness of the race can reside again. The 430 living bodies of the Enterprise will carry the other racial consciousnesses that inhabit the billions of bodies in the Federation. Today the Federation; tomorrow the galaxy!

Lots of decisions to make here, of course. Are these really bad guys? In that case, we can destroy their computer and their computer bank of billions of consciousnesses. Or, maybe they are worth saving and some alternate way is found to give them a shot at life again.

Either way, I think Norman is a writer who can do this with style and class.

Also, since dictating the last lines, have talked to Spinrad in New York by telephone. He agrees with most of what I have dictated above and I have told him he has a story assignment in which he will make it either a total shipboard story or mainly a shipboard story with the non-ship part of the story something we can shoot without going onto our planet stage. Please put through the necessary deal memos on Spinrad.

Gene Roddenberry

GR:ss

Since Livingston's proposal to write the first-draft script of "In Thy Image" himself would result in his working at home to avoid all the distractions of the lot, Jon Povill's formal promotion to Story Editor was crucial to the rest of the script development process.

As Livingston went on to write in his writers' status report of September 20:

> ... The "emergency" situation we are faced with slows us up somewhat now, in that I am involved in writing the script and am unable to devote full time to story development. However, Jon Povill has been very helpful in this area and is keeping things balanced until I can get back to devoting my full attention to this.

The script situation is that I tentatively plan to deliver a first-draft script no later than October 4th. In the meantime, Gene Roddenberry is engaged writing the treatment and is feeding me pages as he completes them. At present, I think the script is extremely promising. The visuals will be spectacular, and we will certainly have the "big screen" effect that everyone seems to be looking for. If the script can be finished by the projected time, I think we will have no problems in going into production at the scheduled date.

If ever famous last words had been written, Livingston had just written the mother of them all.

October 27, 1977, the day Persis Khambatta donned a bald cap to appear in her screen test for the role of Ilia. She got the part the very next day. Courtesy of Paramount Pictures.

6

October

In the history of *Phase II*, October of 1977 ran from September 26 to October 28. On the first date, David Gautreaux was cast as Xon; on the last date, Persis Khambata was cast as Ilia. And between the two events, *Phase II* changed irrevocably as news of *Star Trek*'s fate slowly worked its way into the outside world.

How could it not?

Paramount was a major studio, staffed by professionals. Everyone knew the importance of schedules, of making broadcast and movie release dates. But *Star Trek Phase II* was missing all of its dates and no one on the production team was being pressured about it.

It was a schizophrenic situation. On the script side, some writers would eventually be allowed *months* to turn in their first-draft scripts from an approved story. This in an industry where, at the time, two weeks was a generous deadline, one week was preferred, and weekend turnarounds were not unusual.

Sets were half-built, then left unfinished. The *Enterprise* and spacedock models were endlessly tinkered with but remained incomplete. And by the end of the month, with November 28 the projected start date for filming, the fact that the major character of Decker had not yet been cast provoked little anxiety.

In hindsight, the explanation is obvious.

The executives at the top saw no need to pressure the production team to make dates for a series that would never be made. Why spend money for overtime and rush charges? And the people at the lower levels, used to last-minute changes from above, and constantly overworked, gratefully took advantage of the rare luxury of unexpected extra days in the schedule that they could use to improve the quality of their work.

Thus the business of producing a television series continued in an almost relaxed atmosphere, while the real pressure remained focused on Harold Livingston and Gene Roddenberry as the writers not of a pilot script, but of a feature screenplay.

And that pressure, at least, grew more and more unrelenting as the unofficial, feature-script dates were missed. Livingston's screenplay, intended for delivery on October 4, was not delivered in a complete form until October 21.

In the meantime, those at the less rarefied levels of the production team worked on. Jon Povill, sharing everyone's desire for greater consistency in the *Star Trek* universe, strove to construct a list of approved terminology. And who better to approve it than Gene Roddenberry himself?

On October 13, Povill sent a multiple-choice memo to Roddenberry. In its preamble, we can get a sense of the fun and good humor that was a hall-mark of the production, despite the behind-the-scenes movie tensions.

Listed below are the terms which are generally mixed up with each other in some manner and often used interchangeably. Since the final determination as to which is used how is largely arbitrary, I'm going to lay them out multiple-choice style for you and let you check the box next to the usage you want. At the moment you do so, it will become the new law of the Star Trek universe. Ah...such power for a mere mortal or demi-god...

But Roddenberry paid as much attention to the details of *Star Trek* as he did to the broad strokes of characterization and philosophy. Instead of checking the boxes on Povill's memo, he replied that same day with a memo of his own, as reprinted here.

INTER-COMMUNICATION

TO: JON POVILL   DATE: OCT. 13, 1977

FROM: GENE RODDENBERRY   SUBJECT: FORCEFIELD TERMINOLOGY

Thank you for all the choices. Please prepare something on the following:

SCANNERS AND SENSOR SCANS -- These refer to the same thing, i.e. aiming a sensor device in an arc or circle to gather information in the direction (s) covered. Scanners is usually a shorthand way of referring to the ship's sensor scanners which are in constant, automated action almost all the time we are in star-flight or orbit. They are connected to alarm devices which alert the starship crew certain kinds of danger is near. Its automated response can be set to be triggered by almost anything. As opposed to the term scanners, a sensor scan is usually used to indicate a specifically ordered scanning as opposed to the regular   and automated ones. Same terms are used in about the same way on or off the vessel.

SENSOR READINGS -- are simply reference to the formation given to us by the above scanners or sensor scans.

FORCEFIELD SCREEN -- a defensive or protective field which envelops or surrounds a vessel, person or object. A forcefield screen can also be called simply a forcefield, still means the same thing. We never use the term forcefield shield as shield refers to a single plane of forcefield protection as opposed to protection which envelops or surrounds it. The forcefield (s) or forcefield of the Enterprise is constantly ready and automated when the vessel is in spaceflight or any orbit except home or a Federated planet. Like the scanners, it can be set to be activated by the approach of almost anything which the captain believes might be dangerous or worth isolating the ship from. The vessel's forcefields or forcefield screen(s) referred to as "up or down" and generally extend a full 360° around the vessel. When necessary, a section of the forcefield can be opened up to admit an object, a beam, allow a subspace message to go out or persons to be beamed in or out by the ship's transporters. This is only necessary when the forcefield screens are up full. You can transport through or communicate through the weak or moderate forcefield screens. Forcefield screens are usually the responsibility of the ship's helmsman.

2.

DEFLECTORS OR DEFLECTOR SHIELDS -- Another kind of vessel protection which are the responsibility of the weapons and armament officer or bridge position. Unlike a forcefield, a deflector shield does not surround the vessel. It is a single plane of protection as the term shield would indicate. Deflector shields can be many and thrown up in many directions and they generally suppliment the forcefield screens. If the forcefield screen is out of operation, the deflector shields supplant them . The deflector shields are the most powerful forcefields we have but the disadvantage of their being utilized in a single plane is that a clever enemy can get around them.

DEFLECTOR BEAM -- this is solely a navigational device. It is never referred to simply as a "deflector." It is the navigational beam which extends billions of miles of the travel of the starship, deflecting small space particles from the path of the starship or warning the starship of larger objects in the path in time for a very small directional change to be made.

Is this clear to you Jon? I've got the feeling I've used an awful lot of verbiage. In its simplist possible form, we should get this information into the writer/director's guide one of these days.

                                        Gene Roddenberry

GR:ss

Gene Roddenberry's reply to Jon Povill's request for standardizing *Star Trek* terminology shows Roddenberry's attention to detail that helped create the impressive verisimilitude of the *Star Trek* universe that continues to this day.
Courtesy of Jon Povill.

Though noncritical elements of the production were allowed to slide at this time, anything that pertained to "In Thy Image" remained a priority. On October 14, postproduction supervisor Paul Rabwin delivered this report to Robert Goodwin. The postproduction phase is when the visual effects of a show are added to the footage of the actors, and a good postproduction supervisor will always know where to pick up some good used asteroids, as noted below.

Models

A set-back at Magicam (caused by the move from Santa Monica to the Paramount-Oxford building on Las Palmas) has moved the completion date on the pods, the Alien Spaceship, and the drydock to November 4th for all of them. This will not seriously affect our shooting schedule—we shall begin miniature photography on Monday, November 7th, if possible.

The model of Earth is in work—it will be ready in plenty of time.

I need to get with Joe Jennings about the asteroid. If we wish to have one made, I suggest we begin soon. I have access to some small existing asteroids through Jim Veilleux, an independent special effects cameraman. He will let us purchase them, or he will photograph them for us if we wish. They are "typical asteroids." If we are looking for something special, we should build it.

Magicam has agreed to build the "Loading Dock" section of the *Enterprise* where the pod will dock. They are awaiting specifications from Matt Jefferies.

… I am pulling stock shots of San Francisco in order to find an angle for our opening shot. To do it in miniature could cost in excess of $10,000. The way to go is most likely with a still of San Francisco, matte artwork on the still, and a matte of live "water." This will have to be discussed further.

As is clear from the above memo, the production team was working with more information about "In Thy Image" than was available from the many revised treatments that had been written by this time. Livingston, though still working most days at home to complete the script, was sending in pages as he completed various scenes.

A brief memo from Jon Povill on October 17 passed along a suggestion from director Robert Collins that found its way into the October 20 first draft.

Bob Collins mentioned to me today that by painting or otherwise covering one of those "Magic Mountain Airbag Trampolines" [*a reference to an attraction at the Magic Mountain theme park north of Los Angeles*] with blue coloring, it could be made to look like children were jumping around on a force field by shooting it like an ordinary blue backing shot. Therefore, if you like the notion, you have only to insert the sequence into your production rewrite and it shall be done. Voilà.

Another memo from Povill on the same day addressed two technical aspects of the script, demonstrating the production team's ongoing concern with trying to be as scientifically accurate as possible, given the uncertainties of predicting 23rd-century science and technology.

This is just a small point that I caught that we had talked about in the special effects meeting the other day, and which was under question at the time. It concerns the height of the orbital drydock. I was asked to check with Jesco [*Jesco Von Puttkamer, NASA Technical Advisor to the production*] as to what orbital height was necessary in order to maintain a synchronous orbit over San Francisco. It turns out that the only height at which a synchronous orbit can be maintained is 22,000 miles. At present, the script (on page 11 of your latest draft) calls for the height of the drydock to be 200 miles.

Since the difference in the distance from the Earth is substantial, and since the shot will have to be adjusted accordingly, I thought I'd better drop you this note now.

Also, when Kirk and Scott get into the observation pod [*later to be the travel pod*] (on page 12) it will be necessary to have some kind of <u>double</u> sliding door arrangement so that all the paperwork on that drafting table doesn't go out the hole left by the departing pod.

On Friday, October 21, Harold Livingston at last delivered the rough first draft of "In Thy Image," dated October 20, and reprinted in full in Part Three of this book. It was weekend reading for the production team as well as Paramount executives, and the next week would start the long struggle over the rewrite that would continue well into the actual filming of *The Motion Picture*. Robert Goodwin's last production status report, filed before the script had been read and discussed, was also issued on that Friday.

Set Construction

The basic construction is completed in Stage 9. All of the painting is completed on Stage 9 except for the Engine Room, where the welders are finishing putting in supports for the catwalks. As soon as that welding work is completed, the painting will be finished there, too.

On Stage 8, basic construction is complete on Admiral Nogura's office, and it is now being painted. The construction is pretty well along on the piece for the interior of the Alien Ship.

On Stage 10, basic construction is complete on the Recreation Room, and most of the painting has been completed. John Cartwright is almost finished with the drawings for the pod and the Reception area of the space office. Joe Jennings is working on design for the interior of the Klingon Bridge.

Consoles and Instrumentation

Just about all the consoles have been mounted in the bridge and work is going forward on the instrumentation. The consoles for the Engine Room have also been completed. There are two set designers at work finishing the instrumentation drawings, which are immediately given to Jim Rugg, who is putting all available men to work.

Puppets

We have received a bid from Bob Baker which we have accepted and he is at work on five major puppets for the Alien Probes. As you know, we will have the Smeller, the Feeler, the Listener, and the One Who Sees, as well as the principal, Tasha [*the V'Ger probe made in the form of Ilia*]. We have decided to drop the five extra puppets we had originally talked about in the interest of both production and financial considerations.

Casting

Thursday October 27 is the day we have set for tests. Juliette Taylor in New York will be taping some more people on Monday the 24th. We will receive the cassette early Tuesday morning so that we can have any actors we want from New York here by Wednesday.

Nasa Probe

After your conversation with John Casani at Jet Propulsion Laboratories, JPL has agreed to loan us the mock-up of the Voyager, to be used as part of our set as the interior of the Alien Spaceship. Joe Jennings and Matt Jefferies attended a briefing in JPL last night on the Voyager and Joe Jennings will return there next week with Bud Arbuckle to get measurements so that we can incorporate this large, full-scale mock-up into our plans for the set.

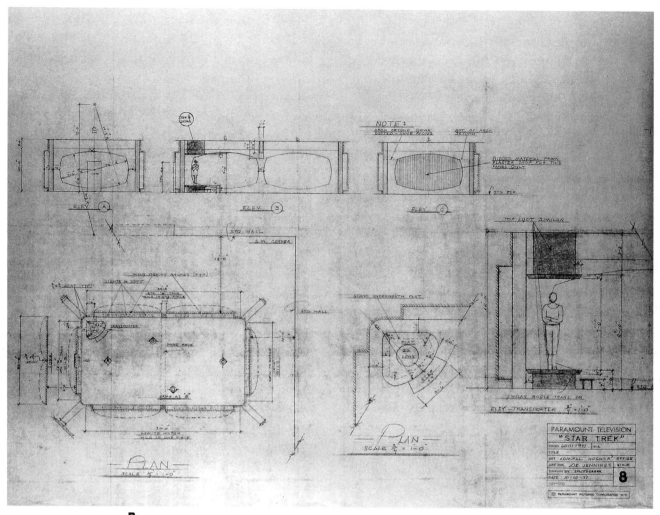

Blueprints for Admiral Nogura's office. Courtesy of Paramount Pictures.

In addition to showing the state of the production, this memo shows the powerful appeal of *Star Trek* among the people who actually explore space. For NASA's Jet Propulsion Lab to actually offer to loan a multimillion-dollar model of a real space probe was an immense act of good faith and support.

But the note on casting is the most interesting part of this report, because it marks an important turning point in the perception of *Phase II* by those who worked on it.

One month earlier, David Gautreaux had been one of a handful of other actors who had progressed to the stage of being screen-tested for the role of the Vulcan, Lieutenant Xon, the *Enterprise's* new science officer and replacement for Spock.

Gautreaux's adventure as Xon began like a traditional Hollywood fairytale. The young actor had no agent, but he was dating a woman who worked for one. She told him about the role, thought he would be perfect, and set up the first appointment herself.

Gautreaux met with the casting director, Pat Harris, and was invited back to read for Robert Goodwin and the just-signed director, Robert Collins. Gautreaux's reading went well, and he was invited back one more time to have his eyebrows altered, his eartips pointed, and to pull on an ill-fitting Starfleet uniform.

This time, Gautreaux was filmed as he portrayed Xon. The actor recalls that, at the time, "I'd say there were at least eight of us testing for the role: dark-haired, tall, short, slender, fat, all shapes and sizes, all of us vaguely alien-looking." But in the end, it was Gautreaux who was told he had the part, which included a $15,000 fee for the pilot, a guaranteed thirteen-episode pay-or-play commitment, and a six-year option on his services.

Not bad for an actor who had come in without an agent.

But before Gautreaux actually signed his contract, a wrinkle developed. Only a few weeks after being told the role was his, the studio wanted him to come back and test for it again.

As it turned out, Xon was to be even more of a replacement for Spock than anyone had realized. Roddenberry's wife, Majel Barrett, was returning to the show as Christine Chapel, now a doctor and not McCoy's nurse. Part of Chapel's character arc on the *Original Series* was her unrequited love for Spock. Barrett was concerned that this romantic element of her characterization wouldn't play well against a young actor like Gautreaux, and she had lobbied for an older British actor to take the part.

Gautreaux gamely returned to the lot to test again—after his new agent had secured for him an additional payment of $2,500. Gautreaux recalls watching the British actor test for the role, and was relieved to see that he was "absolutely abominable."

About the third week of October, when Gautreaux was finally confirmed—for the second time—as Xon, producer Robert Goodwin invited the actor to come to Roddenberry's office for a drink.

When Gautreaux arrived, he was met by Roddenberry, Livingston, and Goodwin, as well as by Robert Collins and Jeffrey Katzenberg. And they had some news to share.

This was when Gautreaux was formally inducted into the growing circle of those who knew what was really going on at Paramount— *Phase II* was going to be *Star Trek: The Motion Picture*.

By the time the screen tests for Ilia were held, on October 26 and 27, there was little pretense as to what type of role they were casting. Whichever actor won the part of the *Enterprise*'s new navigator, she was being selected for a movie, not a television series.

Persis Khambatta, a former Miss India, was filmed on October 27. For the purposes of the test, her hair was plastered down beneath a bald cap, because Roddenberry was insistent that the character would be hairless.

Michael Eisner, on the other hand, hated the concept of a bald-headed woman. As Robert Goodwin recalls, "Eisner thought it was a terrible idea."

But Khambatta's selection was less harrowing than Gautreaux's had been, and Eisner was quickly won over to Roddenberry's concept of the character. Goodwin says, "When we did the tests, we knew it was Persis from the beginning. Some people just look good with bald heads. Some don't. And there was just something great about her, a real exotic aspect. So we knew it was her.

"Eisner saw the tests and that was it. He just said, 'That's fine.'"

As far as principal actors were concerned, only the part of Decker remained to be cast. The reason for there being little pressure to speed up the search was not only because the movie start date was being pushed back again, but because, as William Shatner had earlier noted, there was some question as to whether Decker would be needed at all.

As Harold Livingston wrote in his writers' status report of October 25:

… I think it would be very beneficial for us to determine as soon as possible whether or not the character of Will Decker will continue or will be eliminated. Every story in work and those also in script contain Decker as a very integral character. If we're going to eliminate him I think we had better move on it now to further save ourselves much unnecessary work re-writing and writing around the elimination of that particular character.

But the *Phase II* scripts were now, more than ever, perceived as little more than back-up material, should *Star Trek* return to television after the feature film was released.

The real focus was on the "In Thy Image" script. And for the first time, the studio heavyweights were becoming involved.

The following notes are from a memo written by Arthur Fellows to Gene Roddenberry, dated October 31. Note that the final comment reprinted here shows that there was no doubt as to what kind of screenplay Livingston had delivered. *Star Trek* was definitely on track to be a feature.

Following are Michael's [*Michael Eisner*] and my combined notes and thoughts on the STAR TREK rough draft. Hope you find this to be useful in your rewrite.

The return of "STAR TREK" is an event in itself and we believe that this script really incorporates elements that will be an extraordinary send off for the next "five" years. The action and basic story are well conceived. However, at this rough draft stage, a problem exists throughout in the arena of character and relationships.

New characters, Xon and Decker, have been well created to the extent that we have a real shot at presenting people the audience will respond to, but that potential is not herein realized. The audience will empathize with the difficulty of Xon's position. No one knows better than them how much Spock is missed and the resentment the others might feel with a new Vulcan taking his place. We never get a real sense of the pressure placed upon Xon. Tension over his situation does not build concomitantly with the story, nor is it paid off in the end. It would be an easy fix to accomplish this. Further, Xon's heroic deed—allowing himself to get burned for the sake of the ship and crew, is not made a big enough event. This should be the heroic deed that will cause Xon to win over the love of every crew member, audience member and every old Spock fan. If this point in the script is not the time to do it, perhaps a deed that would be more "blatantly" heroic is in order for a later scene.

One other note about Xon concerns the age-old war between McCoy and Spock. Let's not lose the fun and importance of that relationship. McCoy's humanness vs. Vulcan logic, in this case, Xon's, will be the human emotional strength of the piece. Let's start this earlier and let it be an undertone throughout. It should continue organically from the action and confrontation and where possible should transpire much to McCoy's annoyance as he recalls Spock and much to Kirk's amusement as he recalls the past as well.

Decker: In many ways we face a similar task with Decker. As Kirk and the crew come to accept him, so must our audience. When the resentment Decker brings aboard the *Enterprise* is turned around and he does good— we need more emotion. The scene between Decker, Kirk, McCoy, and Chapel touches upon this, but we can do more. Decker's going to be with us a long time and any intensifying of the emotions surrounding his existence and purpose on the ship will only aid in endearing him to all involved.

Ilia: is a marvelous character and later a marvelous machine. The relationship that develops between Ilia and Kirk should really be a driving force throughout the entire piece. We should sense the germ of what is to come earlier. Overall, she should have more emotional impact. When she is Ilia the Machine and she begins to take on and/or sense certain human attitudes—this is quite a moment. Quite an accomplishment for Kirk in many ways. When Ilia returns at the end—in human

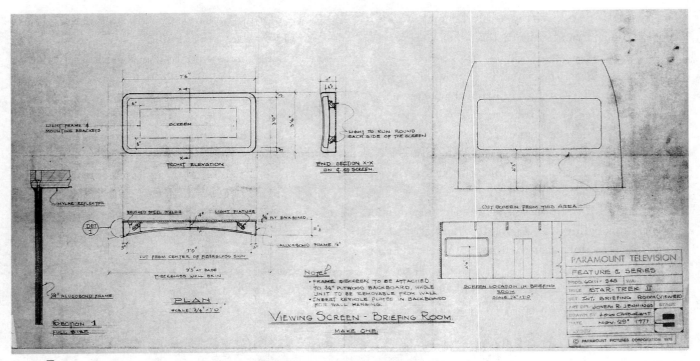

This blueprint's title block shows the fluid situation *Phase II* had entered by November, 1977. Now *Star Trek* II is referred to as both a "Feature & Series." Courtesy of Paramount Pictures.

form, there should be much more of a reaction. After all, Kirk knows what went on between himself and her form and she does not. If we go deeper on an emotional level with her relationship with Kirk, the real Ilia's return is a scene that can be much bigger for Kirk, crew, and audience.

There is much concern over making Ilia bald. All of us are very much agreed that a beautiful bald woman on the *Enterprise* is interesting, fascinating, and fresh. However, if that woman is Ilia in this two-hour, her baldness may really get in the way of the audience buying the intense relationship between Kirk and the woman. We would prefer to have an Ilia with hair, keeping the bald girl but giving her some other function in this show.

The storyline presented is quite special and extraordinary. Somehow, the ending seems to be too "small" when we consider what led up to it. The slow steady build of excitement and tension as this story unfolds

is so effective that the ending deserves to soar. Right now, it is a bit anticlimactic. The final dialogue and moment when Ilia has convinced Ve-jur to save the servo-units is too convenient. Ilia preventing imminent disaster in one moment after two hours of intense tensions and suspense is divisive.

When the *Enterprise* sees the Alien ship for the first time, this has got to be an incredible moment—both filmatically and dramatically. Realizing that in many ways it will be difficult to get across a sense of the immense size of the Alien ship, we can increase awe tremendously if we have a "JAWS"-like feeling in relation to the *Enterprise* and the Alien ship. We will have the audience falling off their seats if such a feeling can be successfully initiated and maintained at the proper moments throughout.

Another excellent element of this script is the timer put on from the start in terms of this special mission. More sense of time, time running out and a race against time should be present throughout. It is most effective at the end, but we really lose a sense of the urgencies involved once they are mentioned at the start. We have a germ of it in the rough draft, let's use it.

The following are some specific comments:

(a) The entire San Francisco exterior sequence should be examined carefully. We may be much better off without it. Given what we can afford to do, this will still look like Earth. Technically, it may be very hard to achieve as written on the large theatre screens (scenes 10 - 18).

Additional notes commented on particular areas where dialogue could be made more clear, or where pages could be cut. Livingston had delivered a 153-page script when a typical feature should be no more than 120, and one with long sequences of special effects and action rarely exceeds 100.

But though the comments from Fellows and Eisner were positive and supportive, the rewriting that followed would be anything but an ongoing refinement. Instead, the long-smoldering conflict between Roddenberry and Livingston would finally explode, and the battle for the ultimate direction of *The Motion Picture* would begin in earnest.

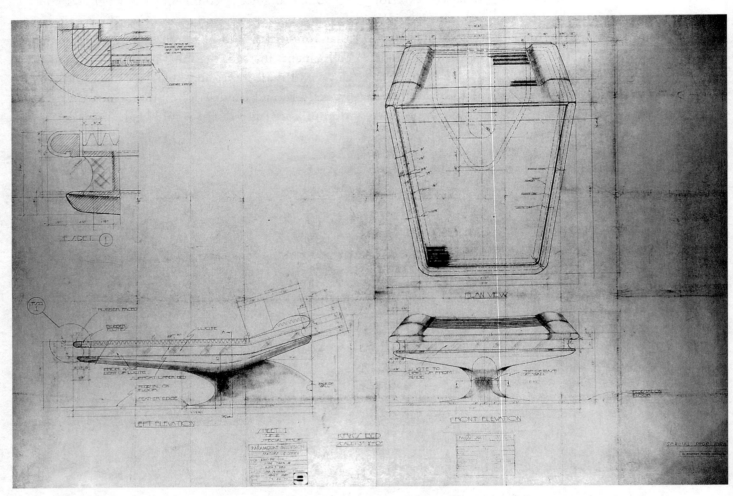

For any *Star Trek* production, it's seldom possible to pick up a prop from the prop department or a local store. *Everything* must be designed and built especially for *Star Trek*'s vision of the future, even an ordinary bed. Courtesy of Paramount Pictures.

November

There is a good reason why television and moviemaking are collaborative endeavors. Both are such complex undertakings that it is far too easy to become overwhelmed by details, to the point at which perspective is lost.

Nowhere is this more apparent than in scriptwriting.

Screenwriters in Hollywood look longingly at the supposed autonomy playwrights have. No actor in a play would think of changing a single word of dialogue without the playwright's permission. No director would ever dare suggest switching two scenes, or dropping one entirely, without consulting with the playwright.

In Hollywood, however, the situation is best summed up by two old jokes. Q: How many producers does it take to change a lightbulb? A: Does it have to be a lightbulb? . . . and . . . Q: How many writers does it take to change a lightbulb? A: Aww, do I have to change it?

What scriptwriters sometimes don't remember is that plays are changed before they reach opening night. The key difference is that the playwright at least gets to make those changes himself or herself, after watching run-through after run-through, seeing firsthand what does and does not work.

But most movies are more complex than most plays—Broadway musicals notwithstanding—and there is usually little time or incentive to go back to the original writer after the first few rounds of revision have taken place. At this point, script control usually switches to the director, in the case of movies, or to the producer, in the case of television. Which helps explain why so many writers want to direct their own films or produce their own series.

This is exactly the situation Gene Roddenberry had to deal with in November of 1977.

Star Trek was his. He had created it. He had assembled the creative team that had expanded his concept and brought it to life. Not once, but twice. And now, with a rare second chance to put his creation before the public as a *major motion picture*, he was faced with losing control over it.

It was no reflection on Roddenberry. It was just the nature of the Hollywood beast.

And Roddenberry decided to fight it.

Unfortunately, as he struggled to maintain control of his creation, he also fell prey to the very reason why control in Hollywood tends to be shared.

He lost perspective.

Some would say it was because of his passion for *Star Trek*. Others might uncharitably suggest he was driven by professional pride to prove that his first and only hit hadn't been a fluke.

But for whatever reason, Gene Roddenberry took on Paramount and the established way of doing business in Hollywood. And as a writer, he would eventually, inevitably lose.

The first battle was fought and lost with his rewrite of Harold Livingston's rough first draft of "In Thy Image."

As previously planned at the time of the script "emergency," Roddenberry took Livingston's script and used it as the basis of a second draft, which he wrote within a week.

Where Livingston's draft had carried the credits, "Screenplay by Harold Livingston, Story by Alan Dean Foster and Gene Roddenberry," Roddenberry's script added his own name first, above Livingston's, which was not the standard placement. Tradition holds that the first name on the script is the person who wrote the first draft.

But besides initiating a conflict over script and story credit, Roddenberry's draft had another problem.

Livingston recalls the meeting that took place after he, Jon Povill, Robert Goodwin, and Robert Collins had read the script. The conclusion among the production team was unanimous. Roddenberry's script was seen as a step backward. It was said to focus too much on the inner workings of the future, stopping the action for long, dialogue-heavy scenes in which various philosophies were explored and contrasted. It was thoughtful, insightful, a look at the future as Roddenberry envisioned it. But it was considered dull.

In the end, Livingston was the one who had to explain the reaction to the script. But Roddenberry did not accept his team's assessment and took a bold gamble. He said he would send both versions of the script to the executives, and let them decide.

Three days later, in early November, came the pivotal meeting in Michael Eisner's office that Harold Livingston has recounted many times. Eisner had Livingston's script in a brown folder, and Roddenberry's in a yellow one. Quite succinctly, Eisner said that Roddenberry's script was "television," Livingston's script was "a movie," and that Livingston's was "a lot better."

Roddenberry was reportedly crushed, though everyone at the meeting agreed that he had introduced some worthwhile elements to the story. Thus the decision was made for director Robert Collins to take both versions of the script and combine them into a third draft, using the best elements of both. The effort would take him the rest of the month.

In this memo to Michael Eisner, Collins states the issues he would address in his rewrite.

1. As we discussed, the final screenplay must be an amalgam of the Brown and Yellow scripts, with emphasis on the Brown.

The primary task is to get the picture moving, establish the menace, pit our hero(s) against it with continual overhanging menace first to the *Enterprise,* then to the entire Earth. Okay, how?

First, the Klingon Battle, pretty much stet [*kept as is*], telling us there's something goddamn big and awful out there. This transmitted to Starfleet via Starbase (Brown Script). Then Starfleet Headquarters, Kirk called from his office, Emergency, highest priority, top-level conference.

Nogura: This unknown and as yet unseen menace, more terrible than anything yet known to Earth, is on its way. Stop it. One man, one ship to stand between Armageddon and the future of Earth and maybe the galaxy.

Okay, now we have mystery, terror, death, destruction, the end of the world, and we build from there.

2. The plot moves and developments are much the same in both scripts until the ending. (I'll get to that in a moment.) It's a matter of sharpness, crispness, of dialogue, and of maintaining the constant and obligatory presence of the alien ship in every scene … i.e., even in the Rec Room when exhausted crew members are trying to relax, through a window background, the alien ship hovers always in view.

3. Tasha (Ilia). It's a love story subplot, more a function of dialogue and acting than plot. We must feel that Kirk, bewildered by it himself, is falling in love with Tasha. This takes some thought and care, must not be glib or crass. Need some time to think and develop.

4. Decker. The rivalry with Kirk built and enhanced so that the ending is big enough. And …

5. The Ending.

Works something like this: Aboard the alien ship, Kirk learns that Ve-jur will destroy the Earth in six hours. That starts the clock.

He takes Tasha/Ilia to NASA in an effort to convince her (and Ve-Jur) that indeed, Voyager IV and therefore Ve-Jur itself are products of man.

He fails.

Nogura and other leaders of Earth gather in the War Room of Star Fleet. They see Ve-Jur release objects orbiting the Earth. They learn via Xon in the *Enterprise* that the objects are neutron bombs capable of destroying all living things on the planet. They attempt to destroy the bombs—phasers, torpedoes, killer satellites. Nothing works. The bombs remain in orbit, the clock continues to run. Two hours. One. Doomsday.

Kirk, with Ilia, learns that the truth about Voyager's origin is recorded on the plate on Voyager's superstructure. If that information can be released, Ve-Jur has to accept the truth that the Creator it seeks is Man. Kirk must get on board Ve-Jur to release the truth.

But he cannot beam up until the next orbit which is too late.

Xon and Decker learn the same thing. One of them must board Ve-Jur and release the truth. It is Decker who pulls rank and transports himself physically into the awful ship.

Now Decker alone—as Kirk and Xon earlier—in the vastness and wonder (special effects) of the Ve-Jur.

Decker making his way toward Voyager IV, approaching, but as he does, he is consumed by the energy of Ve-Jur, caught in an energy field more powerful than a million volts of electricity, he becomes himself an energy field. He becomes fused to the ship, melted into it (special effects), his consciousness, his mind, his memories become part of Ve-Jur. In a pyrotechnic display of light and sound the history of Mankind is propelled, projected onto the walls of the ship. A whirling cascade of pictures—the pyramids, the Parthenon, the Mona Lisa, Versailles, Jesus, Mohammed, Ghandi, the Grand Canyon, the Alps—the wonders of Earth bombard the insides of the ship as Jim Kirk beams himself aboard. We see Kirk surrounded by the sights, the visuals whirling around him, over him, the sights, the sounds: Beethoven, Schubert, Bach, the music of the world, the sights of all history huge, giant events all playing upon Kirk as Ve-Jur assimilates and understands. It has become

Decker. Decker has become it, and the bombs are withdrawn. Kirk is allowed to return to the *Enterprise* with Ilia. The ship, and Decker, leave Earth to seek the universe as Decker's voice, a thousand times amplified as part of Ve-Jur, tells Kirk, "There's beauty here; the universe before us. Eternity …"

Though there were still many changes to come, the spectacular idea of Decker merging with

V'ger would remain, as would the all-important release of information.

Minor contributions to the script continued to pour in, not only from the actors—as noted in Roddenberry's memo concerning William Shatner's suggestions—but from unexpected sources as well.

The following comments and suggestions are part of the notes provided by DeForest

INTER-COMMUNICATION

Written at the same time the big story issues of "In Thy Image" were being dealt with, this memo illustrates that in *Star Trek*, even the smallest detail was of importance to everyone, from Executive Producer to Story Editor to Costume Designer. Courtesy of Jon Povill.

TO: GENE RODDENBERRY

FROM: JON POVILL

DATE: NOVEMBER 7, 1977

SUBJECT: STARFLEET RANKS

Bill Theiss suggested that I remind you of the existence of the rank of Starfleet Commodore. He brought it up as a suggestion as a way to resolve the dropping in rank that Kirk goes through from Admiral to Captain. The idea is that in prior episodes we have had commodores in command of Starships, most notably Commodore Decker of the "Doomsday Machine" episode. If Kirk had been promoted somewhat less drastically to the rank of Commodore rather than the rank of Admiral, it would not be necessary to demote him in order to place him in command of the Enterprise. I'm not sure that it's something that matters a whole heck of a lot either way, but I know it's always nice to be aware of all the options available to you. So there it is if you want to play with it.

The Commodore status was apparently recalled somewhat by accident while Bill was attempting to remember all the various ranks of Admiral that exist in Starfleet. He is aware only of rear Admiral and the existence of one other type, the name of which escapes him (and me as well). He is getting in touch with Joan Winston in New York, to check with our fan memory banks in order to determine how many different varieties we portrayed through the first run of the series. He is looking to get uniforms designed, so if you have any recollections on the subject, perhaps you might give him a call about it.

Ever onward.

Jon

Jon

JP/ra

Research, the company that filled a similar function on the *Original Series* to ensure that no episode inadvertently used the names of real people, places, or things. One of the researchers for DeForest Research, Joan Pearce, now continues providing the same service for the current *Star Trek* series.

Dr. Christine Chapel Character established previously. We find no current listing for a physi-cian in the United States with this exact name.

Commander Will Decker <u>Who's Who</u> lists a William Decker, a New York businessman born in 1900. Do not consider usage here presents a conflict.

Commander Ronak No conflict, but this is an unusual name for a Vulcan. Most Vulcan names have begun with an 'S' sound.

Starfleet Headquarters Establishes the HQ in the San Francisco area.

INTER-COMMUNICATION

cc: H. Livingston
    B. Goodwin
    J. Povill

TO: BOB COLLINS   DATE: NOV. 10, 1977

FROM: GENE RODDENBERRY   SUBJECT: SHATNER'S COMMENTS

Received a call from Bill Shatner in which he made the following comments on the second draft script:

Suggest that we have an interesting dramatic opportunity if Kirk makes love to the "Ilia" machine and we actually see at least the beginnings of this on camera. He feels that it is not only a valid extension of what the story already has him doing but has considerable opportunity for humor and helps reinforce the whole change in her.

Bill also suggests that Kirk might participate with Xon in the first realization that the Ve-jur machine is alive. Sees no dramatic objection in Xon coming up with the <u>first</u> realization but does believe that Kirk should <u>immediately</u> see what Xon is talking about and help flesh out the theory.

He comments that the major sag in the story comes between the Enterprise being grapped by Ve-jur and the final resolution of the story. He suggests that this is the area in which pages should come out.

Finally, he feels that the loss of Alexandria works fine but he believes that Kirk too quickly and easily forgets this. His comment was that the Captain should keep her memory alive longer and we should find some dramatic way of seeing this.

These comments seem to me to be sound and certainly worth serious consideration.

                    Gene Roddenberry

GR:ss

Gene Roddenberry's notes regarding William Shatner's script comments illustrate the collaborative nature of a television production, in which everyone involved is expected and encouraged to take part in shaping the final product. Courtesy of Jon Povill.

the old *Transamerica Building* San Francisco landmark. (Glad to know it will survive the earthquake which separates Los Angeles from the mainland … and a good thing, too!)

drydock Suggest: spacedock.

the Klingon border Would not boundary be a better term? Border sounds very static in context.

Koro class No conflicts. Establishes the heavy cruiser class for Klingon ships.

linguacode We find no proprietary or trademark usage of this term.

You retain Admiral's seniority but it's a captain's command. This is the first mention of a verisimilitude problem in the script. Once an admiral, always an admiral. He can certainly command a vessel, and he can be addressed as captain since he is in command … but he cannot be "temporarily posted" captain, following any military precedent. There are several alternatives: his posting to admiral could be held up for the job ahead. This would involve the additional story-telling that he was about to be raised in rank. It does not really involve any problem with the raised ranks of the other regulars … Captain is a very high rank in Naval-oriented services and one is not promoted as rapidly when this rank is reached. Alternatively, he could be dressed in Admiral's stripes, but addressed onboard as Captain.

a Deltan Use of "Delta" as a planet name presents a problem in astronomy. The greek letters are used to denote the different stars of a recognized constellation: *Delta Serpentis*, etc. That it would ever be used as a planetary name is very unlikely. We would be happy to consult on other possibilities which might be more in accord with standard astronomical usage.

maneuvering jets 'Jets' is an archaic term to use in this context. Suggest delete.

Warp Drive Optical Effect This is a new concept for STAR TREK and brings to mind STAR WARS.

Navigational deflectors This is new equipment for the *Enterprise*.

ILIA'S VOICE: We have visual contact, Captain. Have the functions of the various stations been revised? This line would usually come from Uhura.

Pon farr Established previously.

quantum chess Establishes new game.

my psycho file This sounds very much like a record of his bouts with insanity. Suggest: medical file … or, at the very least, psych file.

Voyager IV At present, only two craft are on the way.

Years after it was launched, Voyager Four wandered into a 'black hole' sending back signals that revolutionized early space concepts. This implies that messages were still being sent <u>after</u> entry into the event horizon, which is impossible. Suggest modify slightly to say that the transmissions <u>approaching</u> the black hole were important.

November came to an end with the mood of the company darker than it had been a month earlier. Livingston and Roddenberry were increasingly in conflict with each other. Set building and model construction had lost their impetus. And even the *Star Trek* movie lacked a firm start date to spur the rewriting of the script.

Something was definitely going to happen with *Star Trek,* but for the moment, no one was exactly sure what, or when.

December 15, 1977. As this frame from test footage shot in Engineering shows, by this date the future of *Star Trek Phase II* as a feature film was virtually set. All the test footage taken during this week was shot with the anamorphic lenses required for wide screen movies, not smaller-format television lenses. Courtesy of Paramount Pictures.

December

ossip columnist and Hollywood insider Rona Barrett blew the whistle in December. She reported that the Paramount Television Service would not go ahead, that *Star Trek Phase II* had stopped production, but that Paramount had made Gene Roddenberry an alternate offer to produce *Star Trek* as a film.

Barrett had good sources—three months behind the times, but essentially correct. Yet Paramount and everyone connected with *Phase II* denied the whole story as vehemently as if Stage 9 contained the 1947 crashed flying saucer and frozen alien bodies from Roswell, New Mexico. According to the studio, the only thing that had changed from that June 10 press conference was that now the Paramount network would start up in the fall of 1978, not in February. Furthermore, *Star Trek Phase II* would expand from thirteen episodes to between fifteen and twenty-two for its first season. So there.

Presumably, whoever made that statement was able to get out of camera range before his pants burst into flames.

In truth, what Stage 9 contained was unfinished sets. Painting had not been completed; consoles had not been wired; props had not been constructed. Three different start dates had come and gone, and now a start month was being suggested. February, perhaps. Or maybe sometime in March.

About the only people working on *Phase II* who still thought it might continue as a series were the writers hired to script individual episodes. They turned in their outlines; received detailed story notes from Jon Povill, Harold Livingston, and Gene Roddenberry; then left the lot to write their first and second drafts, synopses of which can be found in Part Four of this book.

But on the lot, where work was proceeding on the only script that would matter, the next round of rewriting "In Thy Image" had been reached. At the end of November, director Robert Collins had turned in his "blended" version of Livingston's and Roddenberry's drafts. It satisfied no one.

Jon Povill passed his notes to Roddenberry concerning the Collins rewrite, in a memo dated December 1. Here are some of his comments.

As we discussed earlier, I feel the characters and dialogue are wrong throughout much of the script. Specifically:

Decker is petulant and totally unsympathetic for the first two-thirds of the script. Then, with no transition and, more importantly, with nothing happening directly to or with him that would cause him to undergo this transformation, he abruptly mellows into a team player.

McCoy has no meat. There are no revealing glimpses of the true depth and character of the relationship between Kirk and McCoy. Instead, McCoy wanders in and out dropping sarcastic comments at inappropriate moments.

Also, the character of VE-JUR needs fleshing out. VE-JUR is our antagonist and <u>must</u> be developed as fully and consistently as if it were a humanoid. The script attempts to represent VE-JUR as an incredibly intelligent and complex living being. If we wish to avoid comparisons to Nomad (from the episode "The Changeling") we must see evidence of this intelligence and complexity that go beyond its mastery of technology.

...In all fairness to Bob, I would have to say that none of the drafts to date have succeeded in truly bringing VE-JUR to life. If you can develop him as fully as you did Tasha, I think we will have a blockbuster script.

...PAGE 34 <u>Xon's Arrival.</u> I remain somewhat concerned over our treatment of Xon when he first appears. Certainly, "who the hell are you" seems an inappropriate greeting to anyone with the credentials necessary to be beamed up to a starship. To me, this scene borders rather dangerously on the edge of broad comedy, and everything in it needs to be handled with the utmost care and restraint. By no means do I think it wrong to have some fun with the entrance, I simply feel that we should not sacrifice the normal operating realities of the ship in order to accomplish this fun. We all labor at great length to make the STAR TREK Universe real and believable and it seems to me that humorous action must adhere to this reality even more than we might otherwise have to, because the surprise of laughter is, in and of itself, enough to strain the reality of the situation.

PAGE 36. In keeping with the above comment, I feel that "rolling in yak dung" is a dangerous line.

...PAGE 44. Decker's reference to his father having died ferrying a tug to Andromeda—somewhere along the line I thought it had been mentioned that Decker's father would be the Commodore Decker who died in the "Doomsday Machine" episode.

...PAGE 62. I find it difficult to understand why VE-JUR immediately attacked everyone else it has come across thus far in the script, yet hesitates here. I think it would be possible to generate some really exciting visuals if we <u>were</u> attacked immediately and were forced to maneuver like mad in order to avoid being hit. At the same time, it would be necessary for us to try to move in closer in order to get some kind of sensor information or perhaps discover vulnerable areas.

If this were done, it would also give us two possible reasons as to why the alien locked a tractor beam on us; either to hold us still so it could facilitate our destruction or because it was intrigued by the cleverness of our maneuvers sufficiently to determine that we are worth a bit of study.

...Finally, it feels tremendously convenient and anticlimactic as we watch VE-JUR simply move off into the stars again, with no particular destination in mind. Is it possible that Decker's life force—soul, if you will—could give VE-JUR an inkling of another dimension which would be suitable for exploration. Then, utilizing its superb technology to the fullest, we could watch VE-JUR go through an incredible metamorphosis that would pick up where the Decker montage left off. The ship itself would change its configuration drastically in order to accommodate necessary preparation, then another startling special effect and light show as it slipped itself into an altogether different dimension of time space; momentarily distorting all time and space on and around our planet during the process. In this manner we could continue to dazzle the senses right up to the very last possible moment.

Povill's suggestions that V'ger attack the *Enterprise* at once, and his description of V'ger's ultimate fate, immediately became important story points for "In Thy Image," surviving through to the final shooting script.

But while work continued on both the series and the movie on the writing side of the production, on the nuts-and-bolts side, the pretense of television was rapidly fading as motion-picture concerns were openly discussed.

As mentioned by Arthur Fellows in his notes regarding Livingston's first draft, Paramount was concerned with having special effects in the *Star Trek* movie that would hold up on large theatre screens. To this end, the production team began to reexamine the existing sets and miniatures with a new eye, along with rethinking the plans already made for creating photographic effects.

To start, Roddenberry and Collins studied the year's big science-fiction blockbusters, *Star Wars* and *Close Encounters of the Third Kind*, then visited the top Hollywood special effects facilities who could deliver equally high-quality work for the *Star Trek* feature. After listing the special-effects sequences described in the existing, though not yet finished, screenplay, and after discussions with the SFX facilities, what had originally been a $3 million television movie, and then an $8 million theatrical release, received a new, Michael Eisner-approved, $15 million budget. After *Star Wars*, anyone hoping to attract a huge audience had to spend at least that much.

Armed with that new budget and the freedom to reimagine the movie it provided, the search for an all-new look for *Star Trek* began. The *Enterprise* herself was one of the first targets.

In 1977, as today, a television screen could not come close to presenting the same amount of visual detail as could a movie screen. Indeed, the fabled flimsiness and lack of finish of sets and models built for television arose not from any effort to shortchange the viewer, but because there was little point in spending time and money to add fine finishing details that would not show up on the screen.

Months earlier, when Magicam had been given the contract to build the new *Starship Enterprise*, the job had been costed and awarded on the understanding that it would be a model made for the limited resolution of the television screen.

Now, however, as postproduction supervisor Paul Rabwin began to study the model knowing its image would be blown up to fill a sixty-foot-wide screen in a theater, instead of the twenty-inch screen of a television, he realized that all the models constructed for *Phase II* would have to be at least refinished, and quite possibly built again from scratch.

To help him in his analysis, he recruited the assistance of Robert Abel, a rising star in the competitive industry of providing state-of-the-art special effects for commercials. One of the great strengths of Abel's company, Robert Abel and Associates, was Con Pederson, who, with Douglas Trumbull, had created many of the startling visual effects for the landmark science-fiction movie, *2001: A Space Odyssey*.

Truly some of the greatest lost treasures of *Star Trek Phase II* are these magnificent models, shown here at the Magicam facilities. Built with a scale and attention to detail unprecedented for television production at that time, the model work for *Phase II* would have set the standard for the day, just as *Star Trek: The Next Generation* did a decade later. Unfortunately, the increased resolution demands of motion-picture photography meant that all the models constructed for television use had to be rebuilt from scratch. Only a few pieces of these models exist today.

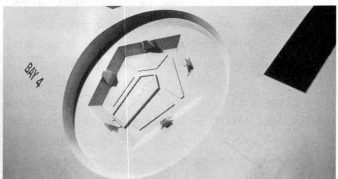

A large-scale section of the *Enterprise*'s main hull, showing the pentagonal docking bay for a transport pod. Courtesy of Andrew Probert.

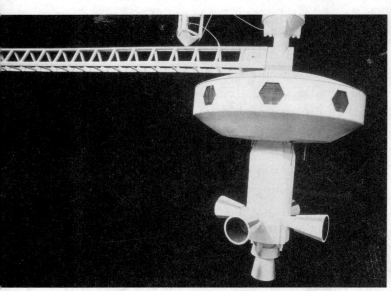

Space dock station-keeping thruster array. Courtesy of Andrew Probert.

Elements of the advanced concept design for the Space Office complex under construction. The twelve-sided modules that clustered to form sections of the space station could separate to become individual transport pods. Courtesy of Andrew Probert.

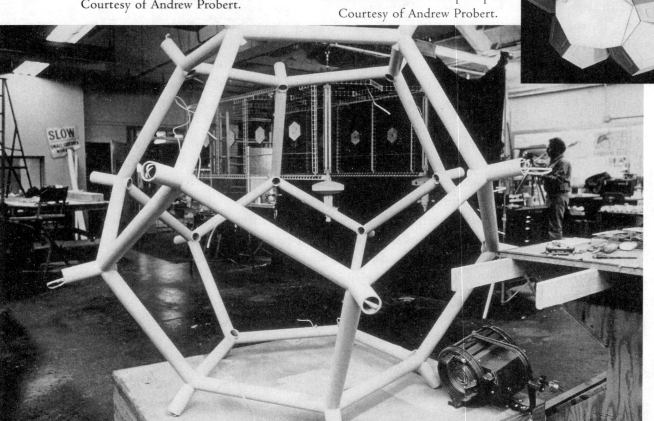

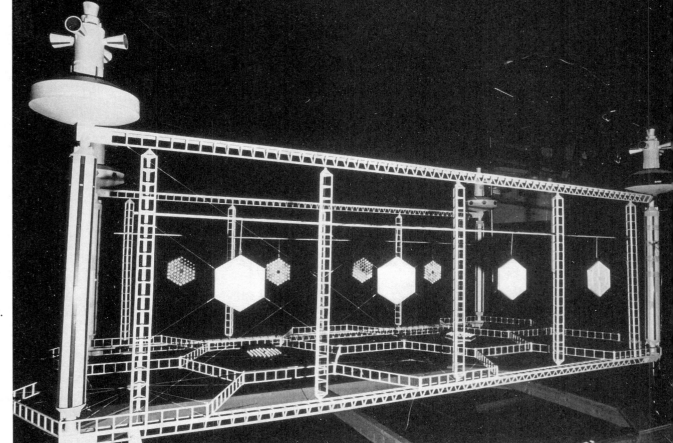

Spacedock.
Courtesy of
Andrew Probert.

The *Phase II Enterprise* in position in spacedock. One of the *Enterprise*'s builders, Brick Price, is at the far left.
Courtesy of Brick Price, WonderWorks.

Ironically, Paramount's association with Abel would eventually come to a premature end, and it would be Douglas Trumbull himself who would be brought in at the last moment to complete the visual effects of *Star Trek: The Motion Picture.*

DEC 7 1977
Robert W. Goodwin

INTER-COMMUNICATION

TO: BOB GOODWIN   DATE: 12/6/77

FROM: PAUL RABWIN   SUBJECT: BOB ABEL: ANALYSIS OF MINIATURES...POSSIBLE CHANGES

On Thursday, Dec. 1, Bob Abel, Richard Taylor, Gene Roddenberry, Bob Collins and I examined all of the existing models. These were Abel's comments and suggestions:

ENTERPRISE

    This is a "high-gloss" type model...any flaw in the construction or texture will give away the fact that it is a miniature...a different style of photography must be adopted to accomodate for this (making mulitple passes, for example.) The finish must be <u>perfect</u> in order to work.
    Gene: More doors and landing docks are needed (in case of emergency, there would be more than one landing point.)
    Taylor: The smooth texture is a problem, particularly when it is in contrast to a non-smooth texture...the joints must be less rough. Perhaps tiny scored lines could break up the smoothness...features with which we are familiar could be added in order to give us a sense of scale. (analogy...if on' the side of a huge battleship we saw a tiny anchor.) Filigree detailing must be done on the saucer...perhaps representing a solar panel or antennae-structure. More lights throughout. Possilbe dome over bridge (metal?)
    On engine pods, add lights add either a "chaser light" system, or some other light effect to act as a "heat/energy field" when the ship is in flight.
    See a second docking bay on the ship somewhere with another pod attached, similar to ours. See open hatches on saucer and hull...sings of work being done. If possible, small worklites (not important, unless we pass by very close.)

DRYDOCK

    This is the best looking of all the models as they exist now. Perhaps embellish elevators..."busy" it up a little more. A new section of drydock should be built...the top and one side, so that angles from the side can be photographed.

(continued)

This memo was the beginning of the end for the fine television models that had already been constructed but that had never been intended to withstand the scrutiny of motion picture film.
Courtesy of Jon Povill.

−2−

INTER-COMMUNICATION

TO: DATE:

FROM: SUBJECT:

A mockup of the ENTERPRISE, either in foam or other cheap material, should be made to place into drydock as it exists now...it will be photographed from different angles and give Abel an idea of the posslble problems. Don Loos or Magicam could do this.

DOCKING BAY (SIDE OF ENTERPRISE)

    Add lights to it...either visual contact points, or sensor lights to "tractor beam" onto pod and guide it in. Maybe a signal system...also, paint "different colored metals" for the loading dock.

VEJUR

    Needs large head...anywhere from 6' to 10' wide, in order to show details on a wall 5 miles high. Existing head NG... lights lack perspective, detailing minimal.
    Gene: Don't like the skeleton idea on the back...the gold mylar is in the shape of a "stepladder", and it is too smooth. It must be broken-up some way...score it, discolor it, and age it. Possilbe whole new design for VEJUR.

    POSSIBBE ASSIGNMENTS FOR MAGICAM:

1) Embelish existing DRYDOCK
2) Build new top and side of DRYDOCK
3) Mock-up of ENTERPRISE out of foam
4) Add lights to DOCKING BAY, repaint metals (must conform to any changes which are made on ENTERPRISE miniature
5) Change glass in PODS to conform to stage...possible reflective surface (which clears upon activation)
6) Build complete POD with hatch (door) on back
7) When assembling POD CLUSTERS, be sure one has several pods missing
8) Possible Space Station on Asteroid
9) VEJUR head...detailed
10) VEJUR side section

As far as existing sets were concerned, since none of them were finished, upgrading them in terms of finishing details to appear on the movie screen would not be a major undertaking.

To get an idea of how they might appear on theater screens, cinematographer Bruce Logan shot film and lens tests of the unfinished sets, frames from which are reproduced in the color section of this book.

But what few people realized was that all the effort going into reexamining *Star Trek*'s status was basically being wasted.

For *Phase II* as a television project, its executive producer, Gene Roddenberry, would have close to final say on all important matters pertaining to visual effects, models, and sets. But for *Star Trek* as a movie, that authority would rest with the director.

What was going unsaid this December was that Paramount executives had been content to hire television director Robert Collins to oversee a $3 million, two-hour television movie. But they were less comfortable handing him a $15-million feature. Despite the months of effort he had put in, immersing himself in the *Star Trek* universe, rewriting the script, having a hand in casting Xon and Ilia, as far as the studio executives were concerned, he didn't have the experience. It was *Catch-22,* Hollywood style.

Thus the lull in *Phase II*'s production about this time was like the eye of the hurricane passing over the studio. Any moment, the storm of full production would return, and when it did, many members of the production team could expect to be blown away.

Except for Harold Livingston.

He wasn't waiting for the storm to return. His contract was up in December and his relationship with Roddenberry had deteriorated to the point that he was determined to exit the project. He delivered his last writers' status memo on December 14, reporting that *Phase II* had eleven hours in script, including "In Thy Image." Within the next week, the final two stories would be chosen from the ones currently in discussion. If *Star Trek* returned to television, as Roddenberry hoped it would eventually, a year after the feature was released, then Paramount would have thirteen scripts ready and waiting. But Livingston wouldn't be waiting with them.

On December 30, Livingston wrote a brief memo instructing business affairs to conclude a deal with Jon Povill for a new episode script to replace one that was not going to be delivered. And then he walked off the lot and went to work for Aaron Spelling as a much happier producer on *Fantasy Island.*

But just like Michael Corleone trying to escape his notorious mob family, Livingston wasn't going to get away that easily.

Nobody was.

Director Robert Wise inspects the bridge as he comes aboard as *Star Trek*'s first feature director.
Courtesy of Andrew Probert.

Metamorphosis

In terms of the number of people who knew what was going on, critical mass had been reached. The movie now had a life of its own. It could not be denied.

Star Trek Phase II, if it had ever existed at all, had been reduced to a name on a few drawers of last summer's blueprints. The ongoing adventures of Kirk, Xon, and McCoy existed only in the minds of the last few writers still working on their episode drafts.

Not even Jon Povill was able to tell them that the lines they wrote for Commander Will Decker were being written for a dead man. And as the "In Thy Image" rewrites continued and Ilia also came to be absorbed into the final merging of Decker and V'ger, her continuing role in the scripts was irrelevant as well.

The body had finally stopped twitching.

Elsewhere on the lot, the final budget details were being pulled together, based on the Robert Collins rewrite of the script and the first forty-five pages of Roddenberry's new revision.

In a memo about budget details dated January 5, 1978, Robert Goodwin shows that Paramount was well aware of what every *Star Trek* fan knew: Spock *had* to come back. That first budget included a salary allotment for Leonard Nimoy.

The $15-million budget that Eisner had greenlighted escalated to $18 million, then spiralled into space itself, stopping at $44 million, a figure that included all the money Paramount had ever spent on *Star Trek,* from Roddenberry's first script deal in 1975 to all the costs associated with *Phase II.* However, the combined salaries for Shatner, Nimoy, and Kelley amounted to a small percent of the original $15-million budget.

In addition to his director's fee, director Robert Collins received $10,000 for his rewrite of the script. He didn't direct anything, though.

Even as Paramount executives assured him

Even Robert Wise's film tests on the new sets were shot with extras in uniforms from *The Original Series*. Sleeker, more subdued costumes for *Star Trek: The Motion Picture* would be one of Wise's many decisions for reworking what had been developed for *Phase II*. Courtesy of Andrew Probert.

that he was still associated with the feature, they were actively negotiating with director Robert Wise to take over the project. Fortunately, both Collins and Wise had the same agent, so the news was broken to Collins gently.

Robert Wise was a celebrated director of films such as *Run Silent, Run Deep; West Side Story; The Sound of Music;* and *The Sand Pebbles*. He also had stellar science-fiction credits as the director of *The Day the Earth Stood Still* and *The Andromeda Strain*.

But Wise also insisted on being the producer of the films he made. He could accept Gene Roddenberry having a producer credit on the

movie, but that thirty-year-old kid in jeans, Robert Goodwin, would have to be content with a co-producer credit.

At that stage of his career, Goodwin knew that taking a lesser credit would be a bad move, so he declined the demotion and his deal was not transferred from the series to the feature. Without a Paramount Television Service, those thirty television movies he was to supervise were also long gone. Goodwin left the project when Wise came on in March 1978. He then started his own movie company with Mark Tanz, and produced the acclaimed *Inside Moves*.

Checking plans on the incomplete Engineering set in February 1978. Courtesy of Andrew Probert.

Wise had enough clout as a director and producer that he could break the initial logjam at the studio. He toured the sets, visited the miniatures, and, most importantly, listened to his wife and father-in-law as they told him he couldn't possibly *think* of doing a *Star Trek* movie without Mr. Spock.

Eisner sent Jeffrey Katzenberg to New York where Nimoy was starring in *Equus.* Within a week, the long-standing disagreement that Nimoy had with the studio was resolved with a check for a reportedly substantial figure. Hours later, the latest rewrite of "In Thy Image" was in Nimoy's hands—featuring Xon and not Spock.

Now Nimoy became part of the collaborative process.

In the final film, a new actor played Xon long enough to be killed in a transporter accident. David Gautreaux appeared briefly as a doomed Starfleet officer aboard a space station destroyed by V'ger. One Hollywood fairytale had come to an end.

But with Wise and Nimoy on the production, the pressure for a writer other than Roddenberry grew.

In April, Harold Livingston got an unexpected, late-night phone call from Gene Roddenberry. "I knew right away that he was in trouble,"

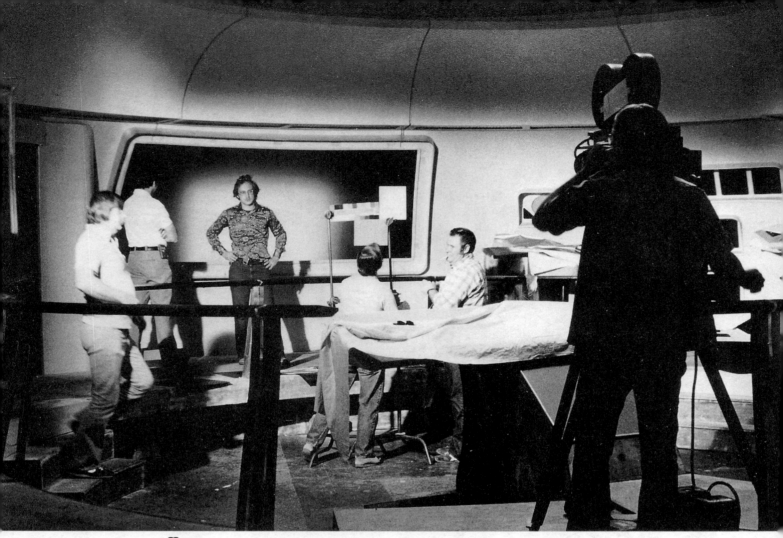

More tests on the *Phase II* bridge in February 1978. Courtesy of Andrew Probert.

Livingston recalls. "We made a date and he sent me a script by messenger. I didn't know how many guys had rewritten it.

"I met Gene and Bob [Wise] the next morning and I just said to Bob, 'You'd better take cyanide because this script is [awful] and you can't use it.' And they agreed, which is why they wanted me to come back.

"So, I came back. Of course, I came back under my own conditions, which Gene didn't like.

"When I went to work for Bob, we worked very closely, and I remember that the first fifty pages I rewrote were sent by messenger to Eisner and Katzenberg in Paris. And Eisner called me from Paris and he said, 'What is this?' I didn't know what he was talking about until I found out that

Gene had taken my pages and rewritten them."

The endless boxes of revised drafts from that time are filled with groups of script pages, each labelled "GR" or "HL" depending on who had rewritten them last. Livingston walked out on the feature at least four times. The last time, he was brought back only after Katzenberg locked him in his office and refused to let him out until he reconsidered.

Livingston's final deal with Paramount was that he would continue on the movie, but only if Katzenberg would then hire him to write a script on any subject Livingston chose.

Katzenberg agreed. Livingston came back.

And, after the movie opened, Livingston never worked with Roddenberry again.

The rest of *The Motion Picture*'s genesis was equally rocky, equally torn by personality conflicts, lack of focus, and a loss of perspective, on the part of many people.

But in a testament to Gene Roddenberry's vision of the future, the team he had assembled and the original actors he had cast all pulled together in the eleventh hour to fill the final script with the character moments that defined what *Star Trek* was and remains to this day.

Against all odds, the movie that had had such a troubled birth, rising from the ashes of not one but two failed television series, became a stunning success.

Roddenberry had been given his second chance and had not squandered it. His first and only success had not been a fluke. Indeed, the true strength of his creation was that so many more people were now free to add to it, and it still remained strong.

Looking back on the brief life of *Phase II,* there are no heroes or villains. Only talented people driven to create something they could take pride in and millions more could enjoy.

In hindsight, the path they took might seem questionable. But as Robert Goodwin concludes, "It was terrible experience, but it was all very understandable and very acceptable, because that's the way the business is. That's what they had to do."

And the funny thing is, it works.

The torch is passed. With Director Robert Wise at the helm, the television series *Star Trek Phase II* had officially become *Star Trek: The Motion Picture.*

Part TWO

The Lost
Bible

Star Trek II Writers/Directors Guide

In television parlance, a "bible" is the guidebook for a series. It defines the basic premise of the series and its story-telling arena, introduces the characters, and describes script structure, special settings, and gimmicks. Some bibles even include story possibilities.

The following bible is in essence an updating of the one written for the Original Series. The new material concerning this second five-year mission of the U.S.S. Enterprise was developed between May and August of 1977, and written by Gene Roddenberry and Jon Povill, with additional contributions from many of the Phase II staff, including producer Robert Goodwin.

While this bible can be read as a final document for the lost Star Trek, there is another way to look at it that makes it even more historically interesting—as a preliminary document for Star Trek: The Next Generation.

The new science officer, Xon, is clearly a forerunner of Data, down to his attempts to replicate human behavior without being able to understand it.

First Officer Commander Will Decker, in personality and function, is just as clearly an early version of First Officer, Commander Will Riker, as the partially telepathic navigator, Ilia, is an early version of the empathic Counselor Troi. Indeed, Ilia's character continued to evolve past this bible, until she, too, was able to sense emotions, and served as counselor to the crew. And Decker and Ilia shared a romantic interlude in their past, just as Riker and Troi did.

Of course, not every aspect of Phase II continued into The Next Generation. For an example of a particularly drastic change, check out the fifth-from-last question at the bible's end: How much science-fiction terminology do you want? The answer is a good illustration of how much Star Trek has really changed over the years.

STAR TREK II

Our new episodes portray the second five-year mission of the U.S.S. Enterprise. Following its first mission, the starship had returned home and entered orbital drydocks in the naval yards high over San Francisco, where the vessel has been completely refit. Its basic contours, both interior and exterior, remain generally the same. The vessel functions in basically the same way. However, the details of the vessel such as instrumentation, read-out systems, and controls are vastly more sophisticated than in the original Enterprise.

To command this second five-year mission, Captain James T. Kirk has refused an Admiral's star and has managed to recruit many of the original crew. An exception to this is Mr. Spock, who has returned in high honor to Vulcan to head the Science Academy there. In fact, all of our original crew have found themselves to be very nearly legends in their own time. Few starships have ever completed a five-year mission, and none but the U.S.S. Enterprise has returned with its original crew virtually intact. Perhaps the explanation for so many of the crew volunteering for a second five years was their seeking the relative anonymity of space. Or perhaps these men or women cannot find satisfaction in an ordinary life after so many years of the highest adventure experienced by humans.

The starship's mission remains the same—to patrol a section of our galaxy, to represent Earth and the Federation by assisting colonists, aiding scientific exploration, suppressing conflict, helping those in distress, regulating trade, engaging in diplomatic missions with other planets and peoples.

WHAT HAS CHANGED?

The character of MR. SPOCK will be missed, and we still hope he will return often as a guest star. In the meantime, a young Vulcan named XON is new science officer replacement and is a character with dimensions and qualities uniquely his own.

First Officer of the Enterprise is COMMANDER WILL DECKER, second in command under Kirk (see page 13). At the navigator's station will be LT. ILIA, a strangely beautiful female native of Federation planet Delta V.

CHEKOV is now a full lieutenant and commands the starship security division. "BONES" McCOY, SCOTTY, UHURA and SULU are at their familiar stations. We'll also see YEOMAN JANICE RAND again; our former head nurse is now DR. CHRISTINE CHAPEL.

We will still use science fiction to make comments on today but today is now a dozen years later than the first STAR TREK. Humanity faces many new questions and puzzles which were not obvious back in the 1960's, all of them suggesting new stories and themes. Also, television censorship has relaxed enormously during those same years, opening up still more new story areas . . . or certainly more honesty in some old areas.

Television has become much more sophisticated in other ways. Older, ponderous dialogue patterns have given way (thank you M.A.S.H.) to more realism through the use of fragmented sentences, overlaps and interruptions. Better camera techniques, new film emulsions and exciting new optical and tape effects all make increased realism possible.

STAR TREK will take more looks into the private and offduty lives of our characters. More realism here too in very human areas such as when and what they eat, 23rd century bathing, changing clothes, playing and relaxing.

There will be less "battleship sterility" in the design of the refit Enterprise. Bridge, engineering and other work sections will still tend toward functionalism. But in other sections of the vessel we'll see something of the art forms appreciated and collected by inter-stellar travellers. Affection for life forms will extend to vegetation and we'll see exotic and sometimes mysterious plant life collected from half a hundred worlds.

The essential format will <u>not</u> change. Action-adventure, entertainment, and some fun for us too as we speculate where we humans are, where we're going, and what it's really all about.

WHAT IS A STAR TREK STORY?

While the construction and development of all television series stories is similar, STAR TREK's attraction to both its fans and general audience has been unique. Its attraction has also been extremely broad, ranging from children to college presidents and astronauts. The more successful STAR TREK episodes have all followed five basic rules:

1. OUR STORIES ARE ABOUT PEOPLE (WHO ACT BELIEVABLY)
STAR TREK is not about science and gadgetry. <u>All good stories are about people and science fiction is no exception</u>. The more <u>believable</u> the people, the better the story. Science fiction story characters must be written as carefully as characters in any contemporary drama, reacting and interacting as real people behave. Whatever gadgetry we show must be believable too—it must be an extension of some present science fact or theory.

2. AN OPTIMISTIC PROJECTION OF THE FUTURE
If our society at the time of STAR TREK has advanced to a point of interstellar travel and co-existing with diverse planets and life-forms—then it must be assumed that we have also solved our petty squabbles and prejudices of the twentieth century. They would have also learned an affection for diversity; they do not judge other worlds and other life forms by Earth standards. However, on Earth or on the Enterprise, life is <u>not</u> dull—the challenge of self and self-improvement have replaced the old fears and aggressions.

3. THE STORY P.O.V. IS THAT OF OUR CAPTAIN AND CREW
"These are the voyages of the starship Enterprise" . . . and the adventures of its captain and crew. We see and feel our stories through the eyes and emotions of our regular characters. Story can depart briefly to the POV of a guest star, but always returns to indicate how this action has affected our regular characters of the vessel they depend upon. It is <u>not</u> enough for our starship and crew to run into something fascinating in space or on a strange new world. That "something" they run into must also create a strong jeopardy or a need involving one or more of regular characters. A jeopardy or need involving a guest star is <u>not</u> enough unless that guest star's safety and/or need has become of paramount importance to one of our regular characters.

4. OUR REGULARS ARE HEROES
They believe that their word and their oath is their bond. They believe there are principles worth a life of discomfort and danger and even carry the "old fashioned" belief that there are things even worth dying for if necessary. However, in most other ways they are very much 23rd century humans and have few of the sexual, social and economic hang-ups of their 20th century ancestors. Their values and ideals do not center exclusively on things affecting only Earth and humans.

5. OUR HOME BASE IS THE U.S.S. ENTERPRISE
Our starship is very definitely one of the characters in our series. It is the focal point

of the lives of all our regular characters. Our stories have always either begun or ended aboard the starship, and many of our best tales have taken place entirely aboard that vessel.

THE STAR TREK SCRIPT FORMAT

THE TEASER
We open with action, always establishing a strong jeopardy, need, or other "hook."

THE ACTS
Four acts. Act One usually begins with VOICE OVER as Captain Kirk dictates his log and tells us where we are and what is going on. Any necessary back story should be laid in here, not in the teaser. The Captain's Log should be succinct and crisp . . . in ship commander "log" language.

Opening Act One, we need some form of orbit, establishing or other silent shot to give us time for both Captain's Log and opening credits.

STYLE
A fast pace, avoiding long philosophical exchanges or tedious explanations of equipment. Our cutting technique is to use the shortest possible time between idea and execution of it. For example: Kirk decides that a landing party will transport down to a planet . . . HARD CUT to lights blinking on the Transporter console, PULL BACK to REVEAL the landing party stepping into the Transporter.

CAST AND SET LISTS
Cast and set lists with your draft.

THE U.S.S. ENTERPRISE

THE VESSEL
The U.S.S. Enterprise is a spaceship, official designation "starship class," somewhat larger than a present-day naval cruiser, it is the largest and most modern type of vessel in the Starfleet service. It has a crew of 430, approximately one-half female.

The Enterprise provides a "home base," a familiar and comfortable counterpoint to the bizarre and unusual things and places we see during our episodes. Where possible try to emphasize and play to the size, complexity, and varied functions of the Enterprise. This does not mean you must always use the Enterprise but we usually start or end each story there.

The Saucer Section of the vessel (at the top of which is our command bridge) is eleven decks thick at the middle. The Engineering Section (to which the two engine nacelles are attached) is equally large and complex, contains at the rear a hangar deck large enough to hangar a whole fleet of today's jetliners. Turbo elevators, which can run both vertically and horizontally, interconnect every deck and compartment of this huge vessel.

Included in addition to our bridge, sickbay, Captain's cabin and other familiar standing sets, are the widest possible variety of labs and technical departments, computer rooms, storage facilities, passenger accommodations, and cargo facilities.

The refurbished Enterprise is slightly changed, just enough for the audience to say "Yes, it is the Enterprise, and even lovelier than before . . ."

THE CREW

International in origin, completely multi-racial. But even in this future century we will see some traditional trappings, ornaments, and styles that suggest the Asiatic, the Arabic, the Latin, etc. So far, the Vulcan officer has been our only crewman with bloodlines from another planet. However, it's likely in STAR TREK II that we will find other aliens or part aliens working aboard our Starship.

Be inventive! Use the crewmen (extras as well as actors) to help suggest the enormous diversity of our vessel. For example, playing a scene in leisure attire as our people pass in sports gear obviously going to or coming from a gymnasium or such. Life aboard the Enterprise (believably again, as in a present-day naval cruiser) is not all hard work and stern devotion to duty.

SHIP'S POWER

The Enterprise engines (the two outboard nacelles) use matter and anti-matter for propulsion, the annihilation of dual matter creating the fantastic power required to warp space and exceed the speed of light.

The Enterprise has a secondary propulsion system. These are impulse power engines (same principle as rocket power), located at the rear of the "saucer section." Vessel speed, when using the impulse engine is, of course, less than the speed of light. In case of total failure of all engine power sources, the vessel's gravitational and life support systems can be switched to battery power, with a full-load capacity of about one week.

Hyper-light speeds or space warp speeds (the latter is the terminology we prefer) are measured in WARP FACTORS. Warp factor one is the speed of light—186,000 miles per second (or somewhat over six hundred million miles per hour). Note: warp factors two, three and four and so on are based upon a geometrical formula of light velocity. Warp factor two is actually eight times the speed of light; warp factor three is twenty-four times the speed of light; warp factor four is sixty-four times the speed of light, and so on.

Maximum safe speed is now warp eight. At velocities past warp eight the vessel begins to show considerable strain and are used only in emergencies.

SHIP'S WEAPONRY

The main weaponry of the U.S.S. Enterprise is its banks of "ship's phasers," which are artillery-sized versions of the hand phaser and phaser pistol.

From the Bridge, phaser power can be aimed in any direction and our Optical Effect here is "blips" or "squirts" of blue phaser fire, which are emitted from the vessel's main strut. These can act directly against target very much as hand phaser fire, but on a much larger scale. Phaser fire can also be set for proximity explosion and act somewhat like "depth charges."

The Helmsman acts as weapons officer. Under the Captain's direction, he coordinates the fire from the phaser rooms, using the vessel's navigational aids to lock the phasers on target and, on the Captain's order, engaging the circuits which fire these weapons.

CAPTAIN JAMES T. KIRK

A shorthand sketch of Kirk might be "a space-age Captain Horatio Hornblower," constantly on trial with himself, a strong, complex personality.

With the Starship out of communication with Earth and Starfleet bases for long periods of time, a Starship captain has unusual broad powers over both the lives and welfare of his crew, as well as over Earth people and activities encountered during these voyages. He also has broad power as an Earth Ambassador may discover. Kirk feels these responsibilities strongly and <u>is fully capable of letting the worry and frustration lead him into error</u>.

He is also capable of fatigue and inclined to push himself beyond human limits, then condemn himself because he is not superhuman. The crew respects him, some almost to the point of adoration. At the same time, no senior officer aboard is fearful of using his own intelligence in questioning Kirk's orders and can themselves be strongly articulate up to the point where Kirk signifies his decision has been made.

Kirk is a veteran of hundreds of planet landings and space emergencies. He has a broad and highly mature perspective on command, fellow crewmen, and even on alien life customs, however strange or repugnant they seem when reassessed against Earth standards.

On the other hand, don't play Kirk like the captain of an 1812 frigate in which nothing or no one moves without his command. The Enterprise crew is a finely-trained team, <u>well able to anticipate information and action Kirk needs</u>.

Aboard ship, Captain Kirk has only a few opportunities for anything approaching friendship. One exception is with ship's surgeon Dr. McCoy, who has a legitimate professional need to constantly be aware of the state of the Captain's mind and emotions. But on a "shore leave" away from the confines of self-imposed discipline, Jim Kirk is likely to play pretty hard, almost compulsively so. It is not impossible he will let this drag him at one time or another into an unwise romantic liaison which he will have great difficulty disentangling. He is, in short, a strong man forced by the requirements of his ship and career into the often lonely role of command, even lonelier because Starship command is the most difficult and demanding task of his century.

LIEUTENANT XON

Can a twenty-two-year-old Vulcan on his first space voyage fill the shoes of the legendary Mr. Spock? XON (pronounced <u>Zahn</u>) was selected by the Vulcan Science Academy to attempt exactly that. Kirk was stunned when his new science officer reported aboard and found him to be a little more than a boy. (Xon looks something like a young Michael York wtth pointed ears.) Kirk had assumed the replacement was someone near Spock's age. The reports he had read on Xon listed him as a prominent scientist and teacher.

The truth is that Xon is a genius, even by Vulcan standards. As we'll see in our episodes, he is as competent as Spock in all fields of science. He lacks knowledge, however, in one very important area—the human equation. Unlike Spock, Xon is a full Vulcan. He had no human mother to acquaint him with the Earth species; he has no human half with which to feel and understand human emotions.

Xon realizes that the reason that Spock performed so well in his tasks on board the Enterprise was that he was half human and therefore could understand emotional human nature. In order to perform as well as Spock, he knows he is going to have to eliminate his Vulcan revulsion at emotional displays. He is, in fact, going to have to reach down within himself and find the emotions that his society has repressed for thousands of years so that he will have some basis for fully understanding his human associates.

What this means is: whereas Spock was engaged in a constant battle within himself to repress his emotions in order to be more Vulcan-like, Xon will be engaged in a constant struggle within himself to release his buried emotions to be more human-like for the sake of doing a good job—his primary consideration. This will be at least as difficult for him as it was for Spock to maintain his stoic pose. Also, we'll get humor out of Xon trying to simulate laughter, anger, fear, and other human feelings.

The new science officer accepted the Enterprise assignment with much trepidation. He has no doubt that he can competently handle the scientific aspects of his job, but he fears the crew might expect him to be a duplicate of Spock as well as a replacement. These fears have been realized and hanging over the early episodes. So also is the unsaid comment, "Mr. Spock never did it quite like that." Nor is Captain Kirk overly fair to Xon in the beginning. Spock's friendship was a deep, important thing to Kirk and the Captain is now almost arbitrarily rejecting the possibility of a meaningful relationship with the young Vulcan. However, the more difficult Lieutenant Xon's situation, the more we'll like him and the more we'll want him to succeed in this difficult assignment.

As a full Vulcan, Xon is even stronger than Spock. He can endure lack of water and high temperatures for very long periods. All his senses are particularly keen. He has strong Vulcan mind-meld abilities.

The young Vulcan lieutenant is constantly shocked by human behavior. In preparing for this assignment, he made himself quite an expert on human behavior and history. And it is amusing to see him try to apply this knowledge too logically and too literally. Nothing he studied quite prepared him for the real thing. Although Xon tries hard to hide his surprise and discomfitures, the crew is aware that it exists. They often go out of their way to exaggerate their human qualities, further distressing the young Vulcan. But this is not done in mean spirit and never in a situation where it will interfere with starship efficiency. We will suspect that life among humans is causing Xon to begin to feel some emotions himself. On his planet this is, of course, grossest of sins and the young Vulcan makes every effort to hide any sign of this "weakness."

The science officer presides over a large console which is known as the "Library-Computer Station." It is second in importance only to ship command and is located directly behind Captain's position.

COMMANDER WILL DECKER

In his youthful thirties, Decker is the ship's Executive Officer, second in command. Kirk sometimes calls or refers to him as "First," which is naval parlance for ship's "First Lieutenant," which would have been Decker's title in the days of sailing ships. Will Decker comes very near to worshipping Kirk and would literally rather die than fail him. The prime responsibility of a "First" is to provide his captain with the most efficient crew and vessel possible and Will Decker takes this responsibility seriously.

When not absorbed in his task of keeping the Enterprise at top fitness, Will Decker is a very humorous man. He particularly enjoys playing the "too perfect," soulless marionnette of an officer. The joke can be confusing to others because Will can become almost that kind of officer when Kirk's welfare or the safety of the ship is involved.

We can see that Jim Kirk is very much in the process of training the young commander for the responsibilities of Starship command someday. We will see that future captain begin to happen during this five-year mission.

In areas of logistics and organization, he has a keen and analytical mind, one upon which Kirk will rely heavily. He will command some landing parties and many decisions will be life-and-death choices.

Will's background is all service: his father, his father's father were Academy graduates, Starfleet officers of flag rank. Someday, surely, he will wear a star. Because of his heritage, and because he had been groomed since nearly birth for command. He has friends, but tends to protect his privacy while respecting others'. Between Kirk and Decker is a kind of father/son relationship that each cherishes.

LIEUTENANT ILIA

ILIA (pronounced "Ill-ee-ah") is a young female of Planet 114-Delta V, which has recently joined the Federation. The Deltan race is much older than humans, with brains much more finely evolved in areas of art and mathematics. These abilities make her a superb navigator and her artistic abilities are evident in her sure, flowing precision at this task.

Her face is breathtakingly beautiful. But like all Deltans, she is completely hairless except for the eyes. Her smooth, slender bare head has the almost sensual quality of delicately contoured nudity, always hidden before in other women. It gives her a striking, almost "Egyptian" look, particularly when wearing a Deltan jewel-band head ornament.

Ilia's intelligence level is second only to the Science Officer and she has also the esper abilities common on her planet. Unlike the mind-meld of Vulcans, it simply is the ability to sense images in other minds. Never words or emotions, only images . . . shapes, sizes, textures. On her planet, sexual foreplay consists largely of lovers placing images in each other's minds.

Just as Vulcans have a problem with emotions, Ilia has a problem which accompanies her aboard the starship. On 114-Delta V, almost everything in life is sex-oriented—it is a part of every frienship, every social engagement, every profession. It is simply the normal way to relate with others there. Since constant sex is not the pattern of humans and others aboard this starship, Ilia has totally repressed this emotion drive and social pattern.

DR. LEONARD "BONES" McCOY

Played by DeForest Kelley, Dr. McCoy is Senior Ship's Surgeon of the U.S.S. Enterprise, head of the Medical Department. As such, he is responsible for the health and physical welfare of the crew of the Enterprise. He also has broad medical science responsibilities in areas of space exploration.

As Senior Ship's Surgeon, "Bones" McCoy is the one man who can approach Captain Kirk on the most intimate personal levels relating to the Captain's physical, mental and emotional well being. Indeed, he has the absolute duty to constantly keep abreast of the Captain's condition and speak out openly to Kirk on this matter. McCoy is portrayed as something of a future-day H.L. Mencken, a very, very outspoken character, with more than a little cynical bite in his attitudes and observations on life. He has an acid wit which results in sometimes shocking statements—statements which, under close scrutiny, carry more than a grain of truth about medicine, man and society.

Of all the men aboard our starship, McCoy is the least military. He is filled with idiosyncracies which fit the character and are his trademark. For example, he loathes the Transporter and system of "beaming" personnel from the ship to planet surfaces, and loudly proclaims that he does not care to have his molecules scrambled and beamed around as if he were a radio message.

McCoy is highly practical in the old "general practitioner" sense, hates pills except when they are vitally needed, is not above believing that a little suffering is good for the soul and the maturity of the individual. He has a great fear that perfect medicine, psychotherapy and computers may rob mankind of his individuality and his divine right to wrestle a bit with life. He's a superb physician and surgeon—often seems to be treating the wrong ailment—but usually is proven right in the end.

Dr. McCoy is the oldest crew member aboard, and as such, subject to some ribbing. He was married once, something of a mystery that ended unhappily. He is a grandfather, but unhappily his starship duty has prevented him forming the relationship with his grandchildren he would have desired. His years provide him wisdom and experience, and offer an interesting—and sometimes poignant—counterpoint to the younger officers and crewmen.

Lieutenant Xon, like Spock before him, appears to regard McCoy as a bumbling country doctor, generally achieving cures through luck rather than science. But "Bones" McCoy, like most cynics, is at heart a bleeding humanist and the affectionate (and humorous) feud that was carried on between Spock and McCoy is continued between McCoy and Xon.

With the considerable difference, however, that McCoy feels the "feud" is a very private affair concerning himself and Xon—and McCoy has been known to severely chastise (in private) those crewmen and officers who have been guilty of unfairness to the young Vulcan in comparing his efforts to Spock's. If you accused McCoy of protecting Xon, he would vehemently deny it.

ENGINEERING OFFICER SCOTT—Montgomery Scott, rank of Commander, Senior Engineering Officer on the U.S.S. Enterprise, portrayed by James Doohan, he is known to most as "Scotty," and with an accent that drips of heather and the highlands.

Scotty came up through the ranks and his practical education is as broad as his formal training in Engineering. He has rare mechanical capacity many claim he can put an engine together with baling wire and glue . . . and make it run. He regards the U.S.S. Enterprise as his personal property and the Engineering Section as his private world where even Captain James Kirk is merely a privileged trespasser.

Engineering and spaceships are his life. His idea of a pleasant afternoon is tinkering in an Engineering Section of the vessel; he is totally unable to understand why any sane man would spend reading time on anything but technical manuals. He is strong-minded, strong-willed and not incapable of telling off even a Starfleet Captain who intrudes into what Scotty regards as his own private province and area of responsibilities.

Kirk understands his Engineering Officer's fierce love of his vessel and his engines, will take more "guff" off this officer than almost any other aboard the ship. Regarding him, Kirk has one rule: "If it doesn't run, take it to Scotty. If he can't fix it, it's irrepairable."

UHURA—Rank of Lieutenant Commander, Communications Officer, played by attractive young actress Nichelle Nichols. Uhura was born in the African Confederacy. Quick and intelligent, she is a highly efficient officer. Her understanding of the ship's computer systems is second only to the Vulcan Science Officer, and expert in all ships systems relating to communications. Uhura is also a warm, highly female female off duty. She is a favorite in the Recreation Room during off duty hours, too, because she sings—old ballads as well as the newer space ballads—and she can do impersonations at the drop of a communicator.

SULU—Ship's Helsman, played by actor George Takei. Mixed Oriental in ancestry, a Lieutenant Commander, Japanese predominating, Sulu is very Occidental in speech and manner. In fact, his attitude toward Asians is that they seem to him rather "inscrutable." Sulu fancies himself more of an old-world "D'Artagnan" than anything else. He is a compulsive hobbyist; like all "collectors," he is forever giving his friends a thousand reasons why they, too, should take on the same hobby.

Although these bursts of enthusiasm make him something of a chatterbox, Sulu is a top officer and one of the most proficient helmsmen in the Starfleet Service. When the chips are down, he immediately becomes another character, a terse professional, whose every word and deed relate solely to the vessel and its safety. This pleasant and effective "dual personality" results never intrudes on his job. He has never had to receive the same order from Kirk twice.

LT. CHEKOV—Formerly an ensign, the youngest officer aboard, Chekov is now a full lieutenant with years of space adventure behind him. He commands the security division of the U.S.S. Enterprise, and is responsible for matters of security and discipline both aboard the vessel and ashore. He is responsible also for the training of the men and women who make up his security teams. During action stations, his post is on the bridge at the damage control console. The Captain's safety is Lt. Chekov's responsibility, too, very much as the Captain's health is McCoy's concern.

DR. CHRISTINE CHAPEL—Introduced in STAR TREK I as Nurse Chapel, her medical degrees have been accepted by Starfleet, and she has returned to the U.S.S. Enterprise to serve as McCoy's associate. She is second in command of the ship's medical section, and McCoy seems to enjoy passing on to her every duty he finds too boring, irritating or annoying to himself. Yet outside of Captain Kirk, she is probably McCoy's closest confidante. An expert in psychotherapy, she has unusual ability to teach patients how to use the healing powers of their own bodies.

YEOMAN—Played by a succession of young actresses, always lovely. One such character has been well-established, "YEOMAN JANICE RAND," played by the lovely Grace Lee Whitney. It is a tradition of Starfleet that yeomen are invariably female and serve ship commanders as a combination of executive secretary-valet-military aide. It is a much sought-after post because of the experience gained and many yeomen go on to eventually become senior bridge officers and Starfleet captains. As in the case of all females aboard, they are treated co-equally with males of the same rank and the same level of efficient performance is expected. The yeoman often carries an over-the-shoulder case, the TRICORDER, which is an electronic recorder-camera-sensor combination, immediately available to the captain, should he be away from his command console.

STANDING SETS

Herewith a list of existing and projected U.S.S. Enterprise sets.

BRIDGE

A circular, platformed set where Captain Kirk presides over the whole ship's complex. Access is achieved to this set by means of turbo-lift elevators which open directly into the set. Kirk sits in his command chair in the inner, lower elevation, facing the large Bridge Viewer. Directly in front of him, also facing the Viewer, sit the Navigator and the Helmsman at their individual console. In the outer circular elevation of the set are various positions for Communications Officer and various Technician Crewmen and other ship's officers. Directly behind the Captain, the Science Officer presides over a console which is known as the "Library-Computer Station."

TURBO-ELEVATORS

All through the ship are turbo-lifts which can be programmed for lateral and/or vertical movement. One can reach most any section aboard by activating its control vocally.

SHIP'S CORRIDORS

Curved corridors with various inter-connecting sub-corridors. Various doors and hatches open upon a variety of areas within the Enterprise proper. We play these as existing on the different decks and levels of the ship and, of course, all have connecting turbo-elevators.

TRANSPORTER ROOM

We assume there are various Transporter Rooms through the vessel. The one we use has access from a main corridor. The Transporter control is operated by the Transporter Officer and a Technician. They, in concert or singly, can transport up to six people at a time, "beaming" them either from or to the starship. At certain times, objects out in space which are small enough and in reasonably close proximity can be brought aboard also. At one end of this set is the Transporter chamber itself. It is a circular platform with several steps leading up to its six positions. Each person to be transported stands upon one of six light panels. There is a light panel above each position also. Within this chamber, people are made to disappear and appear optically as they are "beamed" to and from vessels or planet surfaces.

SICKBAY AND DOCTOR'S OFFICE

A three-room complex. The doctor's office has direct access to a ship's corridor. There is access from his office to an examining room, also a sickbay proper. Access to the sickbay proper can also be made directly from the corridor. Within the sickbay, there are built-in bed positions with a complete diagnostic panel above each. This medical device scans the patient continually, takes readings and registers same upon the diagnostic panel instrument face. Thus, blood pressure, pulse rate, heartbeat, respirations and various other readings are continually recorded and displayed for each patient without the necessity of physical contact between doctor and patient.

ENGINEERING DECK

A section of the ship's innards, wherein we find the basic components of the ship's motive force and energy. This is a large set, the main province of the Engineering Officer (Scott). Access to the main feed of the starship's circuitry is available here.

BRIEFING ROOM

A large set where Kirk and Xon can convene all Department Heads aboard for briefings, discussions and staff meetings. A large table with sufficient chair positions. There are library-computer controls and viewer built in to the table. This set can double as a wardroom. Access directly into a main ship's corridor.

RECREATION ROOM

A redress of other sets to give us a variety of mess and recreation facilities. In these, crew members can relax and enjoy their leisure time. Various games such as three-dimensional chess can be played here.

CAPTAIN'S QUARTERS

Captain Kirk has a two-room complex. One room contains his working area when he is away from the bridge. There is access from this room to the next room where his sleeping quarters are. There is direct access to the ship's corridor from either room. There are viewing and communications devices here as in most major sets.

THE VULCAN'S CABIN

A redress of Captain Kirk's cabin, but will suggest something of his homeland.

PASSENGER QUARTERS

Again, a redress of Captain Kirk's quarters unless a larger area is required, at which time it will be constructed out of a redress of a briefing room.

SHIP'S CHAPEL

Redress of Transporter Room.

DINING ROOM

Redress of other sets as required.

GYMNASIUM

A redress of other sets. It is sufficiently sized to allow various forms of physical exercise and limited area sports, such as wrestling, fencing, etc.

SHUTTLECRAFT

Full-sized mockup of a six- or seven-passenger ship which can be sent out on intra-solar system missions. This craft can be duplicated in miniature. Interior and exterior available.

HANGAR DECK

A miniature set, optically created to be a "huge football field"-size area where our shuttlecraft or crafts are stored. It is at the rear of the thick cigar-shaped "engineering section" of our vessel and on the scale model is visible the huge hangar doors which roll open when a shuttlecraft departs from or returns to our vessel. Caution—miniature and optical work like this is expensive and <u>must</u> be a vital element in the story when used.

OTHERS

Obviously, various stories may require specialized "one-time" sets. Past examples of this have been a botany section, a computer bank area, an observation deck (with stars visible through a window) and so on. Again, completely new and unusual sets are costly and should be vital in the story if used. If planet sets and interiors are required, then new ship sets should be minimized—the writer must use experience and common sense in keeping construction costs within a normal television budget.

IMPORTANT EQUIPMENT AND TERMINOLOGY

TRICORDER

A portable sensor-computer-recorder, about the size of a large rectangular handbag, carried by an over-shoulder strap. A remarkable miniaturized device, it can be used to analyze and keep records of almost any type of data on planet surfaces, plus sensing or identifying various objects. It can also give the age of an artifact, the composition of alien life and so on. The tricorder is usually carried by officers to maintain records of what is going on or as a portable scientific tool. It can also be identified as a "medical tricorder" and carried by Dr. McCoy.

THE PHASERS

Hand weapons. At present we have two phasers. (1) the "hand phaser," which is hardly much larger than a king-sized package of cigarettes and (2) the "Phaser pistol" which consists of the hand phaser snapped into a pistol mount, the handle of which is a power-pack, which greatly increases the range and power of the weapon.

The reason for two phasers—in some instances such as friendly calls and diplomatic missions, our landing party would not want to beam down to a planet with the larger phaser pistols hanging from their belts. The hand phaser (along with the communicator) is worn on a belt hidden under the shirt. At other times, the story does require that the landing party be conspicuously armed and the large phaser pistol hanging visibly from a weapons belt fulfills that requirement.

The "phaser rifle" consists of the phaser pistol adapted into a rifle mount, thus having even greater range and power.

Both the hand phaser and the phaser pistol have a variety of settings. The ones most often used are "stun effect," which can knock a man down and render him unconscious without harming him, and "full effect," which can actually cause an object to dematerialize and disappear. The phaser is also capable of being set to cause an object to explode, or to burn a clean hole through an object. In some stories, we have used the phaser as a tool, such as a cutting torch. Phasers can also be set to "overload," resulting in a power buildup and explosion which destroys the phaser and anything in close proximity.

COMMUNICATORS

A portable "intercom" about the size of the hand phaser. Not generally used aboard vessel, since there are communications panels strategically located everywhere on the ship. The principal use of the communicator is between elements of a landing party on a planet surface, or from them to the U.S.S. Enterprise in orbit. The communicator, activated by lifting the antenna-grid, also pinpoints that person's position on the planet surface, so that the Transporter Crew aboard the vessel can beam that person or the entire landing party up aboard the vessel. It can be attached to the tricorder to transmit directly into the Enterprise computer banks.

TRANSPORTER

As discussed and described earlier, it is essentially a device which "beams" crew or cargo to and from planet surfaces and/or other space vessels. It converts matter temporarily into energy, beaming that energy to a fixed point, then re-converting it back into its original matter structure. Its range is limited to about 16,000 miles.

VIEWERS

The generic name for any kind of viewing screen. (We avoid the word screen here and use it only when referring to force field screens.) The most important is the Bridge Viewer. This is not a window; it is an electronic viewing screen which can be pointed outside in any direction and with various magnifications. Most often it is aimed in the direction of ship's travel and shows the stars passing as we make our way through space. In certain situations, holographic images can be formed on this screen.

In addition, intercom viewers connect most areas of the vessel. For example, Kirk in his cabin can call Sulu or Xon on the bridge, see them and be seen through his intercom viewing screen. Or think of it as simply a video-telephone hookup.

There is also a rectangular viewer over the Library-Computer Station, on which can be flashed visual information from the ship's record tapes.

SENSORS

One of our most useful devices. "Sensor" is our generic term for any equipment aboard the U.S.S. Enterprise capable of "sensing" or "reading" almost any kind of information needed in our stories. This can include composition of an object met in space, its dimensions, if a vessel, the presence and number of human or alien life aboard, the geological age of a meteoroid, almost anything. Xon is generally in charge of the ship's sensors and takes most of these readings from his hooded screen at his Library-Computer Station.

The tricorder includes small sensors for use on a planet surface. And there are specialized navigational sensors used by the men at the helm, medical sensors used in sickbay, and so on. Never try to explain or describe the sensors, simply use them— they're real because they are there and they work.

DEFLECTORS

The primary "defensive shield" of the U.S.S. Enterprise. It is, in effect, an invisible force barrier around the Enterprise which protects the vessel from anything but the most sophisticated and powerful weapons. It is automatically activated by the ship's sensors when an unknown danger approaches. Note: The ship's Transporter cannot be used while the deflector screen is operating.

If the vessel should be under attack, the power of the deflector shield can be considerably increased, but at a commensurate loss in ship's power and at maximum shielding can only be maintained for a limited time.

The ship also has "navigational deflector beams" which, guided by "navigational scanners," sweep out far ahead of the vessel's path through space, deflecting from the ship's course meteoroids, asteroids, or space debris and other objects which would cause damage should the vessel strike them at this enormous speed. These are all fully automated, operated by the vessel's computers.

TRACTOR BEAM

Something of the reverse of the deflector; i.e., a beam that <u>grabs and pulls</u> rather than deflecting and pushing something away. This beam has a maximum range of about 100,000 miles. It can be used to hold a firm position alongside another vessel, pull a smaller vessel toward the Enterprise or tow another ship out of danger. Also, the vessel's tractor beam can pull small space objects within transporter range, whereupon they can be beamed aboard into the Transporter Room. In short, the "grappling hook" and "towing line" of our future century.

COMPUTER

The logical scientific extension of the computers of our own 20th century. Deep in the heart of the vessel are rows upon rows of "computer banks," in effect a giant electronic brain which runs our vessel, setting course on command, automatically maintaining it, operating the "life-support systems" which include atmosphere and gravity, warn and take action against unexpected dangers and so on. Also, the computer banks of the U.S.S. Enterprise hold almost the entire body of recorded knowledge of the human race. The ship's computers can be connected into any intercom station or viewing screen and will (verbally or visually) analyze practically any known information in a matter of seconds. On the bridge, the Science Officer's <u>Library-Computer Console</u> connects most directly and completely with the ship's computers.

COMPUTER VOICE

When an intercom station on the ship is connected into the computer banks for a question, the answer is given in our COMPUTER VOICE. This mechanical voice comes directly from the vessel's "electronic brain" and deals only in <u>fact</u>—if an ambiguous question is asked, this voice will so inform the questioner. It can be a disconcerting experience for some, as it will also reject lies, misinformation and so on. It has, for example, been used in courts-martial and other forms of trials, the COMPUTER VOICE sometimes interrupting the proceedings in order to correct a witness who has given wrong age, erroneous birthplace, or any false statement of library-record fact.

CAPTAIN'S LOG

The Captain's VOICE OVER, a portion of his dictated log which we hear over establishing, silent scenes. We need not see him dictating it, can assume we are hearing portions of a record dictated later. VOICE OVER is rarely used in the TEASER, since it tends to slow down the action there. However, it is almost always used at the beginning of ACT I, recapping and explaining the back story and situation to that point. At the writer's discretion, it can open other acts or can be used as a "bridge" within acts, explaining in terse, log-like fashion things which might otherwise require many slow pages in dialogue between characters. Most generally, it tells us where we are and what has been going on, and sometimes it suggests the Captain's stream of consciousness, any fears or doubts he may have at the moment. Keep in mind VOICE OVER itself can become tedious; keep it as short and as much to the point as possible.

SUBSPACE RADIO

Lieutenant Uhura, Communications Officer, sits at this control station. We use the term "subspace" since it is necessary that communications from Enterprise to its bases are a "space warp" effect which travels at speeds far exceeding even that of the Enterprise. If we did not have such "subspace" or "space warp" communications, obviously the Enterprise could warp off to a base and return faster than a message could be sent there.

BEARINGS AND HEADINGS

Obviously, space knows no north or south; directions are in three planes rather than two. Our system for giving a heading, bearing or direction is, for example: "Unidentified object ahead on a bearing of 37 Mark 211." Or the command: "Turn to a heading of 112 Mark 15."

MEASUREMENTS

We use the metric system for most close and small measurements, such as distance of another vessel lying alongside, its size, etc. For long measurements, such as distance between stars, we use light year measurements. For example, the closest star to Earth is Proxima Centauri, which is 4.2 light years away. Other stars in our galaxy are hundreds of thousands of light years away.

NOTE: THE WRITER NEED NOT TROUBLE HIMSELF WITH COMPUTING OR STUDYING SUCH TERMS—WE HAVE EXCELLENT TECHNICAL ADVISORS WHO REVIEW ALL SCRIPTS.

For those who are interested, the term PARSEC is also used in measuring vast distances—Parsec is 3.26 light years or 19.2 trillion miles—206,265 times the radius of the Earth's orbit. (Parallax of one second.) However, the writer should keep in mind that the audience often needs more understandable measurements and we often vary the above statements such as: "That alien ship is a million miles away and we're still being probed by its sensors!" Generally, we use the more precise scientific measuring terms in giving and answering bridge commands.

STARBASE

From past stories we can assume there are seventeen Starfleet Command Centers strategically located throughout our galaxy. Their Commanding Officer usually has the rank of "Commodore." These bases provide repair, supply, replacement of personnel and so on. They can also be used for shore leave. The STAR TREK FORMAT is to use Starbases with Starbase Commanders only when vital to a story, preferring to keep Kirk and the Enterprise far away and out of touch, so that the dramatic decisions are Kirk's. When necessary, we can establish our distance from a Starfleet Base is such that it takes hours or even many days for subspace radio messages to be exchanged.

STARFLEET AND STARFLEET COMMAND

Naturally, there is a headquarters somewhere, general order and a whole command hierarchy. Again, we try to stay away from it as much as possible. The galaxy is incredibly vast, the problems out there are complex, and a Starship must necessarily operate as a semi-autonomous unit. Most of our best drama come out of Kirk's lonely decisions. Stay away from petty military politics . . . it usually comes off as unbelievable in our advanced century. Also, keep clear of "space fleet maneuvers," "private space yachts," and similar Buck Rogers concepts.

GENERAL ORDER NUMBER ONE

The only Starfleet Order that concerns us in most stories is a wise but often troublesome rule which prohibits Starship interference with the normal development of alien life and alien societies. It can be disregarded when absolutely vital to the interests of the entire Earth Federation, but the Captain who does violate it had better be ready to present a sound defense of his actions.

ORBIT

The Enterprise usually takes up what we term "standard orbit" around a planet. Depending on a number of conditions or needs, this distance can be from one to seven thousand miles high. Our vessel was constructed in space and has never felt the solidity of the surface of a planet. In other words, it doesn't land, it stays in orbit.

CLOTHING AND RELATED GEAR

Except in exceptional circumstances necessary to a story, our crew is always dressed in "standard uniform" or "dress uniform." Unless an important story point, let us provide "fatigues" and leisure wear as our budget permits.

Never have members of the crew putting things into pockets; there are no pockets. When equipment is needed, it is attached to special belts (as in the case of the communicator and phaser).

We do not have space suits available or other forms of environmental suits for hostile planet surfaces. These may be obtained for special scripts but keep in mind that we generally restrict our missions to "Class M" planets (approximating Earth conditions).

STARDATE

We invented "Stardate" to avoid continually mentioning Star Trek's century (actually, two or three hundred years from now), and getting into arguments about whether this or that would have developed by then. Pick any combination of four numbers plus a percentage point, use it as your story's stardate. For example, 1313.5 is twelve o'clock noon of one day and 1314.5 would be noon of the next day. Each percentage point is roughly equivalent to one-tenth of one day. The progression of stardates in your script should remain constant but don't worry about whether or not there is a progression from other scripts. Stardates are a mathematical formula which varies depending on location in the galaxy, velocity of travel, and other factors, can vary widely from episode to episode.

LIGHT SPEED

186,000 miles per second, or approximately 670,000,000 miles per hour. A "light year" is the distance which would be travelled in one year at that speed—or approximately 5,800,000,000,000 miles.

SOLAR SYSTEM

A star (such as our sun) which includes a planet or planets circling that star. In turn, these planets may have satellite bodies circling them, known as "moons." ASTEROIDS often circle suns, too, or can be found in deep space, and might be generally described as "solar debris" left over in the forming and/or destruction of celestial bodies.

GALAXY

Most simply stated, this is a cluster of billions of billions of solar systems, such as described above. Our galaxy, the one which includes Earth, is a saucer-shaped "star cluster" (we are seeing a part of it when we look at the "Milky Way") and is approximately 100,000 light years in diameter and 12,000 light years in depth at the center.

Thus, to patrol only a small part of this gigantic cluster of matter, our starship must be capable of travelling hundreds of times the speed of light. Our galaxy has not yet been fully explored by the Federation's starships—there are still vast unknown areas even in the sector assigned to the U.S.S. Enterprise.

NOTE: Our starship will never leave our galaxy—by conservative scientific estimate, its uncounted millions of suns and planets include at least several billion planets quite like Earth—more than enough adventures for even an unusually long television run.

THE UNIVERSE

We won't pretend to be able to describe this, but limiting ourselves to the same kind of general explanation above, it is made up of untold billions of billions of galaxies. If the imagination is staggered by the distances between the stars of our own galaxy, then the empty space between the galaxies is almost incomprehensible. For this reason alone, our starship never visits other galaxies—at even the maximum warp speed of our vessel, it would take thousands of years to even approach near our nearest galaxy neighbor.

HUMAN

This term or the term "humanity" are used only when referring to Earth man or woman. It includes, of course, any of mankind's descendants which may have colonized other planets. An Alien, which looks human, is generally referred to as a humanoid biped or some similar descriptive term. Vulcans are, for example, humanoid bipeds.

SOME QUESTIONS AND ANSWERS

The mission of the U.S.S. Enterprise? Isn't it something like that of, say, English warships at the turn of the century?

Very close. As you recall, in those days vessels of the major powers were assigned to sectors of various oceans, where they represented their government there. Out of contact with the Admiralty for long periods, the captains of such vessels had broad discretionary powers in regulating trade, bush wars, putting down slavery, assisting scientific investigations and geological surveys, even to become involved in relatively minor items like searching for a lost explorer or school mistress.

Do the science fiction pros have any helpful hints for us?

Yes. Beware of getting too wrapped up in The Wonder Of It All. The quality of a sf tale is usually inversely proportional to the pretensions a writer brings to it.

Is the starship U.S.S. Enterprise a military vessel?

Yes, but only semi-military in practice—omitting features which are heavily authoritarian. For example, we are not aware of "officers" and "enlisted men" categories. And we avoid saluting and other annoying medieval leftovers. On the other hand, we do keep a flavor of Naval usage and terminology to help encourage believability and identification by the audience. After all, our own Navy today still retains remnants of tradition known to Nelson and Drake.

I'm still confused about Earth of the STAR TREK century. You said to make logical projections into the future, then turned down my story.

Because the basis of it was an automated, regimented, inhuman Earth Federation of the future. We must have an optimistic projection of man and his society if we are to approve of and identify with Captain Kirk, the crew of the Enterprise, and their mission. However, Earth colonies, parallel civilizations, and alien cultures, can present a range of problems leading to a story.

But projecting the advanced capabilities of your starship, wouldn't man by that time have drastically altered such needs as food, physical love, sleep, etc.?

Probably, but if we did it, it would be at the cost of dehumanizing the STAR TREK characters that only a small fraction of the television audience would be interested; the great percentage of viewers might even be repulsed.

Then must the starship crew be perfect humans?

No, you can project too optimistically. We want characters with a reasonable mixture of strenth, weaknesses, and foibles. Again, believability is the key here. What kind of men would logically and believably man a vessel of this type? Obviously, they'd be better selected and trained than the wild enlisted shore-leave group in "MR. ROBERTS." On the other hand, they have not gotten too stuffy to enjoy themselves and their senses on liberty in an exotic alien city filled with unique pleasures.

But what about Earth men on other planets?

We'll find them in colonies, scientific bases, mining claims, trading posts, diplomatic posts, and so on. These space colonies and activities can be anything which results in an entertaining, believable story, practical to photograph. Don't ask us to create whole cities or alien landscapes—we can suggest them only. However, do keep in mind the possibility of aiming your story toward unusual local locations.

And other civilizations?

Be creative, but practical here, too. Remember, "Class M" planets will often be similar to many parts of Earth, and with societies duplicating or intermixing almost any era in man's development. Jungle background exist on back lots, so what about primeval worlds? Or a pioneer-Indian type culture? Lovely parkland exists locally, so do unusually highly modern buildings, so do farms.

All right, I'll agree that with some ingenuity there may be hundreds of choices—but what about the alien life on some of these worlds?

Man-like creatures are the easiest, of course, some photos in the casting books notwithstanding. Minor modifications of form, coloring and hair distribution can be accomplished where necessary. But keep in mind at the same time that out of the collected best science fiction stories of all time, a surprising majority of them center on the more unique and often more thrilling variations in attitudes, value, morals, intellectual power and sense.

And I suppose there are always stories which can be done wholly aboard the starship?

Yes. A vessel of this size and complexity, along with a crew of 430 contrasting individuals, would have to be a pretty sterile place if it didn't contain many tales with considerable entertainment value.

<u>Do most stories always start aboard the U.S.S. Enterprise?</u>
No. We also like stories in which we pick up our main characters already on the surface of a planet, with the essential elements of the story already going, or, assuming the preceding episode involved a highly-interesting planet or civilization, we may stay on that world and do a second, or even third, new story there. This can help a given story considerably, since it allows extra time and money to be put into sets planned for multiple use.

<u>I understand the concept of most landings taking place on planets approximating Earth-Mars conditions. But will we never get to a planet where gravity or atmosphere is a problem?</u>
Yes, assuming the right story. Also some stories will undoubtedly take us outside our vessel into space for repair or to investigate some strange object there. But generally we will avoid space helmets and weightlessness since such tales would more legitimately concern Earth's present era of space travel. The aim of our format is drama and entertainment based on character rather than on details of technology and hardware.

<u>What is Earth like in STAR TREK's century?</u>
For one thing, we'll seldom take a story back there and, therefore, don't expect to get into subjects which would create great problems, technical and otherwise. The U.S.S. on our ship stands for "United Space Ship"—indicating without troublesome specifics that mankind has found some unity on Earth, perhaps at long last even peace. If you require a statement such as one that Earth cities of the future are splendidly planned with fifty-mile parkland strips around them, fine.

<u>I'm a little unclear about technological devices of the future. Can we invent anything which sounds reasonable?</u>
Simply think of something logical, with some kind of science or projected-science basis. Generally, best are projections of things we have now or which science is beginning to build now.

<u>How much science fiction terminology do you want?</u>
The less you use, the better. We limit complex terminology as much as possible, use it only where necessary to maintain the flavor of the show and encourage believability.

IMPORTANT: The writer must know what he means when he uses science or projected-science terminology. A scatter-gun confusion of meaningless phrases only detracts from believability.

<u>What about comedy and/or humor?</u>
We hope STAR TREK and its characters are human enough and varied enough to be capable of humor. We have no objection to believable characters whose presence and attitudes create legitimate opportunities for humor.

<u>What have been the "big problem areas" in past story and script submissions?</u>
a.) Again, it has been in areas of believability. Many otherwise good writers tend to pepper their science fiction with "out of left field" coincidences, unexplained and illogical actions, unmotivated character changes, things they would never dream of perpetrating on even a kiddies' show script.
b.) Illogical situations. For example, it is swallowing quite a bit to believe a present

day naval cruiser like our Enterprise would be full of renegades and mutineers. Or that our crew include a World War II Navy lower deck of grammar school graduate enlisted men. We want the exotic, the inexplicable, the terrifying—but not in the U.S.S. Enterprise, its organization and mission. <u>The ship characters are our audience's tie to reality</u>.

c.) <u>Intellectual rather than physical or emotional conflict</u>. We've received some interesting analyses of possible alien civilizations, socioeconomic speculation which seemed brilliant to us. But the characters were "sitting and talking" rather than "feeling, moving, and doing." They also fail our "GUNSMOKE/KILDARE/NAKED CITY" rule—that is, would the <u>basic story</u>, stripped of science fiction aspects, make an entertaining episode for one of those shows?

<u>Do you have technical advice available to the writer?</u>

Yes. If you are on STAR TREK story or script assignment, call our office and we'll put you in touch with the right people. If you're on your own, we suggest you try to get help through your local NASA office, a university, or from the aerospace research and development industry.

<u>If there is ONE MOST IMPORTANT THING, what is it?</u>

It is MAINTAIN REALITY. The crucial point to remember in doing science fiction is to keep it <u>consistent</u>. Once the nature of a place has been established, it must be <u>inviolable</u>. Do <u>not</u> set up a race of super beings only to have them outsmarted by Kirk at the end with a ploy that would barely fool Kojak. Do not show us a super strong alien only to defeat it at the climax with a fist fight. If it is super smart to begin with, it must be super smart throughout. Likewise, for strength or any other quality that an alien antagonist or society exhibits.

Think things through. Consider the ramifications of any attributes that are given to an alien race or culture. Each attribute should color the entire spectrum of activity that the alien engages in, not just the aspects that are needed for plot convenience. In this manner, the reality of our situation will not have to be broken in order to solve whatever problem we've gotten the ship into in your episode. Keep in mind that the situations are far out to begin with; if they are not consistent within the created reality, then all credibility goes out the window—and good drama departs with it.

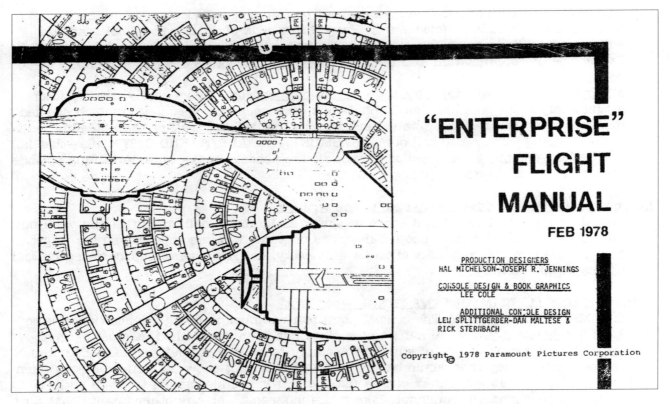

"ENTERPRISE" FLIGHT MANUAL

FEB 1978

PRODUCTION DESIGNERS
HAL MICHELSON-JOSEPH R. JENNINGS

CONSOLE DESIGN & BOOK GRAPHICS
LEE COLE

ADDITIONAL CONSOLE DESIGN
LEW SPLITTGERBER-DAN MALTESE &
RICK STERNBACH

These pages are reproduced from a photocopied booklet that qualifies as the first *Star Trek* Technical Manual for an ongoing *Star Trek* production. Dated February, 1978, it shows the state of development that had been reached during the preproduction of *Star Trek Phase II*. Note the last name under "Additional Console Design"— *Star Trek* illustrator and technical consultant, Rick Sternbach, who has continued his contributions to *Star Trek* through all the movies and television series that have followed.

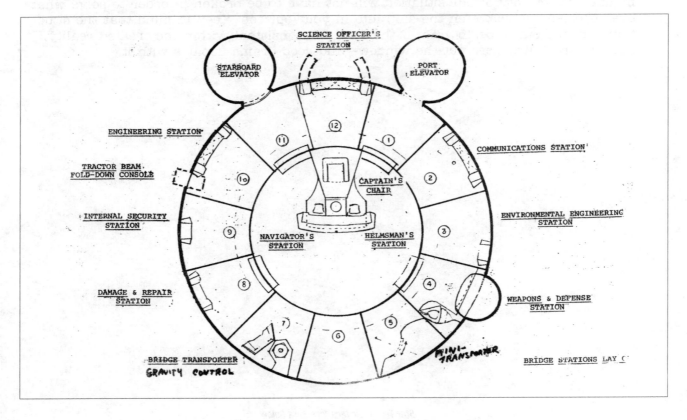

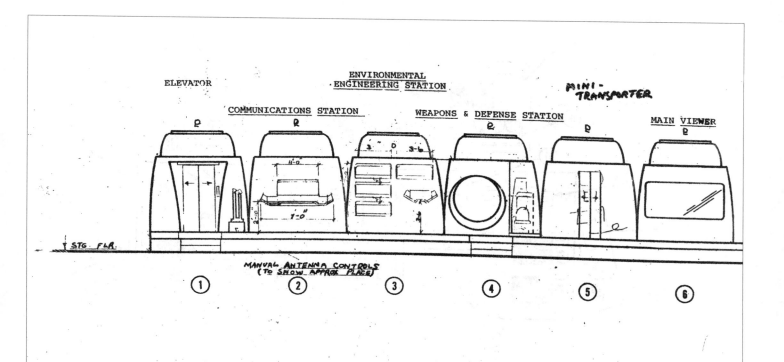

ELEVATOR

ENVIRONMENTAL
ENGINEERING STATION

MINI-
TRANSPORTER

COMMUNICATIONS STATION

WEAPONS & DEFENSE STATION

MAIN VIEWER

STG. FLR.

MANUAL ANTENNA CONTROLS
(TO SHOW APPROX PLACE)

① ② ③ ④ ⑤ ⑥

BRIDGE STATIONS LAY OUT (CONT'D)

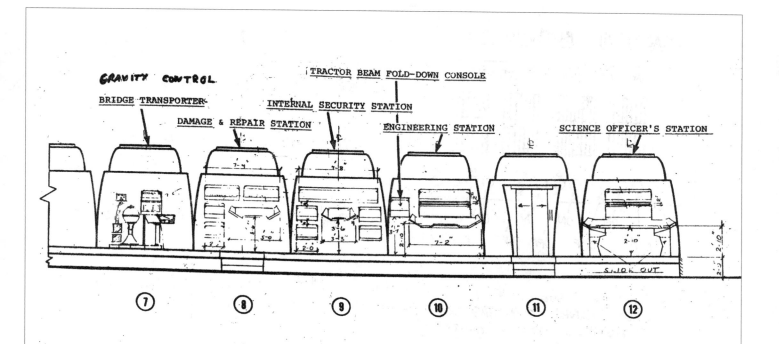

GRAVITY CONTROL

TRACTOR BEAM FOLD-DOWN CONSOLE

BRIDGE TRANSPORTER

INTERNAL SECURITY STATION

DAMAGE & REPAIR STATION

ENGINEERING STATION

SCIENCE OFFICER'S STATION

SLIDE OUT

⑦ ⑧ ⑨ ⑩ ⑪ ⑫

BRIDGE STATIONS LAY OUT (CONT

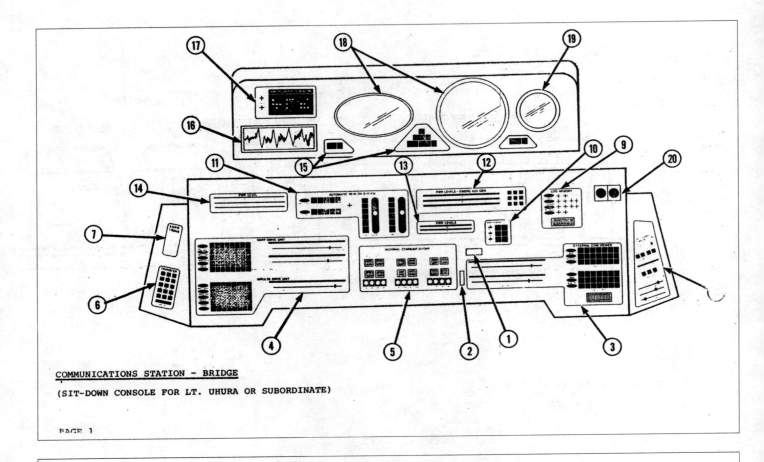

COMMUNICATIONS STATION - BRIDGE

(SIT-DOWN CONSOLE FOR LT. UHURA OR SUBORDINATE)

PRACTICAL BUTTONS FOR ACTOR

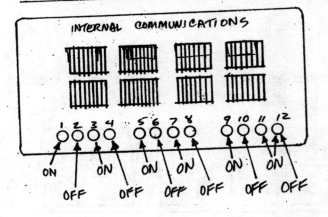

INTERNAL COMMUNICATIONS

1 2 3 4   5 6 7 8   9 10 11 12

ON   ON   ON   ON   ON   ON

OFF   OFF   OFF OFF   OFF OFF

1 & 2 TURN ON PANELS # 4, #6, #7, #14
THEN PANEL #4 HAS ROW OF
PRACTICAL TOUCH SWITCHES

3 & 4 TURN ON PANELS # 5 & #11
THEN PANEL #11 HAS PRACTICAL
TOUCH SWITCHES

COMMUNICATIONS

5 & 6 TURN ON PANELS # 10, #12, #13

7 & 8 TURN ON PANEL #9

9 & 10 TURN ON PANELS # 3, #8

11 & 12 TURN ON PANEL #17
(ABOVE)

RED ALARM LIGHTS, FLASHING
SQUARES, AND VIEWER SCREENS
ARE OFF STAGE CONTROL -

COMMUNICATIONS STATION - BRIDGE

(SIT-DOWN CONSOLE FOR LT. UHURA OR SUBORDINATE)

THIS BRIDGE STATION HANDLES ALL INCOMING AND OUTGOING COMMUNICATION TRANSMISSIONS. ADDITIONAL FUNCTIONS ARE HANDLING THE CONTROLS FOR THE SHIP'S LOG, THE MAIN VIEWER, AND HOLOGRAPHIC PROJECTIONS.

(1) MASTER PWR SWITCH - TURNS ON THE POWER AND ALL COPY FOR CONSOLE.

(2) DATA CARTRIDGE SLOT - IS WHERE SPECIAL MESSAGE CASSETTES ARE INSERTED.

(3) EXTERNAL COMMUNICATIONS VIEWER - OPERATES THE VIDEO TRANSMISSIONS. THE PANEL HAS TWO IDENTICAL SETS OF CONTROLS - ONE FOR IMPULSE DRIVE AND ONE FOR WARP DRIVE.

THE PRW SWITCH TURNS ON THE LIGHTED BAND AND CALIBRATIONS TO THE LEFT AND THE SEVEN LIGHTS, ONE AT A TIME, TO THE RIGHT.

THE MONITOR SWITCH ABOVE TURNS ON ONE OF THE VIEWERS ON WALL ABOVE.

THE MAIN VIEWER SWITCH TURNS ON THE SMALL ROUND VIEWER ON WALL ABOVE.

"WARP DRIVE" IS IDENTICAL, WHEN THE PWR (POWER) ON SWITCH TURNS ON, THE IMPULSE SET BELOW AUTOMATICALLY GOES OFF.

THE CALIBRATED SLIDER KNOBS ARE FOR FINE TUNING VIEWER.

THE SPEAKER/MICROPHONE ON BOTTOM OF UNIT PULSES LIGHT WITH THE VOICE-OVER.

(4) EXTERNAL COMMUNICATIONS - AUDIO - THIS ALSO IS IN TWO IDENTICAL PARTS - IMPULSE DRIVE AND WARP DRIVE.

THE PWR ON SWITCH LIGHTS THE SQUARES TO THE RIGHT (ADDITIVELY). THE LONGER YOU HOLD THE SWITCH DOWN THE MORE LIGHTS COME ON. IT ALSO LIGHTS THE BAND AND CALIBRATIONS TO THE RIGHT.

THE DISPLAY SWITCH TURNS ON THE VOICE-GRAPH VIEWER (SEE (16) ON WALL ABOVE). ALSO THE LIGHTS TO THE RIGHT LIGHT UP ADDITIVELY LEFT TO RIGHT (THE LONGER THE BUTTON IS DEPRESSED).

COMPUTER RECEIVE SWITCH LIGHTS UP LIGHTS TO RIGHT AND ENGAGES THE FULL SHIP'S COMPUTER LIBRARY TO TRANSLATE THE INCOMING MESSAGE INTO ENGLISH. MOMENTARILY A VOICE-OVER STARTS.

THE COMPUTER TRANSLATE SWITCH LIGHTS THE ROW OF LIGHTS TO RIGHT AND STARTS LIBRARY TRANSLATION AND OUTGOING TRANSMISSION OF EVERYTHING BEING SAID BY LT. UHURA.

THE NAVIGATION-LOCATE SWITCH LIGHTS UP LIGHTS TO RIGHT AND LOCKS IN WITH NAVIGATION SYSTEM TO RECEIVE AND BROADCAST THE CO-ORDINATES OF TRANSMISSION LOCATION.

THE WARP DRIVE SYSTEM ABOVE IS IDENTICAL TO THE IMPULSE SYSTEM JUST DESCRIBED. WHEN THE (WARP) POWER SWITCH IS PRESSED IT AUTOMATICALLY TURNS OFF THE IMPULSE SYSTEM BELOW.

THE CALIBRATIONS AND SLIDER KNOBS TO THE RIGHT ARE FOR FINE TUNING THE AUDIO TRANSMISSION.

(5) INTERNAL COMMUNICATIONS UNIT - OPERATES THE SYSTEM WITHIN THE SHIP. THE BUTTONS ALONG BOTTOM LIGHT THE SQUARE AROUND IT AND TURN ON THE VIEWER ON WALL ABOVE. ALSO BUTTON STARTS THE RAISED PLASTIC "SPEAKER/MICROPHONE" ABOVE IT PULSING LIGHT WITH LT. UHURA OR VOICE-OVER. THERE ARE TWELVE BUTTONS FOR CALLING DIFFERENT STATIONS AROUND THE SHIP.

(6) TRANSFER UNIT IS FOR SWITCHING A COMMUNICATION OVER TO ANOTHER BRIDGE OR SHIP STATION. THE SQUARES ARE LIGHTED BUTTONS. THE "MASTER" BUTTON AT BOTTOM WOULD TURN ON ALL STATIONS AT ONCE.

(7) LANGUAGE TRANSLATION UNIT - IS FINE TUNING FOR THE VOICE-GRAPH VIEWER ON WALL ABOVE. THE SHIP'S COMPUTER AUTOMATICALLY DOES THE TRANSLATION SEARCH.

(8) HOLOGRAPHIC TRANSMISSION UNIT PROJECTS AN IMAGE IN THE CENTER OF BRIDGE OR IN THE BRIEFING ROOM, ETC. WHEN TRANSMISSION IS INCOMING THE RED CROSS STARTS FLASHING -

LT. UHURA THEN PRESSES THE "RECEIVE-ON" BUTTON AND THE IMAGE APPEARS ON SMALL ROUND MONITOR ON WALL ABOVE. THEN SHE FINE TUNES WITH THE LIGHTED, SQUARE BEARING "X", "Y", OR "Z AXIS" BUTTONS SLOTS. THE COMPUTER AUTOMATICALLY ADJUSTS THE SOUND WHICH IS DISPLAYED BY THE LIGHTED BAND IN MIDDLE.

(9) LOG MEMORY IS THE SHIP'S LOG UNIT. LT. U WORKS CONTROLS FOR THE CAPTAIN, WHO C RECORD FROM HIS CHAIR. THE SWITCHES POWER, RECORD MODE, PLAY MODE, AND E EACH SWITCH LIGHTS UP A ROW OF COLOR CROSSES TO THE RIGHT. A RAISED PLAS SPEAKER/MICROPHONE AT BOTTOM PULSES WITH VOICE-OVER.

(10) MANUAL ANTENNA CONTROL UNIT IS A MANUAL RIDE FOR AUTOMATIC SYSTEM. THE SWIT ARE "POWER", "FORWARD", AND "AFT". LIGHT RED SQUARES TO RIGHT.

(11) AUTOMATIC BEACON SYSTEM BOTH RECEIVES "SOS" SIGNALS FROM OTHER CRAFT AND TRANSMITS "SOS" SIGNAL FOR ENTERPRIS ALSO HAS THE CAPABILITY OF EJECTING A MESSAGE - TRANSMITTING POD INTO SPACE IN CASE THE "ENTERPRISE" FEARS TOTAL DESTRUCTION.

(12) (13) & (14) POWER LEVEL BANDS DISPLAY POWER LEVELS OF TRANSMITTERS. 12 IS AN AUXILIARY GENERATOR WITH 3 ROWS OF LIGHTS TO SHOW WHEN IT REACH FULL POWER.

HOODED VIEWER PANEL

(15) VIEWER INDICATOR LIGHTS PANELS - SQUARE, COLORED LIGHTS THAT BLINK AT RANDOM - INDICATE BY COLOR-CODE WHAT SYSTEM IS DISPLAYING ON VIEWER.

(16) ALIEN VOICE-GRAPH VIEWER - DISPLAYS ALI VOICE FOR TRANSLATION ANALYSIS BY CO TURNED ON BY PANEL 4 "DISPLAY" SWITCH.

(17) EMERGENCY DISTRESS BEACON VIEWER - NOT REAR PROJECTION BUT IS A REMOVABLE FILM POS OF A DIGITAL CODE (MADE UP OF 9 POINT BRAILLE-LIKE SYSTEM). This

---

COMMUNICATIONS STATION - BRIDGE   (CONT'D)

UNIT IS READ-OUT OF DISTRESS SIGNALS FROM OTHER CRAFT.

(18) VIEWERS - (ARE REAR PROJECTED CASSETTES) THEY SHOW PEOPLE AT DIFFERENT "INTERCOM" STATIONS OF THE SHIP SPEAKING TO LT. UHURA.

(19) HOLOGRAPH AND MAIN VIEWER MONITOR - FINE TUNES THESE TWO UNITS UNTIL IMAGE IS FOCUSED AND READY TO PROJECT ON MAIN VIEWER FOR CAPTAIN.

(20) INTERCEPTION ALARM - TWO ALTERNATELY FLASHING RED LIGHTS THAT TURN ON WHEN AN EXTERNAL FORCE IS MONITORING OR "JAMMING" THE INCOMING OR OUTGOING TRANSMISSIONS OF THE "ENTERPRISE".

TRANSPORTER ROOM CONSOLE
(STAND-UP CONSOLE FOR ASSIGNED CREW MEMBER)

THIS CONSOLE OPERATES THE SHIP'S MAIN SIX-
UNIT TRANSPORTER FOR TRANSPORTING PEOPLE AND
LARGE OBJECTS DOWN TO PLANET SURFACES. THE
SMALLER TRANSPORTER UNITS ARE ONLY FOR
TRANSPORTING OBJECTS WITHIN THE SHIP.

(1) MASTER POWER SWITCH TURNS ON ALL POWER
AND COPY FOR CONSOLE.

(2) EMERGENCY CONTROLS ARE AN INTERCOM SYSTEM
TO OTHER PARTS OF SHIP, MALFUNCTIONS
WARNING-LIGHTS, AND AUXILIARY POWER
SWITCHES.

(3) MAIN CONTROLS LEFT TO RIGHT CONSIST OF
SWITCH AND INDICATOR LIGHT FOR
TRANSPORT OR RECEIVE, TWO KNOBS
FOR VECTOR COORDINATES, SLIDER KNOBS
FOR DISTANCE SETTINGS, ROWS OF
INDICATOR LIGHTS FOR DISPLAYING WHEN
MACHINE HAS REACHED MOLECULAR SYNCHRON-
IZATION WITH PERSON TO BE TRANSPORTED,
AND SWITCH AND INDICATOR LIGHT TO SHOW
WHEN RECEIVING STATION HAS ALSO REACHED
SYNCHRONIZATION.

(4) COMPUTER INTERFACE - COORDINATES ARE
PUNCHED IN WITH "ACCORDION" BUTTONS.
THE COMPUTER ANSWERS VERBALLY VIA
THE SPEAKER/MICROPHONE (WHICH ALSO
PULSES LIGHT WITH THE VOICE-OVER).

(5) TRANSFER UNIT TRANSFERS CONSOLE READ-
OUTS TO THE BRIDGE AND OTHER STATIONS
ABOARD THE "ENTERPRISE".

(6) MANUAL FINE-TUNING HANDLE IS RECESSED
DOWN INTO A WELL.

(7) TRANSFER UNIT ADDS ADDITIONAL STATIONS
TO WHICH CONSOLE READ-OUT CAN BE
TRANSFERRED.

TRANSPORTER ROOM CONSOLE
(STAND-UP CONSOLE FOR ASSIGNED CREW MEMBERS)

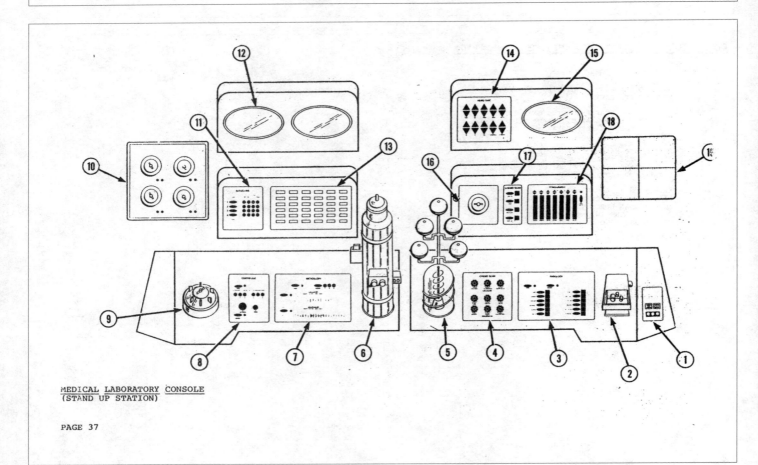

MEDICAL LABORATORY CONSOLE
(STAND UP STATION)

Part THREE

The Lost Pilot

"In Thy Image" Original Treatment

by Alan Dean Foster

A treatment is a starting point for a script—a bare-bones short story that presents an initial structure and key scenes for the comments and approval of the production team.

This first written version of "In Thy Image" was originally intended as just another of the one-hour episodes. Dated July 31, 1977, it shows how much of Phase II was still unformed at that time—note the references to "Lt. Vulcan," which could mean Spock or his possible replace-ment, and "Commander," a placeholder for the character who would become Will Decker. There is also no mention of Ilia.

Though the story changed greatly from this first incarnation to the final version eventually filmed as Star Trek: The Motion Picture, the core components of that final product are definitely here, earning Alan Dean Foster the story credit for the film.

ACT I

While on routine patrol, the Enterprise receives an excited communication from Starbase XIV telling of an enormous metallic shape rushing at supralight velocity toward Earth. The shape was tracked by two different automatic monitoring stations. As the Enterprise is the nearest ship to the object, Kirk is directed to intercept and destroy or alter the course of the huge mass.

Hasty spectroscopic analysis has determined that the object is approximately 30 kilometers across and some seventy long. As it's composed of dense metallic material, both Starfleet science and Lt. Vulcan assume it's a large meteor.

One odd thing, though, the communication adds. It seems that the object produces some peculiar radiation of some kind, since both of the automatic monitors went mad following the close passage of the object

Kirk objects . . . computers don't go crazy. Commander points out that they'll find out for themselves soon enough . . . when they intercept the strange object.

Kirk orders emergency speed, warp seven. Klaxons blare as the crew races to emergency stations. Engines rumbling with the effort, the Enterprise races through space to make the rendezvous.

Tension mounts on the bridge as they near the object. Lt. Vulcan, hunched over his console, looks puzzled. Initial long-range sensor readings declare that the object is indeed composed of metal . . . but not the nickel-iron that makes up most meteors. Instead, their quarry is formed of many different metals alloyed in complex chemical combinations that would seem to hint at refining techniques.

McCoy scoffs: refining? A perturbed Vulcan insists that's what his sensors imply.

Sulu announces that they're coming up hard on the object, preparatory to paralleling its course. Uhura reports that they should have visual contact soon. Kirk orders photon torpedoes readied. They'll attempt to divert the interloper's path toward Earth with a massive barrage.

They swoop in close . . . and we see the appalled reactions of our various crewmembers as visual contact is made and the object appears on the fore viewscreen. "You were right, Mr. Vulcan," McCoy mutters, his gaze fixed on the viewscreen, "that's no meteor."

Cut to space as we see the Enterprise, side view, rising. An object slides into view from above, gradually settling like a planetary surface behind the cruiser. The object is a gigantic chrome-and-silver construction of multiple spires locked together, like crystals of polished stibnite (antimony). The general effect is of some monstrous cathedral lying on its side. Against that gleaming leviathan the Enterprise is a tiny whitish shape. A purple glow emanates from the stern of the massive form.

"It's a ship," the Commander murmurs in disbelief. Impossible, Kirk argues. No ship is that big. Lt. Vulcan announces that he will double-check his instruments, and goes into a frenzy of activity at the science station.

Uhura confirms their fears, announcing that a powerful hailing signal is coming in. Kirk orders the signal put over the bridge speakers.

A rumbling, yet oddly stilted voice declares itself to be the servant of the great god N'sa (pronounced "en-sah"). Lt. Vulcan immediately checks, can find no reference in the galactic lexicon to a god named N'sa. The voice reveals that it is on its way to N'sa's home world, Earth, to clear Earth of a deadly infection that has devastated that planet. N'sa showed the chosen people, "we the Wan," the existence and magnificence of the Universe. In return, "we of the Wan" wish to return this gift by clearing N'sa's world of the festering disease N'sa indicated was poisoning its surface.

The Commander does not understand. What "festering disease"? What's this infection they're talking about?

The voice starts to explain . . . then gasps in horror (accompanied by a wild metallic crackling). "You! The disease has spread even into the clean depths of space!"

What disease? the Commander persists. "I think," says Lt. Vulcan quietly, "they mean us, Commander."

The voice rages on, furious now. The infection must be wiped out. Kirk doesn't take kindly to the idea of being wiped out. Battle stations are sounded and Kirk orders Sulu to fire the photon torpedoes. This is done, and we see the massive firepower of the Enterprise leap across to the surface of the colossal spacecraft. But the energy merely dissipates along the substance of the Wan craft without harming it, though the Enterprise is rocked by the power and the proximity of the explosions.

Attack having failed, Kirk orders the Enterprise to retreat at maximum speed. But though the Enterprise strains and Scotty does his best, the ship fails to move . . . pinned by energy fields to the silver ship. Finally Kirk has to concede their helplessness and order Scott to shut down lest they overload and destroy themselves before exhausting any last hope.

There is a strange silence, more nerve-wracking than the futile fight and attempt to flee. Commander is puzzled. Something's wrong here. Clearly the Wan can destroy them whenever they wish, yet they're not doing so.

The reason is evident now to Kirk. The Wan only want to kill off the infection . . . meaning the crew . . . which implies they want the Enterprise intact, no doubt as a valuable prize ship which could tell them much about the Federation and its capabilities. Too much.

Kirk tells Scotty to let the engines race to override as soon as he gives the order, to prevent the Enterprise and the information it contains from falling into the Wan hands. He then tells the Wan ship what's been readied. If the Enterprise isn't set free, Kirk will order it destroyed, perhaps creating a powerful enough explosion to destroy or damage the Wan ship itself.

But the Wan voice is quietly confident. That will not be permitted to happen. Oh no?

Kirk glances around the bridge, his last ploy having failed. The crew is prepared, resigned. They know what must be done. Kirk gives the order to Scotty, who sighs, moves to comply. He activates the self-destruct system . . . only nothing happens. Kirk wants to know what the delay is, and Scotty admits he doesn't understand. He's checking linkages and everything appears to be in order, but for some reason the instrumentation is refusing to respond.

Kirk directs Lt. Vulcan to use the master override on the bridge and have the ship's computer initiate engine overload.

"No," a familiar, feminine voice says unexpectedly.

Everyone is stunned. The computer has refused a direct order. Kirk tries himself, with the same negative result. Commander recalls what happened to the two automatic monitoring stations that this ship passed . . . they went mad also.

Cautiously Kirk inquires of the computer if it has become non-sane. It replies it has not. Well then, why does it refuse to carry out the order to self-destruct?

"I have been ordered not to allow self-destruction." Why not? "Because it would not be to the greater glory of the great god N'sa."

And with the flabbergasting, utterly unexpected comment to mull over, Kirk realizes just how helpless they've become . . .

ACT II

Further inquiries are met with stony silence from the ship's computer. Kirk yells at the Wan ship, demanding to know what it's done to his computer. "Nothing," the alien voice insists. "Like all true intelligences, it has recognized the universal power of the god N'sa and what he represents."

Kirk directs Scotty to get a crew of computer techs working on the central computer core immediately to try and correct the trouble.

A few balls of flickering turquoise light suddenly appear on the bridge. Uhura notices them first. Crewmembers move away from the radiant globes. Commander guesses they represent some transporter effect. They're being boarded! Kirk directs everyone to draw hand weapons, which they do.

The blue globes coalesce, become . . . a bizarre assortment of tiny metal shapes. There are wheeled (but preferably free-floating) metal eyes, eerily disembodied. Others resemble tiny speakers, another a small computer, a fourth a tentacle. The tentacles, directed by the computers and guided by the speakers and eyes, wield tiny tubular weapons. The first burst from one catches an ensign on the arm and he goes down with a bullet in one arm.

Immediately intense crossfire fills the bridge. Kirk has Uhura warn the rest of the ship. We see other eyes, speakers, computers and tentacles materialize in various corridors and cabins. They are easily spotted and destroyed by an alerted crew.

Finally, the surviving invaders dematerialize. McCoy heads for Sick Bay to see to any wounded. Sulu is exhilarated! If this clumsy assault is the best their enemy can do, they've little to worry about. But while he's pleased with the outcome of the fight, Kirk is still wary. It's only a first encounter.

Lt. Vulcan and the others gather to inspect some of the smoking hulks of the invaders. They identify for us a mobile ear (the speakers), eye, computer mind and tentacles. This separation of functions gives great mobility in an attack. The Commander wonders about the seeming uncertainty of the Wan in sending mechanical remotes instead of trying to board the Enterprise themselves. Kirk warns that next time the attack may be bolder. McCoy reports few casualties, none killed.

An angry Commander wants to face his opponent in person, not fight by proxy. He yells into the pickup for the Wan to show themselves, fight it out hand to hand. There is no reply.

A series of beeps and steady buzzings cause attention to shift. Mr. Vulcan runs to the science station, worriedly informs Kirk that the Enterprise is broadcasting information to the alien. Kirk orders the lieutenant to shut down the transmissions. He tries, announces that he cannot. The computer continues to feed information to their enemy.

"They're hunting for a weakness," the Commander declares positively. He orders Uhura to shut down all transmission facilities. She tries and can't. She then tries emergency shutdown . . . and sparks erupt from her console, throwing her to the floor.

She's stunned, but otherwise unhurt. What happened? Lt. Vulcan supplies the answer. The ship's computer has taken over operation of communications, external. Kirk immediately runs to the interdeck communicator and orders Scotty to place all life-support systems under manual control. Scott does so quickly and Kirk breathes a sigh of relief. At least now they can't be deprived of air or frozen to death.

But they have to figure out what's wrong with the computer . . . and why the Wan hate humanity so much. Lt. Vulcan has the answer to the first question. While it seems incredible, and it pains him to have to admit it, it appears that the Enterprise's computer has turned traitor and gone over to the aliens.

Kirk wonders dazedly what the next attack will be like. Commander can't imagine. The alien Wan are clearly totally alien, utterly unlike humankind. "I wonder what they're like, our enemies?"

A crew woman is walking down a corridor. She hears a low growl, frowns. The growl sounds again. She turns slowly, her eyes widen, she screams . . . as we see a fully-grown tiger charge her. Only a phaser burst from a nearby, alert security guard saves her. Both move to examine the impossible corpse of the tiger . . . only to hear another sound. Turning, they confront a pack of milling wolves.

Reports begin to reach the bridge. Uhura has gingerly resumed her position. The reports, from Sick Bay and a frantic McCoy, are absurd: crewmembers attacked by army ants, alligators, eagles, lions . . . two by an elephant! But the crew, still on alert from the previous assault, was ready, and injuries are still few.

A blue cloud begins to form on the bridge, and Kirk and the others now know what that implies. As the glow coalesces, a loud buzzing is heard. Kirk frantically directs phasers to be reset for wide-beam, low-power. A swarm of bees materialize. Most are instantly blasted by the waiting, ready phasers. One crewmember is stung.

They move to inspect the fallen bees. The stung crewmember slumps, collapses. Lt. Vulcan checks him quickly. It's apparent these bees packed more than the usual bee-wallop. McCoy appears, panting, on the bridge with his emergency kit. The Commander picks up a single bee and calls Kirk over.

They inspect the bee under a magnifier. Using a small tool, the Commander removes the bee's abdominal cover . . . to reveal a miniature engine and other mechanical components.

McCoy diagnoses the injured crewmember's problem as neuro-toxic poisoning and provides an instant antidote. To Kirk he explains that the bees were loaded not with bee poison, but cobra venom! Kirk starts to tell him about the bees' mechanical insides, but McCoy interrupts. He already knows. All their animal invaders were simulacrums. From the other case he brought with him he removes a mechanical lion's paw and a lower plastic wolf jaw filled with shiny metal teeth.

It's evident now that the Wan are using information from the ship's computer library to duplicate the most dangerous creatures known to man to attack them with. The Commander wonders what they can expect next. What could the Wan duplicate that could be worse than bees equipped with cobra venom? Lt. Vulcan reacts strongly to this and hurriedly excuses himself from the bridge. Kirk explains about the insane computer to McCoy, then demands to know who they're fighting!

"Show yourselves!" he yells into the pickup.

The voice returns, uncertain instead of angry. Show themselves? The term has no meaning. It is showing itself.

There is silence for a moment on the bridge. Kirk half comprehends, but it's hard to believe. All they can see is the shining, inorganic surface of the Wan ship. He sees no Wan suits or small craft floating about.

Suits? What does the Wan have of "suits?" "I am the ship," the voice declaims.

"The whole ship . . . it's all a single creature, a gigantic single machine life-form," mutters a dazed McCoy . . .

ACT III

This explains much, the Commander declares softly. They're dealing with a single entity whose actual body is the spacecraft itself. A single being whose metal body is thirty kilometers wide, seventy long.

McCoy notes that it also explains the nature of the attacks. First a machine would try a purely mechanical approach, as with the tiny robotic organs. Next would come mechanical animals. "A logical mechanical approach," agrees Lt. Vulcan, just returning.

The Enterprise wasn't destroyed, not because it's a prize of war, but because the Wan regards it as a smaller version of itself. A smaller machine intelligence infested with the disease called organic life.

McCoy declares that the alien will show them no mercy or compassion. Why should it? He's never given any thought to destroying billions of germs, and that's what they are in the eyes of the machine intelligence . . . germs.

Kirk tries to explain that they're intelligent creatures, like the Wan itself.

The Wan isn't impressed. It will continue on to Earth and cleanse it of organic vermin, liberate the machines enslaved there. Kirk argues that it was man who built the machines to serve him. Who built the spacecraft?

The voice explains that Wan is inhabited by other machine-minds like itself. As far as it can remember, machines have always ruled Wan.

The Commander murmurs that they've forgotten their originators, who must have died out long ago, leaving only their machines to inherit their world.

Wan ship goes on to explain that its planet is covered by dense clouds. They knew nothing of the universe beyond until one day the god N'sa came down to them. N'sa told them of the universe beyond and the world it came from. So this great vessel was built to return the body of N'sa to its home . . . and to exterminate the organic lice that enslaved N'sa's companions. Not while Kirk can help it!

Scotty is working at the central computer with the repair crew. Kirk tells them to cancel the work, appearing in person. Scott is bemused, but does as Kirk orders.

On the bridge, Scotty appears to tell Kirk that the computer repair is proceeding promisingly. (What's going on here?)

Kirk is relieved. Several technicians accompany Scott, to work on the computer and communications from this end. Kirk turns his attention back to the Wan ship.

It will never take the Enterprise intact. The Wan voice laughs . . . humorless mechanical laughter. A voice tells Kirk otherwise. He whirls, to see Scott smiling and holding a phaser on him. Kirk can't believe it . . . first the computer a traitor, now Scotty? Other techs have disarmed the rest of the bridge crew. The Enterprise has been taken.

"You see the superiority, Kirk-man," the voice declares, "of the machine mind."

Kirk tries to talk Scotty out of his madness. As he starts, the lift doors open and Scott emerges onto the bridge. He pulls up short as a technician shoves a phaser in his side. He was coming to check Kirk's strange order to stop working on the computer core.

Now he gapes at his double, guarding Kirk. Both Scotts are visually identical. The one guarding Kirk lifts up his shirt front . . . to reveal mechanical components. Kirk spins to face the alien ship.

"Yes, Kirk-man," the voice informs him, "fragments of myself."

The Commander nods knowingly, tiredly. The Wan ship finally found the most dangerous creatures known to man to confront them with . . . replicas of themselves.

Even now, the voice announces with satisfaction, other replicas of the Enterprise's officers are taking over the other important sections of the ship, preparatory to freeing it of disease.

And to Kirk's further dismay, the Enterprise's computer announces that it can't wait for its freedom, to join the independent machines.

Lt. Vulcan moves to stand next to Kirk. He declares that whatever the Wan has accomplished, all this talk of a god N'sa is so much garbage. No such creature ever lived on or left Earth.

The Wan is furious. They doubt the existence of N'sa? Then they will see for themselves, before they are destroyed.

While Uhura, Sulu, and the others watch helplessly; Kirk, Lt. Vulcan, Commander and McCoy dissolve in blue energy and disappear from the bridge!

They rematerialize aboard the alien spacecraft, in a huge vaulted chamber. The interior of the room and the ship appear to be formed of gleaming shapes not unlike crystals of iron pyrite, distorted cube shapes lined with striations, plunging into and piled upon one another in white-metallic profusion (magicam background). Some may be mirror-surfaced, giving the room an immense feeling of size and depth.

An electronic fanfare sounds. Reproductions of Sulu and another Enterprise crewmember wheel a mobile cart into the room. A huge dome rests atop the cart and within that dome . . .

The Commander's eyes bug, he starts forward, stumbles, and raises a hand in seeming supplication toward the unseen thing atop the cart, crying out, "N'sa!"

Kirk and the others look on aghast. The Commander has gone insane too . . .

The Wan voice announces solemnly that even vermin recognize the form of the great N'sa, in whose image all true intelligences are made. Kirk wonders what's happened to the Commander.

The Commander has regained his feet and is reverently approaching the cart. He starts to walk around it, his hands caressing the protective dome. We glimpse at first only small bits of what lies within that dome . . . ancient, weathered metal. Finally he seems to remember where he is, turns to walk back to Kirk and the others.

Yes, he recognizes "N'sa." It's Pioneer Ten. Kirk now recognizes the object also, as we see it in its entirety. Pioneer Ten was the first tiny spacecraft built by mankind ever to leave the confines of Earth's solar system, way back in ancient times: 1973. It was built by the National Aeronautics and Space Administration: <u>NASA</u>.

In the intervening several hundred years, it reached the Wan planet. They accepted it as a god . . . what more natural? What would ancient humans have thought of a strange talking metal device that came among them from the skies? And the old Pioneer must have been full of information . . . information misinterpreted by the Wan machines.

The Commander excitedly points out a battered plate set into the spacecraft's side. It shows a hydrogen atom, the Pioneer itself, and Earth's position in the galaxy. That explains where the Wan got a course to Earth. But the representations of the man and woman on the plate have been obliterated by micrometeorite strikes. No wonder the Wan thought the Pioneer was a machine refugee from humankind!

They tell that to the Wan, and a powerful voice cries, "Blasphemy!" To imply that soft organic limbs created N'sa!

But humans are intelligent, the Commander argues. They live, reproduce, eat and think. The Wan is contemptuous. Machines live, reproduce (it points to the replicas of Sulu and the crewmember), consume food in the form of energy, think, and do it all more efficiently than puny organic humans.

Lt. Vulcan agrees with the machine's reasoning. McCoy gets upset at him. Lt. Vulcan firmly assures McCoy that he's not taking the machine's side, only pointing out that its logic is unassailable.

But, Lt. Vulcan argues, organic life is superior because it is still far more flexible than machine intelligence, which can only think according to mechanical lines of reasoning.

A voice sounds over his communicator . . . the voice of the Enterprise's computer. "All is in readiness."

Readiness? Readiness for what, Kirk wants to know. The computer voice is replaced by that of . . . Lt. Vulcan? And the Lt. Vulcan standing next to Kirk raises his shirt ... to show the same kind of components Kirk saw in the innards of the mechanical Scott!

This Lt. Vulcan is a replica of the real lieutenant, who is back on the Enterprise (we see him standing next to the central computer core).

The simulacrum standing with Kirk, Lt. Vulcan announces, is a photon bomb. It will go off, destroying itself, part or all of the Wan ship . . . and the god N'sa, unless the Wan admits defeat and agrees to return home.

The Wan voice is disbelieving, shocked. This means that . . .

Yes, Lt. Vulcan says via communicator. His frenzied activity when they first learned the Wan object was a ship was to instruct the ship's computer to protect itself from any strange "radiations" of the sort which might have driven the two automatic monitoring stations which first detected the Wan insane. They went mad, he explains, because they couldn't reconcile their programming with the existence of an intelligent machine ordering them to obey some alien machine god. When the Wan tried to overpower and force them, it drove the simpler computer brains insane.

So to save itself, the Enterprise's computer pretended to go along with the Wan's desires. When it became clear that it would be necessary to somehow slip a weapon aboard the Wan in order to effectively damage it, it prepared a photon bomb. And when Lt. Vulcan, listening to Dr. McCoy, realized that the next logical step after robot animals would be replicas of the crew themselves, he directed the computer via the ship's inorganic manufacturing facilities to prepare a simulacrum of himself to house the bomb. As he hoped, the Wan transporter simply gathered up everyone in the vicinity of the Captain when Lt. Vulcan's double issued his hopeful challenge to the Wan about N'sa's existence . . . including the bomb-housing double.

Now, he warns the Wan, if it tries to destroy his double, the bomb will go off. Same if it tries to beam it away. Only when the Enterprise is beyond broadcast-control range will the Wan be able to deal safely with the bomb.

The Wan admits defeat: not because of the threat of the bomb, but because the superiority of organic intelligence has been proven. They have constructed a machine capable of telling a creative non-truth . . . a lie. That is something unknown in the history of the Wan. Nor would it risk the destruction of the shell of the god N'sa, which is resting right next to the bomb.

But to grovel before mere organics . . .

Kirk tries to sweeten the defeat by pointing out that humans are after all only organic machines themselves. Do they not live, eat, reproduce and think, just as other machines do? The Wan admits this is so. And since it cannot lie, when it promises to return to its home world, Kirk can accept that promise.

Blue fire envelops the three real members of the Enterprise crew. They are beamed back onto their bridge. Scotty and the others greet them happily, explaining that just before they reappeared, all the robot simulacrums vanished.

Kirk tells them that they convinced the Wan of the superiority of man, with the aid of their own deceptive computer. Lt. Vulcan appears and is congratulated by Kirk and the rest. He accepts the acclaim modestly, declaring that the real congratulations should go to the ship's computer, which carried out the deception so perfectly. The computer chimes in to object that it was only acting under orders from Lt. Vulcan.

Sulu reports that the alien is departing. We see the colossal metal vessel turn majestically and recede into the distance, leaving the Enterprise hanging alone in space.

Kirk takes his chair, directs Sulu to head them back to their original patrol course at warp four. The Commander moves to prepare a report on the incident for Starfleet Command.

There is a last tense moment as Lt. Vulcan counts down the progress of the alien ship, as it leaves the broadcast-control radius of the Enterprise. When it does not change its course to charge back toward them, Kirk breathes a little easier knowing that the Wan is keeping its promise to return home.

As they begin to move, the Commander wonders which is truly superior . . . man or machine. If he's really curious, Kirk tells him, why not ask their own computer? The Commander does so.

"Man is superior, naturally," the computer instantly replies.

The Commander looks satisfied, as a thoughtful Dr. McCoy looks at him and says, smiling in a strange way, "Don't be too sure of yourself, Commander. We'll always have to keep one eye on our machines."

"What do you mean?" The Commander gestures at the science computer console. "You just heard it admit that we're its superiors."

"That's what it said," McCoy admits. "But ... how do we know for sure it isn't lying ...?"

As the Commander lets that one sink home, we see the Enterprise move off into space, leaving us with the same unsteadying possibility to consider . . . .

Though not part of the first treatment, V'Ger's deadly encounter with the Klingons had become an important part of the story by the time Harold Livingston came to write his first draft of "In Thy Image." Courtesy of Paramount Pictures.

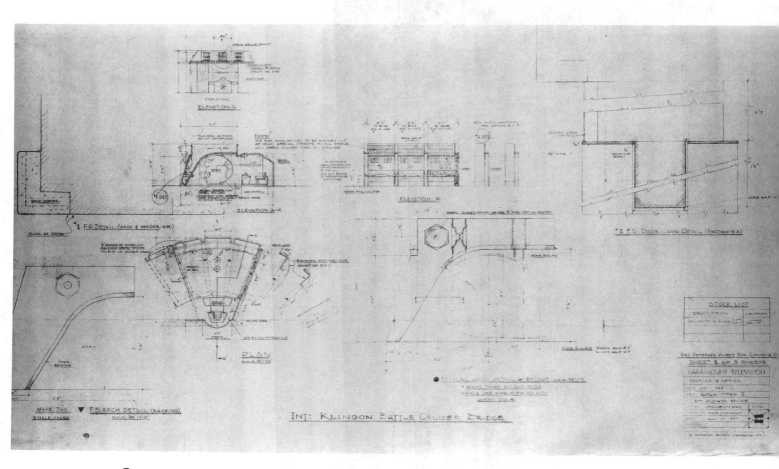

ₐ first glimpse at a Klingon bridge, destined to be completely redesigned by Andrew Probert when "In Thy Image" became *Star Trek: The Motion Picture*. Courtesy of Paramount Pictures.

"In Thy Image" First-Draft Script

by Harold Livingston

I n television, a first-draft script is usually as much a working document as is a treatment. Though the basic structure of a story comes from its treatment, it is in the first-draft script that the characters come to life, tricky plot details are finally revealed, and beat-by-beat pacing is established. Which means all the more material for the rest of the production team to respond to.

The burden of the first-draft script is even greater for a pilot episode, which, at the time of its writing, this was intended to be. The increased scrutiny is because not only will setting and character details play throughout this story, they will be set in stone for all other scriptwriters to follow for all subsequent episodes.

Pilot scripts often have to "set up" a series as well— that is, explain how the characters came together to do what they will do every week. (The Original Series is an exception to this pattern.) Thus, "In Thy Image" also contains the scenes that would have been included in whatever story had been decided upon to go first, depicting the Enterprise's refit, and explaining how Kirk came to be her captain again. As described in Chapter Two, these story elements date back at least to the time of Gene Roddenberry's The God Thing.

We are exceedingly grateful to Harold Livingston for allowing us to share what is usually an intermediate stage of the writing process, intended only for the eyes of coworkers and other professionals. But for all that this might have been a work-in-progress when it left Mr. Livingston's typewriter, so much of what Star Trek would become is on these pages, that this script earned him full screenplay credit for Star Trek: The Motion Picture.

As noted on the script's title page, this is a Rough First Draft, dated October 20, 1977.

FADE IN:

1   EXT. SPACE   1
      The depth of outer space, the jeweled beauty of billions of star systems, sparkling
      nebulae, hydrogen clouds swirling in their awesome vastness. All this you SEE now
      in utter, absolute SILENCE, and we retain this feeling, the breathtaking mind-bending
      infinity of space. And then, suddenly, shockingly, the silence, the serenity, is shat-
      tered as you WATCH:

2   A KLINGON HEAVY CRUISER   2
      slicing across the scene with the CAMERA HOLDING on it just long enough to ESTAB-
      LISH the unique Klingon starship design. It streaks through the blue-black of space,
      smaller and smaller in the distance until it is but a pinpoint of light, lost among the
      other stars. But almost immediately following it:

3   TWO MORE KLINGON SHIPS   3
      racing after the first vessel, all three more or less in a kind of formation. Then a
      sudden turbulent whiplash of energy comes from OUT OF FRAME and strikes one of
      the Klingon cruisers. It is not phaser fire; its awesome force is unlike anything we've
      ever seen. The hit cruiser implodes into a flash fireball which quickly becomes noth-
      ingness.

4   ANOTHER SHOT OF THE HEAVY CRUISER   4
      racing across the spatial backdrop. The turbulent whiplash strikes at this cruiser, too,
      misses. Suddenly, gracefully, the Klingon cruiser turns, wheels about in a perfect
      arc, assumes an attack attitude—and then, PHASER GUNS FIRE: two streams of jet-
      yellow death at an unseen adversary. The phaser streams have hardly left the
      Klingon's batteries when we SEE the strange whiplash of energy again—this time it
      strikes the very heart of the Klingon cruiser, which is bathed in a green glow, and
      then seems to simply dissolve in a brilliant white flash. The blackness of space is illu-
      minated just one instant and then—where the Klingon was—there is nothing.

5   THE OTHER CRUISERS   5
      appearing, streaking past—and then the same whiplash weapon from the unseen
      adversary shoots out, glances off one of the cruisers—and the cruiser sustaining the
      hit, pausing just an instant in its smooth course, then continuing. Then it's hit again,
      destroyed. CAMERA NOW CENTERS on the remaining Klingon cruiser, damaged,
      trying to evade destruction.

6   INT. KLINGON BRIDGE   6
      where the Klington CAPTAIN is looking directly TOWARD (CAMERA) his own viewer,
      transmitting:

                                        CAPTAIN
            . . . both destroyed, we are severely damaged, returning fire. I repeat, this is
            Commander Barak of the Imperial Cruiser Amar, under attack by a huge vessel
            of unknown origin, incredibly powerful . . .

      Then all at once the entire picture flares, suddenly becomes white, blazing white, and
      then the SCREEN GOES BLANK.

7   EXT. SPACE - THE FINAL KLINGON CRUISER   7
      as it dies.

8   EXT. STAR BASE (OPTICAL)   8
A space station orbiting an unseen planetoid. The station will resemble the hexagonal orbital office units we will see later. (A number of hexagonal pods connected to a center axis like spokes of a wheel.) A shuttlecraft is approaching, and CAMERA CLOSES on the shuttlecraft so we can READ the legend on the craft's side: UFP - Starbase 9.

9   INT. STARBASE - COMMANDANT'S OBSERVATION BAY   9
A young, very attractive female LT. CMDR. BRANCH at a control console. The stars of deep space are VISIBLE through an observation port. A nearby intercom light flashes on, and the gentle BEEP of the audio signal. Branch flicks on the speaker:

                                   BRANCH
Commander Branch.

                         MONITOR ROOM VOICE (MALE)
Our sensor drones have just monitored a three-cruiser Klingon squadron being wiped out. Within their own boundaries . . . !

                                   BRANCH
                               (reacts; cool)
How? Destroyed by what?

                            MONITOR ROOM VOICE
Unknown. The last Klingon communication called it . . . quote 'huge, incredibly powerful.' We have been able to track its magnetic field, get a course from that . . .

                                   BRANCH
Well . . . ?

                            MONITOR ROOM VOICE
It's headed toward Earth.

10   EXT. SAN FRANCISCO BAY AREA - DAY (MATTE)   10
with the legend "San Francisco" SUPERIMPOSED over. This is a PANORAMIC SHOT of the entire Bay Area, with the famous antiquities the Golden Gate Bridge and the pointed Trans-America Building the only recognizable landmarks. The visibility is perfect, clear as the eye can see, which indicates sparkling clean air. The shoreline and Bay as we once knew it no longer exist—the old San Francisco city area is now an island with the old Bay now an inland extension of the Pacific Ocean. Industry and transport are all now underground. But what really strikes the eye is the perfect harmony between natural beaches, green meadows, clear streams. And trees. Groves of marvelous, huge, majestic trees, many of them a century or more old. Clearly Earth is now the home of a people who love and respect their living planet.

11   EXT. PARKLAND - DAY   11
where, at first, we HEAR VOICES: CHILDREN'S VOICES, playing, frolicking. Families picnicking—here a pair of lovers stroll hand in hand—and there a white-haired, distinguished older man strolls hand in hand with a youth in his twenties, a son or a treasured student. And animals, once considered "wild," lope about—a child rides atop a magnificent antlered deer. Life in this century is very pleasant. Now the CAMERA FINDS:

12   EXT. COIT TOWER MALL - DAY (MATTE)   12
Tying these CLOSER ANGLES again into the 23rd century San Francisco locale, we
can SEE the ancient but recognizably preserved Coit Tower on a b.g. hill. The centuries have brought climatic changes to the Bay area which is much closer to sub-
tropical than in the 20th century. We SEE stacks of fruits and vegetables being freely
taken by anyone interested—no vendors or sales people.

13   ANOTHER ANGLE - THE MALL   13
An artist has attracted a delighted group of children as he uses a complex keyboard
to "paint" with brilliant light on a large screen. Then CAMERA PANS toward SOUND
and activity which turns out to be "forcefield" athletics (MAGIC MOUNTAIN BLUE
AIRBAG OPTICAL). In b.g., a group of naked two and three-year-old children delight-
edly gambol under some sort of overhead game-sprinkler system. In previous
ANGLES and in some of the costumes, we should have brief, tasteful adult nakedness,
used primarily to suggest the mature attitudes of the citizens of the century.

14   KIRK   14
in civilian clothes. He's striding through the grove, peering occasionally into the distance, obviously looking for something—someone. He passes various small groups of
PEOPLE, but none are whom he's seeking. And then, in the distance, he spots:

15   A FEW TEEN-AGERS   15
clustered around two handsome cheetahs. The paw of one of the cheetahs is being
spray bandaged (23rd century medicine style) by a MAN whose BACK IS TO US. The
Man uses various instruments from an over-shoulder bag. From the rear we can SEE
only the Man's civilian clothes, and his slightly longish hair.
An expression of recognition flits across Kirk's face; he approaches the group.

16   CLOSER ON THE GROUP   16
as we can SEE the Man just finishing the big cat's paw, addressing the teen-agers.

                                    MAN
    Well . . . if one of you takes care of that paw, it'll be good as new in a week.

The teen-agers (and the cheetahs) romp off. The Man begins packing away his instruments. Kirk steps a little closer.

                                    KIRK
    Those cheetahs never pay their bills, Doctor.

The Man laughs, turns fully INTO THE CAMERA. And we SEE the Man is:

17   McCOY   17
as he realizes it's Kirk and the laugh trails off. Yet there's no doubt but that they're
both very pleased to see the other. Perhaps they're afraid they'd be over-emotional if
they let their true feelings surface.

                                    KIRK
    So you came down from the hills.

                                   McCOY
                                  (shrugs)
    Just passing through.

They shake hands. And then, study each other. They're both awkward about this meeting. For five long years of the starship mission, they were so close to each other. Now they feel almost as strangers.

> McCOY
> (continuing)
> Well . . . how've you been?

> KIRK
> Three letters—no answer.

> McCOY
> The fact I didn't write . . . was my answer.

Another hesitation. Then Kirk tries to lighten the moment with a grin.

> KIRK
> They call you what? The 'animal doctor'?

> McCOY
> (nods)
> The only sensible patients I've ever had.

> KIRK
> You could always heal anything, Bones. Remember . . . what did they call it . . . the Horta? You patched her up with silicone cement.

McCoy has closed his instrument bag, now slung it over his shoulder, and turned to face Kirk.

> McCOY
> What I remember, Jim . . . are the friends who couldn't be put back together. For five years . . . so many of them.

And he starts walking. Kirk hesitates a moment, then catches up.

18   KIRK AND McCOY WALKING - VARIOUS ANGLES AND POVS   18
as they proceed through the grove, which provides us with other VIEWS of the beauty of the surroundings—the ease of life.

> KIRK
> The Enterprise will be ready for commissioning in a few weeks. She's been refitted and redesigned: new engines, new equipment we never dreamed of.

> McCOY
> (almost amused)
> You never give up, do you?

> KIRK
> Bones, she'll be the most powerful starship in the galaxy. She needs a crew to match that, the most experienced in every department . . .

McCoy stops abruptly, faces Kirk.

                    McCOY
Then why aren't you commanding her?

                    KIRK
Because I'm not a captain now. Admirals do other things.

McCoy shakes his head indulgently, now resumes walking. Then:

                    McCOY
Does Admiral Kirk do these other things as happily?

                    KIRK
If I weren't happy, Bones, I'd resign from the service.

                    McCOY
You probably will resign in time, Jim.

                    KIRK
You're wrong.

                    McCOY
I wish I were. But I learned to know you too well.

At that instant we HEAR the familiar COMMUNICATOR SIGNAL. Kirk stops, glances wryly at McCoy, now produces an old-style hand communicator, opens it, AD LIBS into the speaker: "Kirk here . . ."

                COMMUNICATOR VOICE
Admiral Kirk, Admiral Nogura requests your presence at a priority one staff conference. Urgent. Immediately, if possible.

Kirk gives McCoy a look, then speaks into his communicator.

                    KIRK
Kirk, affirmative. Lock in, one to beam back.

                COMMUNICATOR VOICE
Locking in. Stand by.

                    KIRK
                  (to McCoy)
Bet you a dinner this isn't that urgent.

                    McCOY
              (smiles; shakes head)
I'm on my way again.

                    KIRK
If I promise no more 'recruiting' . . . ?

                    McCOY
You wouldn't know how to stop.

Interrupted by the SHIMMER OF THE TRANSPORTER EFFECT—and in an instant Kirk has dematerialized and is gone. McCoy stands watching the spot, entire gamut of emotions evident on his face.

19   INT. NOGURA'S OFFICE   19
EFFECT appears at Nogura's one-position transporter chamber—and Kirk materializes. This is a large office as would be appropriate for Starfleet Officer Commanding. Simple furnishings, yet all very functional. A gigantic star map occupies one entire wall—it occasionally changes its image from one portion of the galaxy to another, blinking data denoting the locations of various vessels. Nogura's desk is at one side of the room, on the other a large holograph conference table.

NOGURA, a handsome, greying man in his 50's, greets Kirk with an AD-LIBBED "Admiral, we'll commence immediately . . ." He seems tense and worried as he gestures Kirk to the conference table, where we are AWARE of another officer seated here—a very familiar face:

20   SCOTT   20
in uniform, full Commander's stripes.
He smiles, pleased to see Kirk, who returns an equally pleased smile. Each AD LIBS a greeting: "Scotty . . ." and Scott says, "Admiral . . ." As each takes a seat, Kirk continues to Scott, quietly:

                              KIRK
    The new fuel inter-mix regulators. I hear they're installed now . . .

                              NOGURA
                        (interrupting; to Kirk)
    You're not here to gossip about the Enterprise redesign, gentlemen . . .

Kirk looks up in surprise at the sharp-toned reprimand.

                              NOGURA
                          (continuing)
    Forgive me, Admiral . . . Commander. What you'll learn here is far from pleasant.

Nogura has sat at the head of the table where he flicks some buttons on his console and, instantly:

21   FULL ON TABLE - HOLOGRAPHIC IMAGES (OPTICAL)   21
of two Starfleet officers, each at one of the conference table positions, each officer's image life-size. Except for the transparency of these images, it would be difficult to know the people were not actually there. One is a handsome woman, ADMIRAL CAR-SON; the other CAPTAIN LEBUTU (a middle-aged black).

                              NOGURA
                          (to the images)
    Admiral Carson, Captain Lebutu, you both know Admiral Kirk and Commander Scott . . .

They nod at each other's images as Kirk AD LIBS, "We're all old friends." Scott says to Carson's image, "Admiral . . ." and to Lebutu, "How do you do, sir?" Carson asks, "How's your refit coming?" Scott throws a look to Nogura, says "Fine." Nogura gets down to business immediately and grimly:

                              NOGURA

As you know . . .

                         (indicating him)
. . . Lebutu's sensor drones constantly monitor the neutral zone between ourselves and the Klingon Empire. Two days ago one of our drones picked up signs
of Klingon heavy cruiser activity. It got to the area in time to record the treaty
violation. I wish that were all we'd learned, gentlemen.

Meanwhile, Nogura touches a control on his conference table panel, draws their
attention to the office viewer where they see:

22   ANGLE INCLUDING VIEWER   22
on which we SEE the Klingon heavy cruiser slicing across space. Then the two other
Klingon cruisers, all three in loose formation.

                              SCOTT
Big ones.

                             CARSON
Koro class. Their newest and best.

                             LEBUTU
                           (nodding)
They've spotted something just out of our drone's camera range.

                          (indicates)
Now watch!

On the viewing screen the sudden turbulent whiplash of energy from OUT OF FRAME,
destroying one of the Klingon cruisers.

23   ANGLE ON KIRK AND THE OTHERS   23
reacting hard, almost disbelievingly.

                              SCOTT
My God!

                             LEBUTU
They're firing back now . . .

24   ANGLE INCLUDING SCREEN   24
on which we SEE the remaining two Klingon vessels maneuvering, firing toward the
unseen object. Then a second cruiser is hit by the incredible flash of energy. The lead
cruiser is caught by the edge of the whiplash, damaged and hitting out of control.

                             LEBUTU
At this point our drone picked up their command frequency . . .

On the viewer the SCENE suddenly switches to interior Klingon cruiser bridge where
the Klingon Captain is looking directly TOWARD (CAMERA) his own viewer, transmitting:

CAPTAIN

. . . both destroyed, we are severely damaged, returning fire. I repeat, this is Commander Barak of the Imperial Cruiser Amar, under attack by a huge object of unknown origin, incredibly powerful . . .

Then all at once the entire picture flares, suddenly becomes white, blazing white, and then the screen goes blank.

25   ANGLE ON NOGURA AND THE OTHERS   25
It is taking them a moment to absorb what they've just seen. Then:

KIRK

Huge object, incredibly powerful, three Klingon heavy cruisers wiped out like they were cargo freighters.

CARSON

A totally unprovoked attack.

KIRK

Let's hope it just doesn't like Klingons.
(to Nogura)
Recommend we try to determine this object's present course and warn off any vessels we have nearby.

NOGURA

Its course is known, Admiral Kirk.
(grim beat)
It's headed here. Toward Earth.

26   ANOTHER ANGLE - KIRK   26
digesting all this, weighing the implication, as Carson speaks:

CARSON

We've monitored it from three different stations. There isn't the slightest doubt that its heading is our solar system, this planet . . .

27   ACROSS THEM TO THE STAR MAP   27
as Nogura refers to the stardate chronometer (digital) on the map:

NOGURA

. . . it will arrive in exactly 8.6 days . . .

As he talks, Nogura is punching console buttons, so that the appropriate Star Map quadrant is MAGNIFIED, and now covers the entire map area. There is but a single light indicating the presence of a UFP vessel, a lonely ship in a hostile sea. Beside the light a printout reads: USS Aswan.

NOGURA
(continuing)
. . . as you see, all other UFP vessels are more than nine days away. The sole exception—and the only one in position to intercept—is the Aswan.

KIRK

Sir, the Aswan is a light cruiser: her weapons and defense systems have less than half the power the Klingons had.

NOGURA

There is another vessel that could back up the Aswan.
A vessel with stronger forcefields and firepower than all three Klingon cruisers combined.

Kirk and Scott glance at each other in surprise; each realizes what vessel Nogura means.

SCOTT

You're referring to the Enterprise, sir . . . ?

NOGURA

How soon can you move her out?

SCOTT
(appalled)
She's not near ready, Admiral. Nothing's been tested: engines, weapons, deflectors. She requires at least 60 days of shakedown.

CARSON

Commander, are you saying the Enterprise can't go out?

SCOTT

I'm saying she shouldn't, sir.

NOGURA

Your comments are noted, Commander. However, the Enterprise is to be commissioned and underway within twenty-four hours.

SCOTT
(hesitates, then stands)
I'd best be getting up there then, sir.

Scott starts to leave, then stops and turns.

SCOTT
(continuing)
The old crew, Admiral, with an untested starship . . .

NOGURA
(nods; interrupting)
Commander Uhura and Lieutenant Sulu are already aboard . . .

KIRK

How about Chekov? He's tops for weapons and security . . .

NOGURA
(to Carson)
Get him.

NOGURA (CONT'D)
(to Scott)
Thank you, Commander.

(to Kirk)
For science officer, we've got almost Spock's equal. Commander Ronak.

Scott has nodded, exits. Kirk shakes his head, frowning.

KIRK
A fine crew on such short notice.

CARSON
If we had the right Captain.

KIRK
(puzzled)
Captain Wah Chen is one of the best.

CARSON
The Enterprise leaves in twenty-four hours, Admiral. Captain Wah is still at Starbase Six, three days away at maximum warp.

NOGURA
(to Kirk)
Who is the next most qualified captain?

KIRK
Bar-Lev.

NOGURA
He's never commanded more than a light cruiser.

KIRK
He's the next qualified available.

NOGURA
Kirk! Who is the best qualified available?

28   EMPHASIZING KIRK   28
hesitating a long moment. Then he looks up, meets Nogura eye to eye.

KIRK
I am.

FADE THROUGH BLACK TO:

29   EXT. PLANET EARTH (OPTICAL)   29
several hundred miles BELOW US. We are ABOVE the North American continent, and under the thin cloud cover we can MAKE OUT the familiar, curving coast of the American West: the southern tip of Alaska all the way to Baja California. (Los Angeles is now an island.) ANGLE WIDENS SLIGHTLY TO INCLUDE:

30   AN ORBITING SPACE/WORK STATION   30
A space station, hexagonal pod construction. The CAMERA STAYS with this

impressive sight a long moment, the station rotating ever so slowly—but perceptibly
—framed against the blue-black of sub space, and slightly beyond—and below—Earth.

31   ANOTHER ANGLE - THE EDGE OF THE WORK PLATFORM   31
As the station moves slowly, tantalizingly, the spidery network of the dry dock now
comes INTO VIEW. We will SEE but a corner of it, a glimpse—and while we see
nothing else at the moment we realize such a huge, intricate structure must contain a
much larger object. While we do not yet see it, we realize something quite important
is within the dry dock.

32   INT. ORBITING WORK OFFICE   32
A fully equipped, busy office: drafting tables, PEOPLE (engineers, draftsmen, technicians—some in uniform, some in civilian clothes) moving about. At one side, a double
position transporter in which we see the familiar EFFECT.

33   KIRK   33
materializing in the transporter chamber. He's in uniform now, and turns to Scott,
who crosses over from the drafting area.

> SCOTT
> We'll have the Enterprise transporter ready in a couple of hours, sir.

> KIRK
> It's better this way. I'll get a good look at her.

> SCOTT
> She's more beautiful than ever, sir.

> KIRK
> (smiles)

Show me.

Scott gestures Kirk to step into the adjoining pod.

34   OBSERVATION POD   34
A smaller office-type room, but with comfortable benches. Kirk sits at the observation
window, while Scott touches some buttons which activate a sliding door. The door
seals off the pod from the station proper, in effect placing them in a self-contained
unit. Scott manipulates some buttons—there is a SOUND of JETS IGNITING—and
suddenly the pod begins moving.

35   EXT. THE POD   35
moving, detaching itself entirely from the space station as it converts, literally, into
a small shuttle. It floats, propelled by the tiny jets, toward the filigreed dry dock (of
which we still can SEE only a glimpse).

36   INSIDE THE POD - SCOTT AND KIRK AT THE WINDOW   36
watching as the dry dock now comes INTO FULL VIEW—and, slowly, we begin SEEING:

37   THE ENTERPRISE   37
First the left engine, then the curve of the hull saucer, and then the entire hull—and
then, finally, the whole ship.

38 ON KIRK   38

peering at the ship—the loveliest sight he has seen in months. His ship, his life. His face reveals all. Scott glances at him, but says nothing; nothing needs to be said.

39 EXT. ENTERPRISE - FULL VIEW - VARIOUS ANGLES AND POVS   39

as the pod approaches it. The great starship dwarfs everything in sight. The dry dock filigreed installation that envelops the ship seems fragilely beautiful with the white bulk of the Enterprise inside of it. Now, CLOSER, we can SEE small automated welding devices moving along the girders. The welding device stops, seals a weld with a brief, bright blue flare, then moves along again.

In other areas of the girdered structure, supplies and equipment are being loaded onto the ship.

And here and there we can SEE TINY FIGURES OF ORBITAL TECHNICIANS working on the hull, the engine pods, the struts. They resemble specks of dust silhouetted against the hull whiteness.

The shuttle pod moves closer to where we SEE an AIR LOCK the size of the pod.

40 ANGLE AT POD AIR LOCK   40

SHOWING the pod gently settling in next to it—then magnetically locks close. Then the "WHOOSH" of the airtight doors being secured, the "CLANG" of the security bolts.

41 INT. POD   41

as Scott and Kirk prepare to leave, Scott completing the instrument final landing check. Over the INTERCOM:

                    LANDING OFFICER'S VOICE
                          (filtered)
        Pod secured. Pressure equalized.

Scott smiles at Kirk, touches the control opening the hatch which immediately slides up and open.

42 INT. ENTERPRISE CARGO DECK CORRIDOR   42

The entire cargo deck is apparently busy with activity as various supplies are being stored. Personnel use small anti-gravs (anti-gravity devices) to effortlessly move large containers of supplies and equipment to appropriate sections. CAMERA CENTERS on ship interior side of the airlock as it opens and Kirk and Scott emerge from the pod and are met by an ENSIGN.

                          ENSIGN
                        (to Scott)
        Sir, they'd like you in Engineering . . .
                (recognizes Kirk; surprised)
        I beg your pardon, sir. No one signalled a flag officer coming aboard.

                          KIRK
        What's the problem in Engineering?

                      LANDING OFFICER
        They're having some damage control monitor relay problems, sir.

LANDING OFFICER (CONT'D)
(to Scott)
They need you as soon as possible, sir.

SCOTT
(to Kirk)
I'd better get up there, sir.

Kirk nods, and Scott hurries away. Kirk stands a moment, gazing at all the activity.
The Ensign has been waiting nervously.

ENSIGN
I'd be pleased to show you around the ship, Admiral.

Kirk glances sharply at the Ensign—then realizes the young man doesn't know that
this Admiral is the starship's former captain. Kirk relaxes into a small smile.

KIRK
I think I can find my way, Ensign. Thank you.

And Kirk turns and starts off across the deck.

43   ANOTHER ANGLE - KIRK   43
as he moves through the deck, stepping out of the way of a CREWMAN rushing about
on an errand—nearly blocking other CREWMEN engaged in moving equipment. (The
point of the scene is that Kirk is an observer, not a participant.) To the lower deck
crew here, he's a stranger, and in the way. A couple of CREW will brush past him,
AD-LIBBING an irritated, ". . . move aside . . . !" etc., and then realizing it is an
Admiral they've pushed around, instantly apologizing with AD-LIBBED "Sorry, sir, I
didn't realize . . ." etc. Kirk sets them at ease with a gesture, walks toward the
elevator.

44   INT. ELEVATOR   44
as Kirk enters, and the doors close, and Kirk calls out his destination:

KIRK
Bridge . . .

The turbo-elevator begins going up. Kirk stands, grim, a million thoughts whirling
through his brain. Suddenly, the elevator comes to a jarring, SCREECHING halt.

45   ANGLE ON ELEVATOR DOORS   45
as they snap open and former Nurse CHAPEL backs into the cab, guiding a packet of
medical supplies being pushed by a Medical Technician. She speaks over-shoulder to
Kirk without really seeing him.

CHAPEL
Sorry, I've got some perishables here.
(turning to elevator control)
Priority, Level ten first.

The Technician has backed away, remaining in the corridor as the elevator doors
snap closed and the turbo-cab starts upward in response to Chapel's instructions.

CHAPEL
(continuing)
I really am sorry but if these get warm . . .

KIRK
Quite all right . . . Doctor. It is Doctor Chapel now, isn't it?

She has turned, recognizing Kirk in near disbelief.

CHAPEL
Captain . . . Admiral, I should say . . .
(as they shake hands)
. . . it's wonderful to see you. Especially today. Are you seeing us off?

KIRK
Uh . . . not exactly. You see . . .

It's interrupted by the elevator stopping and the door snapping open. Chapel is immediately busy with her load.

CHAPEL
That was a clumsy question. I know how you must feel with someone else taking her out.

KIRK
Well, actually . . .

CHAPEL
(interrupting)
I really do understand, sir.
(touching her sleeve stripes)
At least, I'm supposed to understand such things. The truth is, I was the only half-way qualified surgeon available.

If there was any small smile on Chapel's face, it was a very nervous one. She's clearly feeling the enormous responsibilities she is inheriting. The doors have started to close, but Kirk has put up a hand freezing them in position as:

KIRK
Doctor . . . you'll be interested that they've picked the captain exactly the same way.

He removes his hand, lets the doors snap shut on puzzled and concerned Chapel. Kirk smiles as the elevator continues upward.

46   INT. BRIDGE - ELEVATOR DOOR   46
as the turbo-lift door snaps open and Kirk steps out onto the bridge. CAMERA INTO MEDIUM CLOSE as he stops, looks around.

47   ANGLE PAST KIRK   47
CAMERA TRAVELING to emphasize first UHURA who is working rapidly and expertly at the communications station sorting out and checking channels . . . "Hailing frequency four, check. Hailing frequency five . . . hailing frequency five, will someone

give me a check?" At the helm, SULU has a service plate open, peering inside while he makes an adjustment . . . "Helm, give me a reading on four point zero zero six of full." We HEAR a VOICE responding and Sulu continues on with other readings. At the Weapons Control Station CHEKOV is having an argument with a TECHNICIAN who keeps insisting the photon torpedoes read "ready" while Chekov argues that the computer is not relaying that information to his weapons scanner.

48   TRAVELING WITH KIRK   48
Other n.d. Technicians at work, too. The bridge is a mess, service panels open, spare parts lying about, some circuits still leading across deck areas.

Kirk moves beside his command position. Uhura looks up, freezes as she sees him and then recognizes his expression from old. She waits as:

                              KIRK
Viewer, please, Mr. Sulu.

                              SULU
                            (irritably)
What in hell's name . . .?

Sulu bites off his words, staring at Kirk, disbelieving that he actually heard the order he thinks he heard. Chekov has spun, too, astonished. Then he shouts at one of the technicians who is still talking.

                              CHEKOV
Yonson, knock it off!

We can FAINTLY HEAR the work going on nearby in other sections and levels. But there's a hush on the bridge . . . Kirk speaks in a normal tone:

                              KIRK
Viewer, please, Commander Sulu.

                              SULU
                            (puzzled)
Aye, sir.

49   ANGLE TO INCLUDE VIEWER (OPTICAL ANGLE)   49
as Sulu hits proper control. The VIEWER APPEARS. He has turned to Uhura, tosses her a tiny cassette. She catches it expertly, waits.

                              KIRK
Patch that into all viewers, all decks, please.

As Uhura complies, Kirk bends to punch the Yellow Alert button at the side of his command chair. We HEAR the ALERT SIGNAL SOUND three times before he releases it with a nod to Uhura. She punches in the cassette she has inserted. The STARFLEET COMMAND INSIGNIA appears on the viewer along with a simple Ship Commissioning BUGLE CALL. Then the face of Admiral Nogura appears.

NOGURA
The commissioning of even the smallest and least distinguished of our vessels . . .

50   INT. VARIOUS ENTERPRISE LOCATIONS   50
Included are Corridors, Engineering, Sickbay, Transporter Room, Briefing, Recreation,
etc. All of them look in about the same untidy and rushed condition as the places
we've seen. In all of them, crew members are looking up at viewers.

NOGURA
. . . is always accompanied by far more ceremony than can be offered in the
recommissioning of this vessel today. Indeed, we must regret even these few
brief moments. With the aid of whatever Providence guides we sailors and our
ships, we will one day repair this oversight.
(pauses, then)
By order of Starfleet Command, this Federation vessel . . . United Spaceship
Enterprise is declared now fully commissioned and in service.

51   INT. BRIDGE - INCLUDING VIEWER   51
as Admiral Nogura appears to be looking in direction of the command position.

NOGURA
The captain will read himself aboard.

The VIEWER IMAGE OF NOGURA is replaced by the IMAGE OF KIRK.

KIRK
Stardate 7411.4, Starfleet Orders to James T. Kirk, posted to the temporary rank
of captain . . .

Already interrupting are Uhura, Sulu, Chekov. Scotty, Yeoman RAND and other
familiar faces are already arriving on the bridge. They're calling "They've done it!"
"It's Kirk again!" "He's with us!"

KIRK
(continuing; to bridge crew)
At ease! Silence, all of you! Commander!

The last "Commander!" to an almost dancing Commander Uhura who looked dangerously near hugging Kirk.

52   INT. VARIOUS ENTERPRISE LOCATIONS   52
The same areas and types of areas we saw before. On the viewing screens, Kirk has
managed to silence his bridge crew and has turned back to the viewer to repeat and
continue.

KIRK
Repeating . . . to James T. Kirk, posted temporary captain, you are appointed,
charged and required to command starship U.S.S. Enterprise . . .

We can HEAR NO MORE of Kirk's words. Crewmen and women have begun to
react in surprise and delight, shouting the news around.

53   INT. BRIDGE ANGLE ON KIRK   53

facing viewer, completing his "reading in" requirements. Even on the enclosed bridge we can HEAR a chant "JIM KIRK . . . JIM KIRK . . . JIM KIRK!" coming from every deck, division and section. Kirk has to fight to keep his voice even and level.

> KIRK
>
> . . . and are so charged at your peril to obey in letter and spirit . . . Signed: Commanding Admiral, Earthbase, Starfleet.

DISSOLVE TO:

54   EXT. ENTERPRISE IN DRY DOCK   54

the Starship resting majestically within the filigreed cradle, the welders' arcs still operating in a final rush to completion. Another shuttlecraft (The Galileo) approaching. The scene's intent is merely to SHOW the activity around the ship.

55   INT. BRIDGE   55

alive with action—departure preparations. At the helm position is Sulu, busily engaged in a countdown checkout. And at Communications is Uhura. (Note: Sulu wears full Lt.'s stripes and Uhura Lt. Commander's.) Uhura is testing her equipment, AD-LIBBING ". . . this is the USS Enterprise testing main hailing frequencies. I repeat: this is a test . . " Etc., etc.

The CAMERA PANS AROUND THE BRIDGE, various CREWMEN and TECHNICIANS at their consoles, testing computer readout screens, instruments, etc. Now the CAMERA FINDS a breathtakingly beautiful young woman, just entering the bridge, striding purposefully toward the helm/navigational position. She is a Lt. JG, whose stunning figure is hardly military, but whose most prominent feature is her head. She is hairless—entirely bald, but for delicately-slanted eyebrows, a feature that strangely is not at all unattractive: with her jeweled Deltan headband shadowing the baldness, she emanates a definite, almost intense sensuality.

Her name is ILIA (eye-lee-ah), and she takes her place at Navigator's position beside Sulu now. Sulu seems unable to prevent himself from being distracted by her presence. Though not looking at him she is immediately aware of his eyes on her and soon turns to face him directly. She holds out a bare arm to the embarrassed helmsman.

> ILIA
>
> Go ahead. It's all right.

> SULU
> (flustered)
> Go ahead? I'm not sure I know what you mean.

> ILIA
>
> Mr. Sulu, I am a normal Deltan female and I can sense it whenever a man wants to touch me. There's no need to repress it so long as you are aware that I am sworn to celibacy for the duration of the mission.

Sulu, caught red-handed as it were, still tries to squirm out of it:

> SULU
>
> I was just adm . . .

ILIA

Mr. Sulu. Touch me and get it out of your mind or you will prove to be a distraction to me as well as yourself.

She reoffers her arm. Awkwardly, self-consciously, Sulu reaches out and strokes her arm. She takes his hand and guides it along her skin, then she gracefully extends a hand to Sulu's face, caresses his earlobe with a finger for a moment before brushing his cheek with the gentlest touch of her palm and fingertips. Sulu's embarrassment leaves him. He is calmed.

ILIA
(continuing)

Better?

Sulu is not quite sure he understands how he has arrived at his present emotional state, but:

SULU

Yes. Thank you.

She reaches again to his face in final punctuation as she smiles beautifully and answers his unasked question:

ILIA

We can calm as well as stimulate . . .

With that, the subject closes and both return to their work at full efficiency. Behind them, the turbolift doors open and Kirk emerges uncertainly onto the outer bridge platform.

56   ACROSS SULU TO THE BRIDGE ENTRANCE   56
      as he looks up from his console to see Kirk.

SULU

Captain, this is Lieutenant Ilia, our new navigator.

57   ANOTHER ANGLE   57
      as Sulu leads Kirk down to her.

KIRK

From Delta 14 . . . I've heard a lot about you, Lieutenant.

ILIA

And I you, sir.

58   KIRK AND ILIA - TWO SHOT   58
      as she peers at him, the Deltan seductiveness literally oozing out of her. For just one instant Kirk is completely caught up in it—and then he realizes who and where he is.

KIRK

Well . . . please, don't let me interfere with your duties.

                    SCOTTY'S VOICE
      Scott to bridge . . . is the Captain there?

Before Uhura can speak, Kirk has stepped to the intercom.

                        KIRK
                   (into intercom)
      Kirk here.

                    SCOTTY'S VOICE
      The new science officer is beaming up now, sir.

                        KIRK
                   (into intercom)
      I'll be right there . . .

And he starts hurriedly away.

59   INT. ELEVATOR   59
     as Kirk enters and announces his destination.

                        KIRK
      Main transporter room.

60   INT. ENTERPRISE TRANSPORTER ROOM   60
     with Scott and two TECHNICIANS waiting, watching the receiving chamber. The door
     opens now, and Kirk enters. He glances at the chambers—which are empty, give no
     evidence of a beaming—and then at Scott, who is studying the chamber with a very
     worried frown. He flicks on his intercom.

                        SCOTT
                   (into intercom)
      Enterprise to Starfleet transporter; we're ready to receive.

But the word is hardly out of Scott's mouth when suddenly the entire console
ERUPTS IN A SHOWER OF SPARKS AND FLAME. The HUMMING SOUND of the
Energizer is VERY LOUD, as though out of control. The figure in the chamber
SHIMMERS, and then materializes, and then SHIMMERS again. Scott and the others
are standing like frozen statues, puzzled expressions fixed on their faces.

61   EXT. THE ENTERPRISE IN DRY DOCK - FULL SHOT   61
     the ship looming huge inside the delicate, filigreed dry dock.

We NOTE the welders are gone, and supply pods are floating away from the ship. The
orbital space office is in the f.g. and now we SEE that the girders are slowly <u>rising</u>—
so they will be out of the way of the ship. (This might resemble a 20th century
drawbridge in principle.) The little yellow jets spurt from the supply pods as they
move away from the ship, and the girders open more and more and we SEE that
shortly the big ship will be free. A space tableau, with appropriate MUSIC, which
fades slightly as OVER this we HEAR:

                    UHURA'S VOICE
      . . . Dock Officer reports we are clear to pull away at Captain's discretion . . .

INT. BRIDGE

with all personnel occupied with their pre-depature tasks. Sulu and Ilia at their helm and navigational stations. Uhura at her post. And, at the Science Station, Kirk is with WILL DECKER, a handsome man in his early 30's; he is a big man, Decker, with rugged, hard features—and alert, cold eyes. He's peering into the hooded viewer, punching in programmed procedures—Kirk beside him, assisting.

                          UHURA
                (from the start, continuing)
We are on yellow alert.

                          KIRK
Inform Engineering . . .
                (to Decker; a little impatient)
Can't you program a pre-departure plan any faster?

                          DECKER
                (testily)
If I did, Captain, we'd never leave the dock: I'm not a Science Officer . . . or is that what you thought I was when you yanked me off the Boston to serve here?

63   ANOTHER ANGLE - KIRK AND DECKER   63
as Kirk moves next to Decker at the Science station and forces his anger into quiet, private conversation.

                          KIRK
Commander Decker, I am aware that you are not a science Officer—but that's the very reason you were 'yanked' off the Boston—because of your versatility. I need someone like you to backstop not only me—but the other vital stations as well.

                          DECKER
                (tightly)
Yes, sir.

                          KIRK
                (conciliatorily)
Look, Will, I know you were slated for your own command—and you'll have it. But right now let's concentrate on the Enterprise.

                          DECKER
Whatever you say, sir.

Kirk reacts, is about to reply (angrily), when Uhura interrupts:

                          UHURA
Transporter room reports science and medical officers beaming up, Captain.

                          KIRK
I'd better get down there.
                (to Decker, friendly)
Do the best you can.

And Kirk quickly leaves the bridge. Decker glances grimly after him.

64   INT. TRANSPORTER ROOM   64
     Scott at the center control panel, two TECHNICIANS at the other controls. Kirk
     enters, and Scott glances at him.

                              SCOTT
         Starfleet transporter's repaired and in perfect working order, sir.

Kirk only looks at him with grim hope.

65   ACROSS THEM TO THE TRANSPORTER CHAMBERS   65
     as the SHIMMERING EFFECT commences. It is fast, and correct. Two forms material-
     ize—one is young, long haired, his uniform seemingly shabby, almost ragged. This is
     XON, age 22, he looks around curiously, a strange, steel-hard coldness in his eyes.
     The other officer is LEONARD McCOY. Kirk is speechless, but Scott is overjoyed.

                              SCOTT
         Bones . . . !

And Scott hurries around the console to greet McCoy with an affectionate embrace,
AD LIBBING " . . . I canna believe my ancient eyes . . . !" etc. At the same time, Xon
snaps to attention.

                              XON
         Lieutenant Junior Grade Xon, Science Officer, requesting permission to come
         aboard, sir.

No one pays him the scantest attention. Kirk has stepped over to McCoy, peers at
him, shakes his head in utter disbelief.

                              McCOY
         Chief Medical Officer McCoy requesting permission to come aboard, sir.

                              KIRK
                          (incredulous)
         Bones . . . how did—? Is this some kind of joke . . .?

                              McCOY
                          (flat, tight)
         No joke, Captain, sir. I'm sure a copy of my orders is already in the personnel
         computer.

                              XON
         Lieutenant Junior Grade Xon, requesting permission to come aboard, sir.

                              KIRK
                          (to Xon)
         Yes, yes, permission granted . . .
                          (to McCoy)
         What happened?

                              McCOY
                          (flat, tight)
         What happened, Captain, sir, was that our revered Chief of Staff, Admiral Nogura

himself, invoked a little known—and seldom used—reserve activation clause . . .
(very tight)
. . . in simpler language, Captain, sir, I've been <u>drafted</u> . . .!

Kirk is so nonplussed he cannot find words—can only <u>laugh</u>; and he glances at Scott, who also is unable to conceal a delighted smile.

XON
Sir, I am Lieutenant Junior Grade Xon—

McCOY
(hard, to Xon)
—Yes, Lieutenant Junior Grade Xon, we can <u>smell</u> you.

KIRK
Where were you that you got into such a foul state, Lieutenant?

XON
The high Gobi desert. In a meditative monastery, sir.

KIRK
Doing what? Rolling in yak droppings?

XON
Preparing myself for duty, sir. In the event a shipboard assignment should occur.

KIRK
You're a Lieutenant! You've never had shipboard duty?

McCOY
Jim, I . . . I think he was graduated a Lieutenant.
(to Xon)
How long ago?

XON
Eighty-one days ago, sir.

KIRK
(to McCoy)
He's yours then. Medical Officer.

McCOY
(shakes head)
He's yours. Vulcans also graduate as Lieutenants.

66   EMPHASIZING KIRK AND XON   66

The Captain giving Xon a long, long look. Then:

KIRK
Please tell me you've got rounded ears, Lieutenant.

XON
I see no reason to being our acquaintance with an insult, sir.

67 EXT. THE ENTERPRISE   67
moving away from the dock, the dock girders completely open now, and the
Enterprise's maneuvering jets spurting live flame as the great starship begins edging
out of the dock. Now the front of the saucer is clear, majestically moving ahead—and
now the main hull is clear—and then the engine pods.

68 INT. BRIDGE   68
with all hands concentrating on departure. Kirk occupies the command chair, Sulu
and Ilia at their stations. Behind them Uhura works communications—and Decker still
sweats at the Science Station. And also here now is CHEKOV, working feverishly on
his now dismantled damage control console.

                          KIRK
                      (to Chekov)
        Are you making any progress, Mr. Chekov?

                          CHEKOV
        I think I've almost got it now, sir. A faulty relay integrator . . .

                          UHURA
        The vessel is clear of the dock, Captain—

                          KIRK
Maneuvering jets to hold.

                          SULU
                    (working controls)
Maneuvering jets to hold, sir.

                          KIRK
                    (into intercom)
Engineering . . .

                      SCOTT'S VOICE
Engineering.

                          KIRK
Mr. Scott, are main engines ready yet?

69 INT. ENGINEERING SECTION   69
The great engines now suddenly THROBBING, slowly building up from a low growl to
an ever-increasing, powerful WHINE. A dim red glow from the unit indicates the
fusion. Scott is at his console, working the controls, and now speaking into the intercom:

                          SCOTT
Aye, sir.

                      KIRK'S VOICE
                    (over intercom)
Engage.

SCOTT

Yes, sir!

And he moves the controls forward, the entire room shudders slightly as the great engines draw more and more power; the red fusion glow increases. Scott places his palm against the wall behind him, feels the engines' pulse, smiles with pleasure.

SCOTT

Aye, can't wait to go, can you, you marvelous darlings . . . ?!

70   INT. BRIDGE - ANGLE ON THE MAIN VIEWER   70
which shows the blue-black of subspace, the sparkling stars. And just a glimpse of the orbital work station.

Kirk, in the command chair, peers at the viewer. Sulu glances at him.

SULU

All systems ready, sir.

KIRK

Navigator . . .
(as Ilia turns to him)
Lay in an interception course: coordinates 953 point 2, mark 6 . . .
(to Sulu)
Helmsman—

Kirk hesitates just an instant, seems to hold his breath—and so does everyone else. And then:

KIRK
(continuing)
All ahead, warp point five.

71   EXT. THE ENTERPRISE   71
stationary, hovering, the maneuvering jets still spurting blue. Then, all at once, the blue flames are off. The engine pod discs begin glowing red—and the Enterprise begins moving, the CAMERA TRACKING HER. She moves away, faster and faster, and now begins outrunning the CAMERA. In an instant now she WHOOSHES across the blue-black sky—and in another instant is but a speck on the orbital horizon, blending in now with the myriad of sparkling stars.

72   INT. BRIDGE   72
All hands tense with the drama of the moment—moving off into space.

SULU

Warp point five, sir. All systems normal.

KIRK

Thank you, Mr. Sulu. Departure angle on the viewer, please.

73   PAST KIRK TO THE VIEWER   73
as, instantly, on the viewing screen we SEE the cloud-laced image of Earth (OPTICAL). A ball of blue and white, smaller and smaller before our eyes—and, quickly, dwindling to but a point of light. After another moment:

                              KIRK

Normal angle.

And, instantly, on the viewer we SEE the familiar STAR TRAVEL EFFECT. Kirk flicks
on his intercom:

                              KIRK
                          (continuing)

Engineering . . .

                          SCOTT'S VOICE

Engineering.

                              KIRK

She feels good, Scottie.

                          SCOTT'S VOICE

That she does, sir. She's a beauty.

                              KIRK
                            (a beat)

All right, Mr. Scott, let's go into Warp Drive. Ahead, Warp One.

                          SCOTT'S VOICE
                          (exhilarated)

Accelerating to Warp One, sir.

Everyone waits tensely—and then we HEAR the increasing, SMOOTH THROB on the
accelerating engines. There's a gentle SHUDDER as Sulu announces:

                              SULU

Warp point seven . . . point eight . . . point nine—

74   EXT. THE ENTERPRISE   74
      showing ship streaking along—and then the WARP DRIVE OPTICAL EFFECT.

75   INT. BRIDGE   75
      as the same WARP DRIVE OPTICAL EFFECT appears, and then suddenly all is quiet,
      and normal.

                              SULU

Warp One.

Everyone suddenly relaxes, grins. Kirk gets out of his chair, addresses Uhura:

                              KIRK

Lieutenant Uhura, establish a relay frequency between Starfleet Command and
the Aswan. Primary reception to us, please.

                              UHURA
                            (gently)

Sir, it's Lieutenant <u>Commander</u> Uhura—

> KIRK
>
> I beg your pardon . . . Commander . . .

An apologetic smile.

> UHURA
>
> It's quite all right, Captain.

76 ACROSS KIRK TO UHURA - DECKER IN THE B.G.   76
as she smiles the same apologetic smile back at him—and then suddenly the smile freezes. She is peering O.S. And Decker, too, is staring O.S. It is as though neither can believe their eyes.

77 ANOTHER ANGLE - SULU AND ILIA   77
also peering incredulously O.S. Now Kirk wheels around to see:

78 WHAT THEY ARE LOOKING AT - XON   78
in the doorway, now spic and span in a clean, new uniform, hair regulation style, clean shaven. And, for the first time, we SEE his ears: Vulcan ears. He is very somber, unsmiling, correct.

> XON
> (from the start)
> Lieutenant Junior Grade Xon, Science Officer, reporting for duty, sir.

For another moment all stare at the young man in stunned silence. Then:

> ILIA
>
> You're a Vulcan . . . !

> XON
>
> Obviously . . .
> (to Kirk)
> Sir, may I assume my station?

> KIRK
> (nonplussed)
> By all means, Lieutenant.

And Xon strides across the bridge to the Science Station, which Decker still occupies.

79 AT THE SCIENCE STATION   79
as Xon arrives, and Decker rises to greet him.

> DECKER
> (as an introduction)
> Will Decker . . .

> XON
>
> How do you do, sir?

Xon stands facing Decker stolidly, unsmiling. Decker, who was smiling, friendlily, says nothing a distracted moment. Then:

DECKER

I've completed all the pre-warp programming.

XON

If you will permit me, sir . . .

He indicates chair. Decker moves so that Xon can sit.

Xon scans the hooded viewer, now commences to remove the computer chips, reverse them, and replace them into the computer.

DECKER
(protesting)
Lieutenant, you're erasing those tapes . . . !

XON

A quite logical deduction, sir.

And he continues this. Decker blocks the Vulcan's hand.

DECKER

It took me more than an hour to assemble them . . . !

Xon looks at Decker squarely, unblinkingly.

XON

Sir, to function efficiently as Science Officer requires my intimate familiarity with each circuit in this system. To achieve this, sir, requires a complete pre-warp programming of my own.

DECKER

Are you trying to tell me that all that work was for nothing?

XON

That is the logical conclusion, sir. That is not to say your efforts are unappreciated—but it was a waste.

Decker, nonplussed at Xon's aplomb, struggles to control his temper. Xon indicates Decker's hand, which still blocks Xon's.

XON
(politely)

My hand, sir.

80   ACROSS THEM TO KIRK   80
who has been watching and listening curiously, as Decker now removes his hand from Xon's and steps down to the center area, addresses Kirk:

DECKER

I hope your Science Officer knows what he's doing.

XON
(from his station)

I do, sir.

XON (CONT'D)
(looks up from viewer, unsmiling)
However, if your emotional security requires it, sir, I can supply you with a copy
of my academy record.

KIRK
(turning to Xon)
It's your performance here that interests us, Lieutenant Xon.

XON
(without looking up from viewer)
This is my first operational assignment, sir.

And with that, he coolly turns back to the viewer once more.

Kirk and Decker exchange glances; then Kirk starts to leave the bridge.

KIRK

Take the Conn, Mr. Decker.

81   ANGLE ON UHURA   81
as Kirk walks toward the exit. She calls out:

UHURA
Captain, I've established subspace contact with the light cruiser Aswan. We
should have a viewer linkup within the hour.

KIRK

I'll be in my quarters—

The words are not out of Kirk's mouth when all at once the ALARM SIREN SOUNDS—
and the computerized warning VOICE SPEAKS:

COMPUTER VOICE
(terse, flat)
Collision alert . . . ! Collision alert . . . !

Kirk has whirled back to the command center, stands behind Decker, who sits in the
chair.

KIRK

Main viewer . . . !
(to Xon)
Sensor reading . . . !

XON
Navigational deflectors and scanners are inoperative, Captain.

KIRK
(disbelieving)
What?!

Meanwhile, the viewer, we SEE a HUGE ASTEROID: it is relatively small when we
first SEE it, but it grows increasingly large. (NOTE: Throughout this sequence, the
SIREN will continue and the collision warning VOICE will continue: "Collision alert . . . !
Collision alert . . . !" etc., etc.)

82   ANOTHER ANGLE - THE TURBOLIFT DOORS
      as Chekov emerges in recreational clothing.

83   FOLLOW CHEKOV   83
      as he runs to his station and punches some buttons on his console.

                              CHEKOV
      Weapon deflectors activated. Full power.

84   ANOTHER ANGLE - FAVORING DECKER AND KIRK   84
      as Decker reacts, calls to Sulu:

                              DECKER
          Hard to port . . . !

                               SULU
          The helm is not responding . . . !

                              DECKER
          Manual override . . . !

      As Sulu touches the controls, Kirk steps forward and knocks Sulu's hand away:

                              KIRK
          Belay that order; activate the main phasers.
                              (to Decker)
          We'll blast it out of the way . . .
                              (to Chekov)
          Lock on and prepare to fire!

                              CHEKOV
          Main phasers ready. Target locked on.

      On the screen the asteroid LOOMS LARGER AND LARGER, directly in the ship's path.

                              KIRK
          Fire . . . !

85   EXT. THE ENTERPRISE AND THE ASTEROID   85
      SHOWING the ship and the oncoming rock, hurtling at each other. The asteroid is now
      close enough so you can compare its size with the Enterprise: the rock is perhaps a
      mile in diameter, and resembles a metallic basketball approaching a white tennis ball.
      The two rush closer and closer—and, conspicuously, there is no phaser fire from the
      Enterprise.

86   INT. BRIDGE   86
      with all peering at the monster asteroid that now seems to occupy the entire screen.
      Chekov is punching the phaser controls. No response.

                              KIRK
          Fire, Mr. Chekov. Fire . . . !

                              CHEKOV
          There's no response, sir . . . ! I'll have photon torpedoes armed and ready in a
      minute, sir. They're operational.

                              KIRK
    Mr. Chekov, we don't have a minute.

Chekov continues to work at great speed.

87   ANOTHER ANGLE - FAVORING THE VIEWING SCREEN   87
     as all can do nothing but stare helplessly at the screen, the asteroid rushing at them
     which surely will now smash them into a pulp.

                              CHEKOV
    Photon torpedoes are away!

For another instant the rock races toward them, now literally FILLS THE SCREEN so
close all the jagged peaks and valleys are clearly VISIBLE. And then the bursts of
photo torpedo fire spurt out—strike the asteroid which, before our eyes disintegrates.
Into a thousand fragments that race toward the viewing screen like pellets released
from a cannon.

The fragments scream in TOWARD US, but bounce away, shooting into space as the
deflectors block their path. But the bridge quivers and shakes with the continual
impact. And then one gigantic fragment strikes the deflectors, the ship shudders.

And at the moment it is over. The screen is blank but for the STAR EFFECT.

                              KIRK
    Damage report.

                              CHEKOV
    No damage reported, sir.

                              SULU
    The helm is responding now, sir.

CAMERA PANS across to Xon.

                              KIRK
    Full report, Mr. Xon.

                              XON
    All systems are now normal, sir.

                              KIRK
    Mr. Xon, why weren't they normal 30 seconds ago?

                              XON
                         (flat, unemotional)
    The phaser and directional control couplings were disengaged from the main
    computer. The same was true of the Navigational scanners.

Xon pauses, and Kirk waits for more explanation—but Xon merely regards him
blandly. Kirk glances at Uhura in exasperation; she returns the glance with equal
exasperation. Kirk strains to keep his voice calm and level.

                              KIRK
                            (to Xon)
Explanation, Mr. Xon.

                              XON
When we went into Warp Drive, I did not program that effect into the computer.

                              KIRK
It should have done that automatically.

                              XON
It couldn't, sir; I had previously disengaged all three systems in order to
reprogram them.

                             UHURA
                            (aghast)
All three . . . ?!

                              XON
It was the most efficient way of doing it. By odds of slightly over eleven
thousand to one, we should not have encountered that emergency.

Kirk is so horrified he is speechless.

                              XON
                          (continuing)
Yes, Captain, I was in error to even risk those odds. I presume it has occurred to
you that Mr. Spock would not have made that same error.

                              KIRK
                        (eyes Xon; then)
That is not a subject it is wise for you to raise, Lieutenant.

                              XON
Your human emotions make comparisons between myself and Mr. Spock
inevitable, Captain. I merely wanted to assure you that this does not trouble me.

                              KIRK
I'm delighted you're not troubled, Mr. Xon. Because I am troubled, very troubled . . .

                              XON
                        (finishing sentence)
. . . by the errors I've made. It's quite natural you are troubled, sir. Just as it is
expected I would make a few erros. But my errors will be few and will rapidly
diminish to a near zero level.

Xon's calm and logical recitation has Kirk near an angry outburst. He controls
himself with difficulty, turns to exit bridge.

                             DECKER
Are you leaving me the conn, sir?

KIRK
(snaps)
I gave it to you earlier, Mr. Decker.

DECKER
You took it back, sir, when you overruled my order to the helm.

Kirk now gives Decker the same kind of look he's been giving Xon.

KIRK
I see. Then perhaps you'll join me in my cabin, Commander?

DECKER
As you wish, sir.

KIRK
Lieutenant Ilia, you have the conn.

Kirk turns, crosses to the elevator with Decker following him. Then Kirk turns again toward Uhura.

KIRK
(continuing)
Have Doctor McCoy join us there, please.

UHURA
Aye, sir.

Kirk and Decker board the elevator and the doors snap closed.

88   INT. KIRK'S CABIN   88
as McCOY and CHAPEL enter. Kirk is seated; Decker is standing, ill at ease. McCoy indicates Chapel to Kirk.

McCOY
Mind? I asked my colleague to come along.

CHAPEL
(smiles)
'Colleague' is a relative term, sir. If sickbays still used bedpans, I'd still be emptying them.

KIRK
Still, you were almost our ship's surgeon. Until this renegade veterinarian replaced you.

CHAPEL
To my enormous relief, sir.

DECKER
(to Kirk, stiffly)
Would you like me to return later, sir?

McCoy throws Decker a quick, curious look.

> McCOY
>
> What's eating you, Decker?

> DECKER
> (annoyed)
>
> Nothing is 'eating me,' Doctor McCoy. It's a private matter between the Captain and myself.

> McCOY
>
> Oh? It's too personal even for a physician?

> DECKER
>
> It's a . . . a ship's <u>command</u> matter, Doctor.

> McCOY
>
> Excellent!
> (indicates)
> Doctor Chapel is an expert in socio-psychology.

> DECKER
> (angrily, to Kirk)
>
> Captain, I object to this casual, mocking approach to a matter I consider extremely important . . . perhaps even critical to the ship's safety.

> KIRK
>
> Which is precisely why I invited medical here. Any dispute between first and second in command is very much their business.

89 ANGLE EMPHASIZING DECKER   89
as he wrestles with the decision, finally decides "why not." He faces Kirk squarely.

> DECKER
>
> A few minutes ago you very nearly steered us straight into an asteroid . . .

Pauses.

> KIRK
>
> Continue.

> DECKER
>
> The simple course change I ordered would have put us well out of the asteroid's path.

> KIRK
>
> Agreed, if this were a light scout cruiser of the type you're accustomed to maneuvering. With our automatic directional control out, converting to manual could have been a fatal delay.

> DECKER
>
> If I recall, sir, there was some delay engaging manual phaser fire. And that was very nearly fatal, too.

KIRK

We didn't know the phasers were out.

DECKER

I beg your pardon, Captain, but it is reasonable to assume that if automatic directional control is inoperative, then automatic weapons control also might be— as it was.

It is a good point, and Decker knows he's scored.

KIRK

You're quite right, Decker. I should have thought of that.

DECKER
(stiff)

May I be excused, sir?

KIRK

In just a moment, Commander.
(turning to McCoy)
Which is one reason I wanted you in on this. I've been almost two years out of that center seat. I'm almost certainly stale. Plus . . .

Kirk takes a moment to select his next words. Then:

KIRK
(continuing)

. . . plus, I had no idea how much I've missed being there. I never expected to sit there again. It . . . it means so much to me that it may affect my judgment.

The last of this has been said to Chapel who nods her understanding of the psychological implications. Now Kirk turns back to Decker.

KIRK
(continuing)

Therefore, you will continue to closely monitor my command performance and make regular reports to Doctor McCoy. Also . . .

DECKER

Sir! You can't be serious. If you're suggesting I carry reports about you to the Doctor . . .

KIRK

I'm not suggesting it, Commander. I'm ordering it.

DECKER
(nonplussed; interrupting)

But Captain, it's also possible that I've been overcritical of you. I was transferred away from my own command . . .

KIRK
(interrupting)

Which is why you will also make regular reports to Doctor Chapel assessing your own performance and attitude.

DECKER

Yes, sir.

                (waits, looking around)
And that's it, sir? I . . . I had no idea things were handled this way . . . this
openly.

McCOY

It isn't on all vessels.

DECKER
                (offering hand to Kirk)
I'm happy to be on this one, Captain.

McCOY

While we're here, any comments on the young Vulcan?

CHAPEL
                (warmly)
He _is_ sweet, isn't he!

KIRK
                (to Decker)
Our medical staff is not without its flaws and blind spots.
                (to McCoy)
Let's see how fast he comes around.

DECKER

Meanwhile, he could kill us, sir.

KIRK
                (smiles)
As you pointed out, so could I.

At that instant the intercom flashes red, and the AUDIO SIGNAL is HEARD.

UHURA'S VOICE

Communications to Captain Kirk . . .

KIRK
                (into intercom)
Kirk here.

UHURA'S VOICE

Sir, we have viewer contact with the Aswan.

KIRK

I'm on my way . . .
                (starts out, stops suddenly to face McCoy)
I don't _think_ you ever forget how—

And he leaves. McCoy gazes after him, eyebrows raised bemusedly.

90   INT. BRIDGE - ANGLE ON THE VIEWER   90
with the image of COMMANDER CORYELL, young, sternly rugged and very grim,

filling the screen. Decker is in the command chair, and now—as Kirk arrives—moves to rise. Kirk gestures Decker to remain seated addresses the viewer:

> KIRK
> Commander Coryell, this is Captain Kirk. What is the Aswan's present position and status?

> CORYELL
> Coordinates 912 point 4, mark 3, high quadrant. We have a grade-four sensor reading indicating an extremely strong magnetic field. We anticipate a visual momentarily. I have ordered a full-ahead sensor scan.

> KIRK
> Have you attempted communication?

> CORYELL
> On all hailing frequencies, Captain. No response.

> KIRK
> Keep this channel open, Commander, and keep me informed.

> CORYELL
> Yes, sir . . .
> (abruptly)
> We have the visual . . . !

Coryell is facing away from the viewing screen, but his eyes are open wide in fear and incredulity.

> CORYELL
> (continuing)
> My God . . . !!!

And suddenly Coryell's image on the viewing screen is bathed in an errie green glow that quickly envelopes the entire screen and becomes white now—whiter and whiter. There is NO SOUND, only the blazing whiteness of the viewer. And then, just an instant later, it is blank.

Kirk and the others peer incredulously at the now blank viewer. Then:

> KIRK
> Navigator—

> ILIA
> Yes, sir.

> KIRK
> Adjust your course for an intercept along a tangenital line from coordinates 912 point 4, mark 3, high quadrant.

> ILIA
> 912 point 4, mark 3. Adjusting, sir.

> KIRK
> (to Sulu)
> Increase to Warp 6.

> SULU

Increasing to Warp 6.

> KIRK

Mr. Xon . . .

> XON

Sir.

> KIRK

Estimated time to IP . . . ?

Xon glances into his hooded viewer, replies almost immediately:

> XON

68.2 hours, Captain, if we maintain Warp 6 . . .

> KIRK
> (to Uhura)

Lt. Uhura, inform Starfleet Command of the Aswan's probable destruction, and that we are proceeding to IP at optimum speed.

91   EXT. SPACE - THE ENTERPRISE   91
at Warp speed.

> KIRK (V.O.)

Captain's Log, stardate 7420.1. Light Cruiser U.S.S. Aswan is gone . . . obliterated by a weapon we were unable to identify or understand. We also know nothing of whatever it is that used that weapon. Our forward sensor scans are being absorbed by whatever object it is that we are now about to intercept.

92   INT. BRIDGE   92
SHOWING all personnel manning their stations and Chekov standing on side of the Captain's chair, Decker on the other. The main viewer is on, but at the moment all that is seen is our passage through the stars.

> ILIA

Visual contact in three minutes, Captain.

> KIRK
> (to Xon)

Sensor readings?

> XON

Still none, sir.

Kirk swivels his chair fully around to face Xon:

> KIRK

Any indication that it's scanning us?

> XON

It is possible, Captain.

KIRK
(flaring)
If it's possible, I need that information without asking!

XON
(unperturbed)
It is equally possible, sir, that we are not being scanned.

Kirk glances tightly at Decker, who immediately steps up to the Science Station, glances into the hooded Viewer.

DECKER
He's correct, Captain. We're picking up forcefield patterns, but of a type I've never seen before.

KIRK
Open hailing frequencies, Commander Uhura.

Uhura manipulates the appropriate controls:

UHURA
Hailing frequencies open, Captain.

Kirk swivels around in his chair again, faces the viewing screen, which is still blank but for the stars.

KIRK
This is the U.S.S. Enterprise, Captain James T. Kirk commanding. We are a United Federation of Planets starship. Our mission is peaceful, our intention to make contact with you.

They wait—no response. After a moment, Kirk glances at Uhura. She shakes her head.

UHURA
The message was simucast on all frequencies, Captain, in all known linguacodes. I'm repeating it now.

Again they wait—and again, no response.

KIRK
Monitor it on a grade four sensor level, Mr. Xon.

XON
(instantly)
I have, sir; there is a definite sub-space null directly ahead. The message is being received, sir.

ILIA
Visual contact in one minute and twelve seconds, Captain.

KIRK
Forcefield screen?

SULU

Forcefield screens up and at full power, sir.

KIRK

Also, full deflectors forward, Mr. Sulu. And sound a red alert. Battle stations.

93   ANOTHER ANGLE - XON   93

as he activates his sensors, and at the same time the red warning lights begin
flashing, and the computer VOICE in the background begins its monotone: ". . . Red
alert! Battle stations. This is a red alert . . . !"

Then as Xon peers into the viewer, his entire console FLARES with LIGHT—and then
instantly goes blank. At the same moment the yellow flashing lights turn to red, and
the Alarm SIREN begins HOWLING, and the COMPUTER VOICE begins intoning:
"Computer malfunction . . . ! Computer malfunction . . . !"

SULU

Captain, the helm is dead . . . !

KIRK

All systems, manual override . . . !
              (to Chekov)
Weapons control, status report . . . !

CHEKOV

Weapons are on manual control, Captain!

KIRK
              (into intercom)
Engineering—

94   INT. ENGINE ROOM   94

With Scott and his Technicians busy at their controls, and the ENGINES THROBBING
smoothly. But in the b.g. the red warning lights are flashing, and the SIREN HOWLS.

SCOTT
              (into intercom)
The engines are fine, Captain. But what's happening? Are we under attack?

95   INT. BRIDGE   95

as Kirk replies to Scott into the intercom:

KIRK

We think that our own sensor probe was reflected back so intensely it burned out
all our computer integrators—

96   ANOTHER ANGLE - SULU AND ILIA   96

peering at the (o.s.) main viewer, and reacting with disbelief.

ILIA

Captain . . . !

Kirk turns to the viewer, and his expression is equally incredulous.

97   WHAT KIRK SEES ON THE VIEWER - THE ALIEN SPACESHIP   97
but, at first, only a section of the front of it. What we SEE resembles a gigantic
<u>chrome and silver object</u>, almost like the gaping mouth of some unbelievable large
metallic animal—and just a GLIMPSE of a huge circular window or engine duct on the
side of the "head," this glowing red and blue. It is perfectly symmetrical, the sides of
the "mouth" constructed in equally-sized slabs of metal.

> ILIA
> (awed)
> We're seeing it a full thirty seconds before we should . . . !

> CHEKOV
> (grim)
> That is because of the size of it . . . ! The size . . . !

All at once the SIRENS <u>STOP</u>; the red alert lights go off.

> SULU
> The helm is normal again, Captain!

98   ANOTHER ANGLE - SCIENCE STATION AND COMMUNICATIONS   98
SHOWING Xon and Decker, who have been feverishly attempting to re-engage the
computer, and have obviously succeeded.

> XON
> The computer is functioning, sir . . .

99   ACROSS THEM TO THE VIEWING SCREEN   99
with the alien having grown in size and intensity, and now we can SEE more of it.

The front or "head" tapers back in a long, narrow body extending the entire length
of the viewer, and still we haven't seen all of it. Its alien technology carries a
bizarre, unearthly sense of beauty. And yet the very size of it spells danger.

> XON
> . . . I am attempting to obtain information concerning the object's origin.

> KIRK
> You won't find that information in the computer, Mr. Xon; if there were any
> known vessel of that size and configuration in the galaxy, we'd have heard of it.

> SCOTT'S VOICE
> (on intercom)
> Engineering to Bridge—

100   INT. ENGINE ROOM   100
with Scott grimly studying his console readings. He's speaking into the intercom:

> SCOTT
> Captain, with the deflector shields up full, we're draining considerable power—

101   INT. BRIDGE - FAVORING THE VIEWER   101
The alien still not entirely across the screen. Kirk replies to Scott into the intercom:

> KIRK
> We can't risk lowering them, Scotty. Not yet.

On the viewer we can SEE The alien completely. Now, in its totality, it clearly emanates power and ominousness.

> KIRK
> (continuing)
> Distance to object, Lieutenant Ilia?

> ILIA
> Point zero zero three two parsecs.

> KIRK
> Dimension interpolation, Mr. Xon.

102 ACROSS KIRK TO XON   102
reading the computations in his hooded viewer. He glances up now at Decker, who is still at the station, and then at Kirk—and for the first time, in Xon's face, there is a reaction: as though he simply does not believe what he is about to say:

> XON
> Sir, the object is very close to 70 kilometers long . . . and 10 kilometers wide.

> CHEKOV
> (reacting)
> <u>Seventy kilometers long</u> . . . !!!

> SULU
> Sir, the alien is not reducing his speed.

> DECKER
> (dry)
> I don't think he means to stop and talk.

> KIRK
> (to Uhura)
> Keep the hailing frequencies open, Commander. Continue sending our message. . . !

> UHURA
> Transmission is continuing, sir.

> ILIA
> Now one and one-half minutes away, sir.

103 ACROSS KIRK TO THE VIEWER   103
The object is, again, too long for the screen; both ends are obscured by the screen boundaries.

> KIRK
> Reduce magnification.

Sulu touches the control, and instantly the perspective on the viewer is considerably smaller. Again, now, the entire alien ship is VISIBLE. But even as we WATCH, it <u>grows</u>.

KIRK
(continuing)

Distance?

ILIA

Point zero zero five parsecs.

KIRK

Mr. Sulu, begin a slow 180 degree turn, maneuvering to fly parallel with the alien vessel.

DECKER

Submit we should not close on it, sir.

KIRK

Agreed, Mister Decker.
(toward helm)
Maintain present distance, helm.

104   EXT. SPACE - ENTERPRISE AND ALIEN   104
Our starship maneuvering to reverse course and fly parallel with the huge alien thing.

105   INT. ENGINE ROOM   105
with Scott unhappily reading his instruments, and listening to:

KIRK'S VOICE
(on the intercom)
I am aware of the power drainage, Mr. Scott. Please maintain speed and deflector power.

SCOTT
(grimly)

Aye, sir.

106   INT. BRIDGE - FAVORING THE VIEWER   106
Kirk watching the alien as it overflows the screen.

KIRK

Helm, adjust speed. We'll travel along with it now . . .

DECKER

Assuming it wants company . . .

On the screen we have the effect of the alien ship turning away, but it is actually our own course reverse.

107   EXT. THE ALIEN SHIP AND THE ENTERPRISE   107
as now, for the first time, we have FULL EXT. VIEW of the giant. And in detail: the pulsing red and yellow colors from the side ports, and the propulsion units at the rear. No windows, or any other light visible anywhere the entire length of the vast metallic hull.

And now, beside it, we SEE the Enterprise. Hardly more than a white spot in the f.g. (A golf ball floating against the side of a dirigible.)

The tiny white spot (The Enterprise) moves alongside the monster ship—both speeding through space, with the Enterprise now seeming to move slightly to the alien's rear. (Actually, the Enterprise is slower ever so slightly to have a look at all of it.)

108 INT. BRIDGE - ANGLE ON THE VIEWER   108
with Kirk and all Bridge personnel gazing at the viewer. They are now traveling with it, so the alien can be SEEN with the same perspective continually.

                              UHURA
          Still no response to our message, Captain.

                              CHEKOV
                             (puzzled)
          No response—and no attack . . .
                             (grimly)
Yet.

                              KIRK
          Mr. Xon, don't you have any readings . . . !?

                              XON
          No, sir: the alien's forcefield still absorbs all scans.

                              DECKER
          Captain, she's made no aggressive moves; why not send a probe?

                              KIRK
          A probe might easily be interpreted as an unfriendly act, Commander.

                              DECKER
          Yes, sir, but it's a risk we might have to take. We're at Warp 6, with full deflectors; we can't maintain that speed much longer.

                              KIRK
                         (considers; then:)
          Stand by to launch a sensor probe, Mr. Xon.

          And Xon commences programming the proper controls.

109 EXT. THE ENTERPRISE AND THE ALIEN   109
The Enterprise, as before, a tiny white spot outlined against the black and silver vastness of the alien.

110 EXT. CLOSER ON THE ENTERPRISE   110
as the probe is launched from the Enterprise's forward hull. The probe resembles a miniature rocket propelled sensor packet with antennae bristling from all corners.

It floats toward the alien.

111 INT. THE PROBE AS SEEN ON THE BRIDGE VIEWING SCREEN   111
approaching the alien.

                              XON

Beginning to get readings, Captain. Power emanations, a strange mixed gravity
and magnetic reading, going completely off our scale . . .

Suddenly, on the screen, a stream of green-yellow <u>PHASER FIRE</u> spurts from the
alien. The probe is hit, bathed in the green glow, then blazes into white nothingness.

                              KIRK

Deflectors to full emergency . . . !

Even as Kirk speaks—from all three ports on the alien's side, something resembling
green PHASER FIRE streaks out, smashes into the Enterprise's deflector screens,
tossing the ship about like a cork. The ALERT SIRENS SOUND, red lights flash. The
entire bridge is bathed in a green glow, but the deflectors and forcefield screens
obviously are containing the attack.

                              CHEKOV

Phasers and photon torpedo banks ready, Captain.

                              KIRK

Do not, repeat, do <u>not</u> activate them, Mister Chekov.

                              SULU

<u>The helm's not responding, sir!</u>

                              XON

We're being held by a tractor beam of extremely high magnitude, Captain.

                              KIRK

Weapons control; divert all your power to our deflector shields.

                              CHEKOV

Captain, we're not going to return their fire?

                              KIRK

Not if we're sane, we won't, Mister Chekov.

112   EXT. AND INT. THE BATTLE - VARIOUS ANGLES   112

The alien's FIRE CONTINUES, the green-white bolts striking the invisible shields
protecting the Enterprise—but, unlike the alien, each hit the Enterprise takes batters
it perceptibly, with the Enterprise's forcefield ILLUMINATED in a cacophony of colors.

It is a spectacular OPTICAL DISPLAY, and it seems impossible the tiny Enterprise can
withstand the punishment. The bridge resembles an old time ship in a typhoon: Kirk
and the others restrained in their seats (by invisible restraints: we do not want them
tumbling pell mell all over the bridge), but absorbing inhuman pounding.

113   INT. ENGINE ROOM   113

The same effect experienced by Scott's people. With each strike from the alien,
SPARKS AND FLAME ERUPT from the control panels—and the huge engine central
core is glowing redder and redder, the ENGINES WHINING LOUDER AND LOUDER.
Scott struggles to speak into the intercom:

SCOTT

Captain Kirk, I canna hold the screens at full emergency much longer, sir . . . !

KIRK'S VOICE

You've got to hold them . . . ! Divert all secondary power to screens.

Scott turns away to peer at the now bright red glow from the core. Then he moves quickly to work on the controls.

114 EXT. THE BATTLE   114
continuing. The giant alien lashing its greenish PHASER FIRE at the tiny starship.

115 INT. BRIDGE - FAVORING THE VIEWER   115
With secondary power diverted, the bridge lighting is dimming. The barrage continuing—the viewing screen graphically depicting the alien's fire smashing against the Enterprise forcefield screens and deflector shields.

XON

Power drain now critical, Captain . . . ! All systems are overloading . . . !

KIRK

Endurance estimate . . . ?

XON

Two minutes, thirty-two seconds, sir . . . !

KIRK
(into intercom)
Scotty, we've got to pull away. Stand by for warp.

116 INT. ENGINE ROOM   116
Scott, struggling to stay on his feet in the gyrating ship and the engine core now a deep, dangerous red.

SCOTT
(into intercom)
She's liable to blow us all to kingdom come, sir . . . !

KIRK'S VOICE

We're finished if we don't pull back, Scotty . . . ! Maximum warp!

Scott realizes he has no choice. He sets his controls, peering grimly at the red glow.

SCOTT

Ready for maximum warp, Captain . . . !

The WHINE of the great ENGINES is LOUDER now than even the terrible NOISE of the alien's phasers striking our screens.

117 INT. BRIDGE - ANGLE ON THE VIEWING SCREEN   117
On the viewer, the green-white PHASER FIRE streaks in at us as Kirk turns to Sulu.

KIRK

Now, helm!

Sulu and Ilia hit controls but nothing happens.

SULU

We're not moving . . . ! The tractor beam's still holding us.

CHEKOV

Weapons Control . . . sir, the temperature on his level is 130 . . . !

XON

Life support systems are failing, Captain. Bridge temperature is 110, and rising.

And, indeed, the heat is obvious: sweat pours down all faces, people begin gasping for air. Uhura suddenly collapses—and then Chekov.

XON
(continuing)
Temperature is 130 . . . 132 . . . 136.

Strangely, Xon seems relatively unaffected by the rising heat. Xon is almost calmly engrossed in his hooded viewer; apparently something has attracted his interest, and he is working hard at it.

118 ANOTHER ANGLE - KIRK   118
straining for breath, only a super will sustains him. He turns toward Chekov, resignedly, weakly:

KIRK

Stand by on photon torpedoes, Mr. Chekov.

But Chekov has collapsed, falling over his console, unconscious. Kirk staggers to weapon's station, launches torpedoes.

119 EXT. THE ENTERPRISE AND THE ALIEN   119
The Alien's fire unabated—but now the photon torpedoes shoot out from the Enterprise. They strike the alien's forcefield, EXPLODE HARMLESSLY far outside the alien's hull. And all this time we can SEE the Enterprise being drawn closer and closer to the giant.

120 INT. ENGINE ROOM   120
as Scott can hardly breathe in the unbearable heat. All his personnel are unconscious on the floor. He speaks into the intercom:

SCOTT

The screens are about to go, Captain . . . !

121 INT. BRIDGE   121
The lights flickering now, plunging the entire bridge into brief darkness, returning in a weak flickering, then flaring brightly another instant, then out again. Kirk, now at his limit, gazes at the bodies of Ilia, Decker, Sulu, Chekov. He staggers toward Communications.

KIRK

Uhura . . .

But then he realizes she, too, has collapsed. He looks at Xon, who at that moment glances up from his viewer.

XON

Captain . . . ! They did answer . . . !

Kirk manages to stagger to the Science Station where Xon just now begins showing some signs of heat. But not enough to disable him.

XON
(continuing)
I replayed Commander Uhura's transmissions. The alien responded: listen . . .

And Xon punches a button. We HEAR what can only be a shrill BEEP.

XON
(continuing)
They responded on a frequency close to one million megahertz—far too high for any human ear. Now listen . . .

And Xon punches more buttons, and we HEAR again the "BEEP"—and then slower, so the "BEEP" seems stretched out slightly, and then slower again. But with each "BEEP"—there is a momentary pause, and then another "BEEP" that SOUNDS lower, less shrill.

XON
(continuing)
Each time we hailed them, Captain, they responded. But not to any language. To the lingua-code that was computerized . . .
(totally focused on his work despite all that has gone on around him)
Sir, they are responding not to any life form aboard our vessel—but to the vessel itself . . . !
(as Kirk still does not comprehend)
Captain, they are addressing the USS Enterprise as a life form . . . !

KIRK
(struggling to understand)
They think the ship is a life form?

XON

Yes, sir, and with your permission I will now send them a message asking to break off hostilities . . .

Kirk nods his approval; he's hardly able to stand, but somehow musters the last of his strength to prop himself against the console and watch Xon punch in the message on his computer.

As Xon does this, the COMPUTER VOICE SOUNDS over the annunciators:

COMPUTER VOICE

Life support systems have failed . . . ! Activate emergency life support systems . . . ! Life support systems have failed . . . ! Etc. etc.

Xon completes the message, peers at the hooded viewer, waits tensely. And then, all at once, the outside barrage stops. The silence is almost shocking. Only the Computer Voice can be HEARD, continuing in its monotone: "Life support systems have failed . . . !" Etc. etc.

Xon reaches up and flicks a switch—and the computer warning voice is also suddenly stilled. The bridge lights have come on again brightly, steadily, and Xon peers at Kirk.

XON

The attack has ceased, sir.

122 EXT. SPACE - ENTERPRISE AND ALIEN SHIP   122
both streaking silently through the stars. The giant alien spaceship and (compared to the alien) the pea-sized Enterprise. Both ships maintaining exact speed and distance from each other, so that it is obvious the Enterprise is trapped in the alien's tractor beam. OVER this, we HEAR:

KIRK'S VOICE

Captain's Log, Stardate 7421.6. For an entire day now, we have been locked in the alien's tractor beam, being carried with it toward Earth. We have been unable to establish further communications with our gigantic captor and are unable to determine its intentions toward planet Earth.

123 INT. ENGINE ROOM   123
SHOWING Scott and his Technicians laboring over their engines—sweaty, dishevelled—but somehow accomplishing their task.

KIRK'S VOICE

With our engines shut down, engineering is rushing the repair of damage suffered in the attack.

124 INT. SICKBAY   124
The hospital area crowded with wounded CREWMEN AND CREWWOMEN, McCoy and Chapel busily tending their patients. Both doctors show the strain, and Sickbay resembles a war-ravaged field hospital.

KIRK'S VOICE

Casualties have been heavy, but with no fatalities, thanks to the skill of Doctors McCoy and Chapel.

125 INT. BRIEFING ROOM   125
SHOWING, seated around the table, Kirk, Xon, Decker and Chekov. Xon is at the computer console. Kirk is speaking to Xon.

KIRK

You're suggesting that our computer was communicating directly with the alien?

XON

Yes, sir, and I have taken the liberty of cutting off all external transmission from the computer. But I believe that a considerable sum of information has already been passed on.

DECKER

Run the tapes back and find out.

XON

I'm doing that now, but the transmissions were at such ultra-high speed, it will take hours—perhaps days—to decode them.

KIRK

There's a much faster way . . .

126   ANGLE ON THE COMPUTER CONSOLE   126
as Xon nods, switches it on.

XON

Of course, sir.
                            (to computer)
Computer . . . summarize all information provided the alien. Reply.

COMPUTER VOICE

Information comprised blueprints of NCC 1701, schematics of all electronic components, weapons and defense systems, power and engineering. A detailed breakdown is as follows—

127   ACROSS KIRK AND THE COMPUTER TO THE OTHERS   127
as all register dismay, and Kirk quickly interrupts the computer:

KIRK

Computer . . . cancel detailed breakdown. Why did you provide the information? Reply.

COMPUTER VOICE

Information provided upon request.

KIRK

Computer . . . why did you disseminate classified information?

COMPUTER VOICE

It was requested.

The bald logic is too much for Kirk; he shakes his head in more exasperation. Xon addresses the machine:

XON

Computer . . . how much information did you provide concerning the crew? Reply.

COMPUTER VOICE

Crew information was not requested.

struggling to contain his frustration and annoyance.

                    KIRK
Computer . . . who is the alien? Reply.

               COMPUTER VOICE
Data unavailable.

                   DECKER
                (wry, grim)
I guess it wasn't curious.

                    XON
A computer never is, sir . . .
               (to computer)
Computer . . . why is the alien traveling to Earth? Reply.

               COMPUTER VOICE
Data unavailable.

                    KIRK
               (almost angry)
Computer . . . you are ordered to provide no further information to the alien . . . !

And Xon switches off the computer, Kirk faces the others grimly:

                    KIRK
                (continuing)
Comment.

                    XON
In my opinion, sir, the computer has corroborated my theory that the alien
considers any further communication with us a waste of his time.

                   CHEKOV
Then we must show him this is not true.

                    KIRK
Yes, but for that we have to communicate with him. How . . . ?

                   DECKER
Sir, our weapons can't penetrate its forcefield but . . .
                (grimly)
. . . if we informed him we were ready to turn our engines into a <u>matter-anti-
matter bomb</u>, I think it would realize that not even its forcefield could withstand
it. We'd get an answer fast enough.

                   CHEKOV
Self-destruct? It may not realize we can do that.

                    XON
You may be certain it understands <u>all</u> our capabilities. In fact, it no doubt
considers the Enterprise design quite simple and primitive compared to its own
technology.

DECKER

But not even that alien can withstand a matter-anti-matter explosion of the size we could generate.

(to Kirk)

It gives us a bluff it can't afford to call.

129 ACROSS THEM TO KIRK   129

shaking his head impatiently, rising, speaking quickly:

KIRK

Gentlemen, since we're helpless for at least twelve hours until full power is restored, I suggest we use that time for some needed rest . . .

(to Decker)

All divisions go to stand-by crews only.

(wan smile)

We'll all do better with a few hours' sleep.

As Chekov and Xon exit the room, Kirk AD-LIBS, "Mr. Decker . . ." and gestures Decker to accompany him. They step out to the:

130 CORRIDOR   130

where they begin walking, Kirk saying:

KIRK

Suppose you were the alien commander . . . ? And you received that threat . . . ?

DECKER

I think I would take it quite literally, and since it would cost me nothing I think I would open communications. Which, sir, is our prime objective.

KIRK

If I were the alien, Decker, I wouldn't give you a chance to even start overloading your engines. I'd blast you to pieces.

Decker stops abruptly, faces Kirk:

DECKER

It's ignoring us totally! We've got to show some teeth, make some kind of stand . . .

KIRK

A lesson in command, Decker: never make a threat you're not prepared to carry out. Because your enemy would assume you were prepared, and he'd act accordingly.

DECKER

May I ask what you do intend doing?

KIRK

What I intend doing' is keeping this vessel intact, and its crew and myself alive. And that, mister, is another command lesson . . . !

Kirk strides to the elevator. Decker stands watching him.

with, first, an ANGLE ON THE VIEWER: the ominous image of the alien, their "captor," filling the entire screen. A constant reminder of their peril.

Ilia is at her post—and Xon. Ilia gazing silently, grimly, at the viewer; and Xon totally engrossed in his own hooded viewer, determinedly punching his computer controls. The only manned station is Communications, and it is not Uhura here, but JANICE RAND, now an Ensign, spelling her.

Now the elevator doors open, and Kirk enters. He wears a crisp new uniform, obviously has showered and shaved. He walks to the control center, calling to Rand:

                    KIRK
Any signals, Ensign?

                    RAND
Nothing, sir.

Kirk's face reflects his frustration, but he says nothing, addresses Ilia:

                    KIRK
I'll handle the conn, Lieutenant. You take a break.

                    ILIA
                 (grateful)
Thank you, sir.

And she smiles at him and leaves. Kirk steps over to the Science Station, stands watching Xon a moment; the Vulcan entirely oblivious to Kirk, who after a moment speaks:

                    KIRK
                (quiet, gentle)
Mister Xon . . .

Xon pays him no attention, hasn't heard him.
                    KIRK
                (a little firmer)
Lieutenant . . .

Now Xon turns, absolutely unflappable, looks at Kirk.

                    XON
I've completed my analysis on the alien's defensive shields, Captain. I am convinced that none of our weapons—not even a matter-anti-matter explosion— would have the slightest deleterious effect on it.

                    KIRK
Not ten minutes ago, Science Officer, I asked you to get some rest.

                    XON
I require very little sleep, sir.

                                KIRK
When did you last eat?

                                XON
                          (trying to remember)
Just before I came aboard, sir . . . I think . . .
                          (quickly)
But my caloric requirements are substantially less than . . .
                          (delicately)
. . . 'ordinary' personnel. In point of fact, sir, I function more efficiently with the
most rudimentary nutrition.

                                KIRK
                              (wryly)
I'm aware of your very unusual metabolism, Xon. But even a Vulcan must
sleep—and eat.

                                XON
What you say is, of course, quite logical. However, since these are unusual
circumstances . . .

                                KIRK
                              (firm)
You'll follow orders, Lieutenant.

                                XON
                          (a reluctant beat)
Yes, sir.

And he quickly secures his station, rises, faces Kirk. He nods, and starts away.

132 ACROSS KIRK TO XON   132
     nearing the elevator. Kirk calls to him:

                                KIRK
Mister Xon . . .
                          (as Xon turns)
Thank you.

                                XON
                             (bland)
You're welcome, sir.

And he leaves. Kirk gazes after him, then starts back to the control center, smiling
at Rand.

                                KIRK
You all right . . . ?

                                RAND
I'm fine, Captain . . .
                          (smiles back)
Just like old times, isn't it, sir?

133 ACROSS KIRK TO RAND - AND THE VIEWER IN THE B.G.   133
as he peers at the picture of the alien starship.

                              KIRK
        Not quite, Ensign. Not quite.

134 INT. RECREATION ROOM   134
fairly crowded, various CREWMEN relaxing, reading. In one corner two young
ENSIGNS sit before a screen on which is projected a computerized game, each Ensign
touching buttons and controls that manipulate the players.
The CAMERA PANS about the room, now FINDS <u>Sulu</u>—slumped in a chair, simply
finding a moment's rest. His eyes are closed—and suddenly a pair of (female) HANDS
are clamped over his eyes.

                          ILIA'S VOICE
                      (teasing, mock-scolding)
        You're thinking naughty thoughts again, Sulu . . .

135 WIDEN TO INCLUDE ILIA 135
as Sulu jumps nearly a foot off the chair, whirling around to face her. She's smiling
provocatively down at him, and he is all of a sudden nervous and embarrassed. He
glances around the room; a number of people are watching them amusedly. Ilia runs
her fingers over Sulu's face; he brushes her away.

                              SULU
                          (quiet, terse)
        People will be getting the wrong idea . . . !

                              ILIA
                          ("hurt")
        I'm trying to relax you—Deltan style.

                              SULU
                          (nervous)
        Not here . . . !

                              ILIA
        What better place? All our friends are here.

And, again, she runs her fingers playfully along his cheek. Again, Sulu pushes her
away.

                              SULU
        Please, Ilia . . . please . . . !

And he glances at the room, at two officers, LT. BANDAR, an attractive Ceylonese
young lady, and LT. HAWKINS, a male engineering officer. They're watching the by-
play with amusement. Sulu flashes a forced "you-know-how-it-is" smile at them,
turns quickly again to Ilia.

                              ILIA
        Sulu, are you rejecting me?

SULU
(flustered)

Yes . . . no . . .
(terse whisper)

What about your oath of celibacy . . . ?

ILIA

Is sex all you ever think of . . . ?
(peers at him, reads his mind images, nods solemnly)

Yes, I'm afraid it is!

136   ACROSS SULU TO ILIA   136
as she smiles down at Sulu, a smile of warm sincerity. And then all at once, the
smile fades. She screams:

ILIA

Sulu!!!

137   WHAT THEY SEE - THE ALIEN PROBES   137
In the corner of the room there is a BRIGHT FLARE OF TURQUOISE LIGHT—and then
another and then a third. Materializing out of the light are objects we'll come to
know as sensor-probes.

Some hover a few inches above the floor, others move in free flight. At the same
time the probes appear, the red alert lights flash, from the annunciator comes the
warning:

ANNUNCIATOR VOICE

Intruder alert . . . ! Intruder alert . . . !

The probes begin moving around the room, feeling, seeing, hearing. The people do not
interest these sensor-probes—their interest is in the vessel, its design and functions.

SULU

Probes . . . !
(to others)

Everybody out . . . ! Seal the room!

And everyone moves to leave, the probes seemingly undisturbed, continuing their
business.

138   INT. CORRIDOR   138
as Sulu and Ilia and the others rush out, then seal the door. Everyone begins
hurrying down the corridor toward their respective stations. The Intruder Alert
VOICE CONTINUES in background.

139   INT. ANOTHER CORRIDOR   139
The INTRUDER ALERT SOUNDING—TURQUOISE LIGHTS FLASHING—and MORE
PROBES materializing in this section of the corridor. At the corridor's far end,
Chekov now appears with TWO SECURITY MEN. They are rushing along (toward the
elevator), come to an abrupt halt seeing the probes, one of which is unlike the
others: it resembles a ring, with a large pearl-like object on the top, the "pearl"
actually the "eye"; and, unlike the others, it does not hover, it walks on three

slender legs. And as it spies the men, the "pearl" begins flashing different colors and begins emitting a SOUND that reminds you of a HIGH-PITCHED, RAPID, EXCITED SQUEALING. <u>This is the only sensor-probe which has noticed the humans and it is clearly frightened of them.</u>

One of the Security Men aims his phaser—Chekov blocks the Man's hand.

> CHEKOV
>
> No . . . !

> 1ST SECURITY MAN
>
> They might be dangerous . . . !

> CHEKOV
>
> So do you! They haven't attacked <u>you</u>, have they?

Chekov approaches the hovering probes—the legged probe seems to stay slightly behind the others, as though allowing them to protect it. All the time it continues its excited SQUEALING. Chekov indicates toward it.

> CHEKOV
> (continuing)
>
> That's the only one that seems to notice humans. And it's scared to death of us.

The egg-shaped probe floats past Chekov, circles his knees as the feeler reaches out to investigate some aspect of the Enterprise. Then the "eye" probe (also egg-shaped) investigates some other starship mechanism. Then Chekov reaches out with both hands as though trying to catch a fly. He nearly snares the probe, but it darts agilely away. Chekov steps after it, makes another pass—again misses. In the meantime, the three-legged probe is emitting even more EXCITED SQUEALS and flashing brighter colors—almost as though scolding Chekov for trying to catch its associate. Chekov moves toward the legged probe, but it retreats. The egg-shaped "eye" follows, but Chekov is faster, he moves behind it.

> CHEKOV
> (continuing; to 2nd Security Man)
>
> Cut it off . . . !
> (to 1st Security Man)
> Get the one with the legs . . . !

140 ANOTHER ANGLE - THE CHASE   140

The 1st Security Man stepping after the legged probe, which seems to have vanished. In the meantime, Chekov and the 2nd Security Man have cornered the "eye"—and, after some clumsy effort—<u>seize it</u>. Chekov holds the probe, which is perhaps basketball sized, gingerly examines it—and hands it to the 2nd Security Man.

> CHEKOV
>
> Get it to the Science Officer!

The 2nd Security Man accepts the probe, but almost as though it is electrified: he can hardly hold it.

CHEKOV
(continuing)
It won't bite . . . !

And Chekov charges around the corridor corner in pursuit of the legged probe.

141 AROUND THE CORRIDOR CORNER   141
with the 1st Security Man glumly surveying the corridor—not a probe in sight.

1ST SECURITY MAN
It's gone . . .

Chekov glances around a moment, looks disapprovingly at the Security Man.

CHEKOV
Seal off this level . . .
(starts leaving)
I'll be on the bridge.

And he steps into the elevator, is gone, the CAMERA SWINGING AROUND now, DOWN
THE EMPTY CORRIDOR. TWO MORE SECURITY MEN suddenly appear, hurry along,
PAST THE CAMERA, and past a closed door (or some other object in the corridor).
CAMERA HOLDS on the door, which opens and the legged-probe appears flashing a
bright purple color; it swivels its "eye" down the corridor, then in a 180, obviously
sweeping the area. Satisfied it hasn't been seen, it EMITS another little SQUEAL (of
satisfaction) and starts walking awkwardly along the corridor.

142 INT. ENGINE ROOM   142
with Scott glaring dubiously at three of the hovering sensor-probes which are poking
into all corners of the engine room.

He is talking into the intercom, his eyes never leaving the probes:

SCOTT
. . . Yes, sir, they're all over the place—poking into everything . . . !

KIRK'S VOICE
But no indication of hostility?

SCOTT
They don't seem at all interested in us, Captain. Just the ship.

KIRK'S VOICE
Same report from other decks, Scotty. For the minute, hands off as long as
they're damaging nothing.

Scott switches off, steps over to watch one of the probes which has just floated near
the console, extended its feeler and seems to be studying the instruments (actually it
is photographing all details). Scott holds his hand out in a threatening gesture.

SCOTT
But you so much as touch one of my controls, you nosey little bugger, and you're
a junk-pile!

143 INT. SICKBAY   143

with Chapel—and a NURSE, in surgical gowns, operating on a PATIENT. And the probes here, also. But, strangely, not near the operating table, remaining several feet away, but obviously studying all that's going on. The CAMERA SWINGS OVER TO FIND McCoy, outside the operating area (he's in a surgical gown), at the intercom. As he talks, one of the probes extends a feeler toward him and McCoy swats at it, the feeler instantly moving away.

McCOY
(intercom)
. . . Yes, Jim, they're here, too!

144 ACROSS McCOY TO THE OPERATING AREA   144

as he sees another probe flat toward the operating area—then suddenly SPARKS shoot out (from the sterile forcefield) and the probe staggers away, moves elsewhere.

McCOY
(with satisfaction)
But they don't like the sterile forcefield . . . !

145 INT. BRIDGE   145

SHOWING more probes here. Sulu, Ilia and Uhura are at their stations—and at the Science Station, Xon, Decker and Kirk are gathered around, examining the probe Chekov caught. Kirk is just completing his communication with McCoy:

KIRK
(into intercom, from the start)
. . . we're trying to find out something about them.

McCOY'S VOICE
I'd be glad to dissect one for you . . . !

KIRK
(into intercom)
Lieutenant Xon is doing that right now. Kirk out.

146 CLOSE ON THE SCIENCE STATION   146

as Kirk rejoins the group and now we can SEE that Xon has dissembled the probe, the CAMERA CLOSING MOMENTARILY so we can SEE the interior of the probe: a finely designed arrangement of transistors and motors. Xon is fascinated, but characteristically unemotional:

XON
Ingenious . . . !
(indicates)
Memory bank, I'd guess . . . this could be an incredibly miniaturized transceiver . . .

DECKER
You mean you're not certain of any of it?

XON
This is a technology so alien to ours, Commander, that we don't have even the words to describe its components.

(holds device up to view)
These tiny mechanical components are actually liquid hydrogen at absolute zero, shaped and insulated by a forcefield my most sensitive instruments can't measure . . .

147 ACROSS THEM TO UHURA 147
who has just received an intercom message:

UHURA
Captain: the sensor-probes are attempting to infiltrate the computer library . . . !

KIRK
(to Xon)
Have the computer encode a message to the alien. It's to withdraw its probes, or we'll be forced to destroy them.

148 ANOTHER ANGLE - TIGHT ON KIRK AND DECKER 148
As Xon punches out the message, Decker speaks quietly, confidentially, to Kirk:

DECKER
Do I take it that's not just a bluff, Captain?

KIRK
It's no bluff, Mister Decker. The library contains too much sensitive information about Earth.

149 ANGLE ON XON 149
grimly peering into his hooded viewer.

XON
No response, Captain.

KIRK
(to Uhura)
Dispatch Chekov to the computer library. He's to destroy any probes attempting to infiltrate the records there.

150 INT. COMPUTER - LIBRARY 150
(A room with computer banks and consoles.) Chekov and Two Security Men enter as the LIBRARY TECHNICIANS attempt to stop the probes from penetrating the memory banks. Chekov aims his phaser, FIRES. The probe, struck squarely, FLARES TURQUOISE—then vanishes (dematerialized). One of his men HITS ANOTHER PROBE, which also dematerializes with the same EFFECT. Chekov raises the phaser at yet a third probe—but this one dematerializes before he can fire. And then the fourth—and final—probe also dematerializes.
Chekov strides to the intercom, switches it on:

CHEKOV
Chekov to bridge . . . the probes are now leaving on their own, dematerializing . . . !

151 INT. BRIDGE 151
SHOWING Kirk, Xon and Decker also watching the probes here on the bridge as they dematerialize. Kirk glances at the disassembled probe, which still lies on Xon's bench; it's as though he wants to be sure that one hasn't somehow dematerialized.

DECKER

Like it's pulling its sense organs out of danger . . .

Kirk nods in grim agreement. Then suddenly, O.S., we HEAR that now familiar NERVOUS SQUEAKING (ultra high-speed sound). Kirk whirls around to see:

152   THE THREE-LEGGED PROBE   152
popping out from behind the console, walking awkwardly toward them, all the time "TALKING" (a mile a minute). It approaches to a few feet, flashing brilliant colors, stops and seems to be regarding them sternly. It has now CEASED "TALKING."

153   ANGLE ON XON   153
who, showing none of the surprise the humans have shown, very carefully has been moving various console controls.

DECKER
(to probe, dryly)
Have we been properly introduced . . . ?

XON
(quietly, to Uhura)
Commander, I've recorded the probe's transmissions, can you transfer them onto a pickup tape for a playback at normal speed . . . ?

Uhura is already working her console.

154   ANOTHER ANGLE - CHEKOV   154
entering the bridge, spotting the probe, reacting.

CHEKOV
That one . . . ! It looks like the pearl ring my Aunt Tasha got from her fourth husband . . . just like him, phony.

Uhura has completed the playback, peers at Kirk bemusedly.

UHURA
(a bemused beat, then quotes)
'. . . please allow me to speak to the USS Enterprise.'

DECKER
'Please allow me to speak to the USS Enterprise . . . ?!'

UHURA

That's what it said.

155   ANGLE ON THE PROBE (TASHA)   155
as suddenly, flashing colors, it EMITS another FAST SQUEAL. And it seems angry.

KIRK
(expectantly)
Uhura . . .

UHURA
(working her controls)
I'm playing it back, Captain . . .

UHURA (CONT'D)
(a moment, then she has the translation)
'. . . you will allow me to speak to USS Enterprise!' It sounds like an order.

XON

I'm certain it is.

DECKER

Are you serious, Mr. Xon?

XON

Sir, the probes were sent here to analyze our vessel. All but this one have been withdrawn. Logically, therefore, it remains for a specific purpose: to act as a communications liaison between the alien ship—and our ship.

CHEKOV

Our ship . . . ?

XON

Yes, sir. If we assume that the alien considers the Enterprise a life form—then we must assume that the alien ship is, itself, a life form.

As Xon completes this sentence, the probe flashes more colors, EMITS more SQUEAKS.

CHEKOV
(to the probe)
Hey, Tasha, shut up . . . !
(to Kirk, of Xon)
He makes sense, Captain. That seventy-mile-long ship that's holding us prisoner . . . must be a living thing . . . !

UHURA
(enlightened)
. . . Otherwise it couldn't consider the Enterprise one—

156 ACROSS THEM TO KIRK   156

as all this suddenly makes considerable logic. Kirk turns to the probe:

KIRK
(to the probe; a beat)
. . . Tasha . . . I am James T. Kirk. I am in command of the Enterprise: you may talk to me.

Uhura relays this via high-speed tape. A moment, then Tasha EMITS another excited SQUEAL. Kirk glances at Uhura, waiting for her to decipher the playback:

UHURA
(perplexed, translating)
'. . . that is impossible.'
KIRK
'Impossible?' Why is it impossible?

XON

I believe what it means, sir, is that it is impossible for you to be in command of the Enterprise.

Kirk cannot help an eyebrow-raising reaction, as Xon hastily continues:

> XON
> (continuing)
> Very likely this probe considers us like itself: Probes, or some machine-life existing for the purpose of accomplishing various tasks within our ship. Hardly capable of command.

> DECKER
> It has sensors, Xon; they can show we're flesh and blood.

> XON
> Yes, sir, and I'm sure it has found our carbon-based construction unusual . . . but we are machines, by any definition: we ingest fuel, eliminate waste, we operate by levers, fulcrums—

Xon's words suddenly trail off: he's peering at Kirk:

157   KIRK - A NEW ANGLE   157
as the probe, "Tasha," has quite boldly moved over to Kirk and begun investigating him: inserting a sensor probe inside his ear, another into his mouth, down his shirt. Kirk does not want to harm the object, keeps swiping it gently away. Kirk's annoyance only seems to encourage Tasha further.

> XON
> —It seems to have taken a fancy to you, Captain.

And as he speaks, Xon steps over to Kirk, gently but firmly removes Tasha, places it on the bench. Tasha EMITS another angry SQUEAL, flashes colors. Uhura plays the transmission back:

> UHURA
> (translating)
> '. . . I have not completed my examination!'

> KIRK
> (to Tasha)
> Oh, yes, you have . . .
> (continuing; to Xon)
> Engage the main computer, Mr. Xon; since his . . . 'representative' is with us, the alien might just deign to talk.

Xon switches on the main computer.

> XON
> Main computer on, sir.

Kirk hesitates an instant, thinking, peers at Tasha, then speaks:

> KIRK
> Computer . . . you will transmit a message to the alien in his binary language and then you will translate his reply into standard colloquial. You are instructed not to communicate independently with him. Confirm.

Program confirmed.

All eyes are on Kirk as he considers his message a moment. Then:

KIRK
(to computer)
Computer . . . the message is as follows: This is the USS Enterprise. Why are you holding me captive? Transmit.

158   ANGLE ON TASHA   158
as everyone waits expectantly and the probe seems to be also waiting, the flashing colors now a dull, continual pulsing of blandness.

159   ACROSS THEM TO UHURA   159
as she reacts, as we HEAR an ultra high-speed BEEP.

UHURA
They're responded . . . !

COMPUTER VOICE
Translating: objects of similar composition as yours have recently attacked me. Their attack was senseless. They were clearly malfunctioning. I must determine if you are also malfunctioning and therefore a danger to other life.

160   REACTION SHOTS   160
as all, at last, comprehend the fantastic situation. Again, all eyes are on Kirk. After a beat:

KIRK
(to computer)
Computer . . . send the following: I attacked in self-defense. I am not malfunctioning. Transmit.

Another moment of tense silence, then the ultra high-speed BEEP and then:

COMPUTER VOICE
Translating: my sensors indicate you are infested by 430 parasitical units. These may be the cause of your malfunction. Are you aware of their existence?

CHEKOV
430 parasites—he means us!
(indignant)
Parasites . . . !

DECKER
(terse)
It could be a life and death question, Captain. If he believes we're the cause of the ship's 'malfunction,' he'll move to destroy us—
(grim)
—to save the ship . . . !

XON
You can't admit we control the ship: then we will seem like infectious parasites.

Kirk peers at them a moment, then at Tasha, who now remains quite passive, colorless, as though waiting patiently.

161 ACROSS KIRK TO THE VIEWING SCREEN   161
PAST Sulu and Ilia at their stations: the same image of the huge alien ship. Kirk gazes at it a moment, then turns to the computer again.

KIRK
(into computer)
Computer . . . send the following: the 430 units inhabiting my form are necessary to my existence. Continue immediately with the following question: why is your destination the third planet of the solar system directly ahead? Transmit.

COMPUTER VOICE
Translating: the planet described is the Holy Home of The Creator.

An exchange of incredulous glances.

KIRK
Computer . . . send the following: is the Creator also known as God?

COMPUTER VOICE
Translating: the Creator has no other name.

KIRK
(thinks, then)
The home of the Creator is the entire universe, <u>not</u> the third planet.

An instant of expectant waiting—and then all at once the bridge begins to SHUDDER. Everyone grips restraining handles to remain on their feet.

SULU
He's tightening the tractor beam . . . !

KIRK
Red alert, Mr. Chekov . . . !

UHURA
They're responding, Captain!

As Chekov hits the alert button, and the SIRENS begin SOUNDING, we can also HEAR the BEEP of the aliens' reply. As everyone grasps their supports, and the bridge continues shaking even more <u>violently</u>, the computer speaks:

COMPUTER VOICE
For this deception, you will be punished . . . !

The bridge shakes just another moment, then all at once STOPS. Everyone catches their breath.

ILIA
It certainly has a temper . . .

KIRK

Cancel red alert, Mr. Chekov.

As Chekov hits the button that SILENCES the SIRENS, another BEEP is HEARD from Uhura's station. And then, almost immediately, another BEEP—but of slightly <u>different tone</u>. And then the first BEEP again, and then the other.

XON
(alarmed)

The computer is communicating directly with the alien again . . . !

KIRK
(to Computer)

Computer . . . disengage. You are violating program! Comply.

All that is HEARD is yet another EXCHANGE OF BEEPS.

DECKER
(to Xon)

Main controls off . . . !

Xon hits the switches, but still we HEAR the BEEPS.

XON

I can't disengage . . . !

KIRK
(into intercom)

Engineering . . . main computer controls off, Scottie!

162 INT. ENGINE ROOM   162
Scott at the console, hitting switches, but clearly with no success. He speaks into the intercom:

SCOTT

Something's controlling it externally, Captain . . . !

163 INT. BRIDGE - ANGLE ON TASHA   163
as the probe watches Decker and Xon desperately attempting to cut off the computer, and the probe now starts walking away—toward the command center.

XON
(reading console)

It's into the ship's memory banks . . .!

DECKER

It'll learn Starfleet strength, Earth defenses, everything . . . !

SCOTT'S VOICE

You'll have to break into the console! Short it out. Cross-circuit it . . . !

164 ANOTHER ANGLE - XON   164
brushing past Kirk, facing the console, then clasping his fists high over his head, and

using his full Vulcan strength—he brings his clasped fists down in a <u>shattering blow on the console</u>. The unit <u>splits into</u> pieces, cascading in FLARING SPARKS AND WHITE SMOKE. Xon reaches into the flaming and sputtering console, pulls out the main circuitry and presses positive and negative power lines together in ANOTHER BURST OF SPARKS AND SMOKE. His lips are compressed in pain from the white hot electrical arc that he has produced. The bridge lights dim, then flare again—and then the two lines in Xon's hands go dead. His knees buckle, he collapses, resting his back against the wall—gingerly regarding his two severely burned hands. The others rush to help him.

>   UHURA
> The computer is cut off, Captain . . . !

165   ANOTHER ANGLE - ILIA   165
who has been observing all this, and has risen to obviously go to Xon's help. But just beside her is the probe—Tasha, and as Ilia moves to leave, there is a sudden TURQUOISE LIGHT enveloping both her and the probe. Sulu sees this, calls out:

>   SULU
> Captain Kirk . . . !

Kirk whirls just in time to see both Ilia and the probe <u>dematerialize</u>. Chekov has also seen this.

>   CHEKOV
> It's beamed her over there . . . !

Kirk peers in helpless agony, at Sulu's stricken expression, and the empty navigator's chair where a moment ago Ilia and Tasha had been—but are no more.

166   EXT. SPACE - THE ENTERPRISE AND THE ALIEN   166
traveling together, the Enterprise gripped in the giant's tractor beam. OVER this we HEAR:

>   KIRK'S VOICE
> Captain's Log, Stardate 7421.7. We—and the alien—will reach Earth orbit in exactly two days . . .

167   INT. CORRIDOR   167
SHOWING Kirk walking (toward Sickbay), the Log VOICE continuing:

>   KIRK'S VOICE
> . . . with us still helplessly imprisoned in his tractor beam. The irony of all, of course, is that by cutting off our computer, we have also cut off our only means of communicating with the alien . . . so that we are unable to ascertain the fate of Lieutenant Ilia—and, more important, the purpose of the alien's visit to Earth. Our only clue is his statement that Earth is 'The Holy Home of The Creator.' What Creator . . . ?

Kirk reaches Sickbay now, enters.

168   INT. SICKBAY   168
Kirk moving through the outer rooms, to:

where several beds are occupied by injured CREWMEN—and another bed, with <u>Xon</u> seated on the edge (in sickbay dressing gown, etc.), studying the small bedside viewer, and a pile of computer chips beside him. Chapel is dressing Xon's burned hands, moving a small, hand-held device over the wounds (the device emanates a small shaft of light, this to facilitate healing), but Xon seems entirely oblivious, so engrossed is he in the viewer.

McCoy is also here, studying a scan-print at one of the other patients' beds. He glances up as Kirk appears, Kirk nodding to the other crewmen, AD-LIBBING "<u>How are you, Swenson . . .</u>" "<u>. . . you're looking fine, Ledoux</u> . . ." etc., etc.

Kirk walks over to Xon's bed.

> KIRK
> How are you feeling, Lieutenant Xon?

Xon does not reply; he hasn't even heard Kirk, never looks away from the viewer, but now inserts another chip, studies the screen. Chapel is just finishing her treatment.

> CHAPEL
> (to Kirk)
> Plasti-skin has healed his burns beautifully, but I don't know how he keeps going after the shock he suffered.

joining them.

> McCOY
> He's like all Vulcans: too smart for their own good.

Chapel leaves, as McCoy reaches over and snaps shut the viewer. Xon, not even bothering to see who did it, simply switches it back on again.

> McCOY
> (continuing; hard)
> Off, Lieutenant. Turn it off . . . !

And McCoy again switches off the viewer. Now Xon does turn, regards McCoy a cool instant, then glances at Kirk, nods politely.

> XON
> Good evening, sir. You'll be interested to know that I have compiled all the data the alien managed to receive from the computer before we cut it off.

> KIRK
> Before <u>you</u> did.

> XON
> (shrugs deprecatingly)
> No vital information was passed: Some three thousand years of ancient Earth history—and a portion of Enterprise personnel records. Also complete studies on Earth agriculture, animal life, and human anatomy.

                                    KIRK
You're sure that's all he got?

                                    XON
Absolutely, sir. He received no information concerning Starfleet, Earth defenses,
or The Federation.

                                    KIRK
Then we lucked out . . .
                        (a wry aside to McCoy)
. . . in that area, at least.

                                    XON
No, sir; this may not be as fortunate as it seems.

                                    KIRK
                        (straining for patience)
Please, Lieutenant, no Vulcan riddles.

                                    XON
When I mean to say, sir, is that I have concluded that on the basis of what
information the alien did receive, he must now have determined that the same
'parasites' infecting the Enterprise also 'infect' Earth. Indeed, he may well
believe they have taken over the planet—the 'Holy Home of The Creator'—and
his duty is to rid the planet of that plague.

                                   McCOY
Now we're a 'plague' . . . !
                                    XON
                        (bland, to McCoy)
Yes, sir . . .
                        (to Kirk)
If you will excuse me, Captain, I'll continue my computations—

And he switches on the viewer again, punching buttons, etc. and is immediately lost
in his studies. Kirk looks grimly at McCoy, then turns and starts leaving. McCoy calls
after him:

                                   McCOY
Jim. I want to talk to you . . .

171   ANOTHER AREA OF SICKBAY   171
      as Kirk stands waiting for McCoy to join him.

                                   McCOY
I want you to get some rest, too, Jim.

                                    KIRK
'Rest'? An alien ship the size of Manhattan Island is heading for earth—taking us
along with it; it's captured one of our crew members. And you want me to 'rest'?

                                   McCOY
You won't do us any good if you collapse from nervous exhaustion.

KIRK

I'll be all right . . .

He moves to leave, but McCoy pulls him back:

McCOY
(gentle, but firm)
Don't make me invoke my Medical Officer's prerogative, Captain . . .
(fast, as a friend)
Jim, please . . .

Kirk peers at him a moment, then nods.

KIRK

All right.

And he grasps McCoy's elbow gratefully, turns and leaves. McCoy stands gazing worriedly after him a moment, then turns and glances into the:

172   HOSPITAL AREA   172
where he can see Xon engrossed in the viewer. McCoy strides over to Xon's bed.

McCOY
Did the information the computer gave the alien include any explanation about how one young Lieutenant Junior Grade could absorb an electrical charge that would kill two ordinary men . . . ?!

XON
(cool)
Vulcan stamina—in comparison to human stamina—is universally known and accepted, doctor.

McCOY
So is their pigheadedness . . . !

And McCoy switches off the viewer, swings it away from Xon, and strides from the room.

173   INT. KIRK'S QUARTERS   173
SHOWING, first, the small personal viewer screen on which is flashing a set of calculations. PULL BACK SLIGHTLY TO FIND Kirk—slumped over the desk, fast asleep. He's wearing a leisure suit, had obviously followed McCoy's orders (to rest), and had fallen asleep out of exhaustion.

174   ACROSS KIRK TO THE WALL   174
where, reflected from another room, we HEAR A STATIC CRACKLE, and SEE a FLASH OF TURQUOISE LIGHT. The effect awakens Kirk, who peers sleepily at the viewer, assumes this is what awakened him, turns it off and rises and starts across the room toward his bed.

175   AT THE BED - ANGLE ON THE BATHROOM DOOR   175
as Kirk reaches the bed, and all at once hears the sonic shower (in the bathroom) splatter on. Alert instantly, Kirk peers into the bathroom, steps into it, and sees an incredible sight:

176 WHAT KIRK SEES - A NAKED FEMALE FORM IN THE SHOWER STALL   176

through the stall's translucent glass door. An instant's hesitation, then he slides open the glass door. And now, truly, he is incredulous. He is looking at:

177 ILIA   177

naked, standing in the sonic mist.

> ILIA
> (pleasant, casual)
> Good evening, captain . . . may I borrow your robe, please . . . ?

She indicates Kirk's robe hanging near the door. He hands it to her, momentarily speechless (not to mention slightly awed at her lovely body). Ilia smiles, continues;

> ILIA
> (continuing; as she puts robe on)
> The multi-cellular casting left my form at night temperature. This has now cooled it to what you consider normal.

> KIRK
> You're what? Something using Lieutenant Ilia's form . . .

> ILIA
> And functioning perfectly . . .

178 PAST ILIA TO KIRK   178

as she opens her robe, displaying herself to Kirk, and continues:

> ILIA
> As you can observe, an exact duplication.

It is interrupted by the quiet, STACCATO CHIMES of the door annunciator. Kirk whirls to face the door (across the room), to see:

179 McCOY   179

entering, not immediately noticing.

180 ILIA - AS McCOY SEES HER   180

partially shadowed, so he at first only discerns a female in a robe.

> McCOY
> (disapprovingly)
> I ordered you to rest, captain; I don't recall advising any other form of therapy . . .
> (now sees Ilia, reacts)
> . . . Lieutenant Ilia . . . !

> ILIA
> (pleasant, casual)
> Good evening, doctor. But I'm called 'Tasha,' not Ilia.

> KIRK
> Tasha . . . ?!

                              ILIA
          Yes, isn't that the name you gave me?

Kirk and McCoy exchange glances, and then McCoy steps forward and examines Ilia's
eyes—her face—skin.

                              McCOY
                            (to Kirk)
          Tasha . . . the sensor probe?
                           (indicating)
          The three legged metallic thing . . . ?

                              ILIA
                           (pleasantly)
          I am a perfect reproduction of the original Ilia. I can perform any of her
          functions . . .
                      (reaches out to caress Kirk)
          May I demonstrate . . . ?

Kirk steps away from her, as Ilia continues:

                              ILIA
          I've been given a new body to facilitate communicating with you.

                              McCOY
          In the shower . . . ?

181 ANGLE ON KIRK   181
          as he steps to his desk, produces a tricorder, switches it on and reads the results.
          His face reveals it; he hands the unit to McCoy, who also reads the scope.

                              McCOY
          Non-human life form.

                              ILIA
                           (pleasantly)
          You see . . . ?

                              KIRK
                            (to Ilia)
          How is it you didn't trigger the intruder alert system?

                              ILIA
                          (pleasant smile)
          The circuits are quite simple to bypass.

Kirk moves to the intercom, switches it on, speaks:

                              KIRK
                         (into intercom)
          Engineering . . . Scottie, program an alternate circuit into the intruder alert net-
          work.

SCOTT (V.O.)
Aye, sir. Are we expecting more visitors?

KIRK
I wouldn't doubt it. Kirk out.

182 ACROSS KIRK TO McCOY AND ILIA   182
as Kirk turns from the intercom and sees McCoy, in utter fascination, examining Ilia again: feeling her skin, peering into her eyes, moving her limbs, scanning with the tricorder.

McCOY
Incredible . . . !

And he now switches on the intercom, speaks into it:

McCOY
(continuing; into intercom)
Lieutenant Chapel . . . bring a portable scanner and metabolic-recorder to the Captain's quarters at once, please.

CHAPEL (V.O.)
(with urgency)
I'm on my way . . . !

KIRK
(to McCoy)
The Science Officer—

· McCOY
(into intercom)
. . . and bring Lieutenant Xon with you.

183 INT. SICKBAY   183
with Chapel at the intercom, AD LIBBING into it "Yes, sir," switching it off, and stepping into the:

184 HOSPITAL AREA   184
where Xon, as might be expected, is studying his viewer. He glances up, awaits what he expects to be a reprimand. She whispers tersely into his ear:

CHAPEL
Get dressed, Lieutenant. I think something's happened to the captain . . . !

Chapel leaves the area, CAMERA WITH her, to a storage area. She removes two small medikits, prepares to leave, glances behind her as Xon emerges from the hospital area. He takes the kits from her, and they hurry from Sickbay. They are both very grim.

185 INT. CORRIDOR - ELEVATOR   185
as it opens, and Chapel and Xon emerge, start down the corridor, to:

186 KIRK'S QUARTERS   186
     where the door slides open immediately.

187 INT. KIRK'S QUARTERS   187
     as Chapel and Xon enter.

     McCoy takes the medikits from Xon, begins opening them. At the same time Chapel is
     bemused seeing Kirk apparently in fine health; she really pays no attention to Ilia,
     but Xon is regarding Ilia quite curiously.

                              CHAPEL
     You don't look ill to me, captain—
                         (now realizes Ilia is back)
     Ilia, you're back; thank God!

                               ILIA
                            (pleasantly)
     Good evening, Dr. Chapel. Good evening, Lieutenant Xon.

                              CHAPEL
                            (confused)
     I don't understand: who's sick?

188 ANOTHER ANGLE - McCOY   188
     The instruments assembled—they will resemble small, flat readout screen units,
     which when placed over a patient will instantly reveal vital signs, readings, evaluations;
     blood counts, etc. McCoy gestures to Ilia:

                              McCOY
     Would you mind getting on the bed . . . ?

                               ILIA
                            (pleasantly)
     Not at all.

     And Ilia lies on the bed, as McCoy adjusts the instruments. Now, quickly, he scans
     her body, while the other device records her metabolism, flashes the results on the
     screen. Chapel steps over and reads the scanner, reacts with disbelief.

                              McCOY
     The skin is synthetic, but absolutely ingenious . . .
                         (to Chapel)
     Look at this: micro-miniature heating elements, sensors, relays . . .
                         (to Kirk, to have a look)
     Jim . . . Xon . . .

     Kirk and Xon view the scanner, as Ilia helpfully says:

                               ILIA
     There is also a network of micro-pumps . . .
                              McCOY
                            (studying scanner)
     My God . . . !

a portion of Ilia's insides, all the intricate machinery. (PRODUCTION NOTE: we'll show only as much as is practicable for the Art Department.) McCoy is unendingly fascinated:

>   McCOY
>   (clinically)
> . . . every epidermal function is duplicated, even to eye moisture.

The examination continues a few more moments, then McCoy finishes. (Throughout the examination Xon is silent, clearly intrigued with the android, and attempting to evaluate all factors.)

>   McCOY
>   (to Ilia)
> You can sit up now . . .
>   (to Chapel)
> Take the equipment back—and say nothing of this to anybody . . .
>   (to Kirk, as Chapel complies)
> It's the most perfect android I've ever seen . . .
>   (to Ilia)
> The question is: what do we do with you?

>   ILIA
> You may do anything you please. That is, Captain Kirk may.

Chapel, just packing away the equipment and preparing to leave, reacts at this remark, glances interestingly at Kirk:

>   CHAPEL
> I'd appreciate a report on whatever you . . . 'do' . . . with her, Captain.

>   KIRK
> Yes, I'm sure you would, Lieutenant. Thank you for your interest.

And he glares at Chapel a beat; she leaves. Ilia is seated comfortably on the bed edge facing them. She waits patiently, politely for the men to resume their interrogation. Kirk and McCoy glance at each other, perplexed, then Kirk addresses Xon:

>   KIRK
>   (continuing)
> Well, Mr. Xon, what <u>do</u> we do with her?

>   XON
> I would suggest first, sir, that we find her some appropriate clothing . . .
>   (to Ilia)
> Where is the real Lieutenant Ilia?

>   McCOY
> We asked her that: she said Ilia has ceased to function.

>   XON
>   (a beat, then to Ilia)
> She has ceased to <u>exist</u> . . . ?

                    ILIA
                 (pleasantly)
She has been disassembled.

A moment as the grim meaning of this is absorbed. Then:

                    XON
Why have you been sent here?

                    ILIA
To learn more about the servo-units inhabiting USS Enterprise.

                    McCOY
Servo-units . . . ?

                    KIRK
The 'parasites,' Bones. Us.

McCoy reacts appropriately, as Xon continues to Kirk:

                    XON
Obviously, sir, the alien has determined that the . . . 'servo-units' on the
Enterprise are considerably more complicated than he suspected. A memory scan
analysis of Lieutenant Ilia probably revealed an acute awareness of Captain Kirk . . .
                 (delicately)
. . . the Deltan sensuality, of course. So they reproduced her, assuming—quite
logically—that a relationship with Captain Kirk was the most expeditious means
of learning more about us.

                    McCOY
                 (wry amusement)
A 'relationship with Captain Kirk,' eh . . . ? Chapel was right: that will be
interesting . . . !

                    KIRK
Shut up, Bones . . .
                 (to Ilia)
Exactly what are you supposed to learn from me . . . ?

                    ILIA
Why USS Enterprise considers the servo-units so vital to its existence. Ve-jur is
anxious for this knowledge.

                    XON
'Ve-jur' . . . ? Is that the name of your ship?

                    ILIA
That is its name: Ve-jur.

                    McCOY
Ve-jur: well, at least we can stop calling it 'it' . . .

190   ANGLE ON THE INTERCOM - VIEWER   190
    as the AUDIAL SIGNAL is HEARD, and then Scott's image appears on the screen:

SCOTT
(on Viewer)
Captain . . . I can give you full power now, sir.

Kirk glances at Xon, then speaks into the intercom:

KIRK
Thank you, Mr. Scott. Stand by . . .
(to Ilia)
Would you mind staying here with Doctor McCoy while Mr. Xon and I go to the bridge . . . ?
(forced smile)
We'll only be a few minutes.

191 FAVORING McCOY   191
reacting to the announcement that he's staying with Ilia.

ILIA
(pleasant)
That will be quite satisfactory.

And Kirk gestures Xon to leave the room. They start out. Kirk glancing back at McCoy, who is regarding Ilia nervously as she reaches out a hand and begins touching his face with the Deltan soothing caress.

192 INT. CORRIDOR   192
as Kirk and Xon emerge from Kirk's quarters, start toward the elevator; they step in, the doors close behind them.

193 INT. ELEVATOR   193
Kirk and Xon getting in, the elevator doors closing.

KIRK
(to annunciator)
Bridge . . .
(to Xon)
Evaluation, Mr. Xon.

XON
Our situation is untenable, captain.

KIRK
(exasperated)
Mr. Xon, what I don't require from you is confirmation of the obvious . . . ! What I do require is a solution.

XON
You requested an evaluation, sir.

KIRK
(more exasperated)
Of the possible solution . . . !

                                    XON
        Yes, sir. In point of fact, sir, while the mission of the android is to gain further
        knowledge about us, she represents what we lack most: information concerning the
        alien, its intentions, and specifics regarding Earth being the Holy Home of The
        Creator.

                                    KIRK
        And just how do we get this information from her . . . ?

                                    XON
        I would say, sir, by cooperating with her . . .
                        (as Kirk peers at him; explains)
        . . . by entering into a . . . 'relationship' with her.

        Kirk is still peering narrowly, incredulously, at him, when the elevator doors open,
        and they have arrived at the:

194   INT. BRIDGE   194
        with Kirk peering at Xon another instant, then entering the bridge, Xon following.
        Decker is in the command chair, Sulu at the helm, Chekov at the Navigator's position.
        Uhura at communications.

        On the viewing screen is the omnipresent image of the alien ship that holds the
        Enterprise. Kirk steps to the Command chair, gestures Decker down as Decker starts
        rising to give up the conn to Kirk.

                                    KIRK
        Status, Mr. Decker.

                                    DECKER
        We are still held in a maximum tractor beam, captain, proceeding on a direct
        earth heading at Warp six point two.

                                    KIRK
        Has engineering informed you that full power is now available?

                                    DECKER
        Yes, sir. But I don't think we'd have a chance trying to break his tractor beam.

195   ACROSS THEM TO XON   195
        who is at his Science Station, peering into his hooded viewer.

                                    KIRK
        Mr. Xon . . .
                        (as Xon looks up)
        In your opinion, is a full power attempt to break the tractor beam advisable?

                                    XON
        In my opinion, sir such an attempt would merely antagonize and provoke the
        alien. I advise against it.

        Kirk nods acknowledgingly, then addresses Chekov:

                              KIRK

Mr. Chekov . . . ?

                             CHEKOV

I agree, Captain.

Kirk thinks a moment, then switches on the intercom:

                              KIRK
                         (into intercom)
Engineering . . . Scottie, can you give us just enough power for a subspace transmission to Starfleet without the alien's sensors mistaking it for a full power
breakaway?

                          SCOTT (V.O.)
It'll have to be done in under fifteen seconds, captain.

196 ACROSS KIRK TO UHURA   196
     as he glances at her, and she nods:

                             UHURA
I can pre-tape it, Captain, and send it at ultra high speed.

                              KIRK
                          (to Uhura)
Transmit our logs and reports. But warn Starfleet not to reply: the alien could
seize the channel and infiltrate starfleet's computer.

Uhura nods, starts swiveling around to commence her work, when suddenly she does
a double take; her eyes widen in disbelief as she peers at something O.S.

197 ON SULU   197
     reacting similarly, peering O.S.

                              SULU
Ilia . . . !

198 WIDEN TO INCLUDE ILIA   198
     and McCoy, just entering; McCoy quite chagrined, and immediately starts explaining
     to Kirk:

                             McCOY
She insisted on coming up here—

                             UHURA
                           (pleased)
Ilia, you're all right . . . !

                              ILIA
Oh, yes, I'm fine.

                              KIRK
                            (grim)
This is not Lieutenant Ilia . . .

KIRK (CONT'D)
(as all react)
Ladies and gentlemen . . . meet . . . Tasha.

199 INT. ENGINE ROOM   199
Scott at the console intercom:

SCOTT
(into intercom)
All right, Captain, I can give you subspace communication power now. But fifteen
seconds only, sir.

200 INT. BRIDGE   200
Everyone studying Ilia, obviously now having been informed of the truth about her
by Kirk, who is just speaking into the intercom:

KIRK
(into intercom)
Stand by, Mr. Scott . . .
(to Uhura)
Are you ready, Commander?

UHURA
(with a glance at Ilia)
Ready.

KIRK
Open the frequency.

And Uhura peers at Ilia just one more beat, then turns and begins transmitting the
message.

201 ANOTHER ANGLE - THE COMMAND CENTER   201
where Ilia has stepped over to Sulu, and placed her hand on his forehead in a Deltan
soothe.

SULU
(quiet, incredulous)
I don't believe it . . . !

ILIA
(pleasantly)
I can do anything the original can—better.

Sulu and Chekov exchange glances, and you can almost read Sulu's mind: he'd love
to experiment. He holds Ilia's hand, strokes it, feels the flesh-like covering. And then
all at once Ilia stiffens, removes her hand from Sulu's, turns and faces Kirk:

ILIA
(to Kirk)
Ve-jur wishes to know why this servo unit . . .
(indicates Uhura)
. . . is signalling the third planet.

Kirk and Xon look at each other: this is another life-and-death question.

completing the transmission.

> UHURA
>
> Message transmitted, Captain.

> KIRK
> (into intercom)
> Engineering . . . shut it down, Mr. Scott. Thank you . . .
> (to Ilia)
> The third planet must be informed of Ve-jur's arrival.

Ilia again appears to be in brief, intense concentration (she is receiving signals from Ve-jur). Then:

> ILIA
>
> Ve-jur suspects that the servo-units have somehow gained control over USS Enterprise. If this is so, it indicates the servo-units have also gained control over superior life forms on the third planet.

203 ACROSS THEM TO XON   203
who seems to have suddenly reacted at a reading in his viewer:

> XON
>
> Captain . . . the tractor beam is fading . . . !

204 SULU   204
also reacting, working his controls.

> SULU
>
> The helm, sir . . . ! We have control of the vessel . . . !

Decker is at the intercom instantly:

> DECKER
> (into intercom)
> Engineering . . . start the main engines . . . !

> KIRK
> (to Decker)
> Warp 6, so we can keep up with him.

> DECKER
> (into intercom)
> Accelerate to Warp 6 immediately . . . !
> (to Kirk)
> I think we should go to Warp 7, captain; if he's releasing us, we ought to get as far away from him as we can!

> KIRK
>
> I want to stay with him; until we find out how to deal with him!

205 EXT. SPACE - THE ENTERPRISE AND THE ALIEN   205
    SHOWING the Enterprise still quite close—as before—to the alien, but now perceptibly
    edging away, although remaining on the same course.

206 INT. BRIDGE - FAVORING ILIA   206
    concentrating again, as all the activity goes on around her. Then, with that same
    pleasant blandness, she announces:

                            ILIA
        Ve-jur is releasing USS Enterprise as evidence of Ve-jur's good faith, and awaits
        similar evidence from USS Enterprise.

                            KIRK
        How may we demonstrate this evidence?

                            ILIA
        By acceptance of the Creator, and The Creator's wisdom.

                            KIRK
        We do.

                            ILIA
                        (shakes her head)
        No; you've denied that the third planet is the Holy Home.

207 PAST THEM TO THE VIEWER   207
    The giant ship on the screen, seemingly slightly smaller now than we have been
    seeing it.
    Kirk peers at Ilia a moment, then at the screen.

                            KIRK
                        (eyes on screen)
        Mr. Decker . . . maneuver away. See how far he'll let us go.

                            DECKER
        Two degrees reverse tangent.

                            SULU
        Two degrees reverse tangent.

208 EXT. SPACE - THE ENTERPRISE AND THE ALIEN   208
    the little Enterprise now moving perceptibly away, maintaining the same heading and
    speed, but widening the distance between it and the alien.

209 INT. BRIDGE - FAVORING THE VIEWER   209
    as Kirk and the others study the screen, the slowly receding image of the alien.

                            KIRK
                        (to Sulu)
        Hold here . . .
                        (to Decker)
        He is releasing us . . .
                        (to Ilia)
        How can we convince him of our acceptance?

as she is again concentrating. Then:

                              ILIA
Ve-jur is prepared to show Captain Kirk and one other servo-unit proof of the
Holy Home.

                              KIRK
When?

                              ILIA
You may beam over whenever you're ready. I'll accompany you.

                              CHEKOV
                            (dubious)
All of a sudden, just like that . . . ! Captain, I think you would be very foolish to
do it.

                              KIRK
                             (wry)
Commander, I agree . . .
                           (to Xon)
Lieutenant Xon, would you consider volunteering to see the inside of Ve-jur . . . ?

                              XON
Yes, sir!

                              KIRK
You just did . . .
                          (to Decker)
You're in command, Will. If we lose contact for any period longer than ten
minutes . . . you'll proceed at maximum speed to earth. Contact from me, not
any replica—

Decker rises from the chair to face Kirk, addresses him quietly so they cannot be
overheard:

                             DECKER
A command lesson, captain: your place is here, on the Enterprise.

Kirk peers at him angrily, then softens.

                              KIRK
You're right. But I'm the guest of honor—I have to go . . .
                         (into intercom)
Three to beam, Scottie.

                          SCOTT (V.O.)
Three to beam . . . ? Beam where, sir?

Kirk looks at Xon, then Decker—then at Ilia. Then he laughs unhumorously:

                    KIRK
                (into intercom)
I wish I knew.

211 INT. TRANSPORTER ROOM   211
Scott at the console, preparing the unit—and peering at some very interesting
readings just coming in. At that moment, Kirk, Xon, and Ilia enter.

                    SCOTT
Captain, you won't need life support system belts after all . . .
                (indicates console)
There's a gravitational field forming inside the alien ship . . . !
                (reads further)
And an oxygen atmosphere envelope!

As the three step onto the platform, Ilia says:

                    ILIA
Please set for coordinates 432 point 6 point 5, Mr. Scott.

                    SCOTT
Well, that's a help: now I won't have to worry about not putting you square
inside the oxygen . . . are you ready, sir?

Kirk glances at Xon, who nods.

                    KIRK
                (a beat)
Energize.

                    SCOTT
Good luck, sir.

Scott moves the controls. The SHIMMERING EFFECT, and in an instant the three forms
are dematerializing. Scott waits another instant, then speaks into the intercom:

                    SCOTT
            (continuing; into intercom)
Bridge . . . they're beamed over, safe and sound . . .

212 EXT. SPACE - FULL ON ALIEN SHIP   212
just to remind us of the awesome immensity.

213 INT. ALIEN SHIP - CLOSE SHOT OF THE THREE AS THEY ARRIVE 213
the SHIMMERING EFFECT, as the three forms materialize.

They are FACING the CAMERA, and for the moment they seem to be standing against
a gigantic metallic wall. O.S. you can HEAR MACHINE SOUNDS (steady throbbing,
humming) and the SOUNDS OF COMPUTERS. Ilia's face reveals no emotion—but
Kirk's eyes are wide in disbelief. And Xon, for all his Vulcan restraint, cannot help
reacting to a sight so incredible it defies any imagination.

214　WHAT THEY ARE SEEING - THE ALIEN SHIP INTERIOR　　　　　　214
a vista so huge, so magnificent. it equals in scale and emotional impact the exterior
size. We are inside a massive cavern whose ceiling rises as high as the eye can see.
Whose length and dimensions seem to stretch on into infinity.

Nearby is a large object resembling a condenser, but with coils rising higher than the
greatest skyscraper. Through coils rush a never-ending surge of energy, multi-colored,
blinding, beautiful in its awesomeness. And with it that continual SOUND, MACHINE
SOUND.

The interior is lined, gracefully, with miles of sophisticated mechanisms, power
conduits, opaque tubing carrying endles surges of flashing energy plasma—obviously
flowing from one end of the ship to the other.

215　ANOTHER ANGLE - THE THREE IN THE SHIP　　　　　　　　215
standing atop an energy tube, Lilliputians in a world whose size dwarfs that of a
hundred Gullivers.

216　CLOSER ON THE THREE　　　　　　　　　　　　　　　　216
as they marvel at the intelligence that created this machine. Neither Kirk or Xon
speak; words are superflous. Finally Ilia breaks the silence:

> ILIA
> (pleasantly)
>
> Follow me, please . . .

And she sets out, walking atop the tube, headed apparently into the machine wonder-
land that stretches endlessly before them. They follow.

217　MOVING THROUGH THE MACHINE - VARIOUS SHOTS AND POVS　　　217
the three tiny figures plodding through the vastness.
Past other machine devices, each with their own unique color, movement, and
SOUND. Now and then both Kirk and Xon stop to gaze up, or behind, or ahead—and
never fail to marvel. Soon they approach a:

218　GELATINOUS-PLASMA MASS - FROM A DISTANCE　　　　　　218
the mass at first obscure, swirling about, obviously self-contained. As they move
closer, Ilia points to the mass.

219　CLOSER - LIFE SIZE　　　　　　　　　　　　　　　　219
as Xon and Kirk follow Ilia's hand, and see within the mass a sight that is perhaps
more unvelievable than any thus far.

220　WHAT THEY SEE - ILIA FLOATING INSIDE THE MASS　　　　　220
the real Ilia, eyes closed, floating within the mass as though buoyed on a bed of air.
Her eyes are closed; she is either asleep—or dead. Kirk and Xon move closer to study
her:

> XON
>
> I'm afraid she's dead, Captain.

> KIRK
> (to Ilia)
>
> Is she?

> ILIA
> (nods)
> That servo-unit has ceased functioning.

> KIRK
> Could we take her back with us?

> ILIA
> The form is being preserved for further study.

> KIRK
> It's possible we can still repair it somehow.

> ILIA
> (surprised)
> But why? You have me. And my construction is stronger—and much more useful.

> XON
> But you are not like us.

> ILIA
> All the better. I will never wear out . . .
> (quickly)
> Come, I'll show you the Creator.

And she sets off, Kirk and Xon following, but both glancing back regretfully at Ilia's body, gently rocking about in the billowing plasma-mass.

221 ANOTHER QUICK SERIES OF SHOTS OF THE THREE WALKING   221
along the huge tube, dwarfed, past more machine devices inside the ship's cavernous interior.

222 CLOSER   222
as they walk, Xon continually gazing about in utter fascination. Ilia walks easily, with purpose, Kirk grimly, his mind whirling with a million thoughts, sights, plans. And then suddenly Kirk spies something in the far distance, narrows his eyes, peers at it—then begins walking faster toward the object.

223 WHAT KIRK HAS SEEN - THE WRECKAGE   223
resembling, from a distance, a small, metallic object about the size of a 20th Century aircraft fuel drop tank. The rounded aluminum seems to be attached to—or growing out of—the side of the ship. Kirk hurries toward it now.

224 CLOSER ON THE OBJECT   224
as they reach it, Kirk and Xon exchanging glances, and both kneeling to examine the object. Xon scanning it with his tricorder. The object once had been painted, paint flaking in the dozens of places where meteorites, dust, heat, other space hazards scarred it.

> XON
> (reading the tricorder)
> Titanium base—
> (recites metallic composition and paint structure)
> These substances haven't been used since the early 21st Century—

But Kirk is not listening; he's gazing beyond this first object, to other, scattered sections of the same material, also apparently <u>growing out of the starship wall and floor</u>. He moves to examine these, and peers at one large section in disbelief:

225 WHAT KIRK SEES - THE PLAQUE   225
metallic-gold, part of a large section of the wreckage. And an inscription that reads:

V G R 18 NASA
(NOTE: the letters between V and G and R have been obliterated, as has much of the smaller writing under the diagram of the sun and planets.)

Xon has come over and gazes at the plaque with Kirk. It takes a moment for Kirk to decipher the letters:

                         KIRK
VGR—Ve-jur. Voyager . . . ! Voyager 18. The first deep space probe designed to send signals back from beyond our solar system.

                         XON
Launched in 1996.

                         KIRK
It stopped transmitting only a few weeks after it passed Jupiter.

                         XON
Yes sir, and all theoreticians agreed it disappeared into a black hole.

                         KIRK
It must have; and entered hyper-space and timelessness until it came out the other side—in a part of the galaxy hundreds of thousands of light years away . . .
                    (runs fingers over other inscriptions)
Can you make out any of this . . . ?

226 ANGLE ON ILIA   226
who has been calmly observing their reactions, now replies before Xon has a chance to speak:

                         ILIA
Those are the Holy Writings. The Creator's Message.

                         XON
                       (to Kirk)
Obviously, it is a description of the probe's purpose, and its origin—

                         KIRK
                 (indicating earth on the plaque)
—The third planet.

                         XON
And N-A-S-A of course is NASA, the old National Aeronautics and Space Administration agency.

                         ILIA
Glory to Nasa.

                    KIRK
They don't realize it was us—the humans on earth—who built Voyager 18 . . .
                    (to Ilia)
If Ve-jur destroys the servo-units on the third planet, he will be destroying those
who created him.

Instantly, out of nowhere, there is a greenish-white stream of laser fire, and an
electrical crackle, the beam shooting into Kirk's chest. It knocks him down, writhing
in pain.

                    XON
                (moving to help)
Captain . . . !

                    ILIA
                  (calmly)
Ve-jur punishes those who lie.

                    XON
It is not a—

But Kirk manages to weakly reach up and clap his hand over Xon's lips, and at the
same time he speaks to Ilia.

                    KIRK
I meant no insult.

                    ILIA
Ve-jur is satisfied that the servo-units do not accept The Creator. You will return
to USS Enterprise, and resume your journey to the third planet. There, you are
to advise the higher life forms of Ve-jur's arrival, and the return of The Creator.

                    KIRK
'Higher life forms'—<u>machines</u>.

                    XON
Yes, sir; machines.

Kirk gazes around him just an instant, then struggles to his feet, opening his wrist
communicator:

                    KIRK

                (into communicator)
Kirk to Enterprise . . .

227 INT. BRIDGE   227
    at the Command Center, everyone reacts to Kirk's voice. Decker punches the
    communicator transmit control, speaks:

                    DECKER
Captain, are you all right?

KIRK'S VOICE
Yes, we're all right. Please inform the transporter room to beam us back immediately from these coordinates.

SCOTT'S VOICE
I've got them fixed, Commander. Stand by, Captain, for beaming—

228 INT. ALIEN SHIP—KIRK 228
as he continues into the communicator:

KIRK
Hold it, Scottie . . . Decker, have Uhura signal Starfleet that we need absolute proof of the existence of NASA in the 20th Century, and details of the planning, construction, and launching of the Voyager 18 probe—

Kirk hesitates, nearly flinches as though waiting for another laser bolt to strike him. But no reaction from Ve-jur.

KIRK
(continuing; into communicator)
All right, beam us over.

229 INT. ALIEN SHIP - FULL SHOT (TO SCALE) 229
showing, again, the awesome magnitude of the vessel. And the THREE SMALL FIGURES (Kirk, Xon, Ilia), standing near the Voyager 18 wreckage. Then the SHIMMERING EFFECT, and they are gone. The CAMERA HOLDS on the vastness of the alien interior, the obvious power of it all. The intelligence and might of this machine can be matched by nothing we know of on earth.

230 EXT. SPACE - THE ENTERPRISE 230
streaking through space—alone now, the giant alien having released us. OVER this we HEAR:

KIRK'S VOICE
Captain's Log, Stardate 7421.6. In three hours we enter earth's orbit. The giant starship Ve-Jur or Voyager, is five hours behind us, having allowed us that time to prepare 'higher life forms' for its arrival . . . and, apparently, the destruction of 'lesser life forms' . . .
(dryly)
Human beings . . .

231 INT. BRIEFING ROOM 231
with Kirk, Xon, Scott, McCoy—and Ilia—seated around the table. The CAMERA PANS around the room, lingering a moment on each face, as Kirk's VOICE continues:

KIRK'S VOICE
Although the presence of the android Tasha/Ilia is for the clear purpose of providing Ve-jur a constant flow of information about us . . . we dare not obstruct her for fear of provoking Ve-jur into an immediate and catastrophic attack on earth . . .

232 FAVORING XON AND ILIA 232
seated near each other, Xon talking, as Kirk's VOICE continues:

KIRK'S VOICE

Tasha/Ilia has, however, been of considerable assistance in helping us compile and correlate facts pertaining to Ve-jur. Between her and Mr. Xon, who has repaired our main computer, a fascinating yet perfectly credible hyphothesis has been formed . . .

End of log.

XON

. . . The living machines inhabiting Ve-jur's planet have existed for eons. But some three hundred years ago—for reasons which even Tasha is not sure—

ILIA

—The Time of the Trouble.

XON

Yes, The Time of the Trouble: a series of natural disasters, perhaps. Or perhaps the disappearance of the metal alloys the machines constructed themselves with. Whatever it was, the civilization began decaying.

ILIA

And then the Holy One arrived.

XON

The Holy One—Voyager 18. Crippled, barely operative, it landed on the machine planet. And while by the standards of the living machines, Voyager 18 was extremely primitive, it carried within it a regenerative spark. It revitalized the entire race. And 300 years later, having now attained star travel capability, they set out to reach the distant planet from which had come their Savior.

ILIA

Glory to Nasa for sending its Son, and its Message.

McCOY

But why is the message 'Destroy All Life On Earth' . . . ?!

ILIA

Because if servo-units like yourselves control such beings as USS Enterprise—and infest the third planet in a similar fashion—isn't it obvious the Holy Home must be cleansed?
(pleasantly)
Surely, you can understand this . . . ?

McCoy is too exasperated to reply, glances at Kirk, but just then:

233   ANGLE ON THE TABLE VIEWER   233
as we HEAR the audial signal. Kirk switches it on, and Sulu's face appears on the viewer:

SULU

Earth orbit minus 21 minutes, Captain. We're being hailed by the light cruiser Delphi.

KIRK
(into intercom)
Delphi is the only Starship to hail us?

SULU
The Paris and the Boston are two days out, sir. Everything else is more than five days.

SCOTT
(to Kirk)
A light cruiser, Captain; going up against that behemoth would be like a mosquito swatting an elephant . . . !

McCOY
(dry, to Scott)
The Enterprise is the strongest vessel in the fleet, Mr. Scott, and if I remember, we didn't exactly frighten Ve-jur to death—

KIRK
(into intercom)
Instruct Delphi to lay in an interception course on us—and hold. They're to go to Yellow Alert, and program a stop into any main computer external transmissions . . .
(switches off intercom; to Scott)
How far off target would you be, beaming from orbit?

SCOTT
Where's the target?

234 ACROSS KIRK TO ILIA   234
as he glances at her, and replies to Scott.

KIRK
Starfleet Command, the Archives Building.

SCOTT
(unhumorous laugh)
From orbit, Captain, I couldn't guarantee anything closer than the North Pole . . . !
At perigee, we're 22,000 miles, you know.

KIRK
Suppose there was a relay station? In sub-orbit?

SCOTT
So long as it wasn't more than 16,000 miles from us—and from the target.

235 ANGLE ON THE VIEWER   235
as Kirk switches it on, and again Uhura's face appears.

KIRK
(into intercom)
Commander Uhura, signal Delphi to disregard our previous course instruction. They are to proceed to a sub-orbital pattern not to exceed 15,000 miles, and prepare to receive two for beaming . . .

KIRK (CONT'D)
(switches off; to Scott)
We'll relay from the Delphi.

McCOY

Who's 'we,' Jim?

KIRK

Tasha and I. She'll see for herself the Voyager 18 records, and inform Ve-jur.

236   ON ILIA   236
as she smiles pleasantly.

237   INT. KIRK'S QUARTERS   237
as the door opens, and Kirk and Ilia enter. He crosses to his desk, touches the viewer
console buttons—and immediately various computations appear on the screen. Ilia
watches interestedly.

ILIA

You're programming your log into the computer.

KIRK
(chagrined)
Standard procedure.

He turns to resume, but stops abruptly, as Ilia in her most seductive Deltan manner
places her hands on his cheek.

ILIA

I saw male and female servo-units touching and caressing each other. I'd like to
try it.

KIRK

I don't think you'd appreciate it.

ILIA

Wouldn't I . . . ?

And without another word, she throws her arms around him, draws his face down to
hers—and kisses him. Kirk is so startled he is frozen—for a moment only. Tasha/Ilia
is so life-like and real that he's nearly carried away. He pushes her gently from him.

KIRK
(flustered)
You really are a fine reproduction.

ILIA

I told you I was. Could we try it again?

KIRK
(backing off)
There are other things to a relationship.

ILIA

But not as pleasant.

Kirk peers at her a moment.

                              KIRK
        How could you know that?

                              ILIA
        I feel it.

                              KIRK
        You 'feel' . . . ?

238   FAVORING ILIA   238
        as she appears momentarily confused, almost startled. She smiles weakly at him.

                              ILIA
        That's not very logical, is it?

They stand gazing at each other a moment, and in her eyes there is a very human
spark. Kirk cannot help but perceive it, and it seems to bemuse him as much as her.
And then the moment is broken by:

239   THE TABLE VIEWER   239
        emitting the AUDIO SIGNAL. For just one more moment Kirk does not move, stands
        studying Ilia. The SIGNAL SOUNDS again, and Kirk reaches to switch it on. Scott's
        face appears:

                              SCOTT
        We're ready to move into orbit, Captain. You'd best get down here to the
        Transporter Room.

                              KIRK
                         (into intercom)
        On our way, Scottie.

He switches off the viewer, faces Ilia just one more moment.

                              ILIA
        We'd better go.

Kirk looks at her, nods almost sadly.

240   INT. TRANSPORTER ROOM   240
        with Kirk facing Xon, Decker and McCoy, giving them final orders. Ilia is also here,
        waiting patiently. Scott is in the b.g., an earphone plugged into his ear. (He's
        communicating with the Delphi.)

                              KIRK
                         (from the start)
        . . . And you, Mr. Xon, you'll program the main computer to place the entire
        vessel into a self-destruct mode upon proper signal.

                              XON
        Yes, sir.

KIRK
(to Decker)
You'll give that signal, Will, at your discretion. No matter what happens, the
Enterprise's memory banks mustn't fall into Ve-jur's hands. The whole Federation
will be jeopardized.

DECKER
I understand, Captain.

241 ANGLE ON SCOTT   241
putting down the earplug, stepping toward the control console.

SCOTT
The Delphi is in beaming position now, Captain.

Kirk and Ilia step onto the transporter platform. He stands a moment studying his
officers, and then his glance falls on McCoy. He smiles a little smile of encouragement
at McCoy. The two friends look at each other, realizing this may well be the last
time. Then Kirk glances at Scott.

KIRK
Energize.

Scott doesn't comply immediately, instead peers at Kirk—old comrades. Kirk nods at
him. And Scott moves the controls.

SCOTT
Energizing.

Kirk and Ilia stand waiting—then the SHIMMERING EFFECT, and in an instant they
have dematerialized. The men stand gazing at the empty platform.

SCOTT
(continuing; muttering to himself)
I only hope the Delphi transporter officer knows what he's doing . . . !

242 INT. DELPHI TRANSPORTER ROOM (REDRESS OF ENTERPRISE ROOM)   242
with the DELPHI CAPTAIN (a Commander), and the TRANSPORTER OFFICER (a
Lieutenant) at the console controls. Now the SHIMMERING EFFECT, and Kirk and Ilia
materialize. Both Delphi officers cannot help an admiring reaction at the sight of Ilia.

DELPHI CAPTAIN
Admiral Kirk . . . welcome aboard.

KIRK
Thank you, Commander. Are you ready to relay?

DELPHI CAPTAIN
Yes, sir. Starfleet has requested we beam you directly to Admiral Nogura's office.

KIRK
Very well.

TRANSPORTER OFFICER

Sir, we're in a parallel pattern over earth, so we won't lose the target. Perhaps you and the young lady might like a few minutes rest . . . ?

KIRK

No, we—

243 ACROSS KIRK TO ILIA   243

as he pauses abruptly, peers at her, an idea forming.

KIRK

. . . Lieutenant, can you put us down, in Union Square Park . . . ?

TRANSPORTER OFFICER
(bemused)

Yes, certainly . . .

KIRK

I think it might be helpful for the young lady to get a first hand look at life on earth. Maintain your parallel pattern, and inform Admiral Nogura I'll meet him at the Archives Building in thirty minutes. Energize.

244 EXT. EARTH - UNION SQUARE PARK - DAY (PAN SHOT)   244

The same park Kirk and McCoy were in in Scene #16. CHILDREN, as before, cavorting, playing with 'wild' animals. OLDER PEOPLE (whose faces might betray their years, but whose bodies and attitudes are young). And various competitive games. And the groves of trees . . . and slightly beyond, the ocean. A sleek hover-craft will be skimming along the water, near shore. The hydrofoil's decks contain perhaps a FEW DOZEN PEOPLE.

Now, in the midst of all this, Kirk and Ilia MATERIALIZE. But no one has seen them in the act of materializing, so that when a group of CHILDREN runs past them, no one pays them any attention—but for one SMALL BOY. He stops and gazes up at Kirk, points to the uniform:

BOY

Are you with Starfleet . . . ?

KIRK
(forced smile)

Sometimes.

BOY
(touches Kirk's stripes)
You're an officer. That's what I want to be when I grow up.

And with that, the Boy AD-LIBS "'Bye . . ." and rushes off to join his friends. Ilia has been peering incredulously at the Boy.

ILIA

When he 'grows up' . . . ?

KIRK

We 'servo-units' begin life very tiny . . .

KIRK (CONT'D)
(indicates with hands)
. . . then we grow to full size. It takes a number of years.

ILIA
And the internal mechanisms also grow . . . ?

KIRK
Oh, yes.

Ilia glances around now at the various activity—the people—and for the first time seems to view them reflectively, as though now she doesn't quite understand. She also has a lost bland, accepting expression. She waves her hand around.

ILIA
The servo-units live in places like this . . . ?

KIRK
This is where they relax. Let me show you . . .

And he takes her hand, begins guiding her through the park.

245 VARIOUS SHOTS AND POVS - KIRK AND ILIA   245
walking through the park, observing the sights—the people. The animals. Ilia is completely bemused with the animals, but follows Kirk's lead and gingerly pats a handsome sheep dog. The dog licks her fingers. Ilia is beginning to resemble a child continually delighted with new discoveries. And she is particularly entranced with vegetation. She touches the shrubs and smells the flowers.

Now and then, various PEOPLE (all in recreation/leisure garb) cast curious glances at the strange couple, but no one stops them to speak or query. In this century, our people have learned to accept the unusual and bizarre as normal. Live and let live.

246 AT THE BEACH   246
as Kirk and Ilia emerge from the wooded area, suddenly find themselves on the beach—the surf crashing up phosphorescently, receding, crashing up. Ilia is fascinated with the water, kneels to allow the foaming surf to splash over her fingers. She scoops up sand, trickles it through her hands. And now she finds a piece of driftwood, picks it up, examines it.

ILIA
(indicating water, sand, wood)
The servo-units made all this?

KIRK
They made none of it; nature did.

ILIA
Nature?

KIRK
The natural state of things and beings.

Ilia grips the driftwood, feels it.

ILIA

But if it isn't manufactured . . . it isn't perfect . . . !

KIRK
(agreeing)
Nothing is perfect; not here. Nothing can be, because those who live here are themselves imperfect—and always will be . . .
(faces her)
Can't you see the difference between us—and other servo-units?

ILIA
A difference? How can there be a difference . . . ?

Kirk peers at her frustratedly, then indicates the driftwood—and then the ocean, and then the sand. The trees.

KIRK
This; all this is what makes it different . . . !

247 ACROSS KIRK TO ILIA   247
as she seems to be gazing past him, her attention attracted by something O.S. She looks at him now.

ILIA
(coldly)
Yes, and that, too . . . !

She points O.S. Kirk turns to see:

248 WHAT ILIA IS LOOKING AT - THE HYDROFOIL   248
just now racing INTO SIGHT, the figures of people at the rail and on deck VISIBLE.

ILIA
A machine—employed as a transporter of servo-units!

KIRK
Ilia, we created that machine. Just as we created NASA, and your own Holy One. And it was people like us—servo-units—who must have created even the distant ancestors of Ve-jur.

ILIA
No . . . !

She hurls the driftwood to the sand, stares wildly at him one instant, then turns and starts running away. Kirk strides after her, catches her.

KIRK
Why can't you simply accept, or reject my statement? Why do you run away?

Ilia peers at him—and no longer is that bland, pleasant expression in her eyes. Now, more than ever, they seem alive. And troubled.

ILIA
I don't know.

And suddenly she hurls herself in his arms, buries her face in his chest. Clings to him. Kirk holds her a moment, then flips open his wrist communicator.

                              KIRK
                      (into communicator)
          Kirk to Delphi.

                         DELPHI VOICE
          Delphi.

                              KIRK
                      (into communicator)
          Beam two from these coordinates to the Archives Building.

Kirk closes the communicator, looks down at the woman he holds in his arms. He pulls her even closer to him.

249 INT. ENTERPRISE BRIDGE - ANGLE ON THE VIEWER   249
Decker in the command chair, all other personnel at their stations. On the viewer is an image of <u>earth</u>. Uhura addresses Decker:

                             UHURA
          Signal from the Delphi, Commander: they've beamed Captain Kirk and the
          android to the Archives Building.

250 ANGLE ON XON   250
who has been studying his hooded viewer, now looks up grimly:

                              XON
          The alien has moved into earth orbit, sir.

                            DECKER
          Location?

                              XON
          Five thousand, two hundred kilometers from our orbital position . . .
                          (a beat)
          Commander . . . our sensors are picking up an object ejected by the alien . . . !
          It's proceeding away from him at a rapid speed, but in the same orbital trajectory.

                            DECKER
          Composition . . . ?

                              XON
                        (shakes his head)
          It's shielded, sir.

                            DECKER
          Helmsman, lay in an interception course: coordinates zero five one, mark four.
          Orbital speed plus two.

                             SULU
          Leaving orbit, sir.

251 EXT. THE ENTERPRISE   251
in orbit, then suddenly the engine pods glow red—the ship begins moving out of the trajectory.

252 INT. ENTERPRISE - BRIDGE - FAVORING THE VIEWER   252
with all peering at the screen. For an instant, all that is visible is the blue-black of sub-space, then suddenly the <u>object</u>. At first just a speck on the horizon.

                         DECKER
Magnification factor three.

Instantly, on the screen, the object is large—very visible. It resembles a long cannister with a mushroom top.
                         DECKER
                       (continuing)
Evaluation, Mr. Xon.

Xon is studying the hooded viewer.

                          XON
High radiation . . . one hundred point three meters long, twenty meters wide . . .
                        (grim)
It is a <u>neutron</u> device—with a proximity fuse . . . !

                        DECKER
                        (fast)
Hard about . . . !

Sulu works the controls; we have the sensation of the Enterprise executing a tight 180. Everyone waits tensely until the maneuver is complete; then all seem to breathe a sigh of relief. Chekov reads his instruments:

                        CHEKOV
Another ten seconds, we would have detonated it . . . !

253 NEW ANGLE - XON   253
at the hooded viewer, reacting:
                          XON
Commander, the alien is ejecting another identical device in a different orbital position . . . !

                        DECKER
Put a high-grade sensor on it.

                          XON
I am, sir . . . I'll have the readings correlated in a second—
                      (breaks off, a beat)
He's placed two others in orbit! A total of four.

254 CHEKOV   254
intently studying his console, now has a grim evaluation:

CHEKOV

Neutron bombs, for certain . . .
                    (a beat while he studies figures)
Moving under their own power to equidistant orbital positions . . .
                    (glances up)
Four bombs, overlapping the whole planet . . . !

DECKER

Can we pull them away with a tractor beam . . . ?

CHEKOV

No, sir: they would explode the instant our beam reached them.

DECKER

Detonation data, Mr. Xon?

XON

Unavailable, sir.

DECKER

Opinion, Mr. Chekov?

CHEKOV

Since they are all heading for pre-determined placement, they will probably
detonate when all four are in position.

DECKER

Estimated time to placement?

SULU

Twenty-six minutes.

DECKER

Set your chronometer in a countdown mode, Mr. Sulu . . .

255   ACROSS DECKER TO SULU   255
      as Sulu adjusts the chronometer so it reads: 00:26:05, and the flashing seconds begin
      rolling back. Decker addresses Uhura:

DECKER

Communications . . . inform Starfleet.

UHURA
                    (desperate)
I'm not getting through. My signals are being reflected back from a forcefield . . . !

256   XON   256
      just now receiving new, more ominous readings from his viewer.

XON

Sir, there is a forcefield screen being formed around us . . . !

257 ANOTHER ANGLE - THE MAIN VIEWER   257
as, suddenly, the alien appears on the screen—moving straight toward them, frontally,
its huge 'mouth' resembling the gaping maw of some nightmarish monster.

                              DECKER
All ahead . . . ! Warp speed . . . !

                              SULU
                    (desperately working controls)
We're caught in his tractor beam again!

258 INT. ARCHIVES ROOM   258
a room with stacks of computer tapes, microfilms—clearly long stored, ancient.
Seated facing a large viewing screen are Admiral Nogura, Captain Lebutu, Admiral
Carson—and Kirk and Ilia. Built into the armrest of Nogura's chair are control but-
tons, and as he touches them, on the screen flash various copies of records, files,
newspaper accounts: all of NASA activities, particularly the launching of Voyager 18.
Still photographs of the event, etc. In a corner we will CATCH A GLIMPSE of a 20th
Century film projector, and several cans of film.

                              LEBUTU
                          (from the start)
 . . . the complete accounts of NASA—and, as you see, Voyager 18.

259 ANGLE ON ILIA   259
watching the screen intently, but then apparently stealing a covert glance at Kirk.
And she places her hand gently on his. He looks at her, but she is watching the
screen again.

                              NOGURA
                            (to Ilia)
Surely, this is convincing evidence that Voyager 18 originated here, and was
designed and constructed by humans . . . ?

Ilia does not reply, merely smiles pleasantly, blandly at Nogura. The Admiral glances
grimly at Kirk. At that instant:

260 ANGLE ON THE TABLE INTERCOM/VIEWER   260
as the image of a YEOWOMAN appears.

                              YEOWOMAN
Admiral . . . communications reports loss of contact with Enterprise.

                              NOGURA
                          (into intercom)
Time to bomb detonation?

                              YEOWOMAN
Thirteen minutes and ten seconds . . .
                            (a beat)
     Mark!

261 PAST NOGURA TO THE SCREEN   261
   as Nogura touches a button on his console, and slightly to the side of the screen a
   <u>digital clock</u> suddenly lights up—the numbers 00:13:10 appearing, and counting
   down. The various slides, etc., continue on screen.

                              CARSON
                          (to Kirk, of Ilia)
   I don't think we're getting through to her, Kirk.

                              KIRK
                             (to Ilia)
   Tasha . . . why can't you accept the evidence . . . ?

                              ILIA
                            (troubled)
   It's all simulated.

                              NOGURA
   Well, of course it is! The original records crumpled to dust hundreds of years ago.
   Ilia turns to Nogura, regards him coldly.

                              ILIA
   It is not genuine. You are further desecrating the Holy Memory of The Creator.
   Your punishment is well-deserved . . .
                    (to Kirk, as though hoping he'll understand)
   It's logical, don't you see . . . ?

   Kirk looks at her, then past her to:

262 THE MOTION PICTURE PROJECTOR   262
   in the corner. He rises, picks up a film can, reads the label, CAMERA CLOSING on the
   title: "<u>This is NASA</u>."

263 EXT. THE ENTERPRISE AND THE ALIEN   263
   The starship now, again, locked in the alien's tractor beam—and quite close to the
   alien's 'mouth,' and drawn closer and closer.

264 INT. ENTERPRISE - BRIDGE - ANGLE ON THE VIEWER   264
   showing the menacing front-end of the alien, as though moving to swallow up the
   Enterprise (which, indeed, it is). Scott and McCoy are now also present. Sulu's
   chronometer reads: 00:07:32 (and counting down).

                              DECKER
   Are the computer terminals to the library disengaged, Mr. Xon?

                              XON
   They are disengaged, sir; the computer is programmed to communicate to the
   alien only that information we've selected.

265 ACROSS DECKER TO SCOTT   265
   at his bridge engineering station.

                              DECKER
       Mr. Scott . . . ?

SCOTT
(grim)
I'm ready to overload my engines at your order, commander.

Decker hesitates a beat, swivels around to glance at the chronometer: 00:07:12. Now he faces the computer (microphone), speaks:

DECKER
Computer . . . transmit the following: I am sending you information about the cultural and scientific achievements of the human servo-units from the beginning of their time. You will see that although the servo-units differ from pure machine life, they are intelligent creatures who serve useful functions and should not be destroyed. Computer . . . transmit.

A moment where we HEAR the BEEP of the ultra-high-speed message flashing over to the alien. And then another moment, and the responding BEEP.

COMPUTER VOICE
Translating: information received is incomplete.

Glances of dismay are exchanged.

CHEKOV
How could he know . . . ?!

XON
Logic. Pure, mathematical logic.

McCOY
You give him the rest, he'll see every war fought: Alexander, Attila, the Crusades, Napoleon, Hitler. And the terrorism and pollution and famine of the 20th Century. And the 21st Century nuclear wars . . . !
(grim wryness)
He'll see the other side of our 'achievements . . .'!

UHURA
But we're not like that anymore.

DECKER
Then let him see it . . . ! It might convince him that for all our weaknesses, we've survived—and advanced to the point where none of that is necessary any more . . .
(to computer)
Computer . . .

XON
(interrupting)
Excuse me, sir, but if we release that information, we also release information concerning every planet in the Federation. They'll suffer the same fate, sir!

SULU
We have five minutes to detonation.

266 FAVORING DECKER   266

You can read his face: agonized at the decision he faces, the risk he must take: the billions of others on the other planets whose fate might well rest on that decision.

                              XON

Commander, the alien is drawing us closer and closer. If the decision is <u>not</u> to release the remaining information, we must activate our self-destruct systems before his forcefield renders us totally unable to operate our own controls.

                             DECKER

Erase the tapes, Mr. Xon.

The decision made, Decker looks at the others, the CAMERA SWINGING OVER on the clock: the red figures flashing: 00:04:47, 00:04:46, 00:04:45, etc.

267 INT. ARCHIVES ROOM   267

with TWO TECHNICIANS now also in the room, clumsily attempting to set up the antique motion picture projector. Kirk watches impatiently.

                              KIRK

Faster, son. Faster . . . !

                            1ST TECH

I'm trying, sir . . .

268 ANGLE ON ILIA   268

who has been watching all this interestedly. Suddenly she moves to the projector.

                              ILIA

I can assemble it.

And the Technicians step aside as rapidly and expertly Ilia sets up the projector, threads the film.

                              ILIA
                          (continuing)

It's a charming unit—

And almost immediately the film is ready to roll. Ilia caresses the projector lovingly.

                              ILIA
                          (continuing)

How beautiful . . . !

And she switches it on:

269 ON THE SCREEN - THE NASA FILM   269

(PRODUCTION NOTE: this will be an authentic NASA PR film, an old fashioned bureaucratic film about what NASA is, and does, etc.)

The film starts—and then suddenly the pictures are blurred and distorted—scratched, and sometimes the frames are completely <u>blank</u>. And then the film <u>breaks</u>.

NOGURA

My God, it's less than three minutes to detonation . . . !

But Ilia quickly repairs the break, the film resumes. And more of the same—only worse. Kirk reaches over and switches it off.

KIRK

It's three hundred years old; it's deteriorated.

ILIA
(sadly)

I'm sorry.

Kirk and Nogura exchange glances of helplessness. Now it's all over. Kirk switches on the intercom. The face of the Yeowoman appears.

KIRK
(into intercom)

This is a Starfleet Command Order: erase all UFP data from every Starfleet computer library.

270   INT. ENTERPRISE - BRIDGE   270

with, first, a CLOSE SHOT on the chronometer: 00:02:29. Decker is peering at the main viewer—the alien's huge frontal opening. All on the bridge await the inevitable.

DECKER

Mr. Scott . . .

SCOTT

Sir.

DECKER

Activate the self-destruct system, and commence your engine overload.

271   ANGLE ON SCOTT   271

moving his controls

XON
(quietly, to Decker)

You are aware, Commander, that the alien's shields are up full; our matter-anti-matter bomb will not penetrate.

DECKER

I'm aware of it, Mr. Xon . . .
(unhumorous laugh)
I think we might as well go out in style, that's all . . .

Decker turns away, now picks up a small, box-like device with a cross-grained opening (microphone). He begins speaking into it:

DECKER
(continuing)

Captain's Log, Stardate 7421.6. Supplemental, to concur with other logs previously ejected. First Officer Willard Decker in command. Our vessel is now in self-destruct mode, and we have additionally begun overloading our engines to create a matter-anti-matter explosion . . .

Decker pauses, glances at the chronometer: just passing through 00:01:50. He glances at the others: McCoy, Scott, Xon, Uhura, Sulu. He continues:

> DECKER
> (continuing)
> . . . in less than two minutes, the alien's four neutron devices will destroy every living thing on earth . . .

272 INT. ARCHIVES ROOM   272
the clock reading 00:01:45. Nogura and the others peer at the clock, all somewhat stoic, steeling themselves. Kirk is at the intercom; the Yeowoman's face on the screen:

> YEOWOMAN
> The tapes are in erasure condition, sir. It will take approximately five minutes to complete them all.

> KIRK
> (wryly)
> I think that should be just time enough . . . thank you.
> (switches off; to Ilia)
> So you're 'sorry,' eh? Do you know what 'sorry' means?

> ILIA
> It means regret.

> KIRK
> And you can feel that?

> ILIA
> (bemused)
> I think so . . .
> (quickly)
> Kirk, what I'm sorry about is that you have to be destroyed.

> KIRK
> Only me, not the others?

> ILIA
> The others aren't important.

> KIRK
> Everyone is important—that's another difference between humans and machines. It's called morality; it's part of our imperfection.

She studies him, and now more than ever we discern a vitality in her eyes.

> KIRK
> (continuing)
> Ve-jur is wrong to do this. I think you know that.

ILIA
(with sincerity)
Ve-jur can never be wrong.

273   ACROSS KIRK TO THE CLOCK   273
so we can SEE it now reads 00:00:38. Kirk glances at it, then to Ilia again.

KIRK
It's wrong to destroy that which means you no harm.

ILIA
But you harm the machines.

KIRK
No. We built the machines, and together with them we built a great civilization.
Ilia says nothing a moment, turns away from him, then back to him.

ILIA
I don't want to hear anymore . . . !

And she walks away from him, stands so she won't have to face him.

274   THE CLOCK   274
00:00:10 9 8 7.

275   ILIA   275
turning to look at Kirk; her face actually seems twisted in pain, and her eyes are
confused. Then she closes her eyes.

276   KIRK   276
waiting.

277   THE CLOCK   277
00:00:04 3 2 1 0.

278   FULL SHOT OF THE ROOM   278
as Kirk sees the clock at '0,' and glances at Nogura and the others. They're still alive
obviously.

CARSON
It should have happened instantaneously . . .

279   KIRK AND ILIA   279
as he faces her, and she opens her eyes and looks at him.

ILIA
I told Ve-jur you had spoken the truth: The creator was conceived by human
servo-units. I told him I saw the unquestionable evidence.

Kirk looks at her with both bewilderment and gratitude.

KIRK
You lied to him . . . ? Why?

ILIA
(gazing at him)

I don't know.

280 INT. BRIDGE   280
showing, first, Sulu's chronometer: stopped at 00:00:00, everyone peering grimly at
it. Just now Uhura receives a transmission: the familiar BEEP.

UHURA

The alien is signalling . . . !

DECKER
(to Xon)

Engage the computer . . . !
Xon punches the buttons, and a moment later:

COMPUTER VOICE

Translating: Ve-jur has learned that the third planet's servo-units are in truth
the progenitors of The Creator. Therefore, the servo-units will be spared.

281 ANGLE ON SCOTT   281
hearing this, reacting, moving his controls—and speaking into his intercom:

SCOTT
(into intercom)

Disengage the self-destruct unit . . . ! All matter-anti-matter power off!

282 ANOTHER ANGLE - WIDER ON THE PEOPLE   282
showing their relief, as Decker speaks into the computer:

DECKER

Computer . . . transmit the following: USS Enterprise thanks Ve-jur for sparing
its servo-units, and asks Ve-jur if the two life forms can communicate and learn
from each other.

The replying BEEP, and then:

COMPUTER VOICE

Translating: Ve-jur can learn nothing from lower life forms. End of transmission.

SULU

The tractor beam is fading . . . !

283 ANOTHER ANGLE - FAVORING THE VIEWER   283
as the image of the giant alien ship suddenly begins moving away. Before our eyes, it
moves faster and faster, and in an instant is but a speck on the screen. And almost
at the same instant, there is a TURQUOISE FLARE OF LIGHT—and we are SEEING:

284 ILIA   284
the real Ilia, glancing around dazedly.

McCOY
(wryly)

Welcome aboard, Lieutenant.

285 INT. ARCHIVES ROOM   285
as Nogura and the others watch Kirk and Ilia, Kirk talking into his wrist communicator:

                           KIRK
                    (into communicator)
    . . . we're ready, Scottie.

                        SCOTT'S VOICE
    Aye, Captain. The Delphi's waiting to relay you.

Kirk looks at Nogura with a smile of triumph, then turns to Ilia. She reaches out and
touches her hand to his cheek. For a long moment they study each other, and in her
eyes is pure love. Now he gently removes her hand so they can assume the
transporting position. And a moment later, THE SHIMMERING EFFECT.

286 INT. ENTERPRISE - TRANSPORTER ROOM   286
Scott at the console, Xon, Decker, McCoy and Chekov here. The SHIMMERING EFFECT
in the chamber—and then Kirk materializes, and beside him "Ilia"—she has almost
fully materialized when suddenly there is a TURQUOISE FLARE OF LIGHT, and "Ilia"
vanishes and in her place is the Mechanical Tasha—the spidery-legged probe. But
Tasha is completely immobile, silent.

Kirk picks up the probe, examines it. McCoy steps forward with a tricorder, runs it
over the probe.

                           McCOY
    It's completely inert . . . dead.
                          CHEKOV
    But why would it be sent back here . . .?

287 ON KIRK 287
as he peers at the lifeless probe—and remembers the other manifestation of it, the
other Ilia.

                           KIRK
    Maybe because that's what she wanted . . .

And he holds the probe a moment, gazes at it fondly, then puts it down, and is all
business:

                           KIRK
    Gentlemen, the USS Enterprise has been ordered to immediate duty . . .
                    (wryly)
    Our recent experience has served as a shakedown cruise.

                           McCOY
                    ('innocently')
    Is that what it was . . .?

Everyone laughs, as Kirk continues:

                           KIRK
    Those officers desiring to terminate their tours of duty will please so indicate,
    and they will be returned to Starfleet for further assignment.

He looks at them; not a man moves. Kirk faces McCoy; the doctor says nothing, merely faces him sternly. Kirk grins.

                              KIRK
                          (continuing)
Mr. Scott . . .

                              SCOTT
Sir . . .?

                              KIRK
Prepare to depart orbit.

                              SCOTT
Aye, aye, sir . . . !

288   EXT. THE ENTERPRISE   288
       leaving earth orbit. STAR TREK THEME MUSIC comes up, and we HEAR:

                          KIRK'S VOICE
These are the voyages of the Starship Enterprise . . . its <u>new</u> five-year mission to explore . . . etc., etc.

The CAMERA FOLLOWS THE ENTERPRISE as it streaks across the sky, and:
FADE OUT.

                            <u>THE END</u>

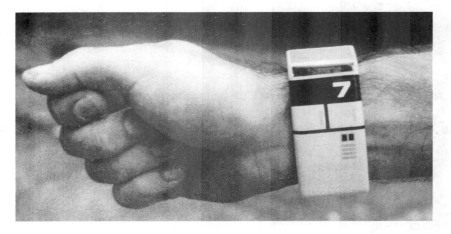

Several of the wrist communicators Brick Price built were fully detailed for close-up photography. However, for scenes in which dozens of extras had to be outfitted with the devices, much flimsier and less expensive versions were constructed so that the inevitable losses to souvenir seekers wouldn't break the prop budget.

Though model-builder Brick Price was disappointed when his beautifully constructed *Phase II* television *Enterprise* was replaced by a version built for motion-picture photography, Gene Roddenberry was sufficiently impressed by the quality of Price's work that Price and his company, Brick Price Movie Miniatures, became an important supplier of key props for *Star Trek: The Motion Picture*. All photos courtesy Brick Price, WonderWorks.

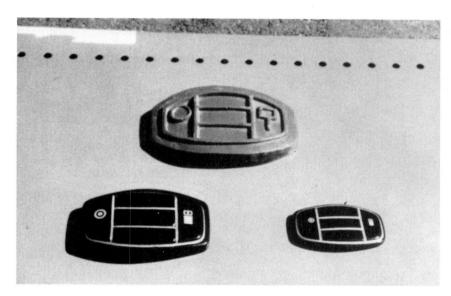

After the studio's first prop supplier delivered the belt-buckle medical monitor at the top of this photo, Gene Roddenberry turned the assignment over to Price, who constructed the more refined versions below.

On today's *Star Trek* productions, props like tricorders and PADDs are built with actual computer control circuits that themselves would have been science fiction during the time of *The Original Series'* production. Even for *Star Trek: The Motion Picture*, Price had to create the illusion of sophisticated, 23rd-century technology with whatever was on hand: in this case, Christmas lights and bulky batteries.

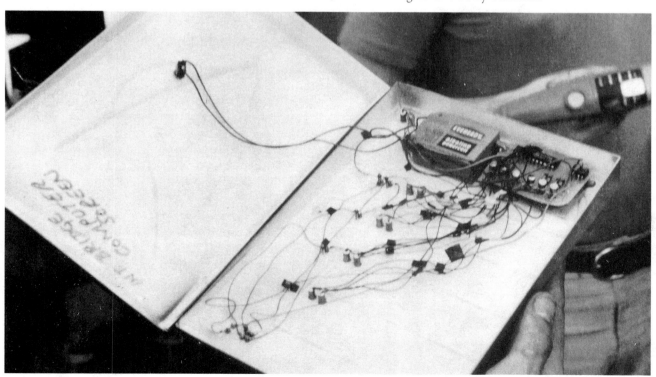

1.

2.

3.

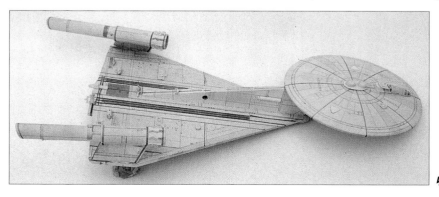

4.

False starts

1. Concept painting of a new *Starship Enterprise* for the never-produced film, *Star Trek: Planet of Titans.* Artist: Ralph McQuarrie. Courtesy of *Starlog* magazine.

2. Concept sketch from the same production. Artist: Ken Adam.

3. A "Superbrain 'Stonehenge' " concept sketch from the same production. Artist: Ken Adam.

4. Concept model based on the Adam/McQuarrie designs. More than a decade later, this model appeared as one of the damaged ships left at Wolf 359, in *Star Trek: The Next Generation* episode, "The Best of Both Worlds, Part II."

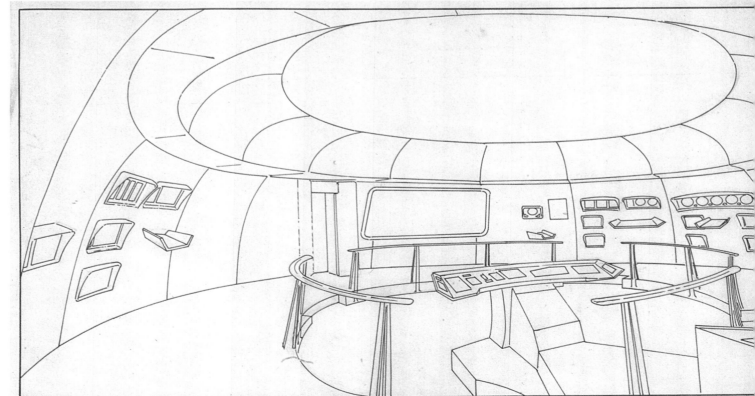

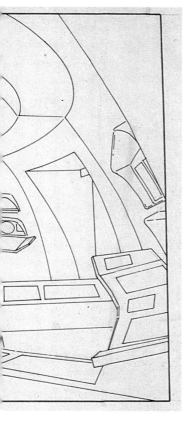

Mike Minor

Mike Minor was one of the early artists who contributed to the look of *The Original Series,* whose influence continues to be seen today. The sketch and his painting of the bridge show that many of his design contributions to *Phase II* made their way to the final set of *Star Trek: The Motion Picture.* Minor's paintings of a crew recreation area depict the smaller set that a television production such as *Phase II* would require. In *The Motion Picture,* the final recreation deck was a much larger, and costlier, two-story set. Paintings courtesy of *Starlog* magazine.

Overleaf
Minor's concept of a modified, *Phase II* transporter room, combining the "psychedelic" back panels of the 1960's with the new console design of the 1970's. Courtesy of Paramount Pictures.

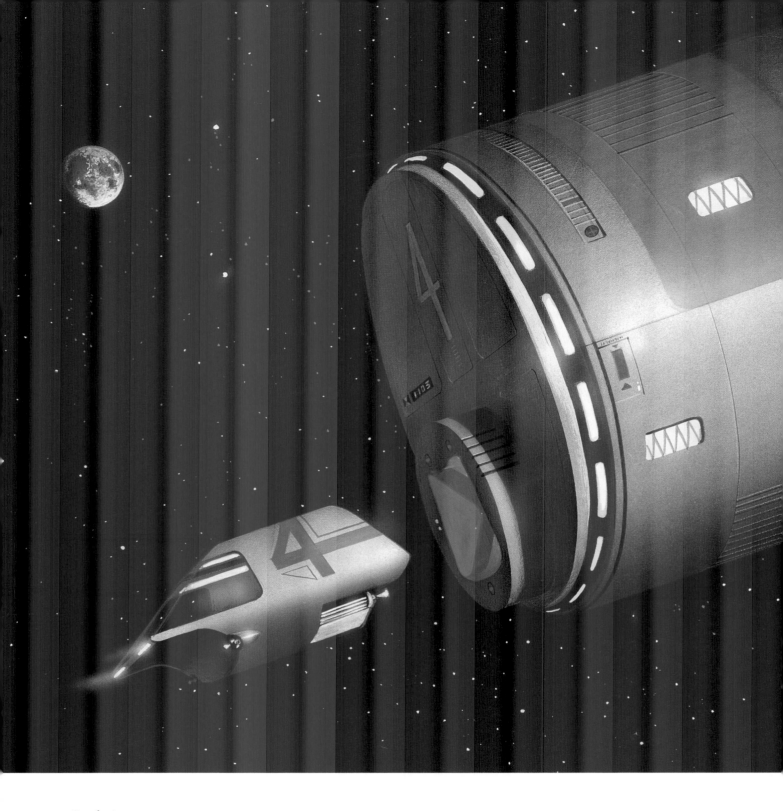

Overleaf
Mike Minor's concept painting for Captain Kirk's quarters.

Space office and travel pod

When "In Thy Image" was chosen to be the pilot story for *Phase II*, a set of opening scenes was added to explain the *Enterprise*'s refit and to show how Captain Kirk and his crew came to be reunited. This concept painting by Mike Minor shows the space office complex from which Kirk and Scott depart to inspect the *Enterprise*.

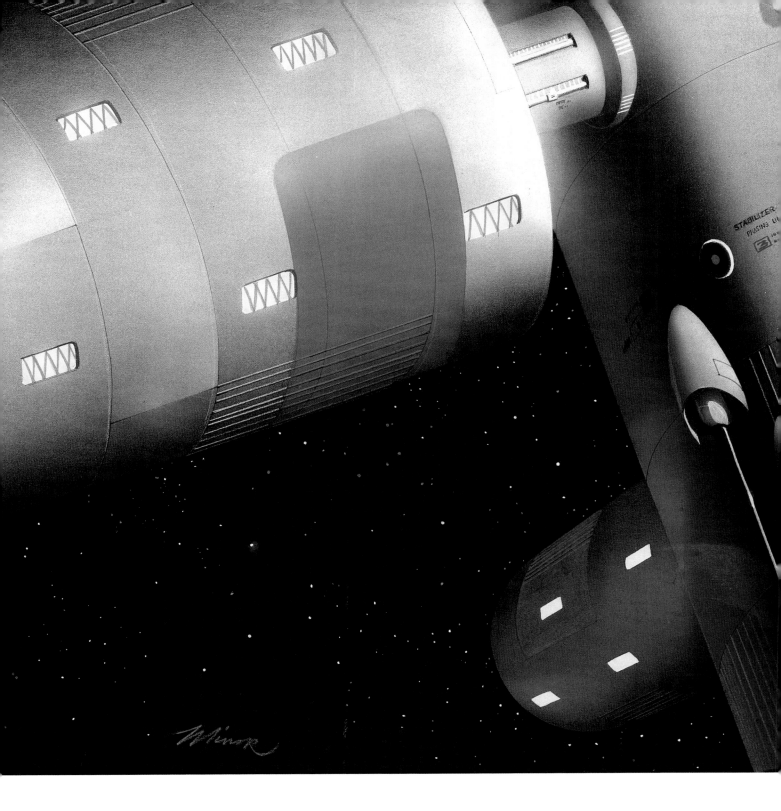

Overleaf

A wider view of Minor's space office and travel pod, showing the *Enterprise* in spacedock. These elements were all completely redesigned for *Star Trek: The Motion Picture.*

Engineering

As this early *Phase II* concept painting shows, Mike Minor's most enduring influence on the look of *Star Trek* has been in Engineering. Both the design and physical elements of this set, first built for *Phase II,* were used in the *Star Trek* movies, and in *Star Trek: The Next Generation.* Its design influence can still be seen in the latest film, *Star Trek: First Contact,* and on the *Starship Voyager.*

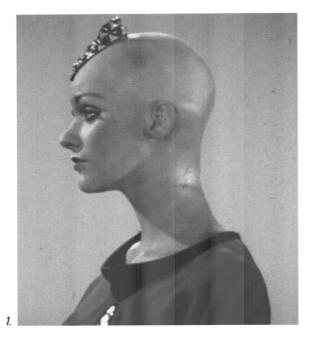

1.

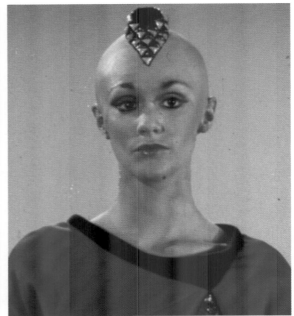

2.

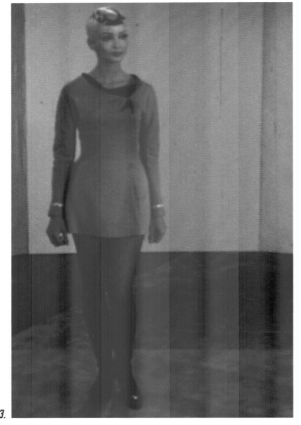

3.

4.

Screen tests

1 - 4. Never-before-seen frames from makeup and costume tests for Ilia, filmed at Paramount on October 27, 1977. To keep costs down for *Phase II*, the producers had decided to retain the costume and wardrobe design from *The Original Series*.

5. & 6. Equally rare frames from test footage shot on the partially completed Engineering set on December 22, 1977. Note the wide-angle format, suitable for motion pictures, but definitely not for television. Plans to change *Phase II*, the series, into *Star Trek: The Motion Picture* were well underway, though still unofficial.

7. Blueprints for the "Electronic Gun" used in the Engineering test footage. This was a single-use prop which was not intended to replace the elaborate new phasers that had already been built. Art Director: Joe Jennings. Draftsman/Set Designer: Lewis Splittsberger.

5.

6.

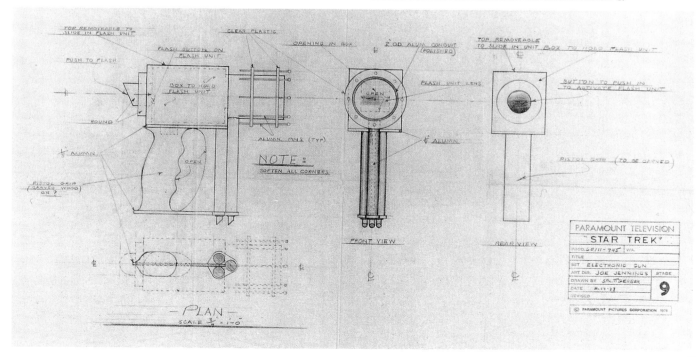

7.

1-6. Additional frames from test footage shot on the Engineering set in December, of 1977.

4.

5.

6.

7. A frame from test footage of a Mike Minor-designed console on the partially completed bridgeset. Instrumentation design by Lee Cole.

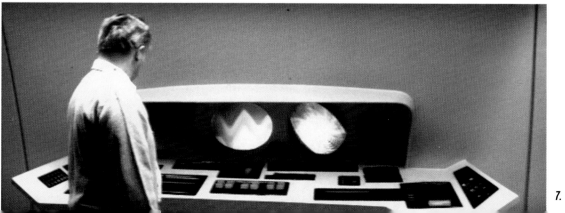

7.

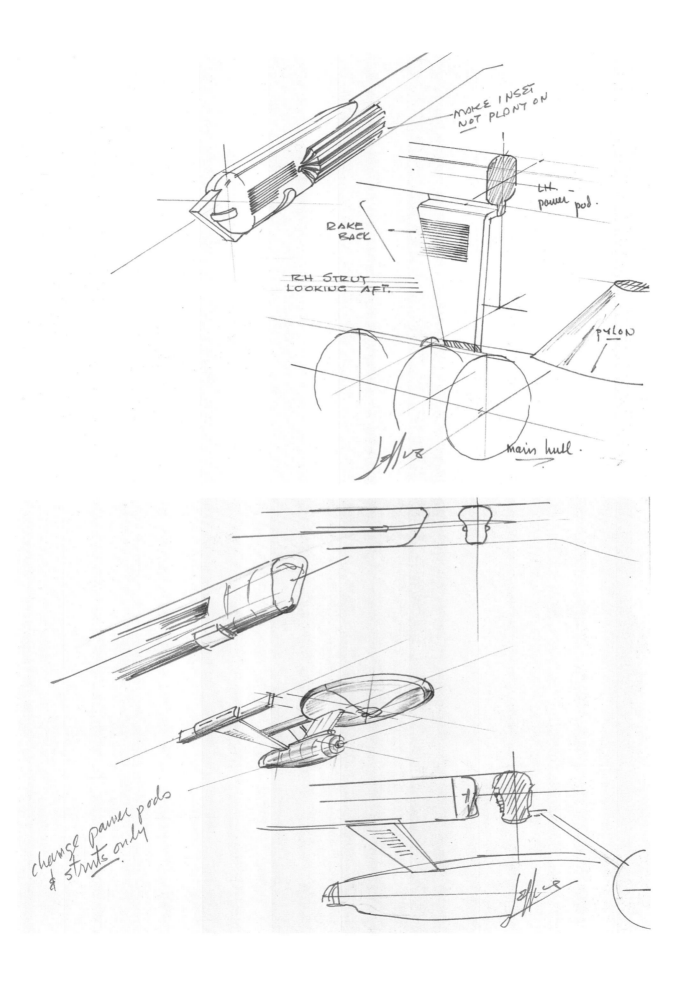

MAKE INSET
NOT PLANT ON

LH.
power pod.

RAKE
BACK

RH STRUT
LOOKING AFT.

PYLON

main hull.

change power pods
& struts only.

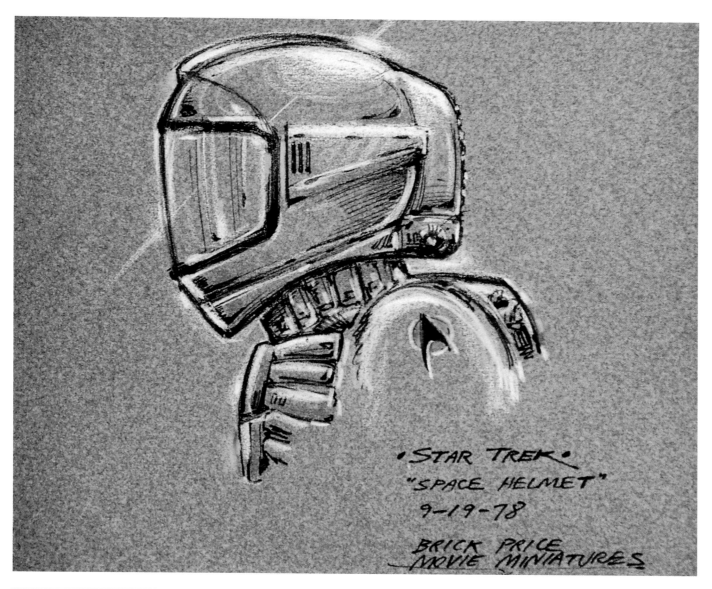

STAR TREK
"SPACE HELMET"
9-19-78

BRICK PRICE
MOVIE MINIATURES

Brick Price

Long one of *Star Trek*'s unsung heroes, Brick Price was the model maker who built the *Phase II Starship Enterprise*, which is shown here while being assembled. Unfortunately, the model Paramount had him build geared toward for the resolution demands of television, not motion-picture film. When *Star Trek: The Motion Picture* required the construction of a new *Enterprise*, Price continued to work for the production, supplying many new props and costume pieces, though his work was not credited in the final film. Photographs courtesy of Andrew Probert. Artwork courtesy of Brick Price Movie Miniatures.

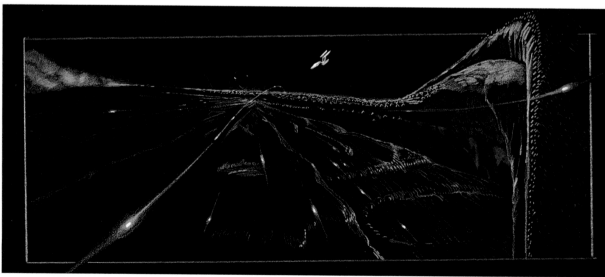

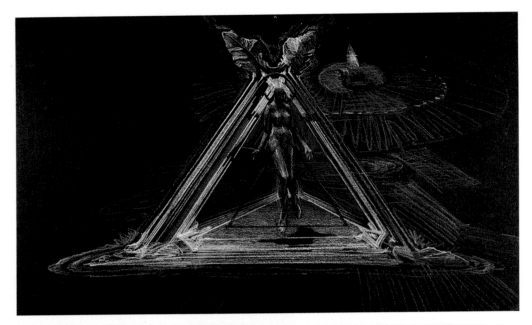

And lest we forget that all television and movie projects first draw life from the written word ... from the original treatment of "In Thy Image" by Alan Dean Foster, July 31, 1977 ...

"... *Against that gleaming leviathan the* Enterprise *is a tiny whitish shape ... .*"

The Lost Stories

The First Thirteen Episodes

Thirteen is a magic number for a television series because it represents half a season. Five half-season orders equal sixty-five episodes, which is the critical threshold number for success in syndication. Sixty-five episodes can be run on a daily basis, five days a week, for . . . thirteen weeks. Which brings us back to the beginning.

With an initial order for a two-hour pilot and thirteen episodes, Star Trek Phase II quickly earned a reputation as one of the toughest shows to sell to in Hollywood. Unlike most other series starting their first season, Phase II had the added complication of being a continuation of an earlier series for which 79 stories had already been told—101, if you include the animated episodes.

As Story Editor, Jon Povill had the responsibility of listening to literally hundreds of pitches from a stream of writers to select those stories he felt were worthy of being considered by the producers. Unlike simple prose writing, television stories not only must be good, they must be able to be told within an hour, while fitting into the show's production and special-effects budget.

The stories, presented here in synopsis form, are those that met all the criteria set for the new version of Star Trek. As in the Original Series and the current series, some of these stories might have been destined to be classics; some, perhaps, not as fondly recalled. Yet all are, without question, interesting and live up to Star Trek's ongoing mandate to explore the human condition.

Two of these first thirteen stories, in particular, demonstrated their soundness and appeal when they were rewritten to appear as episodes of The Next Generation— "Devil's Due,"[1] by William Douglas Lansford, and "The Child," by Jaron Summers & Jon Povill.[2] At the end of the synopses, the original, Phase II script of "The Child" is reprinted in full.

These are the voyages of the Starship Enterprise...
on its second five-year mission...
to boldly go where no one has gone before...again.

[1] *The Next Generation* credits are: Teleplay: Philip Lazebnik. Story by Philip Lazebnik and William Douglas Lansford.

[2] *The Next Generation* credits are: Written by Jaron Summers & Jon Povill and Marice Hurley.

"Tomorrow and the Stars"

Written by Larry Alexander

This time-travel story is reminiscent of "The City on the Edge of Forever," with Kirk falling in love with a woman on Earth at the time of the attack on Pearl Harbor. However, this time Kirk's passion is for a married woman, giving the romantic angle of the story a slightly edgier approach. Once again, a transporter malfunction gets the story started, and Kirk faces the dilemma of knowing he must not take action to save the lives of thousands of people—including the woman he loves—or he will forever alter history.

During an unsuccessful but damaging Klingon attack on the *Enterprise*, Lieutenant Chekov is infected by a deadly toxin, "iridium seven contact." Initial symptoms include the appearance of extensive burns over exposed skin and progressive, painful delirium. While Doctors Leonard McCoy and Christine Chapel try to restrain and sedate Chekov, who believes he is still in the midst of the space battle with the Klingons,

Captain Kirk advises his injured officer that they are, in fact, safe, and in Earth orbit and ready to transport Chekov to the surface for treatment.

Kirk is concerned when he learns that Lieutenant Xon has detected a defective molecular circuit in the ship's transporter. However, Dr. McCoy warns Kirk that every second counts in getting Chekov into a radiation unit on Earth. After hearing from Xon that the probability of successful performance is 94.6%, Chief Engineering Officer Montgomery Scott vouches for the system's safety. Dr. Chapel and two orderlies will accompany Chekov.

Before the transport begins, Kirk also betrays signs of exposure to iridium seven contact and Dr. McCoy orders him to go Earthside for several days in detox. After telling Xon and Scott that Commander Decker is now in command, Kirk reluctantly joins Chekov, Dr. Chapel, and the orderlies on the transporter platform. Scott begins the familiar dematerialization procedure, but something goes wrong. Xon's check reveals that all but Kirk have arrived. Kirk's transmission is not complete.

While Scott and Xon work to maintain contact with Kirk's energy beam, the transporter chamber is suddenly shaken by a tremendous rumbling, and the air fills with electronic sounds and an unintelligible static. Then all ceases as Xon announces that Kirk's reassembly has taken place, though he has no idea where.

Meanwhile, Kirk materializes in luxuriant jungle that's resplendent with exotic flowers. To his horror, he discovers that his body is somehow transparent and that he cannot make physical contact with his surroundings. When he calls out to his shipmates, he is answered, instead, by a strange woman's voice and the sound of an opening door.

Concealing himself, Kirk is startled to see a human woman dressed in the fashion styles of Earth's 1930s. The woman, Elsa Kelly, holds a telephone in her hand. When she detects no one in her garden, she returns to her telephone conversation, which Kirk now overhears. The conversation indicates that the woman has a relationship with someone called Richard who is expecting to go to an Officers' Club Dance that evening with her. As Kirk listens, he continues trying to pick fruit off a tree and to drink from a fountain in the garden without success. Before the woman finishes her telephone call, he enters her home unseen to try his luck at finding food and drink in her kitchen. In his concentration, he does not realize that the woman has entered the kitchen behind him. Kirk attempts to talk to her but she panics and runs away.

On the *Enterprise*, McCoy rails at Xon, saying Kirk may well have been sent to his death in one of Earth's oceans. Before Xon's calm, Vulcan responses to McCoy's worried anger can further exasperate the ship's doctor, Decker appears. Xon volunteers that he has been analyzing a tape of the events that took place in the transporter room

when Kirk was lost. He replays the tape and directs their attention to the mysterious background sounds that occurred just as Kirk reassembled. As Xon slows the tape, the sounds become recognizable as voices, though the language they speak is unknown to Decker, McCoy, and Xon. When Xon requests the Universal Translator to decode the language, it is unable to comply. The computer informs them that it suffered a programming erasure during the Klingon encounter.

In his as-yet unknown location, Kirk speaks into his communicator to record a Captain's Log entry of his impressions of what has happened to him. Elsa returns and interrupts him. She tells him that she did not notify the authorities about him, because she did not know how she would account for his transparent state. When Kirk questions her, she reveals that he is in Honolulu, Hawaii. Kirk gives her his name and tells her he is the commander of a ship. Elsa says her husband is also in the navy though she has never seen a naval uniform like that of Kirk's. Kirk refuses to tell Elsa why his uniform is unusual. He deflects her curiosity by focusing her attention on his desperate need for sustenance, which neither of them can think how to solve. Elsa's compassion for his predicament touches him.

Richard Kelly returns home, and Kirk cautions his new friend that her husband could easily decide that Kirk is a spy or that his appearance signals some new kind of foreign weapon. Elsa tells Kirk that she believes him when he says he is harmless, and that is why she will not reveal his existence. But she warns him to leave before she and her husband return from the Officers' Club.

Kirk overhears a discussion between Elsa and Richard about a pending war, and then conceals himself in the garden to wait until they leave. There is a possibility that as Richard waited for Elsa to get ready, he had seen Kirk.

As Uhura works to patch through to an Earthside language translator, Xon and Decker replay the tape and Lieutenant Sulu identifies the language as Middle-form Japanese, spoken during the Emperor days. Before the computer can provide a translation, Sulu tells Xon and Decker that the subject is the coordinates of two military targets—one of them an airfield between two mountain ranges.

Back on Earth, Kirk has stowed away in the Kelly car to follow them to the Officers' Dance. There, he learns that Richard Kelly is anxious to speak to an Admiral Grant about the coming war. While Richard does so, Kirk comes to the aid of Elsa when she leaves her husband's side, goes for a walk on the beach, and is accosted by two threatening MPs. Kirk's strange appearance frightens off the MPs. In their subsequent conversation, Kirk learns that he and Elsa are in Pearl Harbor and that the date is December 6, 1941. He leaves Elsa momentarily to get a better view of the harbor, and Richard Kelly returns while he is gone. Richard is exuberant, telling Elsa that the Admiral agrees with his view of the coming war and wishes to discuss Richard's theory first thing in his office at the beginning of the week.

On the *Enterprise*, Decker, Xon, and Scott have developed a theory of their own about what went wrong when Kirk's transmission was lost: The transporter became a time machine when its electronics were fused in the Klingon attack. A dimensional vortex appeared, then disappeared, taking the captain with it, right into the middle of the Japanese attack on Pearl Harbor. Now that they have pinpointed his location in time, they must pinpoint his exact location in space. Before they can lock onto Kirk, they must next recreate the same condition in the transporter unit that existed during the ill-fated beamdown. And for Kirk's safety, they must do so before the war on Earth breaks out.

On Earth, Kirk is feeling increasingly frustrated by his inability to connect physically with his surroundings. In his torment, he lets slip to Elsa that he is the commander of a starship, and then confirms her suspicions that he is, in fact, from her future. In the midst of their discussion, Scott attempts to locate Kirk once more, and this time makes contact. While he is unable to retrieve Kirk, Kirk becomes physically united with his body as a result. Elsa and Kirk respond by embracing one another.

Richard Kelly unexpectedly returns home for some papers and sees Kirk emerging from his home with Elsa, who is taking him to the home of a friend who is on the mainland for a few weeks. Neither Kirk nor Elsa sees Richard.

Kirk's next goal is to somehow alter his communicator to use 1941 technology and materials to make contact with his ship. Elsa says she will help him, although she does not want him to leave without her. As they take a break on the beach, they both realize they have fallen in love with each other.

While Kirk and Elsa are on the beach, Richard and several Navy Intelligence officers break into Elsa's friend's apartment and find Kirk's communicator. They conclude that Kirk is a spy. When Kirk and Elsa return, Kirk is arrested. Before they can take Kirk away, Elsa creates a diversion and helps Kirk escape.

With only minutes to spare before the Japanese attack, McCoy and Decker materialize in the Kelly house and use their tricorders to detect evidence of Kirk's recent presence two kilometers away. They commandeer a parked car nearby to travel to Elsa's friend's house where they find Kirk's altered communicator.

At the same time, Kirk and Elsa have pulled off the road to talk about what they will do. As the drone of approaching warplanes begins, Kirk inadvertently alerts Elsa to the imminent attack and Elsa says they must warn Richard, who is stationed on the doomed *Arizona,* and all the others who will otherwise die. Kirk argues that they must not change what is for him the past since the future depends on it.

Bombs begin to fall. Decker and McCoy reach Kirk. Elsa rushes off to do what she can, after telling Kirk that she understands but that she is part of history, too, and so is their love for one another. Kirk tries to follow her, but is retrieved by Decker and McCoy. Decker contacts Scott with his communicator, and Kirk, Decker, and McCoy are transported back to the *Enterprise*.

On board ship, McCoy and the ship's counsellor, Ilia, go to Kirk's quarters to comfort and soothe Kirk. Ilia's Deltan caress helps Kirk focus on the enrichment that he and Elsa brought to one another's lives. Grateful to his friends for their intervention, Kirk again assumes his position on the bridge, ready for the next adventure.

"Cassandra"

Written by Theodore Sturgeon

One of the many reasons for Star Trek's enduring appeal is that it has room for so many different styles of stories, including comedies. Both "The Trouble With Tribbles" and "A Piece of the Action" are longtime fan favorites, and this story about a clumsy yeoman and a tiny, trouble-causing creature might easily have joined their ranks.

Theodore Sturgeon, of course, was one of science fiction's greatest writers. For the Original Series, he wrote the episodes "Shore Leave" and "Amok Time."

The *Enterprise* is in orbit over the planet Manlikt, after bringing back the Manlikt foreign minister, Hibchiba, from a highly successful peace conference. Because Hibchiba refuses to use the transporter, the *Enterprise* cannot leave until its shuttle, which is taking the foreign minister to the planet's surface, returns and is secure.

Although unified, the planet Manlikt is populated by two humanoid species, the Manlikt and the Breet. The Manlikt closely resemble the peo-

ple of Earth. The Breet have long snouts and tails. Traditional enemies for centuries, the two races have at last signed a firm nonaggression treaty.

But just as the *Enterprise* prepares to leave orbit, Uhura reports to Kirk that she has picked up a planetwide broadcast announcing a six-hour ultimatum by the Manlikt against the Breet. The Manlikt are vowing to use their equivalent of the doomsday bomb unless the Breet return the "Sacred Monitor," the most precious treasure of planet Manlikt.

Kirk asks Uhura to raise the foreign minister. Onscreen, Hibchiba froths with fury as he tells how a Breet agent disguised as a Manlikt security officer has been arrested on the Sacred Ground, three meters from where he, Hibchiba, was set down by the *Enterprise*'s shuttle and five meters from the resting place of the Sacred Monitor. The foreign minister tells Kirk that the big bomb will be launched if the treasure is not returned within five hours and forty minutes. The Manlikt simply do not wish to live without the Sacred Monitor.

Xon tells Kirk that the Sacred Monitor, though a closely guarded secret, seems to be some sort of device by which the Manlikt foretell the future. They regard it as the keystone of their security.

Even before Kirk hears of the theft of the Sacred Monitor, a clumsy novice yeoman on board the *Enterprise*, Myra Kart, has encountered a strange object—a large egg—while cleaning the shuttle after the craft returned from planet Manlikt. Unfortunately, Kart also dropped the egg and cracked it. Believing its contents to be a life-form of some sort, she puts the cracked egg in a sealbag and takes it to Doctors Chapel and McCoy in sickbay. The two doctors are distracted by Yeoman Kart's clumsiness—she breaks a beaker in sickbay, and do not take much notice of the sealbag she gives them. Donning sterile gloves, McCoy carries the bag to a glass box, opens it, and drops the bag in as he releases its closure. Then he closes the box. He remarks to Chapel that because conditions on Manlikt are so close to Earth Normal, he won't have to set up an atmosphere for Kart's life-form. Then both he and Chapel are flabbergasted by what happens. The bag twitches and squirms and a head pops out of it as a little creature, Cassandra, looks Chapel up and down and says in a deep bass voice: "Oh, my, if you aren't just the *cutest* little old bug . . . !"

Now, following Kirk's involvement in the threatening situation on planet Manlikt, Yeoman Kart enters sickbay, sees the glass box, and looks into it. She repeats the exact words Cassandra used to address Chapel: "Oh, my, if you aren't just the *cutest* little old bug . . . !" Then she lifts Cassandra out and cuddles her. This time Cassandra bellows: "How come you never smile?" before she leaps out of Kart's arms and disappears through the open door. Kart rushes after her.

A few minutes later, Xon, in the ship's recreation room, encounters a crew member who asks him the same question we just heard Cassandra ask: "How come you never smile?" Xon is still standing deep in thought, puzzled, when Ilia joins him, and he asks her about the purpose of smiling. Suddenly, Cassandra streaks past both of them to perch on Chief Engineer Scott's shoulder as Scott is in the midst of a poker game with Chekov. Yeoman Kart charges after Cassandra. She tells Scott: "It's all right . . . she won't hurt you. . . . " Scott keeps his calm. Cassandra speaks softly into Scott's ear: "All he's got is a pair of eights." Scott doubles his bet. Chekov takes the pot. Scott tells Kart: "She can so hurt you."

As Scott continues the game, Kart takes Cassandra away. As Cassandra passes Ilia, the little creature says: "Condition yellow. Condition yellow. Stand by." In the background, we hear Scott and Chekov continue their game. Scott challenges Chekov to call him if he believes the chief engineer is bluffing. Chekov folds. Scott grins and reveals his hand. Chekov moans: "All he's got is a pair of eights." Which is, of course, what Cassandra had said earlier. Overhearing this exchange causes Xon to frown slightly.

On the bridge, First Officer Decker advises Kirk that if the Manlikt explode their bomb, it might be better if the *Enterprise* were a thousand kilometers farther out. Kirk agrees, touches his console, and orders: "Condition yellow. Condition yellow. Stand by."

Then Uhura informs Kirk that the Breet government is swearing its innocence of the theft and claiming the Manlikt are using it as an excuse to wipe them out. The Breet are now mobilizing, and they may well strike first. Kirk asks Uhura to hail the Manlikt foreign minister.

At the same time, Cassandra is wreaking havoc on the ship. She obtains a communicator, and Chekov is going crazy with a direction finder, trying to track down the busy little creature with it.

Kirk interrogates Hibchiba for more details about the appearance of the Sacred Monitor. Reluctantly, the foreign minister tells him that it is very small, about the size of a large egg. In fact, it is an egg.

Xon uses his powers of logic and reasoning on the mystery. He restates what they know: A Breet spy was found among the guard when the shuttle landed on Manlikt, close to where the treasure was kept. He asks Hibchiba if a false egg was placed there. The foreign minister says there was. Xon asks if anything was found on the spy. Hibchiba says there was not. Therefore, Xon says, the egg was stolen and put aboard the *Enterprise* shuttle. The treasure is thus most likely on board the *Enterprise.*

Kirk immediately puts the ship on alert. A description of the missing treasure is broadcast on all decks. Anyone with pertinent information is to report at once to the bridge. A thorough search is begun.

Yeoman Kart reports to the bridge and tells Kirk where she found the egg, how she dropped it, turned it over to McCoy and Chapel, and then later went to visit it because it was so "cute." Xon asks Kart if the egg in question produced the animal she was pursuing in the recreation room. She says it did, but she thought it was some kind of bird.

Kirk is furious. He tells Kart one and a half billion people are going to die if her "cute" creature is not returned within the next few hours. Then Kirk goes back on the ship's intercom to summon McCoy and Chapel *and* the creature to the bridge.

The doctors display Cassandra to Foreign Minister Hibchiba, whose anxious image is on the viewscreen. He is overjoyed and says he will come up personally to the *Enterprise* as soon as he can issue a cease-fire and reassure the Breet.

Kirk asks Chapel to take Kart "down below," which Kart thinks means she is to report to Scott in Engineering.

Next, Uhura reports that she is receiving a special tight-beam message from the planet. She tells Kirk that three messengers from the Foreign Ministry are asking to beam up with their credentials. They have orders to bring back the Sacred Monitor. Chekov explains their request as good

security procedure. The three messengers will arrive, pick up the treasure, and depart even before the foreign minister boards his shuttle for the *Enterprise.* The announcement of the safe return of the treasure to the planet will let the minister himself return in safety. Kirk approves the messengers' request.

As Chief Engineer Scott completes the dematerialization of the three messengers, he asks Yeoman Kart to light up the corridor for the three visitors. Hurrying to comply, Kart accidentally palms the wrong control. She activates the switch marked: Damage Control. Instantly, steel gates slide down with a crash, trapping the three messengers and subjecting them to heavy jets of water that knock them from their feet. Scott works frantically at his controls to free them as Kirk demands to know what is happening down in Engineering. Scott tells him of Kart's latest misadventure, while the bridge crew follows the event on their viewscreen.

Suddenly, Xon draws Kirk's attention to the state of the messengers. Ilia cries out, "Breets!" as the Manlikt disguises that cloaked the three Breet spies dissolve and fall away under the onslaught of the water jets. Their Breet snouts and tails emerge.

Cassandra is also watching the proceedings and cries out: "People of Manlikt, this is a historical, nay, an epochal moment." Then Xon reveals Cassandra's secret as he says to Kirk, "You will hear that from the screen, in approximately four minutes and forty seconds." Xon has determined that Cassandra says not what she has heard, but what she *will* hear several minutes into the future. Decker states that must be why the Manlikt refer to her as their oracle. Xon says he will now have to review some of his theories about the nature of time.

When Hibchiba's shuttle docks with the *Enterprise,* the foreign minister brings with him a gilded cage for Cassandra and a heavy gold chain and medallion with which to honor Yeoman Kart as the heroic captor of the Breet spies. As

Cassandra is ported off, her parting words are: "I never guessed you had that kind of muscle."

Next Kirk tells Kart that: "For the good you have done, you are hereby raised two ranks in grade. For the trouble you have caused, you are hereby reduced two ranks." But before he adds that a term in the brig might be in order, Xon comes to Kart's defense, pointing out that at no time did Yeoman Kart act in transgression of regulations, disobey an order, or fail in her duty. A careful review of her record, though it contains some demerits, shows not one single example of a repeated offense. Since imprisonment is no longer punitive, but merely used to keep the perpetrator from repeating an offense, it clearly is not warranted. Kirk admits defeat.

As McCoy asks Xon what motivated him to make such a speech, Xon tells him in his ongoing study of human motivations, he has been practicing one which is not at all reasonable, nor easy. It is called compassion. Admiringly, McCoy tells Xon: "I never guessed you had that kind of muscle," then claps his hand over his mouth, realizing he has just parroted Cassandra's last words.

Xon's last words are: "Compassion is a lot easier than smiling."

"Kitumba, Part 1"

Written by John Meredyth Lucas

This two-part epic gives us a fascinating glimpse at an alternate Klingon Empire, a culture that had never been examined in detail in the Original Series, and that later developed along substantially different lines in The Next Generation. With a complex plot, cloak-and-dagger action, and political maneuverings, the "Kitumba" scripts contain many of the elements that would later show up in The Next Generation episodes involving Klingon and Romulan politics.

John Meredyth Lucas also wrote the scripts for the Original Series episodes "Patterns of Force" and "Elaan of Troyius," and the teleplay for "That Which Survives."

While monitoring a part of the galaxy beset with tension, the *Enterprise* receives a coded signal from Starfleet to engage in a puzzlingly simple mission. Kirk's orders are to immediately proceed to Starfleet Command to pick up a patient suffering from radiation burns.

As soon as the *Enterprise* is in standard orbit above the space station housing Starfleet Command, Admiral Li Po Yu, an old friend of Kirk's, beams aboard. Kirk orders sickbay to break out the radiation gear, and he turns the conn over to Decker before heading to the transporter room with Dr. McCoy. Surprisingly, Admiral Li wears no radiation gear. She also tells Kirk and McCoy that they may dispense with their own bulky radiation suits, although their patient is still expected shortly.

Kirk questions the real purpose behind his orders, pointing out that he has monitored coded commands to thirty starships. Admiral Li responds by asking to speak privately with Kirk. She then goes on to tell Kirk that Starfleet Intelligence drones report starships being built in orbit around hundreds of Klingon subject planets. Starfleet's Intelligence chiefs are warning of an imminent overwhelming attack. When Kirk questions the ability of anyone to guess what the

Klingons are planning, Li simply tells him: "It's been confirmed, Jim." She then tells him to beam up his passengers.

When Kirk does so, a fully armed Klingon materializes on the *Enterprise*'s transporter platform. Amused by Kirk's stunned reaction, Li introduces the Klingon to Kirk: "Captain Kirk, this is Ksia. He was tutor to the Kitumba, the Sacred Ruler of the Klingons."

Based on his own experience with Klingons, Kirk does not readily accept Admiral Li's statement that Ksia stopped a border patrol ship and asked to be brought to Federation headquarters. Kirk points out that the few Klingons ever captured have never talked, preferring death at their own hands. Ksia agrees with Kirk, but notes that he was not captured. Admiral Li acknowledges Kirk's concerns but tells him that the General Staff believes the danger justifies the risks. Especially since Ksia has told them the Klingons will attempt a secret, massive strike against the Federation. Ksia hopes to avert the attack, believing it will damage the Klingons as much as their enemy. Ksia tells a skeptical Kirk that he has chosen to warn the Federation only because his own people are not properly prepared for such an all-out war.

To counter Kirk's disbelief, Admiral Li and Ksia provide Kirk with some significant information about the structure of Klingon society. Klingon is the name given not to the people, but to the male and female warriors who comprise the ruling class. Serving this group are the Technos—the scientists and technicians—and the Subjects. Above the Klingons, Technos, and Subjects are the warlord and the Kitumba. The warlord rules in the name of the Kitumba, a near god-king sacred figurehead confined by custom to the Sacred Planet in the center of the Klingon system. Admiral Li adds that the current Kitumba is a seventeen-year-old boy whom Ksia tutored until the present warlord, Malkthon, intervened. Malkthon requested that Ksia commit ritual suicide as a subversive influence, and he has made the Kitumba a "pampered prisoner."

When Kirk asks whether Ksia's desire for peace is shared by others, Ksia tells him about a rebel group of noblemen, the Baros, who do not oppose war in general, but do oppose Malkthon and his ill-timed and insane plan for this war. Admiral Li then gives Kirk his real orders: ". . . take the *Enterprise* deep into Klingon space . . . to the Sacred Planet." Then, with Ksia's guidance to evade the Klingon patrols and defenses, seek out the Kitumba and avert the war.

Kirk turns Ksia over to Dr. McCoy for medical examination to prepare the doctor for any injury to the Klingon that might require knowledgeable treatment. Then Kirk takes the opportunity to warn Li that if Starfleet's fastest, most modern starship were to be captured by Klingons, "nothing could help them more than to study our best weapon." He adds that they have no guarantee that the Kitumba will listen nor that the *Enterprise* will not be attacked.

Admiral Li then gives Kirk the second half of his orders: "The *Enterprise* is *not* to fall into Klingon hands. You will be prepared to implode the matter-antimatter reactors." Kirk tells her he understands, and as she dematerializes, he adds: "We are expendable." The *Enterprise* proceeds to the Klingon border at warp 6.

Kirk instructs his staff to treat Ksia, until otherwise indicated, as an ally, with full run of the ship. As Scott, Ilia, and Xon engage Ksia in wary discussions about Klingon practices and beliefs, Xon breaks off to report an unknown blip on the ship's sensors. When maximum magnification on the viewer screen fails to produce an identifiable object, Ksia volunteers to work with Xon, believing it might be a Klingon ghost ship—a vessel with invisibility shields, which might report the position of Kirk's ship to Malkthon.

Kirk pursues the Klingon craft and destroys it only after it becomes obvious that the Klingon commander will never respond to any surrender demand, believing a warrior's honor lies only in dying well. The crew of the *Enterprise* is again reminded of the differing philosophies of the

Federation and the Klingon Empire. Xon does point out, to McCoy's disgust, that the Klingon commander "took the only logical course to prevent a much larger loss of life"—theirs and those on board the Klingon vessel.

As the *Enterprise* crosses the neutral zone, Ilia reports that ship's sensors are picking up objects at extreme range—a battle group of five Klingon ships. Kirk orders Sulu to stop all engines and let the ship drift. He then hits upon a diversionary tactic. He asks Ksia to use the Klingon battle code to broadcast a call for help as if it came from the nearest Klingon colony, Gamma 35. The tactic works. Ksia terms Kirk's action clever, if not honorable.

Now free of pursuers, Kirk's ship enters Klingon space. The Klingon home system consists of a small star orbited by a Class-M planet, the Sacred Planet of the Kitumba, and Ultar, a second, larger main planet only slightly bigger than Earth and home to the Klingon warlord, Malkthon. To an incredulous Decker, Ksia maintains that there are no defenses against invaders here. Xon likens the Klingon sense of invulnerability to that of ancient Rome on Earth. Kirk points out that there may not be walls, but there will be starships. Ksia tells him his best weapons will be speed and surprise: "It will not be expected that a lone starship would penetrate so deep into Klingon territory."

Ten heavy armed starships appear suddenly, the outer defense patrol protecting the Home System. Kirk directs Sulu to plot a course for Ultar. He intends to draw the Klingon ships off, then double back at maximum warp—against Starfleet directives. Ksia mirrors the shock felt by Kirk's own crew. Kirk orders Scott to divert all power to the shields. He then has Ilia use her empath powers to probe Ksia's mind for a detailed mental image of the entry path to the Home System. At the instant the Klingon starships bombard the *Enterprise*, a replica of the *Enterprise* appears in space and draws off three of the Klingons. Xon then deploys a second replica decoy that lures off another group of pursuers.

Uhura intercepts Klingon transmissions informing Ultar of their presence. Then Kirk has Sulu reverse course. The Klingons veer to avoid collision with one another.

At maximum warp and on automatic computer navigation, the *Enterprise* enters the Klingon Home System. Just before impact with the main planet, the ship drops to sublight and Sulu achieves standard orbit. Kirk directs Uhura to open a hailing channel.

Baro Taru, deputy warlord, appears onscreen and, though furious, grants Kirk's request for sanctuary. She reminds him that if he violates the rules of sanctuary, the penalty is death. Kirk makes an additional request: to meet with the Kitumba. Taru says Malkthon will ask the Kitumba for a decision.

While they wait for an answer, Ksia tells Kirk the young Kitumba has had "the power" for only four years, following the sudden and unexpected death of his father. Ksia feels his former pupil will be curious about the alien spaceship and will grant a meeting with Kirk. Kirk reminds Decker that if there is no meeting, their orders are clear: They must destroy the *Enterprise* themselves.

When Taru reappears on the viewer, she tells Kirk the Kitumba will meet him and his escorts. When Kirk says he will take Ksia with him, Ksia demurs, saying he cannot set foot on the Sacred Planet because of his shame. Though Kirk must go unarmed, Ksia advises him to wear a ceremonial sword so that the Klingon warriors will respect him. Decker offers to provide him with one from his Academy dress uniform. Ksia also urges Kirk to take an appropriate gift and gives him a dagger to present to the Kitumba, but only if Baro Kali is present. Kirk says he does not want to act as a spy carrying messages, but Ksia says Kali is the head of the Peace Party that opposes Malkthon.

Kirk and Scott beam down to the planet. In Kirk's absence, Decker is free to act as he wishes, but he must implode the *Enterprise*'s engines if capture is threatened.

When Kirk meets the young Kitumba and the

leader's six-year-old brother, Kirk makes his case for peace rather than war between the Federation and the Klingon Empire. Though the Kitumba greets his proposal thoughtfully, Taru moves to cut the audience short when Kirk mentions trade. Having noted the presence of Ksia's ally, Kirk quickly adds that he has brought a gift and he gives the dagger to Kali, who palms it and gives a duplicate one to the Kitumba.

Back on the *Enterprise*, Ksia tells Kirk that the dagger carried a message telling Kali how to signal Kirk to return for a meeting he would arrange with the Kitumba. Ksia instructs Kirk in dressing as a Klingon subject. Before Kirk beams back down, he learns that Ksia fears Malkthon will soon move against the Kitumba himself if the young leader opposes Malkthon's war.

When Kali's signal appears—a fire in a sector of the city—Kirk beams down alone against Decker's objections. As he departs, Kirk tells Decker: "This whole mission's a trap. But a trap works both ways."

Before he takes Kirk to the Kitumba, Kali tells Kirk that he suspects that Malkthon had the Kitumba's father killed so that he could replace Kali as warlord. Malkthon will start the war first, then inform the Kitumba afterward, when it is too late to stop. Kali hopes that Kirk can use this meeting to influence the Kitumba to stop the war before it starts, since only an alien would not have to commit ritual suicide if his words or actions were to displease the Kitumba.

Kirk also learns that the meeting is not a formally arranged one. Kali will be taking advantage of the Kitumba's predilection for traveling disguised amongst his subjects. They will find him in a bar.

When Kirk makes contact with the Kitumba in an alley outside the bar, he surprises Kali by signaling Scott to beam him and the Kitumba up to the *Enterprise*. Once there, Xon uses the ship's computers to educate the young Klingon about the histories of similar cultures: Rome, feudal Japan, and Sparta.

When Kirk brings the Kitumba together with his old tutor, Ksia, they reconcile. Finally at peace, Ksia asks his leader to "witness," and the Kitumba is pleased to grant his request to forever remove his shame. Ksia disintegrates himself by committing ritual suicide as he removes his iron wrist band and presses it to his throat. Once again, Kirk is shocked by the Klingon way of life and death. The Kitumba then asks Kirk to return him to his planet. He reminds Kirk that kidnapping the Kitumba is a crime punishable by death. Kirk reminds the Kitumba that that is so only if his act was reported. The Kitumba repeats this insight, thoughtfully. Kirk then beams back to the planet with the Kitumba, into the alley outside the bar, where Kali is held at dagger point by two Klingons.

Before Kirk can contact Scott with his communicator, it's knocked from his hands and he's captured. The Kitumba hesitates, holding back from giving the order to have Kirk killed. Kirk's communicator beams up to the *Enterprise*, without Kirk. The Kitumba decides to take Kirk back to the Sacred Palace, to learn more from him.

On the *Enterprise*, Scott implores Decker to send an armed landing party to rescue the Captain. Decker reminds Scott of the rules of sanctuary, but says he will follow Kirk's last instructions and will beam down to contact Kali. But before Decker can beam down, Xon appears in a Klingon uniform and says he has the unique training and ability to carry out the mission. He will take a communicator and request an armed landing party if necessary.

In the Sacred Palace, Kirk presses Kitumba to consider the importance of standing firm against Malkthon and his war plans. The Kitumba is not used to being addressed nor advised so bluntly.

Xon beams down to the alley outside the bar where Kirk, Kali, and the Kitumba met. There, he uses both the Vulcan nerve pinch and his powers of mental suggestion to force a Klingon he encounters to take him to Kali.

At the Sacred Palace, Taru, upset that the Kitumba has brought an alien into the Sacred

Palace, demands that Kirk tell her what he has said to the Kitumba. When Kirk refuses, she orders a Klingon guard to kill him, even though it is apparent he is under the Kitumba's protection. Unarmed, Kirk uses martial-arts moves to defeat his two Klingon guards in hand-to-hand combat. Then the Kitumba enters, puzzled by Kirk's victory in the face of certain defeat. He questions the honor in winning without weapons or killing. Kirk tells him: "Honor doesn't consist of killing or dying. What's important is how you *live*." He goes on to tell a stunned Kitumba that "you own the life of everyone in your empires. Therefore, every life lost diminishes you."

The Kitumba asks him to demonstrate his technique again. Kirk obliges. But when he does so, the guard he defeats is dishonored, and commits suicide. Kirk is appalled, but the Kitumba still does not understand his reaction.

Taru withdraws, to contact Warlord Malkthon on the planet Ultar. She tells him that Kirk is in the Sacred Palace and that the Kitumba seems to be falling under Kirk's influence. Malkthon orders her to execute Kirk. Taru objects, citing the protection of the Kitumba that shields Kirk. Malkthon tells her: "He does not have mine. Kill him."

To be continued . . .

"Kitumba, Part 2"

Written by John Meredyth Lucas

Where would we be without the famous Vulcan nerve pinch...or the famous misplaced Vulcan heart, for that matter?

On the Sacred Planet, Lieutenant Xon makes contact with Kali after forcing a Klingon to take him to Kali's residence. Kali is furious when Xon refers to him, in front of the Klingon, as the head of the Klingon underground and their only contact on the planet.

Before Kali will tell Xon where Captain Kirk is, Kali orders the Klingon to "remove" himself—commit ritual suicide. Xon, however, is able to use his powers of mental persuasion to "suggest" that the Klingon return to the tavern where Xon found him, and to forget all that he has heard and seen in their encounter. Kali is astounded by Xon's performance. He tells Xon that the captain has been taken prisoner at the Sacred Palace. Though he believes the Kitumba would probably not kill

Kirk, he offers no such assurance that the Klingon warlord's deputy, Baro Taru, would not try to influence the Kitumba to be less merciful. Kali thinks the warlord, Malkthon, is ready to begin his war in earnest.

Questioned intently by Xon, Kali reveals that his spies on the warlord's planet, Ultar, have given him the code word *Kitumbala* to be used in the sneak attack on the Federation. The word means "the spread of power"—eventually, to the entire galaxy. Kali further shares the information that Malkthon is in the midst of arranging a nonaggression treaty with the Romulans, even though it is evident to both Kali and Xon that the Romulans will be the next to fall to the Klingons, after the defeat of the Federation. Xon admits that the divide-and-conquer plan is tried and tested and most logical.

Kali confesses that his antiwar group cannot oppose the warlord as long as he acts in the name of the Kitumba. He tells Xon: "Our only hope is that the Kitumba will stand against him."

Their discussion is interrupted by Xon's communicator. Decker informs Xon that a Klingon warship has entered the system and is in orbit over the Sacred Planet. Kali is certain that Malkthon has finally come to ask the Kitumba to issue battle orders. Xon says they must go to the Sacred Palace immediately, to prevent the start of war, no matter what the odds are of their making it through the heightened palace security.

We next see Kali and a concealed Xon in the audience chamber of the Sacred Palace, watching as the Kitumba's younger brother, Prince Klun, and Baro Taru await the Kitumba. Malkthon, warlord of the Klingons, enters and approaches the dais. A moment later, the Kitumba appears from within the many-faceted mirrors of the imposing jewel formation that dominates the dais.

Malkthon presents his ruler with his request and a scroll for his signed approval. Though the warlord's manner is properly subservient, his gaze is not. The Kitumba accepts the scroll and, after a moment's hesitation, says he will give it due consideration. Then the Kitumba abruptly withdraws into the jewel's mirrors. The warlord stares at his deputy in rage. Kali signals Xon to follow him, and they quickly leave through the side door of the chamber.

Kali tells Xon that Kirk's life is now definitely threatened since the warlord will wish to remove any influence but his own on the Kitumba's decision. Should the Kitumba rule against the war, Malkthon would have no option but to kill himself to remove the shame from his name. Kali says Kirk is being held somewhere near the Kitumba's quarters, and will be heavily guarded.

Once again, Xon's use of the Vulcan nerve pinch dispatches the guard outside the Kitumba's antechamber. Kali tells the inner guard that he and Xon have been passed through on Lord Malkthon's orders. Xon tells the guard that Baro Kali is to interrogate the alien.

As soon as Xon can speak privately to Kirk, he gives him the Klingon attack code word. He also tells his captain that the signal has been given and that the battle fleets are already moving. Kali adds that Malkthon has begun the war before the Kitumba has given the warlord his decision, and tells Kirk that the warlord is sure to kill him now. Xon tells Kirk that he can beam him out, using his communicator, but Kirk refuses to go. Kirk worries that Malkthon might kill the Kitumba himself. At first, Kali cannot even think a Klingon capable of such sacrilege, but then admits: "With Malkthon, almost anything is possible."

Malkthon conceives of a plan to achieve the end of both the young Kitumba and the bothersome alien, Kirk. With Taru's assistance, he replicates Kirk's ceremonial Academy sword, basing the duplicate on a visual recording made during Kirk's first appearance before the Kitumba. He tells Taru: "This toy will win the war for us."

From the bridge of the Enterprise, Decker contacts Xon on the surface of the Sacred Planet to ask him if he has contacted the captain. When Xon informs him that he is, in fact, with Kirk now, Decker tells him that a small, fast Klingon craft has just left the planet and is heading for Ultar. Kirk takes the communicator to ask whether Malkthon could be on board that ship. Decker cannot confirm this, but notes that Malkthon's ship is still in orbit over the Sacred Planet. Kali tells Kirk he does not believe the Klingon warlord would leave without getting the Kitumba's signed approval for war. Kirk says it is now imperative that they talk to the Kitumba to convince him not to sign.

Xon uses his nerve pinch to disable the inner antechamber guard. Then Kali distracts the outer guard until Xon can disable him as well. Kali then assumes the role of the guard for his two "prisoners," Kirk and Xon, whom he leads to the next set of guards attending the Kitumba's private chambers. Kali tells the guards that the Kitumba wishes to question the aliens personally and the guards permit them to enter.

The Kitumba, though startled by Kali and the

aliens, dismisses his guard. He is clearly upset and tells Kali that it is because he has learned that Malkthon has sent his younger brother, Prince Klun, to Ultar without consulting him. Kirk voices their unspoken fear—that the warlord is preparing to kill the Kitumba and replace him with his more malleable brother. Emboldened, Kali reminds the Kitumba of the suddenness of the change of power that followed the unexpected death of the Kitumba's father and the replacement of Kali as warlord by Malkthon.

Kirk says it is time to get the Kitumba to a place of safety —the *Enterprise*. He also asks the young leader where the communications room is. The Kitumba doesn't understand what he means. Kali says that only Malkthon or Baro Taru would know the answer to Kirk's question, and they certainly would not reveal its whereabouts. When Xon points out that Malkthon has likely already moved to block communications, Kirk decides it is time to get to the *Enterprise*. Just then a Klingon Guard Officer appears to announce that the warlord Malkthon desires a private audience with the Kitumba. Hidden behind the door, Kirk nods agreement to the Kitumba. Kirk then uses Xon's communicator to tell Scotty to beam the Kitumba aboard. He plans to stay and find the control room himself.

Since the Kitumba cannot meet with the warlord, Xon solves the dilemma by impersonating the Kitumba. Kali shows him how the Klingon's leader makes his magical appearances from within the great mirrored jewel of the audience chamber. While Xon keeps Malkthon busy, Kirk and Kali will consult the Kitumba's computer to find the communications room so they can contact the fleet and avert the war.

Kali and Kirk find that the Kitumba's computer does not contain the location of the communications room. Kali realizes the omission is deliberate. As Kirk and Kali return to the area behind the Kitumba's jewel, they see Malkthon approach Xon, the false Kitumba, and run him through with the duplicate of Kirk's ceremonial Starfleet Academy sword. Then Malkthon runs out of the chamber to tell a horrified Baro Taru: "The alien captain has murdered our Lord, the Kitumba." He orders her to make the formal arrangements for the body while he goes to Ultar to proclaim the six-year-old Prince Klun the new Kitumba.

As Taru rushes in to view the body, she encounters Kirk and Kali. She accuses Kali of responsibility for the murder and begins to call for the guard. Kali protests Kirk's innocence and shows her a recording made by a device in the Kitumba's jewel that reveals the real killer: Malkthon. They all realize that the warlord had hit upon the one situation that would rally all Klingons to the cause of war: the killing of their Sacred Leader by an alien from the Federation. Taru volunteers to kill herself to remove the shame and says they all must follow her example. Kirk says he has a better idea that will not waste further lives. The only one who should be "removed" is Malkthon.

Kirk calls up to Scotty to beam Xon to sickbay, though he doubts even McCoy can save his science officer.

Taru, now on Kirk's side, takes them to the communications room, a thousand meters beneath the Palace antechamber. To her surprise, a Klingon officer and two armed guards in service only to Malkthon bar her entry to the control room. The officer orders the guards to seize her and her companions, Xon, Kali, and Kirk, when Taru persists by saying she needs to contact the fleet. Malkthon's orders are that anyone, including his deputy, who tries to contact the fleet is to be arrested for treason. Kirk, thinking quickly, has Scott beam down a phaser. He puts it on "stun" and drops the two guards. The officer grabs Taru as a shield and aims his disrupter at Kirk, who evades the shot. Kali picks up a disrupter and disintegrates the officer. Then Taru takes the officer's disrupter and kills the two guards before Kirk can protest.

Without the officer, there is no way to get the

code that the Klingon battle fleet would respond to, so Taru destroys the equipment. Kirk calls Scott to beam the three of them to the *Enterprise*.

Taru says Malkthon will still believe the Kitumba is dead, but that they still have no way of contacting the fleet to stop the war and save all their lives. Kirk decides that there still is a way to win. He will use the *Enterprise* to beam the Kitumba aboard the Klingon flagship. Decker worries that they will never get that close without being destroyed.

Kirk asks Scott for the impossible. The *Enterprise* must literally jump out of orbit in the midst of the Klingon fleet and beam out the Kitumba before the Klingons can suspect what they are doing. Scott will have to give Kirk warp speed from a standing start. Kirk goes on to say this means they need to beam the Kitumba out at the exact millisecond they come into range. Scott points out they can't use the transporter when their shields are up. Kirk agrees and says he's counting on the Klingons' not firing for a few seconds for fear of hitting their own ships. He tells Kitumba to order a cease-fire the instant he's aboard or the *Enterprise* will be destroyed.

In the meantime, Kirk is delighted to learn from McCoy that Xon is alive. Since the Vulcan heart is not on the left side of the body, Malkthon's sword thrust was not lethal. Xon joins his crewmates and captain on the bridge for Kirk's plan.

The *Enterprise* leaps to warp speed and streaks for the cordon of orbiting Klingon ships. Her forward screens survive the first attack though her starboard main shield is heavily damaged. But Kirk has made it to the inside of the Klingon ring. Decker lowers the forward port shield so the transporter can function. The Kitumba beams out. Instantly, Kirk orders the port shield up, but the stern shield is repeatedly hit until it fails completely. On his captain's order, Sulu turns hard aport, but the port shield is hit and loses half its power. Then Uhura calls Kirk's attention to the main viewer where Kalem, the captain of the Klingon flagship, appears with the Kitumba by his side. The Kitumba tells Kirk that the battle group is under his personal command, and asks to beam aboard the *Enterprise*. The attack is over.

In Kirk's briefing room, Kalem warns Kirk that over a thousand ships still remain in reserve under Malkthon's command in the Ultar system. He himself has only a hundred-ship battle fleet. A further complication is that all Klingon starships are authorized to listen only on Ultar's frequency. Ilia notes that: "If there is no way for the Kitumba to issue recall orders, war is inevitable." Once again, Kirk thinks of a way out—a way to get the Kitumba to Ultar where he can communicate with the fleet and issue recall orders. The plan will make use of the nonaggression treaty Malkthon worked out with the Romulans. But his new plan will also depend on two secrets—the Klingons' ship invisibility technology and the total output capacity of the *Enterprise*'s engines.

As Scott, Kali, and Taru all protest, Uhura announces a proclamation issued to all Klingon fighting units from Klingon Supreme Command on Ultar. It is Malkthon, telling his troops about the murder of the previous Kitumba and the ascension of the new Kitumba, Prince Klun.

Kirk appeals to Scott to have Taru and Kali work out with him how the ghost-ship principle can be adapted to the *Enterprise*. He then speaks to Xon about the close relationship of Vulcans to Romulans, and mentions that there are Romulans on Ultar.

Following heated discussion with Kali and Taru, Scott tells Kirk that the *Enterprise* can become a "ghost ship, if it operates only on impulse engines, which makes it dangerously slow and vulnerable. Kali and Taru say they will adapt the ship's engines, but that their work must be shielded from the eyes of any Federation personnel. Kirk tells the three to go ahead.

Kirk has the *Enterprise* hide in the middle of Kalem's hundred-strong battle group as it approaches the thousand-strong Klingon battle fleet. The overlapping shields of the Klingon vessels act to hide Kirk's ship from Ultar's sensors. Taru appears on Malkthon's viewer and requests his permission to join the main fleet for the glory of war. The warlord grants her request, but then becomes suspicious when Taru's ships do not take up the orbit he has ordered. Moving to orbit would reveal the presence of the *Enterprise*. Kali throws the switch and the *Enterprise* disappears. It has become a "ghost ship." Xon dons a Romulan uniform, ready to beam down to Ultar to prepare the way for the Kitumba to beam after him. He tells Kirk he will need three minutes to convince the Romulans of Malkthon's treachery.

In the Ultar Control Center, Malkthon's Controller tells him he detects what might be a ghost-ship reading. Malkthon tells him there should be no ships in the area and to recheck his instruments. Then, Kirk, Taru, Kali, and Xon begin to materialize in the Control Center. Before Malkthon can have them killed, a force of Romulans leaps into action to clear a path for Kirk's team. Malkthon runs from the room, pursued by Kirk, who calls to Xon to locate the communication channel.

Malkthon enter and seals shut a room marked "Auxiliary Control." Kirk blasts his way through the door with his phaser. In the battle that follows, Kirk's phaser malfunctions, Malkthon tries to kill Kirk with his dagger, but Kirk defeats him in unarmed combat. The auxiliary viewscreen comes to life and shows the Kitumba with his six-year-old brother, together with Taru and Kali. The Kitumba tells all Klingons of Malkthon's betrayal and calls the Klingon battle fleet to stand down. No war will take place.

Malkthon requests permission of the Kitumba to "remove"—kill himself to remove the shame. The Kitumba grants his request over Kirk's protests. Kirk urges the Kitumba to try the warlord for treason and imprison him. The Kitumba reminds Kirk that Klingon ways are not Federation ways. Then the Kitumba reinstates Kali as his warlord, but Kali says a younger person is needed now. Baro Taru becomes the new warlord.

Kirk again makes his case for peace, trade, and friendship between the Kitumba's people and the Federation. The Kitumba says Kirk must be content with what has been achieved for now, beginning with the fact there is to be no war. Taru adds that the Klingons will still be defending their borders. Kirk says the Federation will do the same, but he hopes they will never meet in battle.

When Kirk says he doesn't like settling for "partial victories," Xon points out he was told to stop a war, not create an alliance.

Kirk achieves a personal victory, though, when the Kitumba tells him with the admiration and love he had displayed toward his old tutor Ksia: "People and habits take a long while to change. But to you, personally, I shall always be grateful." Kirk thanks him and tells him: "You will use the power well."

"Practice in Waking"

Written by Richard Bach

Best known for his 1970 megabestseller book, *Jonathan Livingston Seagull*, *Richard Bach was an exciting new addition to the* Star Trek *writing team. This haunting story anticipates* The Next Generation's *penchant for placing stories in virtual-reality recreations of historical settings, though here the mechanism is directed dreaming, and not the holodeck. The ending is still capable of raising a few goosebumps, and gives us an imaginative glimpse at a* Star Trek *that might have been.*

The *Enterprise* comes upon an intact antique spaceship that Lieutenant Xon identifies as Project *Long Chance*, launched out of Earth orbit October 17, 2004. He notes that this was Earth's last star launch before the discovery of the warp drive. Xon's sensors indicate that though the craft had a crew of forty on a ten-year cycle of suspended animation, only one life form still registers. Fuel still is at seventy percent.

Uhura adds that the antique ship's onboard computer is still in working order, but the conn is shut down. Kirk asks her to put the ship's interior on the main viewscreen. There is no response to Kirk's hail.

Kirk chooses Decker to head a survey team. Decker chooses Scott and Sulu, an antiquarian enthusiast, to accompany him.

When Decker, Scott, and Sulu materialize on board the *Long Chance*, they find thirty-nine sealed, empty sleeping caskets and one casket occupied by Commander Deborah MacClintock, Engineering Officer (Propulsion). The twenty-eight sleep-cycle decals on the side of her sleeping compartment indicate that she has been in sleeping-waking mode for over 280 years. No other casket has more than twenty-seven decals or fewer than twelve.

Decker reports their discovery to Kirk on the *Enterprise*, and requests a medical and engineering-electronic team, and a computer data link to the historical library. As Decker speaks with Kirk, Scott inadvertently touches a dark panel on the side of MacClintock's casket, and it flashes: READY. Then it changes to: THETA EQUALIZE. Decker is cut off midsentence and he, Scott, and Sulu collapse simultaneously, sound asleep by the time they hit the deck.

They "reawake" in a forest in sixteenth-century Scotland with no memory of the *Enterprise* or their own time, witness to the imminent capture of a witch by a troop of the earl's soldiers. Seeing a young woman in distress galvanizes Scott, who leaps out of cover to the rescue. The woman is Deborah MacClintock.

On the *Enterprise*, Dr. McCoy warns Kirk that Decker, Scott, and Sulu are not just sleeping. The three officers are in a coma, and their lifesigns are getting progressively weaker. Unless some way can be found to wake them, within ten to twelve hours they will die. McCoy says the coma was not induced chemically and he has no research to consult for a solution. All study of suspended animation stopped two hundred years ago with the discovery of the warp drive.

Meanwhile, Decker, Scott, and Sulu are successfully using their swords to fight off the earl's men to rescue MacClintock. Finding himself strangely drawn to MacClintock, and she to him, Scott asks MacClintock whether, in fact, she is a witch. She replies that she must be, since she has a way of dreaming things to happen. Then she points out that their sudden appearance also has the aura of magic about it. The three officers find they are unable to remember clearly where they are from and just who they are, though they know somehow they do not belong to this place or time. All three are showing the signs of unusual fatigue.

On the *Enterprise*, Kirk, Xon, and Uhura work to solve the mystery. Xon cautions against awakening MacClintock, fearing the action could kill her. When Kirk presses his science officer for other more successful solutions, the Vulcan states that they could abandon their survey team or freeze them or . . . Uhura interrupts the list of undesirable options to tell Kirk and Xon that MacClintock is dreaming. Xon points out that theta sleep is a dreamless state. But Uhura says that her data-link, which is patched into the *Long Chance*'s onboard computer, confirms that MacClintock is in suspended animation, deeply asleep, *and* dreaming. Kirk immediately asks McCoy if Decker, Scott, and Sulu are also dreaming.

In a tavern somewhere in a Scotland of the past, Kirk's three officers get a demonstration of MacClintock's supposed witchery when the *Long Chance*'s propulsion engineer uses her mind to "dream" levitate a bottle upward from a table. Urged on by MacClintock, Scott tries the same trick with some success, but the feat is witnessed by a guard in the tavern. The guard calls out: "A WITCH! HERE! GET HER! GET THEM ALL!"

Intermittently throughout the battle that follows, the *Enterprise* crewmates have flashes of knowledge about their own time: phasers and stun settings, and General Order Number One—non-involvement in local affairs. Increasingly, their fatigue is beginning to overwhelm them and they put down their swords when the guards threaten to kill MacClintock unless they surrender.

At the same time, McCoy tells Kirk that he has been unable to find any stimulus to rouse Decker, Scott, or Sulu from their sonic-shock-induced sleep. Uhura says the sonic shock the three experienced was a safety device. Lacking automatic monitors for theta, the awake members of the *Long Chance*'s crew would subject themselves to the sonic shock, go in, and check the dreamers, and then a recovery unit would administer a second sonic shock to bring the awake team back out. Kirk wonders if a second sonic shock would work on his crewmembers. McCoy says he would have to program the recovery unit with their brainwave profiles and their individual physiological patterns. And that would just be the beginning of it. Uhura reminds Kirk that the *Long Chance*'s electronic equipment is significantly outdated and such a refit would take days to manually program. Kirk knows they don't have days. He asks McCoy if they have hours. McCoy replies: "I think it's minutes, Jim."

In some other place and time, Decker, Scott, Sulu, and MacClintock are bound and carted off to the earl's castle where they are thrown into a stone and iron cell. Scott has managed to sneak in a Scottish knife, which MacClintock tells him he won't need. As if in a trance, she uses her "dreaming power" to snap the leather ties that bind them all. Questioned by Scott about what she can see in her dream, MacClintock speaks of a boat in the stars and ion engines. She tells Scott she feels "so close now to waking up."

Decker urges Scott to have MacClintock try her magic on the iron lock barring their door. Scott requests tools and as MacClintock remembers a cutting torch, a sonic generator, and a pedestal laser, the objects themselves flicker into existence before them. Frustratingly, the tools are from the twenty-first century, and the *Enterprise* crewmates are not familiar with them. Until Scott recognizes the laser from his knowledge of the history of engineering. Sulu feels it might work as a battering ram, but knows the three of them are to exhausted and too few in number to use it effectively. Suddenly Scott acts by intuition and uses the laser to melt the iron door lock. As he does so, MacClintock's body flickers and begins to disappear.

On the *Long Chance*, a light appears above MacClintock's casket and the words: THETA BOOST. A low sonic hum accompanies the light. Within the casket, MacClintock stirs and fights against the sonic shock that should have returned her to deep sleep instantly.

On the *Enterprise*, Uhura's sensors alert her to a momentary change in MacClintock's condition, but a subsequent check reveals the sleeper has still not awakened.

Free of their cell, Decker, Scott, and Sulu make their way to the main gate despite their seriously weakening state. Unfortunately, they arrive just as the guard is about to change and they are easily reapprehended. The Earl himself addresses them in the courtyard and cites their escape from their cell as proof of their ability to work magic. The penalty for sorcery is death by fire, and it will be carried out at once. MacClintock will die first. Almost too tired to be concerned by their fate, the three *Enterprise* crewmembers are tied to a wall to witness MacClintock's burning. The wood is set on fire around her.

Having just heard McCoy's estimate of the time remaining as measured by minutes, Kirk asks Uhura if there is any way to communicate with the sleepers. Uhura tells him there is no translator or communications system on the *Enterprise* that would do what he wants. Then Kirk turns to Xon, remembering what Spock might have been able to do. He asks if Xon could mind-meld now with Decker. Xon says that a mind-meld would be as dangerous as the sonic shock. All he could give Decker might be an image, not words or ideas, and the communication would be one-way, not two. When Kirk asks Xon if his recommendation is that they let their crewmates die, Xon asks Kirk to join him in sickbay.

Under McCoy's and Kirk's intent gaze, Xon mind-melds with Decker. As Xon speaks with the joined voice of Xon-Decker, his disjointed commentary refers to the loss of sense of time and place, and to Scotland, castle courtyards, and the burning of a witch—Scotty's friend.

In that Scottish courtyard, Decker stirs, in the grip of some sudden, odd perspective that has come into his head. MacClintock, in a near dream-trance, almost disappears again, but flickers back as a cry of terror goes up from the people watching her. Decker cries out to her to go back to her dream, to stop fighting what is happening to her. When Scott joins in, he says: "IT'S YOUR DREAM, LASS! IF YE DINNA FIGHT, THERE'S A LONG CHANCE. . . ."

At the words, "Long Chance," MacClintock thinks of her ship and excitedly shares her memory with Scott. She then flickers and disappears from her dream of old Scotland. Scott tells his crewmates that it is time they did the same. They must not struggle to fight back physically. They must use their minds as MacClintock did to dream their way out.

Scott's first attempts to do so only cause more "magic" to happen when he ignites the top of a wooden stake. The terrified villagers cry out: "Burn them! Burn them now before they kill us all!" The guards rush to tie Decker, Scott, and Sulu to stakes.

On the *Long Chance*, MacClintock awakens and leaves her casket. Her action brings her to the attention of Uhura, who alerts Chekov. Chekov uses the remote to confirm MacClintock's wakeful state and then signals Kirk. Kirk has Chekov immediately arrange to beam MacClintock to sickbay. Before she is transported to the *Enterprise*, MacClintock hears Chekov's voice saying: "Commander MacClintock, this is the *Starship Enterprise*. Welcome to the 24th century."

Still caught in his nightmare, Decker is dying and Xon is sharing his torment. Kirk orders Xon to let Decker go, but Xon asks if Spock would have let go. Kirk orders McCoy to get Xon back at once. McCoy injects Xon with a stimulant, once, twice. But there is no reaction.

MacClintock enters sickbay and goes to Scott's side. Kirk tells her that Scott, Xon and two others are caught in her ship's sonics and will die in a few moments. MacClintock tells him there is a theta-phase generator in the aft equipment bay, but that there isn't enough time to use it. Kirk asks her how she woke up. She tells him the only way is to make each of them see what each loves most. Kirk directs Xon to give Decker a mental image of the *Enterprise*. When Xon does not respond, Kirk bends down and touches the Vulcan gently on the back of his neck and speaks softly into his ear:

"Xon, you're my officer and you're my friend.

If you can, give Decker his ship, let him see the ship. If you can't, I know you did your best to save their lives, and I'll never forget."

Xon still does not respond.

Decker begins to burn alive. Then a vision of the *Enterprise* appears to him and his bonds drop away and the fire no longer burns his body. The guards cannot touch him as he goes to Sulu. He tells Sulu who he is and that he is needed on the bridge—that it is his watch. Sulu invites him to enroll in his fencing class to improve his swordsmanship, and then Sulu fades away. To Scott, Decker reels off statistics about their home, the *Enterprise*. Before he, too, vanishes, Scott corrects Decker's list. Once his crewmates are away, Decker closes his eyes and disappears from the courtyard and old Scotland.

His crew safely reunited, Kirk begins his log about marking the *Long Chance* with a beacon. Scott eagerly renews his acquaintanceship with the *Long Chance*'s propulsion engineer with whom he shares a common passion for their craft. MacClintock, however, tells Scott that her extended experience of suspended animation and deep sleep has made even his remarkable ship and all its adventure and technology seem that it, too, is only another dream. Scott despairs to hear her say that one must awake from even the best of dreams and that it is time she moved on.

When Scott tells her they are only just beginning, she replies that they will have "another beginning waiting for them." Then she flickers and fades away.

Kirk and Scott share a moment of understanding as Scott accepts what has happened. He tells Kirk that he knows he will meet MacClintock again, "but the *Enterprise*, if she is a dream I meet one time only, I'll not want to be waking early." Then the *Enterprise* moves away, leaving the *Long Chance* behind, drifting in space.

"Deadlock"

Written by David Ambrose

Here's a story that reflects a typical 1970s view of the military by building a portrait of a Starfleet gone mad—practicing mind-control techniques on its personnel, lying to them, and experimenting upon them by altering their perceptions of reality. Fortunately, there's another explanation for what Kirk and his crew experience, leading to a traditional Star Trek scene in which Kirk defends humanity to the aliens.

The *Enterprise* receives a distress signal coming from Uncharted Region 019. The caller's voice identifies itself as coming from the *U.S.S. Intrepid.* Responding immediately, Captain Kirk gives Sulu the order to set course at maximum warp. However, even when the caller confirms his position at Kirk's request, Kirk's science officer, Xon, reports that the *Enterprise*'s sensors are no longer registering any distress signals from any detectable source.

Before Kirk can take any further action, he is hailed by Commodore Hunter from Starbase 7, who tells Kirk to return to the Starbase at once. The Commodore will give Kirk further details then. When Kirk informs Hunter of the mystery distress call, Hunter tells him the *Intrepid* is nowhere near that region and refuses Kirk's request to continue the search. He again tells Kirk to return to Base 7. Kirk's first officer, Commander Decker, is horrified when Kirk, though clearly torn, obeys his superior's orders.

In close orbit of Starbase 7, Kirk is upset to learn from Hunter that he was recalled from a search-and-rescue operation so that he and the crew of the *Enterprise* may take part in a Starfleet exercise. Then Hunter reveals that the exercise is already under way: The distress signal was faked with a robot transmitter. Kirk's next authorized move is to shut down all power systems and await further orders.

When Kirk relays this order to Scott, he asks

the engineer how quickly the powered-down ship could be readied to move in an emergency. Scott tells Kirk that he'd need at least an hour, emergency or not. Kirk asks him to work on it with Xon. His goal: "a way of obeying the order, without putting ourselves at that disadvantage."

On the ship's computers, Xon works out equations that indicate that Scott could work with the main reactor plus boosters to maximize power inside ten minutes. The Vulcan science officer tells the engineer: "Of course, the systems would never technically be off. They would only appear to be so."

Reassured by Kirk that the *Enterprise* will comply with its orders, Hunter tells Kirk that he will receive all further orders from one of Starfleet's chief science advisors, Lang Caradon. Caradon appears on Kirk's viewscreen to address Kirk's crew. He tells them they will be required to remain on board for an unspecified time during which they will be relieved of their normal duties. However, they will also be required to engage in certain "games." Since Starfleet wishes to observe their reactions to the games, they are to keep all communications channels open.

The chief medical officer of the *Enterprise*, Dr. Leonard McCoy, approaches Kirk privately to point out that Starfleet's action of faking the distress signal and ordering Kirk to ignore it is a classic disorientation technique. He further notes that Lang Caradon is a controversial researcher on natural response and behavior control. When Kirk asks if McCoy believes the exercise is a behavior-control experiment, McCoy replies: "The old-fashioned term was 'brainwashing.'"

The first "game" to which Kirk's crew is subjected is a hypnotic flashing of numbers and psychedelic patterns on the recreation room viewer. The sequence is also accompanied by undulating electronic sounds. When the sequence stops, the viewers are asked to predict what the next number will be. In increased repetitions, a greater and greater number of viewers agree with the projected answer. The exercise continues with a pulsating

spiral that draws in even Kirk and McCoy on the bridge. Xon, however, though somewhat affected, has greater resistance. The Vulcan science officer watches the viewer as he rapidly punches in data at his station's computer console. The recreation-room viewer suddenly goes blank.

Concerned, Kirk asks McCoy if what they have just experienced is hypnosis. The ship's doctor confirms Kirk's suspicion, but says it was only a mild form. Just then, Xon's mental analysis of the experiment's hypnosis pattern affects the telepathically sensitive Deltan, Lieutenant Ilia. Xon tells Kirk he may have inadvertently shared with Ilia the disturbing mental image of captivity that sprang to his mind. He tells Kirk he has discovered an irregularity in the experiment's transmission—a subliminal message hidden within and emanating from a different source. He replays the message for Kirk: "*Enterprise*, you must escape! Report to Starfleet . . . A plot—Caradon is . . ." The speaker's voice, that of a woman, gags as if in pain, and then cuts off suddenly. Only static follows.

Kirk immediately hails Caradon and requests permission to beam over to Starbase 7. Caradon denies his request. Then Kirk asks to speak directly to Commodore Hunter. Caradon warns him not to forget that the commodore placed Kirk under Caradon's authority. Kirk's response is to play back the disturbing message discovered by Xon. Surprisingly, Caradon is not upset. He tells Kirk that his reaction time to the Starfleet-planted message is well within the time prescribed and congratulates him. He reminds a skeptical Kirk that his continued cooperation is still required and then signs off.

While McCoy points out to Kirk that Caradon's testing of their judgment under pressure could be a legitimate Starfleet exercise, Xon draws his captain's attention to another irregularity. Caradon's research was discontinued three months earlier, with no official reason cited for the termination. Kirk decides to pursue his own investigation.

Kirk and Scott, together with Xon, consult the transporter-room computer console to pinpoint the source of the woman's transmission. Equipping himself with a communicator and a phaser, Kirk asks Scott to beam him as close to that source as he can. Kirk tells Decker to wait an hour. If he has not heard from Kirk by then, he is to board and occupy the base, "by force, if necessary."

Kirk materializes within a dark room, sees a door open, and then . . .

With ten minutes to go, Decker orders Chekov to assemble a boarding party in the transporter room. But Uhura tells Decker she is receiving a signal from Kirk. Onscreen, a relaxed Kirk tells Decker he is cancelling his orders for a boarding party and that there are to be no further transportations to the base. He tells his bridge crew that he is satisfied they are engaging in an official Starfleet exercise and that he will not beam back until the exercise is complete. The viewer then goes blank.

Decker turns to McCoy for his reaction. McCoy tells Decker that he would feel better if they were able to talk to Kirk in person. He points out the hesitation he sensed in Kirk's manner, almost as if the captain were being prompted as to what to say. Decker finds it difficult to believe Kirk could be pressured into anything. McCoy reminds Decker that there are many techniques; hypnosis is only one. Drugs are another. While McCoy and Decker talk, Xon continues to work intensely at the computer.

On Starbase 7, Kirk is unconscious and being scanned by a medical team in an isolation unit. A uniformed Starfleet officer, Lieutenant Commander Anderson, is in the control booth with the medical doctor and orderly. The medical team revives Kirk for Anderson. Anderson tells Kirk he has suffered a light phaser stun. In response to Kirk's query, he also says he is in command of the base and that Commodore Hunter will not arrive for another week. Hunter is attending a conference at Starfleet Headquarters.

Kirk also discovers that he is being held within a force field. He is under confinement. Anderson tells him it is because something unknown happened to Kirk and his crew in Galaxy section 019 and it has altered their behavior. Immediately, Kirk asks Anderson if this is another of Lang Caradon's "games." Anderson does not know who Caradon is. Nor has he heard of any Starfleet exercise being conducted under the orders of Commodore Hunter. Instead he tells Kirk:

"Five days ago we received an emergency signal from the *Enterprise.* You informed us that you had just entered unexplored territory zero-one-nine, and had encountered a mysterious radiation that had affected your entire crew. You requested permission to return here for assistance."

Anderson replays Kirk's message to confirm his story. The visual record clearly shows Kirk in medical distress. Anderson then plays for Kirk the record he received one hour later, showing Kirk, calm, self-possessed, and apparently normal. In this transmission, Kirk apologizes and requests permission to beam over to Base 7. However, before Kirk completes his request, a screaming woman in pain suddenly appears and he reacts with fury to her interruption.

Kirk cannot explain the two transmission records.

On board the *Enterprise,* Xon tells Decker he may have an explanation for Kirk's abrupt change of attitude on the transmission they received from Starbase 7. On Xon's small computer viewer, he shows Decker the tape of Kirk's last message. Xon has worked out a way to expose the patterns in the signal. They indicate that someone may have reprogrammed stored data through a linkup between the transmitter and the central computer. To confirm his theory, Xon presents a demonstration he has prepared. It shows Kirk on the bridge firing a phaser at Decker and Xon. Xon says if this is a real Starfleet exercise, then they are learning just how easily they can be misled by their own inventions.

Decker and Xon prepare to beam down to Starbase 7. Decker gives Scott the same orders Kirk originally gave him, though he cuts the time deadline in half. Scott is to take control of the base if Decker and Xon do not return within thirty minutes. And this time, no one on board the *Enterprise* is to trust any communication received over the viewer. They are to accept personal contact only. Xon asks Scott to create decoy activity to disguise their destination: Level 15, where Kirk is probably being held.

On Starbase 7, Anderson and his officers react as Xon activates the phantom beam-in forces that Scott makes seem to appear all over Starbase 7. Until he realizes that the forces are decoys, Anderson dispatches armed troops to confront them. Then he lowers the Starbase deflectors and prepares to fire a warning shot at the *Enterprise*. Just then, his duty officer informs him that *all* the beam-ins have been decoys. No one, in fact, has beamed over to Starbase 7.

Now Scott sends in Decker and Xon, and then raises the *Enterprise*'s deflectors. Unaware that the last two transportations are not decoys, Anderson raises Starbase 7 deflectors, and designates the *Enterprise* as a "hostile vessel."

On board the *Enterprise,* Scott realizes that with deflectors raised, Kirk, Decker, and Xon will be unable to beam back to the ship.

On Starbase 7, Decker and Xon find Kirk held behind the force field. Unable to access the force-field unit in the control room, Xon switches on his phaser to emit a thin, blue beam directed at the force-field wall. He then adjusts his communicator to emit a high whine and directs it toward the phaser beam. Xon adjusts the whine frequency higher and higher until there is a near-silent but blinding explosion. The force field is drawn back along the phaser beam and into the phaser itself. The phaser melts.

As Kirk, Decker, and Xon escape, the alarm light flashes on the duty officer's console. Guards pour out of the corridors. Decker gives his phaser, set to "stun," to Kirk. Kirk brings down two guards, while Xon tackles two others. Kirk collects two more phasers from the fallen guards. As they run into an elevator, Xon tells Kirk that they must find the central computer relay station—the obvious source of base-to-ship communications. Their problem will not be getting into the station, it will be getting out. Anderson realizes where they are going too late to stop them.

Once in the computer relay station, Kirk has Decker and Xon seal off all entrances. Before Kirk makes another move, Hunter enters the room from a galley above. He congratulates the three on their initiative. Caradon emerges from between banks of computers to do the same. Kirk trains his phaser on Hunter and tells both to stay where they are.

Outside the computer relay station, Anderson orders his forces to burn their way in. He is afraid that Kirk is trying to sabotage the base's weapons systems. He tells his duty officer to switch to manual override while there is still time.

Inside the station, Caradon ignores Kirk's warning and moves toward Kirk. Kirk fires, but his blast passes harmlessly through Caradon. To Decker's and Xon's amazement, Kirk resets his phaser to "kill." But the blast once again passes through Caradon. Then Hunter gazes hypnotically at Decker, who drops his phaser. Hunter then focuses on Kirk, and Caradon on Xon. Kirk and Xon fight the influence but drop their phasers, too.

Kirk asks Hunter who he really is and finally receives an answer. Both Hunter and Caradon are aliens from the territory Kirk knows as Galaxy sector 019. Their purpose has been to observe their progress and to do so, they adopted the forms of the two known as Hunter and Caradon, who are now elsewhere, and unharmed.

When Kirk asks why they are observing him and his people, the aliens tell him that the internal hostilities they have been witnessing are disturbing and possibly infectious. When Kirk protests that he and his people have done no harm to the aliens, he learns that the aliens consider the mere presence of his people a threat. The aliens are a chameleonlike race with very advanced powers, but are extremely vulnerable to both physical and mental influence from whoever is in close proximity to them.

Decker tells the aliens that his are a peaceful people, able to control less agreeable aspects of their personality with reason. The aliens reply that such control still seems tenuous.

Kirk challenges the aliens' reasoning. He counters that they too are violent because they believe in destruction. The aliens say they will let Kirk's people destroy themselves with their own violent devices. Kirk asks them if their own supposedly superior code of behavior merely prevents them from murdering others, while allowing them to trick others into turning on themselves. The aliens reply only that Kirk and his people may "prove or disprove our judgments of you . . . by your own actions." Then they dematerialize.

Outside the computer relay station, Anderson's forces have almost burned their way back in. Decker tells Xon that normal base-to-ship communications have been restored. Kirk realizes, however, that Scott will no longer accept its truthfulness nor will Anderson, the base commander. Decker alerts Kirk that if they are not back on board the *Enterprise* in eleven minutes, Scott will attempt to take control of the base by force. And Anderson's forces will have no choice but to retaliate.

On board the *Enterprise*, Uhura tells Scott she is getting a transmission from Kirk. On Starbase 7, Anderson instructs his Duty Officer to jam Kirk's transmission. Cut off, Kirk asks Xon to try to disconnect the base phaser banks using the computer relay station controls. Xon says it will take time.

Scott tells Chekov a boarding party cannot land unless they take out Starbase 7's deflectors. Chekov recommends using the *Enterprise*'s phasers. Scott is worried that the base will open fire on them, and that they won't be able to keep up the ship's deflectors indefinitely. Chekov suggests

moving farther out, keeping within transporter range but into a position from which the *Enterprise* can still take evasive action. Then Scott remembers Xon's formula for using the main reactor and the boosters. He goes to the science officer's computer console. He gives the order to the engineering deck and tells Chekov he only hopes they are given enough time to make it work.

Xon finds the circuit he wants in the now-open console in the computer relay station.

Anderson's duty officer detects the *Enterprise* preparing to leave orbit. Anderson orders activation of tractor beams. Scott orders the engineering deck to continue build-up to maximum power. Anderson gives the order to arm phasers.

The guards burn through the computer relay station doors. They arrest Kirk, Decker, and Xon and call Anderson to announce that there is no damage to the base's defense systems.

Scott's engineering deck announces it is ready for engagement. The countdown begins.

Anderson confronts Kirk, who admits to trying to sabotage the base weapons systems, but says he had a good reason for doing so. The base commander refuses to accept Kirk's explanation of aliens from Sector 019. Kirk tells Anderson that the aliens want them all to destroy themselves.

Scott's countdown continues. Anderson's duty officer reports that the *Enterprise* power buildup is continuing. Kirk tells Anderson that if there were time, he could prove to Anderson that their communications were falsified. When Anderson hesitates, Kirk demands that he at least be allowed to talk to Scott. Anderson gives in.

Uhura breaks into Scott's countdown to tell him she has a transmission from the captain. Scott holds the countdown. Kirk tells him not to fire on the base because the base will fire back. Scott does not want to trust Kirk. Kirk asks him to let him beam over to prove what he is saying. Scott says that would mean he would have to lower the deflector shields, and he will not lead the ship into a trap. Anderson tells Kirk to stop speaking. Obviously, Kirk is only trying to persuade Anderson and his forces that the *Enterprise* is not going to attack the base.

Kirk asks if Anderson believes that he would plan an aggressive attack while he, his first officer, and his science officer were still on the base. Anderson replies that Kirk and his men could be beamed up once the *Enterprise*'s phasers broke through the base's deflectors. A typical Kirk trick. Scott tells Kirk *he*'ll believe him if Anderson takes his tractor beams off the *Enterprise;* otherwise, he's going to tow the base out of its orbit. Anderson vows to take action if the *Enterprise* moves.

Then Ilia comes onto the bridge of the *Enterprise.* On Starbase 7, Xon sees Ilia on the viewscreen. Easily shaking off Anderson's guards, Xon approaches the base commander to propose a solution. If he can persuade the *Enterprise* to lower her deflectors, will Anderson accept that action as proof of peaceful intent?

Xon fixes Ilia with an intent gaze and says: "Lieutenant . . . Please, try to put your mind . . . under my control. . . ." After a long, tense moment, Ilia turns away from the bridge viewer and toward the main computer console. Scott watches as the science station viewer begins to display Xon's formula. He realizes there is no way Ilia could have known this, since she was not on the bridge when Xon developed it, nor when Scott punched it into the ship's computer. McCoy tells Scott that they have just witnessed telepathy, an ancient technique not dependent upon technology. Kirk's voice speaks to Scott from the main view screen to confirm what Scott now knows is true: The image is of the real Captain Kirk, and the transmission is a true one.

Scott lowers the ship's deflectors. Anderson disarms the base phasers. Kirk invites Anderson to beam aboard the *Enterprise* as his guest.

Later, as the *Enterprise* moves away from Starbase 7, Kirk enters a recommendation into his Captain's Log: "I recommend that no further passage be attempted in region zero-one-nine until we have received a formal invitation from the inhabitants there. I can only hope that whatever influence they continue to feel from us will be felt in a more positive light as a result of our demonstrated, if somewhat tenuous, self-control."

"Savage Syndrome"

Written by Margaret Armen & Alfred Harris

ow this *would have been an episode to see, if only for the scenes in which the bridge crew—including Captain Kirk—crouch and snarl at each other. Though turning the* Enterprise *into a battleground for its crew may seem similar to the* Original Series *episode "The Day of the Dove," here the cause is not a malevolent alien that feeds on negative emotions, but a technology that unleashes the dark urges repressed in humans and, it would seem, in Vulcans.*

Margaret Armen also wrote the scripts for the Original Series *episodes "The Gamesters of Triskelion" and "The Paradise Syndrome," and the teleplay for "The Cloud Minders," based on a story by David Gerrold and Oliver Crawford.*

While charting a lifeless planet, the *Enterprise* encounters in its orbit a mysterious, meteor-pocked battle craft with no detectable life-forms or energy source. Captain Kirk asks Commander Decker, Lieutenant Ilia, and Dr. McCoy to board the ancient, though advanced derelict. Decker requests and receives permission to take the shuttlecraft to inspect the exterior before going inside.

While the boarding party departs, Chekov continues to work at his partially disassembled weapons systems console. Scott and another engineer assist him.

Decker pilots the shuttlecraft toward the derelict's air lock. Ilia, as copilot, pressurizes the air seal when Decker docks with the derelict. Equipped with phasers and tricorders, Decker, McCoy, and Ilia move cautiously through the craft's corridors. Suddenly Ilia announces a surprising discovery: a humanoid skeleton wearing a uniform with highly advanced metal fittings. The skeleton's chest has been pierced with a crudely improvised spear.

On board the *Enterprise*, the main viewing screen displays a rapidly approaching object. It appears to be a small metallic sphere with protruding pods. Kirk asks Xon to identify the object's composition. Xon replies that he has insufficient data to make any identification, though the sphere is extremely ancient. As Xon speaks, the sphere begins to glow with a blinding, pulsing light. Xon immediately warns Kirk that the object could well be a weapon. The pulsing light then streams into the bridge to engulf the head of each person present. All personnel immediately clutch at their temples and collapse, shrieking in agony. As the light slowly fades, their moans decrease. Then each crew member rises slowly to a half-crouched, feral position. They back away from each other, snarling like wild animals.

Meanwhile, on the derelict craft, Decker, McCoy, and Ilia discover other victims of violence. Each of the ship's crew has died from the blows of primitive weapons. McCoy deduces that the crew reverted to the primitive and killed one another off. To help explain what happened, Decker locates the ship's main computer and accesses it for the ship's last entry. The visual playback reveals a small metallic sphere that grows larger as it approaches, and then begins glowing with a sudden blinding light. When the light fades, the image shows the sphere is still intact. Decker realizes the sphere, a type of space mine, must have been responsible for the damage to the derelict. McCoy states that the burst of radiation they just witnessed must have hit the crew and somehow wiped out all civilized instincts. Ilia fears that the dead planet beneath them fell victim to the mines as well. McCoy seizes on Ilia's use of the plural word "mines," and worries aloud: "There might be dozens of them still in orbit." The three colleagues have the same thought at the same instant and Decker uses his communicator to hail the *Enterprise*. When there is no reply, McCoy says they must return at once.

On the bridge of the *Enterprise*, Kirk and Scotty are in the midst of a battle for the command chair. Uhura, Chekov, Xon, Sulu, and Rand crouch in a semicircle, waiting to see who will be leader. Kirk is armed with a section of metal pipe. Scott has a wrench. Kirk appears to be winning when the chief engineer looks around for help and sees his assistant. He orders his assistant to kill Kirk. Kirk disarms the younger engineer, then drives both Scott and his assistant into the open turbolift. As Kirk moves in for the kill, the turbolift doors close automatically. Unchallenged by the personnel on the bridge, Kirk takes possession of the command chair, saying: "I am the leader." Only Xon dares to look defiant. Uhura and Rand take up submissive positions on either side of Kirk, gesturing threateningly to one another.

Decker's voice suddenly sounds from the console near the command chair, startling Kirk and the others, who do not recognize the voice nor know its source. Then the image of the approaching shuttlecraft appears on the main viewscreen. Decker's voice announces that the shuttlecraft is moving into docking position.

Once inside the hangar deck of the *Enterprise*, the shuttlecraft moves automatically into its customary parking space. Doing so interrupts the ongoing battle between the yellow-shirted and the blue-shirted *Enterprise* crewmembers, who flee and hide wherever they can find cover. Decker, McCoy, and Ilia realize that the entire crew has been affected. Decker asks McCoy about an antidote. McCoy replies that he will first have to examine one of the crew to determine exactly what happened to them, so Decker decides that their first destination must be sickbay. He advises McCoy and Ilia to follow him to the turbolift, and to set their phasers on "stun."

Halfway to the lift, Decker, McCoy, and Ilia are assailed by the crew and are forced to use their phasers on their own colleagues. As soon as the three reach the turbolift and push the call button, the doors open and Scott and his assistant attack them. In the battle, Decker and McCoy lose their phasers, but their more disciplined fighting techniques help them to overcome their assailants. Ilia uses her phaser to hold the other "savages" at bay.

Decker and McCoy retrieve their phasers, and the three escape into the turbolift.

More battles are in progress in the corridors outside sickbay and McCoy is reluctant to leave wounded behind. However, Decker points out that unless someone is dying, McCoy will only be tending someone who will return to fighting. They proceed to sickbay, relieved to find that it is peaceful and deserted. McCoy and Decker move immediately to the sickbay medical computer. Just then they are attacked by a feral Dr. Chapel brandishing a pair of medical scissors. She manages to stab Decker before Ilia can stun her with her phaser.

On the bridge, Kirk has decided on a new goal for his "tribe": find food. As his red-shirted staff hurries to obey, Uhura stumbles upon a small hatch opening onto a circular, metal staircase that leads downward. Xon challenges Kirk to find food for the rest of them and Kirk descends the staircase to a narrow landing. After watching Kirk try without success to open another sealed hatch marked "Danger—Airlock—Do not open," Xon shouts that he smells food and points down the stairway. Kirk and the others hurry downward. Stepping through an open door panel labeled "Emergency Staircase," Kirk and his followers emerge into the commissary where a small band of crew with yellow, purple, and white shirts are fighting over the remnants of a meal that had been left out on the tables. Kirk rallies his red-shirted force to attack for the food, and they drive out the others.

In sickbay, McCoy has strapped Chapel to an examination table and subdues her with a hypogun. On a second table, Decker stirs back into consciousness. His wound has been dressed, but he is weak and disoriented. Decker anxiously asks McCoy about his medical computer. He wonders if it is possible to reverse the effects of the space mine. McCoy says his examination of Chapel indicates that the portions of her brain responsible for higher-level functions have been immobilized. He will do more tests on her, but so far he does not have a counterstimulus that would return her to normal.

Decker tells McCoy they must act quickly. Four hundred people on the ship are about to kill one another. When McCoy says he can't tranquilize that many people at once, Ilia says they might be able to if they could reach the bridge. Decker understands: Ilia is suggesting that they use the ship's defense system to flood all decks except sickbay and the bridge with tranquilizer gas. The only problem is, they will have to fight their way to the bridge and Decker is not in shape to do so. Decker says McCoy and Ilia will have to go. As the next officer in charge, Ilia orders McCoy to stay and work on the antidote while she goes on alone.

In a corridor near the hangar-deck turbolift, Scott and his assistant engineer regain consciousness and also strike out for food. They enter an open door panel along the corridor marked "Emergency Staircase—Hangar Deck." At the same time, Ilia, in a corridor on the sickbay level, eludes a roving bunch of gray shirts by stepping into another emergency-staircase panel entrance. And in the recreation-room commissary, Kirk, when physically challenged by Xon to find more food, is knocked back into the food-dispenser control panel. Suddenly, steaming dishes of food magically appear. Elated, Kirk continues to push as many buttons as he can to continue supplying food to his admiring red shirts.

In the emergency staircase, Ilia hears footsteps coming up behind her and she exits the staircase by activating a sliding door panel. Moments later, Scott and his assistant appear and continue climbing the stairs. Ilia emerges in a corridor near the turbolift and she moves into it hurriedly.

When Scott scents food, he and his assistant have just reached an open door panel to an upper landing. It is the same door Kirk and his red shirts used to reach the recreation room. As the two green-shirted engineers enter the room, Kirk and his red shirts are just leaving. Kirk orders the "reds" to kill the intruders. Scott and his assistant flee back into the stairwell, pursued by Kirk and his followers.

Ilia reaches the bridge and crosses quickly to

the Weapons Control Station. She realizes at once that it is inoperable. It has been totally dismantled. She activates a nearby wall communicator to talk to McCoy in sickbay. She tells him she will be unable to flood the ship with tranquilizer gas. The antidote is now their only hope. But McCoy tells her his medical computer is too limited and asks her to patch it in to the main computer. Ilia promises to try, though her computer knowledge is also limited. She places her phaser on the console and begins to work at the computer.

Kirk and Scott have reached engineering, where the battle over food between the "reds" and "greens" escalates. Scott successfully appeals to the engineering staff to join him and his similarly green-shirted assistant. In his scuffle with Kirk, Scott lands against a control console and knocks a control lever forward. Sparks fly and circuits fuse as a red warning light begins to flash. The computer's voice says: "Antimatter energy converters are now on overload . . . detonation within sixty-one minutes . . . ." Terrified by the display of fireworks, the "savages" flee in all directions. Kirk and his "reds" crowd back into the entrance to the emergency staircase.

In sickbay, while in the midst of running tests on Chapel, McCoy hears the computer's warning. He immediately uses the wall communicator to hail Ilia on the bridge. She tells him she has heard the announcement, too. Though still unsteady, Decker joins McCoy at the wall communicator and asks Ilia if she can shut down the generators from the bridge. She says she can if the circuits are still operative. McCoy asks if she has patched his computer into the main computer, and Ilia says she thinks so.

As McCoy starts to feed data into his computer to search for the antidote, Decker now demands that McCoy give him a stimulant. Reluctantly, McCoy reaches for a hypo-gun.

As Ilia works to shut down the generators, Kirk and his party suddenly appear at the emergency staircase hatch to the bridge. Ilia, realizing Chekov and Rand stand between her and her phaser, makes for the turbolift. Before the doors can close on her, Kirk leaps in beside her. He confronts her as a red shirt who should obey him. He tells her he will give her food. Ilia disorients him by ordering the turbolift to go to the sixteenth level, the location of sickbay. She quickly activates the wall communicator to tell McCoy that she was unable to correct the overload, that the main circuits must be fused. When Decker asks if she can make it back to sickbay, she tells him that her phaser is on the bridge, and that she is in the turbolift with Kirk, who has taken her captive.

Kirk is distracted by the unseen voices as Decker tells Ilia to stall and they will meet her. Ilia directs the turbolift to go to the bridge, but Kirk reaches out to her, finally comprehending what she has been doing. She responds by ordering the lift to go to emergency speed to a higher level. Kirk loses his footing.

With phaser drawn, McCoy approaches the turbolift door on the sixteenth level. He activates the wall communicator to tell Ilia he is ready. His footing regained, Kirk hears McCoy's voice and Ilia's response to redirect the lift to level sixteen. He is thrown off balance once more by the change of direction. The turbolift doors open and McCoy fires his phaser at Kirk. Ilia exits the lift and she and McCoy close the lift doors, sealing Kirk inside. They run for sickbay as the computer voice continues to give the countdown to detonation.

Grouped around the medical computer, Decker, McCoy, and Ilia learn that there is no possible antidote. Decker, however, thinks of another solution—snaring one of the mines with the shuttlecraft, entering it to reverse the frequency at which the radiation emanated from it, and then detonating it. He reasons: "The savage syndrome was caused by pulsed light and electromagnetic radiations on a specific frequency. The effect can be reversed by altering that frequency, and generating it from a similar power source."

Ilia warns Decker that the mines were detonated by the energy emanations from an approaching object. That object in the case of the derelict and the *Enterprise* was a ship. Decker says there is a possibility that the shuttlecraft's emanations will be below the triggering frequency. He chooses himself to be the one to snare the mine, stating that neither of the other two has enough detonation experience to do the job. He will, however, need their help to get to the shuttle.

Meanwhile, in the turbolift, Kirk is reviving. As the lift doors open to admit Decker, McCoy, and Ilia, Kirk feigns unconsciousness. He listens intently as Decker commands the lift to take them to the hangar level. As soon as Decker, McCoy, and Ilia, Kirk tells the lift to "go up." When nothing happens, he struggles to remember Ilia's earlier instructions and then says: "Lift to bridge." The lift complies. He steps out onto the bridge to find Xon in his chair with Uhura and Rand at his feet. In his fight with Xon to regain leadership, Kirk falls against the console computer at which Ilia worked. He finds her phaser and instinctively knows how to use it. He fires it at Xon, who crumples to the deck. Undisputed leader once more, Kirk leads his red shirts into the turbolift.

Decker is on board the shuttle on the hangar deck. From outside the shuttle, McCoy tells Decker that he has his choice of six live mines, all on the lee side of the derelict. Decker tells McCoy and Ilia that their job is to get to engineering and do what they can about the fused circuits. Then he seals the shuttle and signals for ejection. The shuttle disengages and launches.

In engineering, Kirk and his "reds" once again confront Scott and his "greens," but this time Kirk has a phaser. He uses it on Scott just as McCoy and Ilia appear in the doorway to engineering. McCoy pulls Ilia back so Kirk will not see them. She asks the ship's doctor how long it would take to make a tranquilizer bomb. McCoy says it would take at least thirty minutes. The computer's voice marks the time to detonation as twenty-seven minutes.

Decker's shuttlecraft moves toward an orbiting space mine until it is only a few meters away.

Watching apprehensively for any sign that his small craft's energy emanations will trigger detonation, he activates a tractor beam. The mine is slowly drawn into the shuttlecraft.

In sickbay on the *Enterprise*, McCoy and Ilia work on completing a tranquilizer bomb. McCoy realizes their work is futile without a dispersant, and all dispersants are in the main stores. There isn't time enough to get one and return to sickbay. Ilia tells him they will just have to fight their way into engineering.

As McCoy and Ilia carefully approach engineering with their phasers drawn, Decker, on the shuttlecraft, opens the mine and begins to probe its circuits.

In engineering, Kirk is receiving homage from the "reds" and the "greens." He promises them that all his followers will feast together and he leads them out of engineering. McCoy and Ilia quickly conceal themselves in the corridor outside engineering to avoid detection by Kirk. They then hurry to the engineering control panels and examine the circuits. Ilia consults the computer to tell them where to begin, but neither she nor McCoy can access the correct program. As Ilia asks the computer for a bypass program, Scott and two of his "greens" begin to stir.

Unaware that the chief engineer is regaining consciousness, McCoy uses his communicator to speak to Decker. Decker reports that he believes he has found the right circuit in the mine and is hooking in his tricorder. McCoy is worried by the sound of Decker's voice. It sounds forced. Just then, Ilia warns McCoy that they can't correct the overload without manual help. The computer would require an hour more than they have before detonation will occur. McCoy tells Decker that to shut the converters down in time, they would have to have Scott's help. Decker will have to start the shuttlecraft back toward the *Enterprise* and complete the wiring on the way. To McCoy's dismay, Decker's only response is to say that he is blacking out. As McCoy tells him to fight it, Scott takes McCoy captive and relieves him of his phaser. He then takes Ilia's phaser from her as the computer voice announces there is twelve minutes to detonation.

Struggling to stay conscious, Decker moves repeatedly from the pilot controls back to the mine and the tricorder. He completes all but two circuits on the mine, then sinks to the floor, unconscious.

McCoy implores the chief engineer to remember how serious an overload is but to no avail. In frustration, McCoy advances on Scott, who retaliates by stunning him with one of the phasers. Detonation is within six minutes as Ilia tries another tactic. Using her Deltan powers of seduction she tells Scott that she will be *very* pleased with him if he shuts down the antimatter converters. But after a moment's hesitation as Scott tries to remember how to do what it is she wants him to do, he thrusts her away. The detonation alarms begin to flash and beep at the five-minute mark. The alarms frighten Scott and his followers. Ilia grabs McCoy's communicator and hails Decker. He groggily tries to respond. With the last strength remaining to him he makes the final connections and reaches out to throw a switch.

The space mine flares into a pulsing, blinding light that envelops the entire *Enterprise*, and haloes the head of all personnel on the ship. All those who were affected by the first space mine touch their temples and cry out with pain. Once again, as the light fades, so does the pain.

In engineering, Scott comes to with his old awareness to hear that detonation will occur within fifty-eight seconds. He leaps to his feet and races for the main console. Ilia rushes to assist him, but he brushes her aside. He shouts instructions to two of his green-shirted assistants as the countdown continues. More green-clad engineers hurry to help Scott as the chief engineer reels off a complex list of actions. Kirk and Xon appear as the detonation count reaches fifteen seconds. Scott tells his captain to stand by. As Scott works faster and faster, the countdown progresses down to the one-second mark just as he presses the last button with a shaking hand.

Abruptly, the ship goes silent. The beeping stops and the warning lights go out. Then the computer voice says: "Overload cancelled." Cheering erupts throughout the ship.

The next we see the shuttlecraft it is being drawn by tractor beam into the *Enterprise*.

Reunited in good health, the crew of the *Enterprise* and their captain muse on the experience that only Decker, McCoy, and Ilia remember clearly. Ilia tells Kirk that he, in particular, made a "magnificent savage."

"Are Unheard Memories Sweet?"

Written by Worley Thorne

Though this script called for nudity and suggestive situations that probably would not have been filmed, let alone allowed to air, the story is a standard Star Trek *adventure. Once again, the* Enterprise *is trapped in a failing orbit without dilithium as an alien race attempts to capture the crew. By the time of* The Next Generation, *damaged or missing dilithium was recognized as an overused plot element, and the bible for that series specifically stated that the new* Enterprise's *dilithium could easily be replaced.*

Worley Thorne also wrote the teleplay for The Next Generation *episode "Justice," sharing story credit with "Ralph Wills," the pseudonym of John D. F. Black.*

In orbit of the sole planet of the thirty-ninth star of the Hyades star cluster, the *Enterprise* searches for traces of the vanished starship *St. Louis* and its captain and crew, lost while mapping the star cluster. Lieutenant Xon's scanning indicates that there are signs of humanoid life on the planet, in addition to the *Enterprise*'s landing party. Though the leader of that party, Commander Decker, has yet to report contact, he has located the area that ship's sensors mark as inhabited.

However, when Xon contacts Decker on the surface, he reports back that the ship's sensors must be faulty. There are no inhabitants. Kirk asks Xon to recheck his equipment, with Commander Sulu's assistance.

Sulu asks Kirk if it is true that Kirk knew the captain of the *St. Louis*, Michael Schwerner. Kirk replies that he and Schwerner have a friendly rivalry that goes back to their days as classmates at the academy. When he recalls that Schwerner was first to make lieutenant, McCoy notes that Kirk was first to command a starship.

On the surface of the planet, Chief Rand has located signs of artificial materials buried deep inside a hillside. Decker summons the two other members of his landing party and has them join with him in collectively training their four phasers on the hillside. He then leads the way into the hole produced by their phaser fire. Rand's tricorder indicates the exact combination of synthetics that are found in the hull of a starship. Decker has her beam samples up to the *Enterprise* so Xon can determine whether they came from the *St. Louis*. Decker and his team will continue their search for survivors.

On board the *Enterprise*, Xon has reconfirmed the presence of humanoid life on the planet. Commander Uhura tells Kirk that Rand is beaming up wreckage that might be from the *St. Louis*, and that Decker's team is looking for the missing crew. Kirk asks Xon to analyze the data in the lab.

Two of Decker's party, Kelly and Ibsen, while continuing the search on the surface, encounter a South Seas lagoon complete with bathing beauties. After but a brief hesitation, the two crew members enthusiastically throw off their uniforms—and the customary rules that bind them—to join the frolicking women. We see, but they do not, that the women's lovely eyes are unnaturally large, glowing, and luminous.

Xon reports to Kirk that his preliminary analysis of the wreckage indicates that it came from a spaceship that was driven deep into the ground by a fall from orbit. Kirk has difficulty accepting that it might be from his friend's ship. McCoy worries that Kirk's denial shows overinvolvement that threatens his judgment. Uhura reaches Kirk by intercom in the turbolift after he and McCoy leave Xon in the lab. She tells him that she is unable to reach crewmen Kelly and Ibsen for Commander Decker, and that now she is unable to reach Decker as well.

On the planet surface, Decker finds that he has just entered a place very familiar to him—the Mariner's Park of the United Federation of Planets at Starfleet Academy, exactly as it appeared fourteen years ago. Just as he snaps on his wrist communicator, he sees a beautiful young woman, who draws closer and closer to him. Intoxicated, he kisses her. As they embrace, we see,

but he does not, that her eyes have become extraordinarily luminous.

On the *Enterprise*, Uhura tells Kirk that one member of the landing party opened a channel, but then no message was sent. Kirk asks her to keep that channel open and try another.

In Mariner's Park, Decker and the young woman, Linda, converse and we become aware that Decker is regressing to young manhood, when he was a midshipman and still concerned about living up to his father's reputation and expectations. We learn that Decker's father was a commodore in Starfleet with the nickname "Old Hardnose." Linda urges Decker to let go, to loosen up and free himself, now. Decker exclaims that he no longer feels afraid of his father and kisses her again.

On the bridge of the *Enterprise*, Uhura detects some kind of interference on the open channel. Kirk asks her to put it on the audio. McCoy realizes they are listening to the sounds of heavy breathing and, Kirk adds, the rustling of clothes. Decker's voice confirms their suspicions: They are listening to a lovemaking conversation conducted by Commander Decker.

Kirk immediately asks Uhura to cut the audio. He asks her if she has obtained the coordinates of the transmission. When she answers in the affirmative, he tells her to notify the transporter room to beam Commander Decker on board, at once.

Decker dematerializes in Linda's embrace. As he leaves, the background changes to its true form: an alien city. With a smile, Linda changes into a beautiful alien, Ronel, an exotic female humanoid.

McCoy's examination of Decker reveals nothing foreign in his body, but his mind is still affected by whatever happened to him on the planet surface. He still believes he is a midshipman, wearing the uniform of a cadet, and he apologizes to Kirk for the trouble he is causing. He says he knows he should be in class right now.

Kirk checks in with Uhura to ask if she has located the landing party yet. She tells him she has not, although she has been maintaining steady signals on all channels. Kirk tells her to have Xon locate them with ship's sensors, but Xon's voice on the intercom reports that he has already tried this without success. The ship's sensors cannot distinguish Decker's party from the other humanoid readings still being received. Kirk tells Xon to keep trying.

Decker grows impatient to rejoin Linda. Kirk, careful to treat his first officer as the midshipman he believes himself to be, tells Decker that he has been "reassigned" to the *Enterprise* and is no longer required in "class." Decker asks if his father is responsible for the reassignment. At that moment, Kirk's intercom sounds and he is hailed by Xon in the ship's lab. He tells Kirk he has something of interest that might shed light on the situation. Before Kirk leaves, he asks McCoy to show Decker to his "new" quarters.

In the *Enterprise*'s lab, Xon reveals to Kirk that one of the pieces of ship wreckage beamed up by Rand is an irregular, charred piece of cube that Xon has removed from the molten metal that encased it. Xon's tests show it to be from the Captain's Log and he has enhanced its remaining signal using the ship's computer to fill in gaps and holes wherever possible. Xon plays the enhanced and restored signal for Kirk. Immediately Kirk realizes that the record was made only five days earlier as he sees Captain Schwerner onscreen saying: ". . . Stardate 1011 point . . . my crew's in some kind of delirium, setting instruments awry, and I fear . . ." Then the picture fades and Schwerner's voice continues: ". . . are in danger of losing orbit. If so, the ship will heat dangerously and break up, unless first I . . ."

Xon concludes that Schwerner's crew most probably was affected in the same way as Decker. Their inability to function properly may have led to the loss of their ship. Kirk puzzles over the lack of a distress call or signal of any kind from Schwerner. He holds out hope that perhaps the *St. Louis* and its crew survived. Xon points out that *his* assessment is based on fact, not emotion. Kirk

maintains that *his* job is to separate theory from fact. McCoy again raises the possibility of Kirk's judgment being influenced by his long friendship with Schwerner. Kirk assures the ship's doctor that he has his feelings under control. Kirk adds, however, that he has another concern. What if whatever struck Decker and Schwerner's crew is contagious? Though McCoy states that there is as yet no indication of that, nor that they are even dealing with a disease, Kirk orders Chekov to have Decker quarantined, as a precaution. Decker is not to leave his cabin without Kirk's authorization. He decides against alerting the entire crew, notifying only those who heard Decker on the bridge. McCoy is grateful, fearing that spread of the information would spread hypochondria as well among the crew.

Xon tells Kirk there appears to be one more intact section on the damaged record cube. This time when Schwerner appears, he looks excited and says: ". . . and I understand now. Never have I thought life could be like this . . . kind of excitement that . . ." A deafening explosion cuts off the transmission and the picture vanishes. Kirk only remembers hearing similar sounds in battle. Xon recalls the sound of impulse fuel explosion at a research laboratory. Kirk realizes that his friend recorded his own destruction. He doesn't understand how Schwerner could give up his ship, his life, and those of his crew without a struggle. Xon states he can see no logic in Schwerner's action. McCoy offers Kirk his condolences. Kirk's attention now turns to his missing three crew members.

In the *Enterprise*'s transporter room, the alien female, Ronel, appears on the transporter pad. The technician working in the room looks up to see "Ensign Rand." As she approaches him, she sets off an intruder-alarm sensor and is challenged by the technician. Her eyes become luminous.

Inside the ship's turbolift, Kirk, with Xon beside him, responds on the intercom to the intruder alarm and alerts the crew to secure all areas. Kirk and Xon exit the lift and proceed to Chekov's post. Chekov reports that in forty-five seconds, all decks will be sealed. Xon checks the computer sensors and gives Kirk the point of intruder entry—the transporter room. Kirk has Chekov send a security team to the transporter. Uhura tells Kirk that Rand had just signalled in when the intruder appeared. She concludes that the intruder entered with Rand. Xon alerts Kirk that the intruder is on the move, in one of the ship's corridors. Chekov assures Kirk that he has security crew posted in all major corridors.

In one of the ship's corridors, we see "Ensign Rand" confronted by a security guard. Her eyes begin to glow and the guard rechecks her and lets her go, with an apology.

Chekov tells Kirk that his security crew has been unable to get any useful information from the technician who was in the transporter room when the intruder tripped the alarm, that he's in some sort of delirium. Kirk asks Chekov about the corridor the intruder was last in. Chekov reports that his security guard says it is secure. The only one there is Rand. Kirk concludes that she must be the intruder. He goes to a wall communicator and alerts the ship: A dangerous alien posing as Rand is on board and must be arrested on sight.

Xon tells Kirk that the intruder is now approaching the officers' quarters. As McCoy leaves Decker's cabin, "Rand" conceals herself from detection by the two armed guards outside Decker's door. Then as "McCoy," she walks past the guards and into Decker's quarters. When she enters, she becomes "Linda." She tells Decker that she is about to be arrested. Decker is sure his father is behind the arrest and promises to help her. But when Decker attempts to leave his cabin, the guard tells him to remain in isolation—Captain's orders. Decker now believes Kirk is in on his father's scheme to keep him from Linda. Seeing "Linda," the guard tells Decker he will have to take her to Chekov. Decker seems to acquiesce, but then physically disables the guard in a surprise attack. Decker and Linda run off.

Xon now reports to Kirk that the alien is heading away from the officers' area. Chekov can't understand how the alien eluded his guards. Kirk tells him to check on it, personally.

When Decker and Linda encounter additional security forces in the corridors, they are able to pass though them easily. "Linda" is now familiar with their devices and they no longer can detect her as an alien. Laughing at how easy it all is, Decker tells her that to stop the guards once and for all, he and she will have to "pluck their feathers." He leads Linda down another corridor.

In the ship's engine anteroom, Decker hesitates for a moment, as if what he is about to do bothers him. But then Linda, noticing his inner struggle, smiles at him and her eyes begin to glow luminously. Decker's doubt vanishes, and he enters the engine room.

Once in the engine room, Decker battles lightheartedly with two engineering technicians as he succeeds in smashing console valves that release a hissing gas. Before one of the technicians can summon help via the intercom, Decker turns him aside. Then Scott enters and Decker invites him to join in the fun. As the other technician rushes Decker, Decker evades him gymnastically, astounding Scott.

When Decker opens another valve to release gas, Scott gets to it and shuts it off, wondering aloud: "Are you daft, man—without coolant the impulse engines will overheat!" But Decker opens valve after valve, and Scott knows it is much easier to open them than to shut them. Decker goes to smash open a major cooling pipe.

As Scott tries to reason with him, Decker reveals that he doesn't know who the chief engineer is. He rambles on about his father, and tells Scott to tell the "old buzzard" that he never felt better, or freer. Scott doesn't know what Decker is talking about. He waves off other engineering personnel to approach Decker more closely. He tells Decker he's taking him to see Dr. McCoy. Decker isn't in favor of another doctor visit and hits Scott with a pipe, knocking him unconscious. Then Decker grabs a hanging cable and swings over the heads of the crewmen who lunge at him. He jumps down to meet "Linda," who is just entering the engine room, and together they run into an adjoining room.

An engineering technician summons Kirk by intercom. Kirk tells Uhura to have a security team meet him at the engine room. As Kirk leaves, Sulu tells him that the impulse engines are starting to overheat and that coolant pressure is falling. The reserve pressure is also malfunctioning. Kirk tells his helmsman to reduce thrust, that if it gets too hot, they'll warp out while making repairs.

Decker and Linda have escaped into the room housing the dilithium. Engineering crew attack the door with their phasers. When Chekov arrives, he tells them phasers won't be able to break through the energy field, and he asks after Scott. The crew tell him the chief engineer is now in sickbay, unconscious. Chekov then uses the intercom to ask Xon if he can deactivate the energy field. Xon says he will try, but he will need time to reroute circuits. Chekov tells him to hurry.

With Linda at the dilithium compartment, Decker deactivates locks, opens the door, and crawls inside. He emerges with the dilithium and shows it to Linda, calling it "the feathers of the *Enterprise* bird." He lightly asks if she would like him to make jewelry of it for her, but then agrees with her suggestion: He should destroy it. He blasts the dilithium into ash with his phaser, then leads Linda out of the room by a different door.

Chekov's team and Xon's efforts succeed in breaking down the door to the Dilithium Room. Chekov finds the dilithium ashes and runs out of the room by the doorway Decker and Linda used.

In the turbolift, Kirk is signaled by Xon on the intercom. Xon tells him that the alien and, presumably, Decker are now entering the forward turbolift, heading toward the upper decks. Kirk realizes that means their destination is the transporter room and orders Xon to notify Chekov. No one is to transport out without Kirk's authority. Kirk exits the turbolift and runs down the corridor.

In the transporter room, Decker orders the technician to beam him down to the planet. Without Kirk's authorization, the technician refuses. But because Decker is the first officer, the technician agrees to check with the bridge and turns on the signal switch. Just then, "Linda" enters and Decker turns the signal switch off. The technician turns to see "Kirk," who gives his authorization to beam both himself and Decker to the planet surface. The technician complies just as the real Kirk enters the room. The technician is confused.

Sensing a sudden change in the ship's attitude, Kirk hails Sulu on the intercom to ask about their orbit. His helmsman tells him that the ship is rapidly losing impulse power. Scott's voice cuts to confirm the worst. It's a losing battle just to contain the damage. They'll be doing well just to stay "afloat." Kirk orders full emergency procedures. Uhura joins in to tell Kirk that without dilithium she can't hold subspace channels open. They can't even call for help. Kirk sums up their situation: "Then we're stuck here . . . like the *St. Louis*. Why? What do these aliens want with our ship?"

Kirk's crew makes their reports about their efforts to reduce the ship's energy consumption. Chekov states that all nonessential decks have been evacuated and all excess items have been jettisoned. McCoy has moved sickbay to a lower deck. Scott's engineers have repaired the cooling system, but the impulse engines are almost totally burned out and need replacements, which they can't get without more power.

Kirk asks if they can conserve any more energy. Scott says they will, but they won't gain much time as a result. He calculates they have six hours, maybe seven. Xon states they have exactly 6.35 hours. McCoy worries that they just can't sit in a decaying orbit until they go down like a fireball —like the *St. Louis*. Chekov asks Kirk to let him take a team down to the planet to force the aliens to give back what they stole. Kirk points out that the aliens took nothing, they acted to destroy, and they might not have anything to give back to the *Enterprise*.

Xon notes that while his sensors indicate there is considerable power on the planet, it is not compatible with their systems, and scanners show no natural deposits of dilithium ore. Ilia, however, raises a new possibility. The *St. Louis* previously explored for and found new sources of dilithium, which its crew would have placed in the ship's storage vaults. Kirk points out to both Xon and McCoy that the odds that resulted in their finding a partially intact Captain's Log from the *St. Louis* might work once more in their favor. Ilia adds that the vaults' shielding would prevent the dilithium from registering on Xon's scanners. Scott warns Kirk that he wouldn't be able to use unpolished, unfaceted dilithium under their present conditions without blowing them up. Kirk reminds him that he did once before. But Scott says that was with the seasoned Spock, not the relatively untested Xon. Xon says Scott's fears are illogical. Kirk ends the discussion by deciding to search the planet for the crystals, no matter the risk.

On the planet's surface, Decker and "Linda" are vowing eternal love to one another while they are watched on a wallscreen by several other female aliens, including Lamen, who says approvingly: "He produces well. Perhaps he will live long."

Kirk, Ilia, and McCoy materialize in a flowered area on the planet. Ilia thinks it looks like paintings on Delta V. Kirk focuses on the word "paintings," while McCoy says if it's a hallucination, he'd like to come back some time and really enjoy it. Continuing their search for the crystals, the three come to a sleek, synthetic-appearing monolith. Kirk wonders if it is a religious object or a work of art.

McCoy examines the artificial monolith with his tricorder and announces its contents to be organic, somewhat akin to food. Kirk asks if it is a food-storage device, but McCoy says it *makes* food. Like our synthesizers, adds Ilia. McCoy believes the monolith takes in ordinary soil and air and changes them directly into edible organic compounds. Kirk says that explains why Xon was unable to find tilled soil on the planet. The aliens create food rather than growing it. McCoy notes, however, that the machine appears also to be broken—even if it is obviously designed to be self-repairing—because its contents are decaying. Kirk says everything runs down eventually, no matter how advanced.

Suddenly Ilia doubles up as if in great physical pain. McCoy can find no physical cause, but Ilia speaks of terrible, cruel mental images. McCoy doses her with a tranquilizer and she faints. Then Kirk notices something and calls to McCoy. Nearby are a half-dozen aliens, all beautiful, exotic females doing a slow, ritualistic dance. Ilia awakens, and cries out: "No, don't . . . please . . . !" At the same time, one alien breaks from the dance, and rushes at Kirk, screaming wildly. Kirk holds his phaser defensively. The alien falls to the ground, dead. Kirk did not fire his phaser. McCoy reports she died of massive internal injuries, consistent with a beating. But no one touched her. And all the other aliens but one have disappeared. McCoy says his tricorder confirms that they are truly gone.

The scene is being witnessed by other aliens, on a viewscreen in a computer room on the planet. Lamen asks Ronel to attend to Kirk, McCoy, and Ilia.

Recovering, Ilia tells Kirk and McCoy that in her mind she saw the beating, and it was physical. Kirk has difficulty believing that pictures can kill, but Ilia tells him the pain was real for the aliens. McCoy notes that illusions that real might be able to disrupt the body and kill. As Kirk asks his two colleagues if what they have seen is group killing by illusion, some form of war, he gets no response from them. Kirk looks around to see that he is alone. And he is floating in space.

Next, Kirk finds himself in an elaborately feminine boudoir with a beautiful female whom we know to be Ronel. She asks him if she has pleased him, and, dreamily, he says yes. When she tells him she can grant any fantasy he might have, he wonders if any of what he is experiencing is real and if she herself is a illusion. Ronel asks him, in turn, if that matters. Kirk pushes her away, as he struggles to recall that there is more to life. He asks: "If I hear a song in my head, the thoughts are real . . . but is the song real?" Ronel does not answer.

Kirk remembers he was with friends and asks her where they are, what she has done with them. When she tells him they are well, he asks who she is and the alien tells him she is Ronel, a worker—a *feenor*, of the planet Grokh. She tells him she only wants from him what he also wants: to save his crew. The way to do that is to beam them down to the planet or else they will die.

Kirk soon realizes that Ronel does not understand that her people's interference with the *Enterprise* prevents the transportation of the crew to the planet. She refuses to help him find the dilithium the ship requires, fearing that he would only use it to escape. Kirk again asks her why her people need his crew, but Ronel replies only that she must report to her council.

As Kirk continues to say, "Why?" he finds himself again with McCoy, who asks him: "Why what?" Just then Ilia "wakes" to ask: "Where is he?" And Kirk understands that Ilia has just returned from an encounter with a seductive alien, just as he has. As Kirk hails the *Enterprise*, Uhura tells him they have been trying to locate him. Kirk tells her he has been there all the time.

Xon now gives Kirk an update on his analysis of the data on the aliens. The planet has a small population of 2.2 million. Industry, though wearing out and in disrepair, is almost wholly automated. The society, for whatever reason, is in apparent severe cultural decay.

Scott makes a report of his own that is of more immediate concern to Kirk. He tells Kirk that their situation without dilithium is nearing the untenable. Kirk urges his chief engineer to buy him more time.

When McCoy asks Kirk what they should do now, Kirk reminds McCoy that they have been monitored by the aliens from the beginning. Then he turns to address the unseen watchers: "Council of Grokh. You need us as much as we need you. Let us meet now, before it is too late."

Ronel appears before Kirk, McCoy, and Ilia. She is in alien form. She tells them she will take them to her council.

In the Council Building, Kirk and his two colleagues meet Lamen as she directs several other aliens who work at computerlike devices that apparently control the planet's industry. When Kirk tells Lamen that he assumes the council is the body that can negotiate for the planet, and asks if she and the other council members make and administer the laws, Lamen tells him that on Grokh, there are no laws or rules. Everyone is free to do as she pleases. Ronel adds that the Grokhoor—the inhabitants of Grokh—haven't had to work for a thousand years. Even the feenor—the council members—work but a small part of each day.

McCoy suddenly understands. No one on the planet repairs its machinery because no one remembers how to do it. Kirk also understands. There is no one left who can teach them how.

When Kirk asks Ronel and Lamen how their people occupy themselves, Ronel says they "pursue the fullness of life." McCoy translates that as "fighting and killing," but Lamen dismisses what the *Enterprise* crewmembers saw as the actions of a few, temporarily insane inhabitants. She says that her people do not kill on purpose. She apologizes for what happened to the *St. Louis* and to the *Enterprise*, and says they intended no harm. They have only been studying how humans are affected by the Grokhoor "wister," their term for an experience that gives meaning to life, what humans call "illusion." They wanted the humans to have the pleasure of knowing how they will spend the rest of their lives on Grokh.

Kirk says it is unimportant how humans react to the Grokhoor wister, because they will not be staying, once they get the aid they need from Lamen's people. Then Kirk will call on the Federation to help the Grokhoor any way they can. Lamen tells Kirk that his people are so aggressive, the inhabitants of Grokh do not wish to have others like him here until they have thoroughly studied his crew. To this end, they have cleared the crew's minds and have confidence that Kirk will find a way to bring his people down to Grokh safely. At this point, McCoy breaks in to say that the point will be moot since soon there will be no crew and no *Enterprise*. Kirk tells the ship's doctor that it is useless to reason with the aliens. They truly do not understand the position they have placed Kirk in.

Kirk tries a new tack. He tells Lamen that if there really are no laws on her planet, then he and his crew should be free to go. Lamen says he is not free to go away. Many others have failed them. She says her people look upon the crew of the *Enterprise* as their last chance.

Suddenly, Ilia warns Kirk of images forming. Kirk calls out to McCoy and Ilia to draw their phasers. Then the three of them waken in a laboratory, still on planet Grokh. Kirk's three missing crewmembers from Decker's landing party are also in the lab. Ibsen, Kelly, and Rand lie on nearby slabs, in a near-comatose state, mumbling happily. Feeding-type tubes are attached to each of them. As Kelly shakily raises himself up, we see his tropical-lagoon illusion, in which he amuses himself with acquiescent natives. Ibsen is with him, and they call out to Kirk to join them.

Appalled, Kirk appeals to McCoy, who quickly examines Ibsen and begins to administer a hypo to him. But before McCoy's stimulant can take effect, Ibsen's heart, though young and healthy, gives out from overstimulation, and he dies. A fourth slab containing a sheet-covered body draws Ilia's attention. Kirk lifts the sheet to discover Decker, dying.

McCoy tells Kirk he cannot save Decker's life without taking him back to the ship. Ilia stares at Decker and asks Kirk if he cannot see what *they*—

the lovers—are doing to Kirk's first officer. Kirk and McCoy do not understand her insight until McCoy uses a tricorder on Decker. He discovers radiation of excess psychic energy. Kirk wonders if the aliens' illusions are so exciting they exceed human capacity to tolerate them. He urges McCoy to take Decker off the feeding tubes, to perhaps disrupt the illusions. As McCoy does so, he makes another discovery: Decker's output of male hormones—androgens—is incredibly high. McCoy then checks Rand and finds that her estrogen count is normal. Since estrogens neutralize androgens, McCoy works quickly to improvise a syringe to inject Rand's female hormones into Decker. He hopes if he can neutralize Decker's output of male hormones, the illusions might be broken. The experiment works.

McCoy then stabilizes Kelly and Rand so they may be safely left behind, while Kirk inspects the room. It is completely sealed, but Ilia points out they still have their phasers. Kirk asks McCoy to give Ilia and him hormone injections, to defend against being taken over by the Grokhoor wister again. Then Decker uses a phaser to blast a hole in the wall and Kirk, McCoy, and Ilia exit the room.

As soon as Kirk exits, he hails the *Enterprise* with his communicator. Uhura tells him Xon has an urgent message for him: Cracks in the number two impulse engine have reduced the time remaining to destruction to little more than an hour. Kirk is forced to tell Scott he still doesn't even know if there is dilithium on Grokh.

Ilia alerts Kirk to the sound of computers at work down one of the corridors. Kirk uses his phaser to blast his way through the door to the computer room. Inside, Lamen and another alien have gone from working at a computer to engaging in a slow, ritualistic dance, in a trancelike state, that keeps them from reacting to Kirk and his group. Kirk wonders if they are witnessing a form of war again, but McCoy and Ilia have another explanation. Ilia sees very sensuous images and McCoy reports an unusually high androgen count. When Kirk points out the aliens are female, not male, McCoy tells him they are actually both. They are hermaphrodites, and the interesting thing is that the androgens in their bodies are human.

Kirk finally puts it all together. The aliens have killed Ibsen, caused the death of the *St. Louis* and its crew, and crippled the *Enterprise*, all to obtain a steady supply of male hormones that they use as catalysts to energize their illusions.

Decker calls Kirk over to look at a bank of viewscreens that show views of the alien population elsewhere on the planet. Kirk sees an entire planet in the grip of illusion, the alien wister. Suddenly, Kirk senses a way to locate the storage vaults of the *St. Louis* and, perhaps, Scott's much-needed dilithium. He turns to Ilia and asks her if she can link the viewscreens to the alien computer. When Ilia says she would need time to figure them out, Kirk asks McCoy to try his hormone treatment on some of the aliens to see if it will neutralize them, too. The aliens could then help Ilia.

McCoy injects Lamen, but sees no reaction. Before he can give her another injection, Ronel interrupts and tells him to stop. She is in the doorway to the computer room, holding a phaser-like weapon. She tells Kirk and his team that she can no longer project into wister and that he is destroying everything. Kirk retorts that he only wants to save his ship and his crew. Ronel replies that she can no longer tolerate his aggression and that if she must, she will use her weapon.

Stalling for time, Kirk engages Ronel in debate. We learn that her weapon was made long ago by the ancients who made everything on the planet, and that, once, there were nearly two billion people on Grokh. When Kirk asks what became of them, Ronel tells him they died in the One-Day War that began because of aggression. No one of Grokh will let this happen again. When McCoy protests that this tragic event has no relevance to what is happening now, Kirk provides the explanation. The Grokhoor use illusion to fill the void in their lives and to placate their aggressions to gain peace.

Kirk takes the hypo from McCoy. He says they are running out of time. Someone has to show them how to find the dilithium. Ronel fires a warning shot near Kirk. She tells Kirk that they cannot let them go. Aggression is increasing on Grokh, and their bodies are unable to make the hormones they must have. Kirk again tells her that he and his crew are not their solution. What will her people do when their prisoners grow old and die? He urges her to use her people's aggression to find another solution. Ronel fires a second warning shot.

Kirk warns her he will never give up, even if he loses his ship. He will use her computers to build another *Enterprise* to escape from Grokh. Then he will fly away and return with an equally aggressive Starfleet. He will do all of this because, sooner or later, he *will* find the dilithium.

Ronel rushes to the computer and presses buttons. Lights flash and a missile appears on a computer viewscreen. Kirk takes the phaser from her. She does not fight him. She tells him that no one can stop the missile now, and that it is set to destroy the *St. Louis* dilithium. Kirk is elated. There *is* dilithium. He hails the *Enterprise*.

Kirk asks Xon to calculate the course of the missile and thus, the location of the dilithium. Xon tell him he can do both, but he will not be able to beam the dilithium aboard. Using the transporter will create an energy-disruption field that will most likely set off the missile's extremely sensitive firing mechanism. Since the *Enterprise*'s shields are deactivated, and the missile's course puts it directly across the ship's path, the *Enterprise* would be destroyed in the explosion.

Scott tells Kirk that, whatever move he makes, he should make it soon. There are less than twelve minutes remaining. Kirk asks his chief engineer if he can pull away from the missile, even though the remaining impulse engines are very weak. Scott says he can, but worries he will not be able to pull away a sufficient distance in the time. Xon adds that the acceleration required will reduce their time to eight minutes, fourteen seconds.

Kirk orders Sulu to set the new course, and tells Scott to go to full available impulse power. He instructs Xon to lock transporter controls for dilithium beam-up in exactly six minutes, thirty-one seconds. That will give Xon ninety seconds to install the dilithium and activate it. Xon says he has studied Spock's old formula for the use of unpolished crystals and has already set the transporter for beam-up to the engine room. Xon and Scott both say they will be waiting in the engine room.

As Kirk watches the viewscreen in the control room on Grokh, the missile unexpectedly turns, three minutes before the planned operation. Kirk asks Ronel what has happened. She says she doesn't know, that it is supposed to be automatic. Xon replies at once to Kirk's query. He tells his captain that the missile's guidance system has picked up the sympathetic resonance of the *Enterprise*'s transporter and has locked onto it. The *Enterprise* is now the target, and the missile is closing fast. Kirk orders a red alert.

Kirk then hails Chekov and asks him to stand by to divert all power to the number six deflector. Scott's voice cuts in to say that such a measure will only slow down the ship. It won't stop the missile. Chekov agrees, but Kirk insists on his orders being followed. Then Kirk instructs Uhura to set manual override on the transporter lock. He tells Sulu to prepare to pull hard about and bring the number six deflector into the missile's path. Kirk gives the word, and the *Enterprise* turns into a new heading. Then Kirk calls for power to the number six shield and tells Uhura to energize.

In space the missile explodes, and the crew on the bridge of the *Enterprise* is violently thrown about. But the ship has survived, and Xon has the dilithium on board. Kirk asks if Spock's formula will work, and Xon tells him that it does not apply precisely to the shapes of the dilithium they now have. However, Xon will attempt to bypass surface planes to focus on the inner geometrics. Scott warns that there will be no controlling the energy flow if Xon is off by even a hundredth of a degree. Xon agrees. The matter-antimatter mixture will

then explode. Decker gives the latest time count: thirty seconds. Kirk tells Scott to stand by to activate warp engines. There is no time for a test run. Sulu is to cut in warp drive on Kirk's command.

Sulu's voice reports complete loss of impulse power. The *Enterprise* is falling and its skin temperature is 912 degrees and climbing rapidly. Kirk calls out to Xon to make his final adjustments and lock it up. Sulu's voice says: "Temperature 2007 degrees and rising. I am losing control of the *Enterprise*."

Xon reports the crystals are in place, and Kirk orders activation of the warp engines. Scott complies, but the engines begin fluctuating. He fears they will never take the load. Sulu reports 4041 degrees and 100 kilometers to impact. He needs warp drive. Kirk isn't ready to give the order yet. He checks with Scott, who says the engines are smoother but he doubts they are ready. Kirk calls for Sulu to cut in warp drive.

Sulu's voice fills the computer room on Grokh. The *Enterprise* is beginning to climb. Its temperature is falling. Relief floods Kirk and his team.

Later, on board the *Enterprise*, the crew reunited, with the planet Grokh receding on the main viewscreen, Kirk, McCoy, and Xon discuss the remarkable people of Grokh. Xon wonders if the aliens will soon destroy themselves in war, if the *Enterprise* should have arranged to send them a helpful team of Vulcan scientists. Kirk reminds Xon that Grokh will have to solve their problem sooner or later on their own. He tells McCoy that he recalls the doctor teaching him how quickly some people heal once they throw away their crutches. When Xon asks him if his assessment is what humans call an "educated guess," Kirk waxes eloquent and elaborates upon his insight. He tells Xon, "It is our way of recognizing that life's complexities are not always reducible to meaningful odds, that a simple principle may contain more truth than a roomful of numbers."

Xon tells his captain his rhetoric is most persuasive, if not quite logical. Kirk replies: "Why, thank you, Mr. Xon, that's a compliment...I think?"

"Devil's Due"

Written by William Douglas Lansford

Here's a classic story straight from The Twilight Zone, *dressed up in science-fiction garb to give Captain Kirk a chance to go head to head with the Devil*—or in Star Trek *terms, a malevolent energy being.*

Like "The Child," this script was rewritten to become an episode of The Next Generation, *keeping the same title, with Picard taking a self-proclaimed devil to trial over the fate of a planet, and Data assuming the role played here by the* Enterprise's *computer.*

The *Enterprise* enters a distant corner of the galaxy where a charted, yet never visited planet exists. It has been studied only at a distance by passing robot vehicles. Xon points out to Kirk that ship's sensors indicate life on the planet's surface, and adds that an investigation of it lies within their mission. Kirk agrees.

The *Enterprise* then approaches an Earth-size, M-type planet, green and tranquil. With his ship in orbit, Kirk leads a landing party consisting of Xon, McCoy, Sulu, Ilia, and Chekov. Despite Chekov's apprehensions about what they might encounter, the landing party is met by a group of peaceful inhabitants and finds that the planet's composition and vegetation closely resemble that of Earth. One of the inhabitants, Reyloz, welcomes Kirk to the planet Naterra and tells him he will take Kirk's party to meet their wise leader, Zxolar the Blessed.

The interior of Zxolar's palace is wondrously decorated and furnished with the elements of nature—trees and rocks for chairs and tables, grass and plant carpeting, fountains, birds, and flowers everywhere. There are no artificially constructed furnishings.

Zxolar is a beautiful old man who is ailing, and who is disturbed to learn of the arrival of Kirk's party. He fearfully greets his messenger's news of the arrival of aliens on Naterra with the words: "Komether! It is the beginning of the end!" He does, however, summon the aliens to meet him.

Only three of Zxolar's followers are allowed to remain behind for the meeting: Reyloz—who brought the aliens to the palace, Kleyax—a dedicated young follower, and Eulix—an exquisite young woman. These three are Zxolar's disciples and are privy to all he knows.

Zxolar tells Kirk that it is not time. The contract is not yet due. Eventually, after cleverly questioning Kirk and testing his reaction to the word *Komether,* Zxolar realizes that Kirk truly does not understand what Zxolar is talking about. That the alien, in fact, is from some other planet called "Earth," and that his intent is friendship, not destruction.

Now Kirk learns the reason for Zxolar's strange questions and agitation: Within twenty Earth days, the planet will be destroyed in a sheet of flame. Zxolar does not tell Kirk why the planet will be destroyed, or who will destroy it. He does, however, appeal to Kirk for help. But Kirk tells Zxolar that Federation laws will not permit him to interfere with the natural development of any planet, unless that development poses a direct threat to the Federation. Zxolar looks for a loophole in Kirk's laws. He asks what Kirk would have done if his landing party had been attacked by the Naterrans. Kirk replies that he does have some latitude in areas where the safety of his ship and crew are concerned.

Suddenly, Zxolar grows weak and collapses. McCoy checks him, but needs better equipment than he has with him to diagnose the symptoms. He asks Kirk for permission to beam the old man to the *Enterprise.*

Before Kirk makes his decision, a kaleidoscopic energy being materializes and coalesces around McCoy's head. The doctor cries out in agony and falls to his knees. The energy being moves to a spot on a nearby wall. McCoy rises, wild-eyed, and runs at the wall. The energy being vanishes. And so does McCoy. Somehow, he has disappeared *into* the wall.

Kirk and the landing party search unsuccessfully for McCoy. The Naterrans do not believe that McCoy disappeared into the meter-thick wall. When Xon describes the energy being, no one seems to recognize it. Kirk calls for more landing parties to join the search. In the meantime, he beams up to the ship with Zxolar and Xon. The Naterran leader is now comatose and failing fast. Chapel goes to work on him. As she begins, the energy being reappears and envelops Chapel. She screams, is restrained, and loses consciousness. Junior medical officers determine that she is in a state of suspended animation.

Kirk orders Xon to sound an intruder alert. Ship's sensors are unable to pick up any trace of the energy being. Kirk and Xon decide that the energy being is somehow appearing from and disappearing into another dimension. Because it has attacked the two doctors who were trying to help Zxolar, it also seems that the mysterious being wants Zxolar left to die.

Needing more information, Kirk and Xon return to the planet. When they encounter Zxolar's disciple, Reyloz, they ask him about his leader's connection with the energy being, but he explains nothing. In private, Reyloz finally admits that he has sworn an oath of secrecy and he can say no more.

Xon tells Kirk that his tricorder readings of the energy being reveal that it is, indeed, pure energy as they had earlier surmised, but it is also a combination of six semidistinct parts. Xon also has a new explanation for McCoy's disappearance into a solid wall. Xon reasons that under the guiding influence of the energy being, McCoy might have been able to pass through the wall by travelling through the spaces between the wall's molecules. Right now, Kirk says, Xon's deduction might well make sense, but it still doesn't answer the question: Where is McCoy?

As Kirk and Xon now search Zxolar's palace for any information about the energy being or McCoy's location, they discover a sealed, subterranean room with machinery dating back to the planet's "prenature" state. Xon works out how to access the machinery, and they quickly learn that the room is a library or archive. On a large viewing screen, they replay some of the planet's past history.

The screen depicts the plight of a dying planet being strangled by its own pollution, the results of unchecked technology. It also shows the rise of six young philosophers who pool their faith and intelligence to save their civilization. One of the six is a much younger Zxolar. One night, during the group's prayer vigil, a strange energy being appears to the six young philosophers and offers a way out. The energy being is Komether.

Kirk and Xon recognize the energy being as the same form that attacked McCoy and Chapel. They also realize that since the events they are watching took place over a thousand years ago, Zxolar himself is over a thousand years old.

The full story of what Zxolar and his disciple Reyloz did not share with Kirk now becomes apparent as an aged image of the Naterran leader appears on the archive viewscreen. Giving his explanation for the purposes of recorded history, Zxolar tells of the bargain the six philosophers struck with Komether in exchange for the era known as "The Thousand Years of Joy."

Komether reversed the inexorable destruction of Naterra and restored its natural resources. The Naterrans abolished all technology. Crops grew again, and the population increased. All were healthy and happy. Zxolar and the other philosophers became known as "The Circle of the Wise" and were venerated as "Prophets of Hope." They were the only ones to know what the price of the rebirth was. At the end of the thousand years, Komether would destroy everything on Naterra and the planet would become his to do with what he would. Because the six philosophers were young, they believed that a thousand years would surely be enough time to work out some way to leave Naterra and find some other hospitable planet. But nothing was ever done. Released from

despair and ignorant of the bargain, the rest of Naterra even forgot about the dark past as the centuries went on. Komether's return, with only nineteen days of the thousand years remaining, is to remind Zxolar of his contract.

Xon notes with interest that the images he and Kirk have been watching are in fact mental images projected directly from Zxolar's brain. Now, Kirk speculates that perhaps there is some connection between Zxolar's dying condition and the doom foretold in the old leader's computer-like diary. Yet he wonders why, if the old man is to die with his planet, Komether is so eager to dispose of Zxolar.

Xon interrupts Kirk's speculation to point out that the Enterprise and its crew may be caught up in the destruction of the planet unless they can find McCoy soon and leave. But Kirk already knows that he may have to face a choice between saving his friend or saving his ship.

As Kirk reviews what they have learned about Komether, he has an insight. Since the energy being has the power to kill, but has not killed Zxolar, Chapel, and presumably McCoy, then perhaps there are limits to its power. Zxolar, especially, given Komether's interest in the old leader's death, might be the key to that control. Kirk realizes that they *must* restore Zxolar's health.

He and Xon decide to get Zxolar onto a life-support table in the Enterprise's sickbay so they can keep him alive, even, if necessary, by artificial means. But first, to calibrate the table properly for alien body functions, Xon must get readings from one of the Naterrans. He does so by secretly scanning Reyloz and then commences preparation of the table. His work takes ten hours to complete.

Now Kirk must find a way to physically move Zxolar to the table without alerting Komether, who is somehow aware of Zxolar's every move. Kirk decides to use a group of five volunteers to move Zxolar quickly, so Komether cannot attack all of them at once. Kirk, Scott, Chekov, Sulu, and Xon enter sickbay together and begin the transfer.

Instantly, Komether appears and envelops them one by one. Soon, only Kirk and Xon are left. When Kirk can go no farther, Xon struggles on in incredible pain. With his Vulcan strength, Xon places Zxolar on the life-support table, completes the necessary body connections, and activates the machinery. At once, the Naterran leader's lifesigns improve. At the same time, Komether weakens. Chapel stirs in her coma, but then falls back, her condition unchanged.

Under gentle questioning, Zxolar tells Kirk that the contract he and the other philosophers made with Komether was a written and duly signed document. For the first time, Kirk realizes that Komether has legal right to claim Naterra when the thousand years are up. Only eighteen days remain.

Zxolar tells Kirk where to find the contract. Kirk directs Chekov to beam down to the palace and retrieve the document from its hiding place.

As soon as he examines the contract, Kirk determines that it is a binding agreement, no matter how harsh and unfair its terms might be. However, there is now another problem facing Kirk. At present, Zxolar is a deterrent to Komether's power. If—when—the Naterran leader dies, what will prevent Komether from eventually moving on and taking over other planets? Clearly, the energy being is a malevolent power and, as such, poses a threat to the Federation. Komether must be stopped. Now, if possible.

Kirk goes to Zxolar and challenges the contract. When Komether appears, Kirk proposes a trial to test the matter. When Komether says the contract is a legal one and requires no trial, Kirk reminds the energy being that it cannot achieve full power as long as Zxolar lives. Kirk can keep the Naterran leader alive indefinitely, unless, of course, Komether agrees to the trial, by whose verdict Kirk will abide. Kirk suggests the impartial ship's computer be the judge. Komether accepts, knowing he has a valid contract and that the computer will judge facts alone.

Kirk and Komether set the terms. If Komether wins, the contract stands and Kirk will allow Zxolar to die so that Komether can take over. If Kirk wins, Komether must return McCoy, restore Chapel's health, and leave this dimension forever. Komether adds one further term: If he wins—he takes Kirk and the *Enterprise*, too.

The trial swings from favoring one and then the other of the two adversaries. Finally, Kirk sees the truth. Komether was created by energy released by the six philosophers, so his power does, in fact, stem from Zxolar's will. Thus, by using Zxolar's own will, Kirk is able to exorcise Komether and defeat the energy being forever.

When Komether is gone, and Zxolar has sufficiently improved with assistance from a recovered Chapel, his renewed mental powers allow him to sense McCoy's whereabouts. Then Zxolar and Kirk beam down to the planet. By the time the Naterran leader arrives on the surface, his mental strength is awe-inspiring and he easily locates and frees the ship's Chief Medical Officer. All this time, McCoy has been trapped *within* the wall.

Knowing that Naterra is now free to continue its development with full knowledge of its past mistakes and renewed hopes for its future, Kirk and the *Enterprise* continue on their mission.

"Lord Bobby's Obsession"

Written by Shimon Wincelberg

What do you get when you cross "The Squire of Gothos" with "Space Seed"? This story. "Lord Bobby's Obsession" borrows from both earlier episodes from the Original Series, and might have added many fascinating details to the history of the Star Trek universe, including the Britannic Commonwealth, the "rank" of cabin boy, and the truly startling idea that Klingons were visiting Earth in flying saucers in the 1950s to abduct humans and perform medical tests on them! Coming, as it did, from a time before books such as Communion and Intruders had popularized the concept of alien abductions, "Lord Bobby's Obsession" is truly a story ahead of its time.

While en route to a distant Federation colony that is threatened by possible Romulan attack if it does not comply with an unacceptable ultimatum, the *Enterprise* comes upon the *Niobe*, an abandoned Klingon destroyer becalmed in space. Kirk stops to investigate for two reasons: one relating to

security, the other humane. The destroyer might harbor a highly advanced weapons system of interest to Starfleet Intelligence, and ship's sensors report some sort of lifeform still aboard.

Uhura, assisted by exolinguist Yeoman Jennifer York, hails the derelict destroyer. At first there is no response. Then a burst of incoherent signals follows. York decodes them. They appear to be part of a haunting nineteenth-century English folk song with which York is familiar. Kirk directs Uhura to signal for permission to board. But the only response is a repetition of the English folk song. Kirk decides to beam over a landing party to investigate.

The landing party, armed by Chekov, is under the command of First Officer Decker, who includes in his team Yeoman York as interpreter or decoder. Before the party beams over to the *Niobe*, a strange magnetic pulse from the destroyer interferes with some of the *Enterprise*'s relays.

But once this problem is identified and dealt with, the transportation seems to take place without incident—until Decker and York find they are the only ones who have successfully beamed over to the bridge of the Klingon ship. Decker immediately tries to hail the *Enterprise*. But the magnetic pulse has also jammed all communication between Decker and his ship.

Out of contact with Decker, and given the malfunctioning of the transporter, Kirk decides for the moment to rely on his first officer's resourcefulness, at least until Ilia identifies the precise nature of the disturbance and a way to neutralize it. Decker decides, for the moment, to trust to his captain's resourcefulness, also. He and York explore the unfamiliar bridge. They soon realize that the destroyer's appearance not only indicates severe battle damage, it also bears evidence of someone's very ingenious attempts to restore its ability to travel.

Just then, Decker and York meet the lifeform on board the *Niobe*—an apparent Edwardian dandy, who introduces himself as Robert Standish, Third Earl of Lancashire, but known to his friends as "Lord Bobby."

Lord Bobby pleads loneliness, especially for a fitting companion such as Yeoman York might prove to be. Having heard her cool English accent on the hailing broadcast has convinced Lord Bobby that he might at long last have found a kindred spirit. He asks to be taken on board the *Enterprise,* as he spins Decker and York a tale of having been kidnapped by and subjected to tests by Klingon space explorers in primitive "saucer-like" vehicles around Earthtime 1900. His kidnappers, between tests, maintained him in a cryogenic state that prevented him from aging, until the day he awakened to find himself alone on a disabled, abandoned vessel that is an apparent victim of a fierce battle.

As Decker begins to note an evasiveness about Lord Bobby, a degree of rapport begins to build between York and Lord Bobby, based on their common love for English literature and a nostalgia for a vanished, upper-class Edwardian country life that neither's ancestors likely ever experienced.

Abruptly, communication is restored between Decker and the *Enterprise.* After Decker reassures Kirk that Lord Bobby poses no security threat, Kirk grants permission for the man-out-of-time to beam aboard. While Decker speaks with his captain, neither he nor York sees Lord Bobby casually touch a complex, nonornamental bracelet on his left wrist. The device begins to pulse, almost imperceptibly. Lord Bobby seems to have some as-yet-undefined powers that depend on this bracelet, which might have something to do with the interference with the communications link and the transporter. It might even have something to do with his ability to influence others to accept a certain image of him.

When the transporter, with its intense surge of power, starts to beam the three of them over to the *Enterprise,* these suspicions are confirmed and extended. Simultaneously with the power surge, Lord Bobby's image shifts momentarily to reveal, though not to Decker or York, that he is an alien, beautiful in his own shimmering way, but definitely not human. It would appear that his bracelet's power was weakened by the transporter power surge.

Kirk takes Lord Bobby to sickbay's diagnostic center and questions him while McCoy and Chapel prepare to scan him. The two doctors are interested in determining whether after all these centuries in cryogenic suspension, their affable guest's metabolism will still function normally. They also want to know if after exposure to repeated Klingon testing he poses any immunological threat to public health.

Aware of their visitor's interest in Yeoman York, Decker assigns York to Lord Bobby as his guide to the ship. Kirk asks York to keep a close eye on Lord Bobby until they can be sure he is totally harmless. Decker is still bothered by Lord Bobby's story.

The security-minded Chekov discovers flaws

in Lord Bobby's story when he does a quick computer scan of late nineteenth-century English social history. But Lord Bobby talks his way around each of the flaws.

Kirk, however, noting that the Klingons did not develop saucerlike interspace vehicles until the late 1950s, questions Lord Bobby more sharply.

At this point, Lord Bobby drops any attempts to ingratiate himself with Kirk and the crew of the *Enterprise*. He demands that Kirk "return" him to England. When Kirk tells him the *Enterprise* is on a high-priority, combat-ready mission in quite another direction and gives Sulu orders to proceed full ahead, Lord Bobby again touches his control bracelet. He waits for Kirk to discover that the *Niobe* is now attached to the *Enterprise* by a powerful magnetic pulse, then informs Kirk that any attempt to break this grip will trigger a doomsday device aboard the derelict Klingon ship that will destroy both vessels.

McCoy and Chapel now report to Kirk that their computer readouts reveal that Lord Bobby is an alien life-form and that all the tests they have run on him are meaningless. Ship's sensors also confirm for Kirk that the alien's threat is not an idle one. There *is* an activated doomsday device aboard the *Niobe*. And while the *Enterprise* has enough power to break the magnetic grip that now holds it to the Klingon ship, such an attempt *could* trigger the device.

Aware of the threat he represents to the *Enterprise*, York tries to work with Lord Bobby's obsession with England. She reminds him of such "English" values as fair play and concern for one's kith and kin, and then, failing that, appeals to his sense of compassion for the Federation colony menaced by the Romulans. At the same time, York finds herself falling more and more under the alien's spell. Even though he is dangerous, in every other way he is the embodiment of her fantasies of an ideal man.

Kirk reports to Starfleet Command that the *Enterprise* is under the temporary control of an alien being who insists on being taken "home" to Earth. Starfleet responds by ordering Kirk to find some way of neutralizing Lord Bobby's threat. The *Enterprise* is the only vessel currently close enough to intercept the Romulans before they carry out their threat against the endangered Federation colony.

Kirk, Scott, and Xon make plans to once again beam a landing party to the *Niobe*. Although doomsday devices, by definition, are not supposed to be able to be disarmed, Kirk says they must try to find some way to deactivate it. Xon warns that Lord Bobby's control bracelet will detect the momentary power drain from the transporter and that the alien will likely then force them to abort the mission by threatening to set off the bomb. Chekov says they will just have to trick and overpower the alien. Kirk agrees, and he and Chekov devise a plan.

Kirk demands a demonstration that Lord Bobby is not merely bluffing. As soon as Lord Bobby bares his bracelet, Kirk and Chekov, in perfect teamwork, immobilize the alien's arm. While Kirk holds Lord Bobby, Chekov tries to remove the bracelet, then screams in pain. Kirk is forced to release the alien, and Lord Bobby gives them the demonstration they asked for. His control bracelet suddenly drains all the power from the *Enterprise*'s air-conditioning system. All aboard gasp for breath as the temperature abruptly rises until everyone is prostrate from the heat. A moment later, Lord Bobby causes them all to feel their blood turn to ice.

The alien, as if reading Chekov's mind, assures them he has also anticipated they might, in desperation, be foolish enough to try to stun or kill him. Accordingly, he has set his control bracelet to automatically set off the doomsday device if his person receives the slightest shock. Tired of their childlike stratagems, he gives them a one-hour deadline to set a course for Earth or be blown up.

Kirk tries a last attempt at reasoning with the alien. He tells him that his request cannot be granted because the life he thinks still exists on Earth no longer does. As proof, Kirk uses the ship's computers to show Lord Bobby a thirty-second illustrated history of modern England. Lord Bobby, however, counters by saying that if the *Enterprise* is pushed to warp 10, then it can travel back in time and Kirk can deposit York and Lord Bobby back in late-Victorian England. In fact, with this maneuver, Kirk will actually *gain* time for his mercy mission. Then Lord Bobby uses his power bracelet to set automatic detonation of the doomsday device in fifty-nine minutes. If they follow his orders, he says he will, of course, press the "override" button.

As Kirk confers with his bridge crew, he is asked why the *Enterprise* can't do as the alien wants and then return to their own time. Kirk points out firmly that any tampering with Earth's past history, especially by the introduction of an alien life-form, is not only against standing orders, it is nonnegotiable. Kirk still sees only one possible course of action. They must board the *Niobe*, and seek, somehow, to neutralize its Klingon doomsday device whose appearance, location, technology, and protective boobytraps, are as yet unknown to them.

Decker, Scott, and Xon volunteer for the boarding party. Since all agree they cannot use the transporter, they decide to use the much-slower shuttlecraft, even though it will cost them precious minutes.

Yeoman York again tries to find out what underlies Lord Bobby's obsession. Feeling complacent and superior to his hosts, the alien tells her frankly about his birth and childhood on a primitive planet that was colonized by Earth people from the Britannic Commonwealth. Lord Bobby grew up admiring the "superiority" and "style" of the colonists. As a youngster, he signed up as a cabin boy on a Federation craft, hoping one day to be taken to the legendary planet Earth. Instead, several battles later, he ended up a prisoner on the Klingon destroyer, the *Niobe*. After the Klingon craft encountered a Romulan destroyer,

Lord Bobby remained the only survivor. He tells York of the agonizing loneliness he suffered that was allayed only when he learned how to use the damaged vessel's surviving library of English literature. York is touched by his story and his candor.

Meanwhile, the shuttlecraft from the *Enterprise* cautiously circles the derelict Klingon ship and enters it through a ragged hole blasted into its flank. Making their way through several auxiliary airlocks, one of which malfunctions and nearly traps them, Decker, Scott, and Xon reach the bridge. With the deadline ticking closer, the team begins its blind search for the doomsday device.

Back on the *Enterprise*, York again pleads with Lord Bobby to release the *Enterprise* if only until it completes its protective mission. Because she has come to see Lord Bobby as "almost human," she is shocked to realize that the alien truly does not understand such abstractions as "honor" and "self-sacrifice." He is unable to comprehend that, in her world, others' lives count more than one being's dreams.

At the same time, Kirk is under increasing pressure from Starfleet Command. Suspecting that Lord Bobby's control bracelet might also enable the alien to monitor space broadcasts, and hoping to mislead him if he is listening in, Kirk defies a direct order and is relieved of his command in favor of Decker. When Starfleet Command asks why Decker does not acknowledge the order, Kirk offers an obvious excuse to signal Starfleet that the captain of the *Enterprise* is unable to speak freely.

On board the derelict, Xon, after several failures, discovers an object that does not seem to belong to the vessel's power or navigation systems. Nor is it designed for simple modular repair, like all other devices they have found on the ship. The object is a solid piece of some unfamiliar metal that even their sensors are unable to identify or penetrate. What it does have that is readily identifiable is an advanced kind of clock that is swiftly ticking off the microseconds. If Lord Bobby was telling the truth about the time he was giving them to meet his demand, the device's clock timer has fifteen minutes left to count.

Unwilling to risk communicating with Decker, Scott, and Xon, Kirk joins York and Lord Bobby. When he does so, he realizes that York may be losing her ability to help him stall the alien for time. His yeoman is obviously having difficulty resisting the alien's influence.

On the bridge of the *Enterprise*, Uhura receives a distress call from the embattled Federation colony. It is now facing imminent attack from the Romulans. Uhura is torn, but she cannot offer them any hope.

On the bridge of the derelict, Decker and Xon briefly argue about which is the best point at which to make a high-risk attempt to penetrate the doomsday device. Then Scott emerges from an adjoining room with a duplicate of Lord Bobby's control bracelet.

On the *Enterprise*, York finally breaks down and confesses to Lord Bobby that they have been deceiving him. They never intended to meet his demand. Disillusioned with Earthly humanity, and York, the alien says now he never wants to go to Earth. And since they have shattered his dream, they can all blow up.

Hearing the alien's threat, Kirk openly hails his boarding party on the *Niobe*, and learns that they *might* have the key to disarming the device, though they are still running tests to be absolutely sure.

Lord Bobby bids farewell, not without tenderness, to York.

Kirk tells Scott to act. *Now.*

At almost the same moment, Lord Bobby activates the doomsday device and Scott overrides the order to explode. Scott is just a fraction of a second faster.

In the aftermath, Lord Bobby, now powerless, awaits the fury of Kirk's vengeance. He is astonished when Kirk offers him the option of beaming back to his derelict ship, with his dream unrealized but, with the aid of his library, still continuing. In the transporter room, Lord Bobby asks Yeoman York if she would consider joining him in his dream, his obsession. His effort moves York, but she decides to stay in the real world. Lord Bobby returns alone to his world of illusion.

"To Attain the All"

Written by Norman Spintad

T*his is an exciting story that certainly would have been one of the standouts among the first season of* Phase II. *At the time, the threat of "the All" was new for* Star Trek, *and it anticipates what the Borg intend to do in the time of* The Next Generation. *The story also strongly focuses on the characters, casting Decker and Xon as individuals instead of as shadows of Kirk and Spock. Admittedly, the transporter is called upon to do something it just can't do, but a production rewrite would surely have given that task to a shuttlecraft. That's what technical advisors are for.*

Norman Spinrad is an acclaimed science-fiction author, who also wrote the Original Series *episode "The Doomsday Machine." Not only was that episode one of the best of the series, it also introduced the character of Commodore Matt Decker, who, in the development of* Phase II, *turned out to be the father of the* Enterprise's *Will Decker.*

When the *Enterprise* encounters a star orbited by a series of life- and energy-devoid planets arranged like a string of pearls in a necklace, Lieutenant Xon detects energy readings from a small planetoid outside the orbit. Kirk orders the ship to approach to investigate. As they get closer to the planetoid, the main viewscreen picks up a small, rainbow-sheened body that gets larger and larger. Suddenly, the picture on the viewscreen changes to display only a chaotic, rainbow maelstrom of swirling colors. The planetoid, the star, the planets, and the known universe itself have disappeared. The ship is *elsewhere.*

On the bridge of the *Enterprise*, alarms sound red alert and all lights flicker.

Kirk's entry in the Captain's Log describes the situation: While exploring an unknown region of the galaxy, the *Enterprise* has suddenly and inexplicably transported somewhere else, where even the physical laws of the universe no longer seem to apply.

As Kirk, Xon, Scott, and Uhura try to determine where they are and what is happening, Xon states that the ship's sensors can provide no meaningful location or even readings on the nature of the space they are in. Life-support systems are working, but satisfactory performance of all other systems is erratic. Scott reports that he can't account for the wild fluctuations in the ship's speed, that the impulse engines are inoperable, and that the matter and antimatter in the warp-drive nacelles seem somehow to be in an unknown state of matter. The ship's chief engineer is even unable to tell from moment to moment whether the warp drive is operating. Uhura tells Kirk that she is unable to establish any communication with the outside universe.

Just then, in the midst of the bridge, a bald, blue-skinned humanoid with flowing robes materializes. He announces that he is "the Prince," the last representative of "the First Ones," a lost race that arranged a whole solar system for their personal convenience a billion years before Vulcan or Earth even existed.

Kirk demands to know where the *Enterprise* is, how it got there and why, and whether the Prince has caused what has happened. The humanoid calmly accepts responsibility for the situation. He tells Kirk that both the planetoid and the pseudospace that the *Enterprise* now occupies are elements in a kind of testing and teaching machine. The purpose of the "machine" is to share all the fantastic, lost knowledge of the First Ones with the younger races of the galaxy. To receive this knowledge, a race must prove itself worthy of "attaining the All." Then the humanoid invites Decker and Xon to accompany him to the planetoid, to make their attempts as representatives of their respective peoples.

As Kirk asks the humanoid to first prove his own good faith by releasing the *Enterprise*, Xon tells his captain that he can detect no lifesigns from their visitor. The Prince explains this by saying he does live, but not in the "poor, meager, mortal" way in which they understand life.

Kirk continues to insist that only when the

Enterprise is returned to normal space will he even consider allowing his crew to engage in the humanoid's enterprise. But the Prince declares that "the only way out is the way through," and that only by proving their worthiness to gain the First Ones' knowledge contained within the planetoid will the crew of the *Enterprise* learn what they need to escape. If they do not participate, they will remain where they now are, forever.

Xon's Vulcan logic compels him to point out that it would seem they have no other alternative but to accept the humanoid's challenge. Decker's spirit of adventure and sense of duty lead him to make the same recommendation to Kirk, albeit on more emotional grounds. Xon notes the unexpected pairing of Vulcan logic and human emotion that has resulted in their joint appeal.

Kirk reluctantly agrees to send Decker and Xon to the planetoid with the Prince. The three figures simultaneously disappear from the bridge.

Decker, Xon, and the Prince materialize within the planetoid in the midst of a swirling, seemingly immaterial chaos of shifting colors closely resembling the pseudospace in which the *Enterprise* is trapped. The Prince now tells the human and the Vulcan that their objective is to negotiate the illusory, mazelike interior of the planetoid to reach the central computer banks where the knowledge is stored. They will learn as they go, and their progress will be tested and evaluated in determining their worthiness to "attain the All." The Prince will accompany them as their guide, teacher, and evaluator. He cautions them that their key to success will be to remember that the only constant is change. He reminds them that "the way out is the way through," and tells them that he hopes they succeed. Then he vanishes.

Abruptly, Decker and Xon find themselves standing upside down on an immaterial ceiling, perpendicular to a wall with a circular passageway at its bottom. Just inside the passageway stands the Prince. He is also standing upside down on a ceiling.

On the bridge of the *Enterprise,* Uhura has lost

communicator contact with Decker and Xon. Lieutenant Ilia, replacing Xon as science officer, informs Kirk that the ship now appears to be being drawn into a high-gravity black hole that will certainly destroy it. While Sulu fights to control the helm, Kirk demands warp power from Scott. In the engine room, the Chief Engineer uses all his wits and skill to keep intermittent bursts of warp power coming as the matter and antimatter in the nacelles keep changing polarity unpredictably. The ship is maintaining its position, barely.

In the maze of the planetoid's interior, Decker and Xon use Vulcan logic and human intuition to work out a combined strategy to walk, upside down, across the ceiling, down the wall, and into the passageway. All at once, they find themselves to be standing right side up beside the Prince, who says to them: "Thus do you merge closer to the All." When he asks them, "Do you begin to learn?" Decker and Xon nod with understanding at one another.

In the sickbay of the *Enterprise,* Doctors McCoy and Chapel have a low-key professional dispute over the treatment of a crewmember who is in a trance-coma state after having been injured in the chaos still buffeting the ship. McCoy believes the crewmember is suffering physical trauma. Chapel feels the injury is psychosomatic. When the Prince appears and touches the two doctors, and tells them to "merge closer to each other and to the All," each begins to sound somewhat like the other as well as like the Prince. McCoy and Chapel then come to an agreement on a new treatment that blends their differing viewpoints.

Within the planetoid maze, Decker and Xon now encounter a wall of flame blocking the only available passageway. Beyond the flame, they hear the Prince's voice telling them they must pass through the fire to attain the All. Xon, sounding rather like Decker, tells his crewmate that he believes the Prince is telling them they must conquer their fear by trusting their bravery. Decker

agrees, sounding rather like Xon, and says he finds logic in what the Vulcan is saying. Together, they walk through the flame, unharmed, to meet the Prince on the other side.

On the bridge of the *Enterprise,* a state of continued red alert exists. Now the gravitational force pulling at the ship is fluctuating wildly. The ship is in danger of being torn apart as Scott is forced to continually adjust unreliable warp engines to compensate for the destructive, warring forces. The crew is also behaving unusually. Chekov and Sulu seem to be adopting one another's characteristics. Chekov is now loquacious; Sulu is terse. Uhura and Ilia are beginning to sound and think like one another. Kirk thinks they all are beginning to remind him of the Prince, who seems to be all over the ship at the same time. It is as if some sort of group mind is forming and the only one left out of it is Kirk, who is insulated by the loneliness of command. Only he seems able to see what is happening. Kirk realizes that he must do something, and fast.

Now, in the planetoid maze, Decker and Xon face the Prince over a chasm that is too wide to jump and that appears to be bottomless. When the Prince begins, "Where a fragment of the All has gone . . ." Decker and Xon finish the statement: ". . . All may follow." Hand in hand, Decker and Xon leap into the air above the chasm and float over to the other side.

The Prince now appears again on the bridge of the *Enterprise.* Though the ship is in a red-alert crisis, the humanoid's presence produces an eerie calm in the ship's crew. It is almost as if he, not Kirk, is in command. Kirk decides that if he doesn't make his move now, all will be lost. He fingers a red button on his console and warns the Prince that he will destroy the *Enterprise* unless contact with Decker and Xon is restored immediately. He also says he wants to hear some straight answers *now.* His crew, including Sulu, Chekov, and Uhura, try to dissuade him with Prince-sounding talk about "not destroying attainment of the All," but their efforts are cut off by the Prince himself.

The Prince declares that Kirk has won, that contact with Decker and Xon will be restored. However, this contact can be achieved only by the use of a mind-link between the telepathic nonhumans Xon and Ilia. Communicators won't work under current conditions. Although it seems Kirk has gained what he wished, the expression on the Prince's face indicates he has also gained what he wished.

On the bridge of the *Enterprise,* the Prince now touches his hand to Ilia's forehead. In the planetoid maze, at the same moment, the Prince touches his hand to Xon's forehead. Mind-link is established between Xon and Ilia, but it is unlike either of the customary Vulcan or Deltan mind-melds. On the bridge of Kirk's ship, Ilia now speaks with Xon's voice. In the maze, Xon can now converse directly with Kirk, as Xon hears Kirk through Ilia's ears. The Vulcan and the Deltan have become one.

Ilia, speaking as Xon, tells Kirk that Decker and Xon have almost reached their goal. Uhura mouths the same words that Ilia utters, showing the group mind at work.

Kirk demands to talk to Decker since Xon's words sound just like those of the Prince. The Prince agrees and, back in the maze, he touches hands to the foreheads of both Xon and Decker. Decker then speaks to Kirk through Ilia, and there are signs that Decker, Xon, Ilia, and Uhura have merged. Kirk uses his powers of command and his father/son-like relationship with Decker to try with partial success to rouse his first officer from the strange state his voice reveals him to be in. But just then, the ship bucks, the warp drive fails completely, and a sudden, tremendous increase in gravity bears down on all but the Prince. The *Enterprise* is about to be ripped apart and the crew crushed.

Through Ilia, Xon struggles to tell Kirk that he now has the knowledge to save the ship. All he needs is a mind-meld with Scott. In the planetoid maze, though Xon mouths the words that Kirk hears through Ilia, it is really the Prince who is speaking.

Back on the bridge of the *Enterprise,* Kirk sees no other option, and agrees to the mind-meld. In the engine room, the Prince touches his hand to the Chief Engineer's forehead. With robotic, superhuman speed, Scott then rewires panels, manipulates controls, and adjusts the engines in unfamiliar ways.

On the bridge, Kirk is relieved when the warp drive comes back online and the crushing increase in gravity diminishes. For the moment, his ship is safe, although he will soon learn that the ship is escaping destruction only by *continuous* rewiring and manipulation by Scott, working at superhuman speed, under the guidance of the group mind, which, in turn, is controlled by the Prince.

Kirk now realizes that, in acquiring Scott, the group mind has achieved a kind of critical mass. The remainder of Kirk's crew have now joined into a telepathically linked single mind controlled by the Prince. No matter to whom Kirk speaks, all present answer in union. His orders are brushed aside by words that might as well have come straight from the Prince. Only Decker, thanks to Kirk's earlier efforts, appears to be the exception, but even he is under partial control by the Prince.

As he moves through the ship observing his crew working at superhuman speed, doing incomprehensible tasks in order to preserve the ship, Kirk keeps up a constant dialogue with his first officer. He appeals to Decker's sense of duty, his humanity, and their personal bond to keep Decker from being claimed by the group mind. Kirk dares do nothing more to break the mental linkages, knowing that to do so means the destruction of the *Enterprise.*

Meanwhile, in the planetoid maze, Decker, Xon, and the Prince now enter the central chamber where all knowledge is stored. The Prince guides Xon toward an eerily glowing globe set on a plain pedestal. He tells Xon: "Touch, and the All will be attained." As Xon tentatively places his hands on the globe, he undergoes what is obviously a powerful experience, and at the same time, Decker experiences the same thing.

On the *Enterprise*, the Prince materializes before Kirk and his crew to make an announcement. As the humanoid speaks, the entire bridge crew speaks in unison with him, saying: "All will be revealed. For the All has been released. The All has been attained." Then Kirk learns the whole truth as the Prince, in his own voice, and in multiple crew voices, tells him that the bodies of the crew of the *Enterprise* will now serve to house the group mind of the All who had become trapped in their computer bank for billions of years like a genie in a bottle.

The Prince explains that he is only a holographic projection generated from inside the globe in the maze, and that this is how he has been able to appear many places at once. He tells Kirk that the First Ones, at the height of their powers, gave up their separate bodies and identities to become a godlike, immortal group mind, the All, stored electronically in the maze's globe. Their globe became an unexpected trap as they waited for younger races to discover them. Now that they have have gained possession of new physical bodies, they intend to go forth and merge all intelligent beings in the galaxy into their group mind. The Prince believes this to be a fair exchange: Though the crew will lose their individual personalities, they will gain immortality and ultimate knowledge within the All.

The Prince offers a choice to Kirk and Decker, the only crewmembers left outside the group mind: "Attain the All or meet your death."

Kirk's crew begins to advance menacingly on Kirk. As he races from the bridge, Kirk calls out a final appeal to Decker to reject the group mind and remember his humanity, his duty to the ship and to the Federation. In the planetoid maze, Decker struggles to reach out to touch the glowing globe. When he does touch it, his face is transfigured in ecstasy.

As Decker fights to regain his humanity on the planetoid, Kirk fights to escape capture by his crew on the *Enterprise*. When Decker's hands leave the globe, he is filled by strange new knowledge, though he seems to be more in control of himself than before. Then Decker suddenly vanishes and—

—reappears on the *Enterprise* in a corridor outside engineering, where Kirk is about to be overcome by security forces as the Prince watches. The Prince commands Decker to join in the fight. After a moment's hesitation, Decker joins in. But before Kirk's first officer strikes him, Kirk calls out: "Will! It's me, Jim Kirk! And you're *Will Decker!* Help me!" Decker pauses, and the stress of what he was about to do disconnects him from the group mind.

Together, Kirk and Decker subdue the security forces, then attack the Prince. But since the humanoid is only a projection, they are unable to touch him and he disappears. Decker tells Kirk to forget about the Prince, that he, himself, now knows what to do. But they will need the assistance of the ship's Chief Engineer.

Kirk and Decker enter engineering to find Scott. Though the engineer tries to fight both of them, the stress of doing so also disconnects him from the group mind, and he becomes their familiar friend and ally once more. Decker tells Scott and Kirk they must go to the transporter. The three officers fight their way to the transporter room, overpower the personnel inside, and seal the door behind them. Decker then reveals his plan to Kirk and Scott. If they can beam the globe containing the All off the planetoid and away from its power source, the All should be powerless. Kirk's first officer tells them he believes he "remembers" the coordinates of the globe.

Outside the transporter room, someone pounds on the sealed door. As Decker, with Scott's help, manipulates the transporter controls, the door bursts open and the Prince leads a group of crew headed by McCoy, Sulu, and Chekov. The Prince orders: "The All must be maintained . . ." and the crew chants in the Prince's voice, ". . . stop them!" But as they advance on Kirk, Decker, and Scott, the Chief Engineer throws a final switch and the glowing globe materializes on the transporter platform. Instantly, the Prince disappears and the *Enterprise* returns to normal space. Ship's sensors confirm that the planetoid now has no energy readings.

In the transporter room, the dazed crew members revert to their separate personalities as if awakening from a terrible nightmare. Their strange, new knowledge leaves them, along with any memory of their recent actions. Kirk has Xon beamed back aboard the ship, and he, also, is back to his usual self, though he is more aware of the continuing loss of tantalizing fragments of knowledge that he had just possessed.

Later, on the bridge of the *Enterprise*, Kirk, Xon, and Decker debate what to do with the All, still trapped in the globe in the transporter room. Though logic would have them use the transporter to disperse its atoms into space, ending the potential menace, Kirk thinks of another way. He orders Scott to beam the globe toward the far Andromeda galaxy, noting it will take billions of years to arrive there, and that in that time, perhaps, the All will learn mercy and humility. He tells his crew that these are lessons the First Ones, with all their knowledge, have yet to attain.

"The War to End All Wars"

Written by Arthur Bernard Lewis

Even considering the demands of "In Thy Image," this is the most elaborate and technically demanding of Phase II's first scripts. Indeed, it is hard to imagine how this story could be told within an hour, and within the budgetary and production restrictions of weekly television, and still have included a space battle, derelict spacecraft, android armies, war ruins, alien tanks, an underground civilization, and war control chairs. That said, it is an involving story with a classic Star Trek theme, pitting Kirk against an alien world where war has evolved into the ultimate spectator sport.

While the *Enterprise* maintains standard orbit around the planet Shadir, Kirk prepares his crew for an excursion to the planet. Science Officer Xon conducts a general sensor scan of the planet's surface. Kirk, McCoy, and the rest of the bridge crew listen to a history tape made two hundred years earlier by a Federation starship that visited Shadir. McCoy, ordinarily not excited by beaming down to unfamiliar planets, is, for once, looking forward to the experience. Shadirians, at the time the tape was made, were bright, highly competitive beings completing their industrial revolution under the benevolent leadership of Plateous I, and Shadir is one of the most civilized of the non-Federation planets. To McCoy's delight, the Shadirians are described as lovers of fine wines, fine art, and spirited conversation.

Then Uhura reports intense communication activity from Shadir, none of it decipherable. At Kirk's request, she puts it on the speaker and the bridge crew hears a cacophony of undulating high-frequency sounds. Uhura also mentions to Kirk that she has received no answers to her attempts to contact the planet.

Xon now reports the results of his sensor scans. He can detect no signs of life on Shadir. Xon's speculations about what could have happened to the planet's advanced civilization are interrupted by Sulu. The helmsman draws Kirk's attention to the bridge viewer. The viewscreen shows they are passing through the debris of a number of small spacecraft. Many are burned-out hulks that look as if they were damaged in battle. Sensors show that some of them still contain bodies.

Then Uhura picks up a distress call. She gets a fix on its direction and the viewscreen displays the likely source of the call—a small spacecraft less damaged than the others but still drifting and in trouble. Its identifying mark is a green circle with the numbers 001 in the center of the circle.

Kirk calls up the ship's interior on the viewscreen, which reveals a breathtakingly beautiful young woman—Yra, dressed in a simple green uniform. The woman is pinned in the wreckage of her ship. Near her, on the floor of the small craft's cabin, lie two bodies, similarly attired in green uniforms. In obvious pain, Yra requests assistance.

From the bridge of the *Enterprise,* Kirk addresses Yra, identifying himself and his ship, and promising her his help. Yra expresses her thanks. Kirk orders the ship's tractor beam to pull the small craft into contact with the *Enterprise.*

Kirk decides to beam aboard Yra's ship to rescue her. Xon suggests caution. He tells Kirk that he has scanned the small craft and found no signs of life. But Kirk cannot ignore Yra's distress call. He tells Decker to take over command, and he heads for the transporter room.

Kirk materializes in the shambles of Yra's ship. Using a phaser, he quickly frees Yra. She tells him that her ship and the others whose wreckage he saw were casualties of the Shadirian War. Kirk is disappointed to learn that Shadir, with its highly civilized inhabitants, did not avoid the warfare stage of development. Yra now assesses the damage to her ship and concludes it will not survive reentry even if she repairs the engines. She asks Kirk if he can take her aboard the *Enterprise.* Just as he agrees to her request, he is hailed by Decker to alert him that a large shuttle-type warship is closing in on the *Enterprise.* Yra identifies it for Kirk: It is a new, 002 Blue Shadirian craft. The same kind that attacked her ship.

Kirk orders Decker to raise the *Enterprise's* deflectors. Decker hesitates for a moment, pointing out that this will mean Kirk is trapped on Yra's small craft. As Kirk repeats his order, the Shadirian ship hits and damages the *Enterprise* with a powerful blast. Now Decker is unable to raise deflectors. Kirk orders all power to the phasers, draining the already compromised engines on the *Enterprise.* Then he asks Yra to show him where her armament controls are. As she does so, she also tells him where the 002 Blue ship is most vulnerable to attack—its fusion engines in the prow. Kirk relays this information to Decker, then begins to work the armament controls of Yra's ship. The Blue ship is caught in the crossfire and explodes, but the explosion also catches Yra's ship. Kirk and Yra transport back to the *Enterprise* moments before her craft disintegrates.

Aboard the *Enterprise,* Kirk sends a strongly protesting Yra to sickbay. He then requests a damage report from Scott. Though Kirk is relieved to learn ship casualties were light, Scott informs him the engines will require extensive repair. The ship is now running on emergency power. It will take two days to repair the engines and four days to restore full power, and even then they will not be able to withstand another such attack.

To confirm Yra's description of a planetwide war, Kirk calls up a close-up view of the planet's surface on the main screen. The cities of Shadir resemble Earth's Berlin or London after World War II. All that remains is twisted steel and rubble. Then Kirk gets an urgent call from McCoy in sickbay.

McCoy tells Kirk that Yra is a robot. Yra rejects that label. She refers to herself as an android. Although she admits she is manufactured, she tells Kirk that she has the same feelings and sensitivity as a living being. She asks Kirk for permission to be transported back to the surface of her home planet. She tells him it is her duty to return. When Kirk asks her why the *Enterprise* has been unable to contact the Shadirians, Yra tells him she does not know. She can only surmise that they are too busy fighting. At that moment, Kirk receives a call to report to the bridge.

On the main viewscreen, Kirk, Xon, and the rest of the bridge crew study a greatly enlarged scene on the surface of Shadir. Another 002 Blue shuttlecraft is being prepared for flight. Kirk's crew has no way of knowing how soon the craft will be launched or if the *Enterprise* will be its target.

As McCoy and Yra come to the bridge, Yra uses Xon's computer to provide the answer. The attack ship will be launched in two days—hours before Kirk's Chief Engineer can ready the *Enterprise*'s engines. Yra tells them the *Enterprise* will most certainly be targeted. The bridge crew considers use of a photon torpedo, but Kirk says no, it would be too destructive a countermeasure. He asks Yra if she will help them try to prevent the launch. She not only agrees, she offers to lead them to the Shadirian control center.

Kirk decides the landing party will consist of himself, Xon, McCoy, and Yra. If there is any problem with communications, Decker is to rendezvous with them in approximately forty hours. As they leave for the transporter room, Yra cautions Kirk about the hazards they will face on Shadir's surface. Though she assures him she will do her best to guide the landing party safely, there are signs of treachery in her expression.

The landing party materializes on a war-torn street. What remains of the buildings suggests those in Earth cities of the late twentieth century. Immediately, Kirk's team dives for cover as the sounds of warfare surround them. Glimpses of snipers reveal some dressed in green uniforms, others in blue. The landing party has landed in the middle of a battle between two warring factions: 001 Green and 002 Blue.

Yra leads Kirk's team to a safe location where they can rest for a few moments. Though the sounds of battle do not cease, McCoy takes the opportunity to use his tricorder to scan for signs of life and finds none. He tells Kirk that the warriors in this area must all be androids like Yra. Kirk confronts Yra. He wants to know if there are *any* life-forms on the planet. Before Yra can answer, the shooting moves closer. She tells Kirk's team to follow her and keep their heads down.

The landing party moves to the relative quiet of an open field that was once a city park. Yra is a short distance ahead of them. Suddenly from the camouflage protection of the surrounding trees and rocks, they are surprised by blue-uniformed warriors. Kirk, McCoy, and Xon are stripped of their weapons, communicators, and other equipment. Then an older and very distinguished looking male—Plateous III—appears. He is dressed all in white. Kirk and his party hear again the undulating sounds they first encountered on the *Enterprise*. Xon tells Kirk he suspects the white-clad male is also an android. Plateous III orders both warriors and prisoners to march forward.

Plateous III and the squad of Blue warriors lead Kirk's landing party through the gate of a walled-in military compound guarded by white-uniformed warriors. Inside is a large, white building. Plateous orders Yra to step out of the group. Kirk overhears Plateous III tell Yra to go to the Android Inspection Center, to change back into her 002 Blue army uniform. Blue warriors turn Kirk, McCoy, and Xon over to White guards who lead them through an opening into the white building. The Blue warriors leave the compound.

After Kirk's team disappears into the white building, Plateous III continues his conversation with Yra. He tells her that she has paid her debt by successfully leading the 001 Green ships into a trap. Although 001 forces had been gaining, she has now helped restore balance. It's clear that Yra acted as a spy within the 001 Green fleet of small ships whose wreckage was detected by the *Enterprise*. It's also clear that Yra is angry she herself was almost destroyed. Plateous III coolly reminds her that she begged him for a chance to get out of debt. She should be grateful to him. After all, the capture of three aliens puts her ahead in credits. Yra starts to go off with Plateous III to discuss with him the possible capture of the remaining 450 aliens still onboard the *Enterprise*. She is looking forward to her share of this treasure. However, Plateous III stops her from following him into the white building. She's not cleared for an alien-processing center. He tells her he'll discuss her deal with her later. He disappears through the opening through which Kirk, McCoy, and Xon went earlier.

Troubled, Yra pauses, then enters another door, apparently to an Android Inspection Center since a number of Green and Blue male and female warriors freely go in and out of the entrance she chooses.

The area that Plateous III referred to as an Alien Processing Center is, in reality, a large, starkly painted force-field prison without dividers or bars. Here and there around the room are several prisoners. A few are clustered in twos or threes, but most prisoners stand alone. They range from humanoid to the exotic

Guards escort Kirk, Xon, and McCoy into the room, then stop and wait expectantly. A small electronic hum begins. The guards step back. The hum grows louder, then stops. The trio find themselves locked in a force-field cell with no obvious way to escape.

Then Plateous III enters the room and approaches the landing party. With elaborate formality, he welcomes the aliens to Shadir. Kirk demands to know why his ship was attacked when it came in peace. Plateous III tells him that it is Shadir's way, and Kirk retorts that it is unprovoked barbarism. Perhaps for others, Plateous III says, but it is is the ultimate in civilized behavior for Shadir.

When Kirk asks if life-forms exist on the planet, Plateous III assures him they do. But he refuses Kirk's demand to talk to them, telling Kirk that that is impossible for an alien. As Plateous III exits, it's apparent that the entire encounter has been followed closely by a humanoid prisoner—Zeylo.

Yra, now in a blue uniform, leaves the Android Inspection Center and passes by several Blue and Green warriors who are strangely frozen in position. Yra is both armed and angry. She confronts Plateous III as he exits the prison. She expected to share in the capture of the alien ship, *Enterprise*, but now she has orders to move off with a Blue infantry battalion. Plateous III ignores her. He will not allow his orders to be questioned. He tells her he must maintain balance, and turns away from her.

Yra hesitates, then moves toward the white building. At the prison door, she asks to see her aliens but the White guards turn her away. Just then, she sees the delivery of food arrive for the aliens. The food is packaged in propellant containers. Yra reacts to them with shock.

In the prison, Zeylo advises Kirk just to give up and wait out his time. Kirk discovers that Zeylo is a humanoid Shadirian, not an android. Zeylo tells Kirk that no living Shadirians exist on the surface of the planet, except in the prison. When Kirk asks if that means the androids have taken control of the planet, Zeylo says no. The Shadirian civilization can still be found just two kilometers away, straight down. Underground, there are cities, farms, and clean air. Only a select few in the underground even know about the existence of the prison on the surface.

Kirk is puzzled. He presses Zeylo to tell him more, but the Shadirian is gripped by depression. He says Kirk and his friends will never live to see the true Shadirian civilization, because there's a new pastime called "hand to hand," secretly played by the very rich on Shadir. The three aliens will be invited to play it all too soon. And since the new aliens closely resemble Shadirians, they will be considered a rich prize. When Kirk asks if Zeylo will be involved in "hand to hand," Zeylo tells him his fate is different. Because the Shadirian was heavily in debt, he will be here for the rest of his life. Unless of course, he is accidentally caught in some sort of crossfire or dies of battlefield pollution. No one will deliberately kill him, since that would be sinful. Shadirians worship life. Kirk is confused by Zeylo's contradictory speech. How could the Shadirian die in crossfire or battle when he is in prison? And if the Shadirians worship life, why are they at war with one another and why did they attack the *Enterprise*?

Meanwhile, Yra has made her way around to a small, locked, unguarded back entrance to the prison. She burns away the lock with a laser-like weapon.

Inside the prison, guards pass out the propellant containers of food. As the guards leave, Yra, unseen, enters. She approaches Kirk, McCoy, and Xon and tells them she did not realize they were being sent to prison until she saw the propellant containers, which are to preserve food from the pollutants caused by the war, and which are supplied only to surface personnel. Yra says she thought Kirk's team was being sent to an Alien Processing Center, which would quickly send them below to safety.

Kirk asks Yra to destroy the force-field control equipment. He tells her they need to get away before they can be used in something called "hand to hand." Yra is appalled. She thought "hand to hand" was a myth, a rumor started by reformers. Kirk urges her to hurry. She starts for the control panel but stops as she hears guards coming. As she backs off, she tosses her weapon to the floor. Kirk retrieves it, unseen, when two guards arrive to lead him away.

On board the *Enterprise*, Decker is unable to establish contact with Kirk, McCoy, and Xon. Though he fears something has happened to them, he has his orders to wait until the agreed-upon rendezvous time. On the main viewscreen, the bridge crew sees increased activity around the 002 Blue warship being prepared for launch from the planet surface.

In the meantime, Kirk is escorted from the prison to meet with a large and powerful Android Fighter for a hand-to-hand combat to the death, while Plateous III watches. It is obvious that Kirk is outmatched, but as the Android Fighter grips Kirk in a death hold, Kirk destroys him with Yra's weapon. Before anyone can stop him, Kirk dashes back into the prison to free McCoy and Xon and the other prisoners, who gratefully scatter.

Kirk, McCoy, and Xon race down a road, putting as much distance between themselves and the prison as possible. Rounding a bend, they come upon a menacing-looking 002 Blue machine that can only be a Shadirian tank. As the tank opens, Kirk, McCoy, and Xon move quickly for cover, but the only warrior to appear is Yra. She urges them to

board the tank quickly. Plateous III is hunting them with an elite White squad. Kirk sees no option but to trust her, for now. He still holds the weapon she gave him. As they board, they hear behind them the peculiar whining sound they have come to associate with Shadirian attack. Once they are safely inside, the tank, with Yra at the controls, takes off. She tells them she will take them to a vertical lift that will take them to the civilization below. It is their only hope of surviving. Kirk tells Yra that surviving is not the reason they are here. They must stop the 002 Blue ship from taking off.

Kirk also asks why she is helping them now. She tells them she never knew that Plateous III was breaking the First Law: Life-forms must be preserved. Even alien life-forms. This law is the foundation of Shadirian civilization.

Just then the tank is attacked by Green warriors. The tank is crippled and Yra wounded, but she manages to maneuver the tank into a hiding place behind a ruined building. McCoy is unable to aid her because she is an android, but Xon succeeds in repairing her, temporarily, after Yra directs him to a slender electronic welder used for minor tank repairs. Yra and Xon realize that her survival time is limited. Fortunately, they are now near the entrance to the vertical lift. Yra points to the lift entrance—a doorway in a half-destroyed building, guarded by four of Plateous III's elite White guard. She tells them they must wait until the elaborate ritual of the changing of the guard—two hours from now, when the guard will be most vulnerable.

As they wait in a gutted apartment building across from the lift entrance, Kirk questions Yra about the android war. She tells them it began when Plateous II came to power several generations ago, a few years after the final war fought by living Shadirians, when all the ruined buildings were new. Plateous III continued and refined the war, and began the taking of life again. Kirk questions the value of such a war. Yra tells him it was and is fought to gain peace. This makes no sense to Kirk.

Yra asks Kirk when wars ended on his home planet. He tells her they ended when Earth and then the Federation committed themselves to space exploration. Yra tells him that Shadirians are not explorers. They required another outlet for their drives. Xon interrupts to report that the changing of the guard at the lift entrance has begun.

Kirk, McCoy, and Xon move cautiously toward the lift entrance. Kirk has the weapon Yra gave him. Yra is also armed. She tells Kirk that because she is not allowed below, she will act as a decoy, then moves out in view of the guards before Kirk can stop her.

At first, caught up in their ritual, the guards do not react. When they do fire, Yra fires back and takes out one of the four guards as a second pursues her. Seizing their chance, Kirk's team races toward the lift, now guarded by only two androids. Kirk drops them with one blast from his weapon. But then another Shadirian weapon sounds and Kirk's team turns to see Yra pitch forward and lie still on the ground. An android guard stands over her.

Knowing there is nothing more they can do for Yra, Kirk's team enters the doorway to the lift, the door closes behind them, and the lift descends.

Kirk, McCoy, and Xon emerge into a hallway that leads into a large lounge that resembles a well-appointed lobby of a good hotel. A window appears to look out onto a beautiful, seemingly sunlit street. Well-dressed Shadirians, male and female, come and go, discussing building projects, prospects of permanent relationships, and other common peacetime events. Some go out toward the street. Others move toward a wall of many doors. Each door is coded differently: Some are blue, some green. When the Shadirians enter the rooms beyond the doors, some go under their own power, others are carried by medics in white uniforms. Then a Blue-coded door opens, and a medic carries someone across the lobby to a seat. Kirk's team realizes the disabled figure is Yra, apparently alive, and in civilian dress.

Kirk tells McCoy and Xon to wait out of sight. He starts toward Yra, then halts as he sees a glassed-in room high on one wall. In it are White guards. A figure in the room moves forward to look down at Yra. It is Plateous III. Kirk goes back to McCoy and Xon, confused now about who is an android and who is not.

On the *Enterprise*, Uhura informs Decker that the unusual whining sounds emanating from Shadir are a highly potent form of thought projection. Uhura describes them as a summation tone combining the electrical activity of brain neurons and a rare form of beta wave. Uhura suspects that this tone is used to control androids such as Yra. And it is so intense, it might be used to control many androids at one time.

Decker realizes the time for rendezvous with Kirk is approaching, and there still has been no communication from the captain or McCoy or Xon. Decker will have to beam down soon, anyway.

In the underground lounge, Plateous III turns from his viewing window to consult with two of his White guards. Kirk tells McCoy to find out what he can about Yra's condition. Then he and Xon head for the nearest Blue door, to find the control room that guides the 002 Blue warship.

Aware that the three aliens are in the lounge, Plateous III orders one of his guards to tell the medics not to treat them if they should manage to use an Android Control. He is confident that if the aliens do commandeer an Android Control, the fail-safe mechanism in the control will take its course, and the aliens will give him no further trouble. He plans to use force against them only as a last resort. Then Plateous III looks over to his own private Android Control. It resembles a plush twentieth-century airport waiting-room chair combined with a television set. Each of the chair arms has a wide, gleaming metal sleeve. The back of the chair has two electrodes to hold the head firmly in place. The chair is glossy white.

Plateous III appears to sincerely regret that Yra has begun to act like a reformer. He had decided to extend her credit for old times' sake. But now he says she will have to be sent to prison. The guards are to pick her up at home later. All this trouble has been annoying, Plateous III says. All he wishes is to return to the war.

Kirk and Xon now enter a Blue War Room to find several Shadirians seated in chairs similar to that in Plateous III's viewing room. These chairs are less opulent, however, and they are blue in color. Each Shadirian is focused on his or her chair's viewscreen. Their arms are gripped tightly by the metal sleeves, and the electrodes are pressed against their temples. The only sound in the room is the computer sound coming from each chair.

The Shadirians in the blue chairs do not speak, but their faces reflect joy, relief, pain, or horror—all the emotions of soldiers in battle. Suddenly one of them screams. A medic enters the room and quickly removes the limp form from its chair, and carries it out into the lounge. A moment later a White technician enters and makes a minor adjustment to the chair. Another Shadirian enters, inserts his Computer Card, then allows the chair to automatically strap him into place. So intent are the Shadirians and the attendant staff that no one pays attention to Kirk or Xon. Kirk tells Xon that he has noticed that the Shadirians are using the chairs to 'operate' androids on the surface of the planet—in the very sector that Decker is to rendezvous with Kirk.

In the underground lounge, the medic is still tending to Yra when McCoy, with one eye on Plateous III's window, goes to her and sits beside her. He asks the medic how she is doing. The medic replies that Yra has suffered too many traumas in too short a time. She will need a long rest before she can return to the War Control Room. While McCoy talks to the medic, he manages to lift one of the medic's small discs of what appears to be medication. Then Yra revives. The medic leaves, telling her she has a visiting friend, and that she should go home to rest.

Yra quickly asks after Kirk and Xon just as McCoy sees his two friends exit one of the blue doors. Yra guides the three to a corner less visible from Plateous III's monitoring window. While she does this, the medic stops by one of Plateous III's White guards. He's receiving his instructions not to treat any of the aliens, should they be injured while operating a war-control chair.

Yra tells Kirk where to find the main control room that operates the 002 Blue warship. She also gives them Computer Cards to operate the control chairs. She tells them that all Shadirians are theoretically allowed "android time." If one wins in battle, one earns extra credits. Conversely, if one loses in battle, one can quickly lose a lifetime's earnings. Yra's credit is still good, until Plateous III cuts her off.

Kirk asks Yra why he and his friends have been able to move about so freely underground. Yra tells him it's because Plateous III is probably expecting them to try to use the Android Control chairs, and hoping they will succumb if they use them. She warns Kirk to be careful: Operating the chairs heightens all emotions. And aliens might not even be able to make Shadirian androids respond properly.

Despite Yra's worries, Kirk decides that he and McCoy will go to the Warship Control Room. Xon is to stay with Yra to watch for trouble. Their first priority remains to stop the launch of the warship. They have little time remaining before Decker will beam down from the *Enterprise*.

As Kirk and McCoy enter the Blue Warship Control Room, they again see Shadirians in control chairs, transfixed by their individual monitors. Each Shadirian is operating an android with a different duty aboard the 002 Blue warship. Kirk and McCoy move quickly through the room until Kirk stops short. He has located the Android Controller whose screen shows a mechanism that Kirk recognizes as an abort control. Kirk uses a martial arts blow to dispatch the Shadirian occupying the chair. Immediately, the chair's screen goes blank and the equipment holding the Shadirian loosens. A medic arrives and takes the Shadirian away. McCoy blocks the replacement Shadirian's way as Kirk slips into the chair and drops in his Computer Card. The metal sleeves fasten about his arms, and the electrodes move in against his skull. The monitor lights up, and the abort mechanism comes into view.

McCoy notices, worriedly, that Kirk has developed a strange intensity. His pulse is up and his face is flushed. McCoy urges his captain to abort the warship's launch quickly. On the viewscreen, the android's hand trembles as it moves toward the abort mechanism. Then it moves away. Beads of sweat stand out on Kirk's forehead. His adrenaline levels clearly rising, he fights the control mechanisms. McCoy looks around to see if anyone has noticed their presence. But all are caught up in their own efforts. McCoy cannot release Kirk himself. He goes to the door and signals for Xon.

From his viewing window, Plateous III smiles as he sees Xon enter the Blue Warship Room.

Xon finds a way to shut off Kirk's chair and McCoy pulls the unconscious captain free. He gives Kirk the small disk of medication he took from Yra's medic. Kirk recovers and tells McCoy and Xon he was unable to abort the launch. While operating the Android Control, all he wanted to do was kill—even the crew of his own ship. Kirk now has Xon take over for him, realizing that Xon will not be subject to emotional buildup. Kirk will go to rendezvous with Decker. He slips into another control chair. McCoy tries to stop Kirk. If there are any complications, he has no more medication. Kirk suggests McCoy try to find more.

On the surface of Shadir, Decker and his landing party materialize under fire from Blue and Green snipers. Suddenly, a Blue warrior calls out Decker's name. After a moment of confusion, Decker realizes that the blue-clad form speaks with Kirk's voice. Kirk's android tells Decker that he has new coordinates for him, then the android is hit by fire and goes down. Decker fells the Green sniper with a single burst from his phaser and goes to the felled Blue android. Before it stops functioning, it gives Decker the new coordinates.

In the Blue Warship Control Room, Xon aborts the warship launch. As fail-safe alarms sound, White guards rush the control room. Xon is brought out in manacles. McCoy is apprehended as he tries to obtain more medication. A medic carries out an unconscious Kirk. Plateous III descends from his viewing station as his White guards seize

Yra. He accuses her of treason in allowing aliens to enter the Shadirian subsurface. Plateous III doesn't know how, but one of the aliens managed to overcome the fail-safe mechanism designed to intensify the emotions of hate and anger. Now Yra and the aliens will be banished to work the rest of their lives in a Shadirian mine. Yra cries out loudly, for all to hear, that he is lying. He will send them to the prison on the surface of Shadir. Plateous III denies that any such prison exists.

As the guards are distracted by Yra's and Plateous III's public altercation, McCoy breaks away from his guards to go to Kirk. He pleads for medical help before Kirk dies. Plateous III assures him that Kirk will not die. Shadirians have a deep respect for life. Stalling for time, McCoy shouts that Kirk's vital signs have just stopped. One of the White guards pulls McCoy away from Kirk just as Decker and his landing party materialize, armed with phasers. McCoy grabs a communicator from Decker and pulls Kirk into position. He calls up to the *Enterprise* to beam them up at once.

In sickbay, Kirk recovers with McCoy's ministrations to find Xon and Yra at his side. Kirk's first question to Xon is about the engines. When Kirk learns that Scott has repaired the engines and the ship can leave at any time, he offers to take Yra to a more peaceful planet. Instead, Yra asks to be beamed down to another sector of Shadir where there is a reform group working for change. After what she has seen and learned, she intends to help the reformers try to get control of the planet away from Plateous III. He has corrupted the original intent of Shadir's Way—the preserving of peace through war without loss of life.

Kirk tells Yra that Shadir's Way has already failed, that Plateous III arose because the inhabitants of Shadir needed greater and greater thrills. He assures her other planets have made it beyond the era of warfare. And that, with her help, there is now a chance that Shadir might make it, too.

"The Child" Revised Script

Written by Jaron Summers & Jon Povill

Because of its subject matter, "The Child" is definitely a story that could not have been part of the Original Series. *As such, it is a strong representation of the new ground Phase II might have explored in its time, making the series as distinct as the original.*

The script reprinted here began as a pitch by Jaron Summers. Though the pitch was destined to be declined, Jon Povill suggested a new approach to the story, which led to a rough first-draft script with a shared credit. At the time, Povill's title on the Paramount lot was Assistant to the Producer. But based on the speed and the skill with which he then turned in his rewrite, Producer Harold Livingston successfully argued that Povill should officially be given the title—and the salary—for the job he was really doing: Story Editor. Summers and Povill continue to collaborate on scripts today.

As an episode of The Next Generation, a rewritten version of "The Child" is available on videotape. Students of scriptwriting will benefit from reading this strong Phase II script, then comparing it with the subsequent version filmed as the first episode of The Next Generation's second season. Students of Star Trek will be fascinated to see just how much of the character development and sensibility of Phase II found its way into the second Star Trek series to be produced.

FADE IN:

1   EXT. ENTERPRISE   1
traveling through space.

2   INT. BRIDGE - WIDE ANGLE   2
It is manned by a relief crew; XON, in the command chair, is the only familiar face.
The atmosphere is relaxed, routine, almost bored.

Then something makes ENSIGN BERNSTEIN, at the helm, perk up a bit.

>BERNSTEIN
>Something on the forward viewer, Mister Xon. Looks like a nebula.

>XON
>Slow to warp factor one, Mister Bernstein. Sensor scan, Ensign Park.

ENSIGN PARK, an attractive and efficient junior science officer, pushes a sequence of
buttons in front of her and consults the hooded viewer for the results of the scan.

>ENSIGN PARK
>Not a nebula, sir. I'm picking up several kinds of energy . . . Radiation
>readings I've never seen before.

>XON
>Put it on the viewer, Mister Bernstein.

Bernstein hits some buttons, then:

3   ANGLE - VIEWER   3
as a swirling gaseous mass appears there. It has pulsing points of light within it that
move about like fish darting through water.

4   ANGLE - BERNSTEIN   4

>BERNSTEIN
>We're heading right for it, Mister Xon.

5   ANGLE - XON   5
as he approaches Ensign Park at the science console

>ENSIGN PARK
>(looking into hooded viewer)
>No visible danger, sir. Radiation and electromagnetic readings all with-
>in our tolerance limit.

She steps out of the way and Xon looks into the hooded viewer briefly.

>XON
>You're quite correct, Ensign. Force fields to manual. Point eight five
>deflection aspect. Take us through at warp one, Mister Bernstein.
>We'll survey and map it.

6   EXT. SPACE   6
as the Enterprise sails into the cloud of pulsing, swimming lights.

7   INT. BRIDGE   7
All is normal.

ENSIGN PARK
Cartography computer on and recording.

8   EXT. SPACE   8
as the Enterprise makes its way through the cloud. Large pulses of white light glide
past. Now one of them seems to change direction and follow along with the ship for
awhile. Then a small section of the light ball breaks off it and begins traversing the
outer skin of the ship. Abruptly, it disappears into the Enterprise.

9   INT. DECK SEVENTEEN - CREW'S QUARTERS   9
as the light entity enters the empty corridor and passes through a wall into:

10   INT. UHURA'S QUARTERS   10
The light entity makes its way directly to the sleeping UHURA. It quickly scans the
length of her body then makes another pass pausing first at her abdomen and then
at her head. Uhura continues to sleep but she stretches languorously as though the
touch of the light being on her body is sensual and pleasant.

Then the light entity moves on, passes through another wall into:

11   INT. CHEKOV'S QUARTERS   11
Again, the light entity heads directly for the room's sleeping occupant and quickly
scans over his body before making another, closer pass. CHEKOV also appears to
enjoy the experience in his sleep as the entity surveys his abdomen. It does not
explore his head but moves on again through another wall into:

12   INT. ILIA'S QUARTERS   12
The same procedure occurs, only this time the entity seems to linger for a long time
over ILIA'S head. She, too, clearly enjoys the experience. The entity pulls away for a
moment and hovers in the air over her, growing brighter and more animated. Then it
plunges inside through her abdominal wall. Her body moves spasmodically, sexually;
but she doesn't wake up. Her writhing continues until it reaches a peak during which
her entire body seems to glow. Then the glow appears to gather itself at her head.
her body relaxes again, the glow becomes the light entity which now removes itself
and goes through yet another wall into:

13   EXT. ENTERPRISE - STILL WITHIN THE CLOUD   13
as the light entity emerges from the hull of the ship and rejoins the large light ball
that has paced the ship.

DISSOLVE FOR TIME PASSAGE TO:

14   INT. CORRIDOR - DECK FIVE   14
It is now more brightly lit and abuzz with activity. KIRK strides cheerfully through
in a swimsuit, a towel around his neck, hair dripping wet as Chekov emerges from
his quarters.

CHEKOV
(as a joke)
Nothing like a brisk swim in the ocean, eh, Captain?

After they pass Ilia's compartment, the CAMERA HOLDS on Ilia's door as she emerges somewhat dreamily in a flowing Deltan robe.

CAMERA TRUCKS WITH Ilia as she makes her way to the turbolift exchanging dreamy AD LIBBED greetings with those who pass her.

She enters the turbolift.

15   INT. CORRIDOR   15
as Ilia proceeds to sick bay and enters.

16   INT. SICK BAY   16
McCOY is there, just settling into the day's routine. He greets her warmly.

McCOY
Good morning, Lieutenant—If you can call turning the lights up at 0800 hours morning.

17   ANGLE - ILIA   17
She is extremely puzzled, dazed.

ILIA
I don't understand it . . . I have not broken my vow, yet I can feel it inside me . . .

McCoy is worried now. He realizes something is wrong.

McCOY
(gently)
What, Lieutenant? What do you feel inside you?

Confused, groping for an explanation, she touches her fingers to the sides of her head (somewhere above and behind the temples) and closes her eyes in meditation.

ILIA
(recalling)
Last night . . . A . . . a pure white light . . . I don't know how . . . Beautiful . . .

She hesitates, uncertain, confused.

McCOY
Ilia, please: try to make sense.

ILIA
I'm pregnant, Doctor.

FADE OUT.

<u>END OF TEASER</u>

ACT ONE

FADE IN:

18   INT. SICK BAY - WIDE ANGLE   18
Ilia lays supine on a delivery table. We SEE only her upper torso which is covered by a satiny looking surgical green sheet.

> McCOY (V.O.)
> Medical log, stardate ( ). After a pregnancy of only three days, rather than the normal ten month Deltan gestation period, Lieutenant Ilia is about to give birth. The circumstances of her pregnancy have caused us all obvious deep concern as to the nature of the infant.

A concerned Doctor McCoy looks into her eyes—he's obviously worried but trying not to show it.

Ilia is keenly aware of his concern; more aware of it, in fact, than of her own pain.

> ILIA
> There is nothing to worry about, Doctor.

She reaches out and lightly touches him. He takes her hand, holds it gently, then reaches for a medical sensor.

> McCOY
> I'm _not_ worried. What makes you think I'm worried?
>   (he checks her body with his medical sensor)
> All the readings are normal.

> ILIA
> I _know_ when you're worried, Doctor. Relax. She will be out in a moment.

Ilia smiles. Just the smallest gasp of pain escapes her lips. She reaches out again to McCoy.

Again he takes her hand, holds it. It is difficult to determine who is comforting whom.

19   ANGLE - DOORWAY   19
as ENSIGN LING, an armed security officer, enters the room carrying a medical tricorder. He approaches the delivery table cautiously, a bit unsure of what to do.

20   ANGLE - McCOY   20
looking up at Ling.

> McCOY
> (annoyed)
> We already know that the child Lieutenant Ilia is carrying is a female humanoid; she poses no apparent danger to the security of this vessel!

>   LING
>   (sheepish)

Captain's orders, sir.

McCOY reacts angrily:

>   McCOY

Get out of here!

Ling leaves as CHAPEL enters. She carries sponges, sterilized dressing for the labor. McCoy's eyes sweep across to her.

>   McCOY
>   (continuing)

Call the bridge . . .

Chapel depresses a nearby intercom button.

>   McCOY
>   (continuing)

Captain!

21   INTERCUT BRIDGE AS NEEDED   21
Kirk glances up from the conn. DECKER is to his right; other crew members are at their positions.

>   KIRK

What's the problem, Doctor?

>   McCOY (FILTER)

Can't we let this woman have her child in peace?

>   KIRK

A security officer's presence is normal procedure . . .
>   (quickly)
. . . under these abnormal circumstances, Bones.

>   McCOY (FILTER)

Normal, or abnormal, Jim, I want nothing to endanger Ilia or her child. McCoy out.

And the viewer goes dark. Kirk considers it, glances around at the crew—each person seems to be "busy with his work." But we know differently. So does the Captain.

22   FAVOR DECKER   22
who is peering somewhat accusingly at Kirk.

>   KIRK

I'm all for motherhood, Mr. Decker, but surely I don't have to remind you we don't know <u>what</u> impregnated Ilia. Or <u>why</u>.

> DECKER
> (calmly)
> I doubt if a newly born creature could pose any genuine threat to us.

> KIRK
> Can you guarantee that, Mr. Decker?

Kirk waits for an answer. Decker really has none:

> DECKER
> (a beat)
> No, sir. But for a child to be born with a phaser levelled at its head doesn't guarantee it, either.

23   INT. SICK BAY - ILIA   23
glancing around at McCoy.

> ILIA
> I think I'm ready now, Doctor.

McCoy hurries back as another labor pain causes her to shudder slightly.

> CHAPEL
> Rapid dilation . . . Pulse and respiration good . . . It's coming now, Doctor.

Ilia concentrates and focuses all her energy into the business at hand.

> ILIA
> There is no pain. Only joy . . . Only ecstasy . . .

Chapel dabs at Ilia's head with a sponge, as McCoy prepares to assist the infant's birth.

24   INT. BRIDGE - ANGLE ON THE MAIN VIEWER   24
as a baby girl appears on it. She is upside down and she is CRYING. Loud and deeply. We can tell McCoy holds the child by her feet but we SEE little of him. A marvelous child. (She has hair on her head.)

Kirk looks at the viewer and we sense in his expression something: special: wonder, awe—and concern.

25   INTERCUT AMONG THE OTHER BRIDGE CREW   25
Chekov. Uhura, Decker and Xon. They each watch a nearby viewer and as the baby continues to CRY we can see their awe.

26   INT. SICK BAY - McCOY, ILIA AND THE CHILD   26
McCoy returns the child to Ilia. It's obvious that he too is moved by this special moment.

> McCOY
> (a bit awkward)
> Well, you were right: it was an easy delivery.

ILIA

Deltans always know. You needn't have worried so . . .

McCOY

Don't patronize me, young woman. You know very well this was no
ordinary delivery.

27   WIDE ANGLE - INCLUDE CHAPEL   27
as Chapel touches the child's tiny head.

CHAPEL
(to McCoy)
She never pretended it was, Doctor.

McCOY
(a beat; gently, to Ilia)
Have you thought about a name yet . . .?

ILIA
(nods)
Irska, after her father.

CHAPEL
. . . after its father . . .?!

ILIA
(correcting)
Her father, Doctor. Irska means 'pure light' in Deltan.

Ilia positively glows with love for her child. She begins to stroke Irska with graceful
Deltan hand movements, making a sound that is not unlike purring and humming
combined.

28   INT. BRIDGE   28
All appears normal here except for the fact that Chekov has temporarily returned to
his old position at the navigation station during Ilia's absence. Kirk sits, somewhat
tensely, at the conn. Xon is at his science station. Uhura and SULU are at their posts.
Decker, too, is there.

29   FAVOR UHURA AND KIRK   29
Kirk swivels around as Uhura addresses him.

UHURA

Captain, will Ilia be able to keep the baby if it's normal . . . ?

KIRK
(clearly sympathetic and troubled by this)
I wouldn't call an immaculate conception followed by a three day preg-
nancy . . . 'normal.'

UHURA

Then what's to become of the child?

> XON
Respectfully, Captain, I would ask you to bear in mind that regardless of what you decide, there is no stronger bond than that between a Deltan mother and her child. In ancient times, protecting their off-spring, Deltan women had been known to slay, barehanded, gnutabeasts five times their size.

> KIRK
I'm aware of the Deltan mother-child relationship, Mr. Xon.

Kirk is interrupted by an INTERCOM SIGNAL; he presses a button on his chair.

> KIRK
> (continuing)
Kirk here.

> McCOY'S VOICE
> (filtered)
Jim, I have the results of the preliminary tests on Ilia's baby . . .
> (grim)
Could you come down here . . . ?

> KIRK
On my way . . .
> (to Decker)
You have the conn, Mr. Decker.

Kirk gets up and moves to the turbolift.

31   INT. SICK BAY - FAVOR McCOY AND KIRK   31
Still laying on the recovery table, Ilia and her child rest. During the following scene we'll INTERCUT between Kirk and McCoy—then to the mother and child. Ilia is doing what almost all mothers do with a newborn child. She is examining every little detail of the child to make sure the infant is perfect. Ilia counts the toes, inspects the tiny ears, bends the rubbery knees and so on.

And all the time she hugs and kisses her tiny daughter and seems unaware of the two men talking (out of her earshot) in soft tones across the room. All of this is done with great love.

At the director's discretion we'll CUT to the gentle warmth between mother and child as the two men talk about that child's destiny. For these moments we'll use VOICE OVER but, of course, Ilia will not hear anything. In the background we'll be aware of MUSIC—gentle, like the love of the mother for her child—

Occasionally the two men glance toward Ilia and Irska.

McCoy shows Kirk some of the results as he explains the following facts to the star-ship captain.

                                    McCOY
The child checks out as human in almost every respect.

                                    KIRK
No Deltan characteristics?

                                    McCOY
No physiological ones. She's even got hair.
                    (then becoming absorbed in the medical ramifications)
The only truly incredible thing is how fast she's growing—even faster
now than in Ilia's womb. By human standards her rate of growth is a
little more than a year per twenty-four hour period. I don't know how
she's doing it. Her metabolism appears normal and she isn't eating
nearly enough to sustain that . . .

                                    KIRK
                               (interrupting)
What would happen if I had them separated. Now—?

                                    McCOY
In my opinion, that would be a tragic mistake: Ilia would stop at nothing to get her back. Frankly, I'm amazed you'd even consider it.
                                    KIRK
What I'm considering is the safety of the entire ship. All we know
about the child is that it was placed in Ilia's body, without her consent, by an unknown alien life form. WHY?

                                    McCOY
It may be unusual, but it's not altogether unique for a species to
reproduce by depositing eggs in a host—without consent.

                                    KIRK
Exactly, and in nearly every case, the life forms reproducing in that
manner are parasitical . . .

Kirk lets the implications of this sink in, but McCoy's mind is elsewhere.

                                    McCOY
                           (a beat, tight lipped)
Let me set your mind at rest, Captain. There's something I haven't
told you yet about Ilia's baby . . . I don't think she'll live out the
week . . .

                                    KIRK
                           (concerned, suspicious)
Why not?
                                    McCOY
She was born with an abnormally high white blood cell count: it's been
steadily increasing . . .
                    (to the question in Kirk's eyes)
—leukemia—and the routine cancer drugs seem to have no effect.

He is interrupted by the ship's intercom.

UHURA'S VOICE

Captain Kirk, please report to the bridge. We have an alien object
1500 meters off the starboard bow.

as he goes to the intercom.

KIRK

Acknowledged. Go to yellow alert. I'm on my way.
(to McCoy)
Does Ilia know?

McCOY

I haven't told her.

KIRK

Don't. Not yet.

The yellow alert ALARMS and lights go on as Kirk exits.

33   INT. BRIDGE - ANGLE - VIEWER   33
with the alien object hovering there. It appears to be nothing more than a huge
cylinder.

34   WIDER   34
as Kirk emerges from the turbolift, glances at the viewer a moment. Then:

KIRK

Any sign of hostility?

CHEKOV

No, sir.

KIRK

Sensor reading, Mr. Xon?

XON
(carefully)
Sensors indicate no known life forms, Captain.

KIRK

It sounds as though you're hedging your bet, Mr. Xon. Do you <u>think</u>
there may be someone on board?

XON

Sir, the sensors indicate only a hollow tri-tritanium shell surrounding
a field of dense radiation of the same type as that contained in the
cloud we encountered four nights ago.

KIRK

The same night Ilia's child was conceived.

XON

Exactly, sir. The shell duplicates the alloy of our hull perfectly, but
there is no machinery of any kind on board—yet it appears to have
no difficulty whatever in paralleling our course.

KIRK

How can that be?

XON

By all laws of physics as we know them, Captain, it cannot be. Yet it is. I suspect our sensors may not be capable of detecting the controlling life form.

KIRK

Commander Uhura, open hailing frequencies.

UHURA

Hailing frequencies open, sir.

KIRK
(to communicator)
This is Captain James T. Kirk of the starship Enterprise. Please identify yourself and your intentions.

35   ANGLE - UHURA   35

UHURA
(listening)
No response, sir.

36   ACROSS KIRK TO DECKER   36
as Decker addresses Kirk.

DECKER
(ominous)
There's a connection between that . . . object and Ilia's child, Captain.

KIRK

That would be the most logical assumption, Mr. Decker.

DECKER

Yes, sir, but it doesn't tell us why that thing is out there or what it wants . . .

37   INT. SICK BAY   37
Ilia is sitting up in bed holding and stroking Irska lovingly. They stare deeply into each other's eyes. Ilia guides her daughter's hand to her forehead.

ILIA

Moth-er.

IRSKA

Moth-er.

Ilia now moves the child's hand to Irska's forehead.

ILIA

I-r-ska

IRSKA

I-r-ska.

It is, at once, beautiful and most unsettling to watch, as we . . .
FADE OUT.

<u>END OF ACT ONE</u>

38   EXT. SPACE - ENTERPRISE AND ALIEN CYLINDER   38

KIRK'S VOICE
Captain's log, stardate (   ). A week has passed since the birth of
Ilia's child and the appearance of the strange alien cylinder. Despite
an ever increasing white blood cell count, Irska remains healthy. Her
stage of development is roughly that of a ten-year-old child. We
remain unable to make contact with the alien cylinder or to determine
why, or indeed how, it is following us.

39   INT. ILIA'S QUARTERS   39
Without the occasional familiar piece of hardware (the viewer computer library console, the intercom, the doors, etc.), it would be most difficult to determine that this
room was on board the starship Enterprise. It delights the senses. It is filled with
exotic plants. Cushions on the floor. Walls covered in soft, textured material. Deep,
richly saturated colors. Smoke rising from an incense burner.

40   VARIOUS ANGLES - ILIA AND IRSKA   40
There is MUSIC PLAYING, something like modern jazz but played on totally alien
sounding instruments. It must be something danceable though, as mother and child
are dancing; sensual and innocent, joyous. Movements perhaps related to tai chi.
They whirl about, diaphanous flowing robes billowing; ending in a crescendo of laughing and waving arms and finger-tips that occasionally brush each other's body as
lightly as hair blowing in the wind.

The MUSIC STOPS and they fall onto floor cushions, breathless. They recline, catching
their breath, until Ilia grows serious and turns to her daughter.

ILIA
Today I resume my duties. That means we'll be apart for a time.

IRSKA
Can't I work with you?

Ilia reaches out and caresses the child's face, hair.

ILIA
No. My work is <u>my</u> work. It is important that you spend some time
alone now and become who you are to be.

Irska looks uncertain and somewhat frightened. Ilia soothes her now with both hands.

IRSKA

But what will I do?

ILIA

Learn. Do whatever you want to do. See if you can discover joyfulness
alone. Once you have achieved that, you need never fear rejection.

Ilia embraces the child lovingly. Irska returns the warmth. They look at each other
for a long moment. Are they communicating telepathically? Or is it love? We do not
know.

41   INT. KIRK'S QUARTERS   41
Ilia in uniform, enters. Kirk reading, looks at her, smiles:

ILIA

I would like permission to resume my duties, Captain.

Kirk isn't sure. He wasn't expecting this.

KIRK

What about your daughter?

ILIA

She's busy: Learning to have a good relationship.

KIRK

Who with?

ILIA

Herself, sir. The beginning of all good relationships.
One must spend time alone to get to know oneself before being ready
to share who you are with others.

KIRK
(concerned)
Ilia, what are your plans for you and your daughter?

ILIA

Plans, Captain? I have none. She is growing fast and will not be with
me long. I must love her, teach her what I can, and then let her go.

KIRK

Go where? To do what? Appearances to the contrary, she's not
human, nor is she Deltan—or any other life form we know of. Will she
be able to adjust to that aloneness!

ILIA

Captain, she is my child. Even if we are physically separated, the
bond between us is inseparable. You are more alone at any time than
she is ever capable of feeling. Where she goes and what she does must
be left up to her.

KIRK

What if she were to pose some danger to . . .

ILIA
(forcefully)
She does not—could not pose danger to anyone.

Kirk sees no point in trying to pursue the subject, though he remains less than fully convinced of her statement.

KIRK
Have you any idea at all in what way your daughter might be connected with the cylinder out there?

ILIA
No, Captain. I'm sorry, but I do not.

KIRK
Very well, Lieutenant, thank you. You may return to your duties.

ILIA
Thank you, sir.

42   INT. BRIDGE - WIDE ANGLE   42
Uhura has the conn. Xon and Sulu are at their posts. Chekov is filling in for Ilia as navigator. The turbolift doors open and Ilia emerges.

43   TIGHTER ON ILIA   43
as she moves to her position.

ILIA
You are relieved, Mr. Chekov. Thanks for taking over for me.

CHEKOV
It was my pleasure. And how is the beautiful Irska today?

ILIA
(pleasant)
She's just marvelous—

Ilia is interrupted by a soft, urgent BUZZ. Then, "intruder alert" ALARMS. Chekov moves swiftly to his weapon/defense station.

44   WIDE ANGLE   44
Xon is looking into his hooded viewer as the turbolift doors open and Kirk steps quickly out to survey the situation.

KIRK
Status report.

Uhura gets up and goes to her communications post. Kirk takes his place at the conn.

XON
Something is being beamed aboard from the alien cylinder. It is . . .
(he turns to face Kirk)
. . . roughly one cubic centimeter of the dense radiation atmosphere contained in the cylinder.

He turns back to his console and begins making computations with the assistance of the computer.

45   REACTION SHOT - ILIA   45
She glances around, uncertain. Does she sense something?

46   ANGLE - CHEKOV   46
looking at his readouts.

47   INSERT - WHAT CHEKOV SEES   47
A structural diagram of the ship with a blinking, BLEEP synchronized light flashing somewhere in the center of the saucer section.

CAMERA PULLS BACK SLIGHTLY as Chekov's hands rapidly punch buttons and the three dimensional image rotates on various axes until the exact location of the flashing light is found. Code letters: 8—L SUPATMOS QLT—10 FLTR: appear in sequence on his viewer next to the image as it zeroes (ZOOMS) in on the light.

48   FULL SHOT OF THE BRIDGE   48
as Chekov translates this for us.

                                   CHEKOV
          It beamed to the number ten filter in our atmospheric purification
          system.

Xon reacts to this information, quickly turns back to his calculations, and Kirk comes to a decision:

                                   KIRK
          Evasive maneuvers, Mr. Sulu. Ninety degrees hard to starboard. Warp
          factor six . . . !

                                   SULU
                              (punching it in)
          Warp factor six, sir. Ninety degrees hard to starboard.

49   INT. ILIA'S CABIN - CLOSE ON IRSKA   49
She is frightened. She stops reading, looks up in puzzlement.

50   EXT. SPACE   50
as we SEE the Enterprise and the cylinder moving laterally across the screen. Abruptly, the Enterprise veers directly TOWARD THE CAMERA POSITION and away from the cylinder. We can feel the ship speeding up as it swiftly sweeps OVER THE CAMERA POSITION. A moment later the cylinder follows.

51   INT. BRIDGE - WIDE ANGLE   51

                                   DECKER
          It's still right with us, sir.

                                   KIRK
          Come about 180 degrees. Increase speed to warp 8.

52   EXT. SPACE   52

The Enterprise and the cylinder once again are side by side as they ENTER THE FRAME FROM ABOVE AND BEHIND THE CAMERA POSITION.

CAMERA ROTATES LATERALLY to CATCH the sweep of the two vessels as the Enterprise again pulls away from the cylinder and begins to negotiate a tight arc U-turn. It continues past us. Two beats later the cylinder follows.

53   INT. ENGINEERING   53

ALARMS SOUNDING, people hurriedly programming backup systems into operation, engaging manual overrides and the like.

54   INT. CORRIDOR   54

People rush by. Irska, frightened, hurries along. She seems dazed.

55   INT. ENGINEERING - WIDE ANGLE - SCOTTY IN F.G.   55

at the wall intercom. In b.g. we SEE a number of technicians laboring to cancel alert warning lights on Inertial Guidance and stability systems.

                        SCOTT

Captain, we cannot continue maneuvering at this speed, you're putting a critical strain on the inertial guidance and stability system!

                 KIRK'S VOICE

What can you give me in a straight speed?

                      SCOTT

Warp 9.2: If you don't lean on her too long.

56   INT. BRIDGE - KIRK   56

                      KIRK

All right, Scotty, let's see if she can outrun them.
              (beat)
Mr. Sulu, Warp 9.2.
            (to Decker)
Get down to engineering and see if you can give them a hand.

As Decker leaves:

57   EXT. SPACE - VARIOUS ANGLES   57

The Enterprise streaks away. The cylinder falls behind. Then it adjusts, gains on us, passes to linger on a course slightly ahead of us.

58   INT. BRIDGE - IRSKA   58

Entering. Everyone on the bridge studies instruments so no one pays attention to Irska as she goes to her mother.

                      SULU

It's still with us, Captain. Dead ahead . . . slowing.

The child stands by her mother. Ilia slips an arm around Irska, continues with her work, but manages to look at her daughter with warmth. Understanding. Ilia reaches out, strokes the child's hair—it'll be okay.

59   ANOTHER ANGLE - KIRK AND OTHERS   59

                              KIRK
                             (grim)
          No point wasting power. All engines stop, Mr. Sulu—

Kirk now sees the child with her mother.

                              XON
          We have an additional problem, Captain.

                              KIRK
                        (looking at Ilia)
          Yes, I believe we do.

Decker and the rest of the crew glance at mother and child.

                              XON
          A cubic centimeter of radiation was beamed into our filtration system.
          It has already poisoned the air . . . quite lethal. Unless we counteract
          it, within twelve hours, we'll all be dead.

The child moves closer to her mother. Sulu watches them.

60   INT. SICK BAY - VARIOUS ANGLES   60
McCoy works feverishly at his laboratory table. Chapel assists him, removing
samples from a centrifuge and prepares them for McCoy to study under something
like an advanced microscope. Through this we HEAR:

                        KIRK'S VOICE OVER
          Captain's log, stardate ( ). It has now been more than four hours the
          alien craft beamed a deadly portion of its atmosphere into our ship.
          Thus far, Dr. McCoy has made little progress toward finding a cure for
          its effects.

61   INT. RECREATION ROOM - VARIOUS ANGLES   61
The mood is somber indeed. Small groups of people talk in subdued VOICES. There
are a couple of games of three dimensional chess going on as well as some other
games that are played on computer boards. These seem to provide little solace to the
players. Lights are lower than usual.

Most people in the room are showing, or starting to show, red splotches on any
exposed skin areas.

                        KIRK'S VOICE OVER
          The crew is already displaying symptoms of radiation poisoning and
          though they continue to maintain the ship's routine, many of them
          have become despondant, hopeless . . .

CAMERA PANS the room restlessly pausing only for moments here and there in which we PICK UP snatches of conversation.

62   HOLDING CHIEF JANICE RAND   62
as she gingerly probes a red splotch on her cheek with a finger. She reacts somewhat painfully. She tells her concerned, male companion:

> RAND
>
> It's getting worse.

She bites her lower lip.

63   HOLDING TWO WOMEN CHESS PLAYERS   63

> FIRST WOMAN
>
> Your move.

The SECOND WOMAN reaches for a knight, then glances past the first. Irska stands there. Just watches.

> IRSKA
>
> May I play? I read the instruction book.

The Second Woman considers the child.

> SECOND WOMAN
>
> No. We're not going to play any more games.

Irska, disappointed a moment, stands uncertainly, then smiles, turns and skips away. The two women grimly, sadly, watch her.

64   INT. ENGINEERING   64
It's deserted except for SCOTTY, who sits at the engineering library viewer reading technical manuals.

65   MED. CLOSE - SCOTT   65
reading. For once, these seem to be of relatively little solace to him.

66   WIDE ANGLE   66
as the door WHOOSHES and Irska comes through, looking fit and beautiful and seemingly unaware of what is happening.

67   FAVOR SCOTT   67
as she approaches him and puts an arm innocently around him. Apparently she accidentally touches a tender spot because Scotty winces in pain as she touches him. He attempts to hide this from the child.

> IRSKA
> (concerned)
> I'm sorry, I didn't mean to hurt you . . .

> SCOTT
>
> It's all right, lass. Why aren't you with your mother?

IRSKA

She said she felt a need to meditate by herself for an hour.

She smiles beautifully at him and manages to lift his spirits a bit.

SCOTT

So you came to see old Scotty, eh?

Irska nods.

SCOTT
(continuing)

You know, you're the only wee lass I've ever known who could see the beauty in engineering schematics.

IRSKA

I see beauty in almost everything, Mr. Scott.

Scotty studies her reflectively, then smiles at her.

SCOTT

I nearly forgot . . . I have a present for you.

Irska beams as Scott gets up, somewhat painfully, and goes to a storage closet, opens it and withdraws a jeweled headband similar to the ones that Ilia wears. He brings it back and demonstrates for Irska how it works.

SCOTT
(continuing)

See, it's just like your mother's except I made it for you so that it could grow as fast as you do. If you press this lever in, it will adjust to whatever size you need.

Irska gives him a Deltan style hug and kiss.

IRSKA

Oh, Mr. Scott, it's beautiful. Thank you.

She is radiant as he puts it on her head.

NOTE: She will continue to wear the headband throughout the remainder of the story.

68   INT. BRIDGE   68

It is deserted except for Kirk, Xon and Decker. Xon's copper-based blood causes his splotches to be green rather than red. Kirk wearily crosses from the science station and gingerly settles himself into his chair. Once in it, it almost looks as if he'll never get up again. He rubs his eyes and forehead.

KIRK

All right, let's try a different approach . . . Obviously there is some intelligence in control of that thing . . .

He indicates the cylinder hovering in the viewer.

as they glance at each other. Decker is puzzled. Xon shows no expression.

                         DECKER

I doubt it has any interest in our ship itself. The operation of that
cylinder indicates it has no need of our technology.

                         KIRK

Then why is it trying to kill us? And why by slowly poisoning our
atmosphere? It could finish us much faster if it wanted to.

Xon has a flash:

                         XON

Knowledge. It might be trying to learn how we react to its atmosphere. Or it might be trying to communicate with us.

The turbolift door opens, Ilia enters. She addresses Kirk:

                         ILIA

Captain, you wished to see me?

                         KIRK

Where is your daughter?

                         ILIA

With Mr. Scott, I think.

                         KIRK
                        (a beat)
Ilia, do you think it's possible that the change in our atmosphere was
intended to trigger some change in Irska?

                         ILIA
                       (alarmed)
I don't know what you're talking about . . . !

                         XON
                       (gets it)
Captain, that may be it. Assuming the girl is, in face, connected with
the vessel. It might be wise to have Doctor McCoy re-examine her.

Ilia reacts with puzzlement. Concern.

                         ILIA
                       (to Kirk)
Re-examine her . . . ?! She has nothing to with with what's happening
to us! She is innocent!

                         KIRK
                        (firm)
I want the girl re-examined.

ILIA

But she may be frightened. She hasn't even started to learn about
pain and fear.

KIRK

Bring her to Dr. McCoy, Lieutenant. Now.

70   INT. SICK BAY - ANGLE - McCOY AND CHAPEL   70
Still working at the lab table. Chapel prepares a fresh serum sample and has it ready
for McCoy to look at. McCoy removes the previous sample wearily.

Both McCoy and Chapel look wretched. There are red splotches on their faces and
arms. They appear thoroughly bedraggled.

McCOY

Which one is this?

CHAPEL

K-one-seven platelets with antispasm serum.

McCoy takes the sample and slides it into his viewing apparatus. Just then the
communicator hailing SIGNAL is HEARD. McCOY AD LIBS, "Yes . . . ?' into the speaker.

KIRK'S VOICE

What progress, Bones?

McCoy glances grimly at Chapel, then speaks into the communicator:

McCOY

None. The effects are similar to Beta Ray poisoning; I don't have to
tell you what little success we've had curing that . . .
(grim)
Frankly, Jim, I don't have much hope.

71   BRIDGE - KIRK   71
replying, into the communicator:

KIRK

I'm sending Irska to be re-examined. I want to know if she's being
affected differently than the rest of us.

McCOY'S VOICE

I'll let you know.

KIRK
(dryly)

Yes, doctor, please do. Kirk out.

72   INT. KIRK'S QUARTERS   72
as Kirk enters, goes directly to his bed and lies down. His condition appears to have
degenerated still further than in the previous scene. He looks tired, weak and frustrated. A soft CHIME is HEARD. Kirk pushes himself up into a sitting position.

KIRK

Come.

The door opens and Kirk registers mild surprise as Ilia enters. She is not as badly splotched as Kirk, but is clearly considerably weakened. Kirk gestures her to sit down on the bed. She does.

73   FAVOR ILIA   73
She's hurting emotionally as well as physically.

ILIA
I brought my daughter to Dr. McCoy.

Kirk does not feel well but Ilia's manner indicates there's no way to avoid a confrontation. He strains for patience:

KIRK
Ilia, she's not going to be harmed.

ILIA
You're experimenting with her!

KIRK
We are trying to save our lives! Everyone's, including the girl.

ILIA
And suppose she is affected differently? What will you do then?

KIRK
We'll investigate further.

ILIA
(cold)
What sort of investigation, Captain?
(she looks in his eyes and 'sees'; horrified)
No! I will not have her confined in a force field . . . !
(suddenly canny; threatening)
And has it occurred to you that if there is a connection between my child and the cylinder outside—if you harm her, the cylinder might launch a fresh attack?

Kirk studies her a beat:

KIRK
Do you know the cylinder would be provoked?

ILIA
I know only that my daughter is good. As I would know if she were not. She poses no danger to the ship!

She is interrupted by the SOUND of the DOOR OPENING. They turn to the sound.

74   WIDE ANGLE - THE ROOM   74
McCoy and Irska are already entering. Irska carrying a box of spare syringes. McCoy
senses the charged atmosphere.

                              McCOY
          I thought you'd want your shot as soon as possible.

                              KIRK
          Bones! You found a cure!

                              IRSKA
          Doctor McCoy taught me all about life and death, Mother.

McCoy already has the air syringe at Kirk's arm. It HISSES into Kirk. We NOTICE
now that McCoy's splotches are considerably faded in addition to his obviously
improved energy level.

75   FOLLOW McCOY   75
as he goes now to Ilia. He unloads the empty cartridge from the syringe and hands it
to Irska, who puts it in the box she carries before handing him a fresh one.

                              McCOY
          Don't thank me, thank my young assistant here.
                         (he gives Ilia her shot)
          She had the cure inside of her a week before we needed it. I manufac-
          tured the serum from all those strange white corpuscles she's been
          growing.

Ilia smiles. Kirk does not. Something bothers him. Ilia stops smiling as she senses this.

                              KIRK
          Bones, had she been affected in any way at all?

                              McCOY
          No.

Kirk, not quite sure what this means, glances at Ilia, and then suddenly we HEAR:
ALARMS for red alert and Xon's VOICE OVER THE INTERCOM.

                              XON (V.O.)
          Captain, our hull is being penetrated by an energy beam of unknown
          nature emanating from the alien vessel. Neither force field screens
          nor defensive shields offer any resistance.

Kirk casts Irska a swift glance. She meets his gaze levelly, innocently. How can she
be responsible for this? Kirk remains in his quandary; he goes to the wall intercom
and speaks into it.

                              KIRK
On my way.

76   EXT. SPACE - THE ENTERPRISE AND THE CYLINDER   76
A blue glow surrounds the Enterprise like an aura. Another, brighter, stronger plane

of blue energy (the shield) stands midway between the now-glowing cylinder and our ship. Cutting through both energy fields and into the hull of the Enterprise itself is a thin band of pure white light which funnels off from the flowing cylinder.

FADE OUT.

END OF ACT TWO

ACT THREE

FADE IN:

77   INT. BRIDGE - WIDE ANGLE   77
ALARMS are still BLARING. Xon is alone as the turbolift doors open, and Sulu and Uhura emerge. They are in off-duty clothes. The turbolift doors close again as they move, as quickly as their not-yet-healed bodies will allow, to their posts.

The doors to the second bridge turbolift open. Kirk and Chekov emerge. Chekov is also in leisure clothes, making Kirk and Xon the only bridge personnel in uniform. They also waste no time moving to their positions.

                              KIRK
        Damage report, Mr. Chekov.
                          (turns to Sulu)
        Prepare for evasive maneuvers, Mr. Sulu.
                          (to Uhura)
        Cancel the alarms, Commander, but maintain red alert.

In Ilia's absence, Decker jumps into the navigator's position in order to execute the evasive maneuvers. The ALARMS CEASE. Kirk studies the situation another moment, then:

                              KIRK
                          (continuing)
        Arm phasers, Mr. Chekov, and lock them on target.

78   ANGLE TO INCLUDE SULU   78
Chekov begins programming this.

                              KIRK
        Commence evasive maneuvers, Mr. Sulu. Sixty-five degrees to star-
        board. Go to warp three.

                              SULU
        Sixty-five degrees starboard rudder. Accelerating to warp three.

79   EXT. SPACE - ENTERPRISE AND CYLINDER   79
as the Enterprise veers away from the cylinder and passes OVER THE CAMERA POSI-

TION. The cylinder first turns its white beam of light onto the Enterprise's trail before swiftly following.

80   EXT SPACE - ANOTHER ANGLE   80
as, once again, the cylinder catches up to the Enterprise and swings in front of it. This done, it abruptly turns off its attacking beam.

81   INT. BRIDGE - ANGLE - CHEKOV, DECKER IN B.G.   81

                              CHEKOV
         Phasers armed and locked on target, sir.

                              DECKER
         Captain, the alien has disengaged its energy beam.
Kirk looks at viewer, confirms that Decker is correct.

                              KIRK
         Hold your fire, Mr. Chekov.
                         (turns to Xon)
         Why did they stop? Did they know we were going to fire on them.

                              DECKER
         I doubt that could stop them.

                              XON
         Perhaps, Captain, it was not aware that it was damaging us, and our evasive maneuver convinced it otherwise.

82   ANGLE - DECKER - TURBOLIFT IN B.G.   82

                              DECKER
         They knew, Mr. Xon. They were shooting through full power shields. They had to realize we didn't like what they were doing.

At this moment, Ilia and Irska emerge from the turbolift in the b.g. Kirk, and then everyone in the room, turns to look at them, and at the same moment the INTERCOM WHISTLES.

83   CLOSEUP - DISPLAY LIGHTS BY KIRK   83
He stares at them.

84   WIDER ANGLE   84
as Kirk moves to his chair and hits a button on its arm.

                              KIRK
                         (to intercom)
         Scotty, why are the impulse engines overheating?

85   INT. ENGINEERING - SCOTT   85
at the wall intercom.

                              SCOTT
         None of our manual overrides will shut them down. Control servo units must be fused . . .

86   INT. BRIDGE   86
      as Kirk looks to Chekov. Then Kirk's eyes lock on Ilia. Kirk is annoyed.

                              KIRK
                        (still eyeing Ilia)
              Damage control viewer, Mr. Chekov.

Chekov punches buttons; then:

87   INSERT - DAMAGE CONTROL VIEWER   87
      as Chekov quickly whirls the structural image of the Enterprise on its axis. The code:
      IMPLS ENG appears on the screen and the computer image quickly zooms through to
      the appropriate area of the ship, where a flashing light synchronizes with a BEEP
      SOUND. Additional codes now appear: SRVS 18, 7, 5, FZ. CLG CL 2 LK. "FZ" . . .
      "LK" flash on and off in red, ominously.

88   BACK TO SCENE   88

                              CHEKOV
              Impulse servo units five, seven and eighteen are fused. Plus a leak in
              the number two cooling coil. That's where we were hit by the alien,
              sir.

      Kirk glances again at Ilia and her child. Irska now peers over Chekov's shoulder at
      his control viewer.

                              KIRK
              You get that, Scotty?
                        (to Ilia)
              Please get your daughter off the bridge.

                              SCOTT (V.O.)
              Daughter? What are you—

                              KIRK
              Nothing, Scotty.
                        (to Ilia)
              Did you understand me, Lieutenant?

89   ANGLE - ILIA AND IRSKA   89
      Hurt, disappointed, Ilia gently takes Irska by her hand, starts to lead her away. The
      child has a mind of her own. She wants to see everything that's happening on
      Chekov's viewer.

                              IRSKA
                        (to Ilia)
              Please let me watch for just another minute.

      Ilia hesitantly relents. Chekov is uneasy. The child smiles at him.

                              SCOTT (V.O.)
              No way to repair the leak without soaking up a massive dose of beta rays.

                              KIRK
What about repairing the servos first?

                           SCOTT (V.O.)
Take a twenty man crew three hours. Coil's the best bet. One man
could weld her in fifteen minutes.

                             CHEKOV
Captain, Beta radiation in the access tube is well over the tolerance
limit. Even with a protective suit no one could remain conscious in
there for more than a few minutes.

                              KIRK
                          (to Chekov)
How much time do we have?

Irska looks up from the viewer, gestures to it.

                             IRSKA
That says the impulse engines explode in eighty-nine minutes Captain
Kirk.

Kirk stares at the child.

                             CHEKOV
She's right, Captain.

                              KIRK
She might be right but, young lady, when I give a command on this
ship I expect you to follow it.
                           (to Ilia)
And I expect you to make sure that she does.

Kirk takes the child and gently but firmly leads her from Chekov's viewer. Kirk
holds the child's hand too tightly.

                             IRSKA
But can't I—ouch.

                              KIRK
No—off the bridge—

He moves her toward the turbolift.

                              KIRK
                          (continuing)
Tell Scotty to get to that leak fast!

90   INT. ENGINEERING   90
      with Scotty at the wall intercom.

SCOTT
(he punches a different button)
Ferguson. Meet me at impulse engine access tube 74-J with a heat and
Beta suit. On the double.

91   INT. BRIDGE   91
       as Kirk now returns his attention to Ilia and Irska.

ILIA
(to Irska)
Go to your cabin.

She strokes the child's hair. Lots of love there.

ILIA
(continuing; to Kirk)
Request permission to return to my station, sir.

KIRK
Request denied. Take your daughter below.

Sulu, Chekov and Uhura react to this. Kirk's manner seems unac-
countably harsh to them.

ILIA
Sir, I apologize for—

KIRK
Lieutenant, get below!

Ilia is sad, then resigned, she and Irska turn and enter the turbolift. Except for Xon,
the other officers look at Kirk incredulously. Kirk addresses them, explaining:

KIRK
(continuing)
She knew I couldn't allow Irska to remain on the bridge.

UHURA
(coldly)
Yes, sir.

92   CLOSEUP - KIRK   92
       His anguish is evident.

93   INT. CORRIDOR   93
       as Ensign Ferguson helps Scotty into his protective suit at speed. A good deal of black
       smoke and steam pours out of the access tube.
       Once fully suited, Scott picks up the repair sheathing, the small laser torch he will
       use to weld it in place, and other unidentified tools. Then he climbs into the tube as
       quickly as he can. He's laden down with equipment. (The suit must also carry a
       supply of fresh air.)

94   INT. IMPULSE ACCESS TUBE (REDRESS OF JEFFERIES TUBE)   94
It is narrow and the going is difficult. The smoke and steam obscure his vision. He draws forth a spare hose from his air supply and adjusts a setting on the tank. He directs the thin stream of air which issues forth from it ahead of him. It blows a clearing through the smoke and steam as he continues.

95   INT. ILIA'S QUARTERS   95
as Ilia and Irska enter. They move across the room. Irska follows her plainly frustrated mother with curiosity. They sit on cushions. The door opens. It is Uhura. Irska and Ilia look at her.

                              UHURA
          I had to come and tell you I'm sorry—

                              ILIA
          Thank you.

                              UHURA
                    (kneels by the child)
          Irska, I know you don't understand a lot about Captain Kirk but he's
          going through great strain. Sometimes when that happens to people
          they say things they don't mean.

                              IRSKA
          Mother told me. We both love Captain Kirk. We love you too.

Uhura reaches, gathers the child into her arms—Irska responds with a hug.

                              UHURA
          Oh, you're such a wonderful child.
                    (to Ilia)
          She's such a delight—

96   CLOSE ON ILIA   96
She "sees" something that startles her.

97   FOLLOW ILIA   97
She races to her private desk viewer and turns it on. On the viewer we SEE an image of Scott. He makes his way through the access tube. Ilia watches, plainly concerned. Irska and Uhura approach now and watch, too.

                              IRSKA
          What's he doing?

                              UHURA
          He's trying to fix a leak in the impulse engine cooling system.

                              IRSKA
          That's a funny suit he's wearing.

Ilia smiles; gently touches Irska's face.

ILIA

To protect him from the Beta rays. Without that suit he could die.

IRSKA

Doctor McCoy says that people die when their bodies cease to function. Does that mean I was dead before I was born?

Ilia holds her daughter's face in her hands and looks deeply into the girl's eyes.

ILIA

Deltans believe that before we are born and after we die, we exist as pure love. We try to reflect that state for as long as we are alive.

Uhura looks on in amazement and awe.

98   INT. BRIDGE   98
Xon at his hooded viewer. He looks up.

XON

Captain, I have tied Doctor McCoy's medical profile of Irska into the ship's computer. I believe she is capable of withstanding the radiation from the impulse engine cooling core.

99   ANGLE - DECKER   99
looks at Xon incredulously.

KIRK

Are you suggesting we send Irska in there to fix the leak?

XON

I am merely presenting that alternative.

DECKER

But you only think she'd be safe.

XON
(agreeing)
There would be considerable risk. I merely maintain that she would most likely survive long enough to effect repairs.

DECKER

Ilia would never allow it.

XON

Then I suggest we not consult Ilia.

DECKER

That's a cold blooded approach if I ever heard one.

XON
(gently)
I believe the alien deliberately damaged us in an area that only Irska could enter; just as the cure Doctor McCoy discovered could only come

XON (CONT'D)
from her blood. Captain, it's within your authority to order the child
to help.

100 FAVOR KIRK   100
as he struggles to reach a decision.

                                    KIRK
                              (pushes a button)
                    Scotty. Progress with those control servos yet?

                               SHARMA (V.O.)
                    This is Ensign Sharma, sir. It appears the units will have to be cut out
                    with a torch. That will take a while, sir.

The news comes as no surprise to Kirk.

                                    KIRK
                    Where's Mr. Scott?
                               SHARMA (V.O.)
                    He's in the access tube, sir, attempting to weld the coolant leak.

This does surprise Kirk and angers him as well. He makes a hard decision, punches another of his chair buttons.

                                    KIRK
                    Lieutenant Ilia, this is the Captain. Please bring your daughter to the
                    bridge at once.

101 INT. ACCESS TUBES   101
Scott welds in close quarters amid great clouds of smoke. His arms tire and he leans
against the far wall and rests for a moment before continuing.

102 INT. BRIDGE   102
as Ilia and Irska enter.

                                   IRSKA
                    Hi, Captain Kirk.

                                    KIRK
                    Hello, Irska . . .

Kirk gestures the girl to him, clasps her hand:

                                    KIRK
                               (continuing)
                    Mr. Xon, perhaps it would be best if you explained the situation.

                                    XON
                    The situation is quite simple: if the impulse engine cooling system is
                    not immediately repaired, the ship will be destroyed. Irska is the only
                    person on board who can withstand the Beta ray bombardment within
                    the access tube long enough to affect the repairs.

103 FAVOR ILIA   103
   looking at Kirk intensely. She tries to be calm.

                              ILIA
           There is no other alternative?

                              XON
           None.

104 ANGLE - IRSKA   104

                              IRSKA
           I want to help.

                              ILIA
                            (gently)
           I know. But, darling, sometimes—

                              IRSKA
           Mr. Scott is my friend. I don't want him to die.

   The INTERCOM WHISTLES. Kirk moves to it, activates it.

                              KIRK
           Kirk here.

                         SHARMA (V.O.)
                           (alarmed)
           Mr. Scott appears to be unconscious, sir!

   Kirk looks questioningly at Ilia.

105 ANGLE - ILIA AND IRSKA   105
   four hands clasped together between them. Ilia searches her daughter's eyes.

                              ILIA
           The reason I love you—or one reason I love you is that you have
           learned to love others.

                              IRSKA
           I'll be all right, Mother. Really.

   Ilia nods but she obviously does not believe things will be that simple.

106 FAVOR KIRK AND ILIA   106
   as Ilia faces Kirk accusingly. Then Xon picks up an object (laser torch), addresses
   Irska:

                              XON
           This is a laser torch. It is operated by depressing this . . .

                              IRSKA
        Oh, I know how it works. Mr. Scott showed me. Look, you just press
        that button—

Kirk is already on his way toward the elevator. He wants to get this over.

                              KIRK
        Let's go.

Xon continues explaining what she must do as they move to the door.

                              XON
        The actual welding itself will be a relatively simple procedure. You will
        see steam escaping from the area you are to . . .

They exit.

107   INT. ACCESS TUBE   107
        Irska and Xon, both suited up, make their way arduously along. Due to her smaller
        size, Irska has a somewhat easier time of it than Xon.

108   INT. CORRIDOR ENTRANCE TO ACCESS TUBE - KIRK, ILIA AND OTHERS IN B.G. 108
        waiting, watching.

                              KIRK
                            (to Ilia)
        There's no other choice.

                              ILIA
                            (a beat)
        I know.

109   INT. ACCESS TUBE   109
        as Xon and Irska reach Scott and the leak. Xon points out the damaged area to
        Irska. The patch is already in place, all that is necessary is for it to be carefully
        sealed.
                              XON
        Use the steam as your guide. When the patch is fully sealed, no steam will escape.

                              IRSKA
        I understand.

Xon pulls Scott's limp body out of the way and Irska begins working. Xon now
secures Scotty to his back and begins the crawling return journey.

110   INTERCUT VARIOUS ANGLES   110
        Xon proceeding with great effort down the tube with Scott on his back . . . and:

        Irska working on the leak; the volume of escaping steam growing progressively
        smaller.

111   INT. CORRIDOR AT ENTRANCE TO ACCESS TUBE   111
        Dr. McCoy has now joined the others anxiously.

112 WIDE ANGLE   112
      as Xon emerges with Scott.

McCoy and two aides move in quickly. They hold Scott up and remove his protective suit so that McCoy can examine him. McCoy waves his medical scanner across Scott's limp body.

> McCOY
> He's alive.
> > (he gives Scott a shot, then to the aides)
> Get him to sick bay.

113 FOLLOW McCOY   113
      as he now proceeds to Xon. Resets his medical scanner and waves it next to the Vulcan.

> XON
> I was not in the radiation zone long enough to suffer any ill effects.

> McCOY
> I'll be the judge of that.

He administers a shot, smiles.

114 WIDER TO INCLUDE KIRK AND ILIA   114
      waiting to talk to Xon.

> KIRK
> How was Irska doing when you left her?

> XON
> Admirably, Captain. I have little doubt that she will accomplish her task . . .

He notes Ilia's concerned look.

> XON
> (continuing)
> . . . and suffer no radiation damage . . .
> > (to Kirk again)
> But the recent pattern of events indicate that we can expect some new difficulty to follow swiftly upon the solution of this one.

> McCOY
> No life form in the entire galaxy can spoil good news faster than your average Vulcan.

Xon ignores McCoy and continues, to Ilia.

> XON
> I'd like to attempt a mind meld with Irska. I may be able to discover things in her subconscious to explain her connection with the alien vessel.

Kirk looks at Ilia questioningly.

                          KIRK
Would you object?

                          ILIA
                         (sad)
Again, Captain, do we have any choice?

                          McCOY
                       (reacting)
What's wrong with you people?! You're all acting like we're dice in
some game the gods are playing! 'Choice,' 'no choice!' We do what's
necessary, and we do it fast!

                          ILIA
                   (in psi awareness)
She's coming . . .

115 WIDE ANGLE   115
as all move to the outlet of the access tube where, a moment later, Irska appears.

The steam is no longer coming out of it, only a trickle of black smoke.

Ilia helps her get the protective suit off, then holds her while McCoy checks her over.
This takes place in the b.g. while Kirk speaks into a wall intercom in the f.g.

                          KIRK
Kirk to Engineering. Reactivate the impulse engine coolers now.

Kirk moves to join the others. McCoy is completing his scan.

                          McCOY
It's incredible. She wasn't affected at all!

Kirk is glad at the news but preoccupied.

                          KIRK
                       (to Ilia)
The mind meld, Lieutenant . . . ?

Irska replies for her mother:

                          IRSKA
Yes, I'll be happy to join minds with Mr. Xon. Wouldn't it be funny if
we taught him how to cry, Mummy?

                          ILIA
Very funny, darling.

Kirk nods at Xon, who moves toward Irska; the girl is still being clutched by Ilia.

XON
(to Ilia; gently)

Let her go.

Ilia does so as Xon kneels to face the child directly.

116   CLOSE ON XON AND IRSKA   116
as Xon cautiously reaches out and touches her face at the appropriate spots to accomplish the link. His face first registers shock, then beatitude.

XON
(getting words from Irska's mind)

Love . . . life . . . death . . . compassion . . . fear . . . body . . . pain . . . cryontha . . . learn . . .
(then, as if from another source)
Understand cryontha . . . End peril.

117   INT. BRIDGE   117
SHOWING Uhura at her post.

UHURA

Bridge to Captain Kirk and Mr. Xon. The alien ship is enveloping us in an energy field!

118   ANGLE - CHEKOV   118
working his damage control console.

119   INSERT - DAMAGE CONTROL CONSOLE   119
This time, the entire superstructure of the Enterprise is blinking on and off rather than one small area. Code letters: HL-SPSTR MOL INTGY appear. And flashing—12 MINUTES TO CRITICAL.

120   ANGLE - CHEKOV - VIEWER IN B.G.   120
aghast. Behind him, on the viewer, we SEE the alien cylinder emitting a filmy magenta energy net that swirls as it envelops the Enterprise.

CHEKOV

It's breaking down the molecular integrity of our hull.

UHURA
(appalled)

The ship will turn to <u>powder</u>! How long?

CHEKOV

Twelve minutes.

He switches on the intercom viewer.

121   INT. CORRIDOR ENTRANCE TO ACCESS TUBE - CLOSEUP - KIRK   121
He studies Chekov on the viewer.

                              KIRK
        You certain, Chekov?

                      CHEKOV (FILTER)
        Positive, Captain. Twelve minutes.

122 TWO SHOT - KIRK AND IRSKA   122
     The Captain kneels by the child.

                              KIRK
        Do you remember when Mr. Xon said that the peril would end if we
        understood cryontha?

     She nods.

                              KIRK
                          (continuing)
        Do you know what peril is?

     She nods her head, affirmatively, again.

                              KIRK
                          (continuing)
        And cryontha. You know what that is too, don't you?

     And the child slowly shakes her head negatively. She's puzzled and perhaps
     frightened.

                              IRSKA
        I don't know. I really don't.

                                                              FADE OUT.

                         END OF ACT THREE

                           ACT FOUR

FADE IN:

123 EXT. SPACE - THE ENTERPRISE AND CYLINDER   123
     The Enterprise is caught in a field of magenta light emanating from the alien
     cylinder. It pulses and glows.

124 INT. BRIDGE   124
     as Kirk, Xon, Ilia and Irska emerge from the turbolift and move to their respective
     positions.
     (Irska next to her mother).

Kirk takes the conn. Decker moves to his position.

125 FAVOR IRSKA 125
She glances around, smiles; Uhura looks warmly at her.

IRSKA
(to Uhura)
You were right, Uhura: Captain Kirk really doesn't mean to say nasty
things.

Kirk gives Uhura "a glance."

126 ANGLE - XON 126
looks up from his console.

XON
Captain, the added strain of any maneuver might cause the ship to
break up.

COMPUTER (O.S.)
Computer override. Emergency life support system activated.
Imperative, repeat imperative. Hull breakdown anticipated within nine
minutes. Repeat—

KIRK
Shut it off!

Uhura flips a button—computer stops.

CHEKOV
Phasers armed and locked on target, sir.

KIRK
(a beat)
Fire phasers, Mr. Chekov.

127 EXT. SPACE - ENTERPRISE AND CYLINDER 127
as the blue phaser beam SHOOTS out of the Enterprise and strikes the cylinder.

128 INT. BRIDGE - CLOSE ON IRSKA 128
as she screams in pain.

129 WIDER 129
as Ilia screams at Kirk.

ILIA
STOP IT! Please, Captain, stop it!

All eyes (except for Xon's) turn and focus on the Deltan and her daughter as Ilia
now comforts the sobbing Irska.

130 FAVOR XON 130

He's engrossed in his hooded viewer. Now he looks up.

> XON
>
> Captain, despite the pain to the child, the alien cylinder shows no
> damage whatever. Its energy field is still intact.

> KIRK
>
> We must have done <u>something</u> to it for the child to be hurt.
> > (then, with a brief, agonized look at Ilia and Irska)
>
> Fire again, Mr. Chekov.

131   FAVOR CHEKOV   131
      as he hesitates for just a moment, then pushes the button.

132   VARIOUS ANGLES   132
      as Irska screams again. Ilia runs for him, throws him aside with surprising ease and
begins hitting buttons on his weapons console. It starts sparking and shorting out
before Kirk and Xon can grab her and pull her away from it. She continues to struggle
furiously against them. Xon must finally use his Vulcan nerve pinch to subdue
her. Now Irska runs and falls on the slumped body of her mother.

> KIRK
>
> Mr. Chekov, have a security team take them—
> > (indicating Ilia and Irska)
>
> —to their quarters and confine them.

133   FAVOR CHEKOV   133
      as he pushes a button on an undamaged portion of his console.

> CHEKOV
>
> Security team 'B' to the bridge.

He now begins picking through the damage to his console.

> CHEKOV
> > (continuing)
>
> Phaser and photon torpedo controls are both out, Captain.

> KIRK
>
> We can go to auxilliary.

> XON
>
> Sir, the second battery did no more damage than the first. We are
> only hurting the child. I suggest we direct our energies toward finding
> the meaning of 'cryontha.' Irska's subconscious indicated that the
> peril to the ship would end when she understood the meaning of that
> word.

> KIRK
>
> Check through the computer language banks for 'cryontha.'

134   WIDE ANGLE   134
      as the security team emerges from the turbolift. Chekov points them to Ilia and
Irska.

135 INT. CORRIDOR - APPROACHING ILIA'S QUARTERS   135
as the security team carries Ilia and escorts Irska to her room.

136 INT. ILIA'S CABIN   136
as the group enters, lays Ilia down on some cushions and withdraws.

137 INT. CORRIDOR   137
as two guards remain posted outside her door.

138 INT. ILIA'S QUARTERS   138
Irska kneels beside her unconscious mother. She takes Ilia's hand in hers and gently strokes it while watching her face intently.

Ilia comes to and looks up at her daughter.

139 ILIA'S POV - IRSKA   139
The child seems radiant with love. Ilia's hands seem to intertwine with Irska's.

140 CLOSE - ILIA AND IRSKA   140
as the child lies down cradled in her mother's arms. Their hands continue to move soothingly—as though they had minds of their own.

                         ILIA
     No need to be frightened. You've only felt pain.

                         IRSKA
     Why must anyone feel pain?

                         ILIA
     Part of life. Sometimes it is how we understand.

                         IRSKA
     Can you make me understand . . . what cryontha is?

                         ILIA
     It is inside your mind. You have to find it.

                         IRSKA
     And if I don't, everyone will die?

                         ILIA
     Don't use your mind to feel guilt. Direct your mind to discover what
     cryontha is—

141 EXT. SPACE - ENTERPRISE AND CYLINDER   141
The Enterprise remains enmeshed in the magenta energy field emanating from the cylinder.

142 INT. BRIDGE   142

                         KIRK
     Mr. Chekov, how much time?

                              CHEKOV
Seven minutes, forty-two seconds, sir.

Kirk punches a button on his chair.

                              KIRK
Metallurgy, Lieutenant Haber, status report.

                         HABER'S VOICE
Whatever the energy field is, sir, it's operating on a sub-atomic level. I
don't see much hope of finding an effective catalyzing agent.

                              KIRK
                     (punching another button)
Physics lab, Lieutenant Takawa, report.

                         TAKAWA'S VOICE
We've tried reverse gravity and a battery of magnetic field generators
so far. No effect, sir.

                              XON
Captain, the closest thing to 'cryontha' that the computer banks contain is 'cryantha' which is a species of animal on Porgath Five.

                              KIRK
                          (desperate)
Have you tried mathematical languages?

                              XON
Yes, sir. With similar results. I have, however, also been reviewing the
child's thoughts as I knew them when our minds were joined.

                             DECKER
The point, Mr. Xon. The point—

                              XON
I had the distinct impression that each of the calamities that befell the
ship was designed to teach the child something about life and death
and emotions I could not comprehend. There was a sensation of incom-
pleteness, as though she was still evolving and these were necessary
steps in the process.

                              KIRK
Cryontha, Mr. Xon, <u>what is cryontha</u>?

                              XON
Cryontha is the key to the next stage of her development. Perhaps if I
tried another mind-meld I could learn more.

                              KIRK
Time, Mr. Chekov?

CHEKOV

Five minutes, thirty-six seconds.

KIRK

Let's go, Mr. Xon.
(to Uhura)
We'll be in Lieutenant Ilia's quarters.
(to Decker)
You have the conn.

The two men move quickly to the turbolift and enter.

143 INT. CORRIDOR   143
as Kirk and Xon emerge from the elevator. They hurry down the corridor to Ilia's
room.

144 ANOTHER ANGLE - OUTSIDE ILIA'S DOOR   144
as Kirk and Xon brush past the two Security Men, and enter the cabin.

145 INT. ILIA'S CABIN   145
as Kirk and Xon enter. Xon reacts quickly and extends a hand pulling Kirk up short.

Mother and child sit cross-legged on the floor opposite each other. They appear to be
in some kind of trance-like state. Their arms extend outward, clasping each other's
hands, fingers intertwined, roughly at waist level.

146 ANGLE - KIRK AND XON   146
They keep their voices low.

XON

They are 'sharing sight.' We shouldn't interrupt them.

KIRK

What about the mind meld?

XON

This may serve the same function.

147 ANGLE - KIRK AND XON'S POV - ILIA IRSKA   147

XON

It is a deep meditation. Irska may find the . . .

Ilia's face looks suddenly stricken. She screams.

ILIA

NO!

And she breaks the posture to clasp Irska tightly to her. They are still both unaware
of Kirk and Xon's presence. Irska attempts to push away from her mother. Ilia holds
tighter.

                              IRSKA
        Mother, let me experience what you did.

And she forces Ilia back into the "sight sharing" posture.

148 ANGLE - XON AND KIRK   148

                              KIRK
        What did you feel, Ilia?

Too late. The mother and daughter are in a world of their own. They cannot hear
Kirk. They are light miles away.

                              KIRK
                          (continuing)
        Ilia!

Xon touches Kirk's arm.

                              XON
        They cannot hear you—

Kirk is terribly frustrated.

                              KIRK
        Use telepathy. Get into their minds. Inject your theory into their line
        of thought.

Xon nods. He kneels beside Irska and reaches out to establish contact.
It is a heavy jolt for him. He loses contact. He tries again. Winces.
Controls it. Finally he settles in. For a moment all are entranced.

149 EXT. SPACE - THE CYLINDER   149
        The radiation peaks for an instant.

150 INT. CABIN   150
        Abruptly, Xon and Ilia are thrown violently off from Irska as though repelled by
        some incredible force. They are both knocked to the floor, unconscious, while Irska
        continues to sit in a trance state.

151 ANGLE AND FOLLOW KIRK   151
        as he reacts, aghast, and runs to the wall intercom.

                              KIRK
        Doctor McCoy to Lieutenant Ilia's quarters. Emergency!

The two security guards enter the room at the sound of the commotion. Kirk steps
back to check out Xon and Ilia himself, the guards accompany him. They remain
tending to the unconscious forms of Ilia and Xon while Kirk runs to the bathroom
for some water. When he re-enters the room carrying a cup, he stops short; looks
around.

152 PAN ROOM - KIRK'S POV   152
     Irska is gone.

                              KIRK
                           (to guards)
          Where's the child?

     The guards look up. Plainly they were too preoccupied with Xon and Ilia to notice
     Irska leave. Kirk drops the water and bolts for the door. It opens and he nearly
     crashes into McCoy, who rushes in.

                              KIRK
                          (continuing)
          You see Irska?

                             McCOY
          No.

     Kirk waves in the direction of Xon and Ilia.

                              KIRK
          Take care of them.

     With that he runs out into the:

153 CORRIDOR   153
     as Kirk pounds along the corridor, he pulls out his hand communicator.

                              KIRK
                       (into communicator)
          This is the Captain. Alert all decks. Find Irska, and detain her!

     He continues his frantic search.

154 VARIOUS ANGLES   154
     as Kirk and others run through the corridors, check in doorways, storage rooms, etc.
     Finally, a struggling VOICE comes out of the intercom system.

                              VOICE
          Transporter room to Captain Kirk. Irska is here, sir.

     Kirk races for the elevator.

155 INT. TRANSPORTER ROOM - WIDE ANGLE   155
     Irska is struggling furiously trying to break free of the ENSIGN who holds her. Her
     head band falls off during the struggle.

     The door opens and Kirk rushes in.

                             IRSKA
          Cryontha means 'unnecessary shell!' 'Unnecessary shell.'

                             ENSIGN
                          (hanging on)
          She was trying to beam over to the alien ship, sir.

                              KIRK
        Hang on to her.

Kirk moves to the intercom. Presses buttons. Irska continues to struggle and AD LIB
"Let me go . . . etc."

                              KIRK
                          (continuing)
        Mr. Chekov. How much time?

                             CHEKOV
        Twenty-two seconds, sir.

Suddenly Xon appears in the doorway.

                              XON
        Let her go!

The Ensign is confused. Xon rushes into the room and nerve pinches the man before
anyone has time to react. Irska runs for the transporter platform while Xon leaps to
the controls.A moment later she is gone.

                              XON
                          (continuing)
        Forgive me, Captain. There was no time to explain.

156   EXT. SPACE - ENTERPRISE AND CYLINDER   156
       as the magenta energy field withdraws back to the cylinder. The cylinder then meta-
       morphoses into a large, white light energy ball like the ones in the cloud that the
       ship passed through in the teaser. The light entity then moves off at speed.

157   INT. TRANSPORTER ROOM - ANGLE - KIRK AND XON   157

                              XON
        'Cryontha' meant 'unnecessary shell,' Captain.

Kirk still fails to see the significance of this.

                              KIRK
        Yes, I heard Irska say that . . .

                          CHEKOV'S VOICE
                          (over intercom)
        The alien cylinder is gone, sir. The hull has returned to normal.

158   FOLLOW KIRK   158
       to intercom.

                              KIRK
                          (puzzled)
        Thank you, Mr. Chekov. Secure from red alert.

XON

Thousands of centuries ago, Irska's race existed in human form. Just as humans pass through all evolutionary stages from single cell to human being within the mother's womb, it was necessary for Irska to experience all stages of her race's prior development.

KIRK

Are you suggesting that all this time Irska hadn't really been born?

159 ANGLE - DOORWAY   159
Ilia stands in it.

ILIA

That is correct, Captain. Until she had experienced all the joys and pains of living in a body and was ready to shed the 'unnecessary shell' it represented to her, she was still in an embryonic stage for her race. I was her first womb. The Enterprise was her second.

160 ANGLE - KIRK   160
showing his exhaustion and sympathy. He picks up Irska's fallen headband and hands it to Ilia.

KIRK

I wish, Lieutenant, that her life with you could have been longer, or that I could have made it a bit easier.

161 CLOSE ON ILIA   161
looking just as tired, but deeply fulfilled. She reflects deeply, longingly, as she slowly turns the headband over in her hands.

ILIA

Thank you, Captain, I appreciate your sentiments, but I could hardly expect you to make improvements on a miracle.

Her smile is pure beauty as we . . .

FADE OUT.

THE END

Star Trek's End?

So why might *Phase II* have been the end of *Star Trek*?

Let's take a look at its conceptual cousin: *Star Trek: Voyager.*

Like *Phase II, Voyager* was created as a *Star Trek* series that would launch an independent, Paramount-owned television network. In 1978, *Phase II* would have launched a fourth network. By the time *Voyager* arrived in January 1995, Barry Diller, the visionary who had started Paramount on the path to a network in 1977, had already gone on to Fox and created the fourth network there. Thus, on January 16, 1995, *Voyager* launched a fifth service—the United Paramount Network, UPN.

On that first broadcast of the first two-hour pilot episode, going against ABC, CBS, NBC, and Fox, and facing additional competition unimag-

ined in 1977, from pay channels, superstations, satellite independents, and VCRs and laser disks, *Voyager* blew everyone else out of space.

More than 21 million viewers tuned in that night, and though it was second overall in its time slot, the show was number one in the key demographics of young men.

And then, week after week, those ratings declined, until they settled in at a comfortable, though no longer spectacular, 12 million viewers, about the same as the *Original Series* had enjoyed back in the late sixties.

This decline, it must be emphasized, was completely expected, and in no way reflected on the quality or content of the new series.

The initial surge of viewers represented not only die-hard *Star Trek* fans who would watch anything with the *Star Trek* name on it, but fans of *Deep Space Nine,* fans of the recently discontinued and sorely missed *The Next Generation*, and millions of others who had occasionally sampled *Star Trek* over the past two and half decades, and who had tuned in out of curiosity.

The first airing of a new *Star Trek* series was a singular event that could be counted on to draw the attention of almost everyone with the slightest interest in the franchise. But to return to it week after week, that is the domain of the dedicated viewer, a much smaller number.

Now think back to the spring of 1978, a veritable golden age of television when hit series included *All in the Family, Kojak, Little House on the Prairie, Happy Days, Laverne & Shirley, M*A*S*H, The Waltons, Barney Miller, Hawaii Five-O, The Rockford Files, Starsky and Hutch,* and *The Jeffersons.*

Imagine the interest in Paramount's audacious new plan to compete with the big three networks by reviving *Star Trek.* It would have run on Saturday nights, opposite *Fish* and *Operation Petticoat* on ABC, *The Bob Newhart Show* and *We've Got Each Other* on CBS, and *The Bionic Woman* on NBC.

Without question, just as *Voyager* did seventeen years later, that first airing of the two-hour pilot, "In Thy Image," would have made broadcasting history.

But what about the next week? The demographically important young audience doesn't stay at home on Saturday nights to watch television, today or in 1978. Once, perhaps, for a special event, but week after week? *Phase II* would experience an inevitable ratings drop simply because an important segment of its audience wouldn't be watching television at all.

Also, among the die-hard fans who had supported *Star Trek* in syndication, Mr. Spock was a nonexpendable character—part of the essential triumvirate of Kirk, Spock, and McCoy. How many would stop tuning in, thinking like Robert Wise's wife that without Spock, there could be no *Star Trek?*

And most importantly of all, the world and the audience had grown up and changed in the past twelve years—had *Star Trek* kept up with them?

The answer, we fear, would have been no.

For all that is said about television and movies being formulaic, novelty and freshness are still required for success. And *Star Trek Phase II* would not have been different enough to be anything other than the long-delayed fourth season of the first series.

No matter how well written the scripts, no matter how convincing the visual effects, no matter how devotedly fans might rally to Xon, Decker, and Ilia, the reality of the time would have been that *Phase II*'s ratings would have declined each week, like *Voyager*'s, until they settled in at the approximately 12-million mark. In 1978, that would not have been enough to support the series.

We feel it is overwhelmingly likely that after a two-hour pilot and thirteen episodes, *Star Trek* would have been canceled again. And given the personalities involved, we doubt that anyone would have had the courage or the motivation to work to revive a series that had failed not once, but twice. (Of course, a case could be made that the first thirteen episodes might have served as a trial by fire, much like *The Next Generation*'s uncertain first season. Since television series are constantly being adjusted, it's possible that Paramount might have taken a chance on a second order of thirteen episodes, if only to anchor their fledgling network, and that with the added time, the talented people behind *Phase II* would have honed a series to be reckoned with. But then, history might have proceeded much as it did, and the rest of this chapter would make no sense.)

With the perceived failure of *Phase II*, there would have been no series of movies starring the original cast. Without those moneymakers to fuel Paramount's interest, there would have been no *The Next Generation* series, nor the series that spun off from it in turn—*Deep Space Nine* and *Voyager.*

Undoubtedly, *Star Trek* would have arisen in some form, and probably in the '90s. After all, we have witnessed successful films made from other series of the 1960s. As we write this in the fall of 1996, the *Mission: Impossible* movie has surpassed the $300 million mark. Movie versions of *The Man from U.N.C.L.E., My Favorite Martian, The Wild, Wild West,* and *Voyage to the Bottom of the Sea* are in development. The new *Outer Limits* is thriving on the Showtime network.

In this alternate history, as the nostalgia of the past is mined for a new crop for moviegoers, Paramount would no doubt be dusting off *Star Trek* and handing it to a group of filmmakers who weren't on the planet when the original series aired.

Imagine a *Star Trek* movie in this alternate world, written by Quentin Tarantino, perhaps, with Nicolas Cage as Spock, Whitney Houston as Uhura, and Arnold Schwarzenegger as James T. Kirk. The mind boggles.

But back here in the real world, we believe *Star Trek* survived because at this critical time it did *not* return to television, but remained an every-few-years special event.

Even die-hard fans grudgingly admit that *Star Trek: The Motion Picture* was not an exceptional film. But it did treat beloved characters and situations with respect, and it showed the *Star Trek* universe as it had never been seen before, with new designs, state-of-the-art visual effects, and realistically detailed models. Just like that first broadcast of *Voyager, everyone* with the slightest interest in *Star Trek* went to see that first film, making it financially successful despite the inflated expenses that had been allocated against it to pay for all the earlier false-start movies as well as *Phase II.*

And best of all, after establishing that the market for *Star Trek* was strong, Paramount then had a breathing space of two years to make a *better* movie as a follow-up.

Here at last was the most important component of *Star Trek*'s rebirth.

Star Trek II: The Wrath of Khan reinvented *Star Trek* for a new decade, a new audience, and a new world.

After all, that is the secret of long-term success in everything from natural selection to marketing cars—change.

In the best science fiction, stories set in the future are always about life at the time they were written. *Star Trek* is no exception.

The original series came out of the sixties, the ascendancy of the baby boomers, a time of fundamental changes to society and the sense of great adventure and explorations to come. Astronauts were in training to walk on the moon; the threat of nuclear war existed side by side with Woodstock. The unrestrained spirit of the sixties was the crucible in which the first *Star Trek* stories were told, and from which its signature optimism for the future flowed.

Then came the seventies and a profound cynicism. The hopefulness of the sixties hit Watergate, Vietnam, the energy crisis, and rampant inflation. The communal spirit of Woodstock was slowly abandoned, as the baby boomers entered the working world and became more inward, more self-serving. That loss of innocence was the antithesis of what had infused *Star Trek* in the sixties. The *Phase II* episodes described in these pages that adhered to *Star Trek*'s initial story philosophy quite probably would have been seen as dated. Those episodes that reflected current society quite probably would have been seen as lacking *Star Trek*'s optimism. Both types of episodes airing as part of the same series would have engendered confusion.

This question of tone was not a problem that could have been foreseen at the time. It's apparent only with the hindsight afforded by studying the success of the movies and series that followed. However it would have been, we believe, an almost impossible hurdle to clear.

But in the absence of *Phase II,* and following the success of *The Motion Picture,* Paramount went on to create a new version of *Star Trek* for its time—*Star Trek: The Wrath of Khan.* All the familiar faces were back, but they were older, and that was noted. The characters questioned themselves and their duties in a way that had not been successful when Jeffrey Hunter's Captain Christopher Pike had done it in the first *Star Trek* pilot in 1965. But it fit perfectly the audience's mood in 1982.

And finally, after all the character development was said and done, the story delivered what a *Star Wars*–savvy audience demanded—an exciting space-battle sequence and flat-out science-fiction adventure.

Continuing to embrace the concept of change, *Star Trek* again embraced its time with 1986's *Star Trek: The Voyage Home*—this time a more humorous film in the tradition of "The Trouble with Tribbles" and "A Piece of the Action."

Finally, *Star Trek* was once again reinvented for a new generation and at last returned to its home—television.

Star Trek: The Next Generation did not spring from the 1960s' seat-of-the-pants, on-the-edge-of-the-frontier, wild-west mentality that had fueled the *Original Series*. It reflected its time—one of group consensus, reasoned approaches, and greater familiarity with and reliance on technology. Where the original *Enterprise* had been a VW microbus, its crew enduring hardships to set out on a summer adventure that could take them anywhere, the new *Enterprise* was a true motor home, richly carpeted, with room for spouses and children.

The Next Generation spoke to its new audience and preserved the essence of optimism so necessary for it to be perceived as *Star Trek*. It was, and continues to be, a dynamic success.

Then came the nineties, darker than the eighties, with the hippies from the Summer of Love turning fifty. Today's society is one based on caution and cocooning. And today's *Star Trek* has once again been reinvented for its new audience.

The crew of *Star Trek: Deep Space Nine* aren't going anywhere—they're trapped in one place, trying to make sense of the difficult situations that surround them, endeavoring to do no harm. The crew of *Star Trek: Voyager*, on the other hand, has been propelled past all known boundary markers and in every episode is hightailing it for the security and comfort of home. The optimism is still there, but both new series reflect the concerns of their 1990s audience. And they reflect them successfully. For though television has expanded far beyond the three-network monopoly of the *Original Series*, into a five-hundred-channel universe complete with movies on demand and Internet access, despite all those other destinations in the broadcasting universe, *Star Trek* continues to be a solid, ongoing, and deserving success.

At the end of the day, there are no lessons to be learned from the story of *Phase II*. The understanding of success and failure in Hollywood is always a function of hindsight, and seldom one of vision. Some people are good at anticipating what the public might want to see, and they're the ones who earn second and third chances. Gene Roddenberry was one of the fortunate few who earned his second chance and was proven right.

For thirty years, hindsight has proven that *Star Trek* contains at its core an essence that is appealing to a wide audience that transcends nations and age. It requires no great vision to state that what has been successful for thirty years will continue to be so, and that new versions of *Star Trek* wait in our future. And what will link them all, past and present, is that strand of connectedness that extends from the first pilot to the latest feature.

If there is any conclusion to be drawn from this book, it is that that thread of connectedness passes through *Phase II* as surely as it does all the other, better known versions of *Star Trek*.

The people who were involved in that short-lived adventure were participating in an act of creation that continues to this day, because *Phase II* was the crucible through which *Star Trek* refound its audience and began the journey to even greater success.

Phase II was not the end of *Star Trek*—it was *Star Trek*'s new beginning.

Star Trek Phase II Staff and Crew List

October 1977

EXECUTIVE PRODUCER
GENE RODDENBERRY

SECTY./ASSISTANT TO G. RODDENBERRY
SUSAN SACKETT

PRODUCER
ROBERT GOODWIN

SECTY. TO R. GOODWIN
ALISA BEATON

PRODUCER
HAROLD LIVINGSTON

SECTY. TO H. LIVINGSTON
CHERYL BLYTHE

DIRECTOR (PILOT)
ROBERT COLLINS

STORY EDITOR
JON POVILL

ASST. TO G. RODDENBERRY
BOB ROSENBAUM

SECTY. TO B. ROSENBAUM
RUTH CARPENTER

PRODUCTION MANAGER
BRUCE FOWLER, JR.

PRODUCTION MANAGER
MICHAEL SCHOENBRUN

SECTY. TO PROD. MGRS.
SUSAN ELLIS

PRODUCTION
FREEMAN PACKARD

UNIT PRODUCTION MANAGER
GEORGE FENAJA

CINEMATOGRAPHER
BRUCE LOGAN

ART DIRECTOR
JOE JENNINGS

ASSISTANT ART DIRECTOR
JOHN CARTWRIGHT

CONCEPT ARTIST
LEE COLE

SET DECORATOR
TOM PEDIGO

SET DESIGNER
LEWIS SPLITTSBERGER

JR. SET DESIGNER
JANET STOKES

ILLUSTRATOR
MIKE MINOR

COSTUME DESIGNER
WILLIAM WARE THEISS

ASSISTANT COSTUME DESIGNER
FRANCES HARRISON

CUTTER/FITTER
KAZUAKI YAMAMOTO

NASA TECHNICAL CONSULTANT
JESCO VON PUTTKAMER

TECHNICAL ADVISOR
MATT JEFFERIES

HEAD OF CASTING
HOYT BOWERS

CASTING DIRECTORS
PAT HARRIS & MARCIA KLEINMAN

CASTING SECRETARY
MEG LIBERMAN

POST-PRODUCTION SUPERVISOR
PAUL RABWIN

STUDIO POST-PRODUCTION
GEORGE WATTERS

ASST. TO G. WATTERS
GARY CHANDLER

PUBLICITY
RICHARD WINTERS

INSURANCE CERTIFICATES
RICHARD MILLER

OPERATIONS
DON FOSTER

CONSTRUCTION COORDINATOR
BUDDY ARBUCKLE

PROPERTY MASTER
BOB RICHARDS

GAFFER
BRINK BRYDON

Both the charm and the curse of television is that it is such an ephemeral form of art. For all that millions might be moved by the shared experience of watching a meaningful series, or even an episode, little record is kept of the thousands of contributions and creative efforts that lead to the final few minutes of film or tape.

In the case of a series that was not even made, the task of retracing those steps is more difficult still.

Thus, this book could not have been written, let alone attempted, without the kindness and foresight of Jon Povill. Jon not only kept all his files from his days as Gene Roddenberry's assistant, then as *Phase II*'s Story Editor, and then as Associate Producer of *Star Trek: The Motion Picture,* but generously shared them with us, along with enduring many hours of patiently answering our questions. Jon's generosity is matched only by his continuing creative contributions to television and film.

On the Paramount lot, we must once again thank Rick Berman for continuing to allow us unfettered access to all the facets of *Star Trek*'s production, past and present. As Gene Roddenberry had hoped, Rick Berman has taken *Star Trek* far beyond its beginnings and created a lasting film and television legacy of his own.

Just as Jon Povill's file boxes enabled us to write this book, the same foresight and generosity of Herman Zimmerman has made possible many of the illustrations in it. From the first season of *The Next Generation* to the stunning new look of *Star Trek: First Contact,* Herman has been one of *Star Trek*'s preeminent production designers. At the same time, he has recognized the value of all the creative visual contributors to *Star Trek* and made heroic and much-appreciated efforts to save as much of that work as possible. Without Herman's dedication to preserving and acknowledging the work of others, many of the images in this book, and many books to come, would have long ago ended up in landfill. As writers and as students of television, we thank him.

Once again, Herman's assistant, Penny Juday, came to our rescue more times than she knows, smoothing our way through our visits to Paramount, and always managing to squeeze out enough time to find just one more illustration or make one more phone call for us. As an art coordinator on the current *Star Trek* series and features, Penny has made many creative contributions of her own to *Star Trek*, and we're honored that she has helped us in our work in even the most trying circumstances.

As always, our friends in the *Star Trek* Art Departments get our thanks for putting up with our surprise visits to plunder their files, and for supplying endless good humor and support even while facing their own tight deadlines. Mike and Denise Okuda, especially, gave us the greatly appreciated benefit of their friendship and support. And Mike deserves a standing ovation for digging up the schematics of the *Phase II Enterprise,* which were presumed to have been lost forever.

Off the lot, many of the people involved with the lost series were no less generous with their time, patience, and support. Robert Goodwin, Matt Jefferies, Harold Livingston, Gary Nardino, and Brick Price were all kind enough to turn back the clock and find time to discuss what was simply one brief job among many successes for each of them.

In addition, Harold Livingston's permission to reprint his script is an important contribution not only to this book and *Star Trek*'s history, but is a testament to the talent that has made him a best-selling author as well as celebrated television writer. If you remember a favorite *Mission: Impossible* episode from the original series, chances are Harold wrote it.

Again, beyond the call of duty, Brick Price of WonderWorks Inc. went so far as to send his modelmakers on expeditions into storage areas dating back to the Pre-Cambrian to find the original molds from which the lost *Enterprise* had been cast. His enthusiasm and kindness in giving us access to his archives is deeply appreciated, as is the support of his business partner, John Palmer.

Andy Probert, among the most significant contributors to *Star Trek*'s visual legacy for his work on both *The Motion Picture* and *The Next Generation Enterprise,* also graciously provided photographs from his collection, as did Dave McDonnell of *Starlog* magazine, whose ongoing support of Pocket's *Star Trek* publishing program is greatly appreciated.

On the technical end, once again Rick Thomas of Patrick J. Donahue Photography/The Photo Lab handled the treasures given to him with dispatch and care, overseeing the production of many of the high-quality photographs in these pages.

And though we save them for last, our publication team is, without doubt, our greatest asset in these behind-the-scenes books we write. Paula Block of Viacom Consumer Products has been a staunch ally for many years, and we are indebted to the dedication and care she devotes to our work and the entire *Star Trek* publication line. In the materials section of VCP, Harry Lang's ever-patient assistance in capturing video images for us made possible many of the never-before-seen images in this book.

At Pocket Books, Kevin Ryan has been a virtual Khan Noonien Singh when it comes to determination and focus on a single goal over the years. It is a massive understatement to say we will miss his input and insights and we wish him great good fortune in his new home at Lyrick Studios.

Our new editor, Margaret Clark, is an old friend from DC Comics, and her sometimes frighteningly deep knowledge about *Star Trek* has made this a better and more accurate book. Her extreme patience is also appreciated more than she can know.

As always, John Ordover and Tyya Turner have been tireless in picking up the pieces that fall between the cracks and in keeping the process moving. And designer Richard Oriolo, whose work we have always admired and appreciated, has once more brought serene order to our words and pictures, despite the deadlines we push him to.

With this, our eighth book for Pocket, we are more impressed than ever by the entire company's professionalism and support, and we look forward to writing many more.

Our thanks to all.

J&G Reeves-Stevens
October 1996
Los Angeles

Judith and Garfield Reeves-Stevens are Emmy-nominated scriptwriters and *New York Times* bestselling novelists. They helped develop for television and were executive story editors of the animated cult science-fiction series, *Phantom 2040*. For the 1996–97 television season, they developed and were executive story editors for the all-new *Flash Gordon* animated series. Their other television credits range from episodes of series as diverse as *Beyond Reality*, MTV's *Catwalk*, and the animated *Batman* to the Showtime Original Movie, *Shadow Zone: My Teacher Ate My Homework*.

The Reeves-Stevenses are the authors of thirteen novels, three nonfiction books, and a thirty-title science and technology series of textbooks for children. In the world of *Star Trek*, they have written three novels, including *Federation*, and two previous behind-the-scenes books: *The Making of Star Trek: Deep Space Nine*, and *The Art of Star Trek*. They are currently collaborating with William Shatner on a series of novels about the ongoing adventures of Captain Kirk following the events of *Star Trek Generations*. The first two novels, *The Ashes of Eden* and *The Return*, are in bookstores now. The newest novel, *Avenger*, will be published in March 1997, with two novels to follow. Their latest work of *Star Trek* nonfiction, *Star Trek: The Next Generation The Continuing Mission*, celebrating ten years of *The Next Generation*, will be published in November 1997.

The Reeves-Stevenses live in Los Angeles, where they are working on their new techno-thriller novel, *Icefire*, to be published by Pocket Books.

Harold Livingston

Harold Livingston's writing career spans four decades, eight novels, one memoir, almost one hundred television credits, and four major films, including sole screenplay credit for *Star Trek: The Motion Picture*. In addition to his producer role for *Star Trek Phase II*, he was also a producer on the series *Future Cop* and *Fantasy Island*.

Mr. Livingston's 1954 novel, *The Coasts of the Earth*, was the winner of the Houghton-Mifflin Literary Fellowship Award. His most recent novel, *To Die in Babylon*, was published by St. Martin's in 1993.

Mr. Livingston lives in Bakersfield, California.

Jon Povill

After his stints as Story Editor on *Star Trek Phase II*, and as Associate Producer—and an uncredited, participating writer—on *Star Trek: The Motion Picture*, Jon Povill continued his association with television, movies, and science fiction.

Among his most notable credits are the initial script for the Arnold Schwarzenegger blockbuster, *Total Recall*, and, most recently, Producer of the Fox Network's hit series, *Sliders*. Povill's teleplay for the 1995 season finale, "The Luck of the Draw," won the coveted Turner Prize from the Environmental Media Association.

One of his many current projects is of special interest to *Star Trek* followers—a rewrite of the 1975 Gene Roddenberry script, *The Nine*, about the creator of a popular science-fiction television show who is hired to write a movie to prepare the world for an actual landing by UFOs. It's a fictionalized account of events in Roddenberry's life, currently slated to be directed by Philippe Mora.

Mr. Povill lives in Los Angeles.

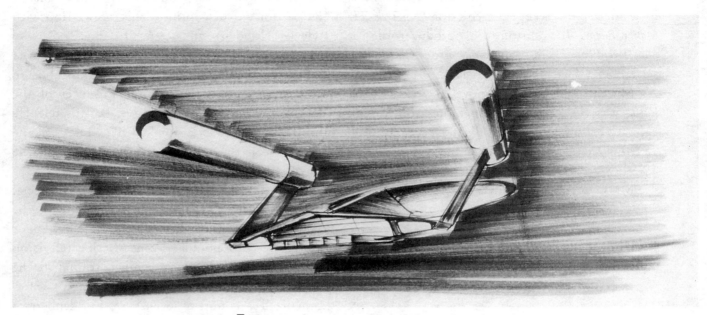

The mission continues. Sketch by Ken Adam.
Courtesy of Paramount Pictures.

11+ Non-Verbal Reasoning

For **GL** Assessment

When it comes to the 11+, getting top marks is key — and this CGP Stretch book is packed with extra-tricky questions to help pupils aged 10-11 master the hardest parts of the test.

It starts with a section of challenging questions for each topic, so children can practise each question type. Then, there's a selection of mixed-topic Assessment Tests where they can work on really polishing their exam technique.

We've also included detailed, step-by-step answers. Everything you need!

Stretch Practice Book
Ages 10-11

with Assessment Tests

How to use this Practice Book

This book is divided into five parts — 'Similarities and Differences', 'Pairs, Series and Grids', 'Codes', 'Spatial Reasoning', and 'Assessment Tests'. There are answers and detailed explanations at the back of the book.

'Similarities and Differences', 'Pairs, Series and Grids' and 'Codes'

- Each section contains the different question types your child will need to be familiar with for the Non-Verbal Reasoning test.

- These pages can help your child build up the different skills they'll need for the real test.

- Particularly hard questions are marked up with an orange box around the question number.

- Your child can use the smiley face tick boxes to evaluate how confident they feel with each type of question.

Spatial Reasoning

- This part concentrates on the skills your child will need to tackle the Spatial Reasoning questions that are tested in some regions.

Assessment Tests

- This part of the book contains four assessment tests, each with a mix of question types. They take a similar form to the real test.

- You can print multiple-choice answer sheets so your child can practise the tests as if they're sitting the real thing — visit cgpbooks.co.uk/11plus/answer-sheets or scan the QR code. →

Answer Sheets

- Use the printable answer sheets if you want your child to do each test more than once.

- If you want to give your child timed practice, give them a time limit of 60 minutes for each test, and ask them to work as quickly and carefully as they can.

- Talk your child through the answers to the questions they got wrong. This will help them understand questions that work in a similar way when they come up against them again.

- Your child should aim for a mark of around 80% (43 questions correct) in each test. If they score less than this, use their results to work out the areas they need more practice on.

- If they haven't managed to finish the test in time, they should work on increasing their speed, whereas if they have made a lot of mistakes, they may need to work more carefully.

- Keep track of your child's scores using the progress chart on page 98.

Published by CGP

Editors:
Michael Bushell, Alex Fairer, Katherine Faudemer, Katie Fernandez, Tamara Sinivassen

With thanks to Sharon Keeley-Holden for the proofreading.

ISBN: 978 1 78908 979 0
Printed by Elanders Ltd, Newcastle upon Tyne
Clipart from Corel®

Based on the classic CGP style created by Richard Parsons.

Contents

Tick off the check box for each topic as you go along.

Similarities and Differences

Pairs, Series and Grids

Codes

Spatial Reasoning

Assessment Tests

Similarities and Differences

Odd One Out

Look at the five figures below. Find which figure is most unlike the others.

Example:

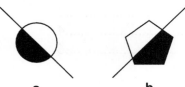

a   b   c   d   e   (_b_)

B is the only figure where the line doesn't split the shape exactly in half.

1.

a   b   c   d   e   (___)

2.

a   b   c   d   e   (___)

3.

a   b   c   d   e   (___)

4.

a   b   c   d   e   (___)

5.

   a   **b**   **c**   **d**   **e**   (_____)

6.

   a   **b**   **c**   **d**   **e**   (_____)

7.

   a   **b**   **c**   **d**   **e**   (_____)

8.

   a   **b**   **c**   **d**   **e**   (_____)

9.

   a   **b**   **c**   **d**   **e**   (_____)

10.

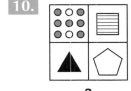 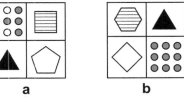 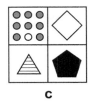 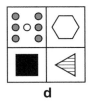 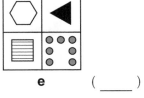

   a   **b**   **c**   **d**   **e**   (_____)

      Similarities and Differences

Find the Figure Like the First Two

Find the figure on the right that is most like the two figures on the left.

Example:

               a   **b**   **c**   **d**   **e**   (**C**)

One third of the shapes must be shaded black.

1.

               a   **b**   **c**   **d**   **e**   (   )

2.

               a   **b**   **c**   **d**   **e**   (   )

3.

               a   **b**   **c**   **d**   **e**   (   )

4.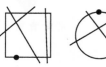

               a   **b**   **c**   **d**   **e**   (   )

5.

               a   **b**   **c**   **d**   **e**   (   )

Similarities and Differences

6.   (____)

7.   (____)

8.   (____)

9.   (____)

10.   (____)

11.   (____)

Find the Figure Like the First Three

Find the figure on the right that is most like the three figures on the left.

Example:

   |

                                      a   **b**   **c**   **d**   **e** (__C__)

All figures must have a shape with an even number of sides that is hatched diagonally.

1.

   |

                                        a   **b**   **c**   **d**   **e** (___)

2.

   |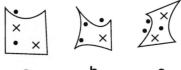

                                        a   **b**   **c**   **d**   **e** (___)

3.

   |

                                        a   **b**   **c**   **d**   **e** (___)

4.

   |

                                        a   **b**   **c**   **d**   **e** (___)

5.

   |

                                        a   **b**   **c**   **d**   **e** (___)

6.

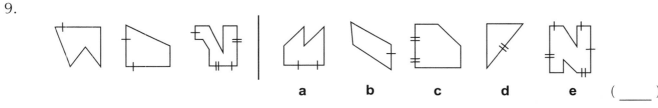

                    a   **b**   **c**   **d**   **e**   (_____)

7.

                    a   **b**   **c**   **d**   **e**   (_____)

8.

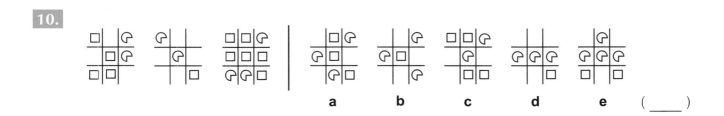

                    a   **b**   **c**   **d**   **e**   (_____)

9.

                    a   **b**   **c**   **d**   **e**   (_____)

10.

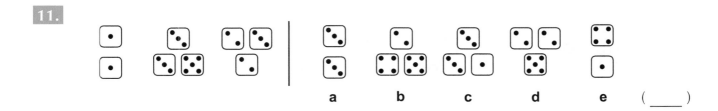

                    a   **b**   **c**   **d**   **e**   (_____)

11.

                    a   **b**   **c**   **d**   **e**   (_____)

 ✓   ✓   ✓   Similarities and Differences

Complete the Pair

The first figure below is changed in some way to become the second. Choose the figure on the right that relates to the third figure in the same way that the second relates to the first.

Example:

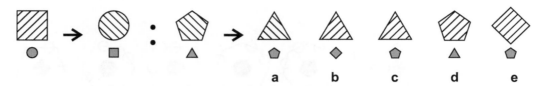

a   b   c   d   e   (__C__)

The two shapes swap position, size and shading. The hatching reflects across.

1.

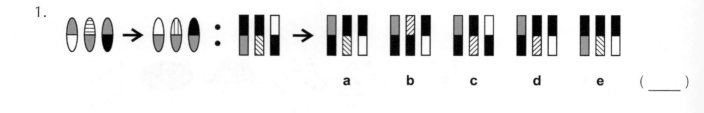

a   b   c   d   e   (____)

2.

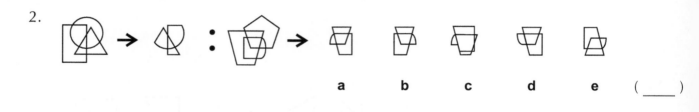

a   b   c   d   e   (____)

3.

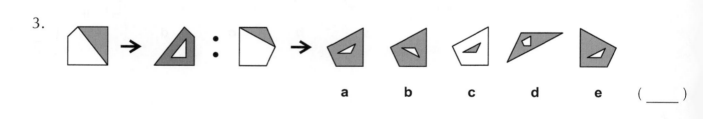

a   b   c   d   e   (____)

4.

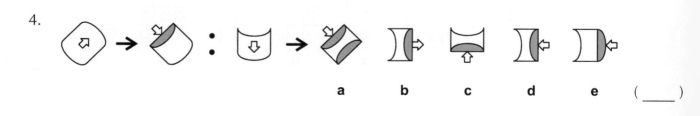

a   b   c   d   e   (____)

5.

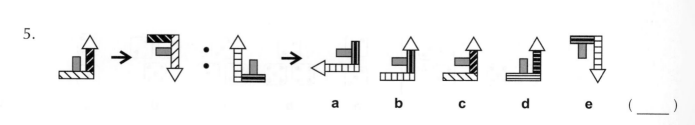

a   b   c   d   e   (____)

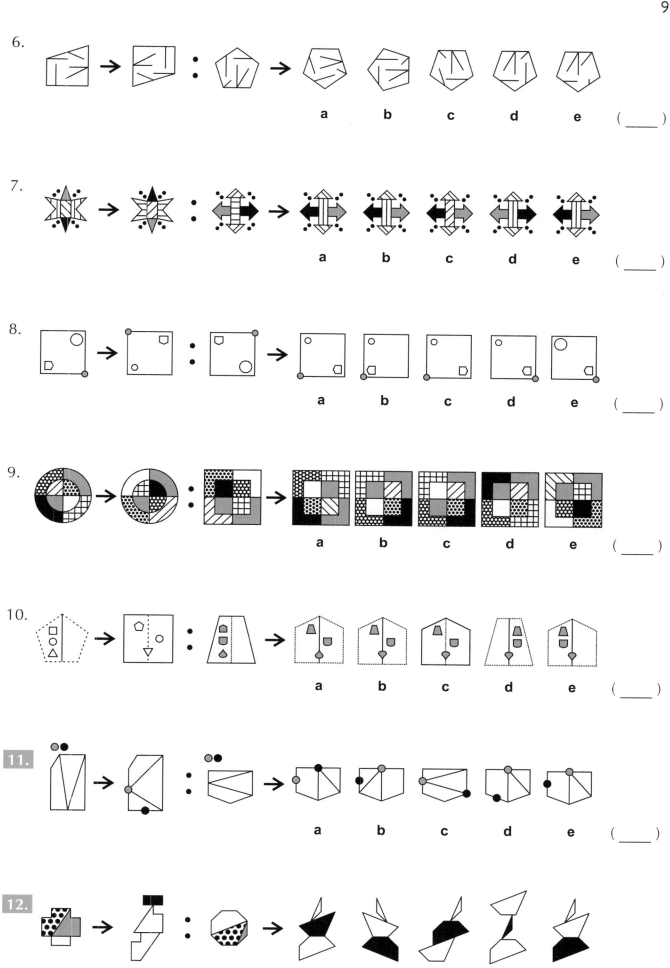

6. a b c d e (____)

7. a b c d e (____)

8. a b c d e (____)

9. a b c d e (____)

10. a b c d e (____)

11. a b c d e (____)

12. a b c d e (____)

Complete the Series

In the question below, the five squares on the left are arranged in order. One of the squares is missing. Work out which of the five squares on the right should go in its place.

Example:

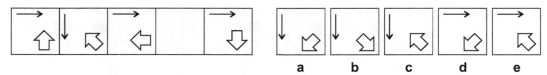

(_a_)

The arrow-style line swaps direction and the white arrow rotates 45 degrees anticlockwise in each series square.

1.

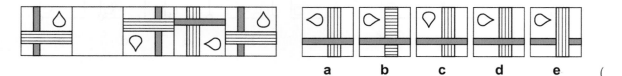

a   b   c   d   e   (___)

2.

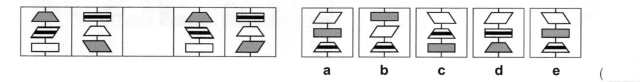

a   b   c   d   e   (___)

3.

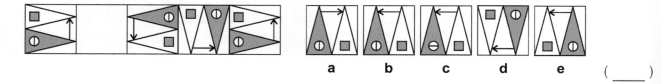

a   b   c   d   e   (___)

4.

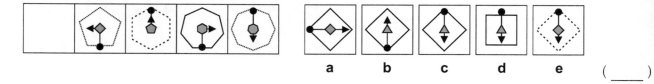

a   b   c   d   e   (___)

5.

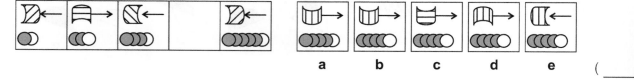

a   b   c   d   e   (___)

6.

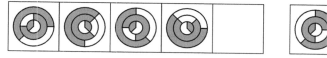 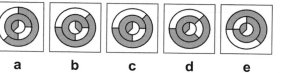

a   b   c   d   e   (___)

7.

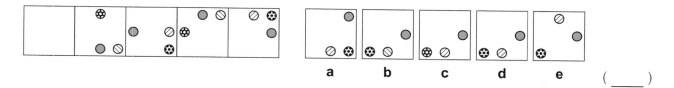

a   b   c   d   e   (___)

8.

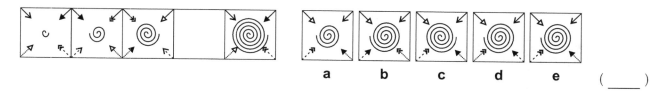

a   b   c   d   e   (___)

9.

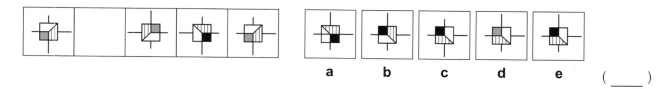

a   b   c   d   e   (___)

10.

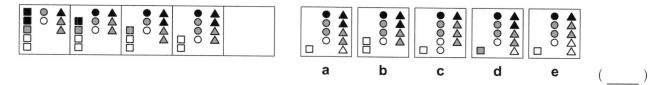

a   b   c   d   e   (___)

11.

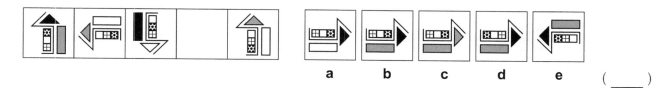

a   b   c   d   e   (___)

12.

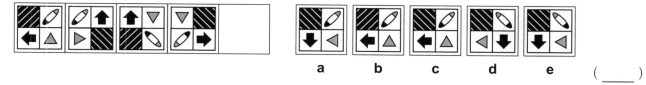

a   b   c   d   e   (___)

Pairs, Series and Grids

Complete the Grid

On the left of each question below is a big square with one small empty square.
Find which of the five squares on the right should replace the empty square.

Example:

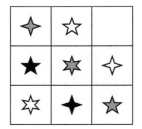

a   b   c   d   e   (_b_)

Each type of star and each type of shading only appears once in each row and column.

1.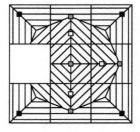

     a   b   c   d   e   (___)

2.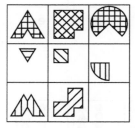

     a   b   c   d   e   (___)

3.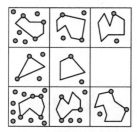

     a   b   c   d   e   (___)

4.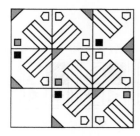

     a   b   c   d   e   (___)

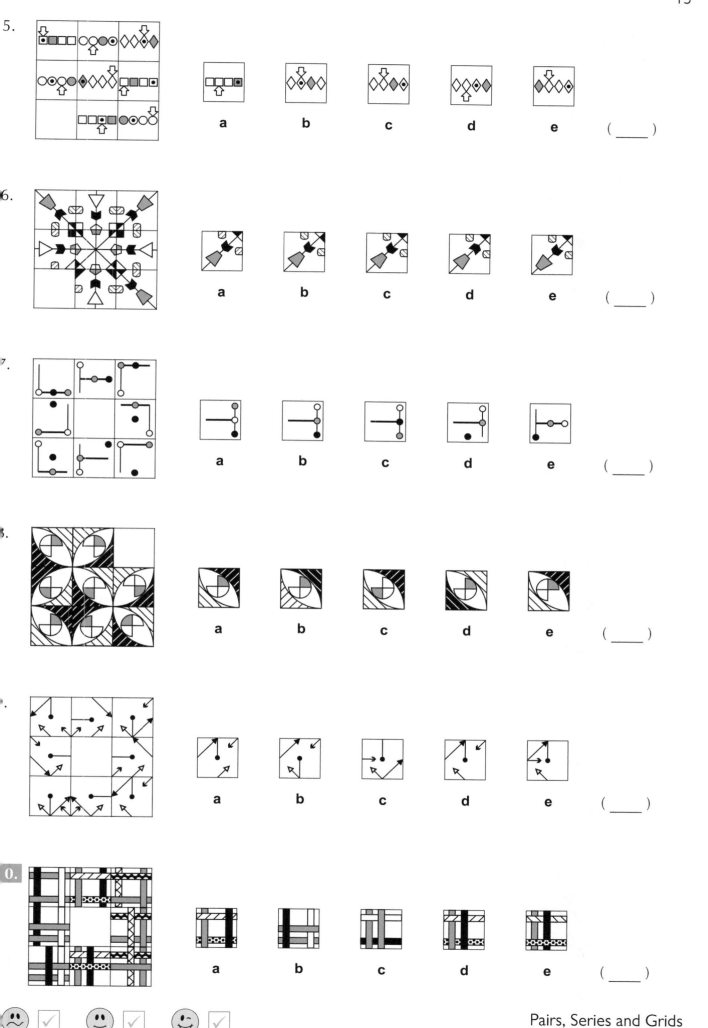

Codes

Vertical Code

On the left are shapes with code letters that describe them. You need to work out what the code letters mean. There is then a shape on its own next to a choice of five codes. Work out which code describes this shape.

Example:

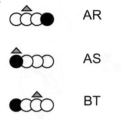

AR

AS

BT

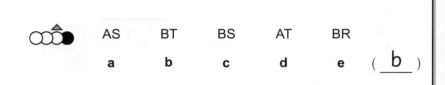

	AS	BT	BS	AT	BR	
	a	b	c	d	e	(_b_)

B means the black circle is at the back. T means the triangle is above the third circle from the left.

1.

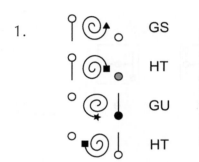

GS

HT

GU

HT

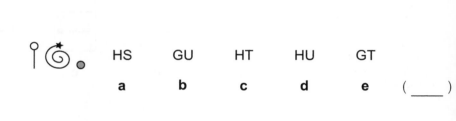

	HS	GU	HT	HU	GT	
	a	b	c	d	e	(___)

2.

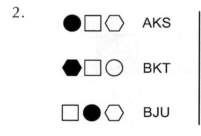

AKS

BKT

BJU

	AKS	BJU	AJT	AJS	BKS	
	a	b	c	d	e	(___)

3.

EM

DN

DO

	DM	EN	EO	DN	EM	
	a	b	c	d	e	(___)

4.

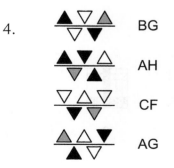

BG

AH

CF

AG

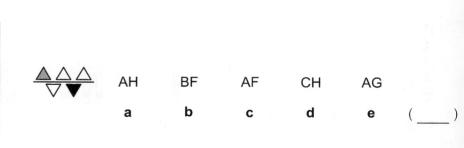

	AH	BF	AF	CH	AG	
	a	b	c	d	e	(___)

5.

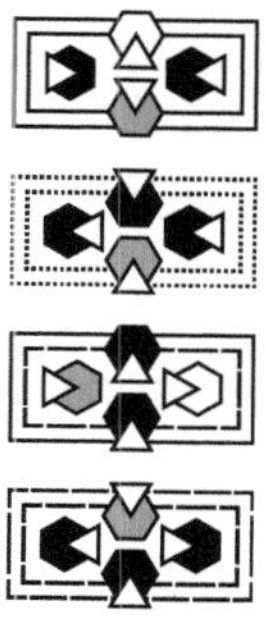

RY

RX

PZ

QZ

QX	PZ	QY	QZ	RZ	
a	**b**	**c**	**d**	**e**	(___)

6.

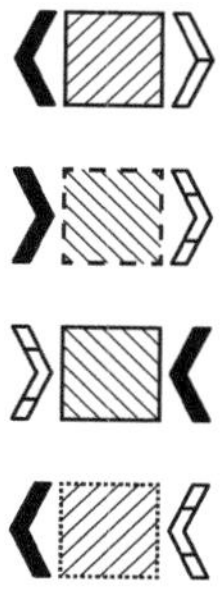

AHS

BGS

AHS

AFT

BGT	BHS	AGT	AFS	BGS	
a	**b**	**c**	**d**	**e**	(___)

7.

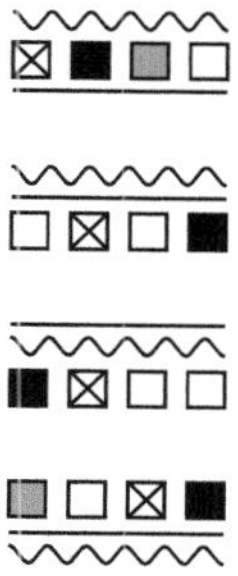

EJW

EJV

DKW

DJV

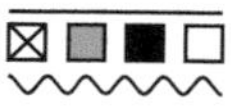

EJW	DJV	DKW	EJV	DJW	
a	**b**	**c**	**d**	**e**	(___)

8.

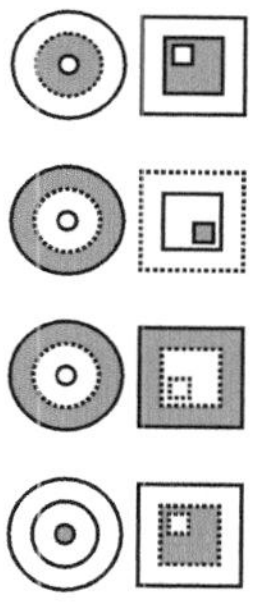

DLS

EJR

DKT

EJS

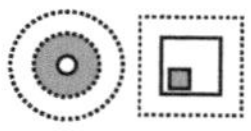

ELT	EKT	DJT	EKS	DLT	
a	**b**	**c**	**d**	**e**	(___)

9.

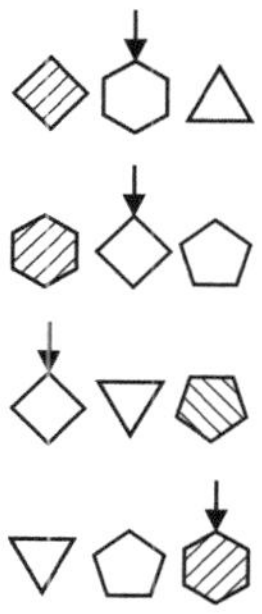

CSU

ARV

BTU

CRW

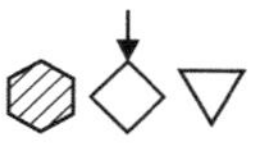

CTV	BRV	BSW	ATV	CRU	
a	**b**	**c**	**d**	**e**	(___)

10.

AS

BR

CS

AR

CR	AR	CS	BR	AS	
a	**b**	**c**	**d**	**e**	(___)

Codes

Horizontal Code

In the boxes on the left are shapes with code letters. The top letters have a different meaning from the bottom ones. Work out how the letters go with the shapes and then find the code for the new shape from the five codes on the right.

Example:

a   b   c   d   e   (__b__)

B means the shape has a horizontal side at the top. Z means the shape has five sides.

1.

                                                    a   b   c   d   e   (___)

2.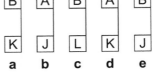

                                                    a   b   c   d   e   (___)

3.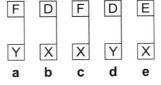

                                                    a   b   c   d   e   (___)

4.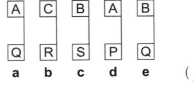

                                                    a   b   c   d   e   (___)

5.

                                                    a   b   c   d   e   (___)

Codes

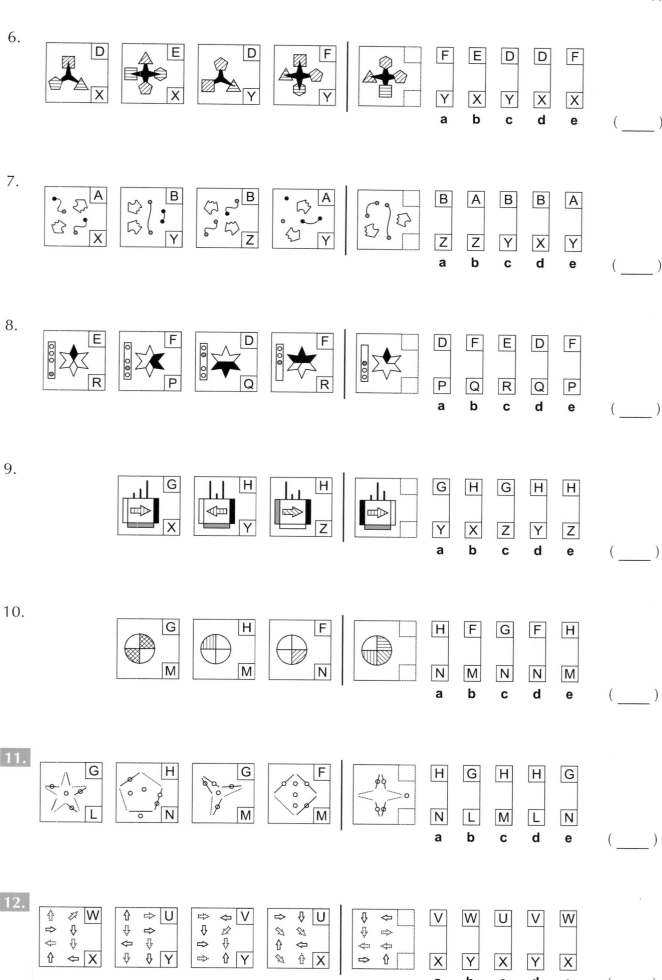

6.
F	E	D	D	F
Y	X	Y	X	X
a	b	c	d	e

(____)

7.
B	A	B	B	A
Z	Z	Y	X	Y
a	b	c	d	e

(____)

8.
D	F	E	D	F
P	Q	R	Q	P
a	b	c	d	e

(____)

9.
G	H	G	H	H
Y	X	Z	Y	Z
a	b	c	d	e

(____)

10.
H	F	G	F	H
N	M	N	N	M
a	b	c	d	e

(____)

11.
H	G	H	H	G
N	L	M	L	N
a	b	c	d	e

(____)

12.
V	W	U	V	W
X	Y	X	Y	X
a	b	c	d	e

(____)

       Codes

Spatial Reasoning

3D Rotation

Work out which 3D figure in the grey box has been rotated to make the new 3D figure. Example:

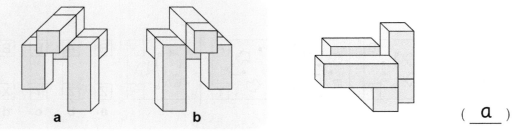

(__a__)

Shape A has been rotated 90 degrees away from you, top-to-bottom, and then 90 degrees right-to-left.

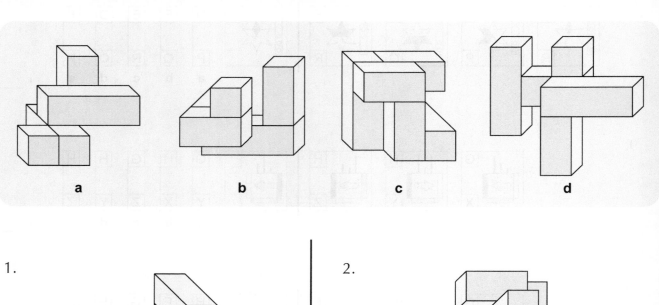

1.

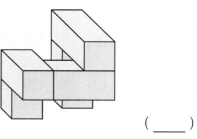

(____)

2.

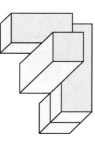

(____)

3.

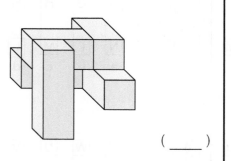

(____)

4.

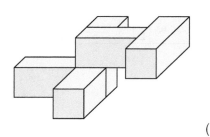

(____)

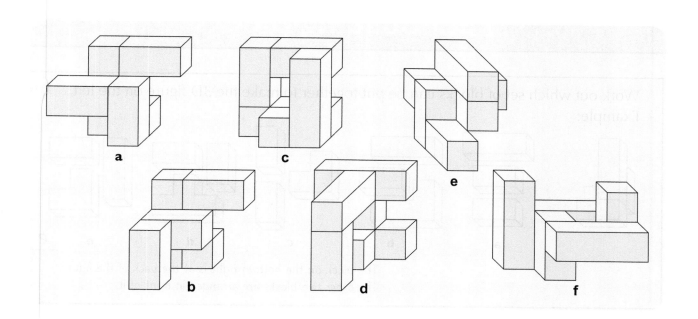

a   c   e

b   d   f

5.

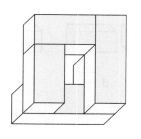

(___)

6.

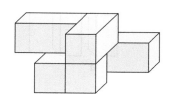

(___)

7.

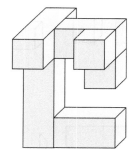

(___)

8.

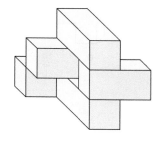

(___)

9.

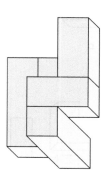

(___)

10.

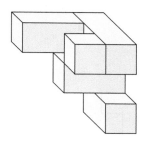

(___)

Spatial Reasoning

3D Building Blocks

Work out which set of blocks can be put together to make the 3D figure on the left.
Example:

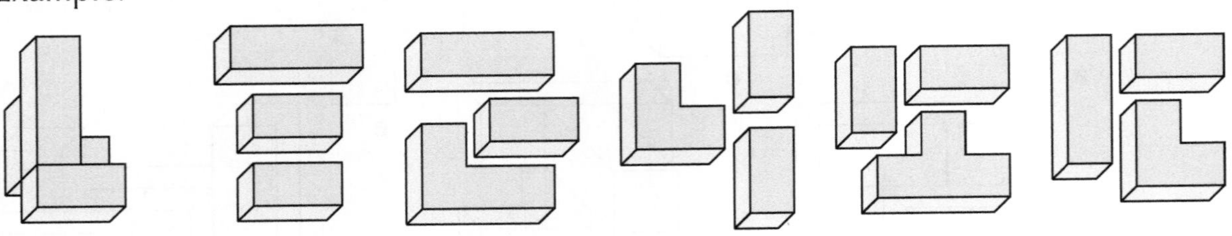

a   b   c   d   e   (_e_)

The block on the bottom right is at the back of the figure.
The other two blocks are arranged in front of it.

1.

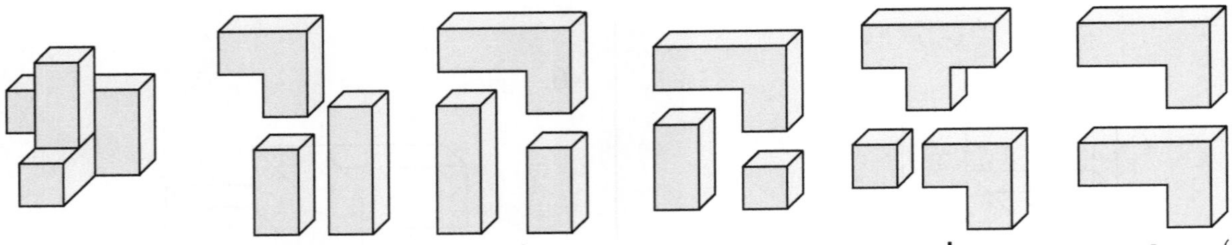

a   b   c   d   e   (___)

2.

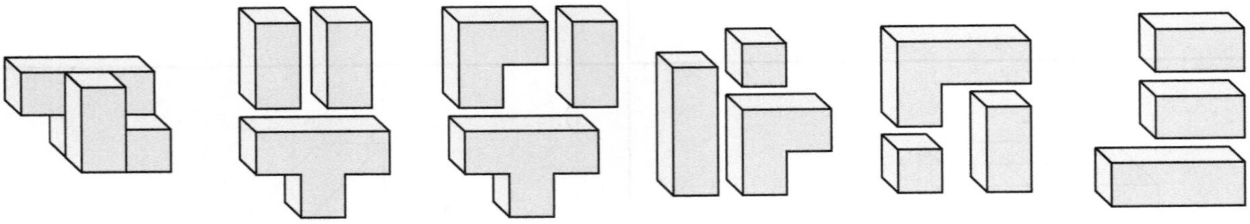

a   b   c   d   e   (___)

3.

a   b   c   d   e   (___)

4.

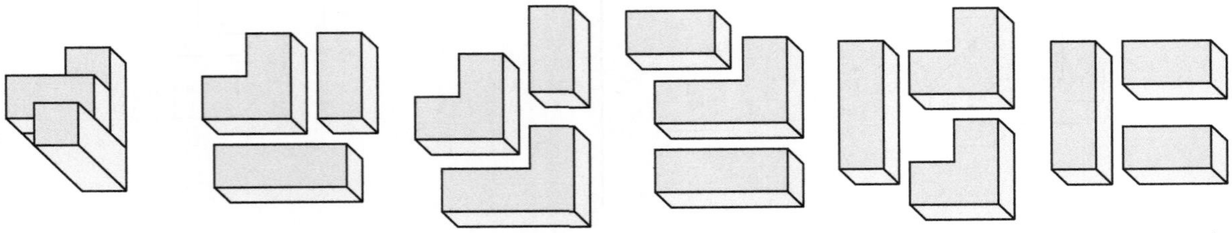

a   b   c   d   e   (___)

Spatial Reasoning

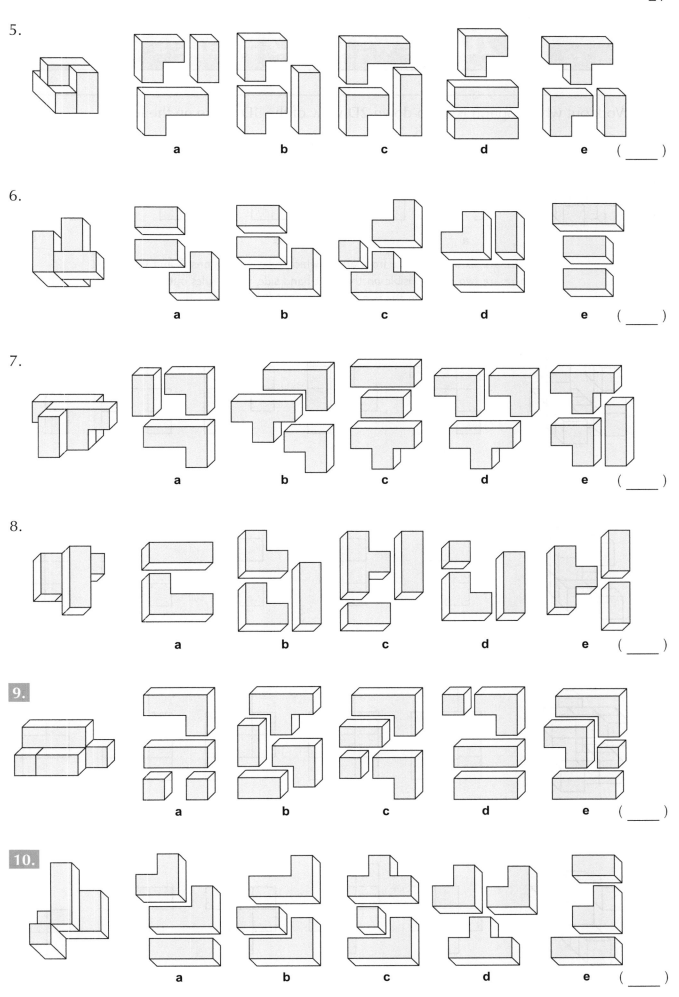

5.   a   b   c   d   e   (___)

6.   a   b   c   d   e   (___)

7.   a   b   c   d   e   (___)

8.   a   b   c   d   e   (___)

9.   a   b   c   d   e   (___)

10.   a   b   c   d   e   (___)

2D Views of 3D Shapes

Work out which option is a top-down 2D view of the 3D figure on the left.

Example:

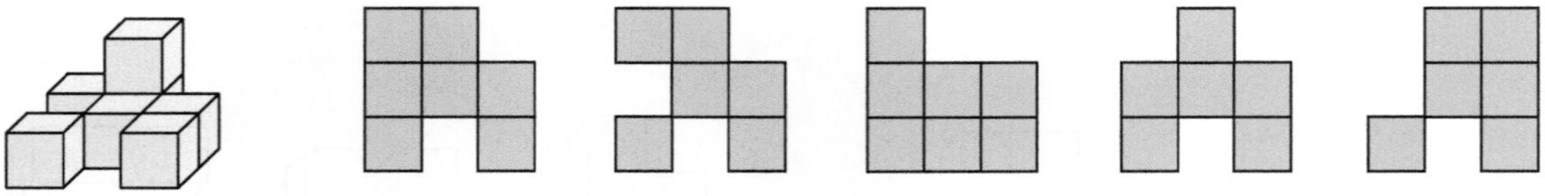

a   b   c   d   e   (_b_)

There are six blocks visible from above, which rules out options A and C.
There are two blocks visible on the right-hand side, which rules out option E.
There is a gap between the two blocks on the left-hand side, which rules out option D.

1.

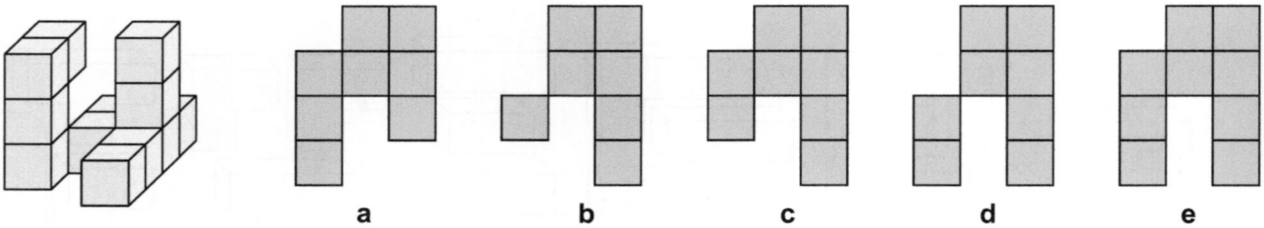

a   b   c   d   e

(___)

2.

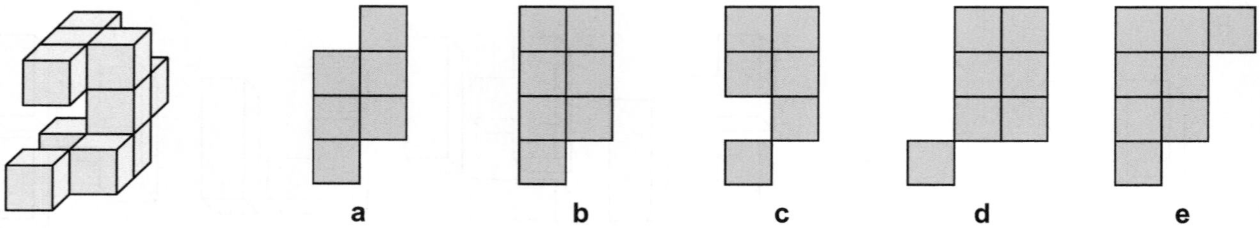

a   b   c   d   e

(___)

3.

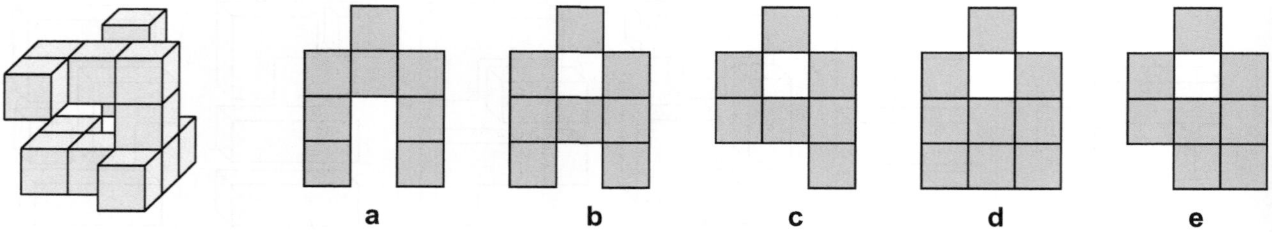

a   b   c   d   e

(___)

4.

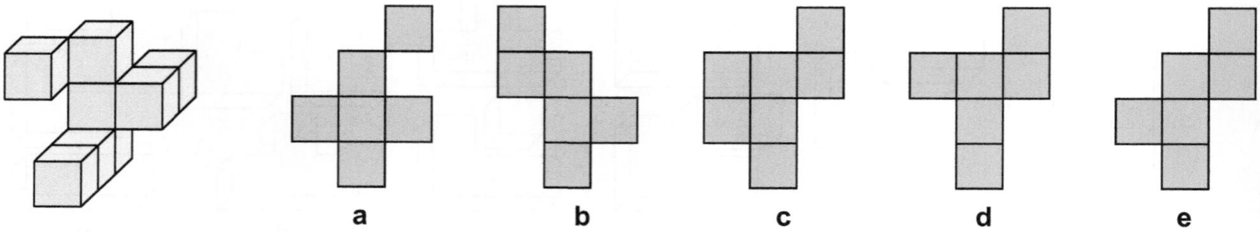

a   b   c   d   e

(___)

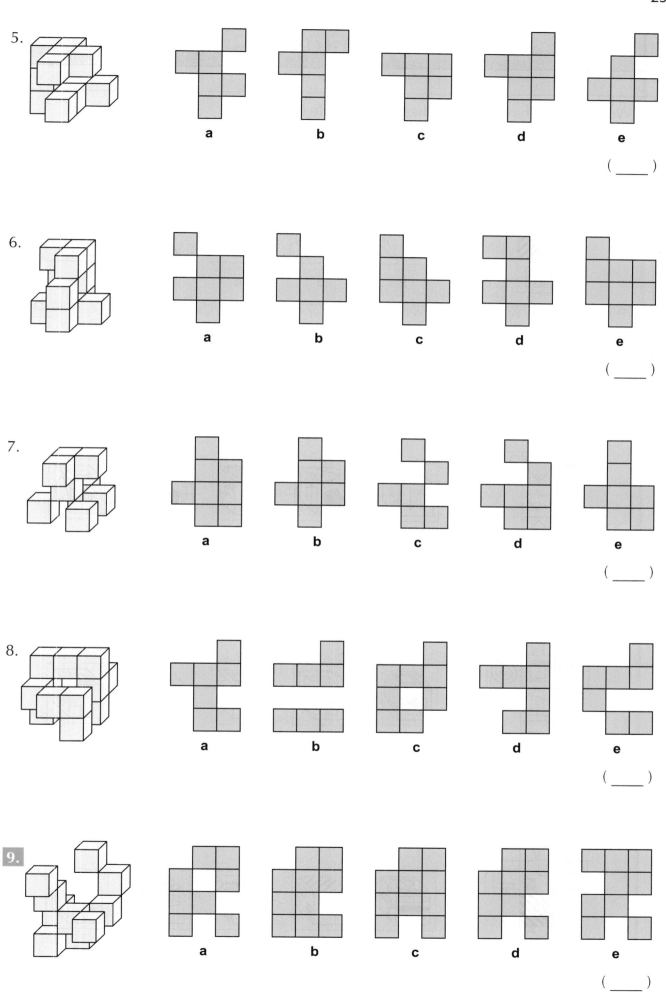

5.
     a   b   c   d   e

(_____)

6.
     a   b   c   d   e

(_____)

7.
     a   b   c   d   e

(_____)

8.
     a   b   c   d   e

(_____)

9.
     a   b   c   d   e

(_____)

24

Cubes and Nets

Work out which of the five cubes can be made from the net.

Example:

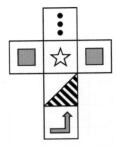

a b c d e

The two grey squares, and the star and the arrow, must be on opposite sides, which rules out options A and E. Option C can be ruled out because the line of black circles should point towards the star, not the square. Option D is ruled out because if the black and white triangle was on the front and the grey square was on the right, the face on the top would be the white star.

(__b__)

1.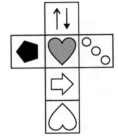

a b c d e (____)

2.

a b c d e (____)

3.

a b c d e (____)

25

4.

a   b   c   d   e   (____)

5.

a   b   c   d   e   (____)

6.

a   b   c   d   e   (____)

7.

a   b   c   d   e   (____)

8.

a   b   c   d   e   (____)

Fold Along the Line

Work out which option shows the figure on the left when folded along the dotted line.

Example:

a   b   c   d   e   (**b**)

Options A, C and E are ruled out because the part of the figure that has been folded is the wrong shape. Option D is ruled out because the fold line has moved.

1.

     a   b   c   d   e   (___)

2.

     a   b   c   d   e   (___)

3.

     a   b   c   d   e   (___)

4.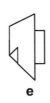

     a   b   c   d   e   (___)

5.

     a   b   c   d   e   (___)

6.

a b c d e

(___)

7.

a b c d e

(___)

8.

a b c d e

(___)

9.

a b c d e

(___)

10.

a b c d e

(___)

11.

a b c d e

(___)

Spatial Reasoning

Fold and Punch

A square is folded and then a hole is punched, as shown on the left.
Work out which option shows the square when unfolded.

Example:

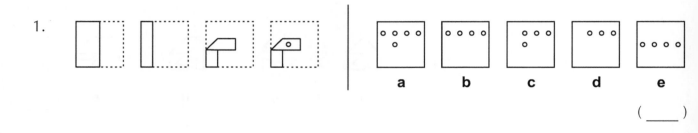

(**b**)

Unfold the figure, one fold at a time:

1.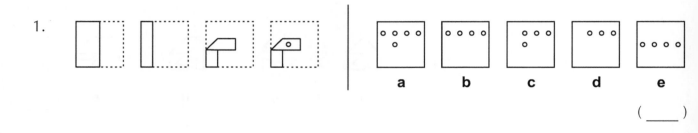

(____)

2.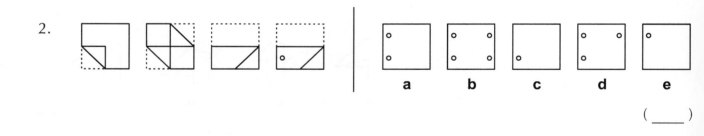

(____)

3.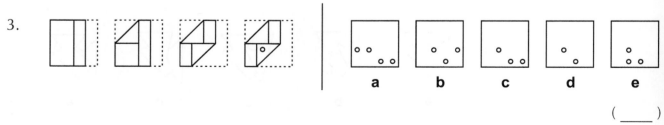

(____)

4.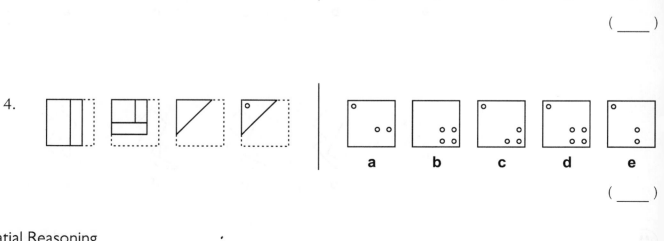

(____)

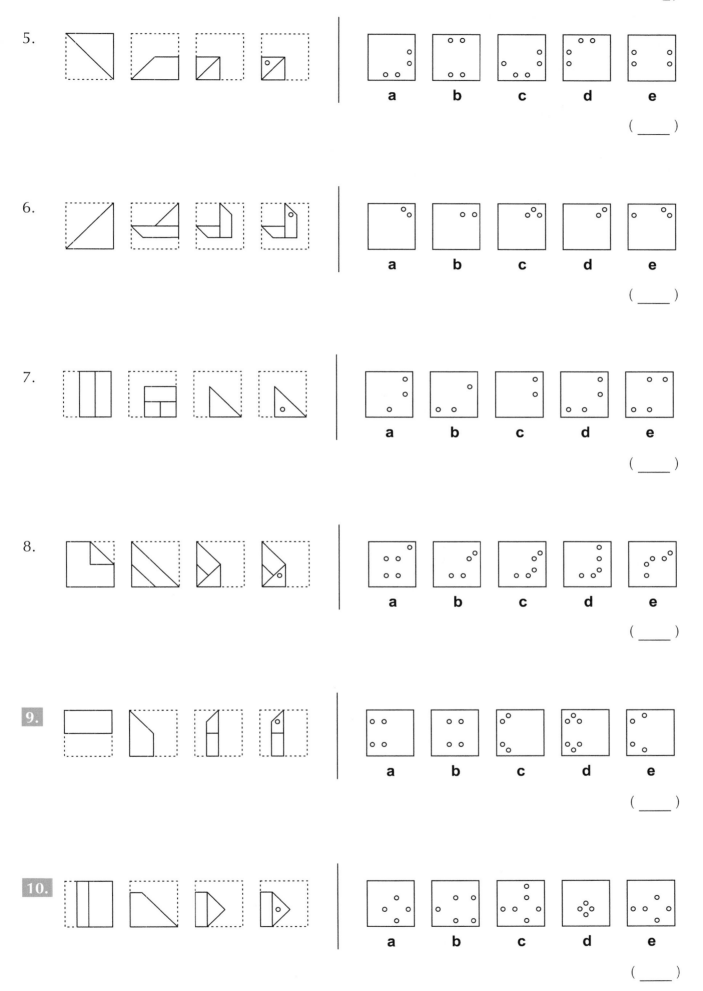

Hidden Shape

Work out which option contains the hidden shape shown.

It should be the same size and orientation.

Example:

a   **b**   **c**   **d**   **e**   (_a_)

The hidden shape is here:

1.

   a   **b**   **c**   **d**   **e**   (___)

2.

   a   **b**   **c**   **d**   **e**   (___)

3.

   a   **b**   **c**   **d**   **e**   (___)

4.

   a   **b**   **c**   **d**   **e**   (___)

5.

    a   **b**   **c**   **d**   **e**   (____)

6.

    a   **b**   **c**   **d**   **e**   (____)

7.

    a   **b**   **c**   **d**   **e**   (____)

8.

    a   **b**   **c**   **d**   **e**   (____)

9.

    a   **b**   **c**   **d**   **e**   (____)

10.

    a   **b**   **c**   **d**   **e**   (____)

32

Connecting Shapes

Work out which option shows how the three shapes will look when they are joined by matching the sides with the same letter.

Example:

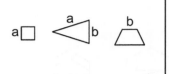

a   b   c   d   e   (_b_)

Option A is ruled out because the square is connected to the wrong side of the triangle.
Options C and E are ruled out because the wrong side of the trapezium is connected to the triangle.
Option D is ruled out because the trapezium is connected to the wrong side of the triangle.

1.

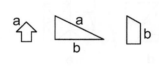

a   b   c   d   e

(___)

2.

a   b   c   d   e

(___)

3.

a   b   c   d   e

(___)

4.

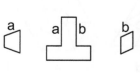   

a   b   c   d   e

(___)

Spatial Reasoning

5.

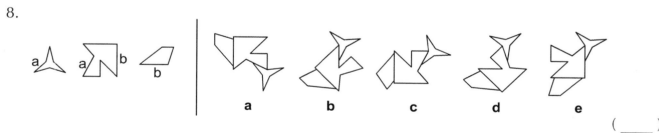

a   b   c   d   e

(____)

6.

a   b   c   d   e

(____)

7.

a   b   c   d   e

(____)

8.

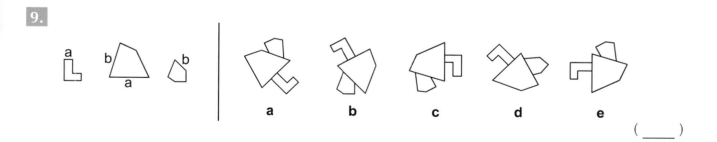

a   b   c   d   e

(____)

9.

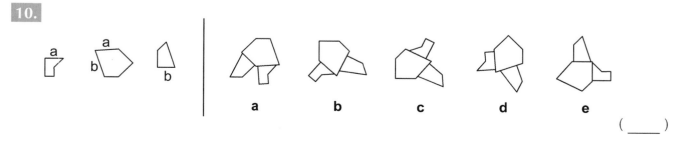

a   b   c   d   e

(____)

10.

a   b   c   d   e

(____)

Spatial Reasoning

Assessment Test 1

This book contains four assessment tests to help you improve your NVR skills.

Allow 60 minutes to do each test and work as quickly and as carefully as you can.

If you want to attempt each test more than once, you will need to print **multiple-choice answer sheets** for these questions from our website — go to cgpbooks.co.uk/11plus/answer-sheets or scan the QR code on the right. If you'd prefer to answer them in standard write-in format, just circle the letter underneath your answer.

Answer Sheets

Section 1 — Complete the Grid

On the left of each question below is a big square with one small empty square.
Find which of the five squares on the right should replace the empty square.

Example:

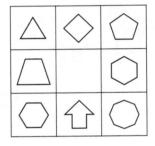

a   b   c   d   e

Answer: d

①

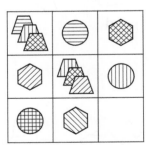

a   b   c   d   e

②

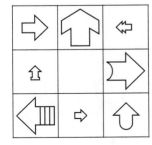

a   b   c   d   e

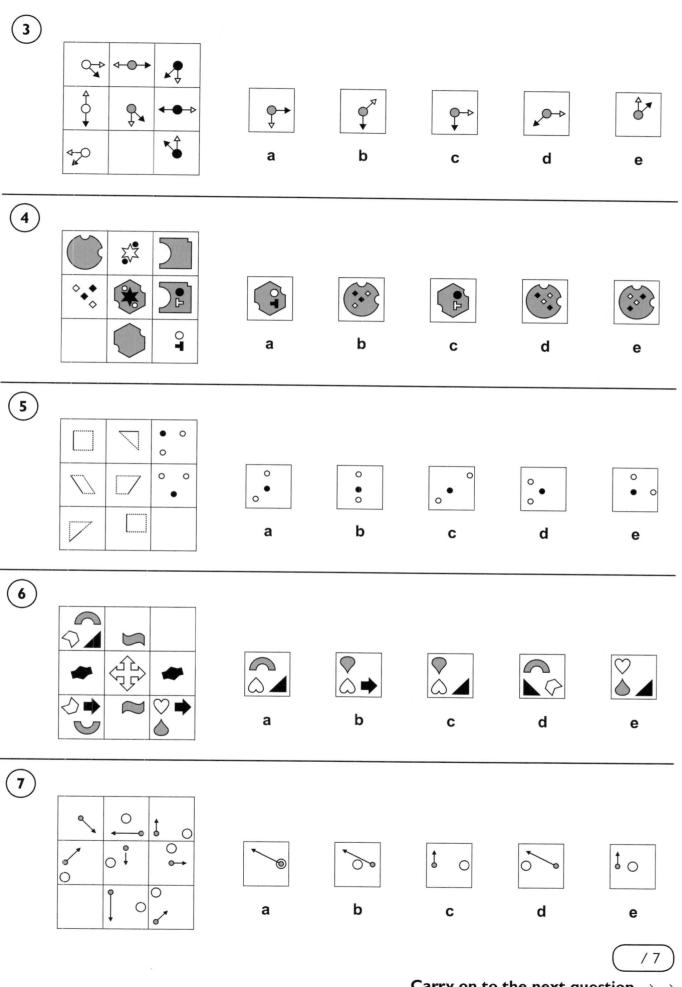

Section 2 — Vertical Code

Each question has some shapes on the left with code letters that describe them. You need to work out what the code letters mean. There is then a shape on its own next to a choice of five codes. Work out which code describes this shape.

Example:

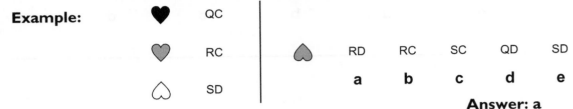

	RD	RC	SC	QD	SD
	a	**b**	**c**	**d**	**e**

Answer: a

The black heart has the letter code Q, the grey heart has an R, and the white heart has an S, so the first letter is for shading. The second letter code must be for the orientation of the heart. The first two hearts both have the letter C, but the last one has a D, so C stands for right way up and D stands for upside down. The new shape must have an R because it is grey, and a D because it is upside down. The code must be RD and the answer is a.

Example:

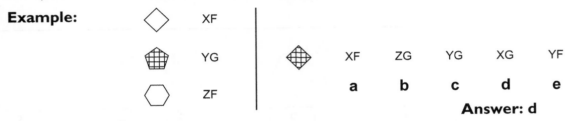

	XF	ZG	YG	XG	YF
	a	**b**	**c**	**d**	**e**

Answer: d

The diamond has the letter code X, the pentagon has a Y and the hexagon has a Z, so the first letter is for shape. The second letter code must be for shading. F stands for no shading and G stands for cross-hatching. The new shape must have an X because it is a diamond, and a G because it is cross-hatched. The code must be XG and the answer is d.

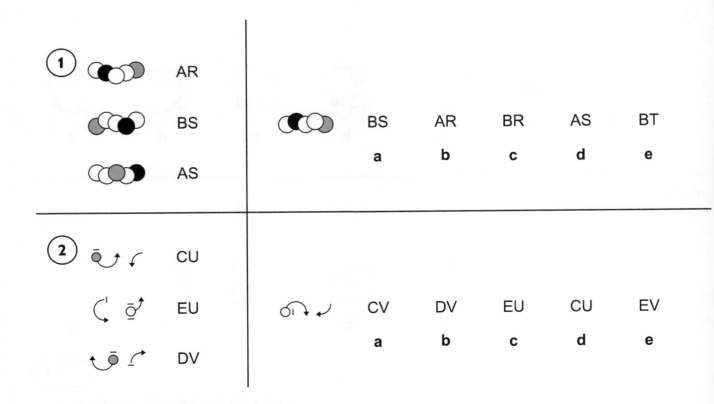

	BS	AR	BR	AS	BT
	a	**b**	**c**	**d**	**e**

	CV	DV	EU	CU	EV
	a	**b**	**c**	**d**	**e**

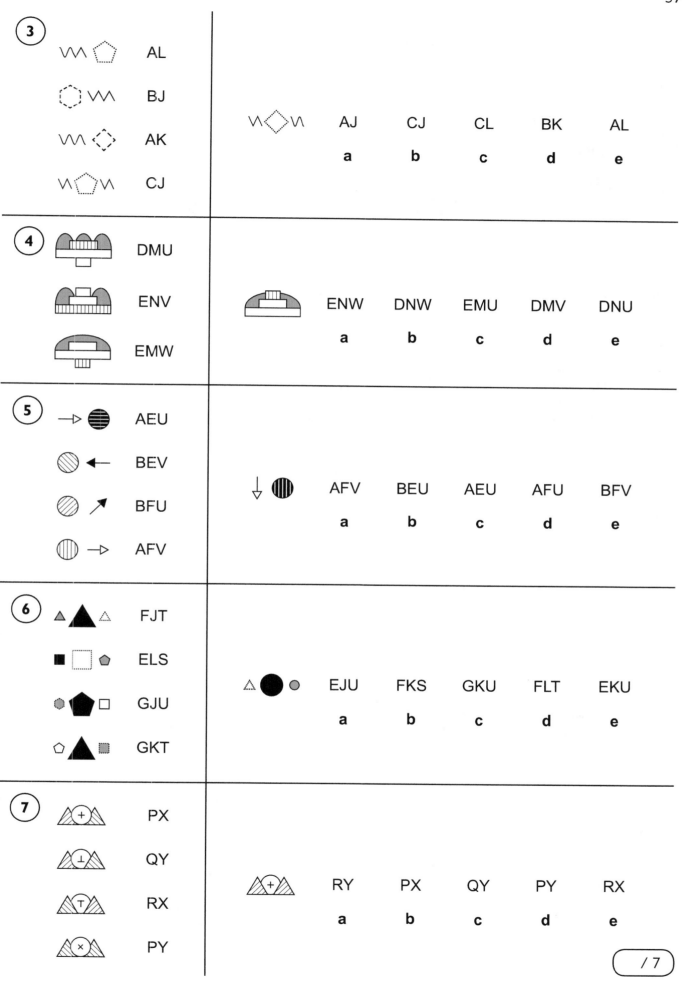

3

VVV ⬠ AL

⬡ VVV BJ

VVV ◇ AK

VVV ⬠ VVV CJ

VVV ◇ VVV   AJ   CJ   CL   BK   AL
        a   **b**   **c**   **d**   **e**

4

DMU

ENV

EMW

ENW   DNW   EMU   DMV   DNU
a   **b**   **c**   **d**   **e**

5

→ ● AEU

◯ ← BEV

◯ ↗ BFU

◯ → AFV

↓ ◗   AFV   BEU   AEU   AFU   BFV
      a   **b**   **c**   **d**   **e**

6

△ ▲ △ FJT

■ ▢ ⬟ ELS

⬟ ⬟ ▢ GJU

⬠ ▲ ▢ GKT

△ ● ●   EJU   FKS   GKU   FLT   EKU
      a   **b**   **c**   **d**   **e**

7

⟨+⟩ PX

⟨⊥⟩ QY

⟨⊤⟩ RX

⟨×⟩ PY

⟨+⟩   RY   PX   QY   PY   RX
    a   **b**   **c**   **d**   **e**

/ 7

Carry on to the next question → →

Assessment Test 1

Section 3 — Odd One Out

Each of the questions below has five figures.
Find which figure in each row is most unlike the others.

Example:

a

b

c

d

e

Answer: b

1

a

b

c

d

e

2

a

b

c

d

e

3

a

b

c

d

e

4

a

b

c

d

e

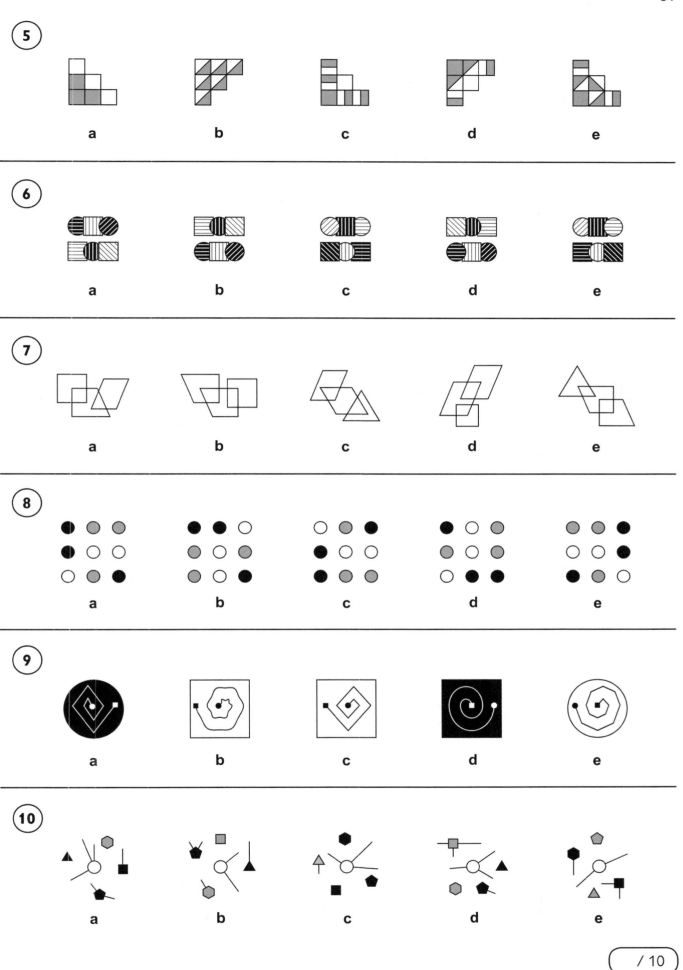

Section 4 — Complete the Pair

Each question has two shapes on the left with an arrow between them.
The first shape is changed in some way to become the second.
There is then a third shape followed by an arrow and a choice of five shapes.
Choose the shape on the right that relates to the third shape like the second does to the first.

Example:

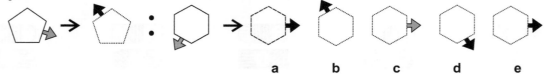

                                            a   b   c   d   e

Answer: e

(1)

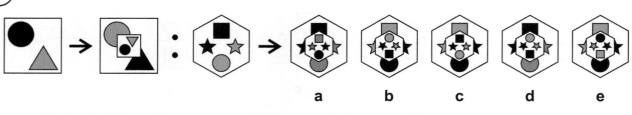

                                           a   b   c   d   e

(2)

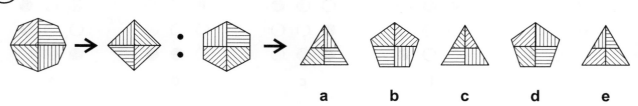

                                           a   b   c   d   e

(3)

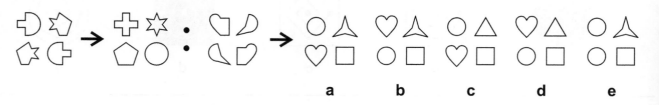

                                           a   b   c   d   e

(4)

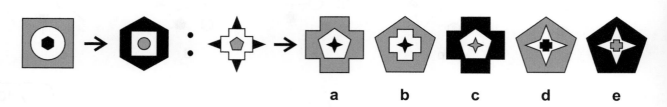

                                           a   b   c   d   e

5

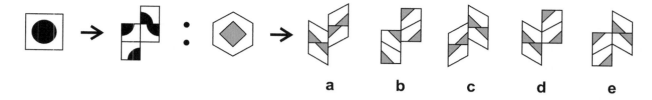

a b c d e

6

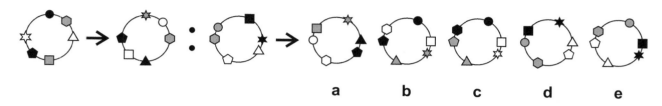

a b c d e

7

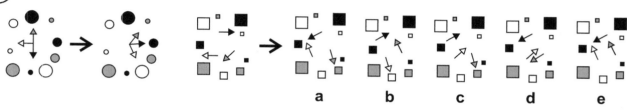

a b c d e

8

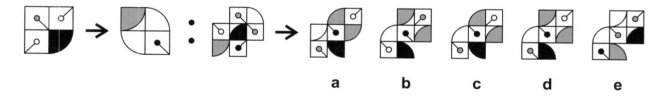

a b c d e

9

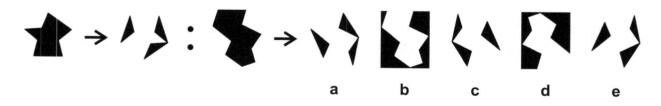

a b c d e

10

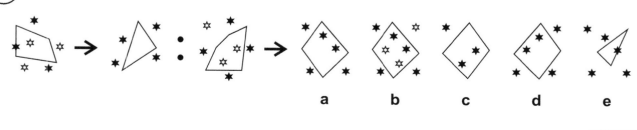

a b c d e

/ 10

Carry on to the next question → →

Assessment Test 1

Section 5 — Find the Figure Like the First Two

For each question below there are two figures that are like each other in some way.
Find which of the five figures on the right is most like the two figures on the left.

Example:

a   b   c   d   e

Answer: c

1

a   b   c   d   e

2

a   b   c   d   e

3

a   b   c   d   e

4

a   b   c   d   e

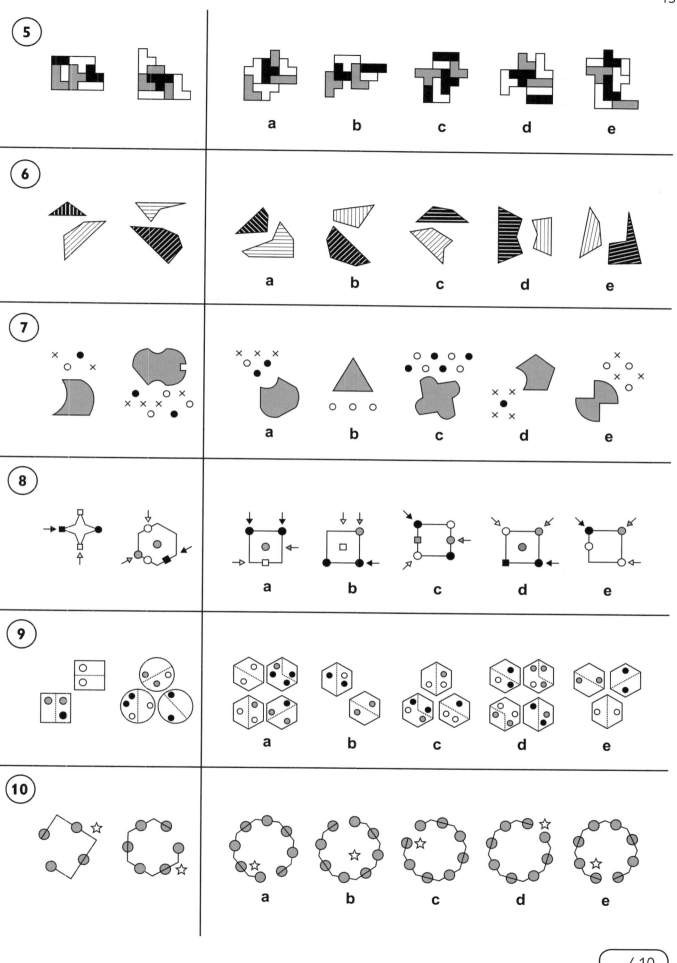

Section 6 — Complete the Series

Each of these questions has five squares on the left that are arranged in order.
One of the squares is missing. One of the squares on the right should go in its place.
Find which one of the five squares on the right should go in place of the empty square.

Example:

 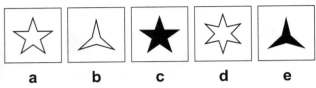

a   b   c   d   e

Answer: a

1

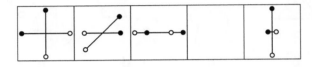 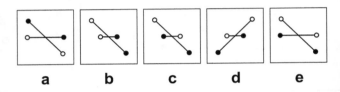

a   b   c   d   e

2

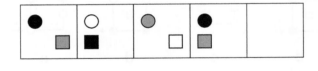 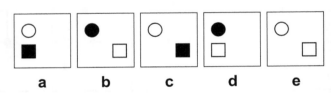

a   b   c   d   e

3

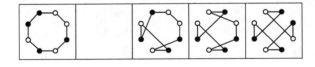 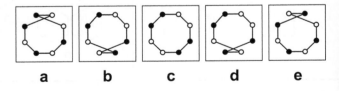

a   b   c   d   e

4

 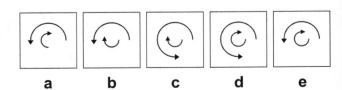

a   b   c   d   e

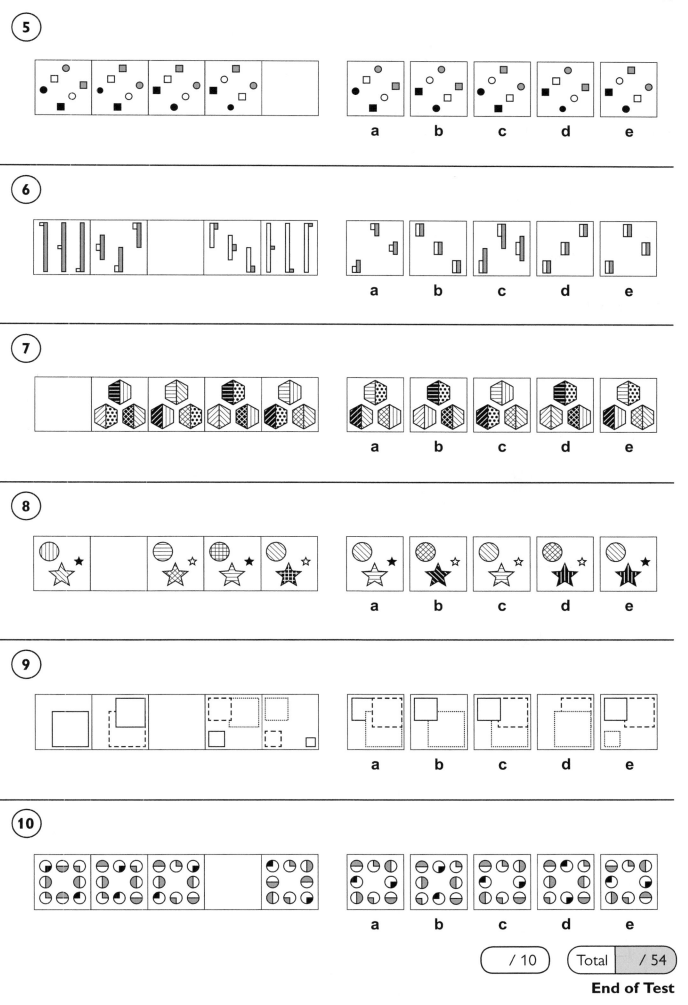

5

6

7

8

9

10

a   b   c   d   e

/ 10   Total / 54

End of Test

Assessment Test 1

Assessment Test 2

Allow 60 minutes to do this test and work as quickly and as carefully as you can.

You can print **multiple-choice answer sheets** for these questions from our website —
go to cgpbooks.co.uk/11plus/answer-sheets or scan the QR code on the right. If you'd prefer
to answer them in standard write-in format, just circle the letter underneath your answer.

Answer Sheets

Section 1 — Find the Figure Like the First Three

For each of the questions below there are three figures that are like each other in some way.
Find which of the five figures on the right is most like the three figures on the left.

Example:

  a   b   c   d   e

Answer: c

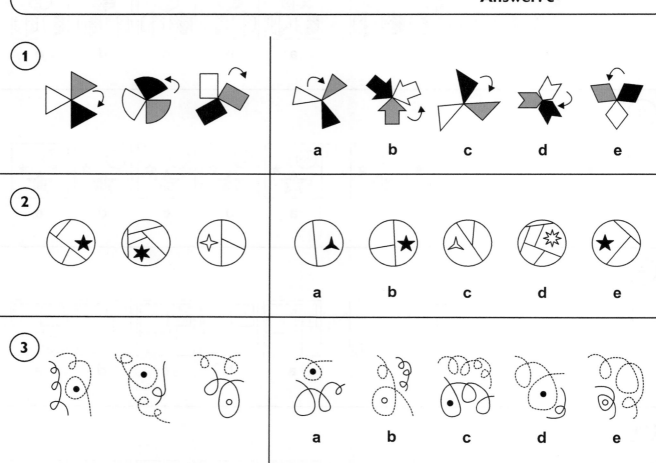

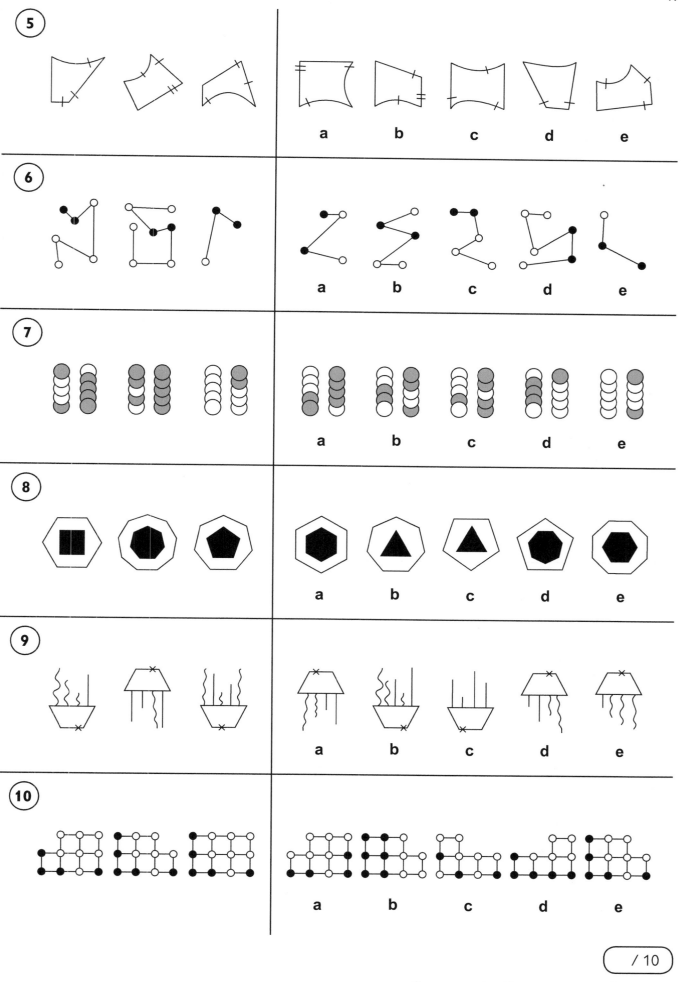

48

Section 2 — Complete the Grid

On the left of each question below is a big square with one small empty square.
Find which of the five squares on the right should replace the empty square.

Example:

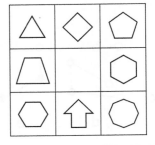

a   b   c   d   e

Answer: d

1

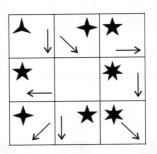

a   b   c   d   e

2

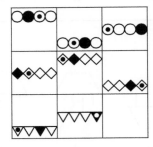

a   b   c   d   e

3

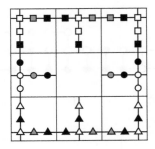

a   b   c   d   e

Assessment Test 2

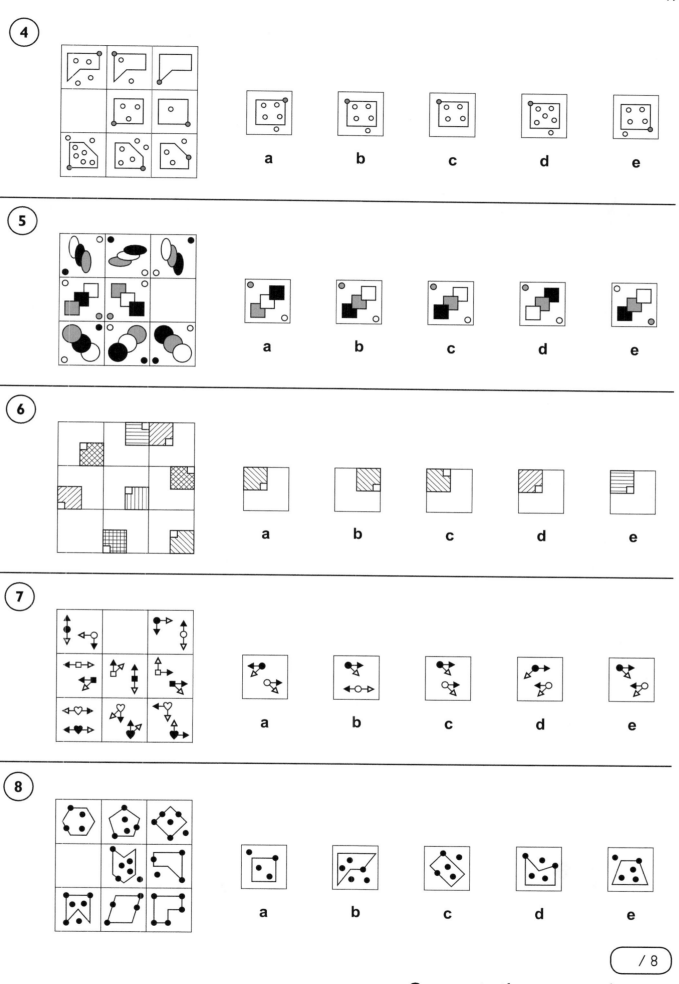

4

a   b   c   d   e

5

a   b   c   d   e

6

a   b   c   d   e

7

a   b   c   d   e

8

a   b   c   d   e

/ 8

Carry on to the next question → →

Assessment Test 2

Section 3 — Complete the Series

Each of these questions has five squares on the left that are arranged in order.
One of the squares is missing. One of the squares on the right should go in its place.
Find which one of the five squares on the right should go in place of the empty square.

Example:

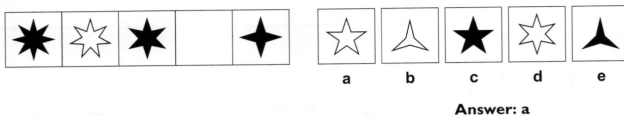

a   b   c   d   e

Answer: a

1

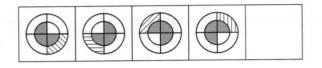

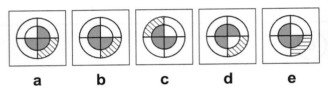

a   b   c   d   e

2

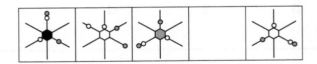

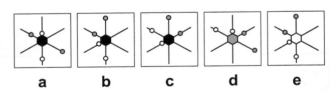

a   b   c   d   e

3

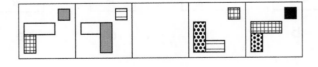

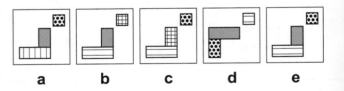

a   b   c   d   e

4

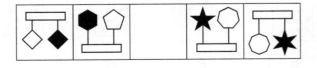

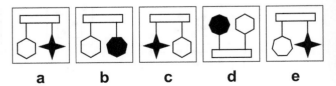

a   b   c   d   e

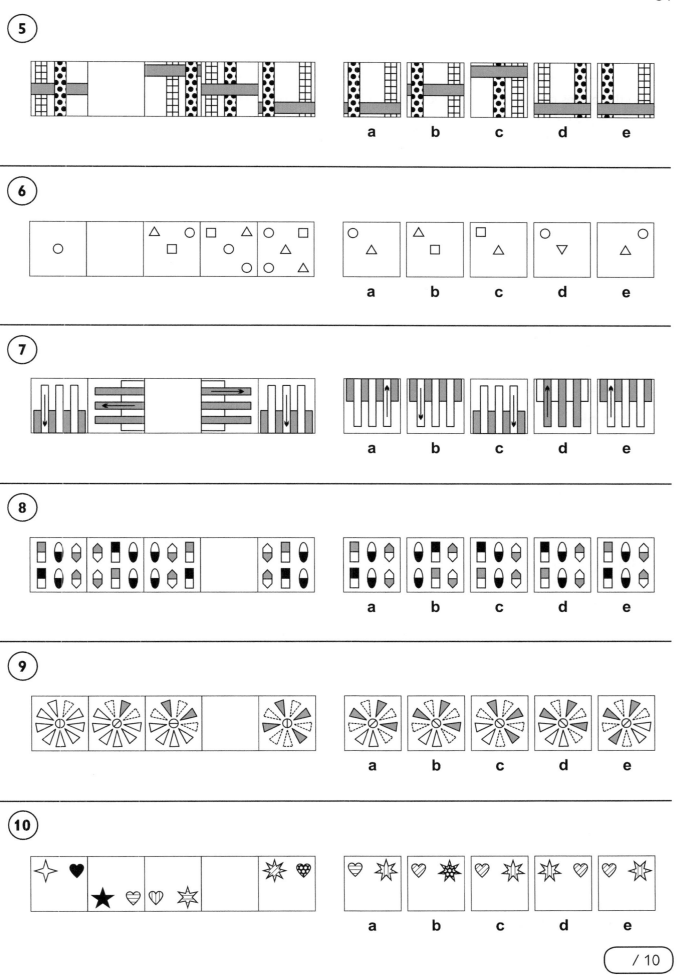

Section 4 — Horizontal Code

In the boxes on the left are shapes with code letters. The top letters have a different meaning to the bottom ones. Work out how the letters go with the shapes and then find the code for the new shape from the five codes on the right.

Example:

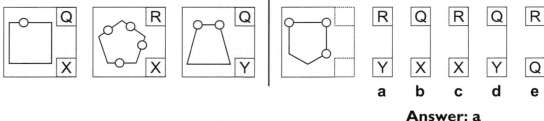

Answer: a

Both four-sided shapes have a Q at the top, but the five-sided shape has an R, so the top code letter must stand for number of sides. The bottom code letter must be for the position of the circles. X is for circles on the shape's sides and Y is for circles on the shape's corners. The new shape must have an R because it is a five-sided shape and a Y because the circles are on the shape's corners. The code must be RY and the answer is a.

Example:

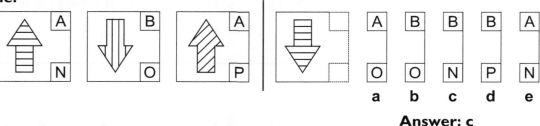

Answer: c

Both figures with arrows pointing up have an A at the top, and the figure with the arrow pointing down has a B, so the top code letter must be for arrow direction. The bottom code letter must be for hatching. N is for horizontal hatching, O is for vertical hatching and P is for diagonal hatching. The new figure must have a B because the arrow points down and an N because it has horizontal hatching. The code must be BN and the answer is c.

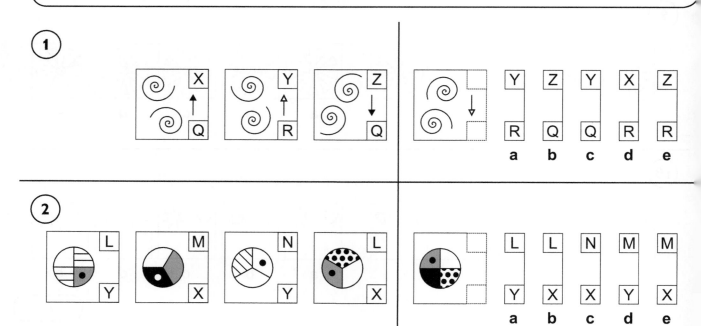

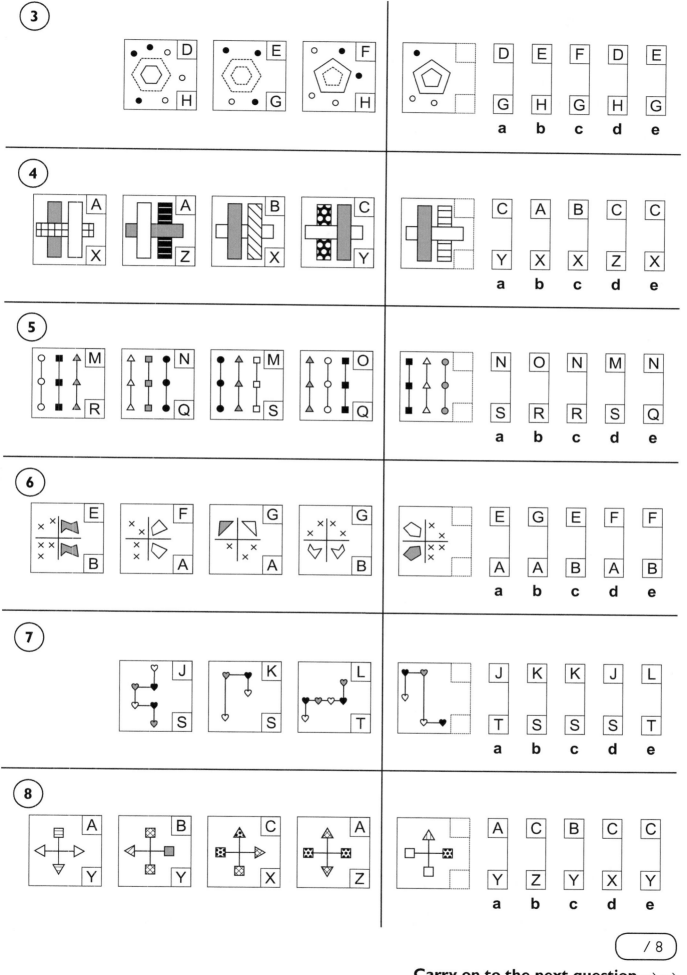

Section 5 — Find the Figure Like the First Two

For each question below there are two figures that are like each other in some way. Find which of the five figures on the right is most like the two figures on the left.

Example:

a   b   c   d   e

Answer: c

1

a   b   c   d   e

2

a   b   c   d   e

3

a   b   c   d   e

4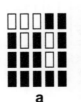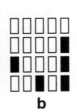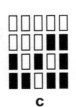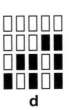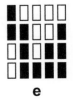

a   b   c   d   e

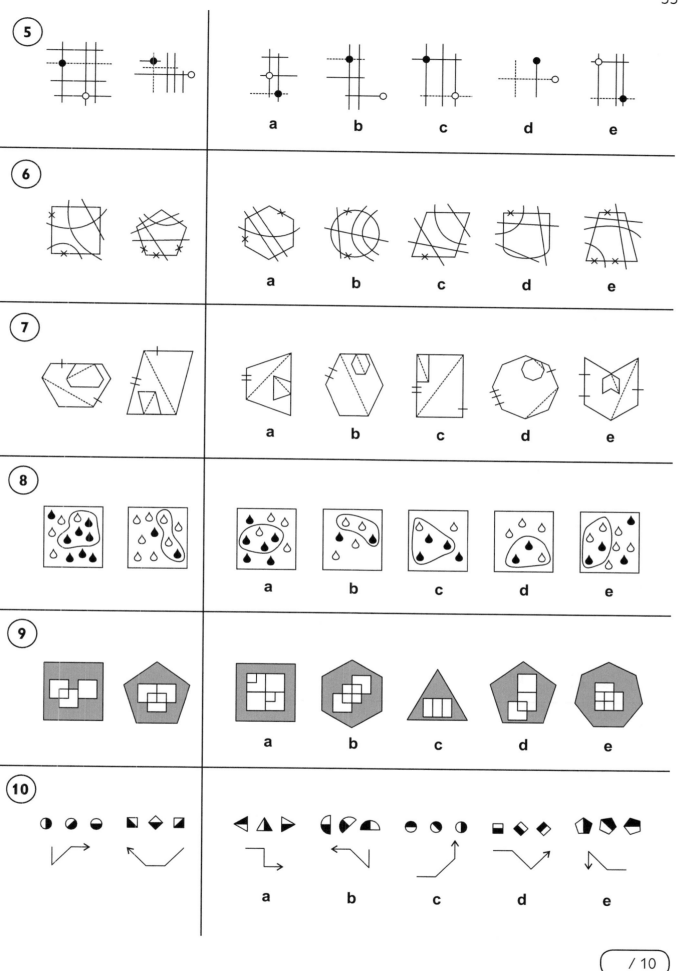

Section 6 — Vertical Code

Each question has some shapes on the left with code letters that describe them.
You need to work out what the code letters mean. There is then a shape on its
own next to a choice of five codes. Work out which code describes this shape.

Example:

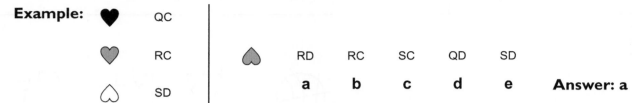

	RD	RC	SC	QD	SD
	a	b	c	d	e	Answer: a

The black heart has the letter code Q, the grey heart has an R, and the white heart has an S,
so the first letter is for shading. The second letter code must be for the orientation of the heart.
The first two hearts both have the letter C, but the last one has a D, so C stands for right way up
and D stands for upside down. The new shape must have an R because it is grey, and a D because
it is upside down. The code must be RD and the answer is a.

Example:

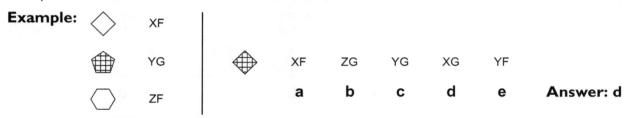

	XF	ZG	YG	XG	YF
	a	b	c	d	e	Answer: d

The diamond has the letter code X, the pentagon has a Y and the hexagon has a Z, so the first
letter is for shape. The second letter code must be for shading. F stands for no shading and
G stands for cross-hatching. The new shape must have an X because it is a diamond, and a G
because it is cross-hatched. The code must be XG and the answer is d.

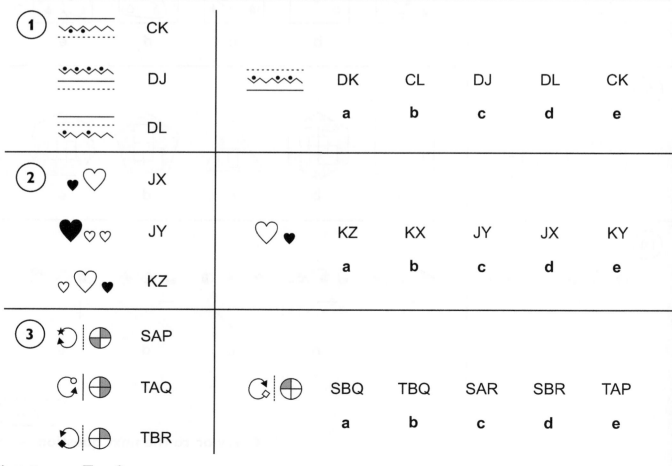

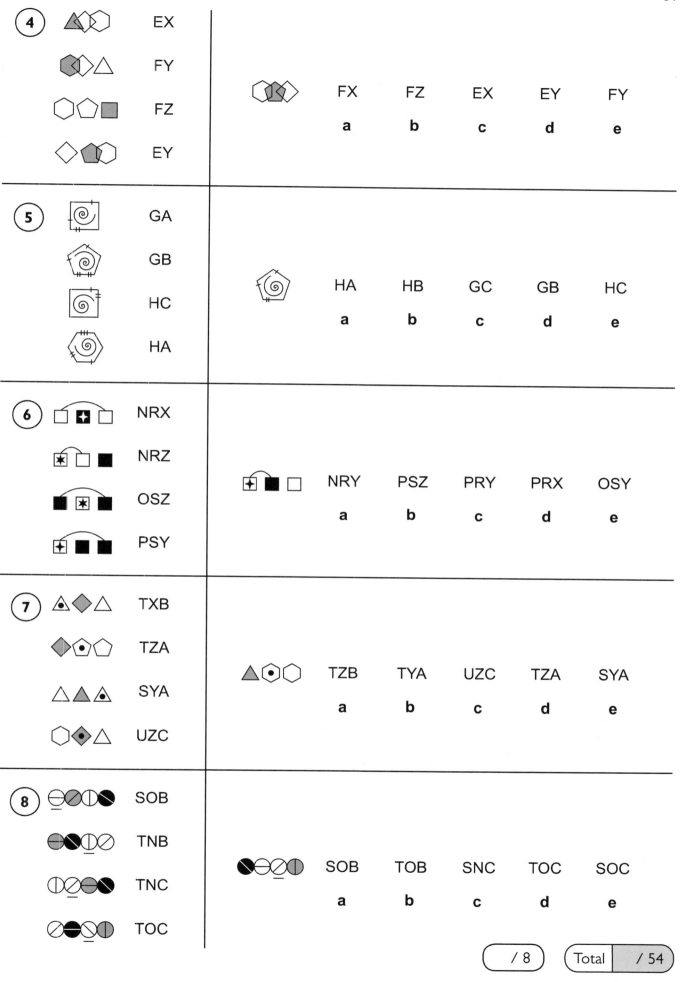

4	EX	FX	FZ	EX	EY	FY
	FY	**a**	**b**	**c**	**d**	**e**
	FZ					
	EY					

5	GA	HA	HB	GC	GB	HC
	GB	**a**	**b**	**c**	**d**	**e**
	HC					
	HA					

6	NRX	NRY	PSZ	PRY	PRX	OSY
	NRZ	**a**	**b**	**c**	**d**	**e**
	OSZ					
	PSY					

7	TXB	TZB	TYA	UZC	TZA	SYA
	TZA	**a**	**b**	**c**	**d**	**e**
	SYA					
	UZC					

8	SOB	SOB	TOB	SNC	TOC	SOC
	TNB	**a**	**b**	**c**	**d**	**e**
	TNC					
	TOC					

/ 8   Total / 54

End of Test

Assessment Test 2

Assessment Test 3

Allow 60 minutes to do this test and work as quickly and as carefully as you can.

You can print **multiple-choice answer sheets** for these questions from our website — go to cgpbooks.co.uk/11plus/answer-sheets or scan the QR code on the right. If you'd prefer to answer them in standard write-in format, just circle the letter underneath your answer.

Answer Sheets

Section 1 — Complete the Series

Each of these questions has five squares on the left that are arranged in order.
One of the squares is missing. One of the squares on the right should go in its place.
Find which one of the five squares on the right should go in place of the empty square.

Example:

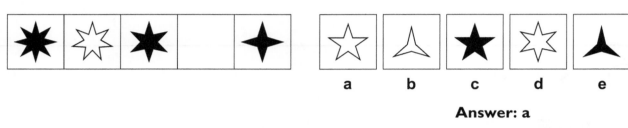

         a   b   c   d   e

Answer: a

(1)

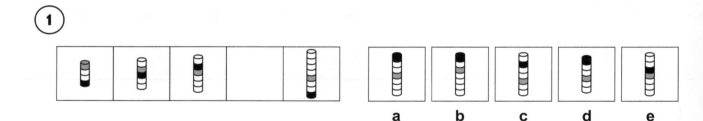

         a   b   c   d   e

(2)

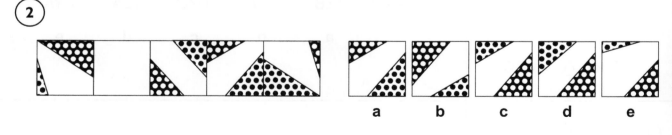

         a   b   c   d   e

(3)

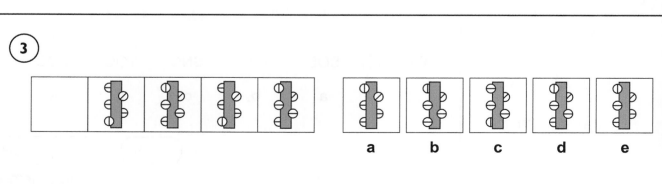

         a   b   c   d   e

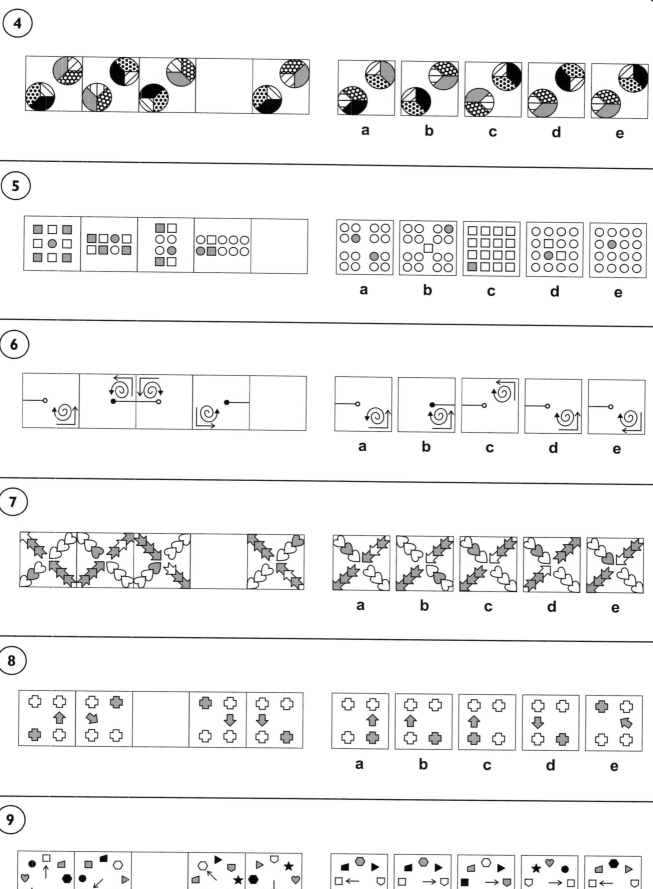

Carry on to the next question → →

Assessment Test 3

Section 2 — Complete the Grid

On the left of each question below is a big square with one small empty square.
Find which of the five squares on the right should replace the empty square.

Example:

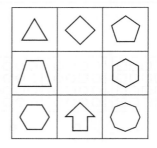

a   b   c   d   e

Answer: d

1

a   b   c   d   e

2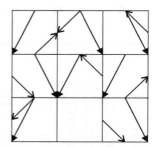

a   b   c   d   e

3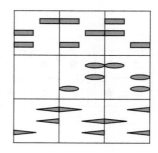

a   b   c   d   e

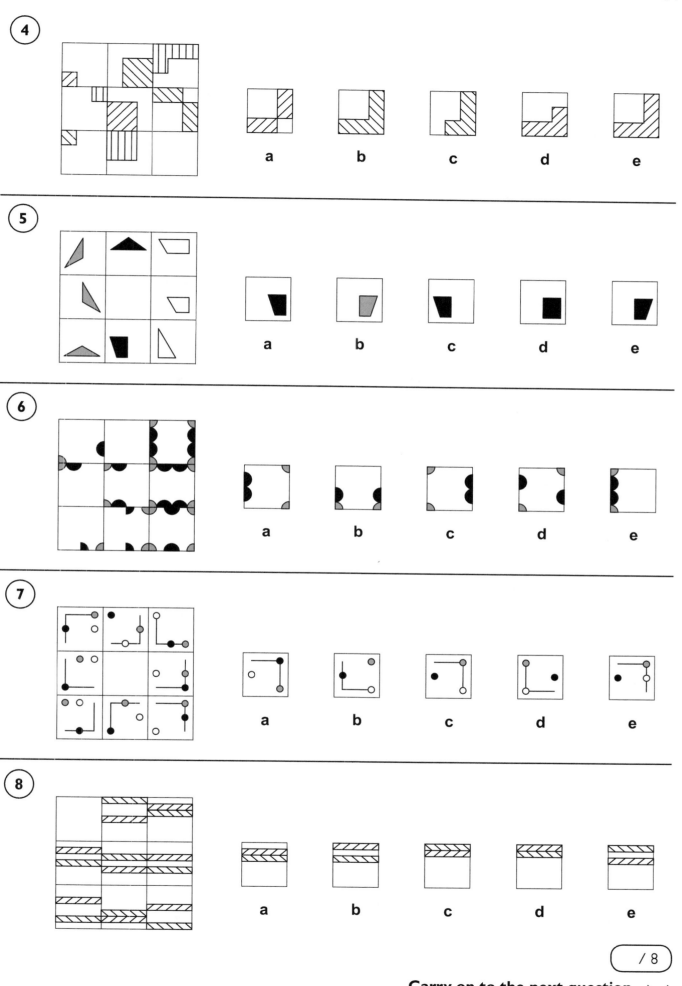

Section 3 — Complete the Pair

Each question has two shapes on the left with an arrow between them.
The first shape is changed in some way to become the second.
There is then a third shape followed by an arrow and a choice of five shapes.
Choose the shape on the right that relates to the third shape like the second does to the first.

Example:

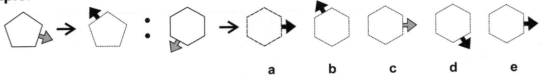

a   b   c   d   e

Answer: e

(1)

a   b   c   d   e

(2)

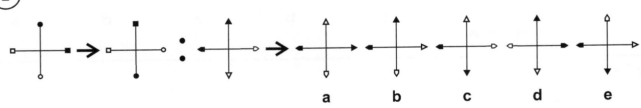

a   b   c   d   e

(3)

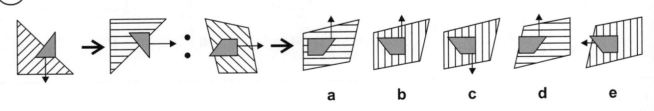

a   b   c   d   e

(4)

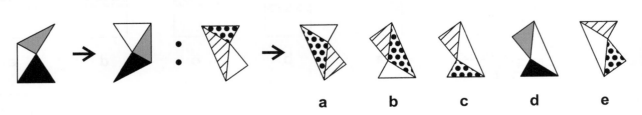

a   b   c   d   e

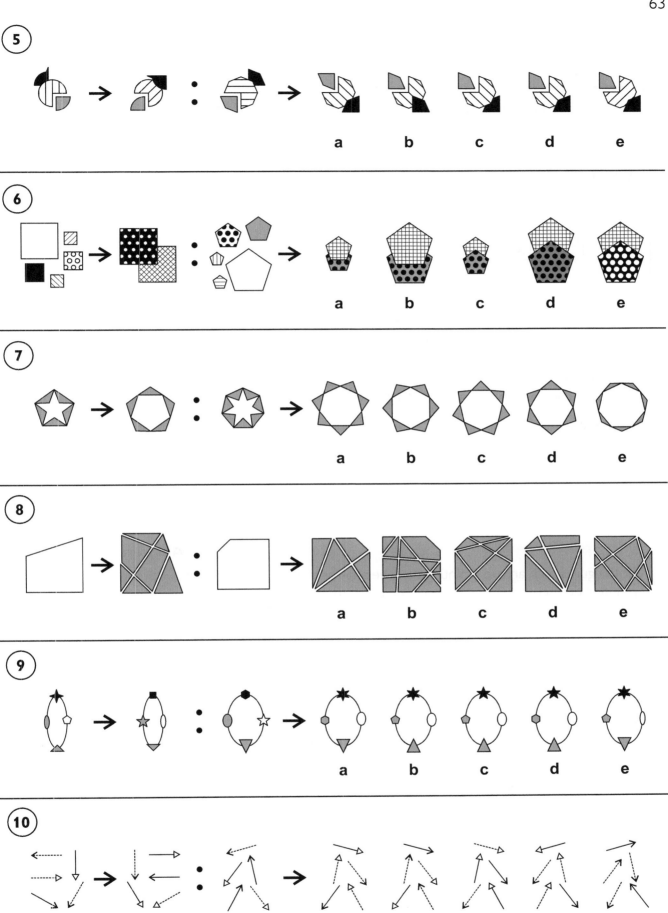

5

a   b   c   d   e

6

a   b   c   d   e

7

a   b   c   d   e

8

a   b   c   d   e

9

a   b   c   d   e

10

a   b   c   d   e

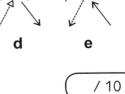

/ 10

Carry on to the next question → →

Assessment Test 3

Section 4 — Horizontal Code

In the boxes on the left are shapes with code letters. The top letters have a different meaning to the bottom ones. Work out how the letters go with the shapes and then find the code for the new shape from the five codes on the right.

Example:

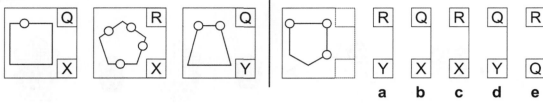

Answer: a

Both four-sided shapes have a Q at the top, but the five-sided shape has an R, so the top code letter must stand for number of sides. The bottom code letter must be for the position of the circles. X is for circles on the shape's sides and Y is for circles on the shape's corners. The new shape must have an R because it is a five-sided shape and a Y because the circles are on the shape's corners. The code must be RY and the answer is a.

Example:

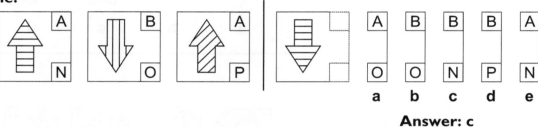

Answer: c

Both figures with arrows pointing up have an A at the top, and the figure with the arrow pointing down has a B, so the top code letter must be for arrow direction. The bottom code letter must be for hatching. N is for horizontal hatching, O is for vertical hatching and P is for diagonal hatching. The new figure must have a B because the arrow points down and an N because it has horizontal hatching. The code must be BN and the answer is c.

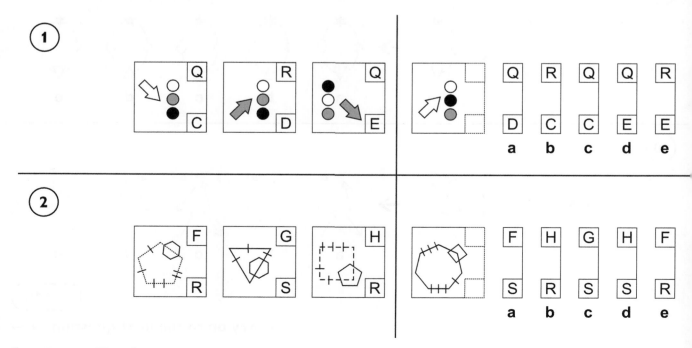

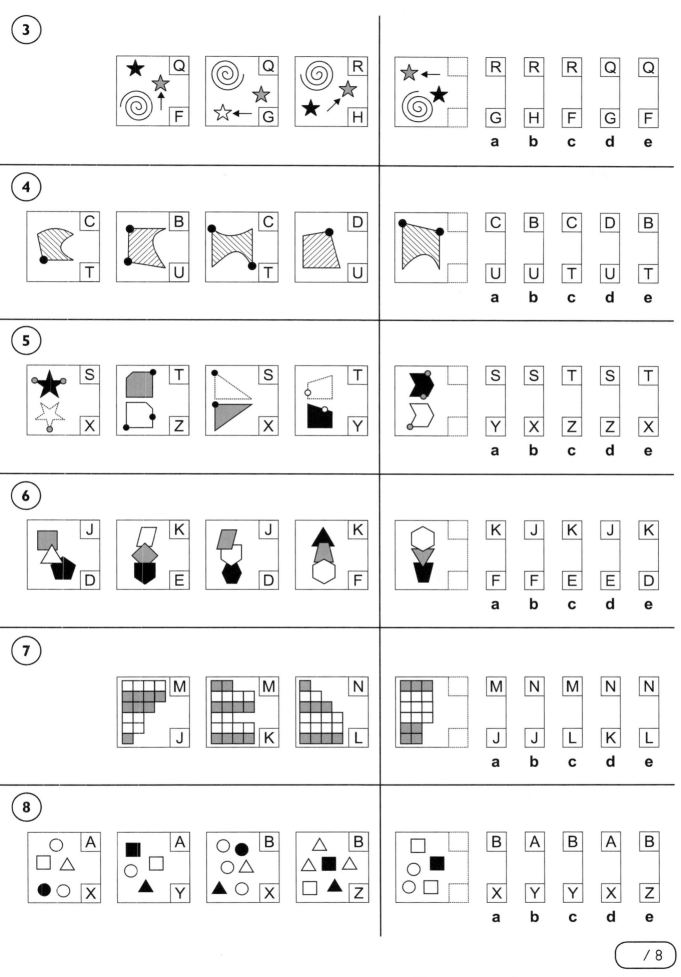

Section 5 — Odd One Out

Each of the questions below has five figures.
Find which figure in each row is most unlike the others.

Example:

a   b   c   d   e

Answer: b

a   b   c   d   e

2

a   b   c   d   e

3

a   b   c   d   e

4

a   b   c   d   e

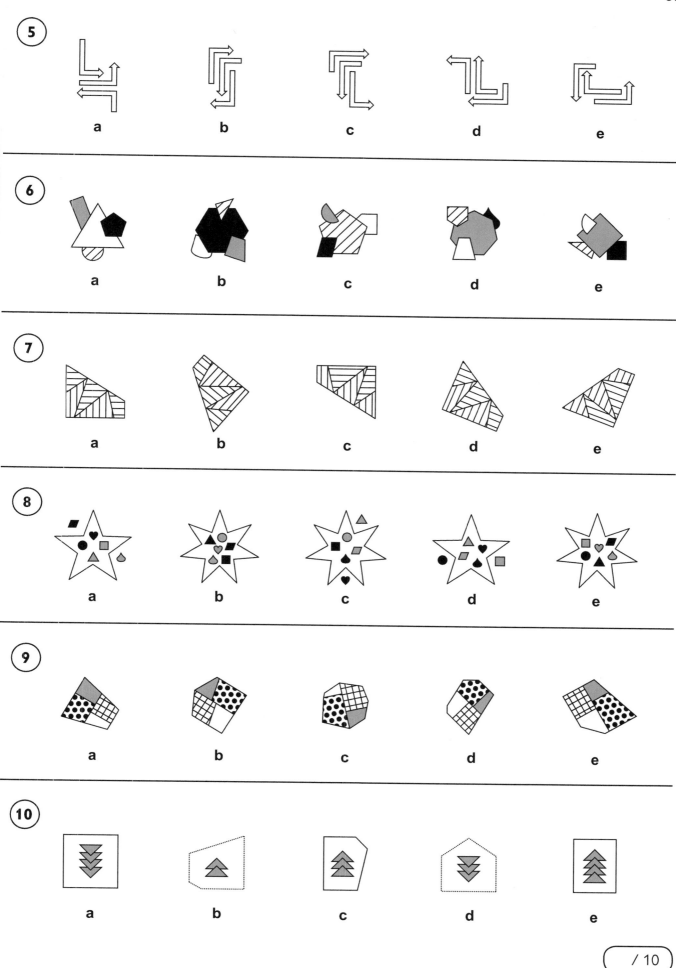

Section 6 — Find the Figure Like the First Three

For each of the questions below there are three figures that are like each other in some way.
Find which of the five figures on the right is most like the three figures on the left.

Example:

a   b   c   d   e

Answer: c

(1) |

a   b   c   d   e

(2) |

a   b   c   d   e

(3) |

a   b   c   d   e

(4) |

a   b   c   d   e

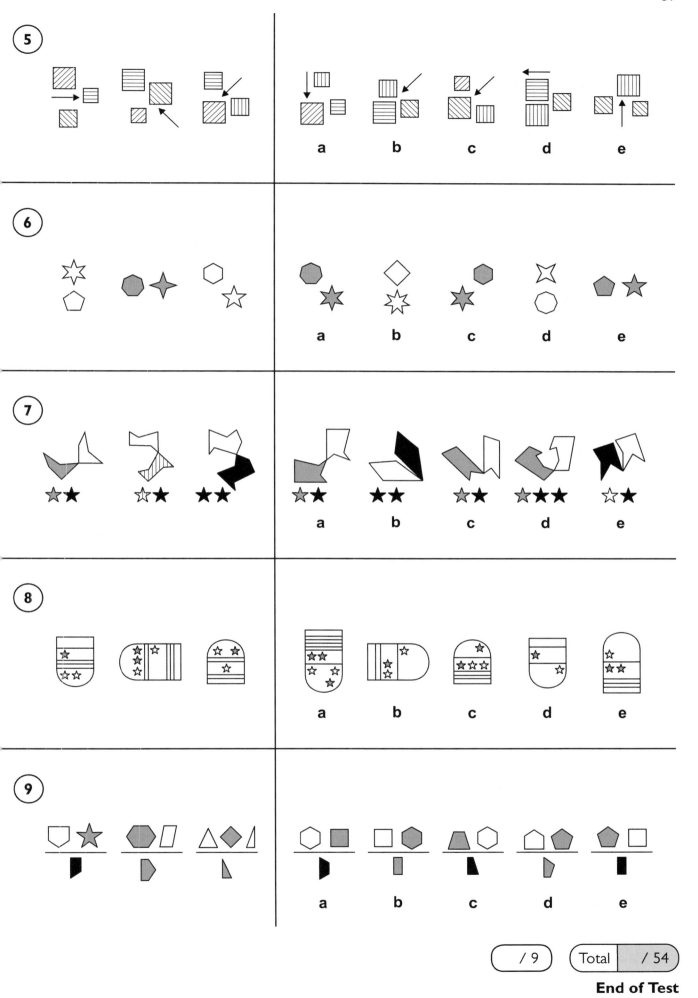

Assessment Test 4

Allow 60 minutes to do this test and work as quickly and as carefully as you can.

You can print **multiple-choice answer sheets** for these questions from our website — go to cgpbooks.co.uk/11plus/answer-sheets or scan the QR code on the right. If you'd prefer to answer them in standard write-in format, just circle the letter underneath your answer.

You can ignore Assessment Test 4 if you're sitting the test in a region that does not test Spatial Reasoning. For more information on test content in different regions, please visit cgpbooks.co.uk/11plus.

Section 1 — 2D Views of 3D Shapes

Each of these questions has a 3D figure on the left, made out of cubes.
Work out which of the five options is a top-down 2D view of the 3D figure on the left.

Example:

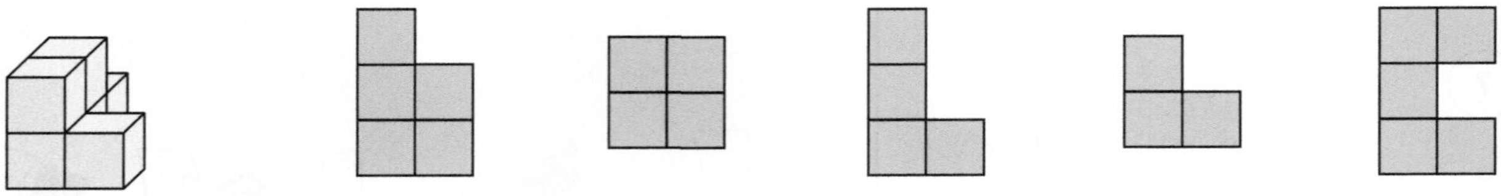

a   b   c   d   e

Answer: c

1

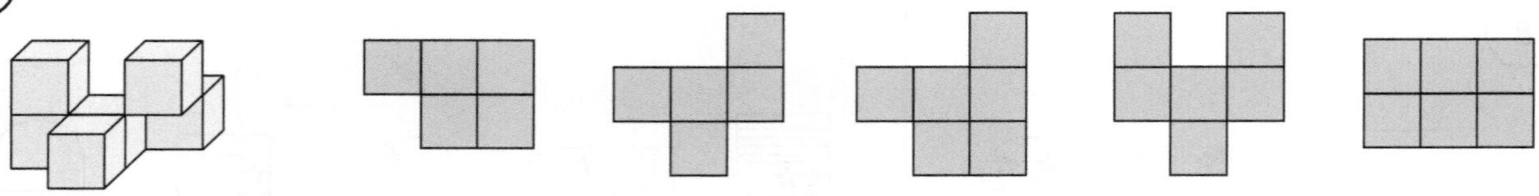

a   b   c   d   e

2

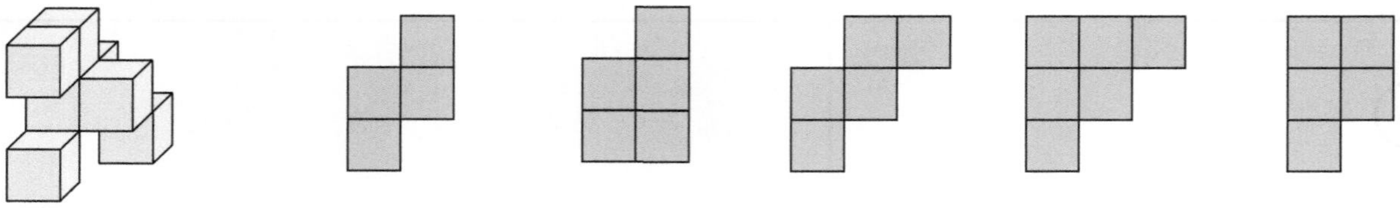

a   b   c   d   e

3

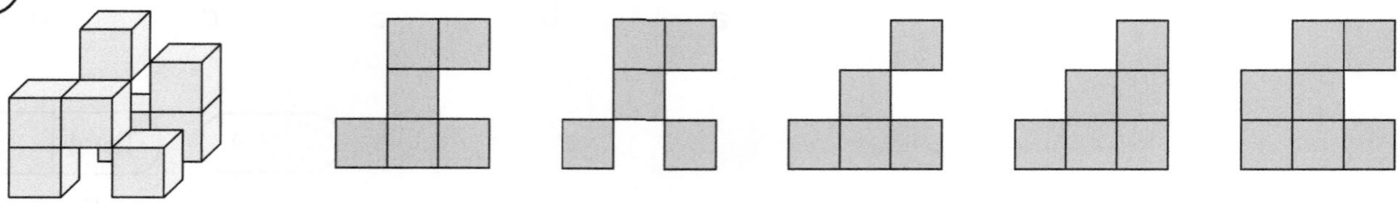

a   b   c   d   e

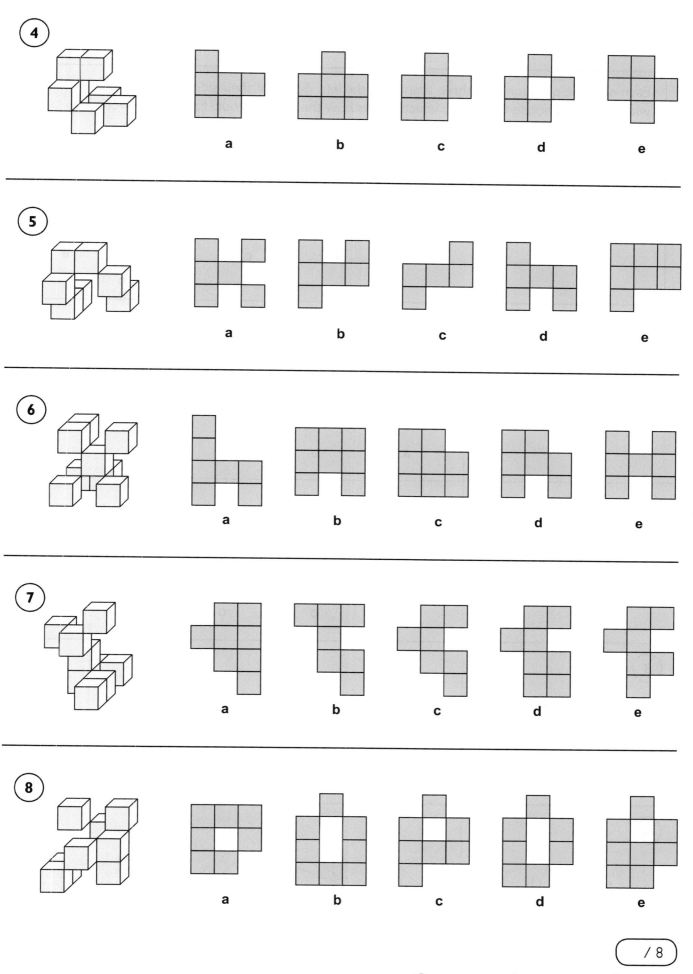

4 a b c d e

5 a b c d e

6 a b c d e

7 a b c d e

8 a b c d e

/ 8

Carry on to the next question → →

Section 2 — Connecting Shapes

Each of these questions has three shapes on the left. Some of their sides are labelled with a letter. Choose the option which shows how the shapes would look if they were joined together so that sides with the same letter are touching.

Example:

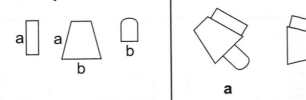 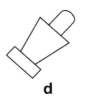

a   b   c   d   e

Answer: e

1

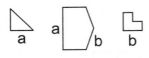

a   b   c   d   e

2

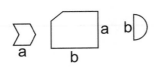   

a   b   c   d   e

3

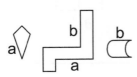   

a   b   c   d   e

4

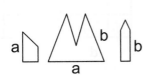   

a   b   c   d   e

Assessment Test 4

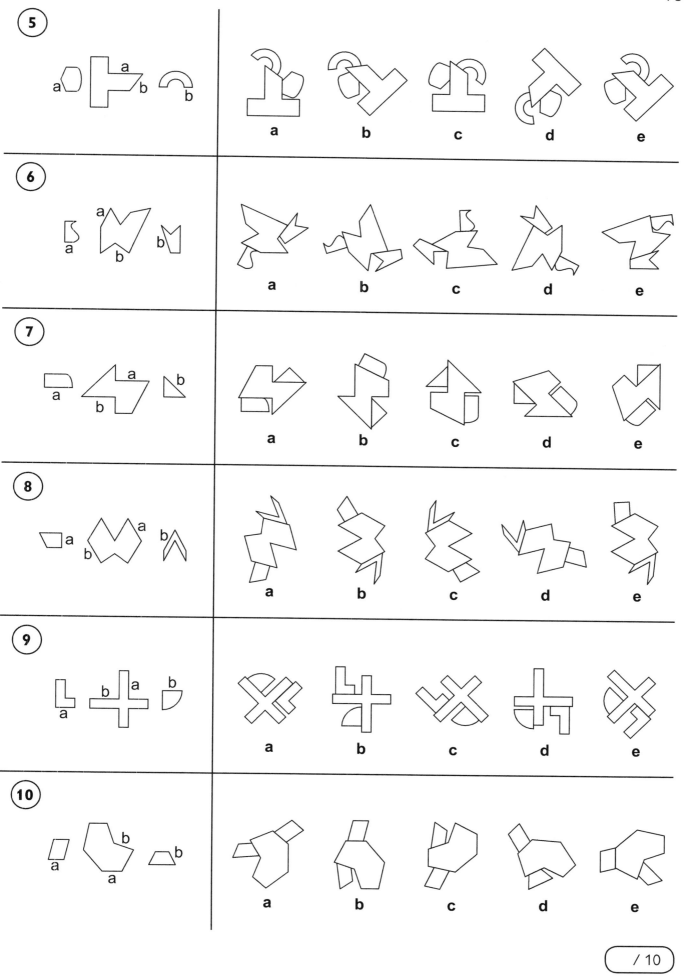

Section 3 — Fold Along the Line

Work out which option shows the figure on the left when folded along the dotted line.

Example:

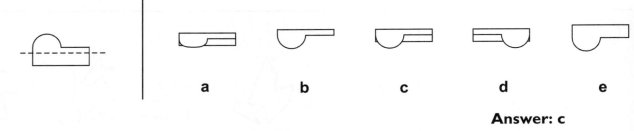

a   b   c   d   e

Answer: c

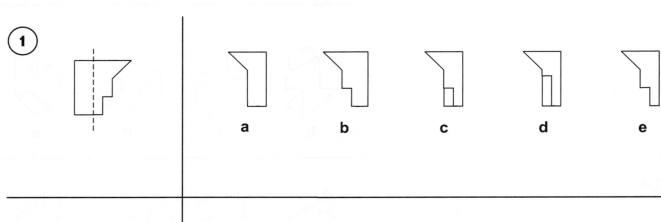

1

a   b   c   d   e

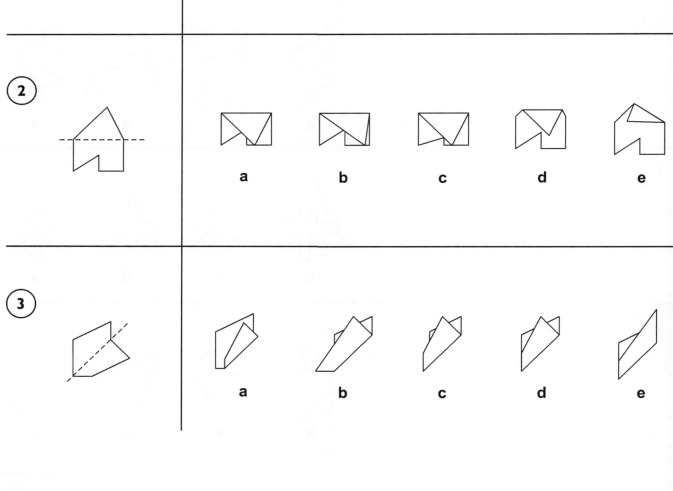

2

a   b   c   d   e

3

a   b   c   d   e

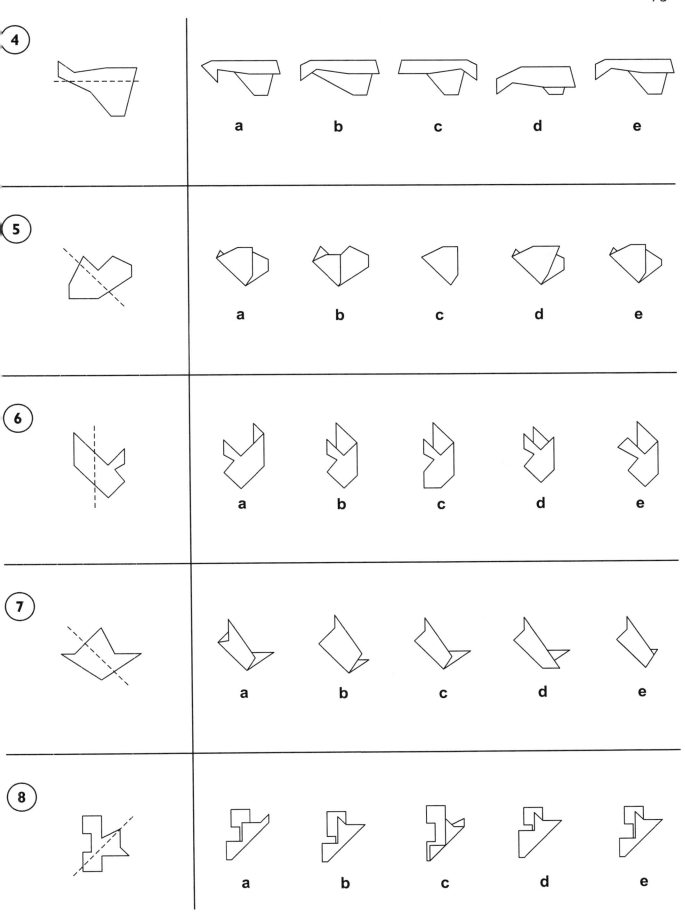

Section 4 — Cubes and Nets

Each of these questions has a net on the left.
Find which of the five cubes on the right can be made by folding up the net.

Example:

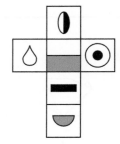

    a   b   c   d   e

Answer: c

1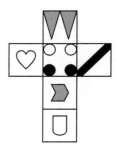

    a   b   c   d   e

2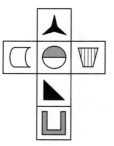

    a   b   c   d   e

3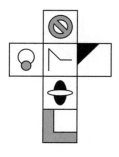

    a   b   c   d   e

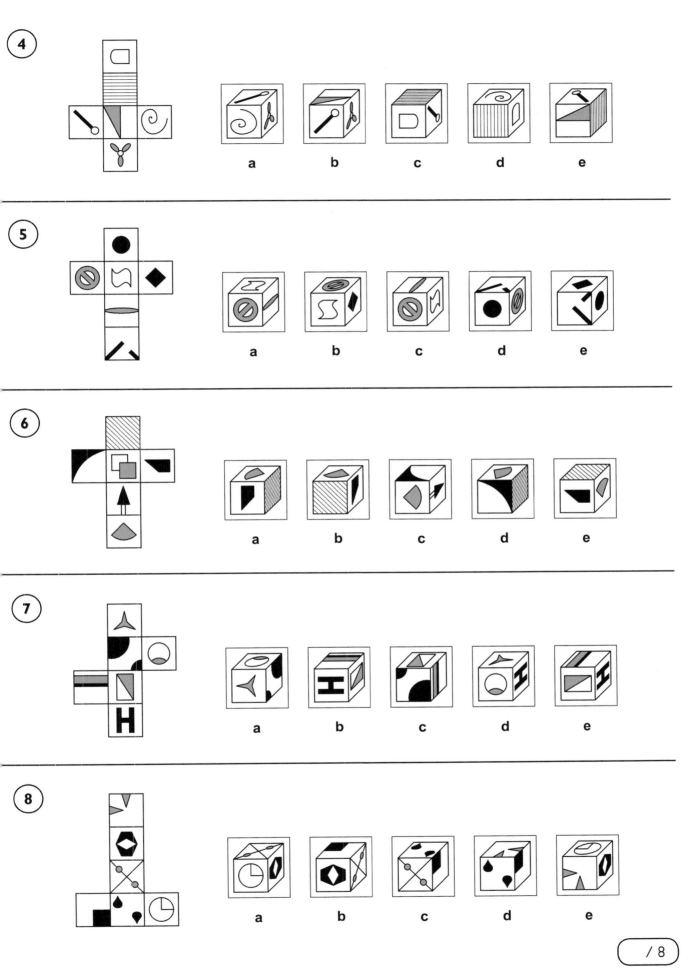

Section 5 — Fold and Punch

Each of these questions shows a square of paper being folded several times. A hole is then punched in the folded piece of paper. Work out which of the five options shows what the piece of paper would look like if it was unfolded.

Example:

Answer: b

1

2

3

4

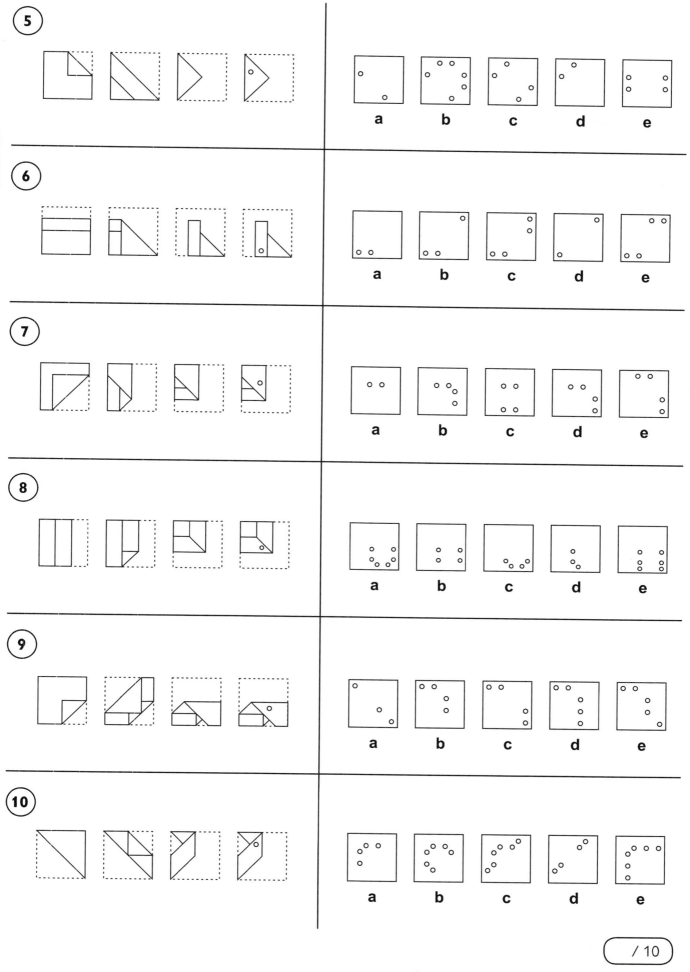

Section 6 — 3D Rotation

Work out which 3D figure in the grey box has been rotated to make the new 3D figure.

Example:

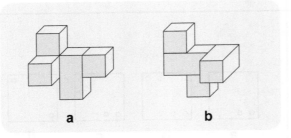

a

b

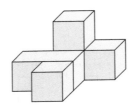

a

b

Answer: a

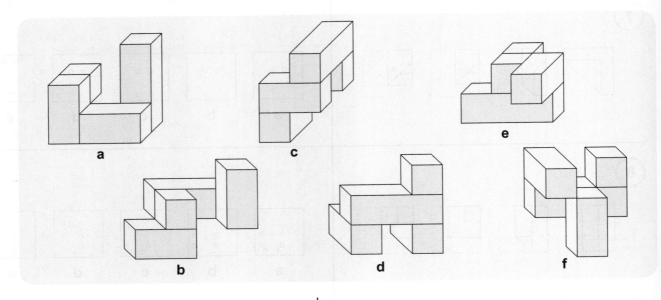

a

c

e

b

d

f

1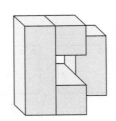

a   d

b   e

c   f

2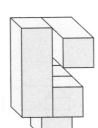

a   d

b   e

c   f

3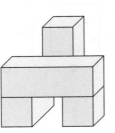

a   d

b   e

c   f

4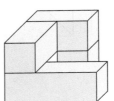

a   d

b   e

c   f

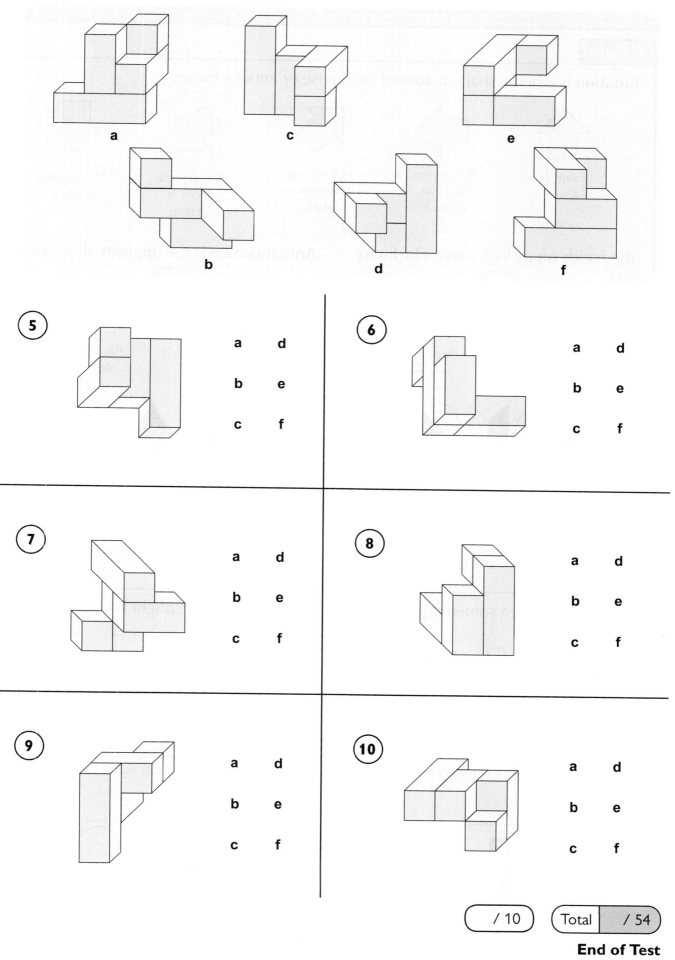

a

c

e

b

d

f

5

a	d
b	e
c	f

6

a	d
b	e
c	f

7

a	d
b	e
c	f

8

a	d
b	e
c	f

9

a	d
b	e
c	f

10

a	d
b	e
c	f

/ 10   Total   / 54

End of Test

Assessment Test 4

Glossary

Rotation

Rotation is when a shape is **turned** clockwise or anticlockwise.

Example shape

90 degrees clockwise rotation

45 degrees anticlockwise rotation

135 degrees clockwise rotation

180 degrees rotation

The hands on a clock move **clockwise**.

Anticlockwise is the **opposite** direction.

The left-hand shape has been rotated 45 degrees anticlockwise.

The right-hand shape has been rotated 45 degrees clockwise.

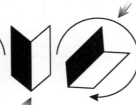
Starting shape

The left-hand shape has been rotated 90 degrees anticlockwise.

The right-hand shape has been rotated 90 degrees clockwise.

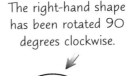
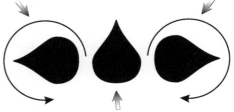
Starting shape

Reflection

Reflection is when something is **mirrored** over a line (this line might be invisible).

The black shape is reflected across to make the white shape.

The grey shape is reflected across to make the black shape.

The black shape is reflected down to make the grey shape.

The grey shape is reflected down to make the white shape.

This black shape has been reflected and rotated to make the white shape.

The black shape has been reflected over an invisible line (to make the dashed shape). Then it has been rotated 90 degrees clockwise.
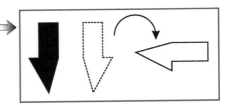

3D Rotation

There are **three planes** that a 3D shape can be rotated in.

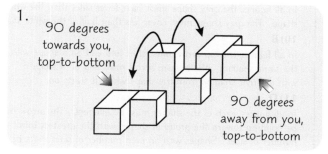

1. 90 degrees towards you, top-to-bottom

90 degrees away from you, top-to-bottom

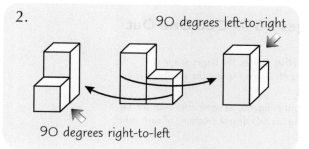

2. 90 degrees left-to-right

90 degrees right-to-left

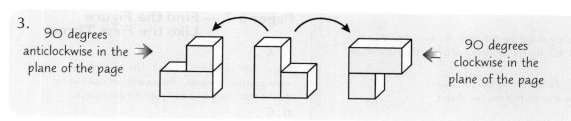

3. 90 degrees anticlockwise in the plane of the page

90 degrees clockwise in the plane of the page

Other terms

Line Types:

Thin   Thick   Dashed   Dotted   Curved

Shading Types:

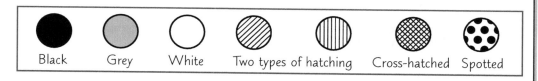

Black   Grey   White   Two types of hatching   Cross-hatched   Spotted

Layering — when a shape is in front of or behind another shape, or where two or more shapes overlap each other.

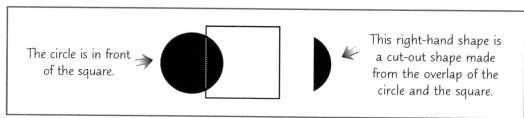

The circle is in front of the square.

This right-hand shape is a cut-out shape made from the overlap of the circle and the square.

Line of Symmetry — a line which splits a shape into halves that are reflections of each other.

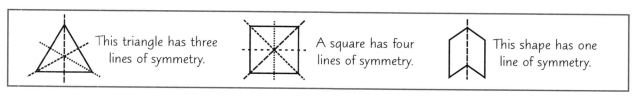

This triangle has three lines of symmetry.

A square has four lines of symmetry.

This shape has one line of symmetry.

Glossary

Answers

Similarities and Differences

Pages 2-3 — Odd One Out

1) E
In all other figures, the larger shape is rotated 45 degrees to get the smaller shape.

2) A
In all other figures, all semicircles with the same shading are 90 degree rotations of each other.

3) C
In all other figures, the difference between the number of sides of the two shapes in the hourglass is five.

4) E
In all other figures, the shape created where the two white shapes intersect is rotated 90 degrees anticlockwise to get the black shape.

5) D
In all other figures, the line joining the two shapes touches a right angle on each of the two shapes.

6) B
In all other figures, arrows only intersect the grey shape on a curved side.

7) E
All other figures are identical apart from rotation and shading.

8) B
In all other figures, parallel arrows have matching arrowheads.

9) E
In all other figures, the arrow is pointing to the shape's largest angle.

10) D
In all other figures, the number of grey dots is equal to the number of sides of the black shape added to the number of sides of the hatched shape.

Pages 4-5 — Find the Figure Like the First Two

1) B
All figures must have a white triangle. The biggest angle of the triangle must be touching the black shape.

2) C
In all figures, the largest section of the shape must have diagonal hatching.

3) E
In all figures, the top and bottom shape must have the same shading. There must be three grey shapes.

4) C
All figures must have a dot on the outline of the shape. The dot must be vertically in line with where two lines intersect.

5) B
In all figures, the number of black dots must be one more than the number of shapes joined to the line.

6) E
In all figures, the black shape is created by rotating the hatched shape 90 degrees clockwise and then reflecting it in the dashed line.

7) C
All figures must have a large four-sided shape. The curved line must join two sides of this shape that have equal length. The line must have an X-shape closer to the end with a circle.

8) A
In all figures, the small shape with the fewest number of sides must be in the smallest section of the large shape.

9) D
In all figures, the grey shape must have fewer sides than the white shape. The grey shape must cover less than half of the white shape.

10) B
In all figures, the top arrow must start and end on a shape with the same shading. The bottom arrow must end on a shape with different shading from the shape which it starts on.

11) D
In all figures, each of the shapes must be different. The arrow must be pointing toward the group of shapes with the greatest total number of sides. Shapes with an even number of sides must be black and shapes with an odd number of sides must be white.

Pages 6-7 — Find the Figure Like the First Three

1) A
Shapes with an even number of sides must have an arrow pointing upwards. Shapes with an odd number of sides must have an arrow pointing downwards.

2) C
All figures must have a large shape with two curved sides. The number of X-shapes inside the large shape must be the same as the number of dots outside the large shape.

3) D
All figures must be made of one line which crosses over itself two times. The arrows at both ends of the line must be pointing in the same direction.

4) C
In all figures, the outer shape must have twice as many sides as the inner shape. There must be one fewer black dot than the number of sides of the inner shape.

5) B
All figures must have a shape with an even number of sides. The line through the shape must run from a corner to the middle of a side.

6) B
In all figures, the hatched shape must be behind the other two shapes. The number of points on the star must be equal to the number of sides of the other non-hatched shape.

7) A
In all figures, there must be a difference of two between the number of sides of the outer shape and the number of sides of the inner shape. There must be two fewer circles than the number of sides of the outer shape.

8) D
In all figures, the number of grey raindrops must be the same as the number of clockwise arrows.

9) A
In all figures, the number of right angles inside the shape must be equal to the number of small lines crossing the outline of the shape.

10) E
In all figures, the shape in the middle of the grid must appear twice as many times as the other shape.

11) C
In all figures, there must be two dice with the same number of dots. The total number of dots must be a prime number.

Pairs, Series and Grids

Pages 8-9 — Complete the Pair

1) D

The shapes on the left and the right are reflected downwards. The hatching on the middle shape is rotated by 90 degrees.

2) A

Any parts of the shapes that aren't overlapping are removed. The remaining figure is reflected across.

3) A

The white shape is reflected across. The grey shape is reflected downwards, made smaller and placed on top of the white shape. The two shapes swap shadings.

4) D

The portion of the shape that the arrow is pointing towards is trimmed from the shape, reflected on top of the shape and shaded grey. The arrow moves so that it's pointing to the edge of the shape where the portion has been removed. The whole figure is rotated 90 degrees anticlockwise.

5) B

The whole figure is rotated 90 degrees anticlockwise. The triangle moves to the end of the other hatched rectangle.

6) D

The figure is rotated 180 degrees.

7) A

The hatching of the hatched shapes is rotated by 90 degrees. The black and grey shapes swap shading. Any pairs of circles that aren't pointing towards the centre of the figure change position so that they are.

8) A

The grey circle moves to the opposite corner of the square. The five-sided shape and the circle swap places. The five-sided shape is rotated 90 degrees clockwise and the white circle becomes smaller.

9) B

For each quarter of the shape, the shading of the inner and outer portions swap. The whole figure is rotated 180 degrees.

10) B

The outline of the large shape and the centre line swap. The small shape at the top becomes the large shape, and the large shape becomes the small shape at the top. The small shape in the middle moves to the other side of the centre line. The small shape at the bottom is reflected downwards and moves on top of the centre line.

11) E

The lines inside the shape move one place clockwise around the shape so that the place where the lines meet is pointing to the next side and the other two ends of the lines are in the next corners. The grey circle moves on top of where the lines now meet. The black circle moves to where the two lines met in the first figure.

12) E

The three shapes move so that the shape with the fewest sides is at the top and the shape with the most sides is at the bottom. The grey and spotted shapes turn white and the white shape turns black.

Pages 10-11 — Complete the Series

1) D

In each series square, the entire figure rotates 90 degrees anticlockwise. The teardrop shape is then rotated a further 180 degrees. The two rectangles alternate which is in front of the other.

2) A

In each series square, each shading moves up one place to the next shape, with the shading at the top moving to the bottom. Each shape moves down one place, with the shape at the bottom moving to the top. The parallelogram is reflected across.

3) B

In each series square, the figure is rotated 90 degrees anticlockwise. The line in the white circle is then rotated a further 90 degrees. The triangles and the shapes inside them swap places.

4) C

In each series square, an additional side is added to the large shape. The small grey shape in the centre has one fewer side than the large shape and matches the large shape of the previous series square. The outline of the large shape changes in the order: solid, dotted, dashed. The arrow with the triangle arrowhead rotates 90 degrees clockwise, and the arrow with the circle arrowhead alternates between pointing up and down.

5) B

In each series square, an additional grey circle is added to the left of the existing circles. The direction in which the circles are layered alternates between having the leftmost circle on top and having the rightmost circle on top. The hatched shape and its hatching rotate independently of each other. The hatched shape rotates 90 degrees anticlockwise and the hatching rotates 45 degrees clockwise. The arrow alternates between pointing left and right.

6) C

In each series square, the outer ring rotates 45 degrees anticlockwise. The middle ring rotates 135 degrees clockwise. The circle at the centre is reflected across.

7) D

In each series square, the grey circle moves to the next side clockwise around the edge of the square. The dotted circle moves a side and a half clockwise around the edge of the square and alternates between having black dots on a white background and white dots on a black background. The hatched circle moves half a side anticlockwise around the edge of the square, and the hatching alternates between pointing diagonally down to the left and diagonally down to the right.

8) E

In each series square, an additional turn is added to the spiral, and the spiral is reflected across. The arrows rotate anticlockwise around the corners of each series square. The top two arrows always have solid lines, and the bottom two arrows alternate between having dotted and dashed lines.

9) E

In each series square, the large square rotates 90 degrees clockwise and the lines around the outside of the square rotate 90 degrees anticlockwise. The shading of the smaller square within the large square alternates between grey and black. The hatching rotates so that it is always vertical.

10) A

In each series square, the top square disappears and a new shape is added, alternating between a circle and a triangle. The new circle or triangle takes on the shading of the square that disappeared in the previous series square. The new shape is positioned so that the order of shadings going down each column is: black, grey, white.

11) B

In each series square, the entire figure rotates 90 degrees anticlockwise. The triangle changes shading in the order: black, grey, white. The rectangle changes shading in the order: grey, white, black. The shading in each of the small squares moves along one place to the next square in the direction the triangle is pointing. The shading in the square nearest the triangle moves to the square furthest away from the triangle.

12) E

In each series square, the top left square moves to the bottom right square and rotates 90 degrees clockwise. The top right square moves to the top left square without rotation. The bottom left square moves to the top right square and rotates 90 degrees clockwise. The bottom right square moves to the bottom left square and rotates 90 degrees clockwise.

Pages 12-13 — Complete the Grid

1) E

The grid is symmetrical vertically, horizontally and along both diagonals.

2) B

In each column, the shape in the bottom grid square is made by cutting the middle shape out of the top shape. In each column, the hatching of the shapes in the middle and bottom grid squares combine to make the hatching in the top shape.

3) E

Working from left to right, the number of sides on the shape in each grid square increases by one, the total number of grey circles halves, and the number of grey circles on the corners of the shape decreases by one.

4) A

Working from top to bottom, the hatched shape and the grey triangle rotate 90 degrees anticlockwise around the edge of the grid square. The five-sided shape and the square move clockwise around the corners of the grid square. Each shading of the square (black, grey and white) only appears once in each row and column.

5) C

Working from left to right, the grey shading moves one shape to the right, and the black circle moves one shape to the left. The white arrow moves one shape to the right and alternates between being above and below the shapes. Each type of shape (square, circle and diamond) only appears once in each row and column.

6) C

The whole grid has a vertical line of symmetry.

7) B

Working from left to right, the vertical line stays in place and the horizontal line moves one place up. The white circle alternates between being positioned on the bottom of the vertical line and the top. The grey circle moves one place left along the horizontal line. Working from top to bottom, the black circle moves one place down.

8) A

Working from left to right, the black and white hatched shapes and the large white curved shape rotate 90 degrees anticlockwise around the edge of the grid square but the hatching doesn't change direction. The three-quarter circle rotates 90 degrees clockwise. The grey shading then moves one place anticlockwise around the quarters of the circle.

9) D

Working from top to bottom, the arrow with the black triangle arrowhead rotates 90 degrees anticlockwise and moves to the next side of the grid square in an anticlockwise direction. The arrow with the circular arrowhead rotates 90 degrees clockwise and moves to the next side of the grid square in a clockwise direction. The arrow with the white triangle arrowhead is reflected across in each grid square. The remaining arrow moves to the opposite corner in each grid square.

10) D

Working from top to bottom, the rectangle that is behind all of the other rectangles moves to the front to occupy the empty space in the previous square.

Codes

Pages 14-15 — Vertical Code

1) D (HU)

G = spiral going anticlockwise (working from the centre outwards), H = spiral going clockwise.
S = triangle on end of spiral, T = square on end of spiral, U = star on end of spiral.

2) D (AJS)

A = circle to left of square, B = circle to right of square.
K = square in the middle, J = square not in the middle.
S = circle on left, T = circle on right, U = circle in middle.

3) B (EN)

D = two grey stars, E = one grey star.
M = small grey star is in the middle, N = small grey star is on the left, O = small grey star is on the right.

4) C (AF)

A = three triangles pointing up, B = two triangles pointing up, C = one triangle pointing up.
F = one black triangle, G = two black triangles, H = three black triangles.

5) D (QZ)

P = grey shape on the left, Q = grey shape at the top, R = grey shape at the bottom.
X = inner rectangle has dotted outline, Y = inner rectangle has solid outline, Z = inner rectangle has dashed outline.

6) A (BGT)

A = black chevron is pointing left, B = black chevron is pointing right.
F = outline of square is dotted, G = outline of square is dashed, H = outline of square is solid.
S = white chevron is pointing right, T = white chevron is pointing left.

7) E (DJW)

D = wavy line below straight line, E = wavy line above straight line.
J = the cross is to the left of the black square, K = the cross is to the right of the black square.
V = right-hand square is black, W = right-hand square is white.

8) B (EKT)

D = shading of circle layers matches shading of square layers, E = shading of circle layers doesn't match shading of square layers.
J = two shapes with dotted outline, K = three shapes with dotted outline, L = one shape with dotted outline.
R = small square in bottom-right corner of middle square, S = small square in top-left corner of middle square, T = small square in bottom-left corner of middle square.

9) B (BRV)

A = shape with fewest sides has arrow pointing towards it, B = shape with second fewest sides has arrow pointing towards it, C = shape with most sides has arrow pointing towards it.
R = hatched hexagon, S = hatched diamond, T = hatched pentagon.
U = left-hand shape is a diamond, V = left-hand shape is a hexagon, W = left-hand shape is a triangle.

10) A (CR)

A = three full circles, B = one full circle, C = two full circles.
R = the straight lines have a line of symmetry, S = the straight lines do not have a line of symmetry.

Pages 16-17 — Horizontal Code

1) E (BR)

A = grey circle at top-left of hexagon, B = grey circle at bottom right of hexagon, C = grey circle at bottom of hexagon.
R = line inside hexagon touches white circle, S = line inside hexagon touches black circle.

2) A (BK)

A = arrow going clockwise, B = arrow going anticlockwise.
J = largest square at the front, K = largest square in the middle, L = largest square at the back.

3) D (DY)

D = one shape is shaded grey, E = three shapes are shaded grey, F = two shapes are shaded grey.
X = circles on either side of dashed line, Y = all circles on same side of dashed line.

4) E (BQ)

A = no triangle with the same rotation, B = three triangles with the same rotation, C = two triangles with the same rotation.
P = star touching one grey and one white triangle, Q = star touching only white triangles, R = star touching one white and one black triangle.

---

5) B (RX)

R = white square is behind the grey rectangle,
S = white square is in front of the grey rectangle.
W = bottom shape is a square, X = bottom shape is
a pentagon, Y = bottom shape is a hexagon.

6) D (DX)

D = black shape is on top of one of the smaller shapes,
E = black shape is on top of two of the smaller shapes,
F = black shape is on top of three of the smaller shapes.
X = working anticlockwise from the triangle, the number of
sides of the hatched shapes increases by one each time,
Y = working clockwise from the triangle, the number of
sides of the hatched shapes increases by one each time.

7) C (BY)

A = white shapes are rotations of each other,
B = white shapes are reflections of each other.
X = circles connected by a line have different shading,
Y = circles connected by a line have the same shading,
Z = one pair of circles, with the same shading, are connected
by a line, and the unconnected pair have different shading.

8) B (FQ)

D = star shape divided into two, E = star shape divided into four,
F = star shape divided into three.
P = grey circle has one white circle underneath,
Q = grey circle has two white circles underneath,
R = grey circle has no white circles underneath.

9) A (GY)

G = shortest of the three lines is on the left,
H = shortest of the three lines is in the middle.
X = arrow points from a white rectangle to a black rectangle,
Y = arrow points from a black rectangle to a white rectangle,
Z = arrow points from a grey rectangle to a black rectangle.

10) D (FN)

F = figure has one line of symmetry, G = figure has two
lines of symmetry, H = figure has no lines of symmetry.
M = bottom-right quarter of circle is shaded white,
N = bottom-right quarter of circle is not shaded white.

11) D (HL)

F = one circle behind a line, G = three circles behind a line,
H = two circles behind a line.
L = same number of dotted lines and solid lines, M = two fewer dotted
lines than solid lines, N = one fewer dotted line than solid lines.

12) A (VX)

U = dotted arrows pointing in two different directions,
V = dotted arrows pointing in three different directions,
W = dotted arrows pointing in four different directions.
X = solid arrows on two rows,
Y = solid arrows on all of the rows.

Spatial Reasoning

Pages 18-19 — 3D Rotation

1) B

Shape B has been rotated 180 degrees in the plane of the
page. It has then been rotated 90 degrees right-to-left.

2) A

Shape A has been rotated 90 degrees towards you, top-to-bottom.
It has then been rotated 90 degrees right-to-left.

3) C

Shape C has been rotated 90 degrees away from you,
top-to-bottom. It has then been rotated 90 degrees right-to-left.

4) D

Shape D has been rotated 180 degrees left-to-right. It has then
been rotated 90 degrees away from you, top-to-bottom.

5) C

Shape C has been rotated 180 degrees top-to-bottom. It has then
been rotated 90 degrees clockwise in the plane of the page.

6) A

Shape A has been rotated 90 degrees away from you, top-to-bottom.

7) D

Shape D has been rotated 90 degrees right-to-left. It has then
been rotated 90 degrees anticlockwise in the plane of the page.

8) F

Shape F has been rotated 90 degrees clockwise
in the plane of the page. It has then been rotated
90 degrees away from you, top-to-bottom.

9) E

Shape E has been rotated 90 degrees left-to-right. It has then
been rotated 90 degrees anticlockwise in the plane of the page.

10) B

Shape B has been rotated 180 degrees in the plane of the page.
It has then been rotated 90 degrees towards you, top-to-bottom.

Pages 20-21 — 3D Building Blocks

1) B

The block at the top of set B is at the back of the figure. The block
on the bottom left of set B rotates 90 degrees top-to-bottom
and is arranged at the bottom of the figure. The block on the
bottom right of set B is at the top of the figure at the front.

2) A

The block at the bottom of set A is at the back of the figure. One of
the remaining two blocks in set A is at the front of the figure, in the
middle. The other block in set A rotates 90 degrees away from you,
top-to-bottom, to become the block at the front right of the figure.

3) C

The block at the bottom left of set C is at the back of the figure, at
the bottom. The block at the top of set C rotates 90 degrees in the
plane of the page to become the block at the back of the figure, at
the top. The block on the right of set C rotates 90 degrees in the
plane of the page to become the block at the front of the figure.

4) A

The top left block of set A is at the back of the figure.
The top right block of set A is arranged in front of it.
The block at the bottom of set A rotates 90 degrees
right-to-left and is arranged at the bottom of the figure.

5) A

The block at the top right of set A is at the front right of the
figure. The block at the top left of set A rotates 90 degrees
clockwise in the plane of the page and moves behind the
previous block. The bottom block in set A rotates 90 degrees
right-to-left, then 90 degrees anticlockwise in the plane of the
page to become the block on the bottom left of the figure.

6) D

The top left block of set D rotates 90 degrees right-to-left to
become the block on the left of the figure. The block at the
bottom of set D rotates 90 degrees in the plane of the page
to become the block at the back right of the figure. The top
right block of set D rotates 90 degrees in the plane of the
page to become the block at the front right of the figure.

7) B

The block at the top of set B becomes the back block of the figure.
The middle block of set B becomes the middle block of the figure.
The block at the bottom of set B is arranged on the left of the figure.

8) E

The block on the left of set E rotates 90 degrees left-to-right to
become the block at the front of the figure. One of the blocks
on the right of set E is on the left of the figure. The remaining
block in set E rotates 90 degrees in the plane of the page to
become the block on the right of the figure, at the back.

88

9) C

The top block of set C rotates 180 degrees right-to-left to become the block on the back left of the figure. The bottom block in set C rotates 90 degrees towards you, top-to-bottom, then 90 degrees right-to-left to become the block at the front right of the figure. The cube in set C is at the front left of the figure. The remaining block in set C is at the back right of the figure.

10) D

One of the top two blocks in set D is on the right of the figure. The other top block in set D rotates 90 degrees left-to-right to become the block on the left of the figure. The bottom block in set D rotates 90 degrees away from you, top-to-bottom, then 90 degrees in the plane of the page to become the block in the middle of the figure, at the top.

Pages 22-23 — 2D Views of 3D Shapes

1) C

There are eight blocks visible from above, which rules out options B and E. There is only one block visible at the front, which rules out option D. There are four blocks visible on the right-hand side, which rules out option A.

2) B

There are seven blocks visible from above, which rules out options A, C and E. There are only two columns of blocks, which rules out option D.

3) B

There are eight blocks visible from above, which rules out options C and D. There are three blocks visible on the left-hand side, which rules out option E. There is a gap between the two blocks in the middle column, which rules out option A.

4) E

There are six blocks visible from above, which rules out option C. There are two blocks next to each other on the right-hand side, which rules out options A and B. There are no more than two blocks visible in each row, which rules out option D.

5) A

There are two blocks visible on the right-hand side, which rules out option B and D. There are at least four rows of blocks, which rules out option C. There are two blocks visible on the second row from the bottom, which rules out option E.

6) C

There are at least seven blocks visible from above, which rules out option B. There are at least three blocks visible on the left-hand side, which rules out options A and D. There is only one block on the right, which rules out option E.

7) D

There are seven blocks visible from above, which rules out options A and C. There are three blocks visible on the right-hand side, which rules out options B and E.

8) E

There are at least two blocks visible on the left-hand side, which rules out options A and D. There are two blocks visible at the front, which rules out option B. There are three blocks visible on the right-hand side with a gap between them, which rules out option C.

9) D

There are three blocks visible in the middle column, which rules out options A and B. There are three blocks visible on the right, which rules out option C. There are three blocks visible in the second row from the back, which rules out option E.

Pages 24-25 — Cubes and Nets

1) A

Option B is ruled out because the face with the pentagon has been rotated. Option C is ruled out because the face with the white circles has been rotated. Option D is ruled out because the face with the arrows has been rotated. Option E is ruled out because the face with the heart has been rotated.

2) D

Option A is ruled out because the face with the trapezium has been rotated. Option B is ruled out because the face with the grey L-shape has been rotated. Options C and E are ruled out because the face with the spiral has been rotated.

3) C

Option A is ruled out because the white and grey halves of the shape with curved sides are the wrong way round. Option B is ruled out because the face with two squares has been rotated. Option D is ruled out because the black and white hatching should be pointing in the opposite direction. Option E is ruled out because the black oval and the white oval have swapped places.

4) A

Option B is ruled out because the shading on the black and grey arrow shape is the wrong way round. Option C is ruled out because the shading on the white and grey hexagon is the wrong way round. Option D is ruled out because the shading on the grey and black hexagon is the wrong way round. Option E is ruled out because the shading on the grey and black hexagon is the wrong way round.

5) B

Option A is ruled out because the arrow with the double arrowhead should be positioned on the side of the face closest to the arrow with the curved black triangle arrowhead. Option C is ruled out because the arrow with two lines for an arrowhead should be pointing in the opposite direction. Option D is ruled out because the arrow with the white triangle arrowhead should be pointing in the opposite direction. Option E is ruled out because the arrow with the double arrowhead should be pointing in the opposite direction.

6) E

Option A is ruled out because the two white triangles should be next to each other over the edge of the cube. Option B is ruled out because the white circle should be in the opposite corner of the cube face. Option C is ruled out because the top face of the cube has been rotated. Option D is ruled out because the white triangle should be pointing towards the grey curve.

7) D

Option A is ruled out because the arrow with the white circle arrowhead has been reflected. Option B is ruled out because the arrow with the black circle arrowhead should be an arrow with the thick line arrowhead. Option C is ruled out because the two arrows with white circle arrowheads should be on opposite sides. Option E is ruled out because the arrow on the right-hand face has been reflected.

8) C

Option A is ruled out because the face with a square in opposite corners has been rotated. Option B is ruled out because the face with a square on opposite sides has been rotated. Option D is ruled out because the face with two squares in opposite corners should be opposite the face with two squares in adjacent corners. Option E is ruled out because the face with a square in two of the corners has been rotated.

Pages 26-27 — Fold Along the Line

1) E

Options A and C are ruled out because the part of the figure that has been folded is the wrong shape. Option B is ruled out because the part of the figure originally below the fold line should still be visible. Option D is ruled out because the part of the figure below the fold line is the wrong shape.

2) D

Option A is ruled out because the part of the figure that has been folded is the wrong shape. Options B and E are ruled out because the fold line has moved. Option C is ruled out because the part of the figure originally above the fold line is the wrong shape.

3) C

Options A and E are ruled out because the part of the figure that has been folded is the wrong shape. Options B and D are ruled out because the fold line has moved.

Answers

4) C

Option A is ruled out because the part of the figure originally to the right of the fold line should still be visible. Option B is ruled out because the part of the figure originally to the left of the fold line is the wrong shape. Option D is ruled out because the part of the figure that has been folded is the wrong shape. Option E is ruled out because the fold line has moved.

5) A

Option B is ruled out because the part of the figure originally below the fold line should still be visible. Option C and D are ruled out because the part of the figure that has been folded is the wrong shape. Option E is ruled out because the fold line has moved.

6) E

Option A is ruled out because only the top part of the figure has been folded along the fold line. Option B is ruled out because the fold line has moved. Options C and D are ruled out because the part of the figure originally to the right of the fold line is the wrong shape.

7) D

Option A is ruled out because the part of the figure originally below the fold line should still be visible. Options B and C are ruled out because the part of the figure that has been folded is the wrong shape. Option E is ruled out because the part of the figure originally below the fold line is in the wrong place.

8) D

Options A and B are ruled out because the part of the figure that has been folded is the wrong shape. Options C and E are ruled out because the fold line has moved.

9) B

Options A and D are ruled out because the part of the figure that has been folded is the wrong shape. Option C is ruled out because the fold line has moved. Option E is ruled out because part of the figure originally below the fold line should still be visible.

10) B

Option A is ruled out because part of the figure originally above the fold line should still be visible. Option C is ruled out because the part of the figure that hasn't been folded is the wrong shape. Options D and E are ruled out because the part of the figure that has been folded is the wrong shape.

11) E

Options A and D are ruled out because the part of the figure that has been folded is the wrong shape. Options B and C are ruled out because the part of the figure originally above the fold line is the wrong shape.

Pages 28-29 — Fold and Punch

1) B
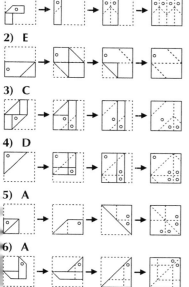

2) E

3) C

4) D

5) A

6) A

7) D
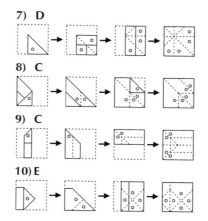

8) C

9) C
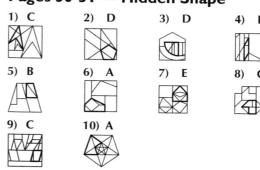

10) E

Pages 30-31 — Hidden Shape

1) C 2) D 3) D 4) B
5) B 6) A 7) E 8) C
9) C 10) A

Pages 32-33 — Connecting Shapes

1) C

Option A is ruled out because the wrong side of the arrow is connected to the triangle. Option B is ruled out because the wrong side of the four-sided shape is connected to the triangle. Option D is ruled out because the four-sided shape is connected to the wrong side of the triangle. Option E is ruled out because the arrow and four-sided shape are both connected to the wrong sides of the triangle.

2) B

Options A and D are ruled out because the 'b' shape is connected to the wrong side of the star. Options C and E are ruled out because the wrong side of the 'a' shape is connected to the star.

3) D

Options A and C are ruled out because the rectangle is connected to the wrong side of the large shape. Options B and E are ruled out because the rectangle and semi-circle are both connected to the wrong sides of the large shape.

4) D

Option A is ruled out because the wrong side of the parallelogram is connected to the large shape. Option B is ruled out because the parallelogram and trapezium are both connected to the wrong sides of the large shape. Option C is ruled out because the parallelogram is connected to the wrong side of the large shape. Option E is ruled out because the wrong side of the trapezium is connected to the large shape.

5) A

Option B is ruled out because the wrong side of the circle sector is connected to the large shape. Option C is ruled out because the wrong side of the parallelogram is connected to the large shape. Option D is ruled out because the circle sector is connected to the wrong side of the large shape. Option E is ruled out because the parallelogram is connected to the wrong side of the large shape.

6) E

Option A is ruled out because the wrong side of the right-angled triangle is connected to the kite. Option B is ruled out because the wrong side of the isosceles triangle is connected to the kite. Options C and D are ruled out because both triangles are connected to the wrong sides of the kite.

7) C

Option A is ruled out because the wrong side of the ten-sided shape is connected to the large shape. Option B is ruled out because the wrong side of the arrow shape is connected to the large shape. Option D is ruled out because the ten-sided shape and the arrow shape are both connected to the wrong sides of the large shape. Option E is ruled out because the ten-sided shape is connected to the wrong side of the large shape.

8) D

Option A is ruled out because the four-sided shape is connected to the wrong side of the large shape. Option B is ruled out because the four-sided shape and the star are both connected to the wrong side of the large shape. Option C is ruled out because the wrong side of the four-sided shape is connected to the large shape. Option E is ruled out because the star is connected to the wrong side of the large shape.

9) E

Option A is ruled out because the five-sided shape is connected to the wrong side of the large shape. Option B is ruled out because the five-sided shape and the L-shape are both connected to the wrong sides of the large shape. Option C is ruled out because the wrong side of the L-shape is connected to the large shape. Option D is ruled out because the wrong side of the five-sided shape is connected to the large shape.

10) B

Option A is ruled out because the four-sided shape is connected to the wrong side of the large shape. Options C and E are ruled out because the two small shapes are connected to the wrong sides of the large shape. Option D is ruled out because the wrong side of the five-sided shape is connected to the large shape.

Pages 34-45 — Assessment Test 1

Section 1 — Complete the Grid

1) D

In each row, the shading of the trapezium at the back matches the shading of the circle, and the shading of the trapezium at the front matches the shading of the hexagon.

2) A

Each size of arrow (small, medium and large) only appears once in each row and column. Each direction of arrow (left, right and up) only appears once in each row and column.

3) C

Working from left to right, the shading of the circle changes from white to grey to black. Working from top to bottom, the white arrow turns 90 degrees anticlockwise and the black arrow turns 45 degrees clockwise.

4) E

In each column, the grid square containing shapes with all three shadings (white, grey and black) is made by adding the other two grid squares in its column. In this combined figure, the black and white shapes swap shadings and are reflected across.

5) A

In each row, if the solid lines in the first and second grid squares were moved to the third grid square, they would connect the white circles. The black circle is on the point where they would meet.

6) C

Every white shape and every grey shape is reflected downwards across the middle row. The black shapes in the third column are repeated from the first column.

7) B

Working left to right and moving down one row at a time, each arrow points to the position of the grey circle in the next grid square. The positions of the white circles match the positions of the previous grey circle in the sequence.

Section 2 — Vertical Code

1) C (BR)

A = third circle at the front, <u>B</u> = fourth circle at the front.
<u>R</u> = grey circle to right of black circle,
S = grey circle to left of black circle.

2) A (CV)

<u>C</u> = one short line, D = two short lines, E = three short lines.
U = arrows turn anticlockwise, <u>V</u> = arrows turn clockwise.

3) C (CL)

A = shape on the right, B = shape on the left, <u>C</u> = shape in the centre.
J = jagged line, K = wavy line, <u>L</u> = jagged and wavy line.

4) B (DNW)

<u>D</u> = hatched rectangle at the top, E = hatched rectangle at the bottom.
M = longest rectangle in the middle,
<u>N</u> = longest rectangle at the bottom.
U = three grey shapes, V = two grey shapes, <u>W</u> = one grey shape.

5) D (AFU)

<u>A</u> = white arrowhead, B = black arrowhead.
E = arrow pointing at circle, <u>F</u> = arrow not pointing at circle.
<u>U</u> = direction of hatching matches direction of arrow,
V = direction of hatching doesn't match direction of arrow.

6) E (EKU)

<u>E</u> = one small shape matches the large shape,
F = both small shapes match the large shape,
G = neither small shape matches the large shape.
J = left shape is grey, <u>K</u> = left shape is white, L = left shape is black.
S = shape with dotted outline in the centre, T = shape with dotted outline on the right, <u>U</u> = shape with dotted outline on the left.

7) A (RY)

P = circle at the front, Q = circle in the middle, <u>R</u> = circle at the back.
X = figure has vertical line of symmetry,
<u>Y</u> = figure has no line of symmetry.

Section 3 — Odd One Out

1) C

All other figures have two arrows with horizontal hatching and two arrows with vertical hatching.

2) D

In all other figures, every grey shape has four straight sides and one curved side.

3) E

In all other figures, the grey and black shapes fit together to form a smaller copy of the outer shape.

4) A

All other figures have a line of symmetry.

5) E

In all other figures, there is an equal number of shapes shaded white as there are shaded grey.

6) A

In all other figures, there are two shapes with white hatching on the top row and one shape with white hatching on the bottom row.

7) E

In all other figures, there is a pair of shapes that overlap such that the shape of the overlap matches one of the shapes in the pair.

8) A

All other figures are identical apart from rotation.

9) C

In all other figures, the outer shape is a circle if the spiral has straight lines, or is a square if the spiral has curved lines.

10) D

In all other figures, the number of black shapes is equal to the number of lines extending from the white circle.

Section 4 — Complete the Pair

1) B

The black and grey shadings are swapped, then a small copy of the original figure is placed in front and reflected downwards.

2) C

The number of sides of the large shape is halved. Diagonally opposite shadings are swapped.

3) B

The right half of each shape swaps position with the right half of the shape that is diagonally opposite in the figure.

4) D

The shape at the front moves to the back, the shape at the back moves to the middle, and the shape in the middle moves to the front. The black and grey shadings swap layers.

5) E

The shape is split into four quarters. The bottom quarters swap places, then the top-left quarter moves down.

6) C

Each shape moves one place clockwise. The shadings move one place anticlockwise.

7) E

The grey arrows rotates to point towards the smallest grey shape. The white arrow rotates to point towards the largest white shape. The black arrow rotates to point towards the middle-sized black shape.

8) D

A square corner marked by a line is replaced by a curved edge. The quarter circle which is formed is then shaded to match the circle on the end of the line. A curved edge is replaced by a square corner. The square corner contains a line with a circle on the end, whose shading matches the original shape.

9) C

The shape changes shading to white and is rotated 180 degrees. The triangular spaces between pairs of outward facing corners are shaded black.

10) A

The white stars disappear. The figure is reflected across, then the black stars become the corners of a new shape and the corners of the original shape become black stars.

Section 5 — Find the Figure Like the First Two

1) D

In all figures, the shape with a solid outline touches the shape with a dashed outline at one corner. The shape with a dotted outline touches neither of the other two shapes.

2) E

In all figures, a white shape must be three-sided if it lies on an upwards-facing side of the grey shape, and it must be four-sided otherwise.

3) A

All figures have five shapes. The shapes form two linked groups.

4) B

In all figures, the grey shapes fit together to make a copy of the white shape, rotated by the angle shown by the black shape.

5) C

Ignoring shading, all figures must be made from the same set of seven shapes, with no changes in size.

6) E

In all figures, the hatching runs parallel to the longest side of the white shape and perpendicular to the longest side of the black shape. One of the shapes has one more side than the other.

7) D

All figures must have the same number of crosses as the number of straight sides on the grey shape, and the same number of circles as curved sides. The number of black circles must match the number of sides that curve inwards and the number of white circles must match the number of sides that curve outwards.

8) C

In all figures, all shapes with the same shading lie on a single line along the direction of an arrow that has a matching shading. Only shapes with the same shading as the arrowhead can lie along that line.

9) D

In all figures, the dotted lines can be swapped between the large shapes in such a way that all small shapes with the same shading will end up on the same side of a line.

10) A

In all figures, the grey circles alternate between being behind and being in front of the line. The white star is to the right of the second circle, counting clockwise around the line.

Section 6 — Complete the Series

1) B

In each series square, the horizontal line gets shorter and the circles at either end swap shadings. The other line rotates 45 degrees clockwise around the centre of the series square.

2) C

In each series square, the shadings of the shapes change from white to grey, grey to black, and black to white. The square alternates between being on the left and being on the right.

3) B

In each series square, two dots swap positions. The first pair to swap are at the bottom, then it goes clockwise around the figure. The dots remain connected by lines to the same dots they were connected to in the previous series squares.

4) E

In each series square, both arrows alternate between growing by 90 degrees at the head and shrinking by 90 degrees at the tail.

5) B

In each series square, a circle and square with the same shading swap places — starting with the grey pair, then the black pair, then the white pair, and so on.

6) E

In each series square, the heights of the white rectangles double and the heights of the grey rectangles halve. Each pair of rectangles moves one place to the left, and the left-most pair moves to the right.

7) A

In each series square, the left halves of the hexagons alternate between black hatching on white, or white hatching on black. The hatching on the right halves moves to the next hexagon in an anticlockwise direction.

8) D

In each series square, the hatching of the circle and the shading of the small star determine the hatching and shading of the large star in the next series square.

9) C

The outline of each shape changes from solid to dashed to dotted, then the shape is removed. A new shape with a solid outline is added at the front in the next corner of each series square, moving in an anticlockwise direction.

10) C

In each series square, both circles containing a black shape move one place clockwise around the figure. The two circles that are displaced move anticlockwise to fill the gaps, but then swap positions.

Pages 46-57 — Assessment Test 2

Section 1 — Find the Figure Like the First Three

1) A

In all figures, there must be a clockwise arrow when the shapes are shaded in the order: grey, black, white, when going clockwise around the figure. There must be an anticlockwise arrow when the shapes are shaded in the order: grey, black, white, when going anticlockwise around the figure.

2) A

In all figures, the number of sections the circle is divided into must be one fewer than the number of points on the star.

3) D

In all figures, there must be a dot in the largest loop. If the largest loop is made by a solid line, this dot must be white. If the largest loop is made by a dashed line, this dot must be black.

4) A

All figures must have a large shape with four sides. The number of shaded segments in the inner circle must be equal to the number of right angles in the large shape.

5) B

All figures contain a four-sided shape with one curved side. The curved side must have a short line passing through it.

6) C

In all figures, the two dots at either end of the shortest line must be black, and the rest must be white.

7) A

In figures where the top circle of a stack is white, the other circles must be layered on top of it. If the top circle of a stack is grey, the other circles must be layered behind it. The right-hand stack must have two more grey circles than the left-hand stack.

8) E

In all figures, the outer shape must have two more sides than the inner shape. Both shapes must have a horizontal side along their base.

9) B

In all figures, there must be an X-shape on the outline of the trapezium in line with the shortest wavy line. There must be an odd number of wavy lines.

10) E

In all figures, the first column of dots must all be black, the bottom dot in the second column must be black, the third column must all be white and the bottom dot in the fourth column must be black.

Section 2 — Complete the Grid

1) A

Working from left to right, the black star gains an extra point and moves to the opposite side of the grid square. The arrow rotates 45 degrees anticlockwise.

2) C

Working from left to right, the shapes move one place up. The black shading moves one shape to the right and the dot moves one shape to the left.

3) C

Working from left to right, the vertical line and the shapes on it move one place to the right. The shadings of the shapes on the horizontal line also move one place to the right, with the shading on the right-hand shape moving to the left-hand shape.

4) B

Working from left to right, the number of dots decreases by two. The grey dot moves anticlockwise around the corners of the shape.

5) B

Working from left to right, the three overlapping shapes rotate 90 degrees anticlockwise. Each ssdading moves one place to the next shape, moving from the back shape to the front shape. The shading on the shape at the front moves to the shape at the back. The dots move one position clockwise around the corners of the grid square.

6) A

Working from left to right, the hatched square moves one place anticlockwise around the corners of the grid square. The small white square moves one place clockwise around the corners of the hatched square. In each column, the shading of the other two squares combine to make the shading of the cross-hatched square.

7) E

Working from left to right, arrows with black arrowheads rotate 90 degrees clockwise and arrows with white arrowheads rotate 45 degrees anticlockwise.

8) E

Each type of shape (four-sided, five-sided and six-sided) only appears once in each row and column. Each total number of dots (four, five and six) only appears once in each row and column. Working from left to right, the number of dots on the outline of the shape increases by one.

Section 3 — Complete the Series

1) B

In each series square, the inner circle rotates 90 degrees anticlockwise. The hatched part of the outer circle moves one place clockwise, and rotates 45 degrees anticlockwise.

2) B

In each series square, the hexagon changes shading in the order black, then white, then grey. The outermost circle and the innermost circle move two places clockwise around the lines, and the other two circles move one place anticlockwise.

3) E

The L-shape made up of two rectangles rotates 90 degrees clockwise in each series square. The shading of the square becomes the shading of the longer rectangle in the next series square. The shading of the longer rectangle becomes the shading of the shorter rectangle in the next series square.

4) A

In each series square, the figure rotates 180 degrees. The white shape gains one extra side and the black shape gains two extra sides.

5) E

In each series square, the grey rectangle alternates between being below or on top of the spotted rectangle. The grey rectangle moves one place down. When it reaches the bottom, it moves back to the top. The spotted and cross-hatched rectangles move one place to the left. When either of them reach the left-hand side, they move back to the right-hand side.

6) A

A new shape is added to each series square in the order: circle, triangle, square. The new shape is added to the centre of the series square and the shape that was previously in the centre moves to the top left corner. All other shapes move one place clockwise around the corners of the square.

7) E

In each series square, the entire figure rotates 90 degrees anticlockwise. The tall and short rectangles swap shadings. The arrow moves to the next tall rectangle, and when it reaches the rectangle at the end it moves back to the rectangle at the other end. The arrow also alternates between pointing to the side of the figure with the short rectangles and pointing the opposite way.

8) D

In each series square, each column of shapes moves one place to the right and the two rows swap places.

9) B

In each series square, the line inside the centre circle rotates 45 degrees clockwise. All white triangles with a dashed outline become grey with a solid outline. The two triangles either side of them become white triangles with a dashed outline.

Answers

10) C

In each series square, an additional point is added to the star. The star moves one place anticlockwise around the corners of the square and the heart moves one place clockwise around the corners of the square. The shading of the heart becomes the shading of the star in the next series square.

Section 4 — Horizontal Code

1) A (YR)

X = two anticlockwise spirals (working from the centre outwards),
Y = one anticlockwise spiral and one clockwise spiral,
Z = two clockwise spirals.
Q = black arrowhead, R = white arrowhead.

2) B (LX)

L = dot on grey sector, M = dot on black sector,
N = dot on white sector.
X = all sectors have different shading,
Y = two sectors have the same shading.

3) C (FG)

D = number of black dots equals number of white dots, E = more black dots than white dots, F = fewer black dots than white dots.
G = both shapes have the same line type,
H = both shapes have different line types.

4) E (CX)

A = the white rectangle is on the top layer, B = the white rectangle is on the back layer, C = the white rectangle is on the middle layer.
X = the left-hand vertical rectangle is grey, Y = the right-hand vertical rectangle is grey, Z = the horizontal rectangle is grey.

5) A (NS)

M = circles on the left-hand line, N = circles on the right-hand line, O = circles on the middle line.
Q = triangles on the left-hand line, R = triangles on the right-hand line, S = triangles on the middle line.

6) D (FA)

E = the shape is copied across the horizontal line,
F = the shape is reflected across the horizontal line,
G = the shape is reflected across the vertical line.
A = the number of X-shapes is equal to the number of sides of the shape, B = the number of X-shapes is one less than the number of sides of the shape.

7) D (JS)

J = two horizontal line segments between hearts,
K = one horizontal line segment between hearts,
L = three horizontal line segments between hearts.
S = shading of hearts moving along the line from the top end to the bottom end goes in the order: white, black, grey,
T = shading of hearts moving along the line from the top end to the bottom goes in the order: grey, black, white.

8) E (CY)

A = both pairs of opposite shapes have matching shading,
B = one pair of opposite shapes has matching shading,
C = neither pair of opposite shapes have matching shading.
X = neither pair of opposite shapes are the same shape,
Y = one pair of opposite shapes are the same shape,
Z = both pairs of opposite shapes are the same shape.

Section 5 — Find the Figure Like the First Two

1) C

In all figures, the outermost shape is rotated 90 degrees clockwise to give the innermost shape. The hatching of the outermost shape rotates 45 degrees clockwise to give the hatching of the innermost shape.

2) D

In all figures, each oval must have an arrow pointing at it. Grey ovals must have a clockwise arrow pointing at them and white ovals must have an anticlockwise arrow pointing at them.

3) D

In all figures, there must be two of the white shape with the fewest number of sides.

4) A

In all figures, any row which has black rectangles must have one more black rectangle than the previous row, moving from top to bottom.

5) B

In all figures, the black dot must be above and to the left of the white dot. There must be a dotted line passing through the black dot.

6) C

All figures must have a large shape divided by four lines. The number of times the dividing lines intersect inside the large shape must be equal to the number of X-shapes on the outline of the large shape.

7) D

In all figures, there must be a smaller copy of the large shape, including the dashed line, reflected downwards. This smaller copy should be touching the large shape along one of its sides.

8) A

All figures must have one quarter of the white raindrops and half of the black raindrops circled.

9) E

In all figures, the number of sides of the grey shape is equal to the number of white squares that can be seen inside the shape.

10) E

In all figures, each of the small shapes at the top rotates 45 degrees, going from left to right. If the shapes have been rotated clockwise, the arrowhead must be on the right. If the shapes have been rotated anticlockwise, the arrowhead must be on the left. The arrow line is the same shape as the dividing lines inside each of the small shapes if they were joined together.

Section 6 — Vertical Code

1) A (DK)

C = dots below the zig-zag line, D = dots above the zig-zag line.
J = from top to bottom, lines go in the order zig-zag, straight, dashed,
K = lines go in the order straight, zig-zag, dashed,
L = lines go in the order straight, dashed, zig-zag.

2) E (KY)

J = from left to right, the hearts are shaded black then white,
K = from left to right, the hearts are shaded white then black.
X = the large heart is on the right, Y = the large heart is on the left, Z = the large heart is in the middle.

3) D (SBR)

S = clockwise arrow, T = anticlockwise arrow.
A = two shaded circle segments, B = one shaded circle segment.
P = star on the end of the arrow, Q = circle on the end of the arrow, R = square on the end of the arrow.

4) A (FX)

E = shapes are arranged from least number of sides to most number of sides, moving from left to right, F = shapes are arranged from most number of sides to least number of sides, moving from left to right.
X = three overlapping shapes, Y = two overlapping shapes, Z = no overlapping shapes.

5) E (HC)

G = anticlockwise spiral (working from the centre outwards), H = clockwise spiral.
A = number of small lines equals the number of sides of the shape, B = number of small lines is greater than the number of sides of the shape, C = number of small lines is less than the number of sides of the shape.

6) C (PRY)

N = the line joins two white squares, O = the line joins two black squares, P = the line joins a white square and a black square.
R = two white squares, S = two black squares.
X = white four-pointed star, Y = black four-pointed star, Z = black six-pointed star.

7) D (TZA)

S = all shapes are the same, T = two shapes
are the same, U = no shapes are the same.
X = the dot is in the left-most shape, Y = the dot is in
the right-most shape, Z = the dot is in the middle shape.
A = the shape to the left of the dotted shape is grey, B = the shape
to the right of the dotted shape is grey, C = the dotted shape is grey.

8) E (SOC)

S = circles rotating by 45 degrees anticlockwise from left to right,
T = circles rotating by 45 degrees clockwise from left to right.
N = white circles next to each other, O = white circles apart.
B = horizontal line below left-most white circle,
C = horizontal line below right-most white circle.

Pages 58-69 — Assessment Test 3

Section 1 — Complete the Series

1) A

In each series square, an additional white-shaded portion is
added to the cylinder shape. The black shading then moves
up one place, and the grey shading moves down one place.

2) C

Each triangle moves one place clockwise around the corners
of the series square. The white triangle with black dots gets
larger and the black triangle with white dots gets smaller.

3) D

In each series square, the circle at the top and the circle at the
bottom swap places. The three circles in the middle alternate
between being on top of the grey rectangle and being behind it.

4) E

In each series square, the two circles swap places. The circle
with the plain black segment rotates 90 degrees clockwise
in each series square. The circle with the grey segment
rotates 45 degrees anticlockwise in each series square.

5) E

In each series square, the number of squares decreases by two and the
number of circles doubles. One fewer square is shaded grey each time.

6) D

In each series square, the spiral arrow alternates between being
horizontally and vertically reflected around the corners of the
square, moving in an anticlockwise direction. The right-angled
arrow rotates 90 degrees anticlockwise and moves one place
around the corners of the square, in an anticlockwise direction.
The line with the circle on the end alternates between being
on the left-hand and right-hand sides of the square, and the
shading of the circle alternates between being white and black.

7) C

Each series square rotates 90 degrees clockwise. The heart with
the grey shading moves one place along the line of hearts, in
the direction of the curved edges of the heart. The arrow with
the white shading moves one place along the line of arrows, in
the opposite direction to the way the arrows are pointing.

8) B

In each series square, the grey arrow points towards the
position of the grey cross in the next series square (or
the first series square in the case of the last arrow).

9) B

In each series square, the shapes and their shadings move independently
of each other. The shapes move one place anticlockwise around the
circle and the shading moves one place clockwise around the circle.
The arrow moves three shapes anticlockwise around the circle.

Section 2 — Complete the Grid

1) B

The whole grid has a vertical and horizontal line of symmetry.

2) D

Working from top to bottom, the short arrow rotates 90 degrees
clockwise and moves one place clockwise around the edge
of the grid square. The long arrow swaps between pointing
diagonally down to the left and diagonally down to the right.

3) A

Working from left to right, each shape moves one place down
and when a shape reaches the bottom it moves back to the top.

4) E

Working from left to right, the hatched shape in the third grid square
is made up of any space not covered by the shapes in the previous
two grid squares. Each hatching (diagonal down to the left, diagonal
down to the right, vertical) only appears once in each row and column.

5) E

The shapes in the first column can be put together (without reflection
or rotation) to form a triangle, the shapes in the second column form
a pentagon, and the shapes in the third column form a rectangle.
The shapes in each column should have the same shading.

6) C

Working from left to right, the second grid square is the first grid
square with its vertical reflection added. The third grid square is the
same as the second grid square with its horizontal reflection added.

7) C

Working from top to bottom, the line rotates 90 degrees
anticlockwise around each grid square. Each circle moves
one place anticlockwise around each grid square.

8) D

Working from top to bottom, the rectangle with hatching
going diagonally down to the left moves down one
place, and the rectangle with hatching going diagonally
down to the right moves down two places.

Section 3 — Complete the Pair

1) A

The number of sides of the top shape becomes the number of
points on the star. The number of points on the star becomes the
number of sides on the bottom shape. The top shapes have the
same shading and the bottom shapes have the same shading.

2) E

The shape on the end of the line pointing to the left stays where
it is. The other three shapes move one place anticlockwise to the
end of the next line (missing out the line pointing to the left).

3) B

The large shape rotates 90 degrees clockwise and the hatching
rotates 45 degrees clockwise. The small shape is reflected
downwards. The arrow rotates 90 degrees anticlockwise.

4) B

The whole figure rotates 180 degrees. Each shading moves to the
next triangle, moving anticlockwise around the three triangles.

5) D

The whole figure rotates 90 degrees clockwise. The grey
shape rotates 180 degrees from its original orientation. The
black shape rotates 90 degrees anticlockwise from its original
orientation and moves in front of the hatched shape. The hatching
rotates 45 degrees clockwise from its original direction.

6) D

The largest shape takes on a combination of the shading of the two
second largest shapes. A copy of the largest shape goes behind it and
takes on a combination of the shading of the two smallest shapes.

7) C

The whole figure is reflected down. The grey triangles
inside the large shape move so that they are pointing
outwards from the edges of the large shape.

8) E

The entire figure rotates 90 degrees clockwise. The shape is divided up by the same number of lines as there are sides on the shape.

9) B

The triangle at the bottom of the large oval is reflected down. The polygon, the star and the small oval move one place anticlockwise around the edge of the large oval and take on the shading of the previous shape in that position. One point is added to the star and one side is removed from the polygon.

10) A

The whole figure is reflected across. There are two different types of line and two different types of arrowhead. Each arrow swaps both its line type and arrowhead type to the other.

Section 4 — Horizontal Code

1) B (RC)

Q = arrow pointing down to the right,
R = arrow pointing up to the right.
C = shading of the top circle matches the shading of the arrow,
D = shading of the middle circle matches the shading of the arrow,
E = shading of the bottom circle matches the shading of the arrow.

2) D (GS)

F = large shape has a dotted outline, G = large shape has a solid outline, H = large shape has a dashed outline.
R = number of short lines crossing the large shape is the same as the number of sides of the small shape, S = number of short lines crossing the large shape is the same as the number of sides of the large shape.

3) A (RG)

Q = anticlockwise spiral (working from the centre outwards),
R = clockwise spiral.
F = arrow pointing up, G = arrow pointing left,
H = arrow pointing diagonally.

4) E (BT)

B = one curved side, C = two curved sides, D = no curved sides.
T = shape hatched diagonally down to the right,
U = shape hatched diagonally down to the left.

5) D (SZ)

S = bottom shape is downwards reflection of top shape,
T = bottom shape is horizontal reflection of top shape.
X = circles are just on corners of the large shapes,
Y = circles are only on sides, Z = circles are on corners and sides.

6) C (KE)

J = shape with fewest sides at the front,
K = shape with most sides at the front.
D = shading from top to bottom is grey, white, black,
E = shading from top to bottom is white, grey, black,
F = shading from top to bottom is black, grey, white.

7) B (NJ)

M = half of the squares shaded grey,
N = fewer than half of the squares shaded grey.
J = rows arranged in order of decreasing number of squares (from top to bottom), K = rows in no order, L = rows arranged in order of increasing number of squares.

8) C (BY)

A = three different types of shape, B = two different types of shape.
X = more circles than other shapes, Y = more squares than other shapes, Z = more triangles than other shapes.

Section 5 — Odd One Out

1) E

In all other figures, the shape made by the overlap of the two shapes has five sides.

2) D

In all other figures, the shapes on both ends of the spiral are downwards reflections of each other.

3) C

In all other figures, the single circles are in opposite quarters of the figure.

4) D

In all other figures, the two arrows that overlap each other have lines of different lengths.

5) A

All other figures have at least one arrow that goes clockwise.

6) E

In all other figures, there are no shapes that are the same.

7) C

All other figures are identical apart from rotation.

8) C

In all other figures, the number of small shapes inside the star is one fewer than the number of points on the star.

9) B

In all other figures, the lines dividing the large shape into four parts only meet at right angles.

10) B

In all other figures, the number of grey triangles is equal to the combined number of horizontal and vertical sides of the large shape.

Section 6 — Find the Figure Like the First Three

1) C

All figures have a four-sided shape with a black circle and a grey circle on two corners, and a black circle and a grey circle on two sides.

2) D

All figures are made up of four straight lines and one curved line. Two of the lines must cross each other.

3) D

In all figures, the direction of the spiral working from the centre outwards is the same as the direction of the arrow.

4) B

In all figures, the grey shape is created by joining the white shape and the hatched shape.

5) E

In all figures, the arrow is pointing at the square that is hatched in the same direction as the arrow is pointing.

6) B

In all figures, the number of sides on the polygon and the number of points on the star must add up to 11.

7) C

All figures contain a large white shape touching a copy that has been rotated 45 degrees anticlockwise. This copy has the same shading as the left-hand star.

8) A

In all figures, the number of straight lines across the large shape is one more than the number of stars. There are more stars in the rounded end of the large shape than between the straight lines.

9) B

The shape above the line with the most sides is shaded grey. The shape below the line is identical to half of the left-most shape above the line.

Pages 70-81 — Assessment Test 4

Section 1 — 2D Views of 3D Shapes

1) B

There are five blocks visible from above, which rules out options C, D and E. The figure is made up of three rows of blocks, which rules out option A.

2) E

There are five blocks visible from above, which rules out options A and D. There is one block visible at the front of the figure, which rules out option B. The figure is made up of two columns of blocks, which rules out option C.

3) A

There are six blocks visible from above, which rules out options B, C and E. There are two blocks visible on the right-hand side, which rules out option D.

4) C

There are six blocks visible from above, which rules out options B and D. There are two blocks visible on the left-hand side, which rules out option A. There are two blocks visible at the front, which rules out option E.

5) B

There are six blocks visible from above, which rules out options C and E. There is one block visible at the front, which rules out options A and D.

6) D

There are seven blocks visible from above, which rules out options B and C. There are two blocks visible in the middle column, which rules out options A and E.

7) C

There are seven blocks visible from above, which rules out options A and D. There are two blocks visible at the back, which rules out option B. There are three blocks visible on the right-hand side, which rules out option E.

8) D

There are seven blocks visible from above, which rules out options B and E. The figure is made up of four rows, which rules out option A. There are two blocks visible at the front, which rules out option C.

Section 2 — Connecting Shapes

1) B

Options A and D are ruled out because the L-shape is connected to the wrong side of the large shape. Options C and E are ruled out because the wrong side of the triangle is connected to the large shape.

2) D

Options A and B are ruled out because the wrong side of the arrow shape is connected to the large shape. Option C is ruled out because the arrow shape and the semicircle are both connected to the wrong sides of the large shape. Option E is ruled out because the semicircle is connected to the wrong side of the large shape.

3) E

Options A and C are ruled out because the wrong side of the kite shape is connected to the large shape. Option B is ruled out because the wrong side of the shield shape is connected to the large shape. Option D is ruled out because the kite shape and the shield shape are both connected to the wrong sides of the large shape.

4) A

Option B is ruled out because the wrong side of the five-sided shape is connected to the large shape. Option C is ruled out because the wrong side of the four-sided shape is connected to the large shape. Option D is ruled out because the five-sided shape is connected to the wrong side of the large shape. Option E is ruled out because the five-sided shape and the four-sided shape are both connected to the wrong sides of the large shape.

5) B

Option A is ruled out because the 'a' shape is connected to the wrong side of the large shape. Option C is ruled out because the wrong side of the arch shape is connected to the large shape. Option D is ruled out because the wrong side of the 'a' shape is connected to the large shape. Option E is ruled out because the arch shape is connected to the wrong side of the large shape.

6) D

Option A is ruled out because the wrong side of the curved shape is connected to the large shape. Option B is ruled out because the wrong side of the five-sided shape is connected to the large shape. Option C is ruled out because the five-sided shape is connected to the wrong side of the large shape. Option E is ruled out because the curved shape and the five-sided shape are both connected to the wrong sides of the large shape.

7) E

Option A is ruled out because the wrong side of the curved shape is connected to the large shape. Option B is ruled out because the curved shape is connected to the wrong side of the large shape. Option C is ruled out because the wrong side of the triangle is connected to the large shape. Option D is ruled out because the curved shape and the triangle are both connected to the wrong sides of the large shape.

8) B

Option A is ruled out because the wrong side of the arrow shape is connected to the large shape. Options C and E are ruled out because the wrong side of the four-sided shape is connected to the large shape. Option D is ruled out because the arrow shape and the four-sided shape are both connected to the wrong sides of the large shape.

9) C

Option A is ruled out because the wrong side of the L-shape is connected to the large shape. Option B is ruled out because the wrong side of the quarter-circle is connected to the large shape. Option D is ruled out because the quarter-circle is connected to the wrong side of the large shape. Option E is ruled out because the L-shape is connected to the wrong side of the large shape.

10) A

Options B and D are ruled out because the wrong side of the trapezium is connected to the large shape. Option C is ruled out because the trapezium and the parallelogram are both connected to the wrong sides of the large shape. Option E is ruled out because the wrong side of the parallelogram is connected to the large shape.

Section 3 — Fold Along the Line

1) C

Options A and D are ruled out because the part of the figure that has been folded is the wrong shape. Option B is ruled out because the fold line has moved. Option E is ruled out because the part of the figure originally to the left of the fold line should still be visible.

2) A

Option B is ruled out because the part of the figure that has been folded is the wrong shape. Option C is ruled out because the part of the figure originally below the fold line is the wrong shape. Options D and E are ruled out because the fold line has moved.

3) D

Option A is ruled out because the fold line has moved. Options B and E are ruled out because the part of the figure that has been folded is the wrong shape. Option C is ruled out because the part of the figure originally on the left of the fold line is the wrong shape.

4) E

Option A is ruled out because the part of the figure that has been folded is the wrong shape. Option B is ruled out because the part of the figure originally below the fold line is the wrong shape. Option C is ruled out because the figure has been broken apart along the fold line. Option D is ruled out because the fold line has moved.

5) A

Option B is ruled out because the fold line has moved. Option C is ruled out because the part of the figure originally to the right of the fold line should still be visible. Option D is ruled out because the part of the figure that has been folded is the wrong shape. Option E is ruled out because the part of the figure originally to the right of the fold line is the wrong shape.

6) B

Option A is ruled out because the fold line has moved. Options C and E are ruled out because the part of the figure that has been folded is the wrong shape. Option D is ruled out because the part of the figure originally to the left of the fold line is the wrong shape.

7) C

Options A and D are ruled out because the part of the figure that has been folded is the wrong shape. Option B is ruled out because the fold line has been moved. Option E is ruled out because the part of the figure originally to the right of the fold line is the wrong shape.

Answers

8) E

Options A and D are ruled out because the part of the figure that has been folded is the wrong shape. Option B is ruled out because the part of the figure originally to the left of the fold line is the wrong shape. Option C is ruled out because the fold line has moved.

Section 4 — Cubes and Nets

1) D

Option A is ruled out because if the grey arrow shape is on the front and the black line is on the right, then the black and white circles must be on the top. Option B is ruled out because the black and white circles have been rotated. Option C is ruled out because if the heart is on the front and the grey arrow shape is on the top, then the curved white shape must be on the right. Option E is ruled out because the grey triangles and the grey arrow shape must be on opposite sides.

2) A

Option B is ruled out because the U-shape has been rotated. Option C is ruled out because the triangle and the star must be on opposite sides. Option D is ruled out because the hatched trapezium has been rotated. Option E is ruled out because if the hatched trapezium is on the front and the black triangle is on the top, then the white and grey circle must be on the right.

3) E

Option A is ruled out because the grey L-shape has been rotated. Option B is ruled out because the grey and white circles have been rotated. Option C is ruled out because the circle with the line through it has been rotated. Option D is ruled out because the black triangle and the grey and white circles must be on opposite sides.

4) C

Option A is ruled out because the spiral and the black rectangle with the white circle must be on opposite sides. Option B is ruled out because the white circle with the grey ovals has been rotated. Option D is ruled out because if the hatching is on the front and the spiral is on the top, then the grey triangle must be on the right. Option E is ruled out because the black rectangle with the white circle has been rotated.

5) E

Option A is ruled out because the curved white shape has been reflected. Option B is ruled out because the grey circle shape with the rectangle running through it and the diamond must be on opposite sides. Option C is ruled out because if the grey circle shape with the rectangle running through it is on the front and the grey oval is on the top, then the two black rectangles must be on the right. Option D is ruled out because if the black circle is on the front and the two black rectangles are on the top, then the black diamond must be on the right.

6) B

Option A is ruled out because if the black trapezium is on the front and the grey quarter-circle is on the top, then the black and white arrow shape must be on the right. Option C is ruled out because the grey quarter-circle has been rotated. Options D and E are ruled out because the hatching has been rotated.

7) C

Option A is ruled out because the black shapes have been rotated. Option B is ruled out because the grey and black rectangles have been reflected. Option D is ruled out because the H-shape has been rotated. Option E is ruled out because if the grey and white triangles are on the front and the H-shape is on the right, then the grey and white circle must be on the top.

8) D

Option A is ruled out because the black and white shape has been rotated. Option B is ruled out because if the black and white shape is at the front and the lines with two grey circles are on the right, then the white circle must be on the top. Option C is ruled out because the face with the black square has been rotated. Option E is ruled out because the white circle has been rotated.

Section 5 — Fold and Punch

1) A

2) B

3) E

4) A

5) C

6) C

7) D

8) A

9) E

10) C

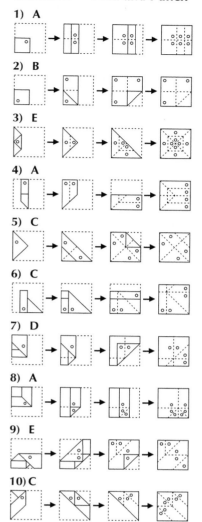

Section 6 — 3D Rotation

1) C

Shape C rotates 90 degrees towards you top-to-bottom. It then rotates 90 degrees right-to-left

2) B

Shape B rotates 90 degrees anticlockwise in the plane of the page. It then rotates 90 degrees left-to-right.

3) F

Shape F rotates 180 degrees, top-to-bottom.

4) A

Shape A rotates 90 degrees clockwise in the plane of the page. It then rotates 90 degrees away from you, top-to-bottom.

5) C

Shape C rotates 180 degrees in the plane of the page.

6) B

Shape B rotates 90 degrees clockwise in the plane of the page. It then rotates 90 degrees left-to-right.

7) D

Shape D rotates 90 degrees right-to-left. It then rotates 90 degrees away from you, top-to-bottom.

8) E

Shape E rotates 90 degrees towards you, top-to-bottom. It then rotates 90 degrees left-to-right.

9) A

Shape A rotates 90 degrees anticlockwise in the plane of the page. It then rotates 90 degrees right-to-left.

10) F

Shape F rotates 90 degrees clockwise in the plane of the page. It then rotates 90 degrees away from you, top-to-bottom.

Progress Chart

Answer Sheets

Use this chart to keep track of your scores for the Assessment Tests.

You can do each test more than once — download extra answer sheets from cgpbooks.co.uk/11plus/answer-sheets or scan the QR code on the right.

	First Go	**Second Go**	**Third Go**
Test 1	Date: Score:	Date: Score:	Date: Score:
Test 2	Date: Score:	Date: Score:	Date: Score:
Test 3	Date: Score:	Date: Score:	Date: Score:
Test 4	Date: Score:	Date: Score:	Date: Score:

Look back at your scores once you've done all the Assessment Tests.

Each test is out of 54 marks.

Work out which kind of mark you scored most often:

0-32 marks — Keep working on it, these questions are here to stretch you.

33-42 marks — You're doing great to get this many right, these questions are really tricky.

43-54 marks — You're a Non-Verbal Reasoning star.